African Stories

by
Doris Lessing

A TOUCHSTONE BOOK
Published by Simon & Schuster Inc.
New York London Toronto Sydney Tokyo Singapore

SPIES I HAVE KNOWN and THE STORY OF A NON-MARRYING MAN were originally published in THE TEMPTATION OF JACK ORKNEY AND OTHER STORIES, and are reprinted by permission of Curtis Brown, Ltd.

First Touchstone Edition, 1981
Published by Simon & Schuster, Inc.
Simon & Schuster Building
Rockefeller Center
1230 Avenue of the Americas
New York, New York 10020

TOUCHSTONE and colophon are registered trademarks
of Simon & Schuster, Inc.

Designed by Cecile Cutler

Manufactured in the United States of America

7 8 9 10 Pbk.

Library of Congress Cataloging in Publication Data

Lessing, Doris May, date.
    African stories.

    (A Touchstone book)
    I. Title.
PR6023.E833A69 1981   823'.914   81-8915
                                                 AACR2
ISBN 0-671-42809-8 Pbk.

Contents

Preface

Most of these stories come from earlier collections. Some have been out of print a long time; others have never appeared in America at all. I am happy to have them around again.

The stories an author likes are not necessarily those chosen by other people. This happens to every writer. Because I was brought up in Southern Africa (Southern Rhodesia) a part of my work has been set there, and the salience of the colour clash has made it inevitable that those aspects which reflect "the colour problem" should have overshadowed the rest. When my first novel, The Grass Is Singing, *came out, there were few novels about Africa. That book, and my second,* This Was the Old Chief's Country, *were described by reviewers as about the colour problem . . . which is not how I see, or saw, them. But then, a decade ago, manifestations of race prejudice in Africa, terribly familiar to those of us who had to live with them, were still a surprise, apparently, to Britain. Or, to put it as cynically as some people feel it, indignation about the colour bar in Africa had not yet become part of the furniture of the progressive conscience. If people had been prepared to listen, two decades earlier, to the small, but shrill-enough, voices crying out for the world's attention, perhaps the present suffering in South Africa and Southern Rhodesia could have been prevented. Britain, who is responsible, became conscious of her responsibility too late; and now the tragedy must play itself slowly out. Mean-while there are dozens of novels, stories, plays about what one happy reviewer called "the colour bore."*

Writers brought up in Africa have many advantages—being at the centre of a modern battlefield; part of a society in rapid, dramatic change. But in a long run it can also be a handicap: to wake up every morning with one's eyes on a fresh evidence of in-humanity; to be reminded twenty times a day of injustice, and always the same brand of it, can be limiting. There are other things in living besides injustice, even for the victims of it. I know an African short-story writer whose gift is for satirical comedy, and he says that he has to remind himself, when he sits down to write, that "as a human being he has the right to laugh." Not only have white sympathizers criticised him for "making comedy out of op-pression," his compatriots do too. Yet I am sure that one day out of Africa will come a great comic novel to make the angels laugh, pressed as miraculously from the bitter savageries of the atrophy as was Dead Souls.

And while the cruelties of the white man towards the black man are among the heaviest counts in the indictment against humanity, colour prejudice is not our original fault, but only one aspect of the atrophy of the imagination that prevents us from seeing our-selves in every creature that breathes under the sun.

I believe that the chief gift from Africa to writers, white and black, is the continent itself, its presence which for some people is like an old fever, latent always in their blood; or like an old wound throbbing in the bones as the air changes. That is not a place to visit unless one chooses to be an exile ever afterwards from an inexplicable majestic silence lying just over the border of memory or of thought. Africa gives you the knowledge that man is a small creature, among other creatures, in a large landscape.

My favourites in This Was the Old Chief's Country *are not neces-sarily those that have been most translated, which are* Little Tembi, The Old Chief Mshlanga, *and* No Witchcraft for Sale. A Sunrise on the Veld, *for instance, and* Winter in July *are both larger stories than the directly social ones.*

All these stories have in common that they are set in Africa, but that is all they have in common. For one thing, while the Old Chief *was a collection of real short stories,* Five *is five long stories, almost short novels. A most enjoyable form this, to write, the long story, although of course there is no way of getting them printed out of book form. There is space in them to take one's time, to think aloud, to follow, for a paragraph or two, on a side-trail—none of which is possible in a real short story.*

Of the four long stories printed here, Hunger *is the failure and, it seems, the most liked.*

It came to be written like this. I was in Moscow with a delegation of writers, back in 1952. *It was striking that while the members of the British team differed very much politically, we agreed with each other on certain assumptions about literature—in brief, that writing had to be a product of the individual conscience, or soul. Whereas the Russians did not agree at all—not at all. Our debates, many and long, were on this theme.*

Stalin was still alive. One day we were taken to see a building full of presents for Stalin, rooms full of every kind of object— pictures, photographs, carpets, clothes, etc., all gifts from his grateful subjects and exhibited by the State to show other subjects and visitors from abroad. It was a hot day. I left the others touring the stuffy building, and sat outside to rest. I was thinking about what Russians were demanding in literature—greater simplicity, simple judgments of right and wrong. We, the British, had argued against it, and we felt we were right and the Russians wrong. But after all, there was Dickens, and such a short time ago, and his characters were all good or bad—unbelievably Good, monstrously Bad, but that didn't stop him from being a great writer. Well, there I was, with my years in Southern Africa behind me, a society as startlingly unjust as Dickens's England. Why, then, could I not write a story of simple good and bad, with clear-cut choices, set in Africa? The plot? Only one possible plot—that a poor black boy or girl should come from a village to the white man's rich town and . . . there he would encounter, as occurs in life, good and bad, and after much trouble and many tears he would follow the path of . . .

I tried, but it failed. It wasn't true. Sometimes one writes things that don't come off, and feels more affectionate towards them than towards those that worked.

The Black Madonna *and* Traitors, *from* Winter's Tales *and* Argosy *respectively, escaped the nets of earlier volumes. I am ad-*

dicted to The Black Madonna, *which is full of the bile that in fact I feel for the "white" society in Southern Rhodesia as I knew and hated it.*

The Pig *and* The Trinket Box *are two of my earliest. I see them as two forks of a road. The second—intense, careful, self-conscious, mannered—could have led to the kind of writing usually described as "feminine." The style of* The Pig *is straight, broad, direct; is much less beguiling, but is the highway to the kind of writing that has the freedom to develop as it likes.*

I hope these stories will be read with as much pleasure as I had in . . . but I mean it. I enjoy writing short stories very much, although fewer and fewer magazines print them, and for every twenty novel readers there is one who likes short stories.

Some writers I know have stopped writing short stories because, as they say, "there is no market for them." Others like myself, the addicts, go on, and I suspect would go on even if there really wasn't any home for them but a private drawer.

—Doris Lessing

African
Stories

The Black Madonna

THERE are some countries in which the arts, let alone Art, cannot be said to flourish. Why this should be so it is hard to say, although of course we all have our theories about it. For sometimes it is the most barren soil that sends up gardens of those flowers which we all agree are the crown and justification of life, and it is this fact which makes it hard to say, finally, why the soil of Zambesia should produce such reluctant plants.

Zambesia is a tough, sunburnt, virile, positive country contemptuous of subtleties and sensibility: yet there have been States with these qualities which have produced art, though perhaps with the left hand. Zambesia is, to put it mildly, unsympathetic to those ideas so long taken for granted in other parts of the world, to do with liberty, fraternity and the rest. Yet there are those, and some of the finest souls among them, who maintain that art is impossible without a minority whose leisure is guaranteed by a hardworking majority. And whatever Zambesia's comfortable minority may lack, it is not leisure.

Zambesia—but enough; out of respect for ourselves and for scientific accuracy, we should refrain from jumping to conclusions. Particularly when one remembers the almost wistful respect Zambesians show when an artist does appear in their midst.

Consider, for instance, the case of Michele.

He came out of the internment camp at the time when Italy was made a sort of honorary ally, during the Second World War. It was a time of strain for the authorities, because it is one thing to be responsible for thousands of prisoners of war whom one must treat according to certain recognized standards; it is another to be faced, and from one day to the next, with these same thousands transformed by some international legerdemain into comrades in arms. Some of the thousands stayed where they were in the camps; they were fed and housed there at least. Others went as farm labourers, though not many; for while the farmers were as always short of labour, they did not know how to handle farm labourers who were also white men: such a phenomenon had never happened in Zambesia before. Some did odd jobs around the towns, keeping a sharp eye out for the trade unions, who would neither admit them as members nor agree to their working.

Hard, hard, the lot of these men, but fortunately not for long, for soon the war ended and they were able to go home.

Hard, too, the lot of the authorities, as has been pointed out; and for that reason they were doubly willing to take what advantages they could from the situation; and that Michele was such an advantage there could be no doubt.

His talents were first discovered when he was still a prisoner of war. A church was built in the camp, and Michele decorated its interior. It became a show-place, that little tin-roofed church in the prisoners' camp, with its whitewashed walls covered all over with frescoes depicting swarthy peasants gathering grapes for the vintage, beautiful Italian girls dancing, plump dark-eyed children. Amid crowded scenes of Italian life, appeared the Virgin and her Child, smiling and beneficent, happy to move familiarly among her people.

Culture-loving ladies who had bribed the authorities to be taken inside the camp would say, "Poor thing, how homesick he must be." And they would beg to be allowed to leave half a crown for the artist. Some were indignant. He was a prisoner, after all, captured in the very act of fighting against justice and democracy, and what right had he to protest?—for they felt these paintings as a sort of protest. What was there in Italy that we did not have right here in Westonville, which was the capital and hub of Zambesia? Were there not sunshine and mountains and fat babies and pretty girls here? Did we not grow—if not grapes, at least lemons and oranges and flowers in plenty?

People were upset—the desperation of nostalgia came from the painted white walls of that simple church, and affected everyone according to his temperament.

But when Michele was free, his talent was remembered. He was spoken of as "that Italian artist." As a matter of fact, he was a bricklayer. And the virtues of those frescoes might very well have been exaggerated. It is possible they would have been overlooked altogether in a country where picture-covered walls were more common.

When one of the visiting ladies came rushing out to the camp in her own car, to ask him to paint her children, he said he was not qualified to do so. But at last he agreed. He took a room in the town and made some nice likenesses of the children. Then he painted the children of a great number of the first lady's friends. He charged ten shillings a time. Then one of the ladies wanted a portrait of herself. He asked ten pounds for it; it had taken him a month to do. She was annoyed, but paid.

And Michele went off to his room with a friend and stayed there drinking red wine from the Cape and talking about home. While the money lasted he could not be persuaded to do any more portraits.

There was a good deal of talk among the ladies about the dignity of labour, a subject in which they were well versed; and one felt they might almost go so far as to compare a white man with a kaffir, who did not understand the dignity of labour either.

He was felt to lack gratitude. One of the ladies tracked him down, found him lying on a camp-bed under a tree with a bottle of wine, and spoke to him severely about the barbarity of Mussolini and the fecklessness of the Italian temperament. Then she demanded that he should instantly paint a picture of herself in her new evening dress. He refused, and she went home very angry.

It happened that she was the wife of one of our most important citizens, a General or something of that kind, who was at that time engaged in planning a military tattoo or show for the benefit of the civilian population. The whole of Westonville had been discussing this show for weeks. We were all bored to extinction by dances, fancy-dress balls, fairs, lotteries and other charitable entertainments. It is not too much to say that while some were dying for freedom, others were dancing for it. There comes a limit to everything. Though, of course, when the end of the war actually came and the thousands of troops stationed in the country had to go home—in short, when enjoying ourselves would no longer be a duty, many were heard to exclaim that life would never be the same again.

In the meantime, the Tattoo would make a nice change for us all.

The military gentlemen responsible for the idea did not think of it in these terms. They thought to improve morale by giving us some idea of what war was really like. Headlines in the newspaper were not enough. And in order to bring it all home to us, they planned to destroy a village by shell-fire before our very eyes.

First, the village had to be built.

It appears that the General and his subordinates stood around in the red dust of the parade-ground under a burning sun for the whole of one day, surrounded by building materials, while hordes of African labourers ran around with boards and nails, trying to make something that looked like a village. It became evident that they would have to build a proper village in order to destroy it; and this would cost more than was allowed for the whole entertainment. The General went home in a bad temper, and his wife said what they needed was an artist, they needed Michele. This was not because she wanted to do Michele a good turn; she could not endure the thought of him lying around singing while there was work to be done. She refused to undertake any delicate diplomatic missions when her husband said he would be damned if he would ask favours of any little Wop. She solved the problem for him in her own way: a certain Captain Stocker was sent out to fetch him.

The Captain found him on the same camp-bed under the same tree, in rolled-up trousers, and an uncollared shirt; unshaven, mildly drunk, with a bottle of wine standing beside him on the earth. He was singing an air so wild, so sad, that the Captain was uneasy. He stood at ten paces from the disreputable fellow and felt the indignities of his position. A year ago, this man had been a mortal enemy to be shot at sight. Six months ago, he had been an enemy prisoner. Now he lay with his knees up, in an untidy shirt that had certainly once been military. For the Captain, the situation crystallised in a desire that Michele should salute him.

"Piselli!" he said sharply.

Michele turned his head and looked at the Captain from the horizontal. "Good morning," he said affably.

"You are wanted," said the Captain.

"Who?" said Michele. He sat up, a fattish, olive-skinned little man. His eyes were resentful.

"The authorities."

"The war is over?"

The Captain, who was already stiff and shiny enough in his laundered khaki, jerked his head back frowning, chin out. He was a large man, blond, and wherever his flesh showed, it was brick-red. His eyes were small and blue and angry. His red hands, covered all over with fine yellow bristles, clenched by his side. Then he saw the disappointment in Michele's eyes, and the hands unclenched. "No it is not over," he said. "Your assistance is required."

"For the war?"

"For the war effort. I take it you are interested in defeating the Germans?"

Michele looked at the Captain. The little dark-eyed artisan looked at the great blond officer with his cold blue eyes, his narrow mouth, his hands like bristle-covered steaks. He looked and said: "I am very interested in the end of the war."

"*Well?*" said the Captain between his teeth.

"The pay?" said Michele.

"You will be paid."

Michele stood up. He lifted the bottle against the sun, then took a gulp. He rinsed his mouth out with wine and spat. Then he poured what was left on to the red earth, where it made a bubbling purple stain.

"I am ready," he said. He went with the Captain to the waiting lorry, where he climbed in beside the driver's seat and not, as the Captain had expected, into the back of the lorry. When they had arrived at the parade-ground the officers had left a message that the Captain would be personally responsible for Michele and for the village. Also for the hundred or so labourers who were sitting around on the grass verges waiting for orders.

The Captain explained what was wanted. Michele nodded. Then he waved his hand at the Africans. "I do not want these," he said.

"You will do it yourself—a village?"

"Yes."

"With no help?"

Michele smiled for the first time. "I will do it."

The Captain hesitated. He disapproved on principle of white men doing heavy manual labour. He said: "I will keep six to do the heavy work."

Michele shrugged; and the Captain went over and dismissed all but six of the Africans. He came back with them to Michele.

"It is hot," said Michele.

"Very," said the Captain. They were standing in the middle of the parade-ground. Around its edge trees, grass, gulfs of shadow. Here, nothing but reddish dust, drifting and lifting in a low hot breeze.

"I am thirsty," said Michele. He grinned. The Captain felt his stiff lips loosen unwillingly in reply. The two pairs of eyes met. It was a moment of understanding. For the Captain, the little Italian had suddenly become human. "I will arrange it," he said, and went off down-town. By the time he had explained the position to the right people, filled in forms and made arrangements, it was late afternoon. He returned to the parade-ground with a case of Cape brandy, to find Michele and the six black men seated together under a tree. Michele was singing an Italian song to them, and they were harmonizing with him. The sight affected the Captain like an attack of nausea. He came up, and the Africans stood to attention. Michele continued to sit.

"You said you would do the work yourself?"

"Yes, I said so."

The Captain then dismissed the Africans. They departed, with friendly looks towards Michele, who waved at them. The Captain was beef-red with anger. "You have not started yet?"

"How long have I?"

"Three weeks."

"Then there is plenty of time," said Michele, looking at the bottle of brandy in the Captain's hand. In the other were two glasses. "It is evening," he pointed out. The Captain stood frowning for a moment. Then he sat down on the grass, and poured out two brandies.

"Ciao," said Michele.

"Cheers," said the Captain. Three weeks, he was thinking. Three weeks with this damned little Itie! He drained his glass and refilled it, and set it in the grass. The grass was cool and soft. A tree was flowering somewhere close—hot waves of perfume came on the breeze.

"It is nice here," said Michele. "We will have a good time together. Even in a war, there are times of happiness. And of friendship. I drink to the end of the war."

Next day, the Captain did not arrive at the parade-ground until after lunch. He found Michele under the trees with a bottle. Sheets of ceiling board had been erected at one end of the parade-ground in such a way that they formed two walls and part of a third, and a slant of steep roof supported on struts.

"What's that?" said the Captain, furious.

"The church," said Michele.

"Wha-at?"

"You will see. Later. It is very hot." He looked at the brandy bottle that lay on its side on the ground. The Captain went to the lorry and returned with the case of brandy. They drank. Time passed. It was a long time since the Captain had sat on grass under a tree. It was a long time, for that matter, since he had drunk so much. He always drank a great deal, but it was regulated to the times and seasons. He was a disciplined man. Here, sitting on the grass beside this little man whom he still could not help thinking of as an enemy, it was not that he let his self-discipline go, but that he felt himself to be something different: he was temporarily set outside his normal behaviour. Michele did not count. He listened to Michele talking about Italy, and it seemed to him he was listening to a savage speaking: as if he heard tales from the mythical South Sea islands where a man like himself might very well go just once in his life. He found himself saying he would like to make a trip to Italy after the war. Actually, he was attracted only by the North and by Northern people. He had visited Germany, under Hitler, and though it was not the time to say so, had found it very satisfactory. Then Michele sang him some Italian songs. He sang Michele some English songs. Then Michele took out photographs of his wife and children, who lived in a village in the mountains of North Italy. He asked the Captain if he were married. The Captain never spoke about his private affairs.

He had spent all his life in one or other of the African colonies as a policeman, magistrate, native commissioner, or in some other useful capacity. When the war started, military life came easily to him. But he hated city life, and had his own reasons for wishing the war over. Mostly, he had been in bush-stations with one or two other white men, or by himself, far from the rigours of civilisation. He had relations with native women; and from time to time visited the city where his wife lived with her parents and the children. He was always tormented by the idea that she was unfaithful to him. Recently he had even appointed a private detective to watch her; he was convinced the detective was inefficient. Army friends coming from L—— where his wife was, spoke of her at parties, enjoying herself. When the war ended, she would not find it so easy to have a good time. And why did he not simply live with her and be done with it? The fact was, he could not. And his long exile to remote bush-stations was because he needed the excuse not to. He could not bear to think of his wife for too long; she was that part of his life he had never been able, so to speak, to bring to heel.

Yet he spoke of her now to Michele, and of his favourite bush-wife, Nadya. He told Michele the story of his life, until he realized that the shadows from the trees they sat under had stretched right across the parade-ground to the grandstand. He got unsteadily to his feet, and said: "There is work to be done. You are being paid to work."

"I will show you my church when the light goes."

The sun dropped, darkness fell, and Michele made the Captain drive his lorry on to the parade-ground a couple of hundred yards away and switch on his lights. Instantly, a white church sprang up from the shapes and shadows of the bits of board.

"Tomorrow, some houses," said Michele cheerfully.

At the end of a week, the space at the end of the parade-ground had crazy gawky constructions of lath and board over it, that looked in the sunlight like nothing on this earth. Privately, it upset the Captain; it was like a nightmare that these skeleton-like shapes should be able to persuade him, with the illusions of light and dark, that they were a village. At night, the Captain drove up his lorry, switched on the lights, and there it was, the village, solid and real against a background of full green trees. Then, in the morning sunlight, there was nothing there, just bits of board stuck in the sand.

"It is finished," said Michele.

"You were engaged for three weeks," said the Captain. He did not want it to end, this holiday from himself.

Michele shrugged. "The army is rich," he said. Now, to avoid curious eyes, they sat inside the shade of the church, with the case of brandy between them. The Captain talked, talked endlessly, about his wife, about women. He could not stop talking.

Michele listened. Once he said: "When I go home—when I go home—I shall open my arms . . ." He opened them, wide. He closed his eyes. Tears ran down his cheeks. "I shall take my wife in my arms, and I shall ask nothing, nothing. I do not care. It is enough to be together. That is what the war has taught me. It is enough, it is enough. I shall ask no questions and I shall be happy."

The Captain stared before him, suffering. He thought how he dreaded his wife. She was a scornful creature, gay and hard, who laughed at him. She had been laughing at him ever since they married. Since the war, she had taken to calling him names like Little Hitler, and Storm-trooper. "Go ahead, my little Hitler," she had cried last time they met. "Go ahead, my Storm-trooper. If you want to waste your money on private detectives, go ahead. But don't think I don't know what *you* do when you're in the bush. I don't care what you do, but remember that I know it . . ."

The Captain remembered her saying it. And there sat Michele on his packing-case, saying: "It's a pleasure for the rich, my friend, detectives and the law. Even jealousy is a pleasure I don't want any more. Ah, my friend, to be together with my wife again, and the children, that is all I ask of life. That and wine and food and singing in the evenings." And the tears wetted his cheeks and splashed on to his shirt.

That a man should cry, good lord! thought the Captain. And without shame! He seized the bottle and drank.

Three days before the great occasion, some high-ranking officers came strolling through the dust, and found Michele and the Captain sitting together on the packing-case, singing. The Captain's shirt was open down the front, and there were stains on it.

The Captain stood to attention with the bottle in his hand, and Michele stood to attention too, out of sympathy with his friend. Then the officers drew the Captain aside—they were all cronies of his—and said, what the hell did he think he was doing? And why wasn't the village finished?

Then they went away.

"Tell them it is finished," said Michele. "Tell them I want to go."

"No," said the Captain, "no. Michele, what would you do if your wife . . ."

"This world is a good place. We should be happy—that is all."

"Michele . . ."

"I want to go. There is nothing to do. They paid me yesterday."

"Sit down, Michele. Three more days, and then it's finished."

"Then I shall paint the inside of the church as I painted the one in the camp."

The Captain laid himself down on some boards and went to sleep. When he woke, Michele was surrounded by the pots of paint he had used on the outside of the village. Just in front of the Captain was a picture of a black girl. She was young and plump. She wore a patterned blue dress and her shoulders came soft and bare out of it. On her back was a baby slung in a band of red stuff. Her face was turned towards the Captain and she was smiling.

"That's Nadya," said the Captain. "Nadya . . ." He groaned loudly. He looked at the black child and shut his eyes. He opened them, and mother and child were still there. Michele was very carefully drawing thin yellow circles around the heads of the black girl and her child.

"Good God," said the Captain, "you can't do that."

"Why not?"

"You can't have a black Madonna."

"She was a peasant. This is a peasant. Black peasant Madonna for black country."

"This is a German village," said the Captain.

"This is my Madonna," said Michele angrily. "Your German village and my Madonna. I paint this picture as an offering to the Madonna. She is pleased—I feel it."

The Captain lay down again. He was feeling ill. He went back to sleep. When he woke for the second time it was dark. Michele had brought in a flaring paraffin lamp, and by its light was working on the long wall. A bottle of brandy stood beside him. He painted until long after midnight, and the Captain lay on his side and watched, as passive as a man suffering a dream. Then they both went to sleep on the boards. The whole of the next day Michele stood painting black Madonnas, black saints, black angels. Outside, troops were practising in the sunlight, bands were blaring and motorcyclists roared up and down. But Michele painted on, drunk and oblivious. The Captain lay on his back, drinking and muttering about his wife. Then he would say "Nadya, Nadya," and burst into sobs.

Towards nightfall the troops went away. The officers came back, and the Captain went off with them to show how the village sprang into being when the great lights at the end of the parade-ground were switched on. They all looked at the village in silence. They switched the lights off, and there were only the tall angular boards leaning like gravestones in the moonlight. On went the lights—and there was the village. They were silent, as if suspicious. Like the Captain, they seemed to feel it was not right. Uncanny it certainly was, but *that* was not it. Unfair—that was the word. It was cheating. And profoundly disturbing.

"Clever chap, that Italian of yours," said the General.

The Captain, who had been woodenly correct until this moment, suddenly came rocking up to the General, and steadied himself by laying his hand on the august shoulder. "Bloody Wops," he said. "Bloody kaffirs. Bloody . . . Tell you what, though, there's one Itie that's some good. Yes, there is. I'm telling you. He's a friend of mine, actually."

The General looked at him. Then he nodded at his underlings. The Captain was taken away for disciplinary purposes. It was decided, however, that he must be ill, nothing else could account for such behaviour. He was put to bed in his own room with a nurse to watch him.

He woke twenty-four hours later, sober for the first time in weeks. He slowly remembered what had happened. Then he sprang out of bed and rushed into his clothes. The nurse was just in time to see him run down the path and leap into his lorry.

He drove at top speed to the parade-ground, which was flooded with light in such a way that the village did not exist. Everything was in full swing. The cars were three deep around the square, with people on the running-boards and even the roofs. The grandstand was packed. Women dressed up as gipsies, country girls, Elizabethan court dames, and so on, wandered about with trays of ginger beer and sausage-rolls and programmes at five shillings each in aid of the war effort. On the square, troops deployed, obsolete machine-guns were being dragged up and down, bands played, and motorcyclists roared through flames.

As the Captain parked the lorry, all this activity ceased, and the lights went out. The Captain began running around the outside of the square to reach the place where the guns were hidden in a mess of net and branches. He was sobbing with the effort. He was a big man, and unused to exercise, and sodden with brandy. He had only one idea in his mind—to stop the guns firing, to stop them at all costs.

Luckily, there seemed to be a hitch. The lights were still out. The unearthly graveyard at the end of the square glittered white in the moonlight. Then the lights briefly switched on, and the village sprang into existence for just long enough to show large red crosses all over a white building beside the church. Then moonlight flooded everything again, and the crosses vanished. "Oh, the bloody fool!" sobbed the Captain, running, running as if for his life. He was no longer trying to reach the guns. He was cutting across a corner of the square direct to the church. He could hear some officers cursing behind him: "Who put those red crosses there? Who? We can't fire on the Red Cross."

The Captain reached the church as the searchlights burst on. Inside, Michele was kneeling on the earth looking at his first Madonna. "They are going to kill my Madonna," he said miserably.

"Come away, Michele, come away."

"They're going to . . ."

The Captain grabbed his arm and pulled. Michele wrenched himself free and grabbed a saw. He began hacking at the ceiling board. There was a dead silence outside. They heard a voice booming through the loudspeakers: "The village that is about to be shelled is an English village, not as represented on the programme, a German village. Repeat, the village that is about to be shelled is . . ."

Michele had cut through two sides of a square around the Madonna.

"Michele," sobbed the Captain, "*get out of here.*"

Michele dropped the saw, took hold of the raw edges of the board and tugged. As he did so, the church began to quiver and lean. An irregular patch of board ripped out and Michele staggered back into the Captain's arms. There was a roar. The church seemed to dissolve around them into flame. Then they were running away from it, the Captain holding Michele tight by the arm. "Get down," he shouted suddenly, and threw Michele to the earth. He flung himself down beside him. Looking from under the crook of his arm, he heard the explosion, saw a great pillar of smoke and flame, and the village disintegrated in a flying mass of debris. Michele was on his knees gazing at his Madonna in the light from the flames. She was unrecognizable, blotted out with dust. He looked horrible, quite white, and a trickle of blood soaked from his hair down one cheek.

"They shelled my Madonna," he said.

"Oh, damn it, you can paint another one," said the Captain. His own voice seemed to him strange, like a dream voice. He was certainly crazy, as mad as Michele himself . . . He got up, pulled Michele to his feet, and marched him towards the edge of the field. There they were met by the ambulance people. Michele was taken off to hospital, and the Captain was sent back to bed.

A week passed. The Captain was in a darkened room. That he was having some kind of a breakdown was clear, and two nurses stood guard over him. Sometimes he lay quiet. Sometimes he muttered to himself. Sometimes he sang in a thick clumsy voice bits out of opera, fragments from Italian songs, and—over and over again—"There's a Long Long Trail." He was not thinking of anything at all. He shied away from the thought of Michele as if it were dangerous. When, therefore, a cheerful female voice announced that a friend had come to cheer him up, and it would do him good to have some company, and he saw a white bandage moving towards him in the gloom, he turned sharp over on to his side, face to the wall.

"Go away," he said. "Go away, Michele."

"I have come to see you," said Michele. "I have brought you a present."

The Captain slowly turned over. There was Michele, a cheerful ghost in the dark room. "You fool," he said. "You messed everything up. What did you paint those crosses for?"

"It was a hospital," said Michele. "In a village there is a hospital, and on the hospital the Red Cross, the beautiful Red Cross—no?"

"I was nearly court-martialled."

"It was my fault," said Michele. "I was drunk."

"I was responsible."

"How could you be responsible when I did it? But it is all over. Are you better?"

"Well, I suppose those crosses saved your life."

"I did not think," said Michele. "I was remembering the kindness of the Red Cross people when we were prisoners."

"Oh shut up, shut up, shut up."

"I have brought you a present."

The Captain peered through the dark. Michele was holding up a picture. It was of a native woman with a baby on her back smiling sideways out of the frame.

Michele said: "You did not like the haloes. So this time, no haloes. For the Captain—no Madonna." He laughed. "You like it? It is for you. I painted it for you."

"God damn you!" said the Captain.

"You do not like it?" said Michele, very hurt.

The Captain closed his eyes. "What are you going to do next?" he asked tiredly.

Michele laughed again. "Mrs. Pannerhurst, the lady of the General, she wants me to paint her picture in her white dress. So I paint it."

"You should be proud to."

"Silly bitch. She thinks I am good. They know nothing—savages. Barbarians. Not you, Captain, you are my friend. But these people they know nothing."

The Captain lay quiet. Fury was gathering in him. He thought of the General's wife. He disliked her, but he had known her well enough.

"These people," said Michele. "They do not know a good picture from a bad picture. I paint, I paint, this way, that way. There is the picture—I look at it and laugh inside myself." Michele laughed out loud. "They say, he is a Michelangelo, this one, and try to cheat me out of my price. Michele—Michelangelo—that is a joke, no?"

The Captain said nothing.

"But for you I painted this picture to remind you of our good times with the village. You are my friend. I will always remember you."

The Captain turned his eyes sideways in his head and stared at the black girl. Her smile at him was half innocence, half malice.

"Get out," he said suddenly.

Michele came closer and bent to see the Captain's face. "You wish me to go?" He sounded unhappy. "You saved my life. I was a fool that night. But I was thinking of my offering to the Madonna —I was a fool, I say it myself. I was drunk, we are fools when we are drunk."

"Get out of here," said the Captain again.

For a moment the white bandage remained motionless. Then it swept downwards in a bow.

Michele turned towards the door.

"And take that bloody picture with you."

Silence. Then, in the dim light, the Captain saw Michele reach out for the picture, his white head bowed in profound obeisance. He straightened himself and stood to attention, holding the picture with one hand, and keeping the other stiff down his side. Then he saluted the Captain.

"Yes, *sir*," he said, and he turned and went out of the door with the picture.

The Captain lay still. He felt—what did he feel? There was a pain under his ribs. It hurt to breathe. He realized he was unhappy. Yes, a terrible unhappiness was filling him, slowly, slowly. He was unhappy because Michele had gone. Nothing had ever hurt the Captain in all his life as much as that mocking *Yes, sir*. Nothing. He turned his face to the wall and wept. But silently. Not a sound escaped him, for the fear the nurses might hear.

The Trinket Box

YES, but it was only recently, when it became clear that Aunt Maud really could not last much longer, that people began to ask all those questions which should have been asked, it seems now, so long ago.

Or perhaps it is the other way about: Aunt Maud, suddenly finding that innumerable nieces and nephews and cousins were beginning to take an interest in her, asking her to meet interesting people, was so disturbed to find herself pushed into the centre of the stage where she felt herself to be out of place, that she took to her bed where she could tactfully die?

Even here, lying on massed pillows, like a small twig that has been washed up against banks of smooth white sand, she is not left in peace. Distant relations who have done no more than send her Christmas cards once a year come in to see her, sit by her bed for hours at a time, send her flowers. But why? It is not merely that they want to know what London in the 'nineties was like for a young woman with plenty of money, although they wake her to ask: "Do tell us, do you remember the Oscar Wilde affair?" Her face puckers in a worried look, and she says: "Oscar Wilde? What? Oh yes, I read such an interesting book, it is in the library."

Perhaps Aunt Maud herself sees that pretty vivacious girl (there is a photograph of her in an album somewhere) as a character in a historical play. But what is that question which it seems everyone comes to ask, but does not ask, leaving at length rather subdued, even a little exasperated—perhaps because it is not like Aunt Maud to suggest unanswerable questions?

Where did it all begin? Some relation returned from a long holiday, and asking casually after the family said: "What! Aunt Maud still alive? Isn't she gone yet?" Is that how people began asking: "Well, but how old is she? Eighty? Ninety?"

"Nonsense, she can't be ninety."

"But she says she remembers . . ." And the names of old "incidents" crop up, the sort of thing one finds in dusty books of memoirs. They were another world. It seems impossible that living people can remember them, especially someone we know so well.

"She remembers earlier than that. She told me once—it must be twenty years ago now—of having left home years before the Boer War started. You can work that out for yourself."

"Even that only makes her seventy—eighty perhaps. Eighty is not old enough to get excited about."

"The Crimean War . . ." But now they laugh. "Come, come, she's not a hundred!"

No, she cannot be as much as that, but thirty years ago, no less, an old frail lady climbed stiffly but jauntily up the bank of a dried-up African river, where she was looking after a crowd of other people's children on a picnic, and remarked: "My old bones are getting creaky." Then she bought herself an ancient car. It was one of the first Ford models, and she went rattling in it over the bad corrugated roads and even over the veld, if there were no roads. And no one thought it extraordinary. Just as one did not think of her as an old maid, or a spinster, so one did not think of her as an old lady.

And then there was the way she used to move from continent to continent, from family to family, as a kind of unpaid servant. For she had no money at all by then: her brother the black sheep died and she insisted on giving up all her tiny capital to pay his debts. It was useless of course; he owed thousands, but no one could persuade her against it. "There are some things one has to do," she said. Now, lying in bed she says: "One doesn't want to be a nuisance," in her small faded voice; the same voice in which she used to announce, and not so very long ago: "I am going to South America as companion to Mrs. Fripp—she is so very very kind." For six months, then, she was prepared to wait hand and foot on an old lady years younger than herself simply for the sake of seeing South America? No, we can no longer believe it. We are forced to know that the thought of her aches and pains put warmth into Mrs. Fripp's voice when she asked Aunt Maud to go with her.

And from the Andes or the Christmas Islands, or some place as distant and preposterous as the Russian-Japanese war or the Morocco scramble seem to be in time, came those long long letters beginning: "That white dressing-jacket you gave me was so useful when I went to the mountains." She got so many presents from us all that now we feel foolish. They were not what she wanted, after all.

Then, before we expected it, someone would write and say: "By the way, did you know I have had Aunt Maud with me since Easter?" So she had come back from the Andes, or wherever it was? But why had she gone *there*? Was Anne having another baby perhaps?

Sitting up in bed surrounded by the cushions and photographs that framed her in the way other people's furniture frame them, always very early in the morning—she wrote letters from five to seven every day of her life—she answered in her tiny precise handwriting: "Jacko's leg is not quite healed yet, although I think he is well on the way to recovery. And then I shall be delighted to avail myself of your kind offer. I will be with you by the middle of . . ." Punctually to the hour she would arrive: the perfect guest. And when she left, because of the arrival of a baby or a sudden illness perhaps five hundred miles away or in another country, with what affectionate heart-warming gratitude she thanked us, until it was easy to forget the piles of mending, the delicious cooking, the nights and nights of nursing. A week after she had left would arrive the inevitable parcel, containing presents so apt that it was with an uneasy feeling that we sat down to write thanks. How did she come to know our most secret wants? And, imperceptibly, the unease would grow to resentment. She had no right, no right at all, to give such expensive presents when she was dependent on relations for her support.

So it was that after every visit a residue of spite and irritation remained. And perhaps she intended that the people she served should never have to feel the embarrassment of gratitude? Perhaps she intended us—who knows?—to think as we sat writing our thank-yous: But after all, she has to live on us, it is after all a kindness to feed and house her for a few weeks.

It is all intolerable, intolerable; and it seems now that we must march into that bedroom to ask: "Aunt Maud, how did you bear it? How could you stand, year in and year out, pouring out your treasures of affection to people who hardly noticed you? Do you realize, Aunt Maud, that now, thirty years or more after you became our servant, it is the first time that we are really aware you were ever alive? What do you say to that, Aunt Maud? *Or did you know it all the time . . .*" For that is what we want to be sure of: that she did not know it, that she never will.

We wander restlessly in and out of her room, watching that expression on her face which—now that she is too ill to hide what she feels—makes us so uneasy. She looks impatient when she sees us; she wishes we would go away. Yesterday she said: "One does not care for this kind of attention."

All the time, all over the house, people sit about, talking, talking, in low urgent voices, as if something vital and precious is leaking away as they wait.

"She *can't* be exactly the same, it is impossible!"

"But I tell you, I remember her on the day the war started—the old war, you know. On the platform, waving goodbye to my son. She was the same, wrinkle for wrinkle. That little patch of yellow on her cheek—like an egg-stain. And those little mauveish eyes, and that funny little voice. People don't talk like that now, each syllable sounding separately."

"Her eyes have changed though." We sneak in to have a look at her. She turns them on us, peering over the puffs of a pink bed-jacket—eyes where a white film is gathering. Unable to see us clearly, afraid—she who has sat by so many death-beds—of distressing us by her unsightliness, she turns away her head, lies back, folds her hands, is silent.

When other people die, it is a thing of horror, swellings, gross flesh, smells, sickness. But Aunt Maud dies as a leaf shrivels. It seems that a little dryish gasp, a little shiver, and the papery flesh will crumble and leave beneath the bedclothes she scarcely disturbs a tiny white skeleton. That is how she is dying, giving the least possible trouble to the niece who waited sharp-sightedly for someone else to use the phrase "a happy release" before she used it herself. "She might not eat anything, but one has to prepare the tray all the same. And then, there are all these people in the house."

"Before she retired, what did she do?"

"Taught, didn't you know? She was forty when her father married again, and she went out and took a post in a school. He never spoke one word to her afterwards."

"But why, why?"

"He was in the wrong of course. She didn't marry so as to look after him."

"Oh, so she might have married? Who was he?"

"Old John Jordan, do you remember?"

"But he died before I left school—such a funny old man!"

Impossible to ask why she never married. But someone asks it. A great-niece, very young, stands beside the bed and looks down with shivering distaste at such age, such death: "Aunt Maud, why did you never marry?"

"Marry! Marry! Who is talking about marrying?" she sounds angered and sullen; then the small eyes film over and she says: "Who did you say is getting married?"

The niece is banished and there are no more questions.

No more visitors either, the doctor says. A question of hours. A few hours, and that casket of memories and sensations will have vanished. It is monstrous that a human being who has survived miraculously and precariously so many decades of wars, illnesses and accidents should die at last, leaving behind nothing.

Now we sit about the bed where she lies and wait for her to die. There is nothing to do. No one stirs. We are all sitting, looking, thinking, surreptitiously touching the things that belonged to her, trying to catch a glimpse, even for a moment, of the truth that will vanish in such a little while.

And if we think of the things that interested her, the enthusiasms we used to laugh at, because it seemed so odd that such an old lady should feel strongly about these great matters, what answer do we get? She was a feminist, first and foremost. The Pankhursts, she said, "were so devoted." She was a socialist; she had letters from Keir Hardie. There had been no one like him since he died. She defended vegetarians, but would not be one herself, because it gave people so much trouble in the kitchen. Madame Curie, Charles Lindbergh, Marie Corelli, Lenin, Clara Butt—these were her Idols, and she spoke of them in agitated defiance as if they were always in need of defence. Inside that tiny shrivelled skull what an extraordinary gallery of heroes and heroines. But there is no answer there. No matter how hard we try, fingering her handkerchief sachet, thinking of the funny flat hats she wore, draped with bits of Liberty cottons, remembering how she walked, as if at any moment she might be called upon to scale a high wall, she eludes us. Let us resign ourselves to it and allow her to die.

Then she speaks, after such long hours of waiting it is as if a woman already dead were speaking. Now, now!! We lean forward, waiting for her to say just that one thing, the perfect word of forgiveness that will leave us healed and whole.

She has made her will, she says, and it is with the lawyer "who has always been so kind" to her. She has nothing to leave but a few personal trinkets . . . The small precise voice is breathless, and she keeps her eyes tight shut. "I have told my lawyer that my possessions, such as they are, are kept in my black trinket box in the cupboard there. He knows. Everything is in order. I put everything right when people became so kind and I knew I was ill."

And that is the last thing she will ever say. We wait intently, shifting our feet and avoiding each other's eyes for fear that our guilty glances may imprint upon our memories of her the terrible knowledge let slip in the order of the words of that final sentence. We do not want to remember her with guilt, oh no! But although we wait, straining, nothing else comes; she seems to be asleep, and slowly we let our limbs loosen and think of the black box. In it we will find the diaries, or the bundle of letters which will say what she refuses to say. Oh most certainly we will find something of that sort. She cannot die like this, leaving nothing. There will be evidence of a consumed sorrow, at the least, something that will put substance into this barrenness. And when at last we look up, glancing at our watches, we see there is a stillness in the tiny white face which means she is dead.

We get up, rather stiffly, because of the hours of sitting, and then after a decent interval open the black box. It is full to the brim with bits of lace and ribbon, scraps of flowery stuffs, buckles, braid, brooches, cheap glass necklaces. Each has a bit of paper pinned to it. "These buttons I thought would do for the frock Alice was making when I was there last month." And: "To little Robin with my fond love. I bought this glass peacock in Cape Town in 1914 for another little boy." And so on, each of us has something. And when we come to the end and search for the diaries and letters there is nothing! Secretively each of us taps at the wood of the bottom— but no, it is solid. And we put back the things and we feel for the first time that Aunt Maud is dead. We want to cry. We would, if it were not absurd to cry for an old woman whom none of us wanted. What would she say if she saw those tears? "One cannot help feeling it would have been more useful to feel for me when I was still alive"? No, she would never say a thing like that; but we can have no illusions now, after that last remark of hers, which revealed the Aunt Maud she had been so carefully concealing all these years. And she would know we were not weeping for her at all.

We cannot leave the black box. We finger the laces, stroke the wood. We come back to it again and again, where it lies on the table in the room in which she is waiting for the funeral people.

We do not look at her, who is now no more than a tiny bundle under the clothes. And slowly, slowly, in each of us, an emotion hardens which is painful because it can never be released. Protest, is that what we are feeling? But certainly a protest without bitterness, for she was never bitter. And without pity, for one cannot imagine Aunt Maud pitying herself. What, then, is left? Are we expected to go on, for the rest of our lives (which we hope will be as long as hers) feeling this intolerable ache, a dull and sorrowful rage? And if we all feel, suddenly, that it is not to be borne, and we must leap up from our chairs and bang our fists against the wall screaming: "No, no! It can't all be for nothing!"—then we must restrain ourselves and remain quietly seated; for we can positively hear the scrupulous little voice saying: "There are some things one does not do."

Slowly, slowly, we become still before the box, and now it seems that we hold Aunt Maud in the hollow of our palms. That was what she was; now we know her.

So it comes to this: we are grown proud and honest out of the knowledge of her honesty and pride and, measuring ourselves against her, we allow ourselves to feel only the small, persistent, but gently humorous anger she must have felt. Only anger, that is permissible, she would allow that. But against what? Against what?

The Pig

THE farmer paid his labourers on a Saturday evening, when the sun went down. By the time he had finished it was always quite dark, and from the kitchen door where the lantern hung, bars of yellow light lay down the steps, across the path, and lit up the trees and the dark faces under them.

This Saturday, instead of dispersing as usual when they took their money, they retired a little way into the dark under the foliage, talking among themselves to pass the time. When the last one had been paid, the farmer said: "Call the women and the children. Everybody in the compound must be here." The boss-boy, who had been standing beside the table calling out names, stood forward and repeated the order. But in an indifferent voice, as a matter of form, for all this had happened before, every year for years past. Already there was a subdued moving at the back of the crowd as the women came in from under the trees where they had been waiting; and the light caught a bunched skirt, a copper armlet, or a bright headcloth.

Now all the dimly-lit faces showed hope that soon this ritual would be over, and they could get back to their huts and their fires. They crowded closer without being ordered.

The farmer began to speak, thinking as he did so of his lands that lay all about him, invisible in the darkness, but sending on the wind a faint rushing noise like the sea; and although he had done this before so often, and was doing it now half-cynically, knowing it was a waste of time, the memory of how good those fields of strong young plants looked when the sun shone on them put urgency and even anger into his voice.

The trouble was that every year black hands stripped the cobs from the stems in the night, sacks of cobs; and he could never catch the thieves. Next morning he would see the prints of bare feet in the dust between the rows. He had tried everything, had warned, threatened, docked rations, even fined the whole compound collectively—it made no difference. The lands lying next to the compound would be cheated of their yield, and when the harvesters brought in their loads, everyone knew there would be less than what had been expected.

And if everyone knew it, why put on this display for the tenth time? That was the question the farmer saw on the faces in front of him; polite faces turning this way and that over impatient bodies and shifting feet. They were thinking only of the huts and the warm meal waiting for them. The philosophic politeness, almost condescension, with which he was being treated infuriated the farmer; and he stopped in the middle of a sentence, banging on the table with his fist, so that the faces centred on him and the feet stilled.

"Jonas," said the farmer. Out on to the lit space stepped a tall elderly man with a mild face. But now he looked sombre. The farmer saw that look and braced himself for a fight. This man had been on the farm for several years. An old scoundrel, the farmer called him, but affectionately: he was fond of him, for they had been together for so long. Jonas did odd jobs for half the year; he drew water for the garden, cured hides, cut grass. But when the growing season came he was an important man.

"Come here, Jonas," the farmer said again; and picked up the .33 rifle that had been leaning against his chair until now. During the rainy season, Jonas slept out his days in his hut, and spent his nights till the cold dawns came guarding the fields from the buck and the pigs that attacked the young plants. They could lay waste whole acres in one night, a herd of pigs. He took the rifle, greeting it, feeling its familiar weight on his arm. But he looked reluctant nevertheless.

"This year, Jonas, you will shoot everything you see—understand?"

"Yes, baas."

"Everything, buck, baboons, pig. And everything you hear. You will not stop to look. If you hear a noise, you will shoot."

There was a movement among the listening people, and soft protesting noises.

"And if it turns out to be a human pig, then so much the worse. My lands are no place for pigs of any kind."

Jonas said nothing, but he turned towards the others, holding the rifle uncomfortably on his arm, appealing that they should not judge him.

"You can go," said the farmer. After a moment the space in front of him was empty, and he could hear the sound of bare feet feeling their way along dark paths, the sound of loudening angry talk. Jonas remained beside him.

"Well, Jonas?"

"I do not want to shoot this year."

The farmer waited for an explanation. He was not disturbed at the order he had given. In all the years he had worked this farm no one had been shot, although every season the thieves moved at night along the mealie rows, and every night Jonas was out with a gun. For he would shout, or fire the gun into the air, to frighten intruders. It was only when dawn came that he fired at something he could see. All this was a bluff. The threat might scare off a few of the more timid; but both sides knew, as usual, that it was a bluff. The cobs would disappear; nothing could prevent it.

"And why not?" asked the farmer at last.

"It's my wife. I wanted to see you about it before," said Jonas, in dialect.

"Oh, your wife!" The farmer had remembered. Jonas was old-fashioned. He had two wives, an old one who had borne him several children, and a young one who gave him a good deal of trouble. Last year, when this wife was new, he had not wanted to take on this job which meant being out all night.

"And what is the matter with the day-time?" asked the farmer with waggish good-humour, exactly as he had the year before. He got up, and prepared to go inside.

Jonas did not reply. He did not like being appointed official guardian against theft by his own people, but even that did not matter so much, for it never once occurred to him to take the order literally. This was only the last straw. He was getting on in years now, and he wanted to spend his nights in peace in his own hut, instead of roaming the bush. He had disliked it very much last year, but now it was even worse. A younger man visited his pretty young wife when he was away.

Once he had snatched up a stick, in despair, to beat her with;

then he had thrown it down. He was old, and the other man was
young, and beating her could not cure his heartache. Once he had
come up to his master to talk over the situation, as man to man;
but the farmer had refused to do anything. And, indeed, what could
he do? Now, repeating what he had said then, the farmer spoke
from the kitchen steps, holding the lamp high in one hand above
his shoulder as he turned to go in, so that it sent beams of light
swinging across the bush: "I don't want to hear anything about
your wife, Jonas. You should look after her yourself. And if you
are not too old to take a young wife, then you aren't too old to
shoot. You will take the gun as usual this year. Good night." And he
went inside, leaving the garden black and pathless. Jonas stood
quite still, waiting for his eyes to accustom themselves to the dark;
then he started off down the path, finding his way by the feel of the
loose stones under his feet.

He had not yet eaten, but when he came to within sight of the
compound, he felt he could not go farther. He halted, looking at
the little huts silhouetted black against cooking fires that sent up
great drifting clouds of illuminated smoke. There was his hut, he
could see it, a small conical shape. There his wives were, waiting
with his food prepared and ready.

But he did not want to eat. He felt he could not bear to go in
and face his old wife, who mocked him with her tongue, and his
young wife who answered him submissively but mocked him with
her actions. He was sick and tormented, cut off from his friends
who were preparing for an evening by the fires, because he could
see the knowledge of his betrayal in their eyes. The cold pain of
jealousy that had been gnawing at him for so long, felt now like an
old wound, aching as an old wound aches before the rains set in.

He did not want to go into the fields, either to perch until he
was stiff in one of the little cabins on high stilts that were built at
the corners of each land as shooting platforms, or to walk in the
dark through the hostile bush. But that night, without going for his
food, he set off as usual on his long vigil.

The next night, however, he did not go; nor the next, nor the
nights following. He lay all day dozing in the sun on his blanket,
turning himself over and over in the sun, as if its rays could cau-
terize the ache from his heart. When evening came, he ate his
meal early before going off with the gun. And then he stood with
his back to a tree, within sight of the compound; indeed, within
a stone's throw of his own hut, for hours, watching silently. He felt
numb and heavy. He was there without purpose. It was as if his

legs had refused an order to march away from the place. All that week the lands lay unguarded, and if the wild animals were raiding the young plants, he did not care. He seemed to exist only in order to stand at night watching his hut. He did not allow himself to think of what was happening inside. He merely watched; until the fires burned down, and the bush grew cold and he was so stiff that when he went home, at sunrise, he had the appearance of one exhausted after a night's walking.

The following Saturday there was a beer drink. He could have got leave to attend it, had he wanted; but at sundown he took himself off as usual and saw that his wife was pleased when he left.

As he leaned his back to the tree trunk that gave him its support each night, and held the rifle lengthwise to his chest, he fixed his eyes steadily on the dark shape that was his hut, and remembered that look on his young wife's face. He allowed himself to think steadily of it, and of many similar things. He remembered the young man, as he had seen him only a few days before, bending over the girl as she knelt to grind meal, laughing with her; then the way they both looked up, startled, at his approach, their faces growing blank.

He could feel his muscles tautening against the rifle as he pictured that scene, so that he set it down on the ground, for relief, letting his arms fall. But in spite of the pain, he continued to think, for tonight things were changed in him, and he no longer felt numb and purposeless. He stood erect and vigilant, letting the long cold barrel slide between his fingers, the hardness of the tree at his back like a second spine. And as he thought of the young man another picture crept into his mind again and again, that of a young waterbuck he had shot last year, lying soft at his feet, its tongue slipping out into the dust as he picked it up, so newly dead that he imagined he felt the blood still pulsing under the warm skin. And from the small wet place under its neck a few sticky drops rolled over glistening fur. Suddenly, as he stood there thinking of the blood, and the limp dead body of the buck, and the young man laughing with his wife, his mind grew clear and cool and the oppression on him lifted.

He sighed deeply, and picked up the rifle again, holding it close, like a friend, against him, while he gazed in through the trees at the compound.

It was early, and the flush from sunset had not yet quite gone from the sky, although where he stood among the undergrowth it was night. In the clear spaces between the huts groups of figures took shape, talking and laughing and getting ready for the dance. Small cooking fires were being lit; and a big central fire blazed, sending up showers of sparks into the clouds of smoke. The tom-toms were beating softly; soon the dance would begin. Visitors were coming in through the bush from other farm compounds miles away: it would be a long wait.

Three times he heard soft steps along the path close to him before he drew back and turned his head to watch the young man pass, as he had passed every night that week, with a jaunty eager tread and eyes directed towards Jonas's hut. Jonas stood as quiet as a tree struck by lightning, holding his breath, although he could not be seen, because the thick shadows from the trees were black around him. He watched the young man thread his way through the huts into the circle of firelight, and pass cautiously to one side of the groups of waiting people, like someone uncertain of his welcome, before going in through the door of his own hut.

Hours passed, and he watched the leaping dancing people, and listened to the drums as the stars swung over his head and the night birds talked in the bush around him. He thought steadily now, as he had not previously allowed himself to think, of what was happening inside the small dark hut that gradually became invisible as the fires died and the dancers went to their blankets. When the moon was small and high and cold behind his back, and the trees threw sharp black shadows on the path, and he could smell morning on the wind, he saw the young man coming towards him again. Now Jonas shifted his feet a little, to ease the stiffness out of them, and moved the rifle along his arm, feeling for the curve of the trigger on his finger.

As the young man lurched past, for he was tired, and moved carelessly, Jonas slipped out into the smooth dusty path a few paces behind, shrinking back as the released branches swung wet into his face and scattered large drops of dew on to his legs. It was cold; his breath misted into a thin pearly steam dissolving into the moonlight.

He was so close to the man in front that he could have touched him with the raised rifle; had he turned there would have been no concealment; but Jonas walked confidently, though carefully, and thought all the time of how he had shot down from ten paces away that swift young buck as it started with a crash out of a bush into a cold moony field.

When they reached the edge of the land where acres of mealies sloped away, dimly green under a dome of stars, Jonas began to walk like a cat. He wanted now to be sure; and he was only fifty yards from the shooting platform in the corner of the field, that looked in this light like a crazy fowl-house on stilts. The young man was staggering with tiredness and drink, making a crashing noise at each step as he snapped the sap-full mealies under heavy feet.

But the buck had shot like a spear from the bush, had caught the lead in its chest as it leaped, had fallen as a spear curves to earth; it had not blundered and lurched and swayed. Jonas began to feel a disgust for this man, and the admiration and fascination he felt for his young rival vanished. The tall slim youth who had laughed down at his wife had nothing to do with the ungainly figure crashing along before him, making so much noise that there could be no game left unstartled for miles.

When they reached the shooting platform, Jonas stopped dead, and let the youth move on. He lifted the rifle to his cheek and saw the long barrel slant against the stars, which sent a glint of light back down the steel. He waited, quite still, watching the man's back sway above the mealies. Then, at the right moment, he squeezed his finger close, holding the rifle ready to fire again.

As the sound of the shot reverberated, the round dark head jerked oddly, blotting out fields of stars; the body seemed to crouch, and one hand went out as if he were going to lean sideways to the ground. Then he disappeared into the mealies with a startled thick cry. Jonas lowered the rifle and listened. There was threshing noise, a horrible grunting, and half-words muttered, like someone talking in sleep.

Jonas picked his way along the rows, feeling the sharp leaf edges scything his legs, until he stood above the body that now jerked softly among the stems. He waited until it stilled, then bent to look, parting the chilled, moon-green leaves so that he could see clearly.

It was no clean small hole: raw flesh gaped, blood poured black to the earth, the limbs were huddled together shapeless and without beauty, the face was pressed into the soil.

"A pig," said Jonas aloud to the listening moon, as he kicked the side gently with his foot, "nothing but a pig."

He wanted to hear how it would sound when he said it again, telling how he had shot blind into the grunting, invisible herd.

Traitors

WE HAD discovered the Thompsons' old house long before their first visit.

At the back of our house the ground sloped up to where the bush began, an acre of trailing pumpkin vines, ash-heaps where pawpaw trees sprouted, and lines draped with washing where the wind slapped and jiggled. The bush was dense and frightening, and the grass there higher than a tall man. There were not even paths.

When we had tired of our familiar acre we explored the rest of the farm: but this particular stretch of bush was avoided. Sometimes we stood at its edge, and peered in at the tangled granite outcrops and great antheaps curtained with Christmas fern. Sometimes we pushed our way in a few feet, till the grass closed behind us, leaving overhead a small space of blue. Then we lost our heads and ran back again.

Later, when we were given our first rifle and a new sense of bravery, we realised we had to challenge that bush. For several days we hesitated, listening to the guinea fowl calling only a hundred yards away, and making excuses for cowardice. Then, one morning, at sunrise, when the trees were pink and gold, and the grass-stems were running bright drops of dew, we looked at each other, smiling weakly, and slipped into the bushes with our hearts beating.

At once we were alone, closed in by grass, and we had to reach out for the other's dress and cling together. Slowly, heads down, eyes half closed against the sharp grass-seeds, two small girls pushed their way past antheap and outcrop, past thorn and gully and thick clumps of cactus where any wild animal might lurk.

Suddenly, after only five minutes of terror, we emerged in a space where the red earth was scored with cattle tracks. The guinea fowl were clinking ahead of us in the grass, and we caught a glimpse of a shapely dark bird speeding along a path. We followed, shouting with joy because the forbidding patch of bush was as easily conquered and made our own as the rest of the farm.

We were stopped again where the ground dropped suddenly to the vlei, a twenty-foot shelf of flattened grass where the cattle went to water. Sitting, we lifted our dresses and coasted down-hill on the slippery swathes, landing with torn knickers and scratched knees in a donga of red dust scattered with dried cow-pats and bits of glistening quartz. The guinea fowl stood in a file and watched us, their heads tilted with apprehension; but my sister said, with bravado: "I am going to shoot a buck!"

She waved her arms at the birds and they scuttled off. We looked at each other and laughed, feeling too grown-up for guinea fowl now.

Here, down on the verges of the vlei, it was a different kind of bush. The grass was thinned by cattle, and red dust spurted as we walked. There were sparse thorn trees, and everywhere the poison-apple bush, covered with small fruit like yellow plums. Patches of wild marigold filled the air with a rank, hot smell.

Moving with exaggerated care, our bodies tensed, our eyes fixed half a mile off, we did not notice that a duiker stood watching us ten paces away. We yelled with excitement and the buck vanished. Then we ran like maniacs, screaming at the tops of our voices, while the bushes whipped our faces and the thorns tore our legs.

Ten minutes later we came slap up against a barbed fence. "The boundary," we whispered, awed. This was a legend; we had imagined it as a sort of Wall of China, for beyond were thousands and thousands of miles of unused Government land where there were leopards and baboons and herds of koodoo. But we were disappointed: even the famous boundary was only a bit of wire after all, and the duiker was nowhere in sight.

Whistling casually to show we didn't care, we marched along by the wire, twanging it so that it reverberated half a mile away down in the vlei. Around us the bush was strange; this part of the farm was quite new to us. There was still nothing but thorn trees and grass; and fat wood-pigeons cooed from every branch. We swung on the fence stanchions and wished that Father would suddenly appear and take us home to breakfast. We were hopelessly lost.

It was then that I saw the pawpaw tree. I must have been staring at it for some minutes before it grew in on my sight; for it was such an odd place for a pawpaw tree to be. On it were three heavy yellow pawpaws.

"There's our breakfast," I said.

We shook them down, sat on the ground, and ate. The insipid, creamy flesh soon filled us, and we lay down, staring at the sky, half asleep. The sun blared down; we were melted through with heat and tiredness. But it was very hard. Turning over, staring, we saw worn bricks set into the ground. All round us were stretches of brick, stretches of cement.

"The old Thompson house," we whispered.

And all at once the pigeons seemed to grow still and the bush became hostile. We sat up, frightened. How was it we hadn't noticed it before? There was a double file of pawpaws among the thorns; a purple bougainvillaea tumbled over the bushes; a rose tree scattered white petals at our feet; and our shoes were scrunching in broken glass.

It was desolate, lonely, despairing; and we remembered the way our parents had talked about Mr. Thompson who had lived here for years before he married. Their hushed, disapproving voices seemed to echo out of the trees; and in a violent panic we picked up the gun and fled back in the direction of the house. We had imagined we were lost; but we were back in the gully in no time, climbed up it, half sobbing with breathlessness, and fled through that barrier of bush so fast we hardly noticed it was there.

It was not even breakfast time.

❦   ❦

"We found the Thompsons' old house," we said at last, feeling hurt that no one had noticed from our proud faces that we had found a whole new world that morning.

"Did you?" said Father absently. "Can't be much left of it now."

Our fear vanished. We hardly dared look at each other for shame. And later that day we went back and counted the pawpaws and trailed the bougainvillaea over a tree and staked the white rosebush.

In a week we had made the place entirely our own. We were there all day, sweeping the debris from the floor and carrying away loose bricks into the bush. We were not surprised to find dozens of empty bottles scattered in the grass. We washed them in a pothole in the vlei, dried them in the wind, and marked out the rooms of the house with them, making walls of shining bottles. In our imagination the Thompson house was built again, a small brick-walled place with a thatched roof.

We sat under a blazing sun, and said in our mother's voice: "It is always cool under thatch, no matter how hot it is outside." And then, when the walls and the roof had grown into our minds and we took them for granted, we played other games, taking it in turn to be Mr. Thompson.

Whoever was Mr. Thompson had to stagger in from the bush, with a bottle in her hand, tripping over the lintel and falling on the floor. There she lay and groaned, while the other fanned her and put handkerchiefs soaked in vlei water on her head. Or she reeled about among the bottles, shouting abusive gibberish at an invisible audience of natives.

It was while we were engaged thus, one day, that a black woman came out of the thorn trees and stood watching us. We waited for her to go, drawing together; but she came close and stared in a way that made us afraid. She was old and fat, and she wore a red print dress from the store. She said in a soft, wheedling voice: "When is Boss Thompson coming back?"

"Go away!" we shouted. And then she began to laugh. She sauntered off into the bush, swinging her hips and looking back over her shoulder and laughing. We heard that taunting laugh away among the trees; and that was the second time we ran away from the ruined house, though we made ourselves walk slowly and with dignity until we knew she could no longer see us.

For a few days we didn't go back to the house. When we did we stopped playing Mr. Thompson. We no longer knew him: that laugh, that slow, insulting stare had meant something outside our knowledge and experience. The house was not ours now. It was some broken bricks on the ground marked out with bottles. We couldn't pretend to ourselves we were not afraid of the place; and we continually glanced over our shoulders to see if the old black woman was standing silently there, watching us.

Idling along the fence, we threw stones at the pawpaws fifteen feet over our heads till they squashed at our feet. Then we kicked them into the bush.

"Why have you stopped going to the old house?" asked Mother cautiously, thinking that we didn't know how pleased she was. She had instinctively disliked our being there so much.

"Oh, I dunno . . ."

❦   ❦

A few days later we heard that the Thompsons were coming to see us; and we knew, without anyone saying anything, that this was no ordinary visit. It was the first time; they wouldn't be coming after all these years without some reason. Besides, our parents didn't like them coming. They were at odds with each other over it.

Mr. Thompson had lived on our farm for ten years before we had it, when there was no one else near for miles and miles. Then, suddenly, he went home to England and brought a wife back with him. The wife never came to this farm. Mr. Thompson sold the farm to us and bought another one. People said:

"Poor girl! Just out from home, too." She was angry about the house burning down, because it meant she had to live with friends for nearly a year while Mr. Thompson built a new house on his new farm.

The night before they came, Mother said several times in a strange, sorrowful voice, "Poor little thing; poor, poor little thing."

Father said: "Oh, I don't know. After all, be just. He was here alone all those years."

It was no good; she disliked not only Mr. Thompson but Father too, that evening; and we were on her side. She put her arms round us, and looked accusingly at Father. "Women get all the worst of everything," she said.

He said angrily: "Look here, it's not my fault these people are coming."

"Who said it was?" she answered.

❦   ❦

Next day, when the car came in sight, we vanished into the bush. We felt guilty, not because we were running away, a thing we often did when visitors came we didn't like, but because we had made Mr. Thompson's house our own, and because we were afraid if he saw our faces he would know we were letting Mother down by going.

We climbed into the tree that was our refuge on these occasions, and lay along branches twenty feet from the ground, and played at Mowgli, thinking all the time about the Thompsons.

As usual, we lost all sense of time; and when we eventually returned, thinking the coast must be clear, the car was still there. Curiosity got the better of us.

We slunk on to the verandah, smiling bashfully, while Mother gave us a reproachful look. Then, at last, we lifted our heads and looked at Mrs. Thompson. I don't know how we had imagined her; but we had felt for her a passionate, protective pity.

She was a large, blond, brilliantly coloured lady with a voice like a go-away bird's. It was a horrible voice. Father, who could not stand loud voices, was holding the arms of his chair, and gazing at her with exasperated dislike.

As for Mr. Thompson, that villain whom we had hated and feared, he was a shaggy and shambling man, who looked at the ground while his wife talked, with a small apologetic smile. He was not in the least as we had pictured him. He looked like our old dog. For a moment we were confused; then, in a rush, our allegiance shifted. The profound and dangerous pity, aroused in us earlier than we could remember by the worlds of loneliness inhabited by our parents, which they could not share with each other but which each shared with us, settled now on Mr. Thompson. Now we hated Mrs. Thompson. The outward sign of it was that we left Mother's chair and went to Father's.

"Don't fidget, there's good kids," he said.

Mrs. Thompson was asking to be shown the old house. We understood, from the insistent sound of her voice, that she had been talking about nothing else all afternoon; or that, at any rate, if she had, it was only with the intention of getting round to the house as soon as she could. She kept saying, smiling ferociously at Mr. Thompson: "I have heard such *interesting* things about that old place. I really must see for myself where it was that my husband lived before I came out . . ." And she looked at Mother for approval.

But Mother said dubiously: "It will soon be dark. And there is no path."

As for Father, he said bluntly: "There's nothing to be seen. There's nothing left."

"Yes, I heard it had been burnt down," said Mrs. Thompson with another look at her husband.

"It was a hurricane lamp . . ." he muttered.

"I want to see for myself."

At this point my sister slipped off the arm of my Father's chair, and said, with a bright, false smile at Mrs. Thompson, "We know where it is. We'll take you." She dug me in the ribs and sped off before anyone could speak.

At last they all decided to come. I took them the hardest, longest way I knew. We had made a path of our own long ago, but that would have been too quick. I made Mrs. Thompson climb over rocks, push through grass, bend under bushes. I made her scramble down the gully so that she fell on her knees in the sharp pebbles and the dust. I walked her so fast, finally, in a wide circle through the thorn trees that I could hear her panting behind me. But she wasn't complaining: she wanted to see the place too badly.

When we came to where the house had been it was nearly dark and the tufts of long grass were shivering in the night breeze, and the pawpaw trees were silhouetted high and dark against a red sky. Guinea fowl were clinking softly all around us.

My sister leaned against a tree, breathing hard, trying to look natural. Mrs. Thompson had lost her confidence. She stood quite still, looking about her, and we knew the silence and the desolation had got her, as it got us that first morning.

"But *where* is the house?" she asked at last, unconsciously softening her voice, staring as if she expected to see it rise out of the ground in front of her.

"I told you, it was burnt down. *Now* will you believe me?" said Mr. Thompson.

"I *know* it was burnt down . . . Well, where was it then?" She sounded as if she were going to cry. This was not at all what she had expected.

Mr. Thompson pointed at the bricks on the ground. He did not move. He stood staring over the fence down to the vlei, where the mist was gathering in long white folds. The light faded out of the sky, and it began to get cold. For a while no one spoke.

"What a godforsaken place for a house," said Mrs. Thompson, very irritably, at last. "Just as well it was burnt down. Do you mean to say you kids play here?"

That was our cue. "We like it," we said dutifully, knowing very well that the two of us standing on the bricks, hand in hand, beside the ghostly rosebush, made a picture that took all the harm out of the place for her. "We play here all day," we lied.

"Odd taste you've got," she said, speaking at us, but meaning Mr. Thompson.

Mr. Thompson did not hear her. He was looking around with a lost, remembering expression. "Ten years," he said at last. "Ten years I was here."

"More fool you," she snapped. And that closed the subject as far as she was concerned.

We began to trail home. Now the two women went in front;

then came Father and Mr. Thompson; we followed at the back. As
we passed a small donga under a cactus tree, my sister called in a
whisper, "Mr. Thompson, Mr. Thompson, look here."

Father and Mr. Thompson came back. "Look," we said, pointing
to the hole that was filled to the brim with empty bottles.

"I came quickly by a way of my own and hid them," said my sister proudly, looking at the two men like a conspirator.

Father was very uncomfortable. "I wonder how they got down
here?" he said politely at last.

"We found them. They were at the house. We hid them for you,"
said my sister, dancing with excitement.

Mr. Thompson looked at us sharply and uneasily. "You are an
odd pair of kids," he said.

That was all the thanks we got from him; for then we heard
Mother calling from ahead: "What are you all doing there?" And at
once we went forward.

After the Thompsons had left we hung around Father, waiting
for him to say something.

At last, when Mother wasn't there, he scratched his head in an
irritable way and said: "What in the world did you do that for?"

We were bitterly hurt. "*She* might have seen them," I said.

"Nothing would make much difference to that lady," he said at
last. "Still, I suppose you meant well."

We drifted off; we felt let down.

                    ℗   ℗

In the corner of the verandah, in the dark, sat Mother, gazing
into the dark bush. On her face was a grim look of disapproval, and
distaste and unhappiness. We were included in it, we knew that.

She looked at us crossly and said, "I don't like you wandering
over the farm the way you do. Even with a gun."

But she had said that so often, and it wasn't what we were waiting for. At last it came.

"My two little girls," she said, "out in the bush by themselves,
with no one to play with . . ."

It wasn't the bush she minded. We flung ourselves on her. Once
again we were swung dizzily from one camp to the other. "Poor
Mother," we said. "Poor, poor Mother."

That was what she needed. "It's no life for a woman, this," she
said, her voice breaking, gathering us close.

But she sounded comforted.

The Old Chief Mshlanga

THEY were good, the years of ranging the bush over her father's farm which, like every white farm, was largely unused, broken only occasionally by small patches of cultivation. In between, nothing but trees, the long sparse grass, thorn and cactus and gully, grass and outcrop and thorn. And a jutting piece of rock which had been thrust up from the warm soil of Africa unimaginable eras of time ago, washed into hollows and whorls by sun and wind that had travelled so many thousands of miles of space and bush, would hold the weight of a small girl whose eyes were sightless for anything but a pale willowed river, a pale gleaming castle—a small girl singing: "Out flew the web and floated wide, the mirror cracked from side to side . . ."

Pushing her way through the green aisles of the mealie stalks, the leaves arching like cathedrals veined with sunlight far overhead, with the packed red earth underfoot, a fine lace of red starred witchweed would summon up a black bent figure croaking premonitions: the Northern witch, bred of cold Northern forests, would stand before her among the mealie fields, and it was the mealie fields that faded and fled, leaving her among the gnarled roots of an oak, snow falling thick and soft and white, the woodcutter's fire glowing red welcome through crowding tree trunks.

A white child, opening its eyes curiously on a sun-suffused landscape, a gaunt and violent landscape, might be supposed to accept it as her own, to take the msasa trees and the thorn trees as familiars, to feel her blood running free and responsive to the swing of the seasons.

This child could not see a msasa tree, or the thorn, for what they were. Her books held tales of alien fairies, her rivers ran slow and peaceful, and she knew the shape of the leaves of an ash or an oak, the names of the little creatures that lived in English streams, when the words "the veld" meant strangeness, though she could remember nothing else.

Because of this, for many years, it was the veld that seemed unreal; the sun was a foreign sun, and the wind spoke a strange language.

The black people on the farm were as remote as the trees and the rocks. They were an amorphous black mass, mingling and thinning and massing like tadpoles, faceless, who existed merely to serve, to say "Yes, Baas," take their money and go. They changed season by season, moving from one farm to the next, according to their outlandish needs, which one did not have to understand, coming from perhaps hundreds of miles North or East, passing on after a few months—where? Perhaps even as far away as the fabled gold mines of Johannesburg, where the pay was so much better than the few shillings a month and the double handful of mealie meal twice a day which they earned in that part of Africa.

The child was taught to take them for granted: the servants in the house would come running a hundred yards to pick up a book if she dropped it. She was called "Nkosikaas"—Chieftainess, even by the black children her own age.

Later, when the farm grew too small to hold her curiosity, she carried a gun in the crook of her arm and wandered miles a day, from vlei to vlei, from *kopje* to *kopje*, accompanied by two dogs: the dogs and the gun were an armour against fear. Because of them she never felt fear.

If a native came into sight along the kaffir paths half a mile away, the dogs would flush him up a tree as if he were a bird. If he expostulated (in his uncouth language which was by itself ridiculous) that was cheek. If one was in a good mood, it could be a matter for laughter. Otherwise one passed on, hardly glancing at the angry man in the tree.

On the rare occasions when white children met together they could amuse themselves by hailing a passing native in order to make a buffoon of him; they could set the dogs on him and watch him run; they could tease a small black child as if he were a puppy

—save that they would not throw stones and sticks at a dog without a sense of guilt.

Later still, certain questions presented themselves in the child's mind; and because the answers were not easy to accept, they were silenced by an even greater arrogance of manner.

It was even impossible to think of the black people who worked about the house as friends, for if she talked to one of them, her mother would come running anxiously: "Come away; you mustn't talk to natives."

It was this instilled consciousness of danger, of something unpleasant, that made it easy to laugh out loud, crudely, if a servant made a mistake in his English or if he failed to understand an order—there is a certain kind of laughter that is fear, afraid of itself.

One evening, when I was about fourteen, I was walking down the side of a mealie field that had been newly ploughed, so that the great red clods showed fresh and tumbling to the vlei beyond, like a choppy red sea; it was that hushed and listening hour, when the birds send long sad calls from tree to tree, and all the colours of earth and sky and leaf are deep and golden. I had my rifle in the curve of my arm, and the dogs were at my heels.

In front of me, perhaps a couple of hundred yards away, a group of three Africans came into sight around the side of a big antheap. I whistled the dogs close in to my skirts and let the gun swing in my hand, and advanced, waiting for them to move aside, off the path, in respect for my passing. But they came on steadily, and the dogs looked up at me for the command to chase. I was angry. It was "cheek" for a native not to stand off a path, the moment he caught sight of you.

In front walked an old man, stooping his weight on to a stick, his hair grizzled white, a dark red blanket slung over his shoulders like a cloak. Behind him came two young men, carrying bundles of pots, assegais, hatchets.

The group was not a usual one. They were not natives seeking work. These had an air of dignity, of quietly following their own purpose. It was the dignity that checked my tongue. I walked quietly on, talking softly to the growling dogs, till I was ten paces away. Then the old man stopped, drawing his blanket close.

"Morning, Nkosikaas," he said, using the customary greeting for any time of the day.

"Good morning," I said. "Where are you going?" My voice was a little truculent.

The old man spoke in his own language, then one of the young men stepped forward politely and said in careful English: "My Chief travels to see his brothers beyond the river."

A Chief! I thought, understanding the pride that made the old man stand before me like an equal—more than an equal, for he showed courtesy, and I showed none.

The old man spoke again, wearing dignity like an inherited garment, still standing ten paces off, flanked by his entourage, not looking at me (that would have been rude) but directing his eyes somewhere over my head at the trees.

"You are the little Nkosikaas from the farm of Baas Jordan?"

"That's right," I said.

"Perhaps your father does not remember," said the interpreter for the old man, "but there was an affair with some goats. I remember seeing you when you were . . ." The young man held his hand at knee level and smiled.

We all smiled.

"What is your name?" I asked.

"This is Chief Mshlanga," said the young man.

"I will tell my father that I met you," I said.

The old man said: "My greetings to your father, little Nkosikaas."

"Good morning," I said politely, finding the politeness difficult, from lack of use.

"Morning, little Nkosikaas," said the old man, and stood aside to let me pass.

I went by, my gun hanging awkwardly, the dogs sniffing and growling, cheated of their favourite game of chasing natives like animals.

Not long afterwards I read in an old explorer's book the phrase: "Chief Mshlanga's country." It went like this: "Our destination was Chief Mshlanga's country, to the north of the river; and it was our desire to ask his permission to prospect for gold in his territory."

The phrase "ask his permission" was so extraordinary to a white child, brought up to consider all natives as things to use, that it revived those questions, which could not be suppressed: they fermented slowly in my mind.

On another occasion one of those old prospectors who still move over Africa looking for neglected reefs, with their hammers and tents, and pans for sifting gold from crushed rock, came to the farm and, in talking of the old days, used that phrase again: "This was the Old Chief's country," he said. "It stretched from those mountains over there way back to the river, hundreds of miles of country." That was his name for our district: "The Old Chief's Country"; he did not use our name for it—a new phrase which held no implication of usurped ownership.

As I read more books about the time when this part of Africa was opened up, not much more than fifty years before, I found Old Chief Mshlanga had been a famous man, known to all the explorers and prospectors. But then he had been young; or maybe it was his father or uncle they spoke of—I never found out.

During that year I met him several times in the part of the farm that was traversed by natives moving over the country. I learned that the path up the side of the big red field where the birds sang was the recognized highway for migrants. Perhaps I even haunted it in the hope of meeting him: being greeted by him, the exchange of courtesies, seemed to answer the questions that troubled me.

Soon I carried a gun in a different spirit; I used it for shooting food and not to give me confidence. And now the dogs learned better manners. When I saw a native approaching, we offered and took greetings; and slowly that other landscape in my mind faded, and my feet struck directly on the African soil, and I saw the shapes of tree and hill clearly, and the black people moved back, as it were, out of my life: it was as if I stood aside to watch a slow intimate dance of landscape and men, a very old dance, whose steps I could not learn.

But I thought: this is my heritage, too; I was bred here; it is my country as well as the black man's country; and there is plenty of room for all of us, without elbowing each other off the pavements and roads.

It seemed it was only necessary to let free that respect I felt when I was talking with old Chief Mshlanga, to let both black and white people meet gently, with tolerance for each other's differences: it seemed quite easy.

Then, one day, something new happened. Working in our house as servants were always three natives: cook, houseboy, garden boy. They used to change as the farm natives changed: staying for a few months, then moving on to a new job, or back home to their kraals. They were thought of as "good" or "bad" natives; which meant: how did they behave as servants? Were they lazy, efficient, obedient, or disrespectful? If the family felt good-humoured, the phrase was: "What can you expect from raw black savages?" If we were angry, we said: "These damned niggers, we would be much better off without them."

One day, a white policeman was on his rounds of the district, and he said laughingly: "Did you know you have an important man in your kitchen?"

"What!" exclaimed my mother sharply. "What do you mean?"

"A Chief's son." The policeman seemed amused. "He'll boss the tribe when the old man dies."

"He'd better not put on a Chief's son act with me," said my mother.

When the policeman left, we looked with different eyes at our cook: he was a good worker, but he drank too much at week-ends— that was how we knew him.

He was a tall youth, with very black skin, like black polished metal, his tightly-growing black hair parted white man's fashion at one side, with a metal comb from the store stuck into it; very polite, very distant, very quick to obey an order. Now that it had been pointed out, we said: "Of course, you can see. Blood always tells."

My mother became strict with him now she knew about his birth and prospects. Sometimes, when she lost her temper, she would say: "You aren't the Chief yet, you know." And he would answer her very quietly, his eyes on the ground: "Yes, Nkosikaas."

One afternoon he asked for a whole day off, instead of the customary half-day, to go home next Sunday.

"How can you go home in one day?"

"It will take me half an hour on my bicycle," he explained.

I watched the direction he took; and the next day I went off to look for this kraal; I understood he must be Chief Mshlanga's successor: there was no other kraal near enough our farm.

Beyond our boundaries on that side the country was new to me. I followed unfamiliar paths past *kopjes* that till now had been part of the jagged horizon, hazed with distance. This was Government land, which had never been cultivated by white men; at first I could not understand why it was that it appeared, in merely crossing the boundary, I had entered a completely fresh type of landscape. It was a wide green valley, where a small river sparkled, and vivid water-birds darted over the rushes. The grass was thick and soft to my calves, the trees stood tall and shapely.

I was used to our farm, whose hundreds of acres of harsh eroded soil bore trees that had been cut for the mine furnaces and had grown thin and twisted, where the cattle had dragged the grass flat, leaving innumerable criss-crossing trails that deepened each season into gullies, under the force of the rains.

This country had been left untouched, save for prospectors whose picks had struck a few sparks from the surface of the rocks as they wandered by; and for migrant natives whose passing had left, perhaps, a charred patch on the trunk of a tree where their evening fire had nestled.

It was very silent: a hot morning with pigeons cooing throatily, the midday shadows lying dense and thick with clear yellow spaces of sunlight between and in all that wide green park-like valley, not a human soul but myself.

I was listening to the quick regular tapping of a woodpecker when slowly a chill feeling seemed to grow up from the small of my back to my shoulders, in a constricting spasm like a shudder, and at the roots of my hair a tingling sensation began and ran down over the surface of my flesh, leaving me goosefleshed and cold, though I was damp with sweat. Fever? I thought; then uneasily, turned to look over my shoulder; and realized suddenly that this was fear. It was extraordinary, even humiliating. It was a new fear. For all the years I had walked by myself over this country I had never known a moment's uneasiness; in the beginning because I had been supported by a gun and the dogs, then because I had learnt an easy friendliness for the Africans I might encounter.

I had read of this feeling, how the bigness and silence of Africa, under the ancient sun, grows dense and takes shape in the mind, till even the birds seem to call menacingly, and a deadly spirit comes out of the trees and the rocks. You move warily, as if your very passing disturbs something old and evil, something dark and big and angry that might suddenly rear and strike from behind. You look at groves of entwined trees, and picture the animals that might be lurking there; you look at the river running slowly, dropping from level to level through the vlei, spreading into pools where at night the bucks come to drink, and the crocodiles rise and drag them by their soft noses into underwater caves. Fear possessed me. I found I was turning round and round, because of that shapeless menace behind me that might reach out and take me; I kept glancing at the files of *kopjes* which, seen from a different angle, seemed to change with every step so that even known landmarks, like a big mountain that had sentinelled my world since I first became conscious of it, showed an unfamiliar sunlit valley among its foothills. I did not know where I was. I was lost. Panic seized me. I found I was spinning round and round, staring anxiously at this tree and that, peering up at the sun which appeared to have moved into an eastern slant, shedding the sad yellow light of sunset.

Hours must have passed! I looked at my watch and found that this state of meaningless terror had lasted perhaps ten minutes.

The point was that it was meaningless. I was not ten miles from home: I had only to take my way back along the valley to find myself at the fence; away among the foothills of the *kopjes* gleamed the roof of a neighbour's house, and a couple of hours' walking would reach it. This was the sort of fear that contracts the flesh of a dog at night and sets him howling at the full moon. It had nothing to do with what I thought or felt; and I was more disturbed by the fact that I could become its victim than of the physical sensation itself: I walked steadily on, quietened, in a divided mind, watching my own pricking nerves and apprehensive glances from side to side with a disgusted amusement. Deliberately I set myself to think of this village I was seeking, and what I should do when I entered it—if I could find it, which was doubtful, since I was walking aimlessly and it might be anywhere in the hundreds of thousands of acres of bush that stretched about me. With my mind on that village, I realized that a new sensation was added to the fear: loneliness. Now such a terror of isolation invaded me that I could hardly walk; and if it were not that I came over the crest of a small rise and saw a village below me, I should have turned and gone home. It was a cluster of thatched huts in a clearing among trees. There were neat patches of mealies and pumpkins and millet, and cattle grazed under some trees at a distance. Fowls scratched among the huts, dogs lay sleeping on the grass, and goats friezed a *kopje* that jutted up beyond a tributary of the river lying like an enclosing arm round the village.

As I came close I saw the huts were lovingly decorated with patterns of yellow and red and ochre mud on the walls; and the thatch was tied in place with plaits of straw.

This was not at all like our farm compound, a dirty and neglected place, a temporary home for migrants who had no roots in it.

And now I did not know what to do next. I called a small black boy, who was sitting on a lot playing a stringed gourd, quite naked except for the strings of blue beads round his neck, and said: "Tell the Chief I am here." The child stuck his thumb in his mouth and stared shyly back at me.

For minutes I shifted my feet on the edge of what seemed a deserted village, till at last the child scuttled off, and then some women came. They were draped in bright cloths, with brass glinting in their ears and on their arms. They also stared, silently; then turned to chatter among themselves.

I said again: "Can I see Chief Mshlanga?" I saw they caught the name; they did not understand what I wanted. I did not understand myself.

At last I walked through them and came past the huts and saw a clearing under a big shady tree, where a dozen old men sat cross-legged on the ground, talking. Chief Mshlanga was leaning back against the tree, holding a gourd in his hand, from which he had been drinking. When he saw me, not a muscle of his face moved, and I could see he was not pleased: perhaps he was afflicted with my own shyness, due to being unable to find the right forms of courtesy for the occasion. To meet me, on our own farm, was one thing; but I should not have come here. What had I expected? I could not join them socially: the thing was unheard of. Bad enough that I, a white girl, should be walking the veld alone as a white man might: and in this part of the bush where only Government officials had the right to move.

Again I stood, smiling foolishly, while behind me stood the groups of brightly-clad, chattering women, their faces alert with curiosity and interest, and in front of me sat the old men, with old lined faces, their eyes guarded, aloof. It was a village of ancients and children and women. Even the two young men who kneeled beside the Chief were not those I had seen with him previously: the young men were all away working on the white men's farms and mines, and the Chief must depend on relatives who were temporarily on holiday for his attendants.

"The small white Nkosikaas is far from home," remarked the old man at last.

"Yes," I agreed, "it is far." I wanted to say: "I have come to pay you a friendly visit, Chief Mshlanga." I could not say it. I might now be feeling an urgent helpless desire to get to know these men and women as people, to be accepted by them as a friend, but the truth was I had set out in a spirit of curiosity: I had wanted to see the village that one day our cook, the reserved and obedient young man who got drunk on Sundays, would one day rule over.

"The child of Nkosi Jordan is welcome," said Chief Mshlanga.

"Thank you," I said, and could think of nothing more to say. There was a silence, while the flies rose and began to buzz around my head; and the wind shook a little in the thick green tree that spread its branches over the old men.

"Good morning," I said at last. "I have to return now to my home."

"Morning, little Nkosikaas," said Chief Mshlanga.

I walked away from the indifferent village, over the rise past the staring amber-eyed goats, down through the tall stately trees into the great rich green valley where the river meandered and the pigeons cooed tales of plenty and the woodpecker tapped softly.

The fear had gone; the loneliness had set into stiff-necked stoicism; there was now a queer hostility in the landscape, a cold, hard, sullen indomitability that walked with me, as strong as a wall, as intangible as smoke; it seemed to say to me: you walk here as a destroyer. I went slowly homewards, with an empty heart: I had learned that if one cannot call a country to heel like a dog, neither can one dismiss the past with a smile in an easy gush of feeling, saying: I could not help it, I am also a victim.

I only saw Chief Mshlanga once again.

One night my father's big red land was trampled down by small sharp hooves, and it was discovered that the culprits were goats from Chief Mshlanga's kraal. This had happened once before, years ago.

My father confiscated all the goats. Then he sent a message to the old Chief that if he wanted them he would have to pay for the damage.

He arrived at our house at the time of sunset one evening, looking very old and bent now, walking stiffly under his regally-draped blanket, leaning on a big stick. My father sat himself down in his big chair below the steps of the house; the old man squatted carefully on the ground before him, flanked by his two young men.

The palaver was long and painful, because of the bad English of the young man who interpreted, and because my father could not speak dialect, but only kitchen kaffir.

From my father's point of view, at least two hundred pounds' worth of damage had been done to the crop. He knew he could not get the money from the old man. He felt he was entitled to keep the goats. As for the old Chief, he kept repeating angrily: "Twenty goats! My people cannot lose twenty goats! We are not rich, like the Nkosi Jordan, to lose twenty goats at once."

My father did not think of himself as rich, but rather as very poor. He spoke quickly and angrily in return, saying that the damage done meant a great deal to him, and that he was entitled to the goats.

At last it grew so heated that the cook, the Chief's son, was called from the kitchen to be interpreter, and now my father spoke fluently in English, and our cook translated rapidly so that the old man could understand how very angry my father was. The young man spoke without emotion, in a mechanical way, his eyes lowered, but showing how he felt his position by a hostile uncomfortable set of the shoulders.

It was now in the late sunset, the sky a welter of colours, the birds singing their last songs, and the cattle, lowing peacefully, moving past us towards their sheds for the night. It was the hour when Africa is most beautiful; and here was this pathetic, ugly scene, doing no one any good.

At last my father stated finally: "I'm not going to argue about it. I am keeping the goats."

The old Chief flashed back in his own language: "That means that my people will go hungry when the dry season comes."

"Go to the police, then," said my father, and looked triumphant.

There was, of course, no more to be said.

The old man sat silent, his head bent, his hands dangling helplessly over his withered knees. Then he rose, the young men helping him, and he stood facing my father. He spoke once again, very stiffly; and turned away and went home to his village.

"What did he say?" asked my father of the young man, who laughed uncomfortably and would not meet his eyes.

"What did he say?" insisted my father.

Our cook stood straight and silent, his brows knotted together. Then he spoke. "My father says: All this land, this land you call yours, is his land, and belongs to our people."

Having made this statement, he walked off into the bush after his father, and we did not see him again.

Our next cook was a migrant from Nyasaland, with no expectations of greatness.

Next time the policeman came on his rounds he was told this story. He remarked: "That kraal has no right to be there; it should have been moved long ago. I don't know why no one has done anything about it. I'll have a chat with the Native Commissioner next week. I'm going over for tennis on Sunday, anyway."

Some time later we heard that Chief Mshlanga and his people had been moved two hundred miles east, to a proper Native Reserve; the Government land was going to be opened up for white settlement soon.

I went to see the village again, about a year afterwards. There was nothing there. Mounds of red mud, where the huts had been, had long swathes of rotting thatch over them, veined with the red galleries of the white ants. The pumpkin vines rioted everywhere, over the bushes, up the lower branches of trees so that the great golden balls rolled underfoot and dangled overhead: it was a festival of pumpkins. The bushes were crowding up, the new grass sprang vivid green.

The settler lucky enough to be allotted the lush warm valley (if he chose to cultivate this particular section) would find, suddenly, in the middle of a mealie field, the plants were growing fifteen feet tall, the weight of the cobs dragging at the stalks, and wonder what unsuspected vein of richness he had struck.

A Sunrise on the Veld

Every night that winter he said aloud into the dark of the pillow: Half-past four! Half-past four! till he felt his brain had gripped the words and held them fast. Then he fell asleep at once, as if a shutter had fallen; and lay with his face turned to the clock so that he could see it first thing when he woke.

It was half-past four to the minute, every morning. Triumphantly pressing down the alarm-knob of the clock, which the dark half of his mind had outwitted, remaining vigilant all night and counting the hours as he lay relaxed in sleep, he huddled down for a last warm moment under the clothes, playing with the idea of lying abed for this once only. But he played with it for the fun of knowing that it was a weakness he could defeat without effort; just as he set the alarm each night for the delight of the moment when he woke and stretched his limbs, feeling the muscles tighten, and thought: Even my brain—even that! I can control every part of myself.

Luxury of warm rested body, with the arms and legs and fingers waiting like soldiers for a word of command! Joy of knowing that the precious hours were given to sleep voluntarily!—for he had once stayed awake three nights running, to prove that he could, and then worked all day, refusing even to admit that he was tired; and now sleep seemed to him a servant to be commanded and refused.

The boy stretched his frame full-length, touching the wall at his head with his hands, and the bedfoot with his toes; then he sprung out, like a fish leaping from water. And it was cold, cold.

He always dressed rapidly, so as to try and conserve his night-warmth till the sun rose two hours later; but by the time he had on his clothes his hands were numbed and he could scarcely hold his shoes. These he could not put on for fear of waking his parents, who never came to know how early he rose.

As soon as he stepped over the lintel, the flesh of his soles contracted on the chilled earth, and his legs began to ache with cold. It was night: the stars were glittering, the trees standing black and still. He looked for signs of day, for the greying of the edge of a stone, or a lightening in the sky where the sun would rise, but there was nothing yet. Alert as an animal he crept past the dangerous window, standing poised with his hand on the sill for one proudly fastidious moment, looking in at the stuffy blackness of the room where his parents lay.

Feeling for the grass-edge of the path with his toes, he reached inside another window further along the wall, where his gun had been set in readiness the night before. The steel was icy, and numbed fingers slipped along it, so that he had to hold it in the crook of his arm for safety. Then he tiptoed to the room where the dogs slept, and was fearful that they might have been tempted to go before him; but they were waiting, their haunches crouched in reluctance at the cold, but ears and swinging tails greeting the gun ecstatically. His warning undertone kept them secret and silent till the house was a hundred yards back: then they bolted off into the bush, yelping excitedly. The boy imagined his parents turning in their beds and muttering: Those dogs again! before they were dragged back in sleep; and he smiled scornfully. He always looked back over his shoulder at the house before he passed a wall of trees that shut it from sight. It looked so low and small, crouching there under a tall and brilliant sky. Then he turned his back on it, and on the frowsting sleepers, and forgot them.

He would have to hurry. Before the light grew strong he must be four miles away; and already a tint of green stood in the hollow of a leaf, and the air smelled of morning and the stars were dimming.

He slung the shoes over his shoulder, veld *skoen* that were crinkled and hard with the dews of a hundred mornings. They would be necessary when the ground became too hot to bear. Now he felt the chilled dust push up between his toes, and he let the muscles of his feet spread and settle into the shapes of the earth; and he thought: I could walk a hundred miles on feet like these! I could walk all day, and never tire!

He was walking swiftly through the dark tunnel of foliage that in day-time was a road. The dogs were invisibly ranging the lower travelways of the bush, and he heard them panting. Sometimes he felt a cold muzzle on his leg before they were off again, scouting for a trail to follow. They were not trained, but free-running companions of the hunt, who often tired of the long stalk before the final shots, and went off on their own pleasure. Soon he could see them, small and wild-looking in a wild strange light, now that the bush stood trembling on the verge of colour, waiting for the sun to paint earth and grass afresh.

The grass stood to his shoulders; and the trees were showering a faint silvery rain. He was soaked; his whole body was clenched in a steady shiver.

Once he bent to the road that was newly scored with animal trails, and regretfully straightened, reminding himself that the pleasure of tracking must wait till another day.

He began to run along the edge of a field, noting jerkily how it was filmed over with fresh spiderweb, so that the long reaches of great black clods seemed netted in glistening grey. He was using the steady lope he had learned by watching the natives, the run that is a dropping of the weight of the body from one foot to the next in a slow balancing movement that never tires, nor shortens the breath; and he felt the blood pulsing down his legs and along his arms, and the exultation and pride of body mounted in him till he was shutting his teeth hard against a violent desire to shout his triumph.

Soon he had left the cultivated part of the farm. Behind him the bush was low and black. In front was a long vlei, acres of long pale grass that sent back a hollowing gleam of light to a satiny sky. Near him thick swathes of grass were bent with the weight of water, and diamond drops sparkled on each frond.

The first bird woke at his feet and at once a flock of them sprang into the air calling shrilly that day had come; and suddenly, behind him, the bush woke into song, and he could hear the guinea fowl calling far ahead of him. That meant they would now be sailing down from their trees into thick grass, and it was for them he had come: he was too late. But he did not mind. He forgot he had come to shoot. He set his legs wide, and balanced from foot to foot, and swung his gun up and down in both hands horizontally, in a kind

of improvised exercise, and let his head sink back till it was pil-
lowed in his neck muscles, and watched how above him small rosy
clouds floated in a lake of gold.

Suddenly it all rose in him: it was unbearable. He leapt up into
the air, shouting and yelling wild, unrecognisable noises. Then he
began to run, not carefully, as he had before, but madly, like a wild
thing. He was clean crazy, yelling mad with the joy of living and a
superfluity of youth. He rushed down the vlei under a tumult of crimson and gold, while all the birds of the world sang about him. He
ran in great leaping strides, and shouted as he ran, feeling his body
rise into the crisp rushing air and fall back surely on to sure feet;
and thought briefly, not believing that such a thing could happen
to him, that he could break his ankle any moment, in this thick
tangled grass. He cleared bushes like a duiker, leapt over rocks;
and finally came to a dead stop at a place where the ground fell
abruptly away below him to the river. It had been a two-mile-long
dash through waist-high growth, and he was breathing hoarsely
and could no longer sing. But he poised on a rock and looked down
at stretches of water that gleamed through stooping trees, and
thought suddenly, I am fifteen! Fifteen! The words came new to
him; so that he kept repeating them wonderingly, with swelling excitement; and he felt the years of his life with his hands, as if he
were counting marbles, each one hard and separate and compact,
each one a wonderful shining thing. That was what he was: fifteen
years of this rich soil, and this slow-moving water, and air that
smelt like a challenge whether it was warm and sultry at noon, or
as brisk as cold water, like it was now.

There was nothing he couldn't do, nothing! A vision came to
him, as he stood there, like when a child hears the word "eternity"
and tries to understand it, and time takes possession of the mind.
He felt his life ahead of him as a great and wonderful thing, something that was his; and he said aloud, with the blood rising to his
head: all the great men of the world have been as I am now, and
there is nothing I can't become, nothing I can't do; there is no
country in the world I cannot make part of myself, if I choose. I
contain the world. I can make of it what I want. If I choose, I can
change everything that is going to happen: it depends on me, and
what I decide now.

The urgency, and the truth and the courage of what his voice
was saying exulted him so that he began to sing again, at the top of
his voice, and the sound went echoing down the river gorge. He
stopped for the echo, and sang again: stopped and shouted. That

was what he was!—he sang, if he chose; and the world had to answer him.

And for minutes he stood there, shouting and singing and waiting for the lovely eddying sound of the echo; so that his own new strong thoughts came back and washed round his head, as if someone were answering him and encouraging him; till the gorge was full of soft voices clashing back and forth from rock to rock over the river. And then it seemed as if there was a new voice. He listened, puzzled, for it was not his own. Soon he was leaning forward, all his nerves alert, quite still: somewhere close to him there was a noise that was no joyful bird, nor tinkle of falling water, nor ponderous movement of cattle.

There it was again. In the deep morning hush that held his future and his past, was a sound of pain, and repeated over and over: it was a kind of shortened scream, as if someone, something, had no breath to scream. He came to himself, looked about him, and called for the dogs. They did not appear: they had gone off on their own business, and he was alone. Now he was clean sober, all the madness gone. His heart beating fast, because of that frightened screaming, he stepped carefully off the rock and went towards a belt of trees. He was moving cautiously, for not so long ago he had seen a leopard in just this spot.

At the edge of the trees he stopped and peered, holding his gun ready; he advanced, looking steadily about him, his eyes narrowed. Then, all at once, in the middle of a step, he faltered, and his face was puzzled. He shook his head impatiently, as if he doubted his own sight.

There, between two trees, against a background of gaunt black rocks, was a figure from a dream, a strange beast that was horned and drunken-legged, but like something he had never even imagined. It seemed to be ragged. It looked like a small buck that had black ragged tufts of fur standing up irregularly all over it, with patches of raw flesh beneath . . . but the patches of rawness were disappearing under moving black and came again elsewhere; and all the time the creature screamed, in small gasping screams, and leaped drunkenly from side to side, as if it were blind.

Then the boy understood: it *was* a buck. He ran closer, and again stood still, stopped by a new fear. Around him the grass was whispering and alive. He looked wildly about, and then down. The ground was black with ants, great energetic ants that took no notice of him, but hurried and scurried towards the fighting shape, like glistening black water flowing through the grass.

And, as he drew in his breath and pity and terror seized him, the beast fell and the screaming stopped. Now he could hear nothing but one bird singing, and the sound of the rustling, whispering ants.

He peered over at the writhing blackness that jerked convulsively with the jerking nerves. It grew quieter. There were small twitches from the mass that still looked vaguely like the shape of a small animal.

It came into his mind that he should shoot it and end its pain; and he raised the gun. Then he lowered it again. The buck could no longer feel; its fighting was a mechanical protest of the nerves. But it was not that which made him put down the gun. It was a swelling feeling of rage and misery and protest that expressed itself in the thought: if I had not come it would have died like this: so why should I interfere? All over the bush things like this happen; they happen all the time; this is how life goes on, by living things dying in anguish. He gripped the gun between his knees and felt in his own limbs the myriad swarming pain of the twitching animal that could no longer feel, and set his teeth, and said over and over again under his breath: I can't stop it. I can't stop it. There is nothing I can do.

He was glad that the buck was unconscious and had gone past suffering so that he did not have to make a decision to kill it even when he was feeling with his whole body: this is what happens, this is how things work.

It was right—that was what he was feeling. *It was right and nothing could alter it.*

The knowledge of fatality, of what has to be, had gripped him and for the first time in his life; and he was left unable to make any movement of brain or body, except to say: "Yes, yes. That is what living is." It had entered his flesh and his bones and grown in to the furthest corners of his brain and would never leave him. And at that moment he could not have performed the smallest action of mercy, knowing as he did, having lived on it all his life, the vast unalterable, cruel veld, where at any moment one might stumble over a skull or crush the skeleton of some small creature.

Suffering, sick, and angry, but also grimly satisfied with his new stoicism, he stood there leaning on his rifle, and watched the seething black mound grow smaller. At his feet, now, were ants trickling back with pink fragments in their mouths, and there was a fresh acid smell in his nostrils. He sternly controlled the uselessly convulsing muscles of his empty stomach, and reminded himself: the ants must eat too! At the same time he found that the tears were streaming down his face, and his clothes were soaked with the sweat of that other creature's pain.

The shape had grown small. Now it looked like nothing recognisable. He did not know how long it was before he saw the blackness thin, and bits of white showed through, shining in the sun—yes, there was the sun, just up, glowing over the rocks. Why, the whole thing could not have taken longer than a few minutes.

He began to swear, as if the shortness of the time was in itself unbearable, using the words he had heard his father say. He strode forward, crushing ants with each step, and brushing them off his clothes, till he stood above the skeleton, which lay sprawled under a small bush. It was clean-picked. It might have been lying there years, save that on the white bone were pink fragments of gristle. About the bones ants were ebbing away, their pincers full of meat.

The boy looked at them, big black ugly insects. A few were standing and gazing up at him with small glittering eyes.

"Go away!" he said to the ants, very coldly. "I am not for you—not just yet, at any rate. Go away." And he fancied that the ants turned and went away.

He bent over the bones and touched the sockets in the skull; that was where the eyes were, he thought incredulously, remembering the liquid dark eyes of a buck. And then he bent the slim foreleg bone, swinging it horizontally in his palm.

That morning, perhaps an hour ago, this small creature had been stepping proud and free through the bush, feeling the chill on its hide even as he himself had done, exhilarated by it. Proudly stepping the earth, tossing its horns, frisking a pretty white tail, it had sniffed the cold morning air. Walking like kings and conquerors it had moved through this free-held bush, where each blade of grass grew for it alone, and where the river ran pure sparkling water for its slaking.

And then—what had happened? Such a swift surefooted thing could surely not be trapped by a swarm of ants?

The boy bent curiously to the skeleton. Then he saw that the back leg that lay uppermost and strained out in the tension of death, was snapped midway in the thigh, so that broken bones jutted over each other uselesssly. So that was it! Limping into the ant-masses it could not escape, once it had sensed the danger. Yes, but how had the leg been broken? Had it fallen, perhaps? Impossible, a buck was too light and graceful. Had some jealous rival horned it?

What could possibly have happened? Perhaps some Africans had thrown stones at it, as they do, trying to kill it for meat, and had broken its leg. Yes, that must be it.

Even as he imagined the crowd of running, shouting natives, and the flying stones, and the leaping buck, another picture came into his mind. He saw himself, on any one of these bright ringing mornings, drunk with excitement, taking a snap shot at some half-seen buck. He saw himself with the gun lowered, wondering whether he had missed or not; and thinking at last that it was late, and he wanted his breakfast, and it was not worth while to track miles after an animal that would very likely get away from him in any case.

For a moment he would not face it. He was a small boy again, kicking sulkily at the skeleton, hanging his head, refusing to accept the responsibility.

Then he straightened up, and looked down at the bones with an odd expression of dismay, all the anger gone out of him. His mind went quite empty: all around him he could see trickles of ants disappearing into the grass. The whispering noise was faint and dry, like the rustling of a cast snakeskin.

At last he picked up his gun and walked homewards. He was telling himself half defiantly that he wanted his breakfast. He was telling himself that it was getting very hot, much too hot to be out roaming the bush.

Really, he was tired. He walked heavily, not looking where he put his feet. When he came within sight of his home he stopped, knitting his brows. There was something he had to think out. The death of that small animal was a thing that concerned him, and he was by no means finished with it. It lay at the back of his mind uncomfortably.

Soon, the very next morning, he would get clear of everybody and go to the bush and think about it.

No Witchcraft for Sale

THE Farquars had been childless for years when little Teddy was born; and they were touched by the pleasure of their servants, who brought presents of fowls and eggs and flowers to the homestead when they came to rejoice over the baby, exclaiming with delight over his downy golden head and his blue eyes. They congratulated Mrs. Farquar as if she had achieved a very great thing, and she felt that she had—her smile for the lingering, admiring natives was warm and grateful.

Later, when Teddy had his first haircut, Gideon the cook picked up the soft gold tufts from the ground, and held them reverently in his hand. Then he smiled at the little boy and said: "Little Yellow Head." That became the native name for the child. Gideon and Teddy were great friends from the first. When Gideon had finished his work, he would lift Teddy on his shoulders to the shade of a big tree, and play with him there, forming curious little toys from twigs and leaves and grass, or shaping animals from wetted soil. When Teddy learned to walk it was often Gideon who crouched before him, clucking encouragement, finally catching him when he fell, tossing him up in the air till they both became breathless with laughter. Mrs. Farquar was fond of the old cook because of his love for her child.

There was no second baby; and one day Gideon said: "Ah, missus, missus, the Lord above sent this one; Little Yellow Head is the most good thing we have in our house." Because of that "we"

Mrs. Farquar felt a warm impulse towards her cook; and at the end of the month she raised his wages. He had been with her now for several years; he was one of the few natives who had his wife and children in the compound and never wanted to go home to his kraal, which was some hundreds of miles away. Sometimes a small piccanin who had been born the same time as Teddy, could be seen peering from the edge of the bush, staring in awe at the little white boy with his miraculous fair hair and Northern blue eyes. The two little children would gaze at each other with a wide, interested gaze, and once Teddy put out his hand curiously to touch the black child's cheeks and hair.

Gideon, who was watching, shook his head wonderingly, and said: "Ah, missus, these are both children, and one will grow up to be a baas, and one will be a servant;" and Mrs. Farquar smiled and said sadly, "Yes, Gideon, I was thinking the same." She sighed. "It is God's will," said Gideon, who was mission boy. The Farquars were very religious people; and this shared feeling about God bound servant and masters even closer together.

Teddy was about six years old when he was given a scooter, and discovered the intoxications of speed. All day he would fly around the homestead, in and out of flowerbeds, scattering squawking chickens and irritated dogs, finishing with a wide dizzying arc into the kitchen door. There he would cry: "Gideon, look at me!" And Gideon would laugh and say: "Very clever, Little Yellow Head." Gideon's youngest son, who was now a herdsboy, came especially up from the compound to see the scooter. He was afraid to come near it, but Teddy showed off in front of him. "Piccanin," shouted Teddy, "get out of my way!" And he raced in circles around the black child until he was frightened, and fled back to the bush.

"Why did you frighten him?" asked Gideon, gravely reproachful.

Teddy said defiantly: "He's only a black boy," and laughed. Then, when Gideon turned away from him without speaking, his face fell. Very soon he slipped into the house and found an orange and brought it to Gideon, saying: "This is for you." He could not bring himself to say he was sorry; but he could not bear to lose Gideon's affection either. Gideon took the orange unwillingly and sighed. "Soon you will be going away to school, Little Yellow Head," he said wonderingly, "and then you will be grown up." He shook his head gently and said, "And that is how our lives go." He seemed to be putting a distance between himself and Teddy, not because of resentment, but in the way a person accepts something inevitable. The baby had lain in his arms and smiled up into his face: the tiny boy had swung from his shoulders and played with him by the hour. Now Gideon would not let his flesh touch the flesh of the white child. He was kind, but there was a grave formality in his voice that made Teddy pout and sulk away. Also, it made him into a man: with Gideon he was polite, and carried himself formally, and if he came into the kitchen to ask for something, it was in the way a white man uses towards a servant, expecting to be obeyed.

But on the day that Teddy came staggering into the kitchen with his fists to his eyes, shrieking with pain, Gideon dropped the pot full of hot soup that he was holding, rushed to the child, and forced aside his fingers. "A snake!" he exclaimed. Teddy had been on his scooter, and had come to a rest with his foot on the side of a big tub of plants. A tree-snake, hanging by its tail from the roof, had spat full into his eyes. Mrs. Farquar came running when she heard the commotion. "He'll go blind," she sobbed, holding Teddy close against her. "Gideon, he'll go blind!" Already the eyes, with perhaps half an hour's sight left in them, were swollen up to the size of fists: Teddy's small white face was distorted by great purple oozing protuberances. Gideon said: "Wait a minute, missus, I'll get some medicine." He ran off into the bush.

Mrs. Farquar lifted the child into the house and bathed his eyes with permanganate. She had scarcely heard Gideon's words; but when she saw that her remedies had no effect at all, and remembered how she had seen natives with no sight in their eyes, because of the spitting of a snake, she began to look for the return of her cook, remembering what she heard of the efficacy of native herbs. She stood by the window, holding the terrified, sobbing little boy in her arms, and peered helplessly into the bush. It was not more than a few minutes before she saw Gideon come bounding back, and in his hand he held a plant.

"Do not be afraid, missus," said Gideon, "this will cure Little Yellow Head's eyes." He stripped the leaves from the plant, leaving a small white fleshy root. Without even washing it, he put the root in his mouth, chewed it vigorously, and then held the spittle there while he took the child forcibly from Mrs. Farquar. He gripped Teddy down between his knees, and pressed the balls of his thumbs into the swollen eyes, so that the child screamed and Mrs. Farquar cried out in protest: "Gideon, Gideon!" But Gideon took no notice. He knelt over the writhing child, pushing back the puffy lids till chinks of eyeball showed, and then he spat hard, again and again, into first one eye, and then the other. He finally lifted Teddy gently into his mother's arms, and said: "His eyes will get better." But

Mrs. Farquar was weeping with terror, and she could hardly thank him: it was impossible to believe that Teddy could keep his sight. In a couple of hours the swellings were gone: the eyes were inflamed and tender but Teddy could see. Mr. and Mrs. Farquar went to Gideon in the kitchen and thanked him over and over again. They felt helpless because of their gratitude: it seemed they could do nothing to express it. They gave Gideon presents for his wife and children, and a big increase in wages, but these things could not pay for Teddy's now completely cured eyes. Mrs. Farquar said: "Gideon, God chose you as an instrument for His goodness," and Gideon said: "Yes, missus, God is very good."

Now, when such a thing happens on a farm, it cannot be long before everyone hears of it. Mr. and Mrs. Farquar told their neighbors and the story was discussed from one end of the district to the other. The bush is full of secrets. No one can live in Africa, or at least on the veld, without learning very soon that there is an ancient wisdom of leaf and soil and season—and, too, perhaps most important of all, of the darker tracts of the human mind—which is the black man's heritage. Up and down the district people were telling anecdotes, reminding each other of things that had happened to them.

"But I saw it myself, I tell you. It was a puff-adder bite. The kaffir's arm was swollen to the elbow, like a great shiny black bladder. He was groggy after a half a minute. He was dying. Then suddenly a kaffir walked out of the bush with his hands full of green stuff. He smeared something on the place, and next day my boy was back at work, and all you could see was two small punctures in the skin."

This was the kind of tale they told. And, as always, with a certain amount of exasperation, because while all of them knew that in the bush of Africa are waiting valuable drugs locked in bark, in simple-looking leaves, in roots, it was impossible to ever get the truth about them from the natives themselves.

The story eventually reached town; and perhaps it was at a sundowner party, or some such function, that a doctor, who happened to be there, challenged it. "Nonsense," he said. "These things get exaggerated in the telling. We are always checking up on this kind of story, and we draw a blank every time."

Anyway, one morning there arrived a strange car at the homestead, and out stepped one of the workers from the laboratory in town, with cases full of test-tubes and chemicals.

Mr. and Mrs. Farquar were flustered and pleased and flattered. They asked the scientist to lunch, and they told the story all over again, for the hundredth time. Little Teddy was there too, his blue eyes sparkling with health, to prove the truth of it. The scientist explained how humanity might benefit if this new drug could be offered for sale; and the Farquars were even more pleased: they were kind, simple people, who liked to think of something good coming about because of them. But when the scientist began talking of the money that might result, their manner showed discomfort. Their feelings over the miracle (that was how they thought of it) were so strong and deep and religious, that it was distasteful to them to think of money. The scientist, seeing their faces, went back to his first point, which was the advancement of humanity. He was perhaps a trifle perfunctory: it was not the first time he had come salting the tail of a fabulous bush-secret.

Eventually, when the meal was over, the Farquars called Gideon into their living-room and explained to him that this baas, here, was a Big Doctor from the Big City, and he had come all that way to see Gideon. At this Gideon seemed afraid; he did not understand; and Mrs. Farquar explained quickly that it was because of the wonderful thing he had done with Teddy's eyes that the Big Baas had come.

Gideon looked from Mrs. Farquar to Mr. Farquar, and then at the little boy, who was showing great importance because of the occasion. At last he said grudgingly: "The Big Baas want to know what medicine I used?" He spoke incredulously, as if he could not believe his old friends could so betray him. Mr. Farquar began explaining how a useful medicine could be made out of the root, and how it could be put on sale, and how thousands of people, black and white, up and down the continent of Africa, could be saved by the medicine when that spitting snake filled their eyes with poison. Gideon listened, his eyes bent on the ground, the skin of his forehead puckering in discomfort. When Mr. Farquar had finished he did not reply. The scientist, who all this time had been leaning back in a big chair, sipping his coffee and smiling with sceptical good-humor, chipped in and explained all over again, in different words, about the making of drugs and the progress of science. Also, he offered Gideon a present.

There was silence after this further explanation, and then Gideon remarked indifferently that he could not remember the root. His face was sullen and hostile, even when he looked at the Far-

quars, whom he usually treated like old friends. They were beginning to feel annoyed; and this feeling annulled the guilt that had
been sprung into life by Gideon's accusing manner. They were beginning to feel that he was unreasonable. But it was at that moment that they all realized he would never give in. The magical
drug would remain where it was, unknown and useless except for
the tiny scattering of Africans who had the knowledge, natives who
might be digging a ditch for the municipality in a ragged shirt and
a pair of patched shorts, but who were still born to healing, heredi-
tary healers, being the nephews or sons of the old witch doctors
whose ugly masks and bits of bone and all the uncouth properties
of magic were the outward signs of real power and wisdom.

The Farquars might tread on that plant fifty times a day as they
passed from house to garden, from cow kraal to mealie field, but
they would never know it.

But they went on persuading and arguing, with all the force of
their exasperation; and Gideon continued to say that he could not
remember, or that there was no such root, or that it was the wrong
season of the year, or that it wasn't the root itself, but the spit from
his mouth that had cured Teddy's eyes. He said all these things one
after another, and seemed not to care they were contradictory. He
was rude and stubborn. The Farquars could hardly recognise their
gentle, lovable old servant in this ignorant, perversely obstinate
African, standing there in front of them with lowered eyes, his
hands twitching his cook's apron, repeating over and over whichever one of the stupid refusals that first entered his head.

And suddenly he appeared to give in. He lifted his head, gave a
long, blank angry look at the circle of whites, who seemed to him
like a circle of yelping dogs pressing around him, and said: "I will
show you the root."

They walked single file away from the homestead down a kaffir
path. It was a blazing December afternoon, with the sky full of hot
rain-clouds. Everything was hot: the sun was like a bronze tray
whirling overhead, there was a heat shimmer over the fields, the
soil was scorching underfoot, the dusty wind blew gritty and thick
and warm in their faces. It was a terrible day, fit only for reclining
on a verandah with iced drinks, which is where they would normally have been at that hour.

From time to time, remembering that on the day of the snake it
had taken ten minutes to find the root, someone asked: "Is it much
further, Gideon?" And Gideon would answer over his shoulder,

with angry politeness: "I'm looking for the root, baas." And indeed, he would frequently bend sideways and trail his hand among the grasses with a gesture that was insulting in its perfunctoriness. He walked them through the bush along unknown paths for two hours, in that melting destroying heat, so that the sweat trickled coldly down them and their heads ached. They were all quite silent: the Farquars because they were angry, the scientist because he was being proved right again; there was no such plant. His was a tactful silence.

At last, six miles from the house, Gideon suddenly decided they had had enough; or perhaps his anger evaporated at that moment. He picked up, without an attempt at looking anything but casual, a handful of blue flowers from the grass, flowers that had been growing plentifully all down the paths they had come.

He handed them to the scientist without looking at him, and marched off by himself on the way home, leaving them to follow him if they chose.

When they got back to the house, the scientist went to the kitchen to thank Gideon: he was being very polite, even though there was an amused look in his eyes. Gideon was not there. Throwing the flowers casually into the back of his car, the eminent visitor departed on his way back to his laboratory.

Gideon was back in his kitchen in time to prepare dinner, but he was sulking. He spoke to Mr. Farquar like an unwilling servant. It was days before they liked each other again.

The Farquars made enquiries about the root from their labourers. Sometimes they were answered with distrustful stares. Sometimes the natives said: "We do not know. We have never heard of the root." One, the cattle boy, who had been with them a long time, and had grown to trust them a little, said: "Ask your boy in the kitchen. Now, there's a doctor for you. He's the son of a famous medicine man who used to be in these parts, and there's nothing he cannot cure." Then he added politely: "Of course, he's not as good as the white man's doctor, we know that, but he's good for us."

After some time, when the soreness had gone from between the Farquars and Gideon, they began to joke: "When are you going to show us the snake-root, Gideon?" And he would laugh and shake his head, saying, a little uncomfortably: "But I did show you, missus, have you forgotten?"

Much later, Teddy, as a schoolboy, would come into the kitchen and say: "You old rascal, Gideon! Do you remember that time you tricked us all by making us walk miles all over the veld for nothing? It was so far my father had to carry me!"

And Gideon would double up with polite laughter. After much laughing, he would suddenly straighten himself up, wipe his old eyes, and look sadly at Teddy, who was grinning mischievously at him across the kitchen: "Ah, Little Yellow Head, how you have grown! Soon you will be grown up with a farm of your own . . ."

The Second Hut

BEFORE that season and his wife's illness, he had thought things could get no worse: until then, poverty had meant not to deviate further than snapping point from what he had been brought up to think of as a normal life.

Being a farmer (he had come to it late in life, in his forties) was the first test he had faced as an individual. Before he had always been supported, invisibly perhaps, but none the less strongly, by what his family expected of him. He had been a regular soldier, not an unsuccessful one, but his success had been at the cost of a continual straining against his own inclinations; and he did not know himself what his inclinations were. Something stubbornly unconforming kept him apart from his fellow officers. It was an inward difference: he did not think of himself as a soldier. Even in his appearance, square, close-bitten, disciplined, there had been a hint of softness, or of strain, showing itself in his smile, which was too quick, like the smile of a deaf person afraid of showing incomprehension, and in the anxious look of his eyes. After he left the army he quickly slackened into an almost slovenly carelessness of dress and carriage. Now, in his farm clothes there was nothing left to suggest the soldier. With a loose, stained felt hat on the back of his head, khaki shorts a little too long and too wide, sleeves flapping over spare brown arms, his wispy moustache hiding a strained, set mouth, Major Carruthers looked what he was, a gentleman farmer going to seed.

The house had that brave, worn appearance of those struggling to keep up appearances. It was a four-roomed shack, its red roof dulling to streaky brown. It was the sort of house an apprentice farmer builds as a temporary shelter till he can afford better. Inside, good but battered furniture stood over worn places in the rugs; the piano was out of tune and the notes stuck; the silver tea things from the big narrow house in England where his brother (a lawyer) now lived were used as ornaments, and inside were bits of paper, accounts, rubber rings, old corks.

The room where his wife lay, in a greenish sun-lanced gloom, was a place of seedy misery. The doctor said it was her heart; and Major Carruthers knew this was true: she had broken down through heart-break over the conditions they lived in. She did not want to get better. The harsh light from outside was shut out with dark blinds, and she turned her face to the wall and lay there, hour after hour, inert and uncomplaining, in a stoicism of defeat nothing could penetrate. Even the children hardly moved her. It was as if she had said to herself: "If I cannot have what I wanted for them, then I wash my hands of life."

Sometimes Major Carruthers thought of her as she had been, and was filled with uneasy wonder and with guilt. That pleasant conventional pretty English girl had been bred to make a perfect wife for the professional soldier she had imagined him to be, but chance had wrenched her on to this isolated African farm, into a life which she submitted herself to, as if it had nothing to do with her. For the first few years she had faced the struggle humorously, courageously: it was a sprightly attitude towards life, almost flirtatious, as a woman flirts lightly with a man who means nothing to her. As the house grew shabby, and the furniture, and her clothes could not be replaced; when she looked into the mirror and saw her drying, untidy hair and roughening face, she would give a quick high laugh and say, "Dear me, the things one comes to!" She was facing this poverty as she would have faced, in England, poverty of a narrowing, but socially accepted kind. What she could not face was a different kind of fear; and Major Carruthers understood that too well, for it was now his own fear.

The two children were pale, fine-drawn creatures, almost transparent-looking in their thin nervous fairness, with the defensive and wary manners of the young who have been brought up to expect a better way of life than they enjoy. Their anxious solicitude wore on Major Carruthers' already over-sensitised nerves. Children had no right to feel the aching pity which showed on their faces whenever they looked at him. They were too polite, too careful, too scrupulous. When they went into their mother's room she grieved sorrowfully over them, and they submitted patiently to her emotion. All those weeks of the school holidays after she was taken ill, they moved about the farm like two strained and anxious ghosts, and whenever he saw them his sense of guilt throbbed like a wound. He was glad they were going back to school soon, for then—so he thought—it would be easier to manage. It was an intolerable strain, running the farm and coming back to the neglected house and the problems of food and clothing, and a sick wife who would not get better until he could offer her hope.

But when they had gone back, he found that after all, things were not much easier. He slept little, for his wife needed attention in the night; and he became afraid for his own health, worrying over what he ate and wore. He learnt to treat himself as if his health was not what he was, what made him, but something apart, a commodity like efficiency, which could be estimated in terms of money at the end of a season. His health stood between them and complete ruin; and soon there were medicine bottles beside his bed as well as beside his wife's.

One day, while he was carefully measuring out tonics for himself in the bedroom, he glanced up and saw his wife's small reddened eyes staring incredulously but ironically at him over the bedclothes. "What are you doing?" she asked.

"I need a tonic," he explained awkwardly, afraid to worry her by explanations.

She laughed, for the first time in weeks; then the slack tears began welling under the lids, and she turned to the wall again.

He understood that some vision of himself had been destroyed, finally, for her. Now she was left with an ageing, rather fussy gentleman, carefully measuring medicine after meals. But he did not blame her; he never had blamed her; not even though he knew her illness was a failure of will. He patted her cheek uncomfortably, and said: "It wouldn't do for me to get run down, would it?" Then he adjusted the curtains over the windows to shut out a streak of dancing light that threatened to fall over her face, set a glass nearer to her hand, and went out to arrange for her tray of slops to be carried in.

Then he took, in one swift, painful movement, as if he were leaping over an obstacle, the decision he had known for weeks he must take sooner or later. With a straightening of his shoulders, an echo from his soldier past, he took on the strain of an extra burden: he must get an assistant, whether he liked it or not.

So much did he shrink from any self-exposure, that he did not even consider advertising. He sent a note by native bearer to his neighbour, a few miles off, asking that it should be spread abroad that he was wanting help. He knew he would not have to wait long. It was 1931, in the middle of a slump, and there was unemployment, which was a rare thing for this new, sparsely-populated country.

He wrote the following to his two sons at boarding-school:

> I expect you will be surprised to hear I'm getting another man on the place. Things are getting a bit too much, and as I plan to plant a bigger acreage of maize this year, I thought it would need two of us. Your mother is better this week, on the whole, so I think things are looking up. She is looking forward to your next holidays, and asks me to say she will write soon. Between you and me, I don't think she's up to writing at the moment. It will soon be getting cold, I think, so if you need any clothes, let me know, and I'll see what I can do . . .

A week later, he sat on the little verandah, towards evening, smoking, when he saw a man coming through the trees on a bicycle. He watched him closely, already trying to form an estimate of his character by the tests he had used all his life: the width between the eyes, the shape of the skull, the way the legs were set on to the body. Although he had been taken in a dozen times, his belief in these methods never wavered. He was an easy prey for any trickster, lending money he never saw again, taken in by professional adventurers who (it seemed to him, measuring others by his own decency and the quick warmth he felt towards people) were the essence of gentlemen. He used to say that being a gentleman was a question of instinct: one could not mistake a gentleman.

As the visitor stepped off his bicycle and wheeled it to the verandah, Major Carruthers saw he was young, thirty perhaps, sturdily built, with enormous strength in the thick arms and shoulders. His skin was burnt a healthy orange-brown colour. His close hair, smooth as the fur of an animal, reflected no light. His obtuse, generous features were set in a round face, and the eyes were pale grey, nearly colourless.

Major Carruthers instinctively dropped his standards of value as he looked, for this man was an Afrikaner, and thus came into an outside category. It was not that he disliked him for it, although his father had been killed in the Boer War, but he had never had anything to do with the Afrikaans people before, and his knowledge of them was hearsay, from Englishmen who had the old prejudice. But he liked the look of the man: he liked the honest and straightforward face.

As for Van Heerden, he immediately recognised his traditional enemy, and his inherited dislike was strong. For a moment he appeared obstinate and wary. But they needed each other too badly to nurse old hatreds, and Van Heerden sat down when he was asked, though awkwardly, suppressing reluctance, and began drawing patterns in the dust with a piece of straw he had held between his lips.

Major Carruthers did not need to wonder about the man's circumstances: his quick acceptance of what were poor terms spoke of a long search for work.

He said scrupulously: "I know the salary is low and the living quarters are bad, even for a single man. I've had a patch of bad luck, and I can't afford more. I'll quite understand if you refuse."

"What are the living quarters?" asked Van Heerden. His was the rough voice of the uneducated Afrikaner: because he was uncertain where the accent should fall in each sentence, his speech had a wavering, halting sound, though his look and manner were direct enough.

Major Carruthers pointed ahead of them. Before the house the bush sloped gently down to the fields. "At the foot of the hill there's a hut I've been using as a storehouse. It's quite well-built. You can put up a place for a kitchen."

Van Heerden rose. "Can I see it?"

They set off. It was not far away. The thatched hut stood in uncleared bush. Grass grew to the walls and reached up to meet the slanting thatch. Trees mingled their branches overhead. It was round, built of poles and mud and with a stamped dung floor. Inside there was a stale musty smell because of the ants and beetles that had been at the sacks of grain. The one window was boarded over, and it was quite dark. In the confusing shafts of light from the door, a thick sheet of felted spider web showed itself, like a curtain halving the interior, as full of small flies and insects as a butcherbird's cache. The spider crouched, vast and glittering, shaking gently, glaring at them with small red eyes, from the centre of the web. Van Heerden did what Major Carruthers would have died rather than do: he tore the web across with his bare hands, crushed the spider between his fingers, and brushed them lightly against the walls to free them from the clinging silky strands and the sticky mush of insect-body.

"It will do fine," he announced.

He would not accept the invitation to a meal, thus making it clear this was merely a business arrangement. But he asked, politely (hating that he had to beg a favour), for a month's salary in advance. Then he set off on his bicycle to the store, ten miles off, to buy what he needed for his living.

Major Carruthers went back to his sick wife with a burdened feeling, caused by his being responsible for another human being having to suffer such conditions. He could not have the man in the house: the idea came into his head and was quickly dismissed. They had nothing in common, they would make each other uncomfortable—that was how he put it to himself. Besides, there wasn't really any room. Underneath, Major Carruthers knew that if his new assistant had been an Englishman, with the same upbringing, he would have found a corner in his house and a welcome as a friend. Major Carruthers threw off these thoughts: he had enough to worry him without taking on another man's problems.

A person who had always hated the business of organisation, which meant dividing responsibility with others, he found it hard to arrange with Van Heerden how the work was to be done. But as the Dutchman was good with cattle, Major Carruthers handed over all the stock on the farm to his care, thus relieving his mind of its most nagging care, for he was useless with beasts, and knew it. So they began, each knowing exactly where they stood. Van Heerden would make laconic reports at the end of each week, in the manner of an expert foreman reporting to a boss ignorant of technicalities —and Major Carruthers accepted this attitude, for he liked to respect people, and it was easy to respect Van Heerden's inspired instinct for animals.

For a few weeks Major Carruthers was almost happy. The fear of having to apply for another loan to his brother—worse, asking for the passage money to England and a job, thus justifying his family's belief in him as a failure, was pushed away; for while taking on a manager did not in itself improve things, it was an action, a decision, and there was nothing that he found more dismaying than decisions. The thought of his family in England, and particularly his elder brother, pricked him into slow burning passions of resentment. His brother's letters galled him so that he had grown to hate mail-days. They were crisp, affectionate letters, without condescension, but about money, bank-drafts, and insurance policies. Major Carruthers did not see life like that. He had not written to his brother for over a year. His wife, when she was well, wrote once a week, in the spirit of one propitiating fate.

Even she seemed cheered by the manager's coming; she sensed her husband's irrational lightness of spirit during that short time. She stirred herself to ask about the farm; and he began to see that her interest in living would revive quickly if her sort of life came within reach again.

But some two months after Van Heerden's coming, Major Carruthers was walking along the farm road towards his lands, when he was astonished to see, disappearing into the bushes a small flaxen-haired boy. He called, but the child froze as an animal freezes, flattening himself against the foliage. At last, since he could get no reply, Major Carruthers approached the child, who dissolved backwards through the trees, and followed him up the path to the hut. He was very angry, for he knew what he would see.

He had not been to the hut since he handed it over to Van Heerden. Now there was a clearing, and amongst the stumps of trees and the flattened grass, were half a dozen children, each as tow-headed as the first, with that bleached sapless look common to white children in the tropics who have been subjected to too much sun.

A lean-to had been built against the hut. It was merely a roof of beaten petrol tins, patched together like cloth with wire and nails and supported on two unpeeled sticks. There, holding a cooking pot over an open fire that was dangerously close to the thatch, stood a vast slatternly woman. She reminded him of a sow among her litter, as she lifted her head, the children crowding about her, and stared at him suspiciously from pale and white-lashed eyes.

"Where is your husband?" he demanded.

She did not answer. Her suspicion deepened into a glare of hate: clearly she knew no English.

Striding furiously to the door of the hut, he saw that it was crowded with two enormous native-style beds: strips of hide stretched over wooden poles embedded in the mud of the floor. What was left of the space was heaped with the stained and broken belongings of the family. Major Carruthers strode off in search of Van Heerden. His anger was now mingled with the shamed discomfort of trying to imagine what it must be to live in such squalor.

Fear rose high in him. For a few moments he inhabited the landscape of his dreams, a grey country full of sucking menace, where he suffered what he would not allow himself to think of while awake: the grim poverty that could overtake him if his luck did not turn, and if he refused to submit to his brother and return to England.

Walking through the fields, where the maize was now waving over his head, pale gold with a froth of white, the sharp dead leaves scything crisply against the wind, he could see nothing but that black foetid hut and the pathetic futureless children. That was the lowest he could bring his own children to! He felt moorless, helpless, afraid: his sweat ran cold on him. And he did not hesitate in his mind; driven by fear and anger, he told himself to be hard; he was searching in his mind for the words with which he would dismiss the Dutchman who had brought his worst nightmares to life, on his own farm, in glaring daylight, where they were inescapable.

He found him with a screaming rearing young ox that was being broken to the plough, handling it with his sure understanding of animals. At a cautious distance stood the natives who were assisting; but Van Heerden, fearless and purposeful, was fighting the beast at close range. He saw Major Carruthers, let go the plunging horn he held, and the ox shot away backwards, roaring with anger, into the crowd of natives, who gathered loosely about it with sticks and stones to prevent it running away altogether.

Van Heerden stood still, wiping the sweat off his face, still grinning with the satisfaction of the fight, waiting for his employer to speak.

"Van Heerden," said Major Carruthers, without preliminaries, "why didn't you tell me you had a family?"

As he spoke the Dutchman's face changed, first flushing into guilt, then setting hard and stubborn. "Because I've been out of work for a year, and I knew you would not take me if I told you."

The two men faced each other, Major Carruthers tall, fly-away, shambling, bent with responsibility; Van Heerden stiff and defiant. The natives remained about the ox, to prevent its escape—for them this was a brief intermission in the real work of the farm—and their shouts mingled with the incessant bellowing. It was a hot day; Van Heerden wiped the sweat from his eyes with the back of his hand.

"You can't keep a wife and all those children here—how many children?"

"Nine."

Major Carruthers thought of his own two, and his perpetual dull ache of worry over them; and his heart became grieved for Van

Heerden. Two children, with all the trouble over everything they ate and wore and thought, and what would become of them, were too great a burden; how did this man, with nine, manage to look so young?

"How old are you?" he asked abruptly, in a different tone.

"Thirty-four," said Van Heerden, suspiciously, unable to understand the direction Major Carruthers followed.

The only marks on his face were sun-creases; it was impossible to think of him as the father of nine children and the husband of that terrible broken-down woman. As Major Carruthers gazed at him, he became conscious of the strained lines on his own face, and tried to loosen himself, because he took so badly what this man bore so well.

"You can't keep a wife and children in such conditions."

"We were living in a tent in the bush on mealie meal and what I shot for nine months, and that was through the wet season," said Van Heerden drily.

Major Carruthers knew he was beaten. "You've put me in a false position, Van Heerden," he said angrily. "You know I can't afford to give you more money. I don't know where I'm going to find my own children's school fees, as it is. I told you the position when you came. I can't afford to keep a man with such a family."

"Nobody can afford to have me either," said Van Heerden sullenly.

"How can I have you living on my place in such a fashion? Nine children! They should be at school. Didn't you know there is a law to make them go to school! Hasn't anybody been to see you about them?"

"They haven't got me yet. They won't get me unless someone tells them."

Against this challenge, which was also an unwilling appeal, Major Carruthers remained silent, until he said brusquely: "Remember, I'm not responsible." And he walked off, with all the appearance of anger.

Van Heerden looked after him, his face puzzled. He did not know whether or not he had been dismissed. After a few moments he moistened his dry lips with his tongue, wiped his hand again over his eyes, and turned back to the ox. Looking over his shoulder from the edge of the field, Major Carruthers could see his wiry, stocky figure leaping and bending about the ox whose bellowing made the whole farm ring with anger.

Major Carruthers decided, once and for all, to put the family out of his mind. But they haunted him; he even dreamed of them; and he could not determine whether it was his own or the Dutchman's children who filled his sleep with fear.

It was a very busy time of the year. Harassed, like all his fellow-farmers, by labour difficulties, apportioning out the farm tasks was a daily problem. All day his mind churned slowly over the necessities: this fencing was urgent, that field must be reaped at once. Yet, in spite of this, he decided it was his plain duty to build a second hut beside the first. It would do no more than take the edge off the discomfort of that miserable family, but he knew he could not rest until it was built.

Just as he had made up his mind and was wondering how the thing could be managed, the boss-boy came to him, saying that unless the Dutchman went, he and his friends would leave the farm.

"Why?" asked Major Carruthers, knowing what the answer would be. Van Heerden was a hard worker, and the cattle were improving week by week under his care, but he could not handle natives. He shouted at them, lost his temper, treated them like dogs. There was continual friction.

"Dutchmen are no good," said the boss-boy simply, voicing the hatred of the black man for that section of the white people he considers his most brutal oppressors.

Now, Major Carruthers was proud that at a time when most farmers were forced to buy labour from the contractors, he was able to attract sufficient voluntary labour to run his farm. He was a good employer, proud of his reputation for fair dealing. Many of his natives had been with him for years, taking a few months off occasionally for a rest in their kraals, but always returning to him. His neighbours were complaining of the sullen attitude of their labourers: so far Major Carruthers had kept this side of that form of passive resistance which could ruin a farmer. It was walking on a knife-edge, but his simple human relationship with his workers was his greatest asset as a farmer, and he knew it.

He stood and thought, while his boss-boy, who had been on this farm twelve years, waited for a reply. A great deal was at stake. For a moment Major Carruthers thought of dismissing the Dutchman; he realized he could not bring himself to do it: what would happen to all those children? He decided on a course which was repugnant to him. He was going to appeal to his employee's pity.

"I have always treated you square?" he asked. "I've always helped you when you were in trouble?"

The boss-boy immediately and warmly assented.

"You know that my wife is ill, and that I'm having a lot of trouble just now? I don't want the Dutchman to go, just now when the work is so heavy. I'll speak to him, and if there is any more trouble with the men, then come to me and I'll deal with it myself."

It was a glittering blue day, with a chill edge on the air, that stirred Major Carruthers' thin blood as he stood, looking in appeal into the sullen face of the native. All at once, feeling the fresh air wash along his cheeks, watching the leaves shake with a ripple of gold on the trees down the slope, he felt superior to his difficulties, and able to face anything. "Come," he said, with his rare, diffident smile. "After all these years, when we have been working together for so long, surely you can do this for me. It won't be for very long."

He watched the man's face soften in response to his own; and wondered at the unconscious use of the last phrase, for there was no reason, on the face of things, why the situation should not continue as it was for a very long time.

They began laughing together; and separated cheerfully; the African shaking his head ruefully over the magnitude of the sacrifice asked of him, thus making the incident into a joke; and he dived off into the bush to explain the position to his fellow-workers.

Repressing a strong desire to go after him, to spend the lovely fresh day walking for pleasure, Major Carruthers went into his wife's bedroom, inexplicably confident and walking like a young man.

She lay as always, face to the wall, her protruding shoulders visible beneath the cheap pink bed-jacket he had bought for her illness. She seemed neither better nor worse. But as she turned her head, his buoyancy infected her a little; perhaps, too, she was conscious of the exhilarating day outside her gloomy curtains.

What kind of a miraculous release was she waiting for? he wondered, as he delicately adjusted her sheets and pillows and laid his hand gently on her head. Over the bony cage of the skull, the skin was papery and blueish. What was she thinking? He had a vision of her brain as a small frightened animal pulsating under his fingers.

With her eyes still closed, she asked in her querulous thin voice: "Why don't you write to George?"

Involuntarily his fingers contracted on her hair, causing her to start and to open her reproachful, red-rimmed eyes. He waited for her usual appeal: the children, my health, our future. But she sighed and remained silent, still loyal to the man she had imagined she was marrying; and he could feel her thinking: *the lunatic stiff pride of men.*

Understanding that for her it was merely a question of waiting for his defeat, as her deliverance, he withdrew his hand, in dislike of her, saying: "Things are not as bad as that yet." The cheerfulness of his voice was genuine, holding still the courage and hope instilled into him by the bright day outside.

"Why, what has happened?" she asked swiftly, her voice suddenly strong, looking at him in hope.

"Nothing," he said; and the depression settled down over him again. Indeed, nothing had happened; and his confidence was a trick of the nerves. Soberly he left the bedroom, thinking: I must get that well built; and when that is done, I must do the drains, and then . . . He was thinking, too, that all these things must wait for the second hut.

Oddly, the comparatively small problem of that hut occupied his mind during the next few days. A slow and careful man, he set milestones for himself and overtook them one by one.

Since Christmas the labourers had been working a seven-day week, in order to keep ahead in the race against the weeds. They resented it, of course, but that was the custom. Now that the maize was grown, they expected work to slack off, they expected their Sundays to be restored to them. To ask even half a dozen of them to sacrifice their weekly holiday for the sake of the hated Dutchman might precipitate a crisis. Major Carruthers took his time, stalking his opportunity like a hunter, until one evening he was talking with his boss-boy as man to man, about farm problems; but when he broached the subject of a hut, Major Carruthers saw that it would be as he feared: the man at once turned stiff and unhelpful. Suddenly impatient, he said: "It must be done next Sunday. Six men could finish it in a day, if they worked hard."

The black man's glance became veiled and hostile. Responding to the authority in the voice he replied simply: "Yes, baas." He was accepting the order from above, and refusing responsibility: his co-operation was switched off; he had become a machine for transmitting orders. Nothing exasperated Major Carruthers more than when this happened. He said sternly: "I'm not having any nonsense. If that hut isn't built, there'll be trouble."

"Yes, baas," said the boss-boy again. He walked away, stopped some natives who were coming off the fields with their hoes over their shoulders, and transmitted the order in a neutral voice. Major Carruthers saw them glance at him in fierce antagonism; then they turned away their heads, and walked off, in a group, towards their compound.

It would be all right, he thought, in disproportionate relief. It would be difficult to say exactly what it was he feared, for the question of the hut had loomed so huge in his mind that he was beginning to feel an almost superstitious foreboding. Driven downwards through failure after failure, fate was becoming real to him as a cold malignant force; the careful balancing of unfriendly probabilities that underlay all his planning had developed in him an acute sensitivity to the future; and he had learned to respect his dreams and omens. Now he wondered at the strength of his desire to see that hut built, and whatever danger it represented behind him.

He went to the clearing to find Van Heerden and tell him what had been planned. He found him sitting on a candle-box in the doorway of the hut, playing good-humouredly with his children, as if they had been puppies, tumbling them over, snapping his fingers in their faces, and laughing outright with boyish exuberance when one little boy squared up his fists at him in a moment of temper against this casual, almost contemptuous treatment of them. Major Carruthers heard that boyish laugh with amazement; he looked blankly at the young Dutchman, and then from him to his wife, who was standing, as usual, over a petrol tin that balanced on the small fire. A smell of meat and pumpkin filled the clearing. The woman seemed to Major Carruthers less a human being than the expression of an elemental, irrepressible force: he saw her, in her vast sagging fleshiness, with her slow stupid face, her instinctive responses to her children, whether for affection or temper, as the symbol of fecundity, a strong, irresistible heave of matter. She frightened him. He turned his eyes from her and explained to Van Heerden that a second hut would be built here, beside the existing one.

Van Heerden was pleased. He softened into quick confiding friendship. He looked doubtfully behind him at the small hut that sheltered eleven human beings, and said that it was really not easy to live in such a small space with so many children. He glanced at the children, cuffing them affectionately as he spoke, smiling like a boy. He was proud of his family, of his own capacity for making children: Major Carruthers could see that. Almost, he smiled; then he glanced through the doorway at the grey squalor of the interior and hurried off, resolutely preventing himself from dwelling on the repulsive facts that such close-packed living implied.

The next Saturday evening he and Van Heerden paced the clearing with tape measure and spirit level, determining the area of the new hut. It was to be a large one. Already the sheaves of thatching grass had been stacked ready for next day, shining brassily in the evening sun; and the thorn poles for the walls lay about the clearing, stripped of bark, the smooth inner wood showing white as kernels.

Major Carruthers was waiting for the natives to come up from the compound for the building before daybreak that Sunday. He was there even before the family woke, afraid that without his presence something might go wrong. He feared the Dutchman's temper because of the labourers' sulky mood.

He leaned against a tree, watching the bush come awake, while the sky flooded slowly with light, and the birds sang about him. The hut was, for a long time, silent and dark. A sack hung crookedly over the door, and he could glimpse huddled shapes within. It seemed to him horrible, a stinking kennel shrinking ashamedly to the ground away from the wide hall of fresh blue sky. Then a child came out, and another; soon they were spilling out of the doorway, in their little rags of dresses, or hitching khaki pants up over the bony jut of a hip. They smiled shyly at him, offering him friendship. Then came the woman, moving sideways to ease herself through the narrow door-frame—she was so huge it was almost a fit. She lumbered slowly, thick and stupid with sleep, over to the cold fire, raising her arms in a yawn, so that wisps of dull yellow hair fell over her shoulders and her dark slack dress lifted in creases under her neck. Then she saw Major Carruthers and smiled at him. For the first time he saw her as a human being and not as something fatally ugly. There was something shy, yet frank, in that smile; so that he could imagine the strong, laughing adolescent girl, with the frank, inviting, healthy sensuality of the young Dutchwoman—so she had been when she married Van Heerden. She stooped painfully to stir up the ashes, and soon the fire spurted up under the leaning patch of tin roof. For a while Van Heerden did not appear; neither did the natives who were supposed to be here a long while since; Major Carruthers continued to lean against a tree, smiling at the children, who nevertheless kept their distance from him, unable to play naturally because of his presence there, smiling at Mrs. Van Heerden who was throwing handfuls of mealie meal into a petrol tin of boiling water, to make native-style porridge.

It was just on eight o'clock, after two hours of impatient waiting, that the labourers filed up the bushy incline, with the axes and picks over their shoulders, avoiding his eyes. He pressed down his anger: after all it was Sunday, and they had had no day off for weeks; he could not blame them.

They began by digging the circular trench that would hold the wall poles. As their picks rang out on the pebbly ground, Van Heerden came out of the hut, pushing aside the dangling sack with one hand and pulling up his trousers with the other, yawning broadly, then smiling at Major Carruthers apologetically. "I've had my sleep out," he said; he seemed to think his employer might be angry.

Major Carruthers stood close over the workers, wanting it to be understood by them and by Van Heerden that he was responsible. He was too conscious of their resentment, and knew that they would scamp the work if possible. If the hut was to be completed as planned, he would need all his tact and good-humour. He stood there patiently all morning, watching the thin sparks flash up as the picks swung into the flinty earth. Van Heerden lingered nearby, unwilling to be thus publicly superseded in the responsibility for his own dwelling in the eyes of the natives.

When they flung their picks and went to fetch the poles, they did so with a side glance at Major Carruthers, challenging him to say the trench was not deep enough. He called them back, laughingly, saying: "Are you digging for a dog-kennel then, and not a hut for a man?" One smiled unwillingly in response; the others sulked. Perfunctorily they deepened the trench to the very minimum that Major Carruthers was likely to pass. By noon, the poles were leaning drunkenly in place, and the natives were stripping the binding from beneath the bark of nearby trees. Long fleshy strips of fibre, rose-coloured and apricot and yellow, lay tangled over the grass, and the wounded trees showed startling red gashes around the clearing. Swiftly the poles were laced together with this natural rope, so that when the frame was complete it showed up against green trees and sky like a slender gleaming white cage, interwoven lightly with rosy-yellow. Two natives climbed on top to bind the roof poles into their conical shape, while the others stamped a slushy mound of sand and earth to form plaster for the walls. Soon they stopped—the rest could wait until after the midday break.

Worn out by the strain of keeping the balance between the fiery Dutchman and the resentful workers, Major Carruthers went off home to eat. He had one and a half hour's break. He finished his meal in ten minutes, longing to be able to sleep for once till he woke naturally. His wife was dozing, so he lay down on the other bed and at once dropped off to sleep himself. When he woke it was long after the time he had set himself. It was after three. He rose in a panic and strode to the clearing, in the grip of one of his premonitions.

There stood the Dutchman, in a flaring temper, shouting at the natives who lounged in front of him, laughing openly. They had only just returned to work. As Major Carruthers approached, he saw Van Heerden using his open palms in a series of quick swinging slaps against their faces, knocking them sideways against each other: it was as if he were cuffing his own children in a fit of anger. Major Carruthers broke into a run, erupting into the group before anything else could happen. Van Heerden fell back on seeing him. He was beef-red with fury. The natives were bunched together, on the point of throwing down their tools and walking off the job.

"Get back to work," snapped Major Carruthers to the men: and to Van Heerden: "I'm dealing with this." His eyes were an appeal to recognise the need for tact, but Van Heerden stood squarely there in front of him, on planted legs, breathing heavily. "But Major Carruthers . . ." he began, implying that as a white man, with his employer not there, it was right that he should take the command. "Do as I say," said Major Carruthers. Van Heerden, with a deadly look at his opponents, swung on his heel and marched off into the hut. The slapping swing of the grain-bag was as if a door had been slammed. Major Carruthers turned to the natives. "Get on," he ordered briefly, in a calm decisive voice. There was a moment of uncertainty. Then they picked up their tools and went to work.

Some laced the framework of the roof; others slapped the mud on to the walls. This business of plastering was usually a festival, with laughter and raillery, for there were gaps between the poles, and a handful of mud could fly through a space into the face of a man standing behind: the thing could become a game, like children playing snowballs. Today there was no pretence at good-humour. When the sun went down the men picked up their tools and filed off into the bush without a glance at Major Carruthers. The work had not prospered. The grass was laid untidily over the roof-frame, still uncut and reaching to the ground in long swatches. The first layer of mud had been unevenly flung on. It would be a shabby building.

"His own fault," thought Major Carruthers, sending his slow, tired blue glance to the hut where the Dutchman was still cherishing the seeds of wounded pride. Next day, when Major Carruthers was in another part of the farm, the Dutchman got his own back in a fine flaming scene with the ploughboys: they came to complain to the boss-boy, but not to Major Carruthers. This made him uneasy. All that week he waited for fresh complaints about the Dutchman's behaviour. So much was he keyed up, waiting for the scene between himself and a grudging boss-boy, that when nothing happened his apprehensions deepened into a deep foreboding.

The building was finished the following Sunday. The floors were stamped hard with new dung, the thatch trimmed, and the walls grained smooth. Another two weeks must elapse before the family could move in, for the place smelled of damp. They were weeks of worry for Major Carruthers. It was unnatural for the Africans to remain passive and sullen under the Dutchman's handling of them, and especially when they knew he was on their side. There was something he did not like in the way they would not meet his eyes and in the over-polite attitude of the boss-boy.

The beautiful clear weather that he usually loved so much, May weather, sharpened by cold, and crisp under deep clear skies, pungent with gusts of wind from the dying leaves and grasses of the veld, was spoilt for him this year: something was going to happen.

When the family eventually moved in, Major Carruthers became discouraged because the building of the hut had represented such trouble and worry, while now things seemed hardly better than before: what was the use of two small round huts for a family of eleven? But Van Heerden was very pleased, and expressed his gratitude in a way that moved Major Carruthers deeply: unable to show feeling himself, he was grateful when others did, so relieving him of the burden of his shyness. There was a ceremonial atmosphere on the evening when one of the great sagging beds was wrenched out of the floor of the first hut and its legs plastered down newly into the second hut.

That very same night he was awakened towards dawn by voices calling to him from outside his window. He started up, knowing that whatever he had dreaded was here, glad that the tension was over. Outside the back door stood his boss-boy, holding a hurricane lamp which momentarily blinded Major Carruthers.

"The hut is on fire."

Blinking his eyes, he turned to look. Away in the darkness flames were lapping over the trees, outlining branches so that as a gust of wind lifted them patterns of black leaves showed clear and fine against the flowing red light of the fire. The veld was illuminated with a fitful plunging glare. The two men ran off into the bush down the rough road, towards the blaze.

The clearing was lit up, as bright as morning, when they arrived.

On the roof of the first hut squatted Van Heerden, lifting tins of water from a line of natives below, working from the water-butt, soaking the thatch to prevent it catching the flames from the second hut that was only a few yards off. That was a roaring pillar of fire. Its frail skeleton was still erect, but twisting and writhing incandescently within its envelope of flame, and it collapsed slowly as he came up, subsiding in a crash of sparks.

"The children," gasped Major Carruthers to Mrs. Van Heerden, who was watching the blaze fatalistically from where she sat on a scattered bundle of bedding, the tears soaking down her face, her arms tight round a swathed child.

As she spoke she opened the cloths to display the smallest infant. A swathe of burning grass from the roof had fallen across its head and shoulders. He sickened as he looked, for there was nothing but raw charred flesh. But it was alive: the limbs still twitched a little.

"I'll get the car and we'll take it in to the doctor."

He ran out of the clearing and fetched the car. As he tore down the slope back again he saw he was still in his pyjamas, and when he gained the clearing for the second time, Van Heerden was climbing down the roof, which dripped water as if there had been a storm. He bent over the burnt child.

"Too late," he said.

"But it's still alive."

Van Heerden almost shrugged; he appeared dazed. He continually turned his head to survey the glowing heap that had so recently sheltered his children. He licked his lips with a quick unconscious movement, because of their burning dryness. His face was grimed with smoke and inflamed from the great heat, so that his young eyes showed startlingly clear against the black skin.

"Get into the car," said Major Carruthers to the woman. She automatically moved towards the car, without looking at her husband, who said: "But it's too late, man."

Major Carruthers knew the child would die, but his protest against the waste and futility of the burning expressed itself in this way: that everything must be done to save this life, even against hope. He started the car and slid off down the hill. Before they had gone half a mile he felt his shoulder plucked from behind, and, turning, saw the child was now dead. He reversed the car into the dark bush off the road, and drove back to the clearing. Now the woman had begun wailing, a soft monotonous, almost automatic sound that kept him tight in his seat, waiting for the next cry.

The fire was now a dark heap, fanning softly to a glowing red as the wind passed over it. The children were standing in a half-circle, gazing fascinated at it. Van Heerden stood near them, laying his hands gently, restlessly, on their heads and shoulders, reassuring himself of their existence there, in the flesh and living, beside him.

Mrs. Van Heerden got clumsily out of the car, still wailing, and disappeared into the hut, clutching the bundled dead child.

Feeling out of place among that bereaved family, Major Carruthers went up to his house, where he drank cup after cup of tea, holding himself tight and controlled, conscious of over-strained nerves.

Then he stooped into his wife's room, which seemed small and dark and airless. The cave of a sick animal, he thought, in disgust; then, ashamed of himself, he returned out of doors, where the sky was filling with light. He sent a message for the boss-boy, and waited for him in a condition of tensed anger.

When the man came Major Carruthers asked immediately: "Why did that hut burn?"

The boss-boy looked at him straight and said: "How should I know?" Then, after a pause, with guileful innocence: "It was the fault of the kitchen, too close to the thatch."

Major Carruthers glared at him, trying to wear down the straight gaze with his own accusing eyes.

"That hut must be rebuilt at once. It must be rebuilt today."

The boss-boy seemed to say that it was a matter of indifference to him whether it was rebuilt or not. "I'll go and tell the others," he said, moving off.

"Stop," barked Major Carruthers. Then he paused, frightened, not so much at his rage, but his humiliation and guilt. He had foreseen it! He had foreseen it all! And yet, that thatch could so easily have caught alight from the small incautious fire that sent up sparks all day so close to it.

Almost, he burst out in wild reproaches. Then he pulled himself together and said: "Get away from me." What was the use? He knew perfectly well that one of the Africans whom Van Heerden had kicked or slapped or shouted at had fired that hut; no one could ever prove it.

He stood quite still, watching his boss-boy move off, tugging at the long wisps of his moustache in frustrated anger.

And what would happen now?

He ordered breakfast, drank a cup of tea, and spoilt a piece of toast. Then he glanced in again at his wife, who would sleep for a couple of hours yet.

Again tugging fretfully at his moustache, Major Carruthers set
off for the clearing.

Everything was just as it had been, though the pile of black
débris looked low and shabby now that morning had come and
heightened the wild colour of sky and bush. The children were
playing nearby, their hands and faces black, their rags of clothing
black—everything seemed patched and smudged with black, and
on one side the trees hung withered and grimy and the soil was hot
underfoot.

Van Heerden leaned against the framework of the first hut. He
looked subdued and tired, but otherwise normal. He greeted Major
Carruthers, and did not move.

"How is your wife?" asked Major Carruthers. He could hear a
moaning sound from inside the hut.

"She's doing well."

Major Carruthers imagined her weeping over the dead child; and
said: "I'll take your baby into town for you and arrange for the
funeral."

Van Heerden said: "I've buried her already." He jerked his
thumb at the bush behind them.

"Didn't you register its birth?"

Van Heerden shook his head. His gaze challenged Major Carruthers as if to say: Who's to know if no one tells them? Major
Carruthers could not speak: he was held in silence by the thought
of that charred little body, huddled into a packing-case or wrapped
in a piece of cloth, thrust into the ground, at the mercy of wild
animals or of white ants.

"Well, one comes and another goes," said Van Heerden at last,
slowly, reaching out for philosophy as a comfort, while his eyes
filled with rough tears.

Major Carruthers stared: he could not understand. At last the
meaning of the words came into him, and he heard the moaning
from the hut with a new understanding.

The idea had never entered his head; it had been a complete
failure of the imagination. If nine children, why not ten? Why not
fifteen, for that matter, or twenty? Of course there would be more
children.

"It was the shock," said Van Heerden. "It should be next month."

Major Carruthers leaned back against the wall of the hut and
took out a cigarette clumsily. He felt weak. He felt as if Van Heerden had struck him, smiling. This was an absurd and unjust feeling, but for a moment he hated Van Heerden for standing there

and saying: this grey country of poverty that you fear so much, will take on a different look when you actually enter it. You will cease to exist; there is no energy left, when one is wrestling naked, with life, for your kind of fine feelings and scruples and regrets.

"We hope it will be a boy," volunteered Van Heerden, with a tentative friendliness, as if he thought it might be considered a familiarity to offer his private notions to Major Carruthers. "We have five boys and four girls—three girls," he corrected himself, his face contracting.

Major Carruthers asked stiffly: "Will she be all right?"

"I do it," said Van Heerden. "The last was born in the middle of the night, when it was raining. That was when we were in the tent. It's nothing to her," he added, with pride. He was listening, as he spoke, to the slow moaning from inside. "I'd better be getting in to her," he said, knocking out his pipe against the mud of the walls. Nodding to Major Carruthers, he lifted the sack and disappeared.

After a while Major Carruthers gathered himself together and forced himself to walk erect across the clearing under the curious gaze of the children. His mind was fixed and numb, but he walked as if moving to a destination. When he reached the house, he at once pulled paper and pen towards him and wrote, and each slow difficult word was a nail in the coffin of his pride as a man.

Some minutes later he went in to his wife. She was awake, turned on her side, watching the door for the relief of his coming. "I've written for a job at Home," he said simply, laying his hand on her thin dry wrist, and feeling the slow pulse beat up suddenly against his palm.

He watched curiously as her face crumpled and the tears of thankfulness and release ran slowly down her cheeks and soaked the pillow.

The Nuisance

Two narrow tracks, one of them deepened to a smooth dusty groove by the incessant padding of bare feet, wound from the farm compound to the old well through half a mile of tall blond grass that was soiled and matted because of the nearness of the clustering huts: the compound had been on that ridge for twenty years.

The native women with their children used to loiter down the track, and their shrill laughter and chattering sounded through the trees as if one might suddenly have come on a flock of brilliant noisy parrots. It seemed as if fetching water was more of a social event to them than a chore. At the well itself they would linger half the morning, standing in groups to gossip, their arms raised in that graceful, eternally moving gesture to steady glittering or rusted petrol tins balanced on head-rings woven of grass; kneeling to slap bits of bright cloth on slabs of stone blasted long ago from the depths of earth. Here they washed and scolded and dandled their children. Here they scrubbed their pots. Here they sluiced themselves and combed their hair.

Coming upon them suddenly there would be sharp exclamations; a glimpse of soft brown shoulders and thighs withdrawing to the bushes, or annoyed and resentful eyes. It was their well. And while they were there, with their laughter, and gossip and singing, their folded draperies, bright armbands, earthenware jars and metal combs, grouped in attitudes of head-slowed indolence, it seemed as if the bellowing of distant cattle, drone of tractor, all the noises of the farm, were simply lending themselves to form a background to this antique scene: Women, drawing water at the well.

When they left the ground would be scattered with the bright-pink, fleshy skins of the native wild-plum which contracts the mouth shudderingly with its astringency, or with the shiny green fragments of the shells of kaffir oranges.

Without the women the place was ugly, paltry. The windlass, coiled with greasy rope, propped for safety with a forked stick, was sheltered by a tiny cock of thatch that threw across the track a long, intensely black shadow. For the rest, veld; the sere, flattened, sun-dried veld.

They were beautiful, these women. But she whom I thought of vaguely as "The cross-eyed one," offended the sight. She used to lag behind the others on the road, either by herself, or in charge of the older children. Not only did she suffer from a painful squint, so that when she looked towards you it was with a confused glare of white eyeball; but her body was hideous. She wore the traditional dark-patterned blue stuff looped at the waist, and above it her breasts were loose, flat crinkling triangles.

She was a solitary figure at the well, doing her washing unaided and without laughter. She would strain at the windlass during the long slow ascent of the swinging bucket that clanged sometimes, far below, against the sides of naked rock until at that critical moment when it hung vibrating at the mouth of the well, she would set the weight of her shoulder in the crook of the handle and with a fearful snatching movement bring the water to safety. It would slop over, dissolving in a shower of great drops that fell tinkling to disturb the surface of that tiny, circular, dully-gleaming mirror which lay at the bottom of the plunging rock tunnel. She was clumsy. Because of her eyes her body lumbered.

She was the oldest wife of "The Long One," who was our most skilful driver.

"The Long One" was not so tall as he was abnormally thin. It was the leanness of those driven by inner restlessness. He could never keep still. His hands plucked at pieces of grass, his shoulder twitched to a secret rhythm of the nerves. Set a-top of that sinewy, narrow, taut body was a narrow head, with wide-pointed ears, which gave him an appearance of alert caution. The expression of the face was always violent, whether he was angry, laughing, or— most usually—sardonically critical. He had a tongue that was feared by every labourer of the farm. Even my father would smile ruefully after an altercation with his driver and say: "He's a man, that native. One must respect him, after all. He never lets you get away with anything."

In his own line he was an artist—his line being cattle. He handled oxen with a delicate brutality that was fascinating and horrifying to watch. Give him a bunch of screaming, rearing three-year-olds, due to take their first taste of the yoke, and he would fight them for hours under a blistering sun with the sweat running off him, his eyes glowing with a wicked and sombre satisfaction. Then he would use his whip, grunting savagely as the lash cut down into flesh, his tongue stuck calculatingly between his teeth as he measured the exact weight of the blow. But to watch him handle a team of sixteen fat tamed oxen was a different thing. It was like watching a circus act; there was the same suspense in it: it was a matter of pride to him that he did not need to use the whip. This did not by any means imply that he wished to spare the beasts pain, not at all; he liked to feed his pride on his own skill. Alongside the double line of ponderous cattle that strained across acres of heavy clods, danced, raved and screamed the Long One, with his twelve-foot-long lash circling in black patterns over their backs; and though his threatening yells were the yells of an inspired madman, and the heavy whip could be heard clean across the farm, so that on a moonlight night when they were ploughing late it sounded like the crack and whine of a rifle, never did the dangerous metal-tipped lash so much as touch a hair of their hides. If you examined the oxen as they were outspanned, they might be exhausted, driven to staggering-point, so that my father had to remonstrate, but there was never a mark on them.

"He knows how to handle oxen, but he can't handle his women."

We gave our natives labels such as that, since it was impossible ever to know them as their fellows knew them, in the round. That phrase summarised for us what the Long One offered in entertainment during the years he was with us. Coming back to the farm, after an absence, one would say in humorous anticipation: "And what has the Long One been up to now, with his harem?"

There was always trouble with his three wives. He used to come up to the house to discuss with my father, man to man, how the youngest wife was flirting with the boss-boy from the neighbouring compound, six miles off; or how she had thrown a big pot of smoking mealie-pap at the middle wife, who was jealous of her.

We grew accustomed to the sight of the Long One standing at the back door, at the sunset hour, when my father held audience after work. He always wore long khaki trousers that slipped down over thin bony hips and went bare-chested, and there would be a ruddy gleam on his polished black skin, and his spindly gesticulating form would be outlined against a sea of fiery colours. At the end of his tale of compliant he would relapse suddenly into a pose of resignation that was self-consciously weary. My father used to laugh until his face was wet and say: "That man is a natural-born comedian. He would have been on the stage if he had been born another colour."

But he was no buffoon. He would play up to my father's appreciation of the comic, but he would never play the ape, as some Africans did, for our amusement. And he was certainly no figure of fun to his fellows. That same thing in him that sat apart, watchfully critical, even of himself, gave his humour its mordancy, his tongue its sting. And he was terribly attractive to his women. I have seen him slouch down the road on his way from one team to another, his whip trailing behind in the dust, his trousers sagging in folds from hip-bone to ankle, his eyes broodingly directed in front of him, merely nodding as he passed a group of women among whom might be his wives. And it was as if he had lashed them with that whip. They would bridle and writhe; and then call provocatively after him, but with a note of real anger, to make him notice them. He would not so much as turn his head.

When the real trouble started, though, my father soon got tired of it. He liked to be amused, not seriously implicated in his labourers' problems. The Long One took to coming up not occasionally, as he had been used to do, but every evening. He was deadly serious, and very bitter. He wanted my father to persuade the old wife, the cross-eyed one, to go back home to her own people. The woman was driving him crazy. A nagging woman in your house was like having a flea on your body; you could scratch but it always moved to another place, and there was no peace till you killed it.

"But you can't send her back, just because you are tired of her."

The Long One said his life had become insupportable. She grumbled, she sulked, she spoilt his food.

"Well, then your other wives can cook for you."

But it seemed there were complications. The two younger women hated each other, but they were united in one thing, that the old wife should stay, for she was so useful. She looked after the children; she did the hoeing in the garden; she picked relishes from the veld. Besides, she provided endless amusement with her ungainliness. She was the eternal butt, the fool, marked by fate for the entertainment of the whole-limbed and the comely.

My father referred at this point to a certain handbook on native
lore, which stated definitively that an elder wife was entitled to be
waited on by a young wife, perhaps as compensation for having to
give up the pleasures of her lord's favour. The Long One and his
ménage cut clean across this amiable theory. And my father, being
unable to find a prescribed remedy (as one might look for a cure of
a disease in a pharmacopoeia), grew angry. After some weeks of
incessant complaint from the Long One he was told to hold his
tongue and manage his women himself. That evening the man
stalked furiously down the path, muttering to himself between
teeth clenched on a grass-stem, on his way home to his two giggling
younger wives and the ugly sour-faced old woman, the mother of
his elder children, the drudge of his household and the scourge of
his life.

It was some weeks later that my father asked casually one day:
"And by the way, Long One, how are things with you? All right
again?"

And the Long One answered simply: "Yes, baas. She's gone
away."

"What do you mean, gone away?"

The Long One shrugged. She had just gone. She had left suddenly, without saying anything to anyone.

Now, the woman came from Nyasaland, which was days and
days of weary walking away. Surely she hadn't gone by herself?
Had a brother or an uncle come to fetch her? Had she gone with a
band of passing Africans on their way home?

My father wondered a little, and then forgot about it. It wasn't
his affair. He was pleased to have his most useful native back at
work with an unharassed mind. And he was particularly pleased
that the whole business was ended before the annual trouble over
the water-carrying.

For there were two wells. The new one, used by ourselves, had
fresh sparkling water that was sweet in the mouth; but in July of
each year it ran dry. The water of the old well had a faintly unpleasant taste and was pale brown, but there was always plenty of
it. For three or four months of the year, depending on the rains, we
shared that well with the compound.

Now, the Long One hated fetching water three miles, four times
a week, in the water-cart. The women of the compound disliked
having to arrange their visits to the well so as not to get in the way
of the water-carriers. There was always grumbling.

This year we had not even begun to use the old well when complaints started that the water tasted bad. The big baas must get the well cleaned.

My father said vaguely that he would clean the well when he had time.

Next day there came a deputation from the women of the compound. Half a dozen of them stood at the back door, arguing that if the well wasn't cleaned soon, all their children would be sick.

"I'll do it next week," he promised, with bad grace.

The following morning the Long One brought our first load of the season from the old well; and as we turned the taps on the barrels a foetid smell began to pervade the house. As for drinking it, that was out of the question.

"Why don't you keep the cover on the well?" my father said to the women, who were still loitering resentfully at the back door. He was really angry. "Last time the well was cleaned there were fourteen dead rats and a dead snake. We never get things in our well because we remember to keep the lid on."

But the women appeared to consider the lid being on, or off, was an act of God, and nothing to do with them.

We always went down to watch the well-emptying, which had the fascination of a ritual. Like the mealie-shelling, or the first rains, it marked a turning-point in the year. It seemed as if a besieged city were laying plans for the conservation of supplies. The sap was falling in tree and grass-root; the sun was withdrawing high, high, behind a veil of smoke and dust; the fierce dryness of the air was a new element, parching foliage as the heat cauterized it. The well-emptying was an act of faith, and of defiance. For a whole afternoon there would be no water on the farm at all. One well was completely dry. And this one would be drained, dependent on the mysterious ebbing and flowing of underground rivers. What if they should fail us? There was an anxious evening, every year; and in the morning, when the Long One stood at the back door and said, beaming, that the bucket was bringing up fine new water, it was like a festival.

But this afternoon we could not stick it out. The smell was intolerable. We saw the usual complement of bloated rats, laid out on the stones around the well, and there was even the skeleton of a small buck that must have fallen in the dark. Then we left, along the road that was temporarily a river whose source was that apparently endless succession of buckets filled by greyish, evil water.

It was the Long One himself that came to tell us the news. Afterwards we tried to remember what look that always expressive face wore as he told it.

It seemed that in the last bucket but one had floated a human arm, or rather the fragments of one. Piece by piece they had fetched her up, the Cross-eyed Woman, his own first wife. They recognised her by her bangles. Last of all, the Long One went down to fetch up her head, which was missing.

"I thought you said your wife had gone home?" said my father.

"I thought she had. Where else could she have gone?"

"Well," said my father at last, disgusted by the whole thing, "if she had to kill herself, why couldn't she hang herself on a tree, instead of spoiling the well?"

"She might have slipped and fallen," said the Long One.

My father looked up at him suddenly. He stared for a few moments. Then: "Ye-yes," he said, "I suppose she might."

Later, we talked about the thing, saying how odd it was that natives should commit suicide; it seemed almost like an impertinence, as if they were claiming to have the same delicate feelings as ours.

But later still, apropos of nothing in particular, my father was heard to remark: "Well, I don't know, I'm damned if I know, but in any case he's a damned good driver."

The De Wets Come to Kloof Grange

THE verandah, which was lifted on stone pillars, jutted forward over the garden like a box in the theatre. Below were luxuriant masses of flowering shrubs, and creepers whose shiny leaves, like sequins, reflected light from a sky stained scarlet and purple and apple-green. This splendiferous sunset filled one half of the sky, fading gently through shades of mauve to a calm expanse of ruffling grey, blown over by tinted cloudlets; and in this still evening sky, just above a clump of darkening conifers, hung a small crystal moon.

There sat Major Gale and his wife, as they did every evening at this hour, side by side trimly in deck chairs, their sundowners on small tables at their elbows, critically watching, like connoisseurs, the pageant presented for them.

Major Gale said, with satisfaction: "Good sunset tonight," and they both turned their eyes to the vanquishing moon. The dusk drew veils across sky and garden; and punctually, as she did every day, Mrs. Gale shook off nostalgia like a terrier shaking off water and rose, saying: "Mosquitoes!" She drew her deck chair to the wall, where she neatly folded and stacked it.

"Here is the post," she said, her voice quickening; and Major Gale went to the steps, waiting for the native who was hastening towards them through the tall shadowing bushes. He swung a sack from his back and handed it to Major Gale. A sour smell of raw meat rose from the sack. Major Gale said with a kindly contempt he used for his native servants: "Did the spooks get you?" and laughed. The native, who had panted the last mile of his ten-mile journey through a bush filled with unnameable phantoms, ghosts of ancestors, wraiths of tree and beast, put on a pantomime of fear and chattered and shivered for a moment like an ape, to amuse his master. Major Gale dismissed the boy. He ducked thankfully around the corner of the house to the back, where there were lights and companionship.

Mrs. Gale lifted the sack and went into the front room. There she lit the oil lamp and called for the houseboy, to whom she handed the groceries and meat she removed. She took a fat bundle of letters from the very bottom of the sack and wrinkled her nose slightly; blood from the meat had stained them. She sorted the letters into two piles; and then husband and wife sat themselves down opposite each other to read their mail.

It was more than the ordinary farm living-room. There were koodoo horns branching out over the fireplace, and a bundle of knobkerries hanging on a nail; but on the floor were fine rugs, and the furniture was two hundred years old. The table was a pool of softly-reflected lights; it was polished by Mrs. Gale herself every day before she set on it an earthenware crock filled with thorny red flowers. Africa and the English eighteenth century mingled in this room and were at peace.

From time to time Mrs. Gale rose impatiently to attend to the lamp, which did not burn well. It was one of those terrifying paraffin things that have to be pumped with air to a whiter-hot flame from time to time, and which in any case emit a continuous soft hissing noise. Above the heads of the Gales a light cloud of flying insects wooed their fiery death and dropped one by one, plop, plop, plop to the table among the letters.

Mrs. Gale took an envelope from her own heap and handed it to her husband. "The assistant," she remarked abstractedly, her eyes bent on what she held. She smiled tenderly as she read. The letter was from her oldest friend, a woman doctor in London, and they had written to each other every week for thirty years, ever since Mrs. Gale came to exile in Southern Rhodesia. She murmured half-aloud: "Why, Betty's brother's daughter is going to study economics," and though she had never met Betty's brother, let alone the daughter, the news seemed to please and excite her extraordinarily. The whole of the letter was about people she had never met and was not likely ever to meet—about the weather, about English politics. Indeed, there was not a sentence in it that would not have struck an outsider as having been written out of a sense of duty; but when Mrs. Gale had finished reading it, she put it aside gently and sat smiling quietly: she had gone back half a century to her childhood.

Gradually sight returned to her eyes, and she saw her husband where previously she had sat looking through him. He appeared disturbed; there was something wrong about the letter from the assistant.

Major Gale was a tall and still military figure, even in his khaki bush-shirt and shorts. He changed them twice a day. His shorts were creased sharp as folded paper, and the six pockets of his shirt were always buttoned up tight. His small head, with its polished surface of black hair, his tiny jaunty black moustache, his farmer's hands with their broken but clean nails—all these seemed to say that it was no easy matter not to let oneself go, not to let this damned disintegrating gaudy easy-going country get under one's skin. It wasn't easy, but he did it; he did it with the conscious effort that had slowed his movements and added the slightest touch of caricature to his appearance: one finds a man like Major Gale only in exile.

He rose from his chair and began pacing the room, while his wife watched him speculatively and waited for him to tell her what was the matter. When he stood up, there was something not quite right—what was it? Such a spruce and tailored man he was; but the disciplined shape of him was spoiled by a curious fatness and softness: the small rounded head was set on a thickening neck; the buttocks were fattening too, and quivered as he walked. Mrs. Gale, as these facts assailed her, conscientiously excluded them: she had her own picture of her husband, and could not afford to have it destroyed.

At last he sighed, with a glance at her; and when she said: "Well, dear?" he replied at once, "The man has a wife."

"Dear me!" she exclaimed, dismayed.

At once, as if he had been waiting for her protest, he returned briskly: "It will be nice for you to have another woman about the place."

"Yes, I suppose it will," she said humorously. At this most familiar note in her voice, he jerked his head up and said aggressively: "You always complain I bury you alive."

And so she did. Every so often, but not so often now, she allowed herself to overflow into a mood of gently humorous bitterness; but it had not carried conviction for many years; it was more, really, of an attention to him, like remembering to kiss him good night. In fact, she had learned to love her isolation, and she felt aggrieved that he did not know it.

"Well, but they can't come to the house. That I really couldn't put up with." The plan had been for the new assistant—Major Gale's farming was becoming too successful and expanding for him to manage any longer by himself—to have the spare room, and share the house with his employers.

"No, I suppose not, if there's a wife." Major Gale sounded doubtful; it was clear he would not mind another family sharing with them. "Perhaps they could have the old house?" he enquired at last.

"I'll see to it," said Mrs. Gale, removing the weight of worry off her husband's shoulders. Things he could manage: people bothered him. That they bothered her, too, now, was something she had become resigned to his not understanding. For she knew he was hardly conscious of her; nothing existed for him outside his farm. And this suited her well. During the early years of their marriage, with the four children growing up, there was always a little uneasiness between them, like an unpaid debt. Now they were friends and could forget each other. What a relief when he no longer "loved" her! (That was how she put it.) Ah, that "love"—she thought of it with a small humorous distaste. Growing old had its advantages.

When she said "I'll see to it," he glanced at her, suddenly, directly, her tone had been a little too comforting and maternal. Normally his gaze wavered over her, not seeing her. Now he really observed her for a moment; he saw an elderly Englishwoman, as thin and dry as a stalk of maize in September, sitting poised over her letters, one hand touching them lovingly, and gazing at him with her small flower-blue eyes. A look of guilt in them troubled him. He crossed to her and kissed her cheek. "There!" she said, inclining her face with a sprightly, fidgety laugh. Overcome with embarrassment he stopped for a moment, then said determinedly: "I shall go and have my bath."

After his bath, from which he emerged pink and shining like an elderly baby, dressed in flannels and a blazer, they ate their dinner under the wheezing oil lamp and the cloud of flying insects. Immediately the meal was over he said "Bed," and moved off. He was always in bed before eight and up by five. Once Mrs. Gale had adapted herself to his routine. Now, with the four boys out sailing the seven seas in the navy, and nothing really to get her out of bed (her servants were perfectly trained), she slept until eight, when she joined her husband at breakfast. She refused to have that meal in bed; nor would she have dreamed of appearing in her dressing-gown. Even as things were she was guilty enough about sleeping those three daylight hours, and found it necessary to apologize for her slackness. So, when her husband had gone to bed she remained under the lamp, re-reading her letters, sewing, reading, or simply dreaming about the past, the very distant past, when she had been Caroline Morgan, living near a small country town, a country squire's daughter. That was how she liked best to think of herself.

Tonight she soon turned down the lamp and stepped on to the verandah. Now the moon was a large, soft, yellow fruit caught in the top branches of the blue-gums. The garden was filled with glamour, and she let herself succumb to it. She passed quietly down the steps and beneath the trees, with one quick solicitous glance back at the bedroom window: her husband hated her to be out of the house by herself at night. She was on her way to the old house that lay half a mile distant over the veld.

Before the Gales had come to this farm, two brothers had it, South Africans by birth and upbringing. The houses had then been separated by a stretch of untouched bush, with not so much as a fence or a road between them; and in this state of guarded inde-pendence the two men had lived, both bachelors, both quite alone. The thought of them amused Mrs. Gale. She could imagine them sending polite notes to each other, invitations to meals or to spend an evening. She imagined them loaning each other books by native bearer, meeting at a neutral point between their homes. She was amused, but she respected them for a feeling she could understand. She made up all kinds of pretty ideas about these brothers, until one day she learned from a neighbour that in fact the two men had quarrelled continually, and had eventually gone bankrupt because they could not agree how the farm was to be run. After this discov-ery Mrs. Gale ceased to think about them; a pleasant fancy had become a distasteful reality.

The first thing she did on arriving was to change the name of the farm from Kloof Nek to Kloof Grange, making a link with home. One of the houses was denuded of furniture and used as a storage space. It was a square, bare box of a place, stuck in the middle of the bare veld, and its shut windows flashed back light to the sun all day. But her own home had been added to and extended, and sur-rounded with verandahs and fenced; inside the fence were two acres of garden, that she had created over years of toil. And what a garden! These were what she lived for: her flowering African shrubs, her vivid English lawns, her water-garden with the goldfish and water lilies. Not many people had such a garden.

She walked through it this evening under the moon, feeling herself grow lightheaded and insubstantial with the influence of the strange greenish light, and of the perfumes from the flowers. She touched the leaves with her fingers as she passed, bending her face to the roses. At the gate, under the hanging white trumpets of the moonflower she paused, and lingered for a while, looking over the space of empty veld between her and the other house. She did not like going outside her garden at night. She was not afraid of natives, no: she had contempt for women who were afraid, for she regarded Africans as rather pathetic children, and was very kind to them. She did not know what made her afraid. Therefore she took a deep breath, compressed her lips, and stepped carefully through the gate, shutting it behind her with a sharp click. The road before her was a glimmering white ribbon, the hard-crusted sand sending up a continuous small sparkle of light as she moved. On either side were sparse stumpy trees, and their shadows were deep and black. A nightjar cut across the stars with crooked trailing wings, and she set her mouth defiantly: why, this was only the road she walked over every afternoon, for her constitutional! There were the trees she had pleaded for, when her husband was wanting to have them cut for firewood: in a sense, they were her trees. Deliberately slowing her steps, as a discipline, she moved through the pits of shadow, gaining each stretch of clear moonlight with relief, until she came to the house. It looked dead, a dead thing with staring eyes, with those blank windows gleaming pallidly back at the moon. Nonsense, she told herself. Nonsense. And she walked to the front door, unlocked it, and flashed her torch over the floor. Sacks of grain were piled to the rafters, and the brick floor was scattered with loose mealies. Mice scurried invisibly to safety, and flocks of cockroaches blackened the walls. Standing in a patch of moonlight on the brick, so that she would not unwittingly walk into a spider-web or a jutting sack, she drew in deep breaths of the sweetish smell of maize, and made a list in her head of what had to be done; she was a very capable woman.

Then something struck her: if the man had forgotten, when applying for the job, to mention a wife, he was quite capable of forgetting children too. If they had children it wouldn't do; no, it wouldn't. She simply couldn't put up with a tribe of children—for Afrikaners never had less than twelve—running wild over her beautiful garden and teasing her goldfish. Anger spurted in her. De

Wet—the name was hard on her tongue. Her husband should not have agreed to take on an Afrikaner. Really, really, Caroline, she chided herself humorously, standing there in the deserted moonlit house, don't jump to conclusions, don't be unfair.

She decided to arrange the house for a man and his wife, ignoring the possibility of children. She would arrange things, in kindness, for a woman who might be unused to living in loneliness; she would be good to this woman; so she scolded herself, to make atonement for her short fit of pettiness. But when she tried to form a picture of this woman who was coming to share her life, at least to the extent of taking tea with her in the mornings, and swapping recipes (so she supposed), imagination failed her. She pictured a large Dutch frau, all homely comfort and sweating goodness, and was repulsed. For the first time the knowledge that she must soon, next week, take another woman into her life, came home to her; and she disliked it intensely.

Why must she? Her husband would not have to make a friend of the man. They would work together, that was all; but because they, the wives, were two women on an isolated farm, they would be expected to live in each other's pockets. All her instincts toward privacy, the distance which she had put between herself and other people, even her own husband, rebelled against it. And because she rebelled, rejecting this imaginary Dutch woman, to whom she felt so alien, she began to think of her friend Betty, as if it were she who would be coming to the farm.

Still thinking of her friend Betty she returned through the silent velt to her home, imagining them walking together over this road and talking as they had been used to do. The thought of Betty, who had turned into a shrewd, elderly woman doctor with kind eyes, sustained her through the frightening silences. At the gate she lifted her head to sniff the heavy perfume of the moon-flowers, and became conscious that something else was invading her dream: it was a very bad smell, an odour of decay mingled with the odour from the flowers. Something had died on the veld, and the wind had changed and was bringing the smell towards the house. She made a mental note: I must send the boy in the morning to see what it is. Then the conflict between her thoughts of her friend and her own life presented itself sharply to her. You are a silly woman, Caroline, she said to herself. Three years before they had gone on holiday to England, and she had found she and Betty had nothing to say to each other. Their lives were so far apart, and had been for so long, that the weeks they spent together were an offering to a friendship that had died years before. She knew it very well, but tried not to think of it. It was necessary to her to have Betty remain, in imagination at least, as a counter-weight to her loneliness. Now she was being made to realise the truth. She resented that too, and somewhere the resentment was chalked up against Mrs. De Wet, the Dutch woman who was going to invade her life with impertinent personal claims.

And next day, and the days following, she cleaned and swept and tidied the old house, not for Mrs. De Wet, but for Betty. Otherwise she could not have gone through with it. And when it was all finished, she walked through the rooms which she had furnished with things taken from her own home, and said to a visionary Betty (but Betty as she had been thirty years before): "Well, what do you think of it?" The place was bare but clean now, and smelling of sunlight and air. The floors had coloured coconut matting over the brick; the beds, standing on opposite sides of the room, were covered with gaily striped counterpanes. There were vases of flowers everywhere. "You would like living here," Mrs. Gale said to Betty, before locking the house up and returning to her own, feeling as if she had won a victory over herself.

The De Wets sent a wire saying they would arrive on Sunday after lunch. Mrs. Gale noted with annoyance that this would spoil her rest, for she slept every day, through the afternoon heat. Major Gale, for whom every day was a working day (he hated idleness and found odd jobs to occupy him on Sundays), went off to a distant part of the farm to look at his cattle. Mrs. Gale laid herself down on her bed with her eyes shut and listened for a car, all her nerves stretched. Flies buzzed drowsily over the window-panes; the breeze from the garden was warm and scented. Mrs. Gale slept uncomfortably, warring all the afternoon with the knowledge that she should be awake. When she woke at four she was cross and tired, and there was still no sign of a car. She rose and dressed herself, taking a frock from the cupboard without looking to see what it was: her clothes were often fifteen years old. She brushed her hair absent-mindedly; and then, recalled by a sense that she had not taken enough trouble, slipped a large gold locket round her neck, as a conscientious mark of welcome. Then she left a message with the houseboy that she would be in the garden and walked away from the verandah with a strong excitement growing in her. This excitement rose as she moved through the crowding shrubs under the walls, through the rose garden with its wide green lawns where water sprayed all the year round, and arrived at her favourite spot among the fountains and the pools of water lilies. Her water-garden was an extravagance, for the pumping of the water from the river cost a great deal of money.

She sat herself on a shaded bench; and on one side were the glittering plumes of the fountains, the roses, the lawns, the house, and beyond them the austere wind-bitten high veld; on the other, at her feet, the ground dropped hundreds of feet sharply to the river. It was a rocky shelf thrust forward over the gulf, and here she would sit for hours, leaning dizzily outwards, her short grey hair blown across her face, lost in adoration of the hills across the river. Not of the river itself, no, she thought of that with a sense of danger, for there, below her, in that green-crowded gully, were suddenly the tropics: palm trees, a slow brown river that eddied into reaches of marsh or curved round belts of reeds twelve feet high. There were crocodiles, and leopards came from the rocks to drink. Sitting there on her exposed shelf, a smell of sun-warmed green, of hot decaying water, of luxurious growth, an intoxicating heady smell, rose in waves to her face. She had learned to ignore it, and to ignore the river, while she watched the hills. They were *her* hills: that was how she felt. For years she had sat here, hours every day, watching the cloud shadows move over them, watching them turn blue with distance or come close after rain so that she could see the exquisite brushwork of trees on the lower slopes. They were never the same half an hour together. Modulating light created them anew for her as she looked, thrusting one peak forward and withdrawing another, moving them back so that they were hazed on a smoky horizon, crouched in sullen retreat, or raising them so that they towered into a brilliant cleansed sky. Sitting here, buffeted by winds, scorched by the sun or shivering with cold, she could challenge anything. They were her mountains; they were what she was; they had made her, had crystallized her loneliness into a strength, had sustained her and fed her.

And now she almost forgot the De Wets were coming, and were hours late. Almost, not quite. At last, understanding that the sun was setting (she could feel its warmth striking below her shoulders), her small irritation turned to anxiety. Something might have happened to them? They had taken the wrong road, perhaps? The car had broken down? And there was the Major, miles away with their own car, and so there was no means of looking for them. Perhaps she should send out natives along the roads? If they had taken the wrong turning, to the river, they might be bogged in mud to the axles. Down there, in the swampy heat, they could be bitten by mosquitoes and then . . .

Caroline, she said to herself severely (thus finally withdrawing from the mountains), don't let things worry you so. She stood up and shook herself, pushed the hair out of her face, and gripped her whipping skirts in a thick bunch. She stepped backwards away from the wind that raked the edges of the cliff, sighed a goodbye to her garden for that day, and returned to the house. There, outside the front door, was a car, an ancient jalopy bulging with luggage, its back doors tied with rope. And children! She could see a half-grown girl on the steps. No, really, it was too much. On the other side of the car stooped a tall, thin, fairheaded man, burnt as brown as toffee, looking for someone to come. He must be the father. She approached, adjusting her face to a smile, looking apprehensively about her for the children. The man slowly came forward, the girl after him. "I expected you earlier," began Mrs. Gale briskly, looking reproachfully into the man's face. His eyes were cautious, blue, assessing. He looked her casually up and down and seemed not to take her into account. "Is Major Gale about?" he asked. "I am Mrs. Gale," she replied. Then, again: "I expected you earlier." Really, four hours late and not a word of apology!

"We started late," he remarked. "Where can I put our things?"

Mrs. Gale swallowed her annoyance and said: "I didn't know you had a family. I didn't make arrangements."

"I wrote to the Major about my wife," said De Wet. "Didn't he get my letter?" He sounded offended.

Weakly Mrs. Gale said: "Your wife?" and looked in wonderment at the girl, who was smiling awkwardly behind her husband. It could be seen, looking at her more closely, that she might perhaps be eighteen. She was a small creature, with delicate brown legs and arms, a brush of dancing black curls. and large excited black eyes. She put both hands round her husband's arm, and said, giggling: "I am Mrs. De Wet."

De Wet put her away from him, gently, but so that she pouted and said: "We got married last week."

"Last week," said Mrs. Gale, conscious of dislike.

The girl said, with an extraordinary mixture of effrontery and shyness: "He met me in a cinema and we got married next day." It seemed as if she were in some way offering herself to the older woman, offering something precious of herself.

"Really," said Mrs. Gale politely, glancing almost apprehensively at this man, this slow-moving, laconic, shrewd South African, who had behaved with such violence and folly. Distaste twisted her again.

Suddenly the man said, grasping the girl by the arm, and gently shaking her to and fro, in a sort of controlled exasperation: "Thought I had better get myself a wife to cook for me, all this way out in the blue. No restaurants here, hey, Doodle?"

"Oh, Jack," pouted the girl, giggling. "All he thinks about is his stomach," she said to Mrs. Gale, as one girl to another, and then glanced with delicious fear up at her husband.

"Cooking is what I married you for," he said, smiling down at her intimately.

There stood Mrs. Gale opposite them, and she saw that they had forgotten her existence; and that it was only by the greatest effort of will that they did not kiss. "Well," she remarked drily, "this is a surprise."

They fell apart, their faces changing. They became at once what they had been during the first moments: two hostile strangers. They looked at her across the barrier that seemed to shut the world away from them. They saw a middle-aged English lady, in a shapeless old-fashioned blue silk dress, with a gold locket sliding over a flat bosom, smiling at them coldly, her blue, misted eyes critically narrowed.

"I'll take you to your house," she said energetically. "I'll walk, and you go in the car—no, I walk it often." Nothing would induce her to get into the bouncing rattle-trap that was bursting with luggage and half-suppressed intimacies.

As stiff as a twig, she marched before them along the road, while the car jerked and ground along in bottom gear. She knew it was ridiculous; she could feel their eyes on her back, could feel their astonished amusement; but she could not help it.

When they reached the house, she unlocked it, showed them briefly what arrangements had been made, and left them. She walked back in a tumult of anger, caused mostly because of her picture of herself, walking along that same road, meekly followed by the car, and refusing to do the only sensible thing, which was to get into it with them.

She sat on the verandah for half an hour, looking at the sunset sky without seeing it, and writhing with various emotions, none of which she classified. Eventually she called the houseboy, and gave him a note, asking the two to come to dinner. No sooner had the boy left, and was trotting off down the bushy path to the gate, than she called him back. "I'll go myself," she said. This was partly to prove that she made nothing of walking the half mile, and partly from contrition. After all, it was no crime to get married, and they seemed very fond of each other. That was how she put it.

When she came to the house, the front room was littered with luggage, paper, pots and pans. All the exquisite order she had created was destroyed. She could hear voices from the bedroom.

"But, Jack, I don't want you to. I want you to stay with me." And then his voice, humorous, proud, slow, amorous: "You'll do what I tell you, my girl. I've got to see the old man and find out what's cooking. I start work tomorrow, don't forget."

"But, Jack . . .'" Then came sounds of scuffling, laughter, and a sharp slap.

"Well," said Mrs. Gale, drawing in her breath. She knocked on the wood of the door, and all sound ceased. "Come in," came the girl's voice. Mrs. Gale hesitated, then went into the bedroom.

Mrs. De Wet was sitting in a bunch on the bed, her flowered frock spread all around her, combing her hair. Mrs. Gale noted that the two beds had already been pushed together. "I've come to ask you to dinner," she said briskly. "You don't want to have to cook when you've just come."

Their faces had already become blank and polite.

"Oh no, don't trouble, Mrs. Gale," said De Wet, awkwardly. "We'll get ourselves something, don't worry." He glanced at the girl, and his face softened. He said, unable to resist it: "She'll get busy with the tin-opener in a minute, I expect. That's her idea of feeding a man."

"Oh Jack," pouted his wife.

De Wet turned back to the washstand, and proceeded to swab lather on his face. Waving the brush at Mrs. Gale, he said: "Thanks all the same. But tell the Major I'll be over after dinner to talk things over."

"Very well," said Mrs. Gale, "just as you like."

She walked away from the house. Now she felt rebuffed. After all, they might have had the politeness to come; yet she was pleased they hadn't; yet if they preferred making love to getting to know the people who were to be their close neighbours for what might be years, it was their own affair . . .

Mrs. De Wet was saying, as she painted her toenails, with her knees drawn up to her chin, and the bottle of varnish gripped between her heels: "Who the hell does she think she is, anyway?

Surely she could give us a meal without making such a fuss when we've just come."

"She came to ask us, didn't she?"

"Hoping we would say no."

And Mrs. Gale knew quite well that this was what they were thinking, and felt it was unjust. She would have liked them to come: the man wasn't a bad sort, in his way; a simple soul, but pleasant enough; as for the girl, she would have to learn, that was all. They should have come; it was their fault. Nevertheless she was filled with that discomfort that comes of having done a job badly. If she had behaved differently they would have come. She was cross throughout dinner; and that meal was not half finished when there was a knock on the door. De Wet stood there, apparently surprised they had not finished, from which it seemed that the couple had, after all, dined off sardines and bread and butter.

Major Gale left his meal and went out to the verandah to discuss business. Mrs. Gale finished her dinner in state, and then joined the two men. Her husband rose politely at her coming, offered her a chair, sat down and forgot her presence. She listened to them talking for some two hours. Then she interjected a remark (a thing she never did, as a rule, for women get used to sitting silent when men discuss farming) and did not know herself what made her say what she did about the cattle; but when De Wet looked round absently as if to say she should mind her own business, and her husband remarked absently, "Yes, dear," when a Yes dear did not fit her remark at all, she got up angrily and went indoors. Well, let them talk, then, she did not mind.

As she undressed for bed, she decided she was tired, because of her broken sleep that afternoon. But she could not sleep then, either. She listened to the sound of the men's voices, drifting brokenly round the corner of the verandah. They seemed to be thoroughly enjoying themselves. It was after twelve when she heard De Wet say, in that slow facetious way of his: "I'd better be getting home. I'll catch it hot, as it is." And, with rage, Mrs. Gale heard her husband laugh. He actually laughed. She realized that she herself had been planning an acid remark for when he came to the bedroom; so when he did enter, smelling of tobacco smoke, and grinning, and then proceeded to walk jauntily about the room in his underclothes, she said nothing, but noted that he was getting fat, in spite of all the hard work he did.

"Well, what do you think of the man?"

"He'll do very well indeed," said Major Gale, with satisfaction. "Very well. He knows his stuff all right. He's been doing mixed farming in the Transvaal for years." After a moment he asked politely, as he got with a bounce into his own bed on the other side of the room: "And what is she like?"

"I haven't seen much of her, have I? But she seems pleasant enough." Mrs. Gale spoke with measured detachment.

"Someone for you to talk to," said Major Gale, turning himself over to sleep. "You had better ask her over to tea."

At this Mrs. Gale sat straight up in her own bed with a jerk of annoyance. Someone for her to talk to, indeed! But she composed herself, said good night with her usual briskness, and lay awake. Next day she must certainly ask the girl to morning tea. It would be rude not to. Besides, that would leave the afternoon free for her garden and her mountains.

Next morning she sent a boy across with a note, which read: "I shall be so pleased if you will join me for morning tea." She signed it: Caroline Gale.

She went herself to the kitchen to cook scones and cakes. At eleven o'clock she was seated on the verandah in the green-dappled shade from the creepers, saying to herself that she believed she was in for a headache. Living as she did, in a long, timeless abstraction of growing things and mountains and silence, she had become very conscious of her body's responses to weather and to the slow advance of age. A small ache in her ankle when rain was due was like a cherished friend. Or she would sit with her eyes shut, in the shade, after a morning's pruning in the violent sun, feeling waves of pain flood back from her eyes to the back of her skull, and say with satisfaction: "You deserve it, Caroline!" It was right she should pay for such pleasure with such pain.

At last she heard lagging footsteps up the path, and she opened her eyes reluctantly. There was the girl, preparing her face for a social occasion, walking primly through the bougainvillaea arches, in a flowered frock as vivid as her surroundings. Mrs. Gale jumped to her feet and cried gaily: "I am so glad you had time to come." Mrs. De Wet giggled irresistibly and said: "But I had nothing else to do, had I?" Afterwards she said scornfully to her husband: "She's nuts. She writes me letters with stuck-down envelopes when I'm five minutes away, and says Have I the time? What the hell else did she think I had to do?" And then, violently: "She can't have anything to do. There was enough food to feed ten."

"Wouldn't be a bad idea if you spent more time cooking," said De Wet fondly.

The next day Mrs. Gale gardened, feeling guilty all the time, because she could not bring herself to send over another note of invitation. After a few days, she invited the De Wets to dinner, and through the meal made polite conversation with the girl while the men lost themselves in cattle diseases. What could one talk to a girl like that about? Nothing! Her mind, as far as Mrs. Gale was concerned, was a dark continent, which she had no inclination to explore. Mrs. De Wet was not interested in recipes, and when Mrs. Gale gave helpful advice about ordering clothes from England, which was so much cheaper than buying them in the local towns, the reply came that she had made all her own clothes since she was seven. After that there seemed nothing to say, for it was hardly possible to remark that these strapped sun-dresses and bright slacks were quite unsuitable for the farm, besides being foolish, since bare shoulders in this sun were dangerous. As for her shoes! She wore corded beach sandals which had already turned dust colour from the roads.

There were two more tea parties; then they were allowed to lapse. From time to time Mrs. Gale wondered uneasily what on earth the poor child did with herself all day, and felt it was her duty to go and find out. But she did not.

One morning she was pricking seedlings into a tin when the houseboy came and said the little missus was on the verandah and she was sick.

At once dismay flooded Mrs. Gale. She thought of a dozen tropical diseases, of which she had had unpleasant experience, and almost ran to the verandah. There was the girl, sitting screwed up in a chair, her face contorted, her eyes red, her whole body shuddering violently. "Malaria," thought Mrs. Gale at once, noting that trembling.

"What is the trouble, my dear?" Her voice was kind. She put her hand on the girl's shoulder. Mrs. De Wet turned and flung her arms round her hips, weeping, weeping, her small curly head buried in Mrs. Gale's stomach. Holding herself stiffly away from this dismaying contact, Mrs. Gale stroked the head and made soothing noises.

"Mrs. Gale, Mrs. Gale . . ."

"What is it?"

"I can't stand it. I shall go mad. I simply can't stand it."

Mrs. Gale, seeing that this was not a physical illness, lifted her up, led her inside, laid her on her own bed, and fetched cologne and handkerchiefs. Mrs. De Wet sobbed for a long while, clutching the older woman's hand, and then at last grew silent. Finally she sat up with a small rueful smile, and said pathetically: "I am a fool."

"But what *is* it, dear?"

"It isn't anything, really. I am so lonely. I wanted to get my mother up to stay with me, only Jack said there wasn't room, and he's quite right, only I got mad, because I thought he might at least have had my mother . . ."

Mrs. Gale felt guilt like a sword: she could have filled the place of this child's mother.

"And it isn't anything, Mrs. Gale, not really. It's not that I'm not happy with Jack. I am, but I never see him. I'm not used to this kind of thing. I come from a family of thirteen counting my parents, and I simply can't stand it."

Mrs. Gale sat and listened, and thought of her own loneliness when she first began this sort of life.

"And then he comes in late, not till seven sometimes, and I know he can't help it, with the farm work and all that, and then he has supper and goes straight off to bed. I am not sleepy then. And then I get up sometimes and I walk along the road with my dog . . ."

Mrs. Gale remembered how, in the early days after her husband had finished with his brief and apologetic embraces, she used to rise with a sense of relief and steal to the front room, where she lighted the lamp again and sat writing letters, reading old ones, thinking of her friends and of herself as a girl. But that was before she had her first child. She thought: This girl should have a baby; and could not help glancing downwards at her stomach.

Mrs. De Wet, who missed nothing, said resentfully: "Jack says I should have a baby. That's all he says." Then, since she had to include Mrs. Gale in this resentment, she transformed herself all at once from a sobbing baby into a gauche but armoured young woman with whom Mrs. Gale could have no contact. "I am sorry," she said formally. Then, with a grating humour: "Thank you for letting me blow off steam." She climbed off the bed, shook her skirts straight, and tossed her head. "Thank you. I am a nuisance." With painful brightness she added: "So, that's how it goes. Who would be a woman, eh?"

Mrs. Gale stiffened. "You must come and see me whenever you are lonely," she said, equally bright and false. It seemed to her incredible that this girl should come to her with all her defences down, and then suddenly shut her out with this facetious nonsense. But she felt more comfortable with the distance between them, she couldn't deny it.

"Oh, I will, Mrs. Gale. Thank you so much for asking me." She lingered for a moment, frowning at the brilliantly polished table in the front room, and then took her leave. Mrs. Gale watched her go. She noted that at the gate the girl started whistling gaily, and smiled comically. Letting off steam! Well, she said to herself, well . . . And she went back to her garden.

That afternoon she made a point of walking across to the other house. She would offer to show Mrs. De Wet the garden. The two women returned together, Mrs. Gale wondering if the girl regretted her emotional lapse of the morning. If so, she showed no signs of it. She broke into bright chatter when a topic mercifully occurred to her; in between were polite silences full of attention to what she seemed to hope Mrs. Gale might say.

Mrs. Gale was relying on the effect of her garden. They passed the house through the shrubs. There were the fountains, sending up their vivid showers of spray, there the cool mats of water lilies, under which the coloured fishes slipped, there the irises, sunk in green turf.

"This must cost a packet to keep up," said Mrs. De Wet. She stood at the edge of the pool, looking at her reflection dissolving among the broad green leaves, glanced obliquely up at Mrs. Gale, and dabbled her exposed red toenails in the water.

Mrs. Gale saw that she was thinking of herself as her husband's employer's wife. "It does, rather," she said drily, remembering that the only quarrels she ever had with her husband were over the cost of pumping up water. "You are fond of gardens?" she asked. She could not imagine anyone not being fond of gardens.

Mrs. De Wet said sullenly: "My mother was always too busy having kids to have time for gardens. She had her last baby early this year." An ancient and incommunicable resentment dulled her face. Mrs. Gale, seeing that all this beauty and peace meant nothing to her companion that she would have it mean, said, playing her last card: "Come and see my mountains." She regretted the pronoun as soon as it was out—*so* exaggerated.

But when she had the girl safely on the rocky verge of the escarpment, she heard her say: "There's my river." She was leaning forward over the great gulf, and her voice was lifted with excitement. "Look," she was saying. "Look, there it is." She turned to Mrs. Gale, laughing, her hair spun over her eyes in a fine iridescent rain, tossing her head back, clutching her skirts down, exhilarated by the tussle with the wind.

"Mind, you'll lose your balance." Mrs. Gale pulled her back. "You have been down to the river, then?"

"I go there every morning."

Mrs. Gale was silent. The thing seemed preposterous. "But it is four miles there and four back."

"Oh, I'm used to walking."

"But . . ." Mrs. Gale heard her own sour, expostulating voice and stopped herself. There was after all no logical reason why the girl should not go to the river. "What do you do there?"

"I sit on the edge of a big rock and dangle my legs in the water, and I fish, sometimes. I caught a barble last week. It tasted foul, but it was fun catching it. And I pick water lilies."

"There are crocodiles," said Mrs. Gale sharply. The girl was wrong-headed; anyone was who could like that steamy bath of vapours, heat, smells and—what? It was an unpleasant place. "A native girl was taken there last year, at the ford."

"There couldn't be a crocodile where I go. The water is clear, right down. You can see right under the rocks. It is a lovely pool. There's a kingfisher, and water-birds, all colours. They are so pretty. And when you sit there and look, the sky is a long narrow slit. From here it looks quite far across the river to the other side, but really it isn't. And the trees crowding close make it narrower. Just think how many millions of years it must have taken for the water to wear down the rock so deep."

"There's bilharzia, too."

"Oh, bilharzia!"

"There's nothing funny about bilharzia. My husband had it. He had injections for six months before he was cured."

The girl's face dulled. "I'll be careful," she said irrationally, turning away, holding her river and her long hot dreamy mornings away from Mrs. Gale, like a secret.

"Look at the mountains," said Mrs. Gale, pointing. The girl glanced over the chasm at the foothills, then bent forward again, her face reverent. Through the mass of green below were glimpses of satiny brown. She breathed deeply: "Isn't it a lovely smell?" she said.

"Let's go and have some tea," said Mrs. Gale. She felt cross and put out; she had no notion why. She could not help being brusque with the girl. And so at last they were quite silent together; and in silence they remained on that verandah above the beautiful garden, drinking their tea and wishing it was time for them to part.

Soon they saw the two husbands coming up the garden. Mrs. De Wet's face lit up; and she sprang to her feet and was off down the path, running lightly. She caught her husband's arm and clung there. He put her away from him, gently. "Hullo," he remarked good-humouredly. "Eating again?" And then he turned back to Major Gale and went on talking. The girl lagged up the path behind her husband like a sulky small girl, pulling at Mrs. Gale's beloved roses and scattering crimson petals everywhere.

On the verandah the men sank at once into chairs, took large cups of tea, and continued talking as they drank thirstily. Mrs. Gale listened and smiled. Crops, cattle, disease; weather, crops and cattle. Mrs. De Wet perched on the verandah wall and swung her legs. Her face was petulant, her lips trembled, her eyes were full of tears. Mrs. Gale was saying silently under her breath, with ironical pity, in which there was also cruelty: You'll get used to it, my dear; you'll get used to it. But she respected the girl, who had courage: walking to the river and back, wandering round the dusty flower-beds in the starlight, trying to find peace—at least, she was trying to find it.

She said sharply, cutting into the men's conversation: "Mr. De Wet, did you know your wife spends her mornings at the river?"

The man looked at her vaguely, while he tried to gather the sense of her words: his mind was on the farm. "Sure," he said at last. "Why not?"

"Aren't you afraid of bilharzia?"

He said laconically: "If we were going to get it, we would have got it long ago. A drop of water can infect you, touching the skin."

"Wouldn't it be wiser not to let the water touch you in the first place?" she enquired with deceptive mildness.

"Well, I told her. She wouldn't listen. It is too late now. Let her enjoy it."

"But . . ."

"About that red heifer," said Major Gale, who had not been aware of any interruption.

"No," said Mrs. Gale sharply. "You are not going to dismiss it like that." She saw the three of them look at her in astonishment. "Mr. De Wet, have you ever thought what it means to a woman being alone all day, with not enough to do. It's enough to drive anyone crazy."

Major Gale raised his eyebrows; he had not heard his wife speak like that for so long. As for De Wet, he said with a slack good-humour that sounded brutal: "And what do you expect me to do about it."

"You don't realize," said Mrs. Gale futilely, knowing perfectly well there was nothing he could do about it. "You don't understand how it is."

"She'll have a kid soon," said De Wet. "I hope so, at any rate. That will give her something to do."

Anger raced through Mrs. Gale like a flame along petrol. She was trembling. "She might be that red heifer," she said at last.

"What's the matter with having kids?" asked De Wet. "Any objection?"

"You might ask me first," said the girl bitterly.

Her husband blinked at her, comically bewildered. "Hey, what is this?" he enquired. "What have I done? You said you wanted to have kids. Wouldn't have married you otherwise."

"I never said I didn't."

"Talking about her as if she were . . ."

"When, then?" Mrs. Gale and the man were glaring at each other.

"There's more to women than having children," said Mrs. Gale at last, and flushed because of the ridiculousness of her words.

De Wet looked her up and down, up and down. "I want kids," he said at last. "I want a large family. Make no mistake about that. And when I married her" —he jerked his head at his wife— "I told her I wanted them. She can't turn round now and say I didn't."

"Who is turning round and saying anything?" asked the girl, fine and haughty, staring away over the trees.

"Well, if no one is blaming anyone for anything," asked Major Gale, jauntily twirling his little moustache, "what is all this about?"

"God knows, I don't," said De Wet angrily. He glanced sullenly at Mrs. Gale. "I didn't start it."

Mrs. Gale sat silent, trembling, feeling foolish, but so angry she could not speak. After a while she said to the girl: "Shall we go inside, my dear?" The girl, reluctantly, and with a lingering backward look at her husband, rose and followed Mrs. Gale. "He didn't mean anything," she said awkwardly, apologizing for her husband to her husband's employer's wife. This room, with its fine old furniture, always made her apologetic. At this moment, De Wet stooped into the doorway and said: "Come on, I am going home."

"Is that an order?" asked the girl quickly, backing so that she came side by side with Mrs. Gale: she even reached for the older woman's hand. Mrs. Gale did not take it: this was going too far.

"What's got into you?" he said, exasperated. "Are you coming, or are you not?"

"I can't do anything else, can I?" she replied, and followed him from the house like a queen who has been insulted.

Major Gale came in after a few moments. "Lovers' quarrel," he said, laughing awkwardly. This phrase irritated Mrs. Gale. "That man!" she exclaimed. "That man!"

"Why, what is wrong with him?" She remained silent, pretending to arrange her flowers. This silly scene, with its hinterlands of emotion, made her furious. She was angry with herself, angry with her husband, and furious at that foolish couple who had succeeded in upsetting her and destroying her peace. At last she said: "I am going to bed. I've such a headache I can't think."

"I'll bring you a tray, my dear," said Major Gale, with a touch of exaggeration in his courtesy that annoyed her even more. "I don't want anything, thank you," she said, like a child, and marched off to the bedroom.

There she undressed and went to bed. She tried to read, found she was not following the sense of the words, put down the book, and blew out the light. Light streamed into the room from the moon; she could see the trees along the fence banked black against stars. From next door came the clatter of her husband's solitary meal.

Later she heard voices from the verandah. Soon her husband came into the room and said: "De Wet is asking whether his wife has been here."

"What!" exclaimed Mrs. Gale, slowly assimilating the implications of this. "Why, has she gone off somewhere?"

"She's not at home," said the Major uncomfortably. For he always became uncomfortable and very polite when he had to deal with situations like this.

Mrs. Gale sank back luxuriously on her pillows. "Tell that fine young man that his wife often goes for long walks by herself when he's asleep. He probably hasn't noticed it." Here she gave a deadly look at her husband. "Just as I used to," she could not prevent herself adding.

Major Gale fiddled with his moustache, and gave her a look which seemed to say: "Oh lord, don't say we are going back to all that business again?" He went out, and she heard him saying: "Your wife might have gone for a walk, perhaps?" Then the young man's voice: "I know she does sometimes. I don't like her being out at night, but she just walks around the house. And she takes the dogs with her. Maybe she's gone further this time—being upset, you know."

"Yes, I know," said Major Gale. Then they both laughed. The laughter was of a quite different quality from the sober responsibility of their tone a moment before: and Mrs. Gale found herself sitting up in bed, muttering: "How *dare* he?"

She got up and dressed herself. She was filled with premonitions of unpleasantness. In the main room her husband was sitting reading, and since he seldom read, it seemed he was also worried. Neither of them spoke. When she looked at the clock, she found it was just past nine o'clock.

After an hour of tension, they heard the footsteps they had been waiting for. There stood De Wet, angry, worried sick, his face white, his eyes burning.

"We must get the boys out," he said, speaking directly to Major Gale, and ignoring Mrs. Gale.

"I am coming too," she said.

"No, my dear," said the Major cajolingly. "You stay here."

"You can't go running over the veld at this time of night," said De Wet to Mrs. Gale, very blunt and rude.

"I shall do as I please," she returned.

The three of them stood on the verandah, waiting for the natives. Everything was drenched in moonlight. Soon they heard a growing clamour of voices from over the ridge, and a little later the darkness there was lightened by flaring torches held high by invisible hands: it seemed as if the night were scattered with torches advancing of their own accord. Then a crowd of dark figures took shape under the broken lights. The farm natives, excited by the prospect of a night's chasing over the veld, were yelling as if they were after a small buck or a hare.

Mrs. Gale sickened. "Is it necessary to have all these natives in it?" she asked. "After all, have we even considered the possibilities? Where can a girl run *to* on a place like this?"

"That is the point," said Major Gale frigidly.

"I can't bear to think of her being—pursued, like this, by a crowd of natives. It's horrible."

"More horrible still if she has hurt herself and is waiting for help," said De Wet. He ran off down the path, shouting to the natives and waving his arms. The Gales saw them separate into three bands, and soon there were three groups of lights jerking away in different directions through the hazy dark, and the yells and shouting came back to them on the wind.

Mrs. Gale thought: "She could have taken the road back to the station, in which case she could be caught by car, even now."

She commanded her husband: "Take the car along the road and see."

"That's an idea," said the Major, and went off to the garage. She heard the car start off, and watched the rear light dwindle redly into the night.

But that was the least ugly of the possibilities. What if she had been so blind with anger, grief, or whatever emotion it was that had driven her away, that she had simply run off into the veld not knowing where she went? There were thousands of acres of trees, thick grass, gullies, *kopjes*. She might at this moment be lying with a broken arm or leg; she might be pushing her way through grass higher than her head, stumbling over roots and rocks. She might be screaming for help somewhere for fear of wild animals, for if she crossed the valley into the hills there were leopards, lions, wild dogs. Mrs. Gale suddenly caught her breath in an agony of fear: the valley! What if she had mistaken her direction and walked over the edge of the escarpment in the dark? What if she had forded the river and been taken by a crocodile? There were so many things: she might even be caught in a gametrap. Once, taking her walk, Mrs. Gale herself had come across a tall sapling by the path where the spine and ribs of a large buck dangled, and on the ground were the pelvis and legs, fine eroded bones of an animal trapped and forgotten by its trapper. Anything might have happened. And worse than any of the actual physical dangers was the danger of falling a victim to fear: being alone on the veld, at night, knowing oneself lost: this was enough to send anyone off balance.

The silly little fool, the silly little fool: anger and pity and terror confused in Mrs. Gale until she was walking crazily up and down her garden through the bushes, tearing blossoms and foliage to pieces in trembling fingers. She had no idea how time was passing; until Major Gale returned and said that he had taken the ten miles to the station at seven miles an hour, turning his lights into the bush this way and that. At the station everyone was in bed; but the police were standing on the alert for news.

It was long after twelve. As for De Wet and the bands of searching natives, there was no sign of them. They would be miles away by this time.

"Go to bed," said Major Gale at last.

"Don't be ridiculous," she said. After a while she held out her hand to him, and said: "One feels so helpless."

There was nothing to say; they walked together under the stars, their minds filled with horrors. Later she made some tea and they drank it standing; to sit would have seemed heartless. They were so tired they could hardly move. Then they got their second wind and continued walking. That night Mrs. Gale hated her garden, that highly-cultivated patch of luxuriant growth, stuck in the middle of a country that could do this sort of thing to you suddenly. It was all the fault of the country! In a civilised sort of place, the girl would have caught the train to her mother, and a wire would have put everything right. Here, she might have killed herself, simply because of a passing fit of despair. Mrs. Gale began to get hysterical. She was weeping softly in the circle of her husband's arm by the time the sky lightened and the redness of dawn spread over the sky.

As the sun rose, De Wet returned alone over the veld. He said he had sent the natives back to their huts to sleep. They had found nothing. He stated that he also intended to sleep for an hour, and that he would be back on the job by eight. Major Gale nodded: he recognised this as a necessary discipline against collapse. But after the young man had walked off across the veld towards his house, the two older people looked at each other and began to move after him. "He must not be alone," said Mrs. Gale sensibly. "I shall make him some tea and see that he drinks it."

"He wants sleep," said Major Gale. His own eyes were red and heavy.

"I'll put something in his tea," said Mrs. Gale. "He won't know it is there." Now she had something to do, she was much more cheerful. Planning De Wet's comfort, she watched him turn in at his gate and vanish inside the house: they were some two hundred yards behind.

Suddenly there was a shout, and then a commotion of screams and yelling. The Gales ran fast along the remaining distance and burst into the front room, white-faced and expecting the worst, in whatever form it might choose to present itself.

There was De Wet, his face livid with rage, bending over his wife, who was huddled on the floor and shielding her head with her arms, while he beat her shoulders with his closed fists.

Mrs. Gale exclaimed: "Beating your wife!"

De Wet flung the girl away from him, and staggered to his feet. "She was here all the time," he said, half in temper, half in sheer wonder. "She was hiding under the bed. She told me so. When I came in she was sitting on the bed and laughing at me."

The girl beat her hands on the floor and said, laughing and crying together: "Now you have to take some notice of me. Looking for me all night over the veld with your silly natives! You looked so stupid, running about like ants, looking for me."

"My God," said De Wet simply, giving up. He collapsed backwards into a chair and lay there, his eyes shut, his face twitching.

"So now you have to notice me," she said defiantly, but beginning to look scared. "I have to pretend to run away, but then you sit up and take notice."

"Be quiet," said De Wet, breathing heavily. "Be quiet, if you don't want to get hurt bad."

"Beating your wife," said Mrs. Gale. "Savages behave better."

"Caroline, my dear," said Major Gale awkwardly. He moved towards the door.

"Take that woman out of here if you don't want me to beat her too," said De Wet to Major Gale.

Mrs. Gale was by now crying with fury. "I'm not going," she said. "I'm not going. This poor child isn't safe with you."

"But what was it all about?" said Major Gale, laying his hand kindly on the girl's shoulder. "What was it, my dear? What did you have to do it for, and make us all so worried?"

She began to cry. "Major Gale, I am so sorry. I forgot myself. I got so mad. I told him I was going to have a baby. I told him when I got back from your place. And all he said was: That's fine. That's the first of them, he said. He didn't love me, or say he was pleased, or nothing."

"Dear Christ in hell," said De Wet wearily, with the exasperation strong in his voice, "what do you make me do these things for? Do you think I want to beat you? Did you think I wasn't pleased: I keep telling you I want kids, I love kids."

"But you don't care about me," she said, sobbing bitterly.

"Don't I?" he said helplessly.

"Beating your wife when she is pregnant," said Mrs. Gale. "You ought to be ashamed of yourself." She advanced on the young man with her own fists clenched, unconscious of what she was doing. "You ought to be beaten yourself, that's what you need."

Mrs. De Wet heaved herself off the floor, rushed on Mrs. Gale, pulled her back so that she nearly lost balance, and then flung herself on her husband. "Jack," she said, clinging to him desperately, "I am so sorry, I am so sorry, Jack."

He put his arms round her. "There," he said simply, his voice thick with tiredness, "don't cry. We got mixed up, that's all."

Major Gale, who had caught and steadied his wife as she staggered back, said to her in a low voice: "Come, Caroline. Come. Leave them to sort it out."

"And what if he loses his temper again and decides to kill her this time?" demanded Mrs. Gale, her voice shrill.

De Wet got to his feet, lifting his wife with him. "Go away now, Mrs. Major," he said. "Get out of here. You've done enough damage."

"I've done enough damage?" she gasped. "And what have I done?"

"Oh nothing, nothing at all," he said with ugly sarcasm. "Nothing at all. But please go and leave my wife alone in future, Mrs. Major."

"Come, Caroline, *please*," said Major Gale.

She allowed herself to be drawn out of the room. Her head was aching so that the vivid morning light invaded her eyes in a wave of pain. She swayed a little as she walked.

"Mrs. Major," she said, "Mrs. Major!"

"He was upset," said her husband judiciously.

She snorted. Then, after a silence: "So, it was all my fault."

"He didn't say so."

"I thought that was what he was saying. He behaves like a brute and then says it is my fault."

"It was no one's fault," said Major Gale, patting her vaguely on shoulders and back as they stumbled back home.

They reached the gate, and entered the garden, which was now musical with birds.

"A lovely morning," remarked Major Gale.

"Next time you get an assistant," she said finally, "get people of our kind. These might be savages, the way they behave."

And that was the last word she would ever say on the subject.

Little Tembi

JANE McCLUSTER, who had been a nurse before she married, started a clinic on the farm within a month of arriving. Though she had been born and brought up in town, her experience of natives was wide, for she had been a sister in the native wards of the city hospital, by choice, for years; she liked nursing natives, and explained her feeling in the words: "They are just like children, and appreciate what you do for them." So, when she had taken a thorough, diagnosing kind of look at the farm natives, she exclaimed, "Poor things!" and set about turning an old dairy into a dispensary. Her husband was pleased; it would save money in the long run by cutting down illness in the compound.

Willie McCluster who had also been born and raised in South Africa was nevertheless unmistakably and determinedly Scottish. His accent might be emphasised for loyalty's sake, but he had kept all the fine qualities of his people unimpaired by a slowing and relaxing climate. He was shrewd, vigorous, earthy, practical and kind. In appearance he was largely built, with a square bony face, a tight mouth, and eyes whose fierce blue glance was tempered by the laughter wrinkles about them. He became a farmer young, having planned the steps for years: he was not one of those who drift on to the land because of discontent with an office, or because of failure, or vague yearnings towards "freedom." Jane, a cheerful and competent girl who knew what she wanted, trifled with her numerous suitors with one eye on Willie, who wrote her weekly letters from the farming college in the Transvaal. As soon as his four years training were completed, they married.

They were then twenty-seven, and felt themselves well-equipped for a useful and enjoyable life. Their house was planned for a family. They would have been delighted if a baby had been born the old-fashioned nine months after marriage. As it was, a baby did not come; and when two years had passed, Jane took a journey into the city to see a doctor. She was not so much unhappy as indignant to find she needed an operation before she could have children. She did not associate illness with herself, and felt as if the whole thing were out of character. But she submitted to the operation, and to waiting a further two years before starting a family, with her usual practical good sense. But it subdued her a little. The uncertainty preyed on her, in spite of herself; and it was because of her rather wistful, disappointed frame of mind at this time that her work in the clinic became so important to her. Whereas, in the beginning she had dispensed medicines and good advice as a routine, every morning for a couple of hours after breakfast, she now threw herself into it, working hard keeping herself at full stretch, trying to attack causes rather than symptoms.

The compound was the usual farm compound of unsanitary mud and grass huts; the diseases she had to deal with were caused by poverty and bad feeding.

Having lived in the country all her life, she did not make the mistake of expecting too much; she had that shrewd, ironical patience that achieves more with backward people than any amount of angry idealism.

First she chose an acre of good soil for vegetables, and saw to the planting and cultivating herself. One cannot overthrow the customs of centuries in a season, and she was patient with the natives who would not at first touch food they were not used to. She persuaded and lectured. She gave the women of the compound lessons in cleanliness and baby care. She drew up diet sheets and ordered sacks of citrus from the big estates; in fact, it was not long before it was Jane who organised the feeding of Willie's two-hundred-strong labour force, and he was glad to have her help. Neighbours laughed at them; for it is even now customary to feed natives on maize meal only, with an occasional slaughtered ox for a feasting; but there was no doubt Willie's natives were healthier than most and he got far more work out of them. On cold winter mornings Jane would stand dispensing cans of hot cocoa from a petrol drum with a slow fire burning under it to the natives before they went to the fields;

and if a neighbour passed and laughed at her, she set her lips and said good-humouredly: "It's good sound commonsense, that's what it is. Besides—poor things, poor things!" Since the McClusters were respected in the district, they were humoured in what seemed a ridiculous eccentricity.

But it was not easy, not easy at all. It was of no use to cure hookworm-infested feet that would become reinfected in a week, since none wore shoes; nothing could be done about bilharzia, when all the rivers were full of it; and the natives continued to live in the dark and smoky huts.

But the children could be helped; Jane most particularly loved the little black piccanins. She knew that fewer children died in her compound than in any for miles around, and this was her pride. She would spend whole mornings explaining to the women about dirt and proper feeding; if a child became ill, she would sit up all night with it, and cried bitterly if it died. The name for her among the natives was The Goodhearted One. They trusted her. Though mostly they hated and feared the white man's medicines,* they let Jane have her way, because they felt she was prompted by kindness; and day by day the crowds of natives waiting for medical attention became larger. This filled Jane with pride; and every morning she made her way to the big stone-floored, thatched building at the back of the house that smelled always of disinfectants and soap, accompanied by the houseboy who helped her, and spent there many hours helping the mothers and the children and the labourers who had hurt themselves at work.

Little Tembi was brought to her for help at the time when she knew she could not hope to have a child of her own for at least two years. He had what the natives call "the hot weather sickness." His mother had not brought him soon enough, and by the time Jane took him in her arms he was a tiny wizened skeleton, loosely covered with harsh greyish skin, the stomach painfully distended. "He will die," moaned the mother from outside the clinic door, with that fatalistic note that always annoyed Jane. "Nonsense!" she said briskly—even more briskly because she was so afraid he would.

She laid the child warmly in a lined basket, and the houseboy and she looked grimly into each other's faces. Jane said sharply to the mother, who was whimpering helplessly from the floor where she squatted with her hands to her face: "Stop crying. That doesn't do any good. Didn't I cure your first child when he had the same

---

* This story was written in 1950.

trouble?" But that other little boy had not been nearly as sick as this one.

When Jane had carried the basket into the kitchen, and set it beside the fire for warmth, she saw the same grim look on the cook-boy's face as she had seen on the houseboy's—and could feel on her own. "This child is *not* going to die," she said to herself. "I won't let it! I won't let it." It seemed to her that if she could pull little Tembi through, the life of the child she herself wanted so badly would be granted her.

She sat beside the basket all day, willing the baby to live, with medicines on the table beside her, and the cookboy and the house-boy helping her where they could. At night the mother came from the compound with her blanket; and the two women kept vigil to-gether. Because of the fixed, imploring eyes of the black woman Jane was even more spurred to win through; and the next day, and the next, and through the long nights, she fought for Tembi's life even when she could see from the faces of the house natives that they thought she was beaten. Once, towards dawn of one night when the air was cold and still, the little body chilled to the touch, and there seemed no breath in it, Jane held it close to the warmth of her own breast murmuring fiercely over and over again: You *will* live, you *will* live—and when the sun rose the infant was breathing deeply and its feet were pulsing in her hand.

When it became clear that he would not die, the whole house was pervaded with a feeling of happiness and victory. Willie came to see the child, and said affectionately to Jane: "Nice work, old girl. I never thought you'd do it." The cookboy and the houseboy were warm and friendly towards Jane, and brought her gratitude pres-ents of eggs and ground meal. As for the mother, she took her child in her arms with trembling joy and wept as she thanked Jane.

Jane herself, though exhausted and weak, was too happy to rest or sleep: she was thinking of the child she would have. She was not a superstitious person, and the thing could not be described in such terms: she felt that she had thumbed her nose at death, that she had sent death slinking from her door in defeat, and now she would be strong to make life, fine strong children of her own; she could imagine them springing up beside her, lovely children con-ceived from her own strength and power against sneaking death.

Little Tembi was brought by his mother up to the house every day for a month, partly to make sure he would not relapse, partly because Jane had grown to love him. When he was quite well, and no longer came to the clinic, Jane would ask the cookboy after him, and sometimes sent a message that he should be fetched to see her. The native woman would then come smiling to the back door with the little Tembi on her back and her older child at her skirts, and Jane would run down the steps, smiling with pleasure, waiting impatiently as the cloth was unwound from the mother's back, revealing Tembi curled there, thumb in mouth, with great black solemn eyes, his other hand clutching the stuff of his mother's dress for security. Jane would carry him indoors to show Willie. "Look," she would say tenderly, "here's my little Tembi. Isn't he a sweet little piccanin?"

He grew into a fat shy little boy, staggering uncertainly from his mother's arms to Jane's. Later, when he was strong on his legs, he would run to Jane and laugh as she caught him up. There was always fruit or sweets for him when he visited the house, always a hug from Jane and a good-humoured, amused smile from Willie.

He was two years old when Jane said to his mother: "When the rains come this year I shall also have a child." And the two women, forgetting the difference in colour, were happy together because of the coming children: the black woman was expecting her third baby.

Tembi was with his mother when she came to visit the cradle of the little white boy. Jane held out her hand to him and said: "Tembi, how are you?" Then she took her baby from the cradle and held it out, saying: "Come and see my baby, Tembi." But Tembi backed away, as if afraid, and began to cry. "Silly Tembi," said Jane affectionately; and sent the houseboy to fetch some fruit as a present. She did not make the gift herself, as she was holding her child.

She was absorbed by this new interest, and very soon found herself pregnant again. She did not forget little Tembi, but thought of him rather as he had been, the little toddler whom she had loved wistfully when she was childless. Once she caught sight of Tembi's mother walking along one of the farm roads, leading a child by the hand and said: "But where's Tembi?" Then she saw the child was Tembi. She greeted him; but afterwards said to Willie: "Oh dear, it's such a pity when they grow up, isn't it?" "He could hardly be described as grown-up," said Willie, smiling indulgently at her where she sat with her two infants on her lap. "You won't be able to have them climbing all over you when we've a dozen," he teased her—they had decided to wait another two years and then have some more; Willie came from a family of nine children. "Who said a dozen?" exclaimed Jane tartly, playing up to him. "Why not?"

asked Willie. "We can afford it." "How do you think I can do everything?" grumbled Jane pleasantly. For she was very busy. She had
not let the work at the clinic lapse; it was still she who did the
ordering and planning of the labourers' food; and she looked after
her children without help—she did not even have the customary
native nanny. She could not really be blamed for losing touch with
little Tembi.

He was brought to her notice one evening when Willie was having the usual weekly discussion with the boss-boy over the farm
work. He was short of labour again and the rains had been heavy
and the lands were full of weeds. As fast as the gangs of natives
worked through a field it seemed that the weeds were higher than
ever. Willie suggested that it might be possible to take some of the
older children from their mothers for a few weeks. He already employed a gang of piccanins, of between about nine and fifteen years
old, who did lighter work; but he was not sure that all the available
children were working. The boss-boy said he would see what he
could find.

As a result of this discussion Willie and Jane were called one day
to the front door by a smiling cookboy to see little Tembi, now
about six years old, standing proudly beside his father, who was
also smiling. "Here is a man to work for you," said Tembi's father
to Willie, pushing forward Tembi, who jibbed like a little calf,
standing with his head lowered and his fingers in his mouth. He
looked so tiny, standing all by himself, that Jane exclaimed com-
passionately: "But, Willie, he's just a baby still!" Tembi was quite
naked, save for a string of blue beads cutting into the flesh of his
fat stomach. Tembi's father explained that his older child, who was
eight, had been herding the calves for a year now, and that there
was no reason why Tembi should not help him.

"But I don't need two herdsboys for the calves," protested Willie.
And then, to Tembi: "And now, my big man, what money do you
want?" At this Tembi dropped his head still lower, twisted his feet
in the dust, and muttered: "Five shillings." "Five shillings a
month!" exclaimed Willie indignantly. "What next! Why, the ten-
year-old piccanins get that much." And then, feeling Jane's hand on
his arm, he said hurriedly: "Oh, all right, four and sixpence. He
can help his big brother with the calves." Jane, Willie, the cookboy
and Tembi's father stood laughing sympathetically as Tembi lifted
his head, stuck out his stomach even further, and swaggered off
down the path, beaming with pride. "Well," sighed Jane, "I never

would have thought it. Little Tembi! Why, it seems only the other day . . ."

Tembi, promoted to a loincloth, joined his brother with the calves; and as the two children ran alongside the animals, everyone turned to look smiling after the tiny black child, strutting with delight, and importantly swishing the twig his father had cut him from the bush as if he were a full-grown driver with his team of beasts.

The calves were supposed to stay all day near the kraal; when the cows had been driven away to the grazing, Tembi and his brother squatted under a tree and watched the calves, rising to run, shouting, if one attempted to stray. For a year Tembi was apprentice to the job; and then his brother joined the gang of older piccanins who worked with the hoe. Tembi was then seven years old, and responsible for twenty calves, some standing higher than he. Normally a much older child had the job; but Willie was chronically short of labour, as all the farmers were, and he needed every pair of hands he could find, for work in the fields.

"Did you know your Tembi is a proper herdsboy now?" Willie said to Jane, laughing, one day. "What!" exclaimed Jane. "That baby! Why, it's absurd." She looked jealously at her own children, because of Tembi; she was the kind of woman who hates to think of her children growing up. But she now had three, and was very busy indeed. She forgot the little black boy.

Then one day a castastrophe happened. It was very hot, and Tembi fell asleep under the trees. His father came up to the house, uneasily apologetic, to say that some of the calves had got into the mealie field and trampled down the plants. Willie was angry. It was that futile, simmering anger that cannot be assuaged, for it is caused by something that cannot be remedied: children had to herd the calves because adults were needed for more important work, and one could not be really angry with a child of Tembi's age. Willie had Tembi fetched to the house, and gave him a stern lecture about the terrible thing he had done. Tembi was crying when he turned away; he stumbled off to the compound with his father's hand resting on his shoulder, because the tears were streaming so fast he could not have directed his own steps. But in spite of the tears, and his contrition, it all happened again not very long afterwards. He fell asleep in the drowsily-warm shade, and when he woke, toward evening, all the calves had strayed into the fields and flattened acres of mealies. Unable to face punishment he ran away, crying, into the bush. He was found that night by his father who cuffed him lightly round the head for running away.

And now it was a very serious matter indeed. Willie was angry. To have happened once—that was bad, but forgivable. But twice, and within a month! He did not at first summon Tembi, but had a consultation with his father. "We must do something he will not forget, as a lesson," said Willie. Tembi's father said the child had already been punished. "You have beaten him?" asked Willie. But he knew that Africans do not beat their children, or so seldom it was not likely that Tembi had really been punished. "You say you have beaten him?" he insisted; and saw, from the way the man turned away his eyes and said, "Yes, baas," that it was not true. "Listen," said Willie. "Those calves straying must have cost me about thirty pounds. There's nothing I can do. I can't get it back from Tembi, can I? And now I'm going to stop it happening again." Tembi's father did not reply. "You will fetch Tembi up here, to the house, and cut a switch from the bush, and I will give him a beating." "Yes, baas," said Tembi's father, after a pause.

When Jane heard of the punishment she said: "Shame! Beating my little Tembi . . ."

When the hour came, she took away her children so that they would not have such an unpleasant thing in their memories. Tembi was brought up to the verandah, clutching his father's hand and shivering with fear. Willie said he did not like the business of beating; he considered it necessary, however, and intended to go through with it. He took the long light switch from the cookboy, who had cut it from the bush, since Tembi's father had come without it, and ran the sharply-whistling thing loosely through the air to frighten Tembi. Tembi shivered more than ever, and pressed his face against his father's thighs. "Come here, Tembi." Tembi did not move; so his father lifted him close to Willie. "Bend down." Tembi did not bend down, so his father bent him down, hiding the small face against his own legs. Then Willie glanced smilingly but uncomfortably at the cookboy, the houseboy and Tembi's father, who were all regarding him with stern, unresponsive faces and swished the wand backwards and forwards over Tembi's back; he wanted them to see he was only trying to frighten Tembi for the good of his upbringing. But they did not smile at all. Finally Willie said in an awful, solemn voice: "Now, Tembi!" And then, having made the occasion solemn and angry, he switched Tembi lightly, three times, across the buttocks, and threw the switch away into the bush. "Now you will never do it again, Tembi, will you?" he said. Tembi stood quite still, shuddering, in front of him, and would not meet his eyes. His father gently took his hand and led him away back home. "Is it over?" asked Jane, appearing from the house. "I didn't hurt him," said Willie crossly. He was annoyed, because he felt the black men were annoyed with him. "They want to have it both ways," he said. "If the child is old enough to earn money, then he's old enough to be responsible. Thirty pounds!"

"I was thinking of our little Freddie," said Jane emotionally. Freddie was their first child. Willie said impatiently: "And what's the good of thinking of him?" "Oh no good, Willie. No good at all," agreed Jane tearfully. "It does seem awful, though. Do you remember him, Willie? Do you remember what a sweet little thing he was?" Willie could not afford to remember the sweetness of the baby Tembi at that moment; and he was displeased with Jane for reminding him; there was a small constriction of feeling between them for a little while, which soon dissolved, for they were good friends, and were in the same mind about most things.

The calves did not stray again. At the end of the month, when Tembi stepped forward to take his four shillings and sixpence wages, Willie smiled at him and said: "Well, Tembi, and how are things with you?" "I want more money," said Tembi boldly. "Wha-a-at!" exclaimed Willie, astounded. He called to Tembi's father, who stepped out of the gang of waiting Africans, to hear what Willie wanted to say. "This little rascal of yours lets the cattle stray twice, and then says he wants more money." Willie said this loudly, so that everyone could hear; and there was laughter from the labourers. But Tembi kept his head high, and said defiantly: "Yes, baas, I want more money." "You'll get your bottom tanned," said Willie, only half-indignant: and Tembi went off sulkily, holding his silver in his hand, with amused glances following him.

He was now about seven, very thin and little, though he still carried his protuberant stomach before him. His legs were flat and spindly, and his arms broader below the elbow than above. He was not crying now, nor stumbling. His small thin shape was straight, and—so it seemed—angry. Willie forgot the incident.

But next month the child again stood his ground and argued stubbornly for an increase. Willie raised him to five and sixpence, saying resignedly that Jane had spoiled him. Tembi bit his lips in triumph, and as he walked off gave little joyous skipping steps, finally breaking into a run as he reached the trees. He was still the youngest of the working children, and was now earning as much as some three or four years older than he: this made them grumble, but it was recognised, because of Jane's attitude, that he was a favourite.

Now, in the normal run of things, it would have been a year, at least, before he got any more money. But the very month following, he claimed the right to another increase. This time the listening natives made sounds of amused protest; the lad was forgetting himself. As for Willie, he was really annoyed. There was something insistent, something demanding, in the child's manner that was almost impertinent. He said sharply: "If you don't stop this non-sense, I'll tell your father to teach you a lesson where it hurts." Tembi's eyes glowed angrily, and he attempted to argue, but Willie dismissed him curtly, turning to the next labourer.

A few minutes later Jane was fetched to the back door by the cook, and there stood Tembi, shifting in embarrassment from foot to foot, but grinning at her eagerly. "Why, Tembi . . ." she said vaguely. She had been feeding the children, and her mind was filled with thoughts of bathing and getting them to bed—thoughts very far from Tembi. Indeed, she had to look twice before she rec-ognised him, for she carried always in the back of her mind the picture of that sweet fat black baby who bore, for her, the name Tembi. Only his eyes were the same: large dark glowing eyes, now imploringly fixed on her. "Tell the baas to give me more money," he beseeched.

Jane laughed kindly. "But, Tembi, how can I do that? I've noth-ing to do with the farm. You know that."

"Tell him, missus. Tell him, my missus," he beseeched.

Jane felt the beginnings of annoyance. But she chose to laugh again, and said, "Wait a minute, Tembi." She went inside and fetched from the children's supper table some slices of cake, which she folded into a piece of paper and thrust into Tembi's hand. She was touched to see the child's face spread into a beaming smile: he had forgotten about the wages, the cake did as well or better. "Thank you, thank you," he said; and, turning, scuttled off into the trees.

And now Jane was given no chance of forgetting Tembi. He would come up to the house on a Sunday with quaint little mud toys for the children, or with the feather from a brilliant bird he had found in the bush; even a handful of wild flowers tied with wisps of grass. Always Jane welcomed him, talked to him, and re-warded him with small gifts. Then she had another child, and was very busy again. Sometimes she was too occupied to go herself to the back door. She would send her servant with an apple or a few sweets.

Soon after, Tembi appeared at the clinic one morning with his toe bound up. When Jane removed the dirty bit of cloth, she saw a minute cut, the sort of thing no native, whether child or adult, would normally take any notice of at all. But she bound it properly for him, and even dressed it good-naturedly when he appeared again, several days later. Then, only a week afterwards, there was a small cut on his finger. Jane said impatiently: "Look here, Tembi, I don't run this clinic for nonsense of this kind." When the child stared up at her blankly, those big dark eyes fixed on her with an intensity that made her uncomfortable, she directed the houseboy to translate the remark into dialect, for she thought Tembi had not understood. He said, stammering: "Missus, my missus, I come to see you only." But Jane laughed and sent him away. He did not go far. Later, when all the other patients had gone, she saw him standing a little way off, looking hopefully at her. "What *is* it?" she asked, a little crossly, for she could hear the new baby crying for attention inside the house.

"I want to work for you," said Tembi. "But, Tembi, I don't need another boy. Besides, you are too small for housework. When you are older, perhaps." "Let me look after the children." Jane did not smile, for it was quite usual to employ small piccanins as nurses for children not much younger than themselves. She might even have considered it, but she said: "Tembi, I have just arranged for a nanny to come and help me. Perhaps later on. I'll remember you, and if I need someone to help the nanny I'll send for you. First you must learn to work well. You must work well with the calves and not let them stray; and then we'll know you are a good boy, and you can come to the house and help me with the children."

Tembi departed on this occasion with lingering steps, and some time later Jane, glancing from the window, saw him standing at the edge of the bush gazing towards the house. She despatched the houseboy to send him away, saying that she would not have him loitering round the house doing nothing.

Jane, too, was now feeling that she had "spoiled" Tembi, that he had "got above himself."

And now nothing happened for quite a long time.

Then Jane missed her diamond engagement ring. She used often to take it off when doing household things; so that she was not at first concerned. After several days she searched thoroughly for it, but it could not be found. A little later a pearl brooch was missing. And there were several small losses, a spoon used for the baby's feeding, a pair of scissors, a silver christening mug. Jane said crossly to Willie that there must be a poltergeist. "I had the thing in my hand and when I turned round it was gone. It's just silly. Things don't vanish like that." "A black poltergeist, perhaps," said Willie. "How about the cook?" "Don't be ridiculous," said Jane, a little too quickly. "Both the houseboys have been with us since we came to the farm." But suspicion flared in her, nevertheless. It was a well-worn maxim that no native, no matter how friendly, could be trusted; scratch any one of them, and you found a thief. Then she looked at Willie, understood that he was feeling the same, and was as ashamed of his feelings as she was. The houseboys were almost personal friends. "Nonsense," said Jane firmly. "I don't believe a word of it." But no solution offered itself, and things continued to vanish.

One day Tembi's father asked to speak to the boss. He untied a piece of cloth, laid it on the ground—and there were all the missing articles. "But not Tembi, *surely*," protested Jane. Tembi's father, awkward in his embarrassment, explained that he had happened to be passing the cattle kraals, and had happened to notice the little boy sitting on his antheap, in the shade, playing with his treasures. "Of course he had no idea of their value," appealed Jane. "It was just because they were so shiny and glittering." And indeed, as they stood there, looking down at the lamplight glinting on the silver and the diamonds, it was easy to see how a child could be fascinated. "Well, and what are we going to do?" asked Willie practically. Jane did not reply directly to the question; she exclaimed helplessly: "Do you realise that the little imp must have been watching me doing things round the house for weeks, nipping in when my back was turned for a moment—he must be quick as a snake." "Yes, but what are we going to do?" "Just give him a good talking-to," said Jane, who did not know why she felt so dismayed and lost. She was angry; but far more distressed—there was something ugly and persistent in this planned, deliberate thieving, that she could not bear to associate with little Tembi, whom she had saved from death.

"A talking-to won't do any good," said Willie. Tembi was whipped again; this time properly, with no nonsense about making the switch whistle for effect. He was made to expose his bare bottom across his father's knees, and when he got up. Willie said with satisfaction: "He's not going to be comfortable sitting down for a week." "But, Willie, there's blood," said Jane. For as Tembi walked off stiffly, his legs straddled apart from the pain, his fists thrust into his streaming eyes, reddish patches appeared on the stuff of his trousers. Willie said angrily: "Well, what do you expect me to do— make him a present of it and say: How clever of you?"

"But *blood*, Willie!"

"I didn't know I was hitting him so hard," admitted Willie. He examined the long flexible twig in his hands, before throwing it away, as if surprised at its effectiveness. "That must have hurt," he said doubtfully. "Still, he deserved it. Now stop crying, Jane. He won't do that again."

But Jane did not stop crying. She could not bear to think of the beating; and Willie, no matter what he said, was uncomfortable when he remembered it. They would have been pleased to let Tembi slip from their minds for a while, and have him reappear later, when there had been time for kindness to grow in them again.

But it was not a week before he demanded to be made nurse to the children: he was now big enough, he said; and Jane had promised. Jane was so astonished she could not speak to him. She went indoors, shutting the door on him; and, when she knew he was still lingering there for speech with her, sent out the houseboy to say she was not having a thief as nurse for her children.

A few weeks later he asked again; and again she refused. Then he took to waylaying her every day, sometimes several times a day: "Missus, my missus, let me work near you, let me work near you." Always she refused, and always she grew more angry.

At last, the sheer persistence of the thing defeated her. She said: "I won't have you as a nurse, but you can help me with the vegetable garden." Tembi was sullen, but he presented himself at the garden next day, which was not the one near the house, but the fenced patch near the compound, for the use of the natives. Jane employed a garden boy to run it, telling him when was the time to plant, explaining about compost and the proper treatment of soil. Tembi was to help him.

She did not often go to the garden; it ran of itself. Sometimes, passing, she saw the beds full of vegetables were running to waste; this meant that a new batch of Africans were in the compound, natives who had to be educated afresh to eat what was good for them. But now she had had her last baby, and employed two nannies in the nurseries, she felt free to spend more time at the clinic and at the garden. Here she made a point of being friendly to

Tembi. She was not a person to bear grudges, though a feeling that he was not to be trusted barred him as a nurse. She would talk to him about her own children, and how they were growing, and would soon be going to school in the city. She would talk to him about keeping himself clean, and eating the right things; how he must earn good money so that he could buy shoes to keep his feet from the germ-laden dust; how he must be honest, always tell the truth and be obedient to the white people. While she was in the garden he would follow her around, his hoe trailing forgotten in his hand, his eyes fixed on her. "Yes, missus; yes, my missus," he repeated continually. And when she left, he would implore: "*When* are you coming again? Come again soon, my missus." She took to bringing him her own children's books, when they were too worn for use in the nursery. "You must learn to read, Tembi," she would say. "Then, when you want to get a job, you will earn more wages if you can say: 'Yes, missus, I can read and write.' You can take messages on the telephone then, and write down orders so that you don't forget them." "Yes, missus," Tembi would say, reverently taking the books from her. When she left the garden, she would glance back, always a little uncomfortably, because of Tembi's intense devotion, and see him kneeling on the rich red soil, framed by the bright green of the vegetables, knitting his brows over the strange coloured pictures and the unfamiliar print.

This went on for about two years. She said to Willie: "Tembi seems to have got over that funny business of his. He's really useful in that garden. I don't have to tell him when to plant things. He knows as well as I do. And he goes round the huts in the compound with the vegetables, persuading the natives to eat them." "I bet he makes a bit on the side," said Willie, chuckling. "Oh no, Willie, I'm sure he wouldn't do that."

And, in fact, he didn't. Tembi regarded himself as an apostle of the white man's way of life. He would say earnestly, displaying the baskets of carefully displayed vegetables to the native women: "The Goodhearted One says it is right we should eat these things. She says eating them will save us from sickness." Tembi achieved more than Jane had done in years of propaganda.

He was nearly eleven when he began giving trouble again. Jane sent her two elder children to boarding-school, dismissed her nannies, and decided to engage a piccanin to help with the children's washing. She did not think of Tembi; but she engaged Tembi's younger brother.

Tembi presented himself at the back door, as of old, his eyes flashing, his body held fine and taut, to protest. "Missus, missus, you promised I should work for you." "But Tembi, you are working for me, with the vegetables." "Missus, my missus, you said when you took a piccanin for the house, that piccanin would be me." But Jane did not give way. She still felt as if Tembi were on probation. And the demanding, insistent, impatient thing in Tembi did not seem to her a good quality to be near the children. Besides, she liked Tembi's little brother, who was a softer, smiling, chubby Tembi, playing good-naturedly with the children in the garden when he had finished the washing and ironing. She saw no reason to change, and said so.

Tembi sulked. He no longer took baskets of green stuff from door to door in the compound. And he did as little work as he need without actually neglecting it. The spirit had gone out of him.

"You know," said Jane half indignantly, half amused, to Willie: "Tembi behaves as if he had some sort of claim on us."

Quite soon, Tembi came to Willie and asked to be allowed to buy a bicycle. He was then earning ten shillings a month, and the rule was that no native earning less than fifteen shillings could buy a bicycle. A fifteen-shilling native would keep five shillings of his wages, give ten to Willie, and undertake to remain on the farm till the debt was paid. That might take two years, or even longer. "No," said Willie. "And what does a piccanin like you want with a bicycle? A bicycle is for big men."

Next day, their eldest child's bicycle vanished from the house, and was found in the compound leaning against Tembi's hut. Tembi had not even troubled to conceal the theft; and when he was called for an interview kept silent. At last he said: "I don't know why I stole it. I don't know." And he ran off, crying, into the trees.

"He must go," said Willie finally, baffled and angry.

"But his father and mother and the family live in our compound," protested Jane.

"I'm not having a thief on the farm," said Willie. But getting rid of Tembi was more than dismissing a thief: it was pushing aside a problem that the McClusters were not equipped to handle. Suddenly Jane knew that when she no longer saw Tembi's burning, pleading eyes, it would be a relief; though she said guiltily: "Well, I suppose he can find work on one of the farms nearby."

Tembi did not allow himself to be sacked so easily. When Willie told him he burst into passionate tears, like a very small child. Then he ran round the house and banged his fists on the kitchen door till Jane came out. "Missus, my missus, don't let the baas send me away." "But, Tembi, you must go, if the boss says so." "I work for you, missus, I'm your boy, let me stay. I'll work for you in the garden and I won't ask for any more money." "I'm sorry, Tembi," said Jane. Tembi gazed at her while his face hollowed into incredulous misery: he had not believed she would not take his part. At this moment his little brother came round the corner of the house carrying Jane's youngest child, and Tembi flew across and flung himself on them, so that the little black child staggered back, clutching the white infant to himself with difficulty. Jane flew to rescue her baby, and then pulled Tembi off his brother, who was bitten and scratched all over his face and arms.

"That finishes it," she said coldly. "You will be off this farm in an hour, or the police will chase you off."

They asked Tembi's father, later, if the lad had found work; the reply was that he was garden boy on a neighbouring farm. When the McClusters saw these neighbours they asked after Tembi, but the reply was vague: on this new farm Tembi was just another labourer without a history.

Later still Tembi's father said there had been "trouble," and that Tembi had moved to another farm, many miles away. Then, no one seemed to know where he was; it was said he had joined a gang of boys moving south to Johannesburg for work on the gold mines.

The McClusters forgot Tembi. They were pleased to be able to forget him. They thought of themselves as good masters; they had a good name with their labourers for kindness and fair dealing; while the affair of Tembi left something hard and unassimilable in them, like a grain of sand in a mouthful of food. The name "Tembi" brought uncomfortable emotions with it; and there was no reason why it should, according to their ideas of right and wrong. So at last they did not even remember to ask Tembi's father what had become of him: he had become another of those natives who vanish from one's life after seeming to be such an intimate part of it.

It was about four years later that the robberies began again. The McClusters' house was the first to be rifled. Someone climbed in one night and took the following articles: Willie's big winter coat, his stick, two old dresses belonging to Jane, a quantity of children's clothing and an old and battered child's tricycle. Money left lying in a drawer was untouched. "What extraordinary things to take," marvelled the McClusters. For except for Willie's coat, there was nothing of value. The theft was reported to the police, and a routine visit was made to the compound. It was established that the thief must be someone who knew the house, for the dogs had not barked at him; and that it was not an experienced thief, who would certainly have taken money and jewellery.

Because of this, the first theft was not connected with the second, which took place at a neighbouring farmhouse. There, money and watches and a gun were stolen. And there were more thefts in the district of the same kind. The police decided it must be a gang of thieves, not the ordinary pilferer, for the robberies were so clever and it seemed as if several people had planned them. Watchdogs were poisoned; times were chosen when servants were out of the house; and on two occasions someone had entered through bars so closely set together that no one but a child could have forced his way through.

The district gossiped about the robberies; and because of them, the anger lying dormant between white and black, always ready to flare up, deepened in an ugly way. There was hatred in the white people's voices when they addressed their servants, that futile anger, for even if their personal servants were giving information to the thieves, what could be done about it? The most trusted servant could turn out to be a thief. During these months when the unknown gang terrorized the district, unpleasant things happened; people were fined more often for beating their natives; a greater number of labourers than usual ran away over the border to Portuguese territory; the dangerous, simmering anger was like heat growing in the air. Even Jane found herself saying one day: "Why do we do it? Look how I spend my time nursing and helping these natives! What thanks do I get? They aren't grateful for anything we do for them." This question of gratitude was in every white person's mind during that time.

As the thefts continued, Willie put bars in all the windows of the house, and bought two large fierce dogs. This annoyed Jane, for it made her feel confined and a prisoner in her own home.

To look at a beautiful view of mountains and shaded green bush through bars, robs the sight of joy; and to be greeted on her way from house to storerooms by the growling of hostile dogs who treated everyone, black and white, as an enemy, became daily more exasperating. They bit everyone who came near the house, and Jane was afraid for her children. However, it was not more than three weeks after they were bought that they were found lying stretched in the sun, quite dead, foam at their mouths and their eyes glazing. They had been poisoned. "It looks as if we can expect another visit," said Willie crossly; for he was by now impatient of the whole business. "However," he said impatiently, "if one chooses to live in a damned country like this, one has to take the consequences." It was an exclamation that meant nothing, that could not be taken seriously by anyone. During that time, however, a lot of settled and contented people were talking with prickly anger about "the damned country." In short, their nerves were on edge.

Not long after the dogs were poisoned, it became necessary for Willie to make the trip into town, thirty miles off. Jane did not want to go; she disliked the long, hot, scurrying day in the streets. So Willie went by himself.

In the morning, Jane went to the vegetable garden with her younger children. They played around the water-butt, by themselves, while she staked out a new row of beds; her mind was lazily empty, her hands working quickly with twine and wooden pegs. Suddenly, however, an extraordinary need took her to turn around sharply, and she heard herself say: "Tembi!" She looked wildly about her; afterwards it seemed to her she had heard him speak her name. It seemed to her that she would see a spindly earnest-faced black child kneeling behind her between the vegetable beds, poring over a tattered picture book. Time slipped and swam together; she felt confused; and it was only by looking determinedly at her two children that she regained a knowledge of how long it had been since Tembi followed her around this garden.

When she got back to the house, she sewed on the verandah. Leaving her chair for a moment to fetch a glass of water, she found her sewing basket had gone. At first she could not believe it. Distrusting her own senses, she searched the place for her basket, which she knew very well had been on the verandah not a few moments before. It meant that a native was lingering in the bush, perhaps a couple of hundred yards away, watching her movements. It wasn't a pleasant thought. An old uneasiness filled her; and again the name "Tembi" rose into her mind. She took herself into the kitchen and said to the cookboy: "Have you heard anything of Tembi recently." But there had been no news, it seemed. He was "at the gold mines." His parents had not heard from him for years.

"But why a sewing basket?" muttered Jane to herself, incredulously. "Why take such a risk for so little? It's insane."

That afternoon, when the children were playing in the garden and Jane was asleep on her bed, someone walked quietly into the bedroom and took her big garden hat, her apron, and the dress she had been wearing that morning. When Jane woke and discovered this, she began to tremble, half with anger, half with fear. She was alone in the house, and she had the prickling feeling of being watched. As she moved from room to room, she kept glancing over her shoulders behind the angles of wardrobe and cupboard, and fancied that Tembi's great imploring eyes would appear there, as unappeasable as a dead person's eyes, following her.

She found herself watching the road for Willie's return. If Willie had been there, she could have put the responsibility on to him and felt safe: Jane was a woman who depended very much on that invisible support a husband gives. She had not known, before that afternoon, just how much she depended on him; and this knowledge—which it seemed the thief shared—made her unhappy and restless. She felt that she should be able to manage this thing by herself, instead of waiting helplessly for her husband. I must do something, I must do something, she kept repeating.

It was a long, warm, sunny afternoon. Jane, with all her nerves standing to attention, waited on the verandah, shading her eyes as she gazed along the road for Willie's car. The waiting preyed on her. She could not prevent her eyes from returning again and again to the bush immediately in front of the house, which stretched for mile on mile, a low, dark scrubby green, darker because of the lengthening shadows of approaching evening. An impulse pulled her to her feet, and she marched towards the bush through the garden. At its edge she stopped, peering everywhere for those dark and urgent eyes, and called "Tembi, Tembi." There was no sound. "I won't punish you, Tembi," she implored. "Come here to me." She waited, listening delicately, for the slightest movement of branch or dislodged pebble. But the bush was silent under the sun; even the birds were drugged by the heat; and the leaves hung without trembling. "Tembi!" she called again: at first peremptorily, and then with a quaver in her voice. She knew very well that he was there, flattening himself behind some tree or bush, waiting for her to say the right word, to find the right things to say, so that he could trust her. It maddened her to think he was so close, and she could no more reach him than she could lay her hands on a shadow. Lowering her voice persuasively she said: "Tembi, I know you are there. Come here and talk to me. I won't tell the police. Can't you trust me, Tembi?"

Not a sound, not the whisper of a reply. She tried to make her mind soft and blank, so that the words she needed would appear there, ready for using. The grass was beginning to shake a little in the evening breeze, and the hanging leaves tremored once or twice; there was a warm mellowing of the light that meant the sun would soon sink; a red glow showed on the foliage, and the sky was flaring high with light. Jane was trembling so she could not control her limbs; it was a deep internal trembling, welling up from inside, like a wound bleeding invisibly. She tried to steady herself. She said: This is silly. I can't be afraid of little Tembi! How could I be? She made her voice firm and loud and said: "Tembi, you are being very foolish. What's the use of stealing things like a stupid child? You can be clever about stealing for a little while, but sooner or later the police will catch you and you will go to prison. You don't want that, do you? Listen to me, now. You come out now and let me see you; and when the boss comes I'll explain to him, and I'll say you are sorry, and you can come back and work for me in the vegetable garden. I don't like to think of you as a thief, Tembi. Thieves are bad people." She stopped. The silence settled around her; she felt the silence like a coldness, as when a cloud passes overhead. She saw that the shadows were thick about her and the light had gone from the leaves, that had a cold grey look. She knew Tembi would not come out to her now. She had not found the right things to say. "You are a silly little boy," she announced to the still listening bush. "You make me very angry, Tembi." And she walked very slowly back to the house, holding herself calm and dignified, knowing that Tembi was watching her, with some plan in his mind she could not conjecture.

When Willie returned from town, tired and irritable as he always was after a day of traffic, and interviewing people, and shopping, she told him carefully, choosing her words, what had happened. When she told how she had called to Tembi from the verges of the bush, Willie looked gently at her and said: "My dear, what good do you think that's going to do?" "But Willie, it's all so awful . . ." Her lips began to tremble luxuriously, and she allowed herself to weep comfortably on his shoulder. "You don't know it is Tembi," said Willie. "Of course it's Tembi. Who else could it be? The silly little boy. My silly little Tembi . . ."

She could not eat. After supper she said suddenly: "He'll come here tonight. I'm sure of it." "Do you think he will?" said Willie seriously, for he had a great respect for Jane's irrational knowledge. "Well, don't worry, we'll be ready for him." "If he'd only let me talk to him," said Jane. "Talk to him!" said Willie. "Like hell! I'll have him in prison. That's the only place for him." "But, *Willie* . . ." Jane protested, knowing perfectly well that Tembi must go to prison.

It was then not eight o'clock. "I'll have my gun beside the bed," planned Willie. "He stole a gun, didn't he, from the farm over the river? He might be dangerous." Willie's blue eyes were alight; he was walking up and down the room, his hands in his pockets, alert and excited: he seemed to be enjoying the idea of capturing Tembi, and because of this Jane felt herself go cold against him. It was at this moment that there was a sound from the bedroom next door. They sprang up, and reached the entrance together. There stood Tembi, facing them, his hands dangling empty at his sides. He had grown taller, but still seemed the same lithe, narrow child, with the thin face and great eloquent eyes. At the sight of those eyes Jane said weakly: "Willie . . ."

Willie, however, marched across to Tembi and took that unresisting criminal by the arm. "You young rascal," he said angrily, but in a voice appropriate, not to a dangerous thief, who had robbed many houses, but rather to a naughty child caught pilfering fruit. Tembi did not reply to Willie: his eyes were fixed on Jane. He was trembling; he looked no more than a boy.

"Why didn't you come when I called you?" asked Jane. "You are so foolish, Tembi."

"I was afraid, missus," said Tembi, in a voice just above a whisper. "But I said I wouldn't tell the police," said Jane.

"Be quiet, Jane," ordered Willie. "Of course we're calling the police. What are you thinking of?" As if feeling the need to remind himself of this important fact, he said: "After all, the lad's a criminal."

"I'm not a bad boy," whispered Tembi imploringly to Jane. "Missus, my missus, I'm not a bad boy."

But the thing was out of Jane's hands; she had relinquished it to Willie.

Willie seemed uncertain what to do. Finally he strode purposefully to the wardrobe, and took his rifle from it, and handed it to Jane. "You stay here," he ordered. "I'm calling the police on the telephone." He went out, leaving the door open, while Jane stood there holding the big gun, and waiting for the sound of the telephone.

She looked helplessly down at the rifle, set it against the bed, and said in a whisper: "Tembi, why did you steal?"

Tembi hung his head and said: "I don't know, missus." "But you must know." There was no reply. The tears poured down Tembi's cheeks.

"Tembi, did you like Johannesburg?" There was no reply. "How long were you there?" "Three years, missus." "Why did you come back?" "They put me in prison, missus." "What for?" "I didn't have

a pass." "Did you get out of prison?" "No, I was there one month
and they let me go." "Was it you who stole all the things from the
houses around here?" Tembi nodded, his eyes cast down to the
floor.

Jane did not know what to do. She repeated firmly to herself:
"This is a dangerous boy, who is quite unscrupulous, and very
clever," and picked up the rifle again. But the weight of it, a cold
hostile thing, made her feel sorry. She set it down sharply. "Look at
me, Tembi," she whispered. Outside, in the passage, Willie was
saying in a firm confident voice: "Yes, Sergeant, we've got him
here. He used to work for us, years ago. Yes."

"Look, Tembi," whispered Jane quickly. "I'm going out of the
room. You must run away quickly. How did you get in?" This
thought came to her for the first time. Tembi looked at the window.
Jane could see how the bars had been forced apart, so that a very
slight person could squeeze in, sideways. "You must be strong," she
said. "Now, there isn't any need to go out that way. Just walk out of
that door," she pointed at the door to the living-room, "and go
through into the verandah, and run into the bush. Go to another
district and get yourself an honest job and stop being a thief. I'll
talk to the baas. I'll tell him to tell the police we made a mistake.
Now then, Tembi . . ." she concluded urgently, and went into the
passage, where Willie was at the telephone, with his back to her.

He lifted his head, looked at her incredulously, and said: "Jane,
you're crazy." Into the telephone he said: "Yes, come quickly." He
set down the receiver, turned to Jane and said: "You know he'll do it
again, don't you?" He ran back to the bedroom.

But there had been no need to run. There stood Tembi, exactly
where they had left him, his fists in his eyes, like a small child.

"I told you to run away," said Jane angrily.

"He's nuts," said Willie.

And now, just as Jane had done, Willie picked up the rifle,
seemed to feel foolish holding it, and set it down again.

Willie sat on the bed and looked at Tembi with the look of one
who has been outwitted. "Well, I'm damned," he said. "It's got me
beat, this has."

Tembi continued to stand there in the centre of the floor, hanging his head and crying. Jane was crying too. Willie was getting
angrier, more and more irritable. Finally he left the room, slamming the door, and saying: "God damn it, everyone is mad."

Soon the police came, and there was no more doubt about what
should be done. Tembi nodded at every question: he admitted

everything. The handcuffs were put on him, and he was taken away in the police car.

At last Willie came back into the bedroom, where Jane lay crying on the bed. He patted her on the shoulder and said: "Now stop it. The thing is over. We can't do anything."

Jane sobbed out: "He's only alive because of me. That's what's so awful. And now he's going to prison."

"They don't think anything of prison. It isn't a disgrace as it is for us."

"But he's going to be one of those natives who spend all their lives in and out of prison."

"Well, what of it?" said Willie. With the gentle, controlled exasperation of a husband, he lifted Jane and offered her his handkerchief. "Now stop it, old girl," he reasoned. "Do stop it. I'm tired. I want to go to bed. I've had hell up and down those damned pavements all day, and I've got a heavy day tomorrow with the tobacco." He began pulling off his boots.

Jane stopped crying, and also undressed. "There's something horrible about it all," she said restlessly. "I can't forget it." And finally, "What did he *want*, Willie? What is it he was *wanting*, all this time?"

Old John's Place

THE people of the district, mostly solidly established farmers who intended to live and die on their land, had become used to a certain kind of person buying a farm, settling on it with a vagabond excitement, but with one eye always on the attractions of the nearest town, and then flying off again after a year or so, leaving behind them a sense of puzzled failure, a desolation even worse than usual, for the reason that they had taken no more than a vagabond's interest in homestead and stock and land.

It soon became recognised that the Sinclairs were just such persons in spite of, even because of, their protestations of love for the soil and their relief at the simple life. Their idea of the simple was not shared by their neighbours, who felt they were expected to measure up to standards which were all very well when they had the glamour of distance, but which made life uncomfortably complicated if brought too close.

The Sinclairs bought Old John's Farm, and that was an unlucky place, with no more chance of acquiring a permanent owner than a restless dog has. Although this part of the district had not been settled for more than forty years, the farm had changed hands so often no one could remember how it had got its name. Old John, if he had ever existed, had become merely a place, as famous people may do.

Mr. Sinclair had been a magistrate before he retired, and was known to have private means. Even if this had not been known—

he referred to himself humorously as "another of these damned cheque-book farmers"—his dilettante's attitude towards farming would have proved the fact: he made no attempt at all to make money and did not so much as plough a field all the time he was there. Mrs. Sinclair gardened and gave parties. Her very first party became a legend, remembered with admiration, certainly, but also with that grudging tolerance that is accorded to spend-thrifts who can afford to think of extravagance as a necessity. It was a week-end affair, very highly organised, beginning with tennis on Saturday morning and ending on Sunday night with a lengthy formal dinner for forty people. It was not that the district did not enjoy parties, or give plenty of their own; rather it was, again, that they were expected to enjoy themselves in a way that was foreign to them. Mrs. Sinclair was a realist. Her parties, after that, followed a more familiar routine. But it became clear, from her manner, that in settling here she had seen herself chiefly as a hostess, and now felt that she had not chosen her guests with discrimination. She took to spending two or three days of each week in town; and went for prolonged visits to farms in other parts of the country. Mr. Sinclair, too, was seen in the offices of estate agents. He did not mention these visits; Mrs. Sinclair was reticent when she returned from those other farms.

When people began to say that the Sinclairs were leaving, and for the most familiar reason, that Mrs. Sinclair was not cut out for farm life, their neighbours nodded and smiled, very politely. And they made a point of agreeing earnestly with Mrs. Sinclair when she said town life was after all essential to her.

The Sinclairs' farewell party was attended by perhaps fifty people who responded with beautiful tact to what the Sinclairs expected of them. The men's manner towards Mr. Sinclair suggested a sympathy which the women, for once, regarded with indulgence. In the past many young men, angry and frustrated, had been dragged back to offices in town by their wives; and there had been farewell parties that left hostility between husbands and wives for days. The wives were unable to condemn a girl who was genuinely unable "to take the life," as the men condemned her. They championed her, and something always happened then which was what those farmers perhaps dreaded most; for dig deep enough into any one of those wives, and one would find a willing martyr alarmingly apt to expose a bleeding heart in an effort to win sympathy from a husband supposed—for the purposes of this argument—not to have one at all.

But this substratum of feeling was not reached that evening. Here was no tragedy. Mrs. Sinclair might choose to repeat, sadly, that she was not cut out for the life; Mr. Sinclair could sigh with humorous resignation as much as he liked; but the whole thing was regarded as a nicely acted play. In corners people were saying tolerantly: "Yes, they'll be much happier there." Everyone knew the Sinclairs had bought another farm in a district full of cheque-book farmers, where they would be at home. The fact that they kept this secret—or thought they had—was yet another evidence of unnecessary niceness of feeling. Also, it implied that the Sinclairs thought them fools.

In short, because of the guards on everyone's tongue, the party could not take wings, in spite of all the drink and good food.

It began at sundown, on Old John's verandah, which might have been designed for parties. It ran two sides of the house, and was twenty feet deep.

Old John's house had been built on to and extended so often, by so many people with differing tastes and needs, that of all the houses in the district it was the most fascinating for children. It had rambling creeper-covered wings, a staircase climbing to the roof, a couple of rooms raised up a flight of steps here, another set of rooms sunk low, there; and through all these the children ran wild till they began to grow tired and fretful. They then gathered round their parents' chairs, where they were a nuisance, and the women roused themselves unwillingly from conversation, and began to look for places where they might sleep. By eight o'clock it was impossible to move anywhere without watching one's feet— children were bedded down on floors, in the bath, on sofas, any place, in fact, that had room for a child.

That done, the party was free to start properly, if it could. But there was always a stage when the women sat at one end of the verandah and the men at the other. The host would set bottles of whisky freely on window-ledges and on tables among them. As for the women, it was necessary, in order to satisfy convention, to rally them playfully so that they could expostulate, cover their glasses, and exclaim that really, they couldn't drink another mouthful. The bottles were then left unobtrusively near them, and they helped themselves, drinking no less than the men.

During this stage Mrs. Sinclair played the game and sat with the women, but it was clear that she felt defeated because she had been unable to dissolve the ancient convention of the segregation of the sexes. She frequently rose, when it was quite unnecessary, to attend to the food and to the servants who were handing it round; and each time she did so, glances followed her which were as ambiguous as she was careful to keep her own.

Between the two separate groups wandered a miserable child, who was too old to be put to bed with the infants, and too young to join the party; unable to read because that was considered rude; unable to do anything but loiter on the edge of each group in turn, until an impatient look warned her that something was being suppressed for her benefit that would otherwise add to the gaiety of the occasion. As the evening advanced and the liquor fell in the bottles, these looks became more frequent. Seeing the waif's discomfort, Mrs. Sinclair took her hand and said: "Come and help me with the supper," thus giving herself a philanthropic appearance in removing herself and the child altogether.

The big kitchen table was covered with cold roast chickens, salads and trifles. These were the traditional party foods of the district; and Mrs. Sinclair provided them; though at that first party, two years before, the food had been exotic.

"If I give you a knife, Kate, you won't cut yourself?" she enquired; and then said hastily, seeing the child's face, which protested, as it had all evening, that such consideration was not necessary: "Of course you won't. Then help me joint these chickens . . . not that the cook couldn't do it perfectly well, I suppose."

While they carved, Mrs. Sinclair chatted determinedly; and only once said anything that came anywhere near to what they were both thinking, when she remarked briskly: "It is a shame. Really, arrangements should be made for you. Having you about is unfair to you and to the grown-ups."

"What could they do with me?" enquired Kate reasonably.

"Heaven knows," acknowledged Mrs. Sinclair. She patted Kate's shoulder encouragingly, and said in a gruff and friendly voice: "Well, I can't say anything helpful, except that you are *bound* to grow up. It's an awful age, being neither one thing or the other." Kate was thirteen; and it was an age for which no social provision was made. She was thankful to have the excuse to be here, in the kitchen, with at least an appearance of something to do. After a while Mrs. Sinclair left her, saying without any attempt at disguising her boredom, even though Kate's parents were among those who bored her: "I've got to go back, I suppose."

Kate sat on a hard kitchen chair, and waited for something to happen, though she knew she could expect nothing in the way of amusement save those odd dropped remarks which for the past year or so had formed her chief education.

In the meantime she watched the cook pile the pieces of chicken on platters, and hand trays and jugs and plates to the waiters, who were now hurrying between this room and the verandah. The sound of voices was rising steadily; Kate judged that the party must be moving towards its second phase, in which case she must certainly stay where she was, for fear of the third.

During the second phase the men and women mingled, pulling their chairs together in a wide circle; and it was likely that some would dance, calling for music, when the host would wind up an old portable gramophone. It was at this stage that the change in the atmosphere took place which Kate acknowledged by the phrase: "It is breaking up." The sharply-defined family units began to dissolve, and they dissolved always in the same way, so that during the last part of each evening, from about twelve o'clock, the same couples could be seen together dancing, talking, or even moving discreetly off into dark rooms or the night outside. This pattern was to Kate as if a veil had been gently removed from the day-time life of the district, revealing another truth, and one that was bare and brutal. Also quite irrevocable, and this was acknowledged by the betrayed themselves (who were also, in their own times and seasons, betrayers) for nothing was more startling than the patient discretion with which the whole thing was treated.

Mrs. Wheatley, for instance, a middle-aged lady who played the piano at church services and ran the Women's Institute, known as a wonderful mother and prize cook, seemed on these occasions not to notice how her husband always sought out Mrs. Fowler (her own best friend) and how his partnership seemed to strike sparks out of the eyes of everyone present. When Andrew Wheatley emerged from the dark with Nan Fowler, their eyes heavy, their sides pressed close together, Mrs. Wheatley would simply avert her eyes and remark patiently (her lips tightened a little, perhaps): "We ought to be going quite soon." And so it was with everyone else. There was something recognised as dangerous, that had to be given latitude, emerging at these parties, and existing only because if it were forbidden it would be even more dangerous.

Kate, after many such parties, had learnt that after a certain time, no matter how bored she might be, she must take herself out of sight. This was consideration for the grown-ups, not for her; since she did not have to be present in order to understand. There was a fourth stage, reached very rarely, when there was an explosion of raised voices, quarrels and ugliness. It seemed to her that the host and hostess were always acting as sentinels in order to prevent this fourth stage being reached: no matter how much the others drank, or how husbands and wives played false for the moment, they had to remain on guard; at all costs Mrs. Wheatley must be kept tolerant, for everything depended on her tolerance.

Kate had not been in the kitchen alone for long, before she heard the shrill thin scraping of the gramophone; and only a few minutes passed before both Mr. and Mrs. Sinclair came in. The degree of Kate's social education could have been judged by her startled look when she saw that neither were on guard and that anything might happen. Then she understood from what they said that tonight things were safe.

Mrs. Sinclair said casually: "Have something to eat, Kate?" and seemed to forget her. "My God, they are a sticky lot," she remarked to her husband.

"Oh, I don't know, they get around in their own way."

"Yes, but what a way!" This was a burst of exasperated despair. "They don't get going tonight, thank heavens. But one expects . . ." Here Mrs. Sinclair's eyes fell on Kate, and she lowered her voice. "What I can't stand is the sameness of it all. You press a button—that's sufficient alcohol—and then the machinery begins to turn. The same things happen, the same people, never a word said—it's awful." She filled her glass liberally from a bottle that stood among the denuded chicken carcasses. "I needed that," she remarked, setting the glass down. "If I lived here much longer I'd begin to feel that I couldn't enjoy myself unless I were drunk."

"Well, my dear, we are off tomorrow."

"How did I stick two years of it? It really is awful," she pursued petulantly. "I don't know why I should get so cross about it. After all," she added reasonably, "I'm no puritan."

"No, dear, you are not," said Mr. Sinclair drily; and the two looked at each other with precisely that brand of discretion which Kate had imagined Mrs. Sinclair was protesting against. The words opened a vista with such suddenness that the child was staring in speculation at this plain, practical lady whose bread and butter air seemed to leave even less room for the romance which it was hard enough to associate with people like the Wheatleys and the Fowlers.

"Perhaps it is that I like a little more—what?—grace? with my sin?" enquired Mrs. Sinclair, neatly expressing Kate's own thought;

and Mr. Sinclair drove it home by saying, still very dry-voiced: "Perhaps at our age we ought not to be so demanding?"

Mrs. Sinclair coloured and said quickly: "Oh, you know what I mean." For a moment this couple's demeanour towards each other was unfriendly; then they overcame it in a gulp of laughter. "Cat," commented Mrs. Sinclair, wrily appreciative; and her husband slid a kiss on her cheek.

"You know perfectly well," said Mrs. Sinclair, slipping her arm through her husband's. "that what I meant was . . ."

"Well, we'll be gone tomorrow," Mr. Sinclair repeated.

"I think, on the whole," said Mrs. Sinclair after a moment, "that I prefer worthies like the Copes to the others; they at any rate have the discrimination to know what wouldn't become them . . . except that one knows it is sheer, innate dullness . . ."

Mr. Sinclair made a quick warning movement; Mrs. Sinclair coloured, looked confused, and gave Kate an irritated glance, which meant: That child here again!

To hear her parents described as "worthies" Kate took, defiantly, as a compliment; but the look caused the tears to suffuse her eyes, and she turned away.

"I am sorry, my dear," said kindhearted Mrs. Sinclair penitently. "You dislike being your age as much as I do being mine, I daresay. We must make allowances for each other."

With her hand still resting on Kate's shoulder, she remarked to her husband: "I wonder what Rosalind Lacey will make of all this?" She laughed, with pleasurable maliciousness.

"I wouldn't be surprised if they didn't do very well." His dryness now was astringent enough to sting.

"How could they?" asked Mrs. Sinclair, really surprised. "I shall be really astonished if they last six months. After all, she's not the type—I mean, she has at least *some* idea."

"Which idea?" enquired Mr. Sinclair blandly, grinning spitefully; and though Mrs. Sinclair exclaimed: "You are horrid, darling," Kate saw that she grinned no less spitefully.

While Kate was wondering how much more "different" (the word in her mind to distinguish the Sinclairs from the rest of the district) the coming Laceys would be from the Sinclairs, they all became aware that the music had stopped, and with it the sounds of scraping feet.

"Oh dear," exclaimed Mrs. Sinclair, "you had better take out another case of whisky. What is the matter with them tonight? Say what you like, but it is exactly like standing beside a machine with an oil-can waiting for it to make grinding noises."

"No, let them go. We've done what we should."

"We must join them, nevertheless." Mrs. Sinclair hastily swallowed some more whisky, and, sighing heavily, moved to the door. Kate could see through a vista of several open doors to the verandah, where people were sitting about with bored expressions which suggested surreptitious glances at the clock. Among them were her own parents, sitting side by side, their solidity a comment (which was not meant) on the way the others had split up. Mr. Cope, who was described as The Puritan by his neighbours, a name he considered a great compliment, managed to enjoy his parties because it was quite possible to shut one's eyes to what went on at them. He was now smiling at Andrew Wheatley and Nan Fowler, as if the way they were interlaced was no more than roguish good fun. I like to see everyone enjoying themselves, his expression said, defiant of the gloom which was in fact settling over everyone.

Kate heard Mrs. Sinclair say to her husband, this time impatiently: "I suppose those Lacey people are going to spoil everything we have done here?" and this remark was sufficient food for thought to occupy her during the time she knew must elapse before she would be called to the car.

What had the Sinclairs, in fact, done here? Nothing—at least, to the mind of the district.

Kate supposed it might be something in the house; but, in fact, nothing had been built on, nothing improved; the place had not even been painted. She began to wander through the rooms, cautious of the sleeping children whose soft breathing could be heard from every darkened corner. The Sinclairs had brought in a great deal of heavy dark furniture, which everyone knew had to be polished by Mrs. Sinclair herself, as the servants were not to be trusted with it. There was silver, solid and cumbersome stuff. There were brass trays and fenders and coal scuttles which were displayed for use even in the warm weather. And there were inordinate quantities of water-colours, engravings and oils whose common factor was a pervading heaviness, a sort of brownish sigh in paint. All these things were now in their packing-cases, and when the lorries came in the morning, nothing would be left of the Sinclairs. Yet the Sinclairs grieved for the destruction of something they imagined they had contributed. This paradox slowly cleared in Kate's mind as she associated it with that suggestion in the Sinclairs' manner that everything they did or said referred in some way to a standard that other people could not be expected to understand, a standard that had nothing to do with beauty, ugliness, evil or goodness. Looked at in this light, the couple's attitude became clear. Their clothes, their furniture, even their own persons, all shared that same attribute, which was a kind of expensive and solid ugliness that could not be classified in any terms that had yet been introduced to Kate.

So the child shelved that problem and considered the Laceys, who were to arrive next week. They, presumably, would be even more expensive and ugly, yet kind and satisfactory, than the Sinclairs themselves.

But she did not have time to think of the Laceys for long; for the house began to stir into life as the parents came to rouse their children, and the family units separated themselves off in the dark outside the house, where the cars were parked. For this time, that other pattern was finished with, for now ordinary life must go on.

In the back of the car, heavily covered by blankets, for the night was cold, Kate lay half asleep, and heard her father say: "I wonder who we'll get this time?"

"More successful, I hope," said Mrs. Cope.

"Horses, I heard." Mr. Cope tested the word.

Mrs. Cope confirmed the doubt in his voice by saying decisively: "Just as bad as the rest, I suppose. This isn't the place for horses on that scale."

Kate gained an idea of something unrespectable. Not only the horses were wrong; what her parents said was clearly a continuation of other conversations, held earlier in the evening. So it was that long before they arrived the Laceys were judged and judged as vagrants.

@   @

Mr. Cope would have preferred to have the kind of neighbours who become a kind of second branch of one's own family, with the children growing up together, and a continual borrowing back and forth of farm implements and books and so forth. But he was a gentle soul, and accepted each new set of people with a courtesy that only his wife and Kate understood was becoming an effort . . . it was astonishing the way all the people who came to Old John's place were so much *not* the kind that the Copes would have liked.

Old John's house was three miles away, a comparatively short distance, and the boundary between the farms was a vlei which was described for the sake of grandness as a river, though most of the year there was nothing but a string of potholes caked with cracked mud. The two houses exchanged glances, as it were, from opposite ridges. The slope on the Copes' side was all ploughed land, of a dull yellow colour which deepened to glowing orange after rain. On the other side was a fenced expanse that had once been a cultivated field, and which was not greening over as the young trees spread and strengthened.

During the very first week of the Laceys' occupation this land became a paddock filled with horses. Mr. Cope got out his binoculars, gazed across at the other slope, and dropped them after a while, remarking: "Well, I suppose it is all right." It was a grudging acceptance. "Why shouldn't they have horses?" asked Kate curiously.

"Oh, I don't know, I don't know. Let's wait and see." Mr. Cope had met Mr. Lacey at the station on mail-day, and his report of the encounter had been brief, because he was a man who hated to be unfair, and he could not help disliking everything he heard about the Laceys. Kate gathered that the Laceys included a Mr. Hackett. They were partners, and had been farming in the Argentine, in the Cape, and in England. It was a foursome, for there was also a baby. The first wagon load of furniture had consisted of a complete suite of furniture for the baby's nurseries and many cases of saddles and stable equipment; and while they waited for the next load the family camped on the verandah without even so much as a teapot or a table for a meal. This tale was already making people smile. But because there was a baby the women warmed towards Mrs. Lacey before they had seen her; and Mrs. Cope greeted her with affectionate welcome when she arrived to make friends.

Kate understood at first glance that it was not Mrs. Lacey's similarity to Mrs. Sinclair that had caused the latter to accept her, in advance, as a companion in failure.

Mrs. Lacey was not like the homely mothers of the district. Nor did she—like Mrs. Sinclair—come into that category of leathery-faced and downright women who seemed more their husbands' partners than their wives. She was a tall, smooth-faced woman, fluidly moving, bronze hair coiled on her neck with a demureness that seemed a challenge, taken with her grace, and with the way she used her eyes. These were large, grey, and very quick; and Kate thought of the swift glances, retreating immediately behind smooth lowered lids, as spies sent out for information. Kate was charmed, as her mother was; as her father was, too—though against his will;

but she could not rid herself of distrust. All this wooing softness was an apology for something of which her parents had a premonition, while she herself was in the dark. She knew it was not the fact of the horses, in itself, that created disapproval; just as she knew that it was not merely Mrs. Lacey's caressing manner that was upsetting her father.

When Mrs. Lacey left, she drew Kate to her, kissed her on both cheeks, and asked her to come and spend the day. Warmth suddenly enveloped the child, so that she was head over ears in love, but distrusting the thing as a mature person does. Because the gesture was so clearly aimed, not at her, but at her parents, that first moment resentment was born with the love and the passionate admiration; and she understood her father when he said slowly, Mrs. Lacey having left: "Well, I suppose it is all right, but I can't say I like it."

The feeling over the horses was explained quite soon: Mr. Lacey and Mr. Hackett kept these animals as other people might keep cats. They could not do without them. As with the Sinclairs, there was money somewhere. In this district people did not *farm* horses; they might keep a few for the races or to ride around the lands. But at Old John's Place now there were dozens of horses, and if they were bought and sold it was not for the sake of the money, but because these people enjoyed the handling of them, the business of attending sales and the slow, shrewd talk of men as knowledgeable as themselves. There was, in fact, something excessive and outrageous about the Laceys' attitude towards horses: it was a passionate business, to be disapproved of, like gambling or women.

Kate went over to "spend a day" a week after she was first asked; and that week was allowed to elapse only because she was too shy to go sooner. Walking up the road beside the paddock, she saw the two men, in riding breeches, their whips looped over their arms, moving among the young animals with the seriousness of passion. They were both lean, tough, thin-flanked men, slow-moving and slow-spoken; and they appeared to be gripping invisible saddles with their knees even when they were walking. They turned their heads to stare at Kate, in the manner of those so deeply engrossed in what they are doing that outside things take a long time to grow in to their sight, but finally their whips cut a greeting in the air, and they shouted across to her. Their voices had a burr to them conveying again the exciting sense of things foreign; it was not the careful English voice of the Sinclairs, nor the lazy South African slur. It was an accent that had taken its timbre from many places and climates, and its effect on Kate was as if she had suddenly smelt the sea or heard a quickening strain of music.

She arrived at Old John's Place in a state of exaltation; and was greeted perfunctorily by Mrs. Lacey, who then seemed to remind herself of something, for Kate once more found herself enveloped. Then, since the rooms were still scattered with packing-cases, she was asked to help arrange furniture and clear things up. By the end of that day her resentment was again temporarily pushed to the background by the necessity for keeping her standards sharp in her mind; for the Laceys, she knew, were to be resisted; and yet she was being carried away with admiration.

Mrs. Sinclair might have brought something intangible here that to her was valuable, and she was right to have been afraid that Mrs. Lacey would destroy it. The place was transformed. Mrs. Lacey had colour-washed the walls sunny yellow, pale green, and rose, and added more light by the sort of curtains and hangings that Kate knew her own mother would consider frivolous. Such rooms were new in this district. As for Mrs. Lacey's bedroom, it was outrageous. One wall had been ripped away, and it was now a sheet of glass; and across it had been arranged fifty yards of light transparent material that looked like crystallized sunlight. The floor was covered right over from wall to wall with a deep white carpet. The bed, standing out into the room in a way that drew immediate notice, was folded and looped into oyster-coloured satin. It was a room which had nothing to do with the district, nothing to do with the drifts of orange dust outside and the blinding sunlight, nothing to do with anything Kate had ever experienced. Standing just outside the door (for she was afraid she might leave orange-coloured footprints on that fabulous carpet), she stood and stared, and was unable to tear her eyes away even though she knew Mrs. Lacey's narrowed grey gaze was fixed on her. 'Pretty?" she asked lightly, at last; and Kate knew she was being used as a test for what the neighbours might later say. "It's lovely," said Kate doubtfully; and saw Mrs. Lacey smile. "You'll never keep it clean," she added, as her mother would certainly do, when she saw this room. "It will be difficult, but it's worth it," said Mrs. Lacey, dismissing the objection far too lightly, as Kate could see when she looked obliquely along the walls, for already there were films of dust in the grain of the plaster. But all through that day Kate felt as if she were continually being brought face to face with something new, used, and dismissed: she had never been so used; she had never been so ravaged by love, criticism, admiration and doubt.

Using herself (as Mrs. Lacey was doing) as a test for other people's reactions, Kate could already hear the sour criticisms which would eventually defeat the Laceys. When she saw the nursery, however, she felt differently. This was something that the women of the district would appreciate. There were, in fact, three rooms for the baby, all conveying a sense of discipline and hygiene, with white enamel, thick cork floors and walls stencilled all over with washable coloured animals. The baby himself, at the crawling stage, was still unable to appreciate his surroundings. His nanny, a very clean, white-aproned native girl, sat several paces away and watched him. Mrs. Lacey explained that this nanny had orders not to touch the baby; she was acting as a guard; it was against the principles which were bringing the child up that the germs (which certainly infested every native, washed or not) should come anywhere near him.

Kate's admiration grew; the babies she had known were carried about by piccanins or by the cook's wife. They did not have rooms to themselves, but cots set immediately by their mothers' beds. From time to time they were weighed on the kitchen scales, for feeding chairs and baby scales had been encountered only in the pages of women's magazines that arrived on mail-days from England.

When she went home that evening she told her mother first about the nurseries, and then about the bedroom; as she expected, the first fact slightly outweighed the second. "She must be a good mother," said Mrs. Cope, adding immediately: "I should like to know how she's going to keep the dust out of that carpet." Mr. Cope said: "Well, I'm glad they've got money, because they are certainly going to need it." These comments acted as temporary breakwaters to the flood that would later sweep through such very modified criticism.

For a while people discussed nothing but the Laceys. The horses were accepted with a shrug and the remark: "Well, if they've money to burn . . ." Besides, that farm had never been properly used; this was merely a perpetuation of an existing fact. The word found for Mrs. Lacey was that she was "clever." This was not often a compliment; in any case it was a tentative one. Mrs. Lacey made her own clothes but not in the way the other women made theirs. She cut out patterns from brown paper by some kind of an instinct; she made the desserts and salads from all kinds of unfamiliar substances; she grew vegetables profusely, and was generous with them. People were always finding a native at the back door, with a basket full of fresh things and Mrs. Lacey's compliments. In fact, the women were going to Old John's house these days as they might have gone to raid a treasure cave; for they always returned with some fresh delight: mail-order catalogues from America, new recipes, patterns for nightdresses. Mrs. Lacey's nightdresses were discussed in corners at parties by the women, while the men called out across the room: "What's that, eh? Let us in on the fun." For a while it remained a female secret, for it was not so often that something new offered itself as spice to these people who knew each other far, far too well. At last, and it was at the Copes' house, one of the women stood up and demonstrated how Mrs. Lacey's nightdresses were cut, while everyone applauded. For the first time Kate could feel a stirring, a quickening in the air; she could almost see it as a man slyly licking his lips. This was the first time, too, that Mr. Cope openly disapproved of anything. He might be laughed at, but he was also a collective conscience; for when he said irritably: "But it is so unnecessary, so *unnecessary*, this kind of thing . . ." everyone became quiet, and talked of something else. He always used that word when he did not want to condemn, but when he was violently uncomfortable. Kate remembered afterwards how the others looked over at him while they talked: their faces showed no surprise at his attitude, but also, for the moment, no agreement; it was as if a child looked at a parent to see how far it might go before forfeiting approval, for there was a lot of fun to be had out of the Laceys yet.

Mrs. Lacey did not give her housewarming party until the place was finished, and that took several weeks. She did all the work herself. Kate, who was unable to keep away, helped her, and saw that Mrs. Lacey was pleased to have her help. Mr. Lacey was not interested in the beautiful house his wife was making; or, at any rate, he did not show it. Provided he was left enough room for books on horses, equipment for horses, and collections of sombreros, belts and saddles he did not mind what she did. He once remarked: "Well, it's your money, if you want to pour it down the sink." Kate thought this sounded as if he wished to stop her; but Mrs. Lacey merely returned, sharply: "Quite. Don't let's go into that again, now." And she looked meaningly at Kate. Several times she said: "At last I can feel that I have a home. No one can understand what that is like." At these moments Kate felt warm and friendly with her, for Mrs. Lacey was confiding in her; although she was unable to see Old John's Place as anything but a kind of resthouse. Even the spirit of Mrs. Sinclair was still strong in it, after all; for

Kate summoned her, often, to find out what she would think of all this. She could positively see Mrs. Sinclair standing there looking on, an ironical, pitying ghost. Kate was certain of the pity; because she herself could now hardly bear to look at Mrs. Lacey's face when Mr. Lacey and Mr. Hackett came into meals, and did not so much as glance at the work that had been done since they left. They would say: "I heard there was a good thing down in Natal," or "that letter from old Perry, in California, made me think . . ." and they were so clearly making preparations for when the restless thing in them that had already driven them from continent to continent spoke again, that she wondered how Mrs. Lacey could go on sewing curtains and ordering paints from town. Besides, Mrs. Sinclair had known when she was defeated: she had chosen, herself, to leave. Turning the words over on her tongue that she had heard Mrs. Sinclair use, she found the right ones for Mrs. Lacey. But in the meantime, for the rest of the district, she was still "clever," and everyone looked forward to that party.

The Copes arrived late. As they climbed out of the car and moved to the door, they looked for the familiar groups on the verandah, but there was no one there, although laughter came from inside. Soon they saw that the verandah had been cleared of furniture, and the floor had been highly polished. There was no light, save for what fell through the windows; but this gave an appearance, not so much of darkness, but of hushed preparedness. There were tubs of plants set round the walls, forming wells of shadow, and chairs had been set in couples, discreetly, behind pillars and in corners.

Inside the room that opened from the verandah, there were men, but no women. Kate left her parents to assimilate themselves into the group (Mrs. Cope protesting playfully that she was the only woman, and felt shy) and passed through the house to the nurseries. The women were putting the children to bed, under the direction of Mrs. Lacey. The three rooms were arranged with camp-beds and stretchers, so that they looked like improvised dormitories, and the children were subdued and impressed, for they were not used to such organisation. What Mrs. Lacey represented, too, subdued them, as it was temporarily subduing their mothers.

Mrs. Lacey was in white lace, and very pretty; but not only was she in evening dress and clearly put out because the other women were in their usual best dresses of an indeterminate floral crepiness that was positively a uniform for such occasions, there was that contrast, stronger now then ever, between what she seemed to want to appear, and what everyone felt of her. Those heavy down-looping, demure coils of hair, the discreet eyelids, the light white dress with childish puffed sleeves, were a challenge, but a challenge that was being held in reserve, for it was not directed at the women.

They were talking with the hurried forced laughter of nervousness. "You have got yourself up, Rosalind," said one of them; and this released a chorus of admiring remarks. What was behind the admiration showed itself when Mrs. Lacey left the nurseries for a moment to call the native nanny. The same sycophantic lady said tentatively, as if throwing a bird into the air to be shot at: "It is a sort of madonna look, isn't it? That oval face and smooth hair, I mean . . ." After a short silence someone said pointedly: "Some madonna," and then there was laughter, of a kind that sickened Kate, torn as she was between passionate partisanship and the knowledge that here was a lost cause.

Mrs. Lacey returned with the native girl; and her brief glance at the women was brave; Kate could have sworn she had heard the laughter and the remark that prompted it. It was with an air of womanly dignity that fitted perfectly with her dress and appearance that she said: "Now we have got the children into bed, we'll leave the girl to watch them and feel safe." But this was not how she had said previously: "Let's get them out of the way, and then we can enjoy ourselves." The women, however, filed obediently out; ignoring the small protests of the children, who were not at all sleepy, since it was before their proper bedtime.

In the big room Mrs. Lacey arranged her guests in what was clearly a planned compromise between the family pattern and the thing she intended should grow out of it. Husbands and wives were put together, yes; but in such a way that they had only to turn their heads to find other partners. Kate was astonished that Mrs. Lacey could have learned so much about these people in such a short time. The slightest suggestion of an attraction, which had merited no more than a smile or a glance, was acknowledged frankly by Mrs. Lacey in the way she placed her guests. For instance, while the Wheatleys were sitting together, Nan Fowler was beside Andrew Wheatley, and an elderly farmer, who had flirted mildly with Mrs. Wheatley on a former occasion, was beside her. Mrs. Lacey sat herself by Mr. Fowler, and cried gaily: "Now I shall console you, my dear—no, I shall be jealous if you take any notice of your wife tonight." For a moment there was a laughing, but uneasy pause, and then Mr. Lacey came forward with bottles, and Kate saw that everything was working as Mrs. Lacey had intended. In half an hour she saw she must leave, if she wanted to avoid that uncomfortable conviction of being a nuisance. By now Mrs. Lacey was beside Mr. Lacey at the sideboard, helping him with the drinks; there was no help here—she had been forgotten by her hostess.

Kate slipped away to the kitchens. Here were tables laden with chickens and trifles, certainly; but everything was a little dressed up; this was the district's party food elaborated to a stage where it could be admired and envied without causing suspicion.

Kate had had no time to do more than look for signs of the fatal aspics, sauces and creams when Mrs. Lacey entered. Kate had to peer twice to make sure it was Mr. Hackett and not Mr. Lacey who came with her: the two men seemed to her so very alike. Mrs. Lacey asked gaily: "Having a good tuck-in?" and then the two passed through into the pantries. Here there was a good deal of laughter. Once Kate heard: "Oh, do be careful . . ." and then Mrs. Lacey looked cautiously into the kitchen. Seeing Kate she assumed a good-natured smile and said, "You'll burst," and then withdrew her head. Kate had eaten nothing; but she did what seemed to be expected of her, and left the kitchen, wondering just what this thing was that sprang up suddenly between men and women—no, not *what* it was, but what prompted it. The word love, which had already stretched itself to include so many feelings, atmospheres and occasions, had become elastic enough for Kate not to astonish her. It included, for instance, Mr. Lacey and Mrs. Lacey helping each other to pour drinks, with an unmistakable good feeling; and Mrs. Lacey flirting with Mr. Hackett in the pantry while they pretended to be looking for something. To look at Mrs. Lacey this evening—that was no problem, for the bright expectancy of love was around her like sunlight. But why Mr. Hackett, or Mr. Lacey; or why either of them? And then Nan Fowler, that fat, foolish, capable dame who flushed scarlet at a word: what drew Andrew Wheatley to her, of all women, through years of parties, and kept him there?

Kate drifted across the intervening rooms to the door of the big living-room, feeling as if someone had said to her: "Yes, this house is yours, go in," but had forgotten to give her the key, or even to tell her where the door was. And when she reached the room she stopped again; through the hazing cigarette smoke, the hubbub, the leaning, laughing faces, the hands lying along chair-arms, grasping glasses, she could see her parents sitting side by side, and knew at once, from their faces, that they wanted only to go home, and that if she entered now, putting her to bed would be made an excuse for

going. She went back to the nurseries; as she passed the kitchen
door she saw Mr. Hackett, Mr. Lacey and Mrs. Lacey, arms linked
from waist to waist, dancing along between the heaped tables and
singing: All I want is a *little* bit of love, a *little* bit of love, a *little* bit
of love. Both men were still in their riding things, and their boots
thumped and clattered on the floor. Mrs. Lacey looked like a species
of fairy who had condescended to appear to cowhands—cowhands
who, however, were cynical about fairies, for at the end of the
dance Mr. Lacey smacked her casually across her behind and said,
"Go and do your stuff, my girl," and Mrs. Lacey went laughing to
her guests, leaving the men raiding the chickens in what appeared
to be perfect good fellowship.

In the nurseries Kate was struck by the easy manner in which
some twenty infants had been so easily disposed of: they were all
asleep. The silence here was deepened by the soft, regular sounds
of breathing, and the faint sound of music from beyond the heavy
baize doors. Even now, with the extra beds, and the little piles of
clothing at the foot of each, everything was so extraordinarily tidy.
A great cupboard, with its subdued gleaming paint, presented to
Kate an image of Mrs. Lacey herself; and she went to open it. Inside it was orderly, and on the door was a list of its contents, neatly
typed; but if a profusion of rich materials, like satin and velvet,
had tumbled out as the door opened, she would not have been in
the least surprised. On the contrary, her feeling of richness restrained and bundled out of the way would have been confirmed,
but there was nothing of the kind, not an article out of place anywhere, and on the floor sat the smiling native nanny, apologizing
by her manner for her enforced uselessness, for the baby was
whimpering and she was forbidden to touch it.

"Have you told Mrs. Lacey?" asked Kate, looking doubtfully at
the fat pink and white creature, which was exposed in a brief vest
and napkin, for it was too hot an evening for anything more. The
nanny indicated that she had told Mrs. Lacey, who had said she
would come when she could.

Kate sat beside the cot to wait, surrendering herself to self-pity:
the grownups were rid of her, and she was shut into the nursery
with the tiny children. Her tears gathered behind her eyes as the
baby's cries increased. After some moments she sent the nanny
again for Mrs. Lacey, and when neither of them returned, she rather
fearfully fetched a napkin from the cupboard and made the baby
comfortable. Then she held it on her knee, for consolation. She did
not much like small babies, but the confiding warmth of this one

soothed her. When the nursery door swung open soundlessly, so that Mrs. Lacey was standing over her before she knew it, she could not help wriggling guiltily up and exclaiming: "I changed him. He was crying." Mrs. Lacey said firmly: "You should never take a child out of bed once it is in. You should never alter a time-table." She removed the baby and put it back into the cot. She was afloat with happiness, and could not be really angry, but went on: "If you don't keep them strictly to a routine, they take advantage of you." This was so like what Kate's own mother always said about her servants, that she could not help laughing; and Mrs. Lacey said good-humouredly, turning round from the business of arranging the baby's limbs in an orderly fashion: "It is all very well, but he is perfectly trained, isn't he? He never gives me any trouble. I am quite certain you have never seen such a well-trained baby around here before." Kate admitted this was so, and felt appeased: Mrs. Lacey had spoken as if there was at least a possibility of her one day reaching the status of being able to profit by the advice: she was speaking as if to an equal.

Kate watched her move to the window, adjust the angle of a pane so that the starlight no longer gleamed in it, and use it as a mirror: there was no looking-glass in the nurseries. The smooth folds of hair were unruffled, but the usually guarded, observant eyes were bright and reckless. There was a vivid glow about Mrs. Lacey that made her an exotic in the nursery; even her presence there was a danger to the sleeping children. Perhaps she felt it herself, for she smoothed her forefinger along an eyebrow and said: "Are you going to stay here?" Kate hesitated. Mrs. Lacey said swiftly: "I don't see why you shouldn't come in. It's your father, though. He's such an old . . ." She stopped herself, and smiled sourly. "He doesn't approve of me. However, I can't help that." She was studying Kate. "Your mother has no idea, no idea at all," she remarked impatiently, turning Kate about between her hands. Kate understood that had Mrs. Lacey been her mother, her clothes would have been graded to suit her age. As it was, she wore a short pink cotton frock, reaching half-way down her thighs, that a child of six might have worn. That frock caused her anguished embarrassment, but loyalty made her say: "I like pink," very defiantly. Her eyes, though, raised in appeal to Mrs. Lacey's, gained the dry reply: "Yes, so I see."

On her way out, Mrs. Lacey remarked briskly: "I've got a lot of old dresses that could be cut down for you. I'll help you with them." Kate felt that this offer was made because Mrs. Lacey truly loved clothes and materials; for a moment her manner to Kate had not been adjusted with an eye to the ridiculous but powerful Mr. Cope. She said gratefully: "Oh, Mrs. Lacey . . ."

"And that hair of yours . . ." she heard, as the door swung, and went on swinging, soundlessly. There was the crisp sound of a dress moving along the passage, and the sweet homely smell of the nursery had given way to a perfume as unsettling as the music that poured strongly through the house. The Laceys had a gramophone and the newest records. Feet were swishing and sliding, the voices were softer now, with a reckless note. The laughter, on the other hand, swept by in great gusts. Peering through the doors, Kate tried to determine what "stage" the party had reached; she saw there had been no stages; Mrs. Lacey had fused these people together from the beginning, by the force of wanting to do it, and because her manner seemed to take the responsibility for whatever might happen. Now her light gay voice sounded above the others; she was flirting with everyone, dancing with everyone. Now there was no criticism; they were all in love with her.

Kate could see that while normally at this hour the rooms would be half empty, tonight they were all there. Couples were moving slowly in the subdued light of the verandah, very close together, or sitting at the tables, looking on. Then she suddenly saw someone walking towards her, by herself, in a violent staggering way; and, peering close, saw it was Mrs. Wheatley. She was crying. "I want to go home, I want to go home," she was saying, her tongue loose in her mouth. She did not see Kate, who ran quickly back to the baby, who was now asleep, lying quite still in its white cot, hands flexed at a level with its head, its fingers curled loosely over. Darling baby, whispered Kate, the tears stinging her cheeks. Darling, darling baby. The painful wandering emotion that had filled her for weeks, even since before the Laceys came, when she had felt held safe in Mrs. Sinclair's gruff kindliness, spilled now into the child. With a fearful, clutching pounce, she lifted the sleeping child, and cuddled it. Darling, darling baby . . . Later, very much later, she woke to find Mr. Lacey, looking puzzled, taking the baby from her; they had been lying asleep on the floor together. "Your father wants you," stated Mr. Lacey carefully, the sickly smell of whisky coming strong from his mouth. Kate staggered up and gained the door on his arm; but it was not as strong a support as she needed, for he was holding on to tables and chairs as he passed them.

For a moment Kate's sleep-dazed eyes could find nothing to hold them, for the big room was quite empty; so, it seemed, was the verandah. Then she saw Mrs. Lacey, dancing by herself down the dim shadowed space, weaving her arms and bending her body, and leaning her head to watch her white reflection move on the polished floor beside her. "Who is going to dance with me?" she crooned. "Who is going to dance?"

"You've worn us out," said a man's voice from Kate's feet; and looking hazily round she saw that couples were sitting around the edges of the space, with their arms about each other. Another voice, a woman's, this time, said: "Oh what a beautiful dress, what a beautiful dress," repeating it with drunken intensity; and someone answered in a low tone: "Yes, and not much beneath it, either, I bet."

Suddenly Kate's world was restored for her by her father's comment at her shoulder: "So unnecessary!" And she felt herself pushed across the verandah in the path of the dancing Mrs. Lacey, whose dim white skirts flung out and across her legs in a crisp caress. But she took no notice of Kate at all; nor did she answer Mr. Cope when he said stiffly: "Goodbye, Mrs. Lacey. I am afraid we must take this child to bed." She continued to dance, humming to herself, a drowsy happy look on her face.

In the car Kate lay wrapped in blankets and looked through the windows at the sky moving past. There was a white blaze of moonlight and the stars were full and bright. It could not be so very late after all, for the night still had the solemn intensity of midnight; that feeling of glacial withdrawal that comes into the sky towards dawn was not yet there. But in the hollow of the veld, where the cold lay congealed, she shivered and sat up. Her parents' heads showed against the stars, and they were being quite silent for her benefit. She was waiting for them to say something; she wanted her confused, conflicting impressions sorted and labelled by them. In her mind she was floating with Mrs. Lacey down the polished floor; she was also in the nursery with the fat and lovable baby; she could feel the grip of Mr. Lacey's hand on her shoulder. But not a word was said, not a word; though she could almost feel her mother thinking: "She has to learn for herself," and her father answering it with a "Yes, but how unpleasant!"

The next day Kate waited until her father had gone down to the lands in order to watch his labourers at their work, and her mother was in the vegetable garden. Then she said to the cook: "Tell the missus I have gone to Old John's Place." She walked away from her home and down to the river with the feeling that large accusing eyes were fixed on her back, but it was essential that she should see Mrs. Lacey that day: she was feverish with terror that Mr. Lacey had given her away—worse, that the baby had caught cold from lying on the floor beside her, and was ill. She walked slowly, as if dragged by invisible chains: if she left behind her unspoken disapproval, in front of her she sensed cruel laughter and anger.

Guilt, knowledge of having behaved ridiculously, and defiance churned through her; above the tumult another emotion rose like a full moon over a sky of storm. She was possessed by love; she was in love with the Laceys, with the house and its new luxuries, with Mrs. Lacey and the baby—even with Mr. Lacey and Mr. Hackett, who took lustre from Mrs. Lacey. By the time she neared the place, fear had subsided in her to a small wariness, lurking like a small trapped animal with bared teeth; she could think of nothing but that in a moment she would again have entered the magical circle. The drowsy warmth of a September morning, the cooing of the pigeons in the trees all about, the dry smell of sun-scorched foliage— all these familiar scents and sounds bathed her, sifted through her new sensitiveness and were reissued as it were, in a fresh currency: around Mrs. Lacey's house the bush was necessarily more exciting than it could be anywhere else.

The picture in her mind of the verandah and the room behind it, as she had seen them the night before, dissolved like the dream it had appeared to be as she stepped through the screen door. Already at ten in the morning, there was not a sign of the party. The long space of floor had been polished anew to a dull gleaming red; the chairs were in their usual circle at one end, against a bank of ferns, and at the other Mrs. Lacey sat sewing, the big circular table beside her heaped with materials and neatly-folded patterns. For a moment she did not notice Kate, who was free to stand and gaze in devoted wonder. Mrs. Lacey was in fresh green linen, and her head was bent over the white stuff in her lap in a charming womanly pose. This, surely, could never have been that wild creature who danced down this same verandah last night? She lifted her head and looked towards Kate; her long eyes narrowed, and something hardened behind them until, for a brief second, Kate was petrified by a vision of a boredom so intense that it was as if Mrs. Lacey had actually said: "What! Not you again?" Then down dropped those lids, so that her face wore the insufferable blank piety of a primitive Madonna. Then she smiled. Even that forced smile won Kate; and she moved towards Mrs. Lacey with what she knew was an uncertain and apprehensive grin. "Sit down," said Mrs. Lacey cordially, and spoiled the effect by adding immediately: "Do your parents know you are here?" She watched Kate obliquely as she put the question. "No," said Kate honestly, and saw the lids drop smoothly downwards.

She was stiff with dislike; she could not help but want to accept this parody of welcome as real; but not when the illusion was destroyed afresh every time Mrs. Lacey spoke. She asked timidly: "How is the baby?" This time Mrs. Lacey's look could not possibly be misinterpreted: she had been told by her husband; she had chosen, for reasons of her own, to say nothing. "The baby's very well," she said neutrally, adding after a moment: "Why did you come without telling your mother?" Kate could not give any comfort. "They would be angry if they knew I was here. I left a message." Mrs. Lacey frowned, laughed with brave, trembling gaiety, and then reached over and touched the bell behind her. Far away in the kitchens of that vast house there was a shrill peal; and soon a padding of bare feet announced the coming of the servant. "Tea," ordered Mrs. Lacey. "And bring some cakes for the little missus." She rearranged her sewing, put her hand to her eyes, laughed ruefully and said: "I've got such a hang-over I won't be able to eat for a week. But it was worth it." Kate could not reply. She sat fingering the materials heaped on the table; and wondered if any of these were what Mrs. Lacey had intended to give her; she even felt a preliminary gratitude, as it were. But Mrs. Lacey seemed to have forgotten her promise. The white stuff was for the baby. They discussed suitable patterns for children's vests: it went without saying that Mrs. Lacey's pattern was one Kate had never seen before, combining all kinds of advantages, so that it appeared that not a binding, a tape or a fastener had escaped the most far-sighted planning.

The long hot morning had to pass at last; at twelve Mrs. Lacey glanced at the folding clock which always stood beside her, and fetched the baby from where he lay in the shade under a big tree. She fed him orange juice, spoon by spoon, without taking him from the pram, while Kate watched him with all the nervousness of one who has betrayed emotion and is afraid it may be unkindly remembered. But the baby ignored her. He was a truly fine child, fat, firm, dimpled. When the orange juice was finished he allowed himself to be wheeled back to the tree without expostulating; and no one could have divined, from his placid look, the baffled affection that Kate was projecting into him.

That done, she accompanied Mrs. Lacey to the nursery, where the cup and the spoon and the measuring-glass were boiled for germs and set to cool under a glass bell. The baby's rooms had a cool, ordered freshness; when the curtains blew out into the room,

Kate looked instinctively at Mrs. Lacey to see if she would check such undisciplined behaviour, but she was looking at the time-table which hung on the inside of the baize door. This time-table began with: "Six A.M., orange juice"; continued through "Six-thirty, rusk and teething ring, seven, wash and dress"; and ended at "five P.M., mothering hour and bed." Somewhere inside of Kate bubbled a disloyal and incredulous laughter, which astonished her; the face she turned towards Mrs. Lacey was suddenly so guilty that it was met with a speculative lift of the smooth wide brows. "What is wrong with you now, Kate?" said Mrs. Lacey.

Soon after, the men appeared, in their breeches and trailing their whips behind them across the polished floors. They smiled at Kate, but for a moment their pupils narrowed as Mrs. Lacey's had done. Then they all sat on the verandah, not at the sewing end, but at the social part, where the big grass chairs were. The servant wheeled out a table stacked with drinks; Kate could not think of any other house where gin and vermouth were served as a routine, before meals. The men were discussing a gymkhana that was due shortly; Mrs. Lacey did not interrupt. When they moved indoors to the dining-room, Kate again felt the incongruity between the orderly charm created by Mrs. Lacey and the casual way the men took it, even destroying it by refusing to fit in. Lunch was a cool, lazy affair, with jugs of frosted drinks and quantities of chilled salads. Mr. Lacey and Mr. Hackett were scribbling figures on pieces of paper and talking together all through the meal; and it was not until it was over that Kate understood that the scene had been like a painted background to the gymkhana which to the men was far more real than anything Mrs. Lacey said or did.

As soon as it was over, they offered their wide, lazy good-humoured grins, and slouched off again to the paddock. Kate could have smiled; but she knew there would be no answering smile from Mrs. Lacey.

In silence they took their places at the sewing-table; and at two o'clock to the minute Mrs. Lacey looked at the clock and brought the baby in for his nap, leaving the nanny crouched on the floor to guard him.

Afterwards Kate's discomfort grew acute. In the district "coming over for the day" meant either one of two things: something was arranged, like tennis or swimming, with plenty to eat and drink; or the women came by themselves to sew and cook and knit, and this sharing of activity implied a deeper sharing. Kate used to think that her mother came back from a day with one of her women friends wearing the same relaxed softened expression as she did after a church service.

But Kate was at a hopelessly loose end, and Mrs. Lacey did not show it only because it suited her book better not to. She offered to sew, and did not insist when Mrs. Lacey rather uncomfortably protested. Mrs. Lacey sewed exquisitely, and anything she could do would be bungling in comparison.

At last the baby woke. Kate knew the time-table said: "Three to five: walk or playpen," and offered to push the pram. Again she had to face up to the shrewd, impatient look, while Mrs. Lacey warned: "Remember, babies don't like being messed about." "I know," said Kate consciously, colouring. When the baby was strapped in and arranged, Kate was allowed to take the handles of the pram. Leading away from the house in the opposite direction from the river was a long avenue of trees where the shade lay cool and deep. "You mustn't go away from the trees," directed Mrs. Lacey; and Kate saw her return to the house, her step quickening with relief; whatever her life was, the delicious, devoted, secret life that Kate imagined, she was free to resume it now that Kate was gone: it seemed impossible this lovely and secret thing should not exist: for it was the necessary complement to the gross practicality of her husband and Mr. Hackett. But when Kate returned at five o'clock, after two hours of steady walking up and down the avenue, pushing the pram and suppressing her passionate desire to cuddle the indifferent baby, Mrs. Lacey was baking tarts in the kitchen.

If she was to be back home before it grew darker, she must leave immediately. She lingered, however, till five past five: during those two hours she had, in fact, been waiting for the moment when Mrs. Lacey would "mother" the baby. But Mrs. Lacey seated herself with a book and left the child to crawl on a rug at her feet. Kate set off on the road home; and this time the eyes she felt follow her were irritated and calculating.

At the gate stood her mother. "You shouldn't have gone off without telling me!" she exclaimed reproachfully. Now, Kate was free to roam as she willed over the farm, so this was unjust, and both sides knew it to be so. "I left a message," said Kate, avoiding her mother's eyes.

Next morning she was loitering about the gate looking out over the coloured slopes to the Laceys' house, when her mother came up behind her, apparently cutting zinnias, but in fact looking for an opportunity to express her grievance. "You would live there, if you could, wouldn't you, dear?" she said, smiling painfully. "All those

fashions and new clothes and things, we can't compete, can we?"
Kate's smile was as twistingly jealous as hers; but she did not go to
the Laceys' that day. After all, she couldn't very well: there were
limits. She remained in that part of the farm which lay beside the
Laceys', and looked across at the trees whose heavy greenness
seemed to shed a perfume that was more than the scent of sun-
heated leaves, and where the grass beckoned endlessly as the wind
moved along it. Love, still unrecognized, still unaccepted in her,
flooded this way and that, leaving her limp with hatred or exalted
with remembrance. And through it all she thought of the baby
while resentment grew in her. Whether she stood with the binoculars stuck to her eyes, hour after hour, hoping for a glimpse of Mrs.
Lacey on the verandah, or watching the men lean against the fence
as the horses moved about them, the baby was in the back of her
mind; and the idea of it was not merely the angry pit that is identi-
fication with suffering, but also a reflection of what other people
were thinking. Kate knew, from a certain tone in her mother's voice
when she mentioned that child, that she was not wholly convinced
by time-tables and hygiene.

The ferment of the last party had not settled before Mrs. Lacey
issued invitations for another; there had only been a fortnight's
interval. Mr. Cope said, looking helplessly across at his wife: "I
suppose we ought to go?" and Mrs. Cope replied guardedly: "We
can't very well not, when they are our nearest neighbours, can we?"
"Oh Lord!" exclaimed Mr. Cope, moving irritably in his chair.
Then Kate felt her parents' eyes come to rest on her; she was not
surprised when Mr. Cope asked: "When does Kate go back to
school?" "The holidays don't end for another three weeks."

So the Copes all went Mrs. Lacey's second party, which began
exactly as the first had done:everything was the same. The women
whisked their children into the improvised dormitory without showing even a formal uneasiness. One of them said: "It is nice to be
free of them for once, isn't it?" and Kate saw Mrs. Lacey looking
humorous before she turned away her face. That evening Mrs.
Lacey wore a dress of dim green transparent stuff, as innocent and
billowing, though as subtly indiscreet as the white one. And the
women—save for Mrs. Cope—were in attempts at evening dress.

Mrs. Lacey saw Kate standing uncertainly in the passage,
grasped her by the shoulder, and pushed her gently into the room
where all the people were. "I shall find you a boy friend," she stated
gaily; and Kate looked apprehensively towards her parents, who
were regarding her, and everyone else, with helpless disapproval.

Things had gone beyond their censure already: Mrs. Lacey was so sure of herself that she could defy them about their own daughter before their eyes. But Kate found herself seated next to a young assistant recently come to the district, who at eighteen was less likely to be tolerant of little girls than an older man might have been. Mrs. Lacey had shown none of her usual shrewdness in the choice. After a few painful remarks, Kate saw this young man turn away from her, and soon she tried to slip away. Mr. Hackett, noticing her, put his arm round her and said, "Don't run away, my dear," but the thought of her watching parents stiffened her to an agony of protest. He dropped his arm, remarked humorously to the rest of the room—for everyone was looking over at them and laughing: "These girlish giggles!" and turned his attention to the bottle he was holding. Kate ran to the kitchens. Soon she fled from there, as people came in. She crept furtively to the baby's cot, but he was asleep; and it was not long before Mrs. Lacey glanced in and said: "Do leave him alone, Kate," before vanishing again. Kate took herself to that set of rooms that Mrs. Lacey had not touched at all. They were still roughly whitewashed, and the cement floors, though polished, were bare. Saddles of various patterns hung in rows in one room; another was filled with beautifully patterned belts with heavy silver buckles and engraved holsters. There were, too, rows and rows of guns of all kinds, carved, stamped, twisted into strange shapes. They came from every part of the world, and were worth a fortune, so people said.

These rooms were where Mr. Lacey and Mr. Hackett liked to sit; and they had heavy leather armchairs, and a cupboard with a private supply of whisky and syphons. Kate sat stiffly on the edge of one of the chairs, and looked at the rows of weapons: she was afraid the men might be angry to find her there. And in fact it was not long before Mr. Lacey appeared in the doorway, gave an exclamation, and withdrew. He had not been alone. Kate, wondering who the lady was, and whether Mrs. Lacey would mind, left the house altogether and sat in the back of their car. Half asleep, she watched the couples dancing along the verandah, and saw how at one end a crowd of natives gathered outside in the dark, pressing their noses to the wire gauze, in curious admiration at the white people enjoying themselves. Sometimes a man and a woman would come down the steps, their arms about each other, and disappear under the trees; or into the cars. She shrank back invisibly, for in the very next car were a couple who were often visitors at their house, though as members of their own families; and she did not want them to have the embarrassment of knowing she was there. Soon she stuck her fingers in her ears; she felt sick, and she was also very hungry.

But it was not long before she heard shouts from the house, and the shouts were angry. Peering through the back window of the car she could see people standing around two men who were fighting. She saw legs in riding breeches, and then Mrs. Lacey came and stood between them. "What nonsense," Kate heard her exclaim, her voice still high and gay, though strained. Almost immediately Kate heard her name called, and her mother appeared, outlined against the light. Kate slipped from the car so that the couple in the next car might not see her and ran to tug at her mother's arm.

"So there you are!" exclaimed Mrs. Cope in a relieved voice. "We are going home now. Your father is tired."

In the car Kate asked: "What were Mr. Hackett and Mr. Lacey fighting about?" There was a pause before Mrs. Cope replied: "I don't know, dear." "Who won?" insisted Kate. Then, when she got no answer, she said: "It's funny, isn't it, when in the day-time they are such friends?" In the silence the sound of her own words tingled in her ears, and Kate watched something unexpected, yet familiar, emerge. Here it was again, the other pattern. It was of Mr. Hackett that she thought as the car nosed its way through the trees to their own farm, and her wonder crystallised at last into exclamation: "But they are so much alike!" She felt as she would have done if she had seen a little girl, offered a doll, burst into tears because she had not been given another that was identical in every way. "Don't bother your head about it," soothed Mrs. Cope. "They aren't very nice people. Forget about it."

The next Sunday was Church Sunday. The ministers came in rotation: Presbyterian, Church of England, Roman Catholic. Sometimes there was a combined service. The Copes never missed the Church of England Sundays.

The services were held in the district hall, near the station. The hall was a vast barn of a place, and the small group of worshippers crowded at one end, near the platform, where Nan Fowler perched to play the hymns, like a thin flock of birds in a very large tree. The singing rose meagrely over the banging of the piano and dissolved in the air above their heads: even from the door the music seemed to come from a long way off.

The Laceys and Mr. Hackett arrived late that day, tiptoeing uncomfortably to the back seats and arranging themselves so that Mrs. Lacey sat between the men. This was the first time they had been to

church. Kate twisted her neck and saw that for once the men were
not in riding things; released, thus, from their uniform, looking
ordinary in brown suits, it was easier to see them as two different
people. But even so, they were alike, with the same flat slouching
bodies and lean humorous faces. They hummed tunelessly, making
a bumblebee noise, and looked towards the roof. Mrs. Lacey, who
held the hymn book for all three of them, kept her eyes on the print
in a manner which seemed to be directing the men's attention to it.
She looked very neat and sober today, and her voice, a pretty con-
tralto, was stronger than anyone's, so that in a little while she was
leading the singing. Again, irresistibly, the subterranean laughter
bubbled in Kate, and she turned away, glancing doubtfully at her
mother, who hissed in her ear: "It's rude to stare."

When the service was over, Mrs. Lacey came straight to Mrs.
Cope and held out her hand. "How are you?" she asked winningly.
Mrs. Cope replied stiffly: "It is nice to see you at Church." Kate saw
Mrs. Lacey's face twitch, and sympathy told her that Mrs. Lacey,
too, was suffering from the awful need to laugh. However, her face
straightened, and she glanced at Mr. Cope and flushed. She stood
quietly by and watched while Mrs. Cope issued invitations to everyone who passed to come home to Sunday lunch. She was expecting
an invitation too, but none was offered. Mrs. Cope finally nodded,
smiled, and climbed into the car. There was suddenly a look of
brave defiance about Mrs. Lacey that tugged at Kate's heart: if it
had not been for the stoic set of her shoulders as she climbed into
the car with her two men, Kate would have been able to bear the
afternoon better. When lunch was over, things arranged themselves
as usual with the men on one side of the room and the women on
the other. Kate stood for a while behind her father's chair; then,
with burning cheeks, she moved over to the women who had their
heads together around her mother's chair. They glanced up at her,
and then behaved as grown-up people do when they wish to talk
and children are in the way; they simply pretend she was not there.
In a few moments Kate sped from the house and ran through the
bush to her place of refuge, which was a deep hollow over which
bushes knotted and tangled. Here she flung herself and wept.

Nobody mentioned the Laceys at supper. People seemed to have
been freed from something. There was a great deal of laughter at
the comfortable old jokes at which they had been laughing for
years. The air had been cleared: something final had happened, or
was going to happen. Later, when these farmers and their wives,
carrying their children rolled in blankets, went to find their cars,

Kate lifted the curtain and looked over at the cluster of lights on the opposite ridge, and wondered if Mrs. Lacey was watching the headlights of the cars swing down the various roads home, and if so, what it was she was thinking and feeling.

Next morning a basket arrived at the back door, full of fresh vegetables and roses. There was also a note addressed to Miss Catherine Cope. It said: "If you have nothing better to do, come and spend the day. I have been looking over some of my old dresses for you." Kate read this note, feeling her mother's reproachful eyes fixed on her, and reluctantly handed it over. "You are not going, surely!" exclaimed Mrs. Cope. "I might as well, for the last time," said Kate. When she heard what it was she had said, the tears came into her eyes, so that she could not turn round to wave goodbye to her mother.

That last day she missed nothing of the four miles' walk: she felt every step.

The long descent on their side was through fields which were now ploughed ready for the wet season. A waste of yellow clods stretched away on either side, and over them hung a glinting haze of dust. The road itself was more of a great hog's-back, for the ditches on either side had eroded into cracked gullies fifteen feet deep. Soon, after the rains, this road would have to be abandoned and another cut, for the water raced turbulently down here during every storm, swirling away the soil and sharpening the ridge. At the vlei, which was now quite dry, the gullies had cut down into a double pothole, so that the drift was unsafe even now. This time next year the old road to the Lacey's would be a vivid weal down the slope where no one could walk.

On the other side the soil changed: here it was pale and shining, and the dews of each night hardened it so that each step was a small crusty subsidence. Because the lands had not been farmed for years and were covered with new vegetation, the scars that had been cut down this slope, too, were healing, for the grasses had filmed over them and were gripping the loose soil.

Before Kate began to ascend this slope she took off her cretonne hat that her mother had made to "go" with her frock, and which stuck up in angles round her face, and hid it in an ant-bear hole, where she could find it on the way home; she could not bear Mrs. Lacey to see her in it.

Being October, it was very hot, and the top of her head began to feel as if a weight were pressing on it. Soon her shoulders ached too, and her eyes dazzled. She could hardly see the bright swift horses in the bushy paddock for glare, and her tight smile at Mr. Hackett and Mr. Lacey was more like a grimace of pain. When she arrived on the verandah, Mrs. Lacey, who was sewing, gave her a concerned glance, and exclaimed: "What have you done with your hat?" "I forgot it," said Kate.

On the sewing table were piles of Mrs. Lacey's discarded frocks. She said kindly: "Have a look at these and see which you would like." Kate blinked at the glare outside and slid thankfully into a chair; but she did not touch the frocks. After a while her head cleared and she said: "I can't take them. My mother wouldn't like it. Thank you all the same." Mrs. Lacey glanced at her sharply, and went on sewing for a while in silence. Then she said lightly: "I don't see why you shouldn't, do you?" Kate did not reply. Now that she had recovered, and the pressure on her head had gone, she was gazing about her, consciously seeing everything for the last time, and wondering what the next lot of people would be like.

"Did you have a nice time yesterday?" asked Mrs. Lacey, wanting to be told who had spent all the day with the Copes, what they had done, and—most particularly—what they had said. "Very nice, thank you," said Kate primly; and saw Mrs. Lacey's face turn ugly with annoyance before she laughed and asked: "I am in disgrace, am I?"

But Kate could not now be made an ally. She said cautiously: "What did you expect?"

Mrs. Lacey said, with amused annoyance: "A lot of hypocritical old fogeys." The word "hyprocrite" isolated itself and stood fresh and new before Kate's eyes; and it seemed to her all at once that Mrs. Lacey was wilfully misunderstanding.

She sat quietly, watching the sun creep in long warm streaks towards her over the shining floor, and waited for Mrs. Lacey to ask what she so clearly needed to ask. There would be some question, some remark, that would release her, so that she could go home, feeling a traitor no longer: she did not know it, but she was waiting for some kind of an apology, something that would heal the injustice that burned in her: after all, for Mrs. Lacey's sake she had let her own parents dislike her.

But there was no sound from Mrs. Lacey, and when Kate looked up, she saw that her face had changed. It was peaked, and diminished, with frail blue shadows around the mouth and eyes. Kate was looking at an acute, but puzzled fear, and could not recognise it; though if she had been able to search inside herself, now, thinking of how she feared to return home, she would have found pity for Mrs. Lacey.

After a while she said: "Can I take the baby for a walk?" It was almost midday, with the sun beating directly downwards; the baby was never allowed out at this hour; but after a short hesitation Mrs. Lacey gave her an almost appealing glance and said: "If you keep in the shade." The baby was brought from the nursery and strapped into the pram. Kate eased the pram down the steps, but instead of directing her steps towards the avenue, where there might possibly have been a little shade, even at this hour, went down the road to the river. On one side, where the bushes were low, sun-glare fell about the grass-roots. On the other infrequent patches of shade stood under the trees. Kate dodged from one patch to the next, while the baby reclined in the warm airless cave under the hood.

She could not truly care: she knew Mrs. Lacey was watching her and did not turn her head; she had paid for this by weeks of humiliation. When she was out of sight of the house she unstrapped the baby and carried it a few paces from the road into the bush. There she sat, under a tree, holding the child against her. She could feel sweat running down her face, and did not lift her hand to find whether tears mingled with it: her eyes were smarting with the effort of keeping her lids apart over the pressure of tears. As for the baby, beads of sweat stood all over his face. He looked vaguely about and reached his hands for the feathery heads of grasses and seemed subdued. Kate held him tight, but did not caress him; she was knotted tight inside with tears and anger. After a while she saw a tick crawl out of the grass on to her leg, and from there to the baby's leg. For a moment she let it crawl; from that dark region of her mind where the laughter spurted, astonishingly, came the thought: He might get tick fever. She could see Mrs. Lacey very clearly, standing beside a tiny oblong trench, her head bent under the neat brown hat. She could hear women saying, their admiration and pity heightened by contrition: "She was so brave, she didn't give way at all."

Kate brushed off the tick and stood up. Carefully keeping the sun off the child—his cheek was already beginning to redden—she put him back in the pram, and began wheeling it back. Whatever it was she had been looking for, satisfaction, whether of pain, or love, she had not been given it. She could see Mrs. Lacey standing on the verandah shading her eyes with her hand as she gazed towards them. Another thought floated up: she vividly saw herself pleading with Mrs. Lacey: "Let me keep the baby, you don't want him, not really."

When she faced Mrs. Lacey with the child, and looked up into the concerned eyes, guilt swept her. She saw that Mrs. Lacey's hands fumbled rapidly with the straps; she saw how the child was lifted out, with trembling haste, away from the heat and the glare. Mrs. Lacey asked: "Did you enjoy the walk?" but although she appeared to want to make Kate feel she had been willingly granted this pleasure, Mrs. Lacey could not help putting her hand to the baby's head and saying: "He's very hot."

She sat down beside her sewing table; and for the first time Kate saw her actually hold her child in her arms, even resting her cheek against his head. Then the baby wriggled round towards her and put his arms around her neck and burrowed close, gurgling with pleasure. Mrs. Lacey appeared taken aback; she looked down at her own baby with amazement in which there was also dismay. She was accepting the child's cuddling in the way a woman accepts the importunate approaches of someone whose feelings she does not want to hurt. She was laughing and protesting and putting down the baby's clutching arms. Still laughing, she said to Kate: "You see, this is all your doing." The words seemed to Kate so extraordinary that she could not reply. Through her mind floated pictures of women she had known from the district, and they flowed together to make one picture—her idea, from experience, of a mother. She saw a plump smiling woman holding a baby to her face for the pleasure of its touch. She remembered Nan Fowler one mail-day at the station, just after the birth of her third child. She sat in the front seat of the car, with the bundled infant on her lap, laughing as it nuzzled to get to her breasts, where appeared two damp patches. Andrew Wheatley stood beside the car talking to her, but her manner indicated a smiling withdrawal from him. "Look," she seemed to be saying—not at all concerned for her stretched loose body and those shameless patches of milk— "as you observe, I can't be really with you for the moment, but I'd like to see you later."

Kate watched Mrs. Lacey pull her baby's arms away from her neck, and then gently place it in the pram. She was frowning. "Babies shouldn't be messed about," she remarked; and Kate saw that her dislike of whatever had just happened was stronger even than her fear of Kate's parents.

Kate got up, saying: "I feel funny." She walked blindly through the house in the direction of the bedroom. The light had got inside her head: that was how it felt; her brain was swaying on waves of light. She got past Mrs. Lacey's bed and collapsed on the stool of the dressing-table, burying her face in her arms. When she lifted her eyes, she saw Mrs. Lacey standing beside her. She saw that her own shoes had left brownish patches on the carpet, and that along the folds of the crystalline drapery at the windows were yellowish streaks.

Gazing into the mirror her own face stared back. It was a narrow face, pale and freckled; a serious lanky face, and incongruously above it perched a large blue silk bow from which pale lanky hair straggled. Kate stood up and looked at her body in shame. She was long, thin, bony. The legs were a boy's legs still, flat lean legs set on to a plumping body. Two triangular lumps stood out from her tight child's bodice. Kate turned in agony from this reflection of herself, which seemed to be rather of several different young boys and girls haphazardly mingled, and fixed her attention to Mrs. Lacey, who was frowning as she listened to the baby's crying from the verandah: this time he had not liked being put down. "There!" she exclaimed angrily. "That's what happens if you give in to them." Something rose in a wave to Kate's head: "Why did they say the baby is exactly like Mr. Hackett?" she demanded, without knowing she had intended to speak at all. Looking wonderingly up at Mrs. Lacey she saw the shadows round her mouth deepen into long blue lines that ran from nose to chin; Mrs. Lacey had become as pinched and diminished as her room now appeared. She drew in her breath violently: then held herself tight, and smiled. "Why, what an extraordinary thing for them to say," she commented, walking away from Kate to fetch a handkerchief from a drawer, where she stood for a while with her back turned, giving them both an opportunity to recover. Then, turning, she looked long and closely at Kate, trying to determine whether the child had known what it was she had said.

Kate faced her with wide and deliberately innocent eyes; inside she was gripped with amazement at the strength of her own desire to hurt the beloved Mrs. Lacey, who had hurt her so badly: it was this that the innocence was designed to conceal.

They both moved away from the room to the verandah, with the careful steps of people conscious of every step, every action. There was, however, not a word spoken.

As they passed through the big room Mrs. Lacey took a photograph album from a bookstand and carried it with her to the chairs. When Kate had seated herself, the album was deposited on her lap;

and Mrs. Lacey said: "Look at these; here are pictures of Mr. Lacey when he was a baby; you can see that the baby is the image of him." Kate looked dutifully at several pages of photographs of yet another fat, smiling, contented baby, feeling more and more surprised at Mrs. Lacey. The fact was that whether the baby did or did not look like Mr. Hackett was not the point; it was hard to believe that Mrs. Lacey did not understand this, had not understood the truth, which was that the remark had been made in the first place as a sort of stick snatched up to beat her with. She put down the album and said: "Yes, they do look alike, don't they?" Mrs. Lacey remarked casually: "For the year before the baby was born I and Mr. Lacey were living alone on a ranch. Mr. Hackett was visiting his parents in America." Kate made an impatient movement which Mrs. Lacy misinterpreted. She said reproachfully: "That was a terrible thing to say, Kate." "But I didn't say it." "No matter who said it, it was a terrible thing." Kate saw that tears were pouring down Mrs. Lacey's cheeks.

"But . . ."

"But what?"

"It isn't the point."

"What isn't the point?"

Kate was silent: there seemed such a distance between what she felt and how Mrs. Lacey was speaking. She got up, propelled by the pressure of these unsayable things, and began wandering about the verandah in front of Mrs. Lacey. "You see," she said helplessly. "we've all been living together so long. We all know each other very well."

"You are telling me," commented Mrs. Lacey, with an unpleasant laugh. "Well?"

Kate sighed. "Well, we have all got to go on living together, haven't we? I mean, when people have *got* to live together . . ." She looked at Mrs. Lacey to see if she had understood.

She had not.

Kate had, for a moment, a vivid sense of Mrs. Sinclair standing there beside her; and from this reinforcement she gained new words: "Don't you see? It's not what people do, it's how they do it. It can't be broken up."

Mrs. Lacey's knotted forehead smoothed, and she looked ruefully at Kate: "I haven't a notion of what I've done, even now." This note, the playful note, stung Kate again: it was as if Mrs. Lacey had decided that the whole thing was too childish to matter.

She walked to the end of the verandah, thinking of Mrs. Sinclair.

"I wonder who will live here next?" she said dreamily, and turned to see Mrs. Lacey's furious eyes. "You might wait till we've gone," she said. "What makes you think we are going?"

Kate looked at her in amazement: it was so clear to her that the Laceys would soon go.

Seeing Kate's face, Mrs. Lacey's grew sober. In a chastened voice she said: "You frighten me." Then she laughed, rather shrilly.

"Why did you come here?" asked Kate unwillingly.

"But why on earth shouldn't we?"

"I mean, why *this* district. Why so far out, away from everything?"

Mrs. Lacey's eyes bored cruelly into Kate's. "What have they been saying? What are they saying about us?"

"Nothing," said Kate, puzzled, seeing that there was a new thing here, that people could have said.

"I suppose that old story about the money? It isn't true. It isn't true, Kate." Once again tears poured down Mrs. Lacey's face and her shoulders shook.

"No one has said anything about money. Except that you must have a lot," said Kate. Mrs. Lacey wiped her eyes dry and peered at Kate to see if she were telling the truth. Then her face hardened. "Well, I suppose they'll start saying it now," she said bitterly.

Kate understood that there was something ugly in this, and directed at her, but not what it could be. She turned away from Mrs. Lacey, filled again with the knowledge of injustice.

"Aren't I ever to have a home? Can't I ever have a home?" wept Mrs. Lacey.

"Haven't you ever had one?"

"No, never. This time I thought I would be settled for good."

"I think you'll have to move again," said Kate reasonably. She looked around her, again trying to picture what would happen to Old John's Place when the new people came. Seeing that look, Mrs. Lacey said quickly: "That's superstition. It isn't possible that places can affect people."

"I didn't say they did."

"What are you saying, then?"

"But you get angry when I do say. I was just thinking that . . ."

"Well?"

Kate stammered: "You ought to go somewhere where . . . that has your kind of people." She saw this so clearly.

Mrs. Lacey glared at her and snapped: "When I was your age I thought of nothing but hockey." Then she picked up her sewing as she might have swallowed an aspirin tablet, and sat stitching with trembling, angry fingers.

Kate's lips quivered. Hockey and healthy games were what her own mother constantly prescribed as prophylactics against the little girl she did not want Kate to be.

Mrs. Lacey went on: "Don't you go to school?"

"Yes."

"Do you like it?"

Kate replied: Yes, knowing it was impossible to explain what school meant to her: it was a recurring episode in the city where time raced by, since there was nothing of importance to slow it. School had so little to do with this life, on the farm, and the things she lived by, that it was like being taken to the pictures as a treat. One went politely, feeling grateful, then sat back and let what happened on the screen come at you and flow over you. You left with relief, to resume a real life.

She said slowly to Mrs. Lacey, trying to express that injustice that was corroding her: "But if I had been—like you want—you wouldn't have been able to—find out what you wanted, would you?"

Mrs. Lacey stared. "If you were mine I'd . . ." She bit off her thread angrily.

"You'd dress me properly," said Kate sarcastically, quivering with hate, and saw Mrs. Lacey crimson from throat to hairline.

"I think I'd better be going home," she remarked, sidling to the door.

"You must come over again some time," remarked Mrs. Lacey brightly, the fear lying deep in her eyes.

"You know I can't come back," said Kate awkwardly.

"Why not?" said Mrs. Lacey, just as if the whole conversation had never happened.

"My parents won't let me. They say you are bad for me."

"Do you think I am bad for you?" asked Mrs. Lacey, with her high, gay laugh.

Kate stared at her incredulously. "I'm awfully glad to have met you," she stammered finally, with embarrassment thick in her tongue. She smiled politely, through tears, and went away down the road to home.

"Leopard" George

GEORGE CHESTER did not earn his title for some years after he first started farming. He was well into middle age when people began to greet him with a friendly clout across the shoulders and the query: "Well, what's the score now?" Their faces expressed the amused and admiring tolerance extorted by a man who has proved himself in other ways, a man entitled to eccentricities. But George's passion for hunting leopards was more than a hobby. There was a period of years when the District Notes in the local paper were headed, Friday after Friday, by a description of his week-end party: "The Four Winds' Hunt Club bag this Sunday was four jackals and a leopard" —or a wild dog and two leopards, as the case might be. All kinds of game make good chasing; the horses and dogs went haring across the veld every week after whatever offered itself. As for George, it was a recognised thing that if there was a chance of a leopard, the pack must be called off its hare, its duiker, its jackal, and directed after the wily spotted beast, no matter what the cost in time or patience or torn dogs. George had been known to climb a *kopje* alone, with a wounded leopard waiting for him in the tumbled chaos of boulder and tree; they told stories of how he walked once into a winding black cave (his ammunition finished and his torch smashed) and finally clouted the clawing spitting beast to death with the butt of his rifle. The scars of that fight were all over his body. When he strode into the post office or store, in shorts, his sleeves rolled up, people looked at the flesh that was raked from shoulder to knuckle and from thigh to ankle with great white weals, and quickly turned their eyes away. Behind his back they might smile, their lips compressed forbearingly.

But that was when he was one of the wealthiest men in the district: one of those tough, shrewd farmers who seem ageless, for sun and hard work and good eating have shaped their bodies into cases of muscle that time can hardly touch.

George was the child of one of the first settlers. He was bred on a farm, and towns made him restless. When the First World War began he set off at once for England where he joined up in a unit that promised plenty of what he called fun. After five years of fighting he had collected three decorations, half a dozen minor wounds, and the name "Lucky George." He allowed himself to be demobilized with the air of one who does not insist on taking more than his fair share of opportunities.

When he returned to Southern Rhodesia, it was not to that part of it he had made his own as a child; that was probably because his father's name was so well known there, and George was not a man to be the mere son of his father.

He saw many farms before finally choosing Four Winds. The agent was a man who had known his father well: this kind of thing still counts for more than money in places where there is space and time for respect of the past, and George was offered farms at prices which broke the agent's businessman's heart. Besides, he was a war hero. But the agent was defeated by George. He had been selling farms long enough to recognise the look that comes into a man's face when he is standing on land that appeals to him, land which he will shape and knead and alter to the scale of his own understanding—the look of the creator. That look did not appear on George's face.

After months of visiting one district after another, the agent took George to a farm so beautiful that it seemed impossible he could refuse to buy it. It was low-lying and thickly covered with trees, and the long fat strip of rich red land was held between two rivers. The house had gardens running away on two sides to vistas of water. Rivers and richness and unspoiled trees and lush grass for cattle— such farms are not to be had for whistling in Africa. But George stood there on a rise between the stretches of water where they ran close to each other, and moved his shoulders restlessly in a way which the agent had grown to understand. "No good?" he said, sounding disgruntled. But by now there was that tolerance in him for George which he was always to make people feel: his standards were different. Incomprehensible they might be; but the agent at last saw that George was not looking for the fat ease promised by this farm. "If you could only tell me what you *are* looking for," he suggested, rather irritably.

"This is a fine farm," said George, walking away from it, holding his shoulders rigid. The agent grabbed his elbow and made him stop. "Listen to me," he said. "This must be one of the finest farms in the country."

"I know," said George.

"If you want me to get you a farm, you'll have to get your mind clear about what you need."

George said: "I'll know it when I see it."

"Have I got to drive you to every free farm in a thousand miles of Africa? God damn it, man," he expostulated, "be reasonable. This is my job. I am supposed to be earning my living by it."

George shrugged. The agent let go his arm, and the two men walked along beside each other, George looking away over the thick dark trees of the river to the slopes on the other side. There were the mountains, range on range of them, rising high and glistening into the fresh blue sky.

The agent followed that look, and began to think for himself. He peered hard at George. This man, in appearance, was what one might expect after such a childhood, all freedom and sunlight, and after five years of such fighting. He was very lean and brown, with loose broad shoulders and an easy swinging way of moving. His face was lean and angled, his eyes grey and shrewd, his mouth hard but also dissatisfied. He reminded the agent of his father at the same age; George's father had left everything familiar to him, in an old and comfortable country, to make a new way of living with new people. The agent said tentatively: "Good to get away from people, eh? Too many people crowded together over there in the Old Country?" exactly as he might have done to the older man. George's face did not change: this idea seemed to mean nothing to him. He merely continued to stare, his eyes tightened, at the mountains. But now the agent knew what he had to do. Next day he drove him to Four Winds, which had just been surveyed for sale. It was five thousand acres of virgin bush, lying irregularly over the lower slopes of a range of *kopjes* that crossed high over a plain where there were still few farms. Four Winds was all rocky outcrops, scrubby trees and wastes of shimmering grass, backed by mountains. There was no house, no river, not so much as a fence; no one could call it a desirable farm. George's face cleared to content as he walked over it, and on it came that look for which the agent had been waiting.

He slouched comfortably all through that day over those bare and bony acres, rather in the way a dog will use to make a new place its own, ranging to pick up a smell here or a memory there, anything that can be formed into a shell of familiarity for comfort against strangeness. But white men coming to Africa take not only what is there, but also impose on it a pattern of their own, from other countries. This accounts for the fine range of variation one can find in a day's travelling from farm to farm across any district. Each house will be different, suggesting a different country, climate, or way of speech.

Towards late afternoon, with the blaze of yellow sunlight falling directly across his face and dazzling into his eyes, and glazing the wilderness of rock and grass and tree with the sad glitter of sunset, George stooped suddenly in a place where gullies ran down from all sides into a flat place among bushes. "There should be water here, for a borehole," he said. And, after a moment: "There was a windmill I caught sight of in Norfolk from a train. I liked the look of it. The shape of it, I mean. It would do well here . . ."

It was in this way that George said he was buying the farm, and showed his satisfaction at the place. The restless, rather wolfish look had gone from the long bony face.

"Your nearest neighbour is fifteen miles away," was the last warning the agent gave.

George answered indifferently: "This part of the country is opening up, isn't it?" And the next day he signed the papers.

He was no recluse after all, or at least, not in the way the agent had suspected.

He went round to what farms there were, as is the custom, paying his respects, saying he had bought Four Winds, and would be a neighbour, though not a near one. And the house he built for himself was not a shack, the sort of house a man throws together to hold off the weather for a season.

He intended to live there, though it was not finished. It looked as if it had been finely planned and then cut in half. There were, to begin with, three large rooms, raftered with that timber that sends out a pungent fragrance when the weather changes, and floored with dark red wood. These were furnished properly, there were no makeshifts here, either. And he was seen at the station on mail-days, not often, but often enough, where he was greeted in the way proper not only to his father's son and to his war record, but because people approved what he was doing. For after both wars there has been a sudden appearance of restless young men whose phrases: "I want to be my own boss," and "I'm not going to spend my life wearing out the seat of my trousers on a stool," though cliches, still express the spirit that opened up the country in the first place. Between wars there is a different kind of immigrant, who use their money as spades to dig warm corners to sleep in. Because of these people who have turned an adventurous country into a sluggish one, and because of the memory of something different, restless young men find there is no need to apologize for striking out for themselves. It is as if they are regarded as a sort of flag, or even a conscience. When people heard that George had bought Four Winds, a bare, gusty, rocky stretch of veld on the side of a mountain, they remarked, "Good luck to him," which is exactly how they speak when a returning traveller says: "There is a man on the shores of Lake Nyasa who has lived alone in a hut by himself for twenty years," or "I heard of someone who has gone native in the Valley—he goes away into the bush if a white person comes near him." There is no condemnation, but rather a recognition of something in themselves to which they pay tribute by proxy.

George's first worry was whether he would get sufficient native labour; but he had expected an anxious time, and, knowing the ropes, he sat tight, built his house, sank his borehole and studied his land. A few natives did come, but they were casual labourers, and were not what he was waiting for. He was more troubled, perhaps, then he let himself know. It is so easy to get a bad name as an employer. A justly dismissed man can spitefully slash a tree on the boundary of a farm where the migrating natives walk, in such a way that they read in the pattern of the gashes on the bark: This is a bad farm with a bad master. Or there may be a native in the compound who frightens or tyrannises over the others, so that they slowly leave, with excuses, for other farms, while the farmer himself never finds out what is wrong. There can be a dozen reasons why a fair man, just to his natives according to the customs of the time, can get a bad name without ever knowing the reason for it.

George knew this particular trouble was behind him when one day he saw coming up the road to his front door an old native who had worked many years for his own father. He waited on the steps, smoking comfortably, smiling his greeting.

"Morning," he said.

"Morning, baas."

"Things go well with you, old Smoke?"

"Things go well, baas."

George tapped out his pipe, and motioned to the old man to seat himself. The band of young men who had followed Smoke along the road, were waiting under some trees at a short distance for the palaver to finish. George could see they had come a long way, for they were dusty, weary with the weight of their big bundles. But they looked a strong lot and good for work, and George settled himself in the big chair he used for audiences with satisfaction growing in him.

"You have come a long way?" he asked.

"A long way, baas. I heard the Little Baas had come back from the war and was wanting me. I have come to the Little Baas."

George smiled affectionately at old Smoke, who looked not a day older now than he had ten years, or even twenty years back, when he had lifted the small boy for rides on the mealie waggon, or carried him, when he was tired, on his back. He seemed always to have been a very old man, with grizzling hair and filming eyes but as light and strong and erect as a youth.

"How did you know I had come back?"

"One of my brothers told me."

George smiled again, acknowledging that this was all he would ever be told of the mysterious way the message had travelled from mouth to mouth across hundreds of miles. "You will send messages to all your brothers to work for me? I need a great many boys."

"I have brought twenty. Later, others will come. I have other relations coming after the rains from Nyasaland."

"You will be my boss-boy, Smoke? I need a boss-boy."

"I am too old, much too old, baas."

"Do you know how old you are?" asked George, knowing he would get no satisfactory answer, for natives of Smoke's generation had no way of measuring their age.

"How should I know, baas? Perhaps fifty. Perhaps a hundred. I remember the days of the fighting well, I was a young man." He paused, and added carefully, having averted his eyes: "Better we do not remember those days, perhaps."

The two men laughed, after a moment during which their great liking for each other had time to take the unpleasantness from the reminder of war. "But I need a boss-boy," repeated George. "Until I find a younger man as capable as you are, will you help me?"

"But I am too old," protested Smoke again, his eyes brightening. Thus it was settled, and George knew his labour troubles were over. Smoke's brothers would soon fill his compound. It must be explained that relationships, among Africans, are not understood as they are among white people. A native can travel a thousand miles in strange country, and find his clan brothers in every village, and be made welcome by them.

George allowed these people a full week to build themselves a village, and another week as earnest of good feeling. Then he pulled the reins tight and expected hard work. He got it. Smoke was too old to work hard himself; also he was something of an old rascal with his drinking and his women—he had got his name because he smoked dagga, which bleared his eyes and set his hands shaking —but he held the obedience of the younger men, and because of this was worth any amount of money to George.

Later, a second man was chosen to act as boss-boy under Smoke. He was a nephew, and he supervised the gangs of natives, but it was understood that Smoke was the real chief. When George held his weekly palavers to discuss farm matters, the two men came up from the compound together, and the younger man (who had in fact done the actual hard work) deferred to the older. George brought a chair from the house to the foot of the great flight of stone steps that led up to the living-rooms, and sat there at ease smoking, while Smoke sat cross-legged on the ground before him. The nephew stood behind his uncle, and his standing was not so much an act of deference to George—though of course it was that too—as respect for his tribal superior. (This was in the early 'twenties, when a more gentle, almost feudal relationship was possible between good masters and their servants: there was space, then, for courtesy, bitterness had not yet crowded out affection.)

During these weekly talks it was not only farm matters that were discussed, but personal ones also. There was always a short pause when crops, weather, plans, had been finished; then Smoke turned to the young man behind him and spoke a few dismissing words. The young man said, "Good night, baas," to George, and went away.

George and Smoke were then free to talk about things like the head driver's quarrels with his new wife, or how Smoke himself was thinking of taking a young wife. George would laugh and say: "You old rascal. What do you want with a wife at your age." And Smoke would reply that an old man needed a young body for warmth during the cold weather.

Nor was old Smoke afraid of becoming stern, though reproachful, as if he momentarily regarded himself as George's father, when he said: "Little Baas, it is time you got married. It is time there was a woman on this farm. " And George would laugh and reply that he certainly agreed he should get married, but that he could find no woman to suit him.

Once Smoke suggested: "The baas will perhaps fetch himself a wife from England?" And George knew then that it was discussed in the compound how he had a photograph of a girl on his dressing-table: old Smoke's son was a cookboy in George's house.

The girl had been his fiancée for a week or so during the war, but the engagement was broken off after one of those practical dissecting discussions that can dissolve a certain kind of love like mist. She was a London girl, who liked her life, with no desire for anything different. There was no bitterness left after the affair; at least, not against each other. George remained with a small bewildered anger against himself. He was a man, after all, who liked things in their proper place. It was the engagement he could not forgive himself: he had been temporarily mad; it was that he could not bear to think of. But he remembered the girl sometimes with an affectionate sensuality. She had married and was living the kind of life he could not imagine any sane person choosing. Why he kept her picture—which was a very artificial posed affair—he did not ask himself. For he had cared for other women more, in his violent intermittent fashion.

However, there was her picture in his room, and it was seen not only by the cookboy and the houseboys but by the rare visitors to the house. There was a rumour in the district that George had a broken heart over a woman in England; and this explanation did as well as any other for George's cheerful but determined self-isolation, for there are some people the word loneliness can never be made to fit. George was alone, and seemed not to know it. What surprised people was that the frame of his life was so much larger than he needed, and for what he was. The three large rooms had been expanded, after a few years, into a dozen. It was the finest house for many miles. Outhouses, storehouses, wash-houses and poultry yards spread about the place, and he had laid out a garden, and paid two boys handsomely to keep it beautiful. He had scooped out the soil between a cluster of boulders, and built a fine natural swimming pool over which bamboos hung, reflecting patterns of green foliage and patches of blue sky. Here he swam every morning at sun-up, summer or winter, and at evening, too, when he came from the day's work. He built a row of stables, sufficient to house a dozen beasts, but actually kept only two, one of which was ridden by old Smoke (whose legs were now too feeble to carry him far) and one which he used himself. This was a mare of great responsiveness and intelligence but with no beauty, chosen with care after weeks of attending sales and following up advertisements: she was for use, not show. George rode her round the farm, working her hard, during the day, and when he stabled her at night patted her as if he were sorry she could not come into the house with him. After he had come from the pool, he sat in the glow from the rapidly fading sunset, looking out over the wild and beautiful valley, and ceremoniously drinking beside a stinkwood table laden with decanters and syphons. Nothing here of the bachelor's bottle and glass on a tin tray; and his dinner was served elaborately by two uniformed men, with whom he chatted or kept silence, as he felt inclined. After dinner coffee was brought to him, and having read farming magazines for half an hour or so, he went to bed. He was asleep every night by nine, and up before the sun.

That was his life. It was his life for years, one of exhausting physical toil, twelve hours a day of sweat and effort in the sun, but surrounded by a space and comfort that seemed to ask for something else. It asked, in short, for a wife. But it is not easy to ask of such a man, living in such a way, what it is he misses, if he misses anything at all.

To ask would mean entering into what he feels during the long hours riding over the ridges of *kopje* in the sunshine, with the grass waving about him like blond banners. It would mean understanding what made him one of mankind's outriders in the first place.

Even old Smoke himself, ambling beside him on the other horse, would give him a long look on certain occasions, and quietly go off, leaving him by himself.

Sloping away in front of the house was a three-mile-long expanse of untouched grass, which sprang each year so tall that even from their horses the two men could not see over it. There was a track worn through it to a small knoll, a cluster of rocks merely, with trees breaking from the granite for shade. Here it was that George would dismount and, leaning his arm on the neck of his mare, stand gazing down into the valley which was in itself a system of other hills and valleys, so high did Four Winds stand above the rest of the country. Twenty miles away other mountains stood like blocks of tinted crystal, blocking the view; between there were trees and grass, trees and rocks and grass, with the rivers marked by lines of darker vegetation. Slowly, as the years passed, this enormous reach of pure country became marked by patches of cultivation; and smudges of smoke showed where new houses were going up, with the small glittering of roofs. The valley was being developed. Still George stood and gazed, and it seemed as if these encroaching lives affected him not at all. He would stay there half the morning, with the crooning of the green-throated wood-pigeons in his ears, and when he rode back home for his meal, his eyes were heavy and veiled.

But he took things as they came. Four Winds, lifted high into the sky among the great windswept sun-quivering mountains, tumbled all over with boulders, offering itself to storms and exposure and invasion by baboons and leopards—this wilderness, this pure, heady isolation, had not affected him after all.

For when the valley had been divided out among new settlers, and his neighbours were now five miles, and not fifteen, away, he began going to their houses and asking them to his. They were very glad to come, for though he was an eccentric, he was harmless enough. He chose to live alone: that piqued the women. He had become very rich; which pleased everyone. For the rest, he was considered mildly crazy because he would not allow an animal to be touched on his farm; and any native caught setting traps for game would be beaten by George himself and then taken to the police afterwards: George considered the fine that he incurred for beating the native well worth it. His farm was as good as a game reserve; and he had to keep his cattle in what were practically stockades for fear of leopards. But if he lost an occasional beast, he could afford it.

George used to give swimming parties on Sundays; he kept open house on that day, and everyone was welcome. He was a good host, the house was beautiful, and his servants were the envy of every housewife; perhaps this was what people found it difficult to forgive him, the perfection of his servants. For they never left him to go "home" as other people's boys did; their home was here, on this farm, under old Smoke, and the compound was a proper native village, and not the usual collection of shambling huts about which no one cared, since no one lived in them long enough to care. For a bachelor to have such well-trained servants was a provocation to the women of the district; and when they teased him about the perfection of his arrangements, their voices had an edge on them. They used to say: "You damned old bachelor, you." And he would reply, with calm good-humour: "Yes, I must think about getting me a wife."

Perhaps he really did feel he ought to marry. He knew it was suspected that this new phase, of entertaining and being entertained, was with a view to finding himself a girl. And the girls, of course, were only too willing. He was nothing, if not a catch; and it was his own fault that he was regarded, coldly, in this light. He would sometimes look at the women sprawled half-naked around the swimming pool under the bamboos—sprawling with deliberate intent, and for his benefit—and his eyes would narrow in a way that was not pleasant. Nor was it even fair, for if a man will not allow himself to be approached by sympathy and kindness, there is only one other approach. But the result of all this was simply that he set that photograph very prominently on the table beside his bed; and when girls remarked on it he replied, letting his eyelids half-close in a way which was of course exasperatingly attractive: "Ah, yes, Betty—now *there* was a woman for you."

At one time it was thought he was "caught" after all. One of his boundaries was shared with a middle-aged woman with two grown daughters; she was neither married, nor unmarried, for her husband seemed not to be able to make up his mind whether to divorce her or not, and the girls were, in their early twenties, horse-riding, whisky-drinking, flat-bodied tomboys who were used to having their own way with the men they fancied. They would make good wives for men like George, people said: they would give back as good as they got. But they continued to be spoken of in the plural, for George flirted with them both, and they were extraordinarily similar. As for the mother, she ran the farm, for her husband was too occupied with a woman in town to do this, and drank a little too much, and could be heard complaining fatalistically: "Christ, why did I have daughters? After all, sons are *expected* to behave badly." She used to complain to George, who merely smiled and offered her another drink. "God help you if you marry either of them," she would say, gloomily. "May I be forgiven for saying it, but they are fit for nothing but enjoying themselves." "At their age, Mrs. Whately, that seems reasonable enough." Thus George retreated, into a paternally indulgent attitude that nevertheless had a hint in it of cruel relish for the girls' discomfiture.

He used to look for Mrs. Whately when he entered a room, and stay beside her for hours, apparently enjoying her company; and she seemed to enjoy his. She did all the talking, while he stretched himself beside her, his eyes fixed thoughtfully on his glass, which he swung lightly between finger and thumb, occasionally letting out an amused grunt. She spoke chiefly of her husband whom she had turned from a liability into an asset, for the whole room would become silent to hear her humorous, grumbling tales of him. "He came home last week-end," she would say, fixing wide astonished eyes on George, "and do you know what he said? My God, he said, I don't know what I'd do without you, old girl. If I can't get out of town for a spot of fresh air, sometimes, I'd go mad. And there I was, waiting for him with my grievance ready to air. What can one do with a man like that?" "And are you prepared to be a sort of week-end resort?" asked George. "Why, Mr. Chester!" exclaimed Mrs. Whately, widening her eyes to an incredibly foolish astonishment, "after all, he's my husband, I suppose." But this handsome, battered matron was no fool, she could not have run the farm so capably if she had been; and on these occasions George would simply laugh and say: "Have another drink."

At his own swimming parties Mrs. Whately was the only woman who never showed herself in a swimming suit. "At my age," she explained, "it is better to leave it to one's daughters." And with an exaggerated sigh of envy she gazed across at the girls. George would gaze, too, non-committally; though on the whole it appeared he did not care for the spare and boyish type. He had been known, however, during those long hot days when thirty or forty people lounged for hours in their swimming suits on the edge of the pool, eating, drinking, and teasing each other, to rise abruptly, looking inexplicably irritated, and walk off to the stables. There he saddled his mare—who, one would have thought, should have been allowed her Sunday's rest, since she was worked so hard the rest of the week—swung himself up, and was off across the hillsides, riding like a maniac. His guests did not take this hardly; it was the sort of thing one expected of him. They laughed—most particularly the women—and waited for him to come back, saying: "Well, old George, you know . . ."

They used to suggest it would be nice to go riding together, but no one ever succeeded in riding with George. Now that the farms had spread up from the valley over the foothills, George often saw people on horses in the early morning, or at evening; and on these occasions he would signal a hasty greeting with his whip, rise in his stirrups and flash out of sight. This was another of the things people made allowances for: George, that lean, slouching, hard-faced man, riding away along a ridge with his whip raised in perfunctory farewell, was positively as much a feature of the landscape as his own house, raised high on the mountain in a shining white pile, or the ten-foot-high notices all along the boundaries saying: Anyone found shooting game will be severely prosecuted.

Once, at evening, he came on Mrs. Whately alone, and as instinctively he turned his horse to flee, heard her shout: "I won't bite." He grinned unamiably at her expectant face, and shouted back: "I'm no more of a fool than you are, my dear."

At the next swimming party she acknowledged this incident by saying to him thoughtfully, her eyes for once direct and cool: "There are many ways of being a fool, Mr. Chester, and you are the sort of man who would starve himself to death because he once overate himself on green apples."

George crimsoned with anger. "If you are trying to hint that there are, there really *are*, some *sweet, charming* women, if I took the trouble to look, I promise you women have suggested that before."

She did not get angry. She merely appeared genuinely surprised. "Worse than I thought," she commented amicably. And then she began talking about something else in her familiar, rather clowning manner.

It was at one of these swimming parties that the cat came out of the bag. Its presence had of course been suspected, and accorded the usual tolerance. In fact, the incident was not of importance because of his friends' reactions to it, but because of George's own reactions.

It was one very warm December morning, with the rains due to break at any moment. All the farmers had their seed-beds full of tobacco ready to be planted out, and their attention was less on the excellence of the food and drink and the attractions of the women, than on the sky, which was filled with heavy masses of dull cloud. Thunder rolled behind the *kopjes,* and the air was charged and tense. Under the bamboos round the pool, whose fronds hung without a quiver, people tended to be irritable because of the feeling of waiting; for the last few weeks before the season are a bad time in any country where rain is uncertain.

George was sitting dressed on a small rock: he always dressed immediately he had finished bathing. The others were still half-naked. They had all lifted their heads and were looking with interested but non-committal expressions past him into the trees when he noticed the direction of their gaze, and turned himself to look. He gave a brief exclamation; then said, very deliberately: "Excuse me," and rose. Everyone watched him walk across the garden, and through the creeper-draped rocks beyond to where a young native woman stood, hand on hips provocatively, swinging herself a little as if wishing to dance. Her eyes were lowered in the insolently demure manner of the native woman; and she kept them down while George came to a standstill in front of her and began to speak. They could not make out from his gestures, or from his face, what he was saying; but after a little while the girl looked sulky, shrugged, and then moved off again towards the compound, which could be seen through trees and past the shoulder of a big *kopje*, perhaps a mile away. She walked dragging her feet, and swinging her hands to loosely clutch at the grass-heads: it was a beautiful exhibition of unwilling departure; that was the impression given, that this was not only how she felt, but how she intended to show she felt. The long ambiguous look over her bare shoulder (she wore native-style dress, folded under the armpits) directed at the group of white people, could be interpreted in a variety of ways. No one chose to interpret it. No one spoke; and eyes were turned carefully to sky, trees, water or fingernails, when George returned. He looked at them briefly, without any hint of apology, then sat himself down again and reached for his glass. He took a swallow, and went on speaking where he had left off. They were quick to answer him; and in a moment conversation was general, though it was a conscious and controlled conversation: these people were behaving as if for the benefit of an invisible observer who was standing somewhere at a short distance and chuckling irresistibly as he called out: "Bravo! Well done!"

What they felt towards George—an irritation which was a reproach for not preserving appearances—was not allowed to appear in their manner. The women, however, were noticeably acid; and George's acknowledgment of this was a faint smile, so diminishing of their self-respect that by that evening, when the party broke up (it would rain before midnight and they would all have to be up early for a day's hard planting), relations were as usual. In fact, George would be able to count on their saying, or implying: "Oh, George! Well, it is all very well for him, I suppose."

But that did not end the matter for him. He was very angry. He summoned old Smoke to the house when the visitors had gone, and this showed how angry he was, for it was a rule of his never to disturb the labourers on a Sunday.

The girl was Smoke's daughter (or grand-daughter, George did not know), and the arrangement—George's attitude towards the thing forbade any other term—had come about naturally enough. The only time it had ever been mentioned between the two men was when shortly after the girl had set herself in George's path one evening when he was passing from swimming pool to house, Smoke had remarked, without reproach, but sternly enough, that a half-caste child would not be welcome among his people. George had replied, with equal affability, that he gave his assurance there would be no child. The old man replied, half-sighing, that he understood the white people had means at their disposal. There the thing had ended. The girl came to George's room when he sent for her, two or three times a week. She used to arrive when George's dinner was finished, and she left at sun-up, with a handful of small change. George kept a supply of sixpences and threepenny bits under his handkerchiefs, for he had noticed she preferred several small coins to one big one. This discrimination was the measure of his regard for her, of her needs and nature. He liked to please her in these little ways. For instance, recently, when he had gone into town and was down among the kaffir-truck shops buying a supply of aprons for his houseboys, he had made a point of buying her a head-cloth of a colour she particularly liked. And once, she had been ill, and he drove her himself to hospital. She was not afraid to come to him to ask for especial favours to her family. This had been going on for five years.

Now, when old Smoke came to the house, with the lowered eyes and troubled manner that showed he knew of the incident, George said simply that he wished the girl to be sent away; she was making trouble. Smoke sat cross-legged before George for some minutes before replying, looking at the ground. George had time to notice that he was getting a very old man indeed. He had a shrunken, simian appearance; even the flesh over his skull was crinkled under the dabs of white wool; his face was withered to the bone; and his small eyes peered with difficulty. At last he spoke, and his voice was resigned and trembling: "Perhaps the Little Baas could speak to the girl? She will not do it again."

But George was not taking the chance of it happening again.

"She is my child," pleaded the old man.

George, suddenly irritable, said: "I cannot have this sort of thing happening. She is a very foolish girl."

"I understand, baas, I understand. She is certainly a foolish girl. But she is also young, and my child." But even this last appeal, spoken in the old wheezy voice, did not move George.

It was finally arranged that George should pay the expenses of the girl at mission school, some fifty miles off. He would not see her before she left, though she hung about the back steps for days. She even attempted to get into his bedroom the night before she was to set off, accompanied by one of her brothers for escort, for the long walk to her new home. But George had locked his door. There was nothing to be said. In a way he blamed himself. He felt he might have encouraged the girl: one did not know, for example, how the matter of the head-cloth might rearrange itself in a primitive woman's mind. He had been responsible, at any rate, for acting in a way that had "put ideas into her head." That appearance of hers at the swimming pool had been an act of defiance, a deliberate claiming of him, a provocation, whose implications appalled him. They appalled him precisely because the thing could never have happened if he had treated her faultily.

During the week after she left, one evening, before going to bed, he suddenly caught the picture of the London girl off his dressing-table, and tossed it into a cupboard. He was thinking of old Smoke's daughter—grand-daughter, perhaps—with an uncomfortable aching of the flesh, for some weeks before another girl presented herself for his notice.

He had been waiting for this to happen; for he had no intention of incurring old Smoke's reproach by enticing a woman to him.

He was sitting on his verandah one night, smoking, his legs propped on the verandah wall, gazing at the great yellow moon that was rising over a long wooded spur to one side of the house, when a furtive, softly-gliding shape entered the corner of his vision. He sat perfectly still, puffing his pipe, while she came up the steps, and across the patch of light from the lamp inside. For a moment he could have sworn it was the same girl, but she was younger, much younger, not more than about sixteen. She was naked above the waist, for his inspection, and she wore a string of blue beads around her neck.

This time, in order to be sure of starting on the right basis, he pulled out a handful of small coins and laid them on the verandah wall before him. Without raising her eyes, the girl leaned over sideways, picked them up, and caused them to disappear in the folds of her skirt. An hour later she was turned out of the house, and the doors were locked for the night. She wept and pleaded to be allowed to stay till the first light came (as the other girl had always done) for she was afraid to go home by herself through the dark bush that was full of beasts and ghosts and the ancient terrors that were her birthright. George replied simply that if she came at all, she must resign herself to leaving when the business of the occasion was at an end. He remembered the nights with the other one, which had been spent wrapped close in each other's arms—*that* was where he had made his mistake, perhaps? In any case, it was not going to be allowed to happen again.

This girl wept pitifully the first night, and even more violently the second. George suggested that one of her brothers should come for her. She was shocked at the idea, so shocked that he understood things were with her as with him: the thing was permissible provided it was possible decently to ignore it. But she was sent home; and George did not allow himself to picture her gliding through the dark shadows of the moonlit path, and whimpering with fear, as she had done in his arms before leaving him.

At their next weekly palaver, George waited for Smoke to speak, for he knew that he would. It was with a conscious determination not to show guilt (a reaction which surprised and annoyed him) that George watched the old man dismiss the nephew, wait for him to get well on his way on the path to the compound, and turn back to face him, in appeal. "Little Baas," he said, "there are things that need not be said between us." George did not answer. "Little Baas, it is time that you took a wife from your own people."

George replied: "The girl came to me, of her own accord."

Smoke said, as if it were an insult that he was forced to say such an obvious thing: "If you had a wife, she would not have come." The old man was deeply troubled; far more so than George had expected. For a while he did not answer. Then he said: "I shall pay her well." It seemed to him that he was speaking in that spirit of honesty that was in everything he said, or did, with this man who had been the friend of his father, and was his own good friend. He could not have said anything he did not feel. "I'm paying her well; and will see that she is looked after. I am paying well for the other one."

"Aie, aie," sighed the old man, openly reproachful now, "this is not good for our women, baas. Who will want to marry her?"

George moved uncomfortably in his chair. "They both came to me, didn't they? I didn't go running after them." But he stopped. Smoke so clearly considered this argument irrelevant that he could not pursue it, even though he himself considered it valid. If he had gone searching for a woman among those at the compound, he would have felt himself responsible. That old Smoke did not see things in this light made him angry.

"Young girls," said Smoke reproachfully, "you know how they are." Again there was more than reproach. In the feeble ancient eyes there was a deeper trouble. He could not look straight at George. His gaze wavered this way and that, over George's face, away to the mountains, down to the valley, and his hands were plucking at his garments.

George smiled, with determined cheerfulness: "And young men, don't you make allowances for them?"

Smoke suddenly flashed into anger: "Young men, little boys, one expects nonsense from them. But you, baas, you—you should be married, baas. You should have grown children of your own, not spoiling mine . . ." The tears were running down his face. He scrambled to his feet with difficulty, and said, very dignified: "I do not wish to quarrel with the son of my old friend, the Old Baas. I ask you to think, only, Little Baas. These girls, what happens to them? You have sent the other one to the mission school, but how long will she stay? She has been used to your money and to . . . she has been used to her own way. She will go into the town and become one of the loose women. No decent man will have her. She will get herself a town husband, and then another, and another. And now there is this one . . ." He was now grumbling, querulous, pathetic. His dignity could not withstand the weight of his grief. "And now this one, this one! You, Little Baas, that you should take this woman . . ." A very old, tottering, scarecrow man, he swayed off down the path.

For a moment George was impelled to call him back, for it was the first time one of their palavers had ended in unkindness, without courteous exchange in the old manner. But he watched the old man move uncertainly past the swimming pool through the garden, along the rockeries, and out of sight.

He was feeling uncomfortable and irritated, but at the same time he was puzzled. There was a discrepancy between what had happened and what he had expected that he felt now as a sharp intrusion—turning over the scene in his mind, he knew there was something that did not fit. It was the old man's emotion. Over the first girl reproach could be gathered from his manner but a reproach that was fatalistic, and related not to George himself but rather to circumstances, some view of life George could not be expected to share. It had been an impersonal grief, a grief against life. This was different; Smoke had been accusing him, George, directly. It had been like an accusation of disloyalty. Reconstructing what had been said, George fastened upon the recurring words: "wife" and "husband"; and suddenly an idea entered George's head that was intolerable. It was so ugly that he rejected it, and cast about for something else. But he could not refuse it for long; it crept back, and took possession of him, for it made sense of everything that had happened: a few months before old Smoke had taken to himself a new young wife.

After a space of agitated reflection George raised his voice and called loudly for his houseboy. This was a young man brought to the house by old Smoke himself, years before. His relations with George were formal, but warmed slightly by the fact that he knew of George's practical arrangements and treated them with an exquisite discretion. All this George now chose to throw aside. He asked directly: "Did you see the girl who was here last night?"

"Yes, baas."

"Is she old Smoke's new wife?"

His eyes directed to the ground, the youth replied: "Yes, baas."

George smothered an impulse to appeal: "I didn't know she was," an impulse which shocked him, and said: "Very well, you can go." He was getting more and more angry; the situation infuriated him; by no fault of his own he was in a cruel position.

That night he was in his room reading when the girl entered smiling faintly. She was a beautiful young creature, but for George this fact had ceased to exist.

"Why did you not tell me you were Smoke's new wife?" he asked.

She was not disconcerted. Standing just inside the door, still in that pose of shrinking modesty, she said: "I thought the baas knew." It was possible that she had thought so; but George insisted: "Why did you come when you knew I didn't know."

She changed her tone, and pleaded: "He is an old man, baas," seeming to shudder with repugnance.

George said: "You must not come here again."

She ran across the room to him, flung herself down, and embraced his legs.

"Baas, baas," she murmured, "don't send me away."

George's violent anger, that had been diffused within him, now focussed itself sharply, and he threw her away from him, and got to his feet. "Get out," he said. She slowly got to her feet, and stood as before, though now sullenness was mingled with her shrinking humility. She did not say a word. "You are not to come back," he ordered; and when she did not move, he took her arm with the extreme gentleness that is the result of controlled dislike, and pushed her out of the front door. He locked it, and went to bed.

He always slept alone in the house, for the cookboy and the houseboys went back to the compound every night after finishing the washing-up, but one of the garden boys slept in a shed at the back with the dogs, as a guard against thieves. George's garden boys, unlike his personal servants, were not permanent, but came and went at short intervals of a few months. The present one had

been with him for only a few weeks, and he had not troubled to
make a friend of him.

Towards midnight there was a knock at the back door, and when
George opened it he found this garden boy standing there, and there
was a grin on his face that George had never seen on the face of a
native before—at least, not directed at himself. He indicated a
shadowy human shape that stood under a large tree which rose
huge and glittering in the strong moonlight, and said intimately:
"She's there, baas, waiting for you." George promptly cuffed him, in
order to correct his expression, and then strode out into the moonlight. The girl neither moved nor looked at him. A statue of grief,
she stood waiting, with her hands hanging at her sides. Those
hands—the helplessness of them—particularly infuriated George.
"I told you to get back to where you belong," he said, in a low angry
voice. "But, baas, I am afraid." She began to cry again.

"What are you afraid of?"

The girl, her eyeballs glinting in the gleams of moonlight that
fell strong through the boughs overhead, looked along to the compound. It was a mile of bush, with *kopjes* rising on either side of
the path, big rocks throwing deep shadows all the way. Somewhere
a dog was howling at the moon; all the sounds of night rose from
the bush, bird noises, insect noises, animal noises that could not be
named: here was a vast protean life, and a cruel one. George, looking towards the compound, which in this unreal glinting light had
shrunk back, absorbed, into the background of tree and rock, without even a glow of fire to indicate its presence, felt as he always
did: it was the feeling which had brought him here so many years
before. It was as if, while he looked, he was flowing softly outwards, diffused into the bush and the moonlight. He knew no terror; he could not understand fear; he contained that cruelty within
himself, shut safe in some deep place. And this girl, who was bred
of the bush and of the wildness, had no right to tremble with fright.
That, obscurely, was what he felt.

With the moonlight pouring over him, showing how his lips were
momentarily curled back from his teeth, he pulled the girl roughly
towards him out of the shade, turned her round so that she faced
the compound, and said: "Go, now."

She was trembling, in sharp spasms, from head to foot. He could
feel her convulse against him, as if in the convulsions of love, and
he pushed her away so that she staggered. "Go," he ordered, again.
She was now sobbing wildly, with her arm across her eyes. George
called to the garden boy who was standing near the house watching

the scene, his face expressing an emotion George did not choose to recognise. "Take this woman back to the compound."

For the first time in his life George was disobeyed by a native. The youth simply shook his head, and said with a directness that was not intended to be rude, but was rather a rebuke for asking something that could not be asked: "No, baas." George understood he could not press the point. Impatiently he turned back to the girl and dismissed the matter by saying: "I'm not going to argue with you."

He went indoors, and to bed. There he listened futilely for sounds of conversation: he was hoping that the two people outside might come to some arrangement. After a few moments he heard the scraping of chains along earth, and the barking of dogs; then a door shut. The garden boy had gone back to his shed. George repressed a desire to go to the window and see if the girl was still there. He imagined that she might perhaps steal into one of the outhouses for shelter. Not all of them were locked.

It was hours before he slept. It was the first night in years that he had difficulty in sleeping. He was still angry, yes; he was uncomfortable because of his false relationship to old Smoke, because he had betrayed the old man; but beyond these emotions was another; again he felt that discrepancy, something discordant which expressed itself through him in a violent irritation; it was as if a fermenting chemical had been poured into a still liquid. He was intolerably restless, and his limbs twitched. It seemed as if something large and challenging were outside himself saying: And how are you going to include *me*? It was only by turning his back on that challenge that he eventually managed to sleep.

Before sunrise next day, before the smoke began to curl up from the huts in the compound, George called the garden boy, who emerged sleepy and red-eyed from the shed, the dogs at his heels, and told him to fetch old Smoke. George felt he had to apologize to him; he must put himself right with that human being to whom he felt closer than he had ever felt to anyone since his parents died.

He dressed while waiting. The house was quite empty, as the servants had not yet come from the compound. He was in a fever of unrest for the atonement it was necessary for him to make. But the old man delayed his coming. The sun was blazing over the *kopjes*, and the smells of coffee and hot fat were pervading the house from the kitchen when George, waiting impatiently on the verandah, saw a group of natives coming through the trees. Old Smoke was wrapped in a blanket, and supported on each side by a young man;

and he moved as if each step were an effort to him. By the time the three natives had reached the steps, George was feeling like an accused person. Nor did any of his accusers look at him directly.

He said at once: "Smoke, I am very sorry. I did not know she was your wife." Still they did not look at him. Already irritation was growing inside him, because they did not accept his contrition. He repeated sternly: "How was I to know? How could I?"

Instead of answering directly, Smoke said in the feeble and querulous tones of a very old man: "Where is she?"

This George had not foreseen. Irritation surged through him with surprising violence. "I sent her home," he said angrily. It was the strength of his own anger that quieted him. He did not know himself what was happening within him.

The group in front of him remained silent. The two younger men, each supporting Smoke with an arm under his shoulders, kept their eyes down. Smoke was looking vaguely beyond the trees and over the slopes of grass to the valley; he was looking for something, but looking without hope. He was defeated.

With a conscious effort at controlling his voice, George said: "Till last night I did not know she was your wife." He paused, swallowed, and continued, dealing with the point which he understood now was where he stood accused: "She came to me last night, and I told her to go home. She came late. Has she not returned to you?"

Smoke did not answer: his eyes were ranging over the *kopjes* tumbled all about them. "She did not come home," said one of the young men at last.

"She has not perhaps gone to the hut of a friend?" suggested George futilely.

"She is not in the compound," said the same young man, speaking for Smoke.

After a delay, the old man looked straight at George for the first time, but it was as if George were an object, a thing, which had nothing to do with him. Then he moved himself against the arms of the young man in an effort towards independence; and, seeing what he wanted, his escort turned gently round with him, and the three moved slowly off again to the compound.

George was quite lost; he did not know what to do. He stood on the steps, smoking, looking vaguely about him at the scenery, the familiar wild scenery, and down to the valley. But it was necessary to do something. Finally he again raised his voice for the servant. When he came, orders were given that the garden boy should be questioned. The houseboy returned with a reflection of the garden boy's insolent grin on his face, and said: "The garden boy says he does not know what happened, baas. He went to bed, leaving the girl outside—just as the baas did himself." This final phrase showed itself as a direct repetition of the insolent accusation the garden boy had made. But George did not act as he would have done even the day before. He ignored the insolence.

"Where is she?" he asked the houseboy at last.

The houseboy seemed surprised; it was a question he thought foolish, and he did not answer it. But he raised his eyes, as Smoke had done, to the *kopjes,* in a questing hopeless way; and George was made to admit something to his mind he had been careful not to admit.

In that moment, while he stood following the direction of his servant's eyes with his own, a change took place in him; he was gazing at a towering tumbling heap of boulders that stood sharp and black against a high fresh blue, the young blue of an African morning, and it was as if that familiar and loved shape moved back from him, reared menacingly like an animal and admitted danger —a sharp danger, capable of striking from a dark place that was a place of fear. Fear moved in George; it was something he had not before known; it crept along his flesh with a chilling touch, and he shivered. It was so new to him that he could not speak. With the care that one uses for a fragile, easily destroyable thing he took himself inside for breakfast, and went through the meal conscious of being sustained by the ceremony he always insisted on. Inside him a purpose was growing, and he was shielding it tenderly; for he did not know what it was. All he knew was, when he had laid down his coffee cup, and rung the bell for the servants, and gone outside to the verandah, that there the familiar landscape was outside of him, and that something within him was pointing a finger at it. In the now strong sunlight he shivered again; and crossed his arms so that his hands cupped his shoulders: they felt oddly frail. Till lately they had included the pushing strength of mountains; till this morning his arms had been branches and the birds sang in them; within him had been that terror which now waited outside, and which he must fight.

He spent that day doing nothing, sitting on his verandah with his pipe. His servants avoided the front part of the house.

Towards sundown he fetched his rifle which he used only on the rare occasions when there was a snake that must be killed, for he had never shot a bird or a beast with it, and cleaned it, very carefully. He ordered his dinner for an hour earlier than usual, and several times during that meal went outside to look at the sky. It was clear from horizon to horizon, and a luminous glow was spreading over the rocks. When a heavy yellow moon was separated from the highest boulder of the mountain by a hairline, he said to the boys that he was going out with his gun. This they accepted as a thing he must do; nor did they make any move to leave the house for the compound: they were waiting for him to return.

George passed the ruffling surface of the swimming pool, picked his way through the rock garden, and came to where his garden merged imperceptibly, in the reaching tendrils of the creepers, with the bush. For a few yards the path passed through short and trodden grass, and then it forked, one branch leading off to the business part of the farm, the other leading straight on through a grove of trees. Through the dense shadows George moved steadily; for the grass was still short, and the tree trunks glimmered low to the ground. Between the edge of this belt of trees and the half mile of path that wound in and around the big boulders of the *kopje* was a space filled with low jagged rocks, that seemed higher and sharper than they were because of the shadows of the moon. Here it was clear moving. The moon poured down its yellow flood; and his shadow moved beside him, lengthening and shortening with the unevenness of the ground. Behind him were the trees in their gulf of black, before him the *kopjes*, the surfaces of granite showing white and glittering, like plates of crusted salt. Between, the broken shadows, of a dim purple colour, dappled with moonlight. To the left of him the rocks swept up sharply to another *kopje;* on the other side the ground fell away into a gulley which in its turn widened into the long grass slope, which, moving gently in the breeze, presented a gently gleaming surface, flattening and lifting so that there was a perpetual sweeping movement of light across miles of descending country. Far below, was the valley, where the lights of homesteads gleamed steadily.

The *kopje* in front of him was silent, dead silent. Not a bird stirred, and only the insects kept up their small shrilling. George moved into the shadows with a sharp tug of the heart, holding his fear in him cold and alive, like a weapon. But his rifle he handled carelessly.

With cautious, directed glances he moved along and up the path as it rose through the boulders on the side of the *kopje*. As he went he prayed. He was praying that the enemy might present itself and be slain. It was when he was on the height of the path so that half a mile behind showed the lit verandah of his house, and half a mile in front the illuminated shapes of the huts in the compound, that he stopped and waited. He remained quite still, and allowed his fear to grow inside him, a controlled fear, so that while his skin crept and his scalp tingled, yet his hands remained steady on the rifle. To one side of him was a large rock, leaning forward and over him in a black shelf. On the other was a rock-encumbered space, girt by a tangle of branches and foliage. There were, in fact, trees and rocks all about him; the thing might come from any side. But this was the place; he knew it by instinct. And he kept perfectly still for fear that his enemy might be scared away. He did not have to wait long. Before the melancholy howling of the moon-struck dogs in the compound had had time to set the rhythm of his nerves, before his neck had time to ache with the continual alert movements of his head from side to side, he saw one of the shadows a dozen paces from him lengthen gradually, and at last separate itself from the rock. The low, ground-creeping thing showed a green glitter of eyes, and a sheen of moonlight shifted with the moving muscles of the flank. When the shape stilled and flattened itself for a spring, George lifted his rifle and fired. There was a coughing noise, and the shape lay still. George lowered the rifle and looked at it, almost puzzled, and stood still. There lay the enemy, dead, not a couple of paces from him. Sprawled almost at his feet was the leopard, its body still tensing and convulsing in death. Anger sprang up again in George: it had all been so easy, so easy! Again he looked in wonder at his rifle; then he kicked the unresisting flesh of the leopard, first with a kind of curiosity, then brutally. Finally he smashed the butt of the rifle, again and again, in hard, thudding blows, against the head. There was no resistance, no sound, nothing.

Finally, as the smell of blood and flesh began to fill him, he desisted, weak and helpless. He was let down. He had not been given what he had come for. When he finally left the beast lying there, and walked home again, his legs were weak under him and his breath was coming in sobs; he was crying the peevish, frustrated tears of a disappointed man.

The houseboys went out, without complaint, into the temporarily safe night to drag the body into the homestead. They began skinning the beast by lamplight. George slept heavily; and in the morning found the skin pegged in the sunshine, flesh side uppermost, and the fine papery inner skin was already blistering and puffing in the heat. George went to the *kopje*, and after a morning's search among thorn and blackjack and stinging-nettle, found the mouth of a cave. There were fresh human bones lying there, and the bones of cattle, and smaller bones, probably of buck and hare.

But the thing had been killed; and George was still left empty, a hungry man without possibility of food. He did not know what satisfaction it was he needed.

The farm boys came to him for instructions; and he told them, impatiently, not to bother him, but to go to old Smoke.

In a few days old Smoke himself came to see him, an evasive, sorrowful, dignified figure, to say he was going home: he was too old now to work for the Old Baas's son.

A few days later his compound was half empty. It was the urgent necessity of attracting new labour that pulled George together. He knew that an era was finished, for him. While not all old Smoke's kinsmen had left, there was now no focus, no authority, in his compound. He himself, now, would have to provide that focus, with his own will, his own authority; and he knew very well the perpetual strain and worry he must face. He was in the position of his neighbours.

He patched things up, as he could; and, while he was re-ordering his life, found that he was behaving towards himself as he might to a convalescent. For there was a hurt place in him, and a hungry anger that no work could assuage.

For a while he did nothing. Then he suddenly filled his stables with horses; and his home became a centre for the horse-loving people about him. He ran a pack of dogs, too, trained by himself; and took down those notices along his boundaries. For "Leopard" George had been born. For him, now, the landscape was simply a home for leopards. Every week-end his big house was filled with people, young, old, male and female, who came for various reasons; some for the hospitality, some for love of George, some, indeed, for the fun of the Sunday's hunting, which was always followed by a gigantic feast of food and drink.

Quite soon George married Mrs. Whately, a woman who had the intelligence to understand what she could and could not do if she wished to remain the mistress of Four Winds.

Winter in July

THE three of them were sitting at their evening meal on the verandah. From behind, the living-room shed light on to the table, where
their moving hands, the cutlery, the food, showed dimly, but clear
enough for efficiency. Julia liked the half-tones. A lamp or candles
would close them into a soft illuminated space, but obliterate the
sky, which now bent towards them through the pillars of the verandah, a full deep sky, holding a yellowy bloom from an invisible
moon that absorbed the stars into a faint far glitter.

Sometimes Tom said, grumbling humorously: "Romantic, that's
what she is"; and Kenneth would answer, but with an abrupt,
rather grudging laugh: "I like to see what I am eating." Kenneth
was altogether an abrupt person. That quick, quickly-checked
laugh, the swift critical look he gave her (which she met with her
own eyes, as critical as his) were part of the long dialogue between
them. For Kenneth did not accept her. He resisted her. Tom accepted her, as he accepted everything. For Julia it was not a question of preference: the two men supported her in their different
manners. And the things they said, the three of them, seemed
hardly to matter. The real thing was the soft elastic tension that
bound them close.

Her liking for the evening hour, before moving indoors to the
brightly-lit room, was expression of her feeling for them. The
mingling lights, half from the night-sky, half from the lamp, softened their faces and subdued their voices, and she was free to feel

what they were, rather than rouse herself by listening. This state was a continuation of her day, spent by herself (for the men were most of the time on the lands) in an almost trance-like condition where the soft flowing of the hours was marked by no necessities of action strong enough to wake her. As for them, she knew that returning to her was an entrance into that condition. Their day was hard and vigorous, full of practical details and planning. At sundown they entered her country, and the evening meal, where the outlines of fact were blurred by her passivity no less than by the illusion of indistinctness created by sitting under a roof which projected shadow-like into the African night, was the gateway to it.

They used to say to her sometimes: "What do you do with yourself all day? Aren't you bored?" She could not explain how it was she could never become bored. All restlessness had died in her. She was content to do nothing for hours at a time; but it depended on her feeling of being held loosely in the tension between the two men. Tom liked to think of her content and peaceful in his life; Kenneth was irritated.

This particular evening, halfway through the meal, Kenneth rose suddenly and said: "I must fetch my coat." Dismay chilled Julia as she realized that she, too, was cold. She had been cold for several nights, but had put off the hour of recognising the fact. Her thoughts were confirmed by Tom's remark: "It's getting too cold to eat outside now, Julia."

"What month is it?"

He laughed indulgently. "We are reaping."

Kenneth came back, shrugging himself quickly into the coat. He was a small, quick-moving, vital man; dark, dark-eyed, impatient; he did everything as if he resented the time he had to spend on it. Tom was large, fair, handsome, in every way Kenneth's opposite. He said with gentle persistence to Julia, knowing that she needed prodding: "Better tell the boys to move the table inside tomorrow."

"Oh, I suppose so," she grumbled. Her summer was over: the long luminous warm nights, broken by swift showers, or obscured suddenly by heavy driving clouds—the tumultuous magical nights —were gone and finished for this year. Now, for the three months of winter, they would eat indoors, with the hot lamp over the table, the cold shivering about their legs, and outside a parched country, roofed by dusty freezing stars.

Kenneth said briskly: "Winter, Julia, you'll have to face it."

"Well," she smiled, "tomorrow you'll be able to see what you are eating."

There was a slight pause; then Kenneth said: "I shan't be here tomorrow night. I'm taking the car into town in the morning."

Julia did not reply. She had not heard. That is to say, she felt dismay deepening in her at the sound of his voice; then she wondered at her own forebodings, and then the words: "Town. In the morning," presented themselves to her.

They very seldom went into the city, which was fifty miles away. A trip was always planned in advance, for it would be a matter of buying things that were not available at the local store. The three of them had made the journey only last week. Julia's mind was now confronting and absorbing the fact that on that day Kenneth had abruptly excused himself and gone off on some business of his own. She remembered teasing him, a little, in her fashion. To herself she would have said (disliking the knowledge) that she controlled jealousy, like many jealous women, by becoming an accomplice, as it were, in Kenneth's adventures: the tormenting curiosity was eased when she knew what he had been doing. Last week he had disliked her teasing.

Now she looked over at Tom for reassurance, and saw that his eyes were expressing disquiet as great as her own. Doubly deserted, she gazed clearly and deliberately at both men; and because Kenneth's bald statement of his intentions seemed to her so gross a betrayal of their real relations, chose to say nothing, but in a manner of waiting for an explanation. None was offered, though Kenneth appeared uneasy. They finished their meal in silence and went indoors, passing through the stripped dining-room, which tomorrow would appear in its winter guise of arranged furniture and candles and bowls of fruit, into the living-room.

The house was built for heat. In the winter cold struck up from the floor and out of the walls. This room was very bare, very high, of dull red brick, flagged with stone. Tomorrow she would put down rugs. There was a large stone fireplace, in which stood an earthenware jar filled with Christ-thorn. Julia unconsciously crossed to it, knelt, and bent to the little glowing red flowers, holding out her hands as if to the comfort of fire. Realizing what she was doing, she lifted her head, smiled wrily at the two men, who were watching her with the same small smile, and said: "I'll get a fire put in." Shaking herself into a knowledge of what she did by action, she walked purposefully to the door, and called to the servants. Soon the houseboy entered with logs and kindling materials, and the three stood drinking their coffee, watching him as he knelt to make the fire. They were silent, not because of any scruples against letting their lives appear falsely to servants, but because they knew speech was necessary, and that what must be said would break their life together. Julia was trembling; it was as if a support had been cut away beneath her. Held as she was by these men, her life made for her by them, her instincts were free to come straight and present themselves to her without the necessity for disapproval or approval. Now she found herself glancing alternatively from Tom, that large gentle man, her husband, whose very presence comforted her into peace, to Kenneth, who was frowning down at his coffee cup, so as not to meet her eyes. If he had simply laughed and said what was needed!—he did not. He drank what remained in the cup with two large gulps, seemed to feel the need of something to do, and then went over to the fireplace. The native still knelt there, his bare legs projecting loosely behind him, his hands hanging loose, his body free and loose save for head and shoulders, into which all his energy was concentrated for the purpose of blowing up the fire, which he did with steady, bellow-like breathing. "Here," said Kenneth, "I'll do that." The servant glanced at him, accepted the white man's whim, and silently left the room, leaving the feeling behind him that he had said: "White men can't make fires"; just as Julia could feel her cook saying, when she was giving orders in the kitchen: "I can make better pastry than you."

Kenneth knelt where the servant had knelt and began fiddling with the logs. But he was good with his hands, and in a moment the sparse beginnings of a fire flowered in the wall; while the crock of prickly red thorn blossoms, Julia's summer fire, was set to one side.

"Now," said Kenneth, rather offhand, rather too loudly: "You can warm your hands, Julia." He gave his quick, grudging laugh. Julia found it offensive; and met his eyes. They were hostile. She flushed, walked slowly over to the fireplace, and sat down. The two men followed her example. For a while they did nothing; that unoffered explanation hung in the air between them. After a while Kenneth reached for a magazine and began to read. Julia looked over at her husband, whose kind blue eyes had always accepted everything she was, and raised her brows humorously. He did not respond, for he had turned again to Kenneth's now purposely bent head.

The fact that Kenneth had not spoken, that Tom was troubled, made Julia, thrown back on herself, ask: "Why should you be so resentful? Surely he has a right to do as he pleases?" No, she answered herself. Not in this way. He shouldn't suddenly withdraw, shutting us out. Either one thing or the other. Doing it this way

means that all our years together have been a lie; he simply repudi-
ates them. But that *was* Kenneth, this continuous alternation between giving and withdrawal. Julia felt tears welling up inside her
from a place that for a long time had remained dry. They were the
tears of trembling insecurity. The thin, cold air in the great stone
room, just beginning to be warmed by the small fire, was full of
menace for Julia. But Kenneth did not speak: he was reading as if
his future depended on the advertisements for tractors; and Tom
soon began to read too, ignoring Julia.

She pulled herself together, and lay back in her chair, making
herself think. She was thinking consciously of her life and what
she was. There had been no need for her to consider herself for so
long, and she hated having to do it.

She was the daughter of a small-town doctor in the North of
England. To say that she had been ambitious would be false: the
word ambition implies purpose; she was rather critical and curious,
and her rebellion against the small-town atmosphere, and the prospect of marrying into it was no more conscious than the rebellion
of most young people who think vaguely: Surely life can be better
than this?

Yet she escaped. She was clever: at the end of her schooling she
was better educated than most. She learned French and German
because languages came easily to her, but mostly because at eighteen she fell in love with a French student, and at twenty became
secretary to a man who had business connections in Germany, and
she liked to please men. She was an excellent secretary, not merely
because she was competent, but because of her peculiar fluid sympathy for the men she worked with. Her employers found that she
quickly, intuitively, fitted herself in with what they wanted: it was
a sort of directed passivity, a receptiveness towards people. So she
earned well, and soon had the opportunity of leaving her home
town and going to London.

Looking back now from the age she had reached (which was
nearly forty) on the life she had lived (which had been varied and
apparently adventurous) she could not put her finger on any point
in her youth when she had said to herself: "I want to travel; I want
to be free." Yet she had travelled widely, moving from one country
to the next, from one job to the next; and all her relations with
people, whether men or women, had been coloured by the brilliance
of impermanence. When she left England she had not known it
would be final. It was on a business trip with her employer, and her
relations with him were almost those of a wife with a husband,

excepting for sex: she could not work with a man unless she offered a friendly, delicate sympathy.

In France she fell in love, and stayed there for a year. When that came to an end, the mood took her to go to Italy—no, that is the wrong way of putting it. When she described it like that to herself, she scrupulously said: That's not the truth. The fact was that she had been very seriously in love; and yet could not bring herself to marry. Going to Italy (she had not wanted to go in the least) had been a desperate but final way of ending the affair. She simply could not face the idea of marriage. In Italy she worked in a travel agency; and there she met a man whom she grew to love. It was not the desperate passion of a year before, but serious enough to marry. Later, she moved to America. Why America? Why not?—she was offered a good job there at the time she was looking for some place to go.

She stayed there two years, and had, as they say, a wonderful time. She was now a little bit more cautious about falling in love; but nevertheless, there was a man who almost persuaded her to stay in New York. At the last moment a wild, trapped feeling came over her: what have I got to do with this country? she asked herself. This time, leaving the man was a destroying effort; she did not want to leave him. But she went south to the Argentine, and her state of mind was not a pleasant one.

Also, she found she was not as efficient as she had been. This was because she had become more wary, less adaptable. Afraid of falling in love, she was conscious of pulling away from the people she worked for; she gave only what she was paid to give, and this did not satisfy her. What, then, was going to satisfy her? After all, she could not spend all her life moving from continent to continent; yet there seemed no reason why she should settle in one place rather than another, even why it should be one man rather than another. She was tired. She was very tired. The springs of her feeling had run dry. This particular malaise is not so easily cured.

And now, for the first time, she had an affair with a man for whom she cared nothing: this was a half-conscious choice, for she understood that she could not have chosen a man whom she would grow to love. And so it went on, for perhaps two years. She was associating only with people who moved her not at all; and this was because she did not want to be moved.

There came a point when she said to herself that she must decide now, finally, what she wanted, and make sacrifices to get it. She was twenty-eight. She had spent the years since leaving school moving from hotel to furnished flat, from one job to the next, from one country to another. She seemed to have a tired affectionate remembrance of so many people, men and women, who had once filled her life. Now it was time to make something permanent. But what?

She said to herself that she was getting hard; yet she was not hard; she was numbed and tired. She must be very careful, she decided; she must not fall in love, lightly, again. Next time, it must matter.

All this time she was leading a full social life: she was attractive, well-dressed, amusing. She had the reputation of being brilliant and cold. She was also very lonely and she had never been lonely before, since there had always been some man to whom she gave warmth, affection, sympathy.

There was one morning when she had a vision of evil. It was at the window of a large hotel, one warm summer's day, when she was looking down through the streets of the attractive modern city in South America, with the crowds of people and the moving traffic . . . it might have been almost any city, on a bright warm day, from a hotel window, with the people blowing like leaves across her vision, as rootless as she, as impermanent, their lives meaning as little. For the first time in her life, the word evil meant something to her: she looked at it, coldly, and rejected it. This was sentiment, she said; the result of being tired, and nearly thirty. The feeling was not related to anything. She could not feel—why should one feel? She disliked what she was—well, it was at any rate honest to accept oneself as unlikable. Her brain remarked dispassionately that if one lived without rules, one should be prepared to take the consequences, even if that meant moments of terror at hotel windows, with death beckoning below and whispering: Why live? Anyway, who was responsible for the way she was? Had she ever planned it? Why should one be one thing rather than another?

It was chance that took her to Cape Town. At a party she met a man who offered her a job as his secretary on a business trip, and it was easy to accept, for she had come to hate South America.

During the trip over she found, with a groan, that she had never been more efficient, more responsible, more gently responsive. He was an unhappy man, who needed sympathy . . . she gave it. At the end of the trip he asked her to marry him; and she understood she would have felt much the same if he had asked her to dinner. She fled.

She had enough money saved to live without working, so for

months she stayed by herself, in a small hotel high over Cape
Town, where she could watch the ships coming and going in the
harbour and think: they are as restless as I am. She lived gently,
testing every emotion she felt, making no contact save the casual
ones inevitable in a hotel, walking by herself for hours of every day,
soaking herself in the sea and the sun as if the beautiful peninsula
could heal her by the power of its beauty. And she ran away from
any possibility of liking some other human being as if love itself
were poisoned.

One warm afternoon when she was walking high along the side
of a mountain, with the blue sea swinging and lifting below, and a
low sun sending a sad red pathway from the horizon, she was overtaken by two other walkers. There was no one else in sight, and it
was inevitable they should continue together. She found they were
farmers on holiday from Rhodesia, half-brothers, who had worked
themselves into prosperity; this was the first holiday they had taken
for years, and they were in a loosened, warm, adventurous mood.
She sensed they were looking for wives to take back with them.

She liked Tom from the first, though for a day or so she flirted
with Kenneth. This was an automatic response to his laughing,
challenging antagonism. It was Kenneth who spoke first, in his
brusque, offhand way, and she felt attracted to him: theirs was the
relationship of people moving towards a love affair. But she did not
really want to flirt; with Kenneth it seemed anything else was impossible. She was struck by the way Tom, the elder brother, listened
while they sparred, smiling uncritically, almost indulgently: his
was an almost protective attitude. It was more than protective. A
long while afterwards she told Tom that on that first afternoon he
had reminded her of the peasant who uses a bird to catch fish for
him. Yet there was a moment during the long hike back to the city
through the deepening evening, when Julia glanced curiously at
Tom and saw his warm blue glance resting kindly on her in a slow,
speculative way, and she chose him, then, in her mind, even while
she continued the exchange with Kenneth. Because of that kindness, she let herself sink towards the idea of marriage. It was what
she wanted, really; and she did not care where she lived. Emotionally there was no country of which she could say: this is my home.

For several days the three of them went about together, and all
the time she bantered with Kenneth and watched Tom. That defensive, grudging thing she could feel in Kenneth, which attracted her,
against her will, was what she was afraid of: she was watching,
half-fearfully, half-cynically, for its appearance in Tom. Then,

slowly, Kenneth's treatment of her grew more offhand and brutal: he knew he was being made use of. There came a point when in his sarcastic frank way he shut himself off from her; and for a while the three of them were together without contact. It had been Kenneth and she, with Tom as urbane onlooker; now it was she, by herself, drifting alone, floating loose, waiting, as it were, to be gathered in; and it was possible to mark the point when Tom and Kenneth looked at each other sardonically, in understanding, before Tom moved into Kenneth's place in his warm and deliberate fashion, claiming her.

He was nicer than she had believed possible. There was suddenly no conflict. He listened to her tales about her life with detached interest, as if they could not possibly concern him. He remarked once, in his tender, protective way: "You must have been hurt hard at some time. That's the trouble with you independent women. Actually, you are quite a nice woman, Julia." She laughed at him scornfully, as an arrogant male who has to make some kind of a picture of a woman so as to be able to fit her into his life. He treated her laughter tolerantly. When she said things like this he found it merely a sort of piquancy, a sign of her wit. Half-laughingly, half-despairingly, she said to Kenneth: "You do realize that Tom hasn't an idea of what I'm like? Do you think it's fair to marry him?"

"Well, why not, if he wants to be married?" returned Kenneth briskly. "He's romantic. He sees you as a wanderer from city to city, and from bed to bed, because you are trying to heal a broken heart or something of the kind. That appeals to him."

Tom listened to this silently, smiling with disquiet. But there were times when Julia liked to think she had a broken heart; it certainly felt bruised. It was restful to accept Tom's idea of her. She said in a piqued way to Kenneth: "I suppose *you* understand perfectly easily why I've lived the way I have?"

Kenneth raised his brows. "Why? Because you enjoyed it of course. What better reason?"

She could not help laughing, even while she said crossly, feeling misunderstood: "The fact is, you are as bad as Tom. You make up stories about women, too, to suit yourself. You like thinking of women as hard and decided, cynically making use of men."

"Certainly," said Kenneth. "Much better than letting yourself be made use of. I like women to know what they want and get it."

This kind of conversation irritated and saddened Julia: it was rather like the froth whipping on the surface of the sea, with the currents underneath dark and unknown.

She did not like being reminded how much better Kenneth understood her than Tom did. She was pleased to get the business of the ceremony over. Tom married her in a purposeful, unhurrying way; but he remarked that it must be before a certain date because he wanted to start planting soon.

Kenneth attended as best man with a glint of malice in his eye, and the air of a well-wishing onlooker, interested to see how things would turn out. Julia and he exchanged a glance of pure understanding, very much against their wills, for their attitude towards each other was now one of brisk friendship. From the security of Tom's arms, she allowed herself to think that if Kenneth were not the kind of man to feel protective towards a woman simply because he enjoyed feeling protective, then it was so much the worse for him. This was slightly vindictive in her; but on the whole good-natured enough—good-nature was necessary; the three of them would be living together in one house, on the same farm, seeing other people seldom.

It was quite easy, after all. Kenneth did not have to efface himself. Tom effortlessly claimed Julia as his wife, from his magnificent, lazy self-assurance, and she was glad to be claimed. Kenneth and she maintained a humorous understanding. He was given three rooms to himself in one wing of the house; but it was not long before they became disused. It seemed silly for him to retire after dinner by himself. In the evenings, the fact that Julia was Tom's wife was marked by their two big chairs set side by side, with Kenneth's opposite. He used to sit there watching them with his observant, slightly sarcastic smile.

After a while Julia understood she was feeling uneasy; she put it down to the fact that she had expected subtle antagonism between the two men, which she would have to smooth over, while in fact there was no antagonism. It went deeper than that. Those first few nights, when Kenneth tactfully withdrew to his rooms, but looking amused, Tom was restless: he missed Kenneth badly. Julia watched them; and saw with a curious humorous sinking of the heart that they were so close to each other they could not bear to be apart for long. In the evenings it was they who talked, in the odd bantering manner they used even when serious: particularly when serious. Tom liked it when Kenneth sat there opposite, looking shrewd and sceptical about this marriage: they would tease each other in a way that, had they been man and woman, would have seemed positively flirtatious. Listening to them, Julia felt an extraordinary unease, as at a perversity. She chose not to think about it.

Better to be affectionately amused at Tom's elder-brother attitude towards Kenneth; there was often something petulant, rebellious, childish, in Kenneth's attitude towards Tom. Why, Tom was even elder-brotherish to her, who had been managing her own life, so efficiently, for years all over the world. Well, and was not that why she had married him?

She accepted it. They all accepted it. They grew into a silent comfortable understanding. Tom, so to speak, was the head of the family, commanding, strong, perhaps a little obtuse, as authority has to be; and Julia and Kenneth deferred to him, with the slightest hint of mockery, to gloss the fact that they were glad to defer: how pleasant to let the responsibility rest on someone else!

Julia even learned to accept the knowledge that when Tom was busy, and she walked with Kenneth, or swam with Kenneth, or took trips into town with Kenneth, it was not only with Tom's consent: more, he liked it, even needed it. Sometimes she felt as if he were urging her to be with his brother. Kenneth felt it and rebelled, shying away in his petulant younger-brother manner. He would exclaim: "Good Lord, man, Julia's your wife, not mine." And Tom would laugh uneasily and say: "I don't like the idea of being possessive." The thought of Tom being possessive was so absurd that Julia and Kenneth began giggling helplessly, like conspiring and wise children. And when Tom had departed, leaving them together, she would say to Kenneth, in her troubled serious fashion: "But I don't understand this. I don't understand any of it. It flies in the face of nature."

"So it does," Kenneth would return easily. He looked at her with a quizzical glint. "You must take things as they come, my dear sister-in-law." But Julia felt she had been doing just that: she had relaxed, without thinking, drifting warmly and luxuriously inside Tom's warm and comfortable grasp: which was also Kenneth's, and because Tom wanted it that way.

In spite of Tom, she maintained with Kenneth a slight but strong barrier, because they were people who could be too strongly attracted to each other. Once or twice, when they had been left alone together by Tom, Kenneth would fly off irritably: "Really, why I bother to be loyal in the circumstances I can't think."

"But what *are* the circumstances?" Julia asked, puzzled.

"Oh *Lord*, Julia . . ." Kenneth expostulated irritably.

Once, when he was brutal with irritability, he made the curious remark: "The fact is, it was just about time Tom and I had a wife." He began laughing, not very pleasantly.

Julia did not understand. She thought it sounded ugly.

Kenneth regarded her ironically and said: "Fortunately for Tom, he doesn't know anything at all about himself."

But Julia did not like this said about her husband, even though she felt it to be true. Instinctively this particular frontier in their mutual relations was avoided in future; and she was careful with Kenneth, refusing to discuss Tom with him.

From time to time during those two years before Tom left for the war, Kenneth investigated (his own word) the girls on surrounding farms, with a view to marrying. They bored him. He had a prolonged affair with a married woman whose husband bored her. To Julia and Tom he made witty remarks about his position as a lover. Sometimes the three of them would become helpless with laughter at his descriptions of himself being gallant: the lady was romantic, and liked being courted. Kenneth was not romantic, and his interest in the lady was confined to an end which he could not prevent himself describing in his pungent, sour, resigned fashion during those long evenings with the married couple. Again, Julia got the uneasy feeling that Tom was really too interested—no, that was not the word; it was not the easy-going interest of an amused outsider that Tom displayed; while he listened to Kenneth being witty about his affair, it was almost as if he were participating himself, as if he were silently urging Kenneth on to further revelations. On these occasions Julia felt a revulsion from Tom. She said to herself that she was jealous, and repressed the feeling.

When the war started Tom became restless; Julia knew that he would soon go. He volunteered before there was conscription; and she watched, with a humorous sadness, the scene (an uncomfortable one) between her two men, when it seemed that Tom felt impelled to apologise to Kenneth for taking the advantage of him in grasping a rare chance of happiness. Kenneth was unfit: the two brothers had come to Africa in the first place because of Kenneth's delicate lungs. Kenneth did not at all want to go to the war. "Lord!" he exclaimed to Tom; "there's no need to sound so apologetic. You're welcome. I'm not a romantic. I don't like getting killed unless in a good cause. I can't see any point in the thing." In this way he appeared to dismiss the war and the world's turmoil. As for Tom, he didn't really care about the issues of the war, either. It was sufficient that there was a war. For both men it was axiomatic that it was impossible England could ever be beaten in a war; they might laugh at their own attitude (which they did, when Julia,

from her liberal travelled internationalism, mocked at them), but
that was what they felt, nevertheless.

As for Julia, she was more unhappy about the war than either of
them. She had grown into security on the farm; now the world,
which she had wanted to shut out, pressed in on her again; and she
thought of her many friends, in so many countries, in the thick of
things, feeling strange partisan emotions which seemed to her absurd. For she thought in terms of people, not of nations or issues;
and the war, to her, was a question of mankind gone mad, killing
each other pointlessly. Always the pointlessness of everything! And
now she was not allowed to forget it.

To do her credit, all her unhappiness and female resentment at
being so lightly abandoned by Tom at the first sound of a bugle
calling adventure down the wind was suppressed. She merely said
scornfully to him: "What a baby you are! As if there hadn't been
the last war! And look at all the men in the district, pleased as
punch because something exciting is going to happen. If you really
cared two hoots about the war, I might respect you. But you don't.
Nor do most of the people we know."

Tom did not like this. The atmosphere of war had stirred him
into a superficial patriotism. "You sound like a newspaper leader,"
Julia mocked him. "You don't really believe a word you say. The
truth is that most people like us, in all the countries I've been in,
haven't a notion what we believe about anything. We don't believe
in the slogans and the lies. It makes me sick, to see the way you all
get excited the moment war comes."

This made Tom angry, because it was true; and because he had
suddenly remembered his sentimental attachment to England, in
the Rupert Brooke fashion. They were on edge with each other, in
the days before he left: he was glad to go, particularly as Kenneth
was being no less caustic. This was the first time the two men had
ever been separated; and Julia felt that Kenneth was as hurt as she
because Tom left them so easily. In fact, they were all pleased
when Tom was able to leave the farm, and put an end to the misery
of their tormenting each other.

But after he had gone, Julia was very unhappy. She missed him
badly. Marrying had been a greater peace than she had imagined
possible for her. To let the restless critical part of one die; to drift;
to relax; to enjoy Africa as a country, the way it looked and the way
it felt; to enjoy the physical things slowly, without haste—learning
all this had, she imagined, healed her. And now, without Tom, she

was nothing. She was unsupported and unwarmed; and she knew
that marrying had after all cured her of nothing. She was still floating rootlessly, without support; she belonged nowhere; and even
Africa, which she had grown to love, meant nothing to her really: it
was another country she had visited as lightly as a migrant bird.

And Kenneth was no help at all. With Tom on the farm she
might have been able to drift with the current, to take the conventional attitude towards the war. But Kenneth used to switch on the
wireless in the evenings and pungently translate the news of the
war into the meaningless chaotic brutality which was how she herself saw it. He spoke with the callous cynicism that means people
are suffering, and which she could hear in her own voice.

"It's all very well," she would say to him. "It's all very well for us.
We sit here out of it all. Millions of people are suffering."

"People like suffering," he would retort, angrily. "Look at Tom.
There he sits in the desert, bored as hell. He'll be talking about the
best years of his life in ten years' time."

Julia could hear Tom's voice, nostalgically recalling adventure,
only too clearly. At the same time Kenneth made her angry, because he expressed what she felt, and she did not like the way she
felt. She joined the local women's groups and started knitting and
helping with district functions; and flushed up when she saw Kenneth's cold angry eyes resting on her. "By God, Julia, you are as bad
as Tom . . ."

"Well, surely, one must be part of it, surely, Kenneth?" She tried
hard to express what she was feeling.

"Just what are you fighting *for?*" he demanded. "Can you tell me
that?"

"I feel we ought to find out . . ."

He wouldn't listen. He flounced off down the farm saying: "I'm
going to make a new dam. Unless they bomb it, it's something useful done in all this waste and chaos. You can go and knit nice
woollies for those poor devils who are getting themselves killed and
listen to the dear women talking about the dreadful Nazis. My God,
the hypocrisy. Just tell them to take a good look at South Africa,
from me, will you?"

The fact was, he missed Tom. When he was approached to sub-
scribe to war charities he gave generously, in Tom's name, sending the receipts carefully to Tom, with sarcastic intention. As the
war deepened and the dragging weight of death and suffering settled in their minds, Julia would listen at night to angry pacing footsteps up and down, up and down the long stone passages of the

house, and, going out in her dressing-gown, would come on Kenneth, his eyes black with anger, his face tense and white: "Get out
of my way, Julia. I shall kill you or somebody. I'd like to blow the
whole thing up. Why not blow it up and be finished with it? It
would be good riddance."

Julia would gently take him by the arm and lead him back to
bed, shutting down her own cold terror at the world. It was necessary for one of them to remain sane. Kenneth at that time was not
quite sane. He was working fourteen hours a day; up long before
sunrise, hastening back up the road home after sundown, for an
evening's studying: he read scientific stuff about farming. He was
building dams, roads, bridges; he planted hundreds of acres of
trees; he contour-ridged and drained. He would listen to the news
of so many thousands killed and wounded, so many factories blown
up, and turn to Julia, his face contracted with hate, saying, "At any
rate I'm building not destroying."

"I hope it comforts you," Julia would remark, mildly sarcastic,
though she felt bitter and futile.

He would look at her balefully and stride out again, away on
some work for his hands.

They were quite alone in the house. For a short while after Tom
left they discussed whether they would get an assistant, for conventional reasons. But they disliked the idea of a stranger, and the
thing drifted. Soon, as the men left the farms to go off to the war,
many women were left alone, doing the work themselves, or with
assistants who were unfit for fighting, and there was nothing really
outrageous in Kenneth and Julia living together by themselves. It
was understood in the district, that for the duration of the war, this
kind of situation should not be made a subject for gossip.

It was inevitable they should be lovers. From the moment Tom
left they both knew it.

Tom was away three years. She was exhausted by Kenneth. His
mood was so black and bitter and she knew that nothing she could
do or say might help him, for she was as bad herself.

She became the kind of woman he wanted: he did not want a
warm, consoling woman. She was his mistress. Their relationship
was a complicating fencing game, conducted with irony, tact, and
good sense—except when he boiled over into hatred and vented it
on her. There were times when suddenly all vitality failed her, and
she seemed to sink swiftly, unsupported, to lie helpless in the
depths of herself, looking up undesirously at the life of emotion
and warmth washing gently over her head. Then Kenneth used to

leave her alone, whereas Tom would have gently coaxed her into life again.

"I wish Tom would come back, oh dear Christ, I wish he'd come back," she would sigh.

"Do you imagine I don't?" Kenneth would enquire bitterly. Then, a little piqued, but not much: "Don't I do?"

"Well enough, I suppose."

"What do you want then?" he enquired briefly, giving what small amount of attention he could spare from the farm to the problem of Julia, the woman.

"Tom," Julia replied simply.

He considered this critically. "The fact is, you and I have far more in common than you and Tom."

"I don't see what 'in common' has to do with it."

"You and I are the same kind of animal. Tom doesn't know the first thing about you. He never could."

"Perhaps that's the reason."

Dislike began welling between them, tempered, as always, by patient irony. "You don't like women at all," complained Julia suddenly. "You simply don't like me. You don't trust me."

"Oh if it comes to liking . . ." He laughed, resentfully. "You don't trust me either, for that matter."

It was the truth; they didn't trust each other; they mistrusted the destructive nihilism that they had in common. Conversations like these, which became far more frequent as time went on, left them hardened against each other for days, in a condition of watchful challenge. This was part of their long, exhausting exchange, which was a continual resolving of mutual antagonism in tired laughter.

Yet, when Tom wrote saying he was being demobilized, Kenneth, in a mood of tenderness, asked Julia to marry him. She was shocked and astonished. "You know quite well you don't want to marry me," she expostulated. "Besides, how could you do that to Tom?" Catching his quizzical glance, she began laughing helplessly.

"I don't know whether I want to marry you or not," admitted Kenneth honestly, laughing with her.

"Well, I know. You don't."

"I've got used to you."

"I haven't got used to you. I never could."

"I don't understand what it is Tom gives you that I don't."

"Peace," said Julia simply. "You and I fight all the time, we never do anything else."

"We don't fight," protested Kenneth. "We have never, as they say, exchanged a cross word." He grimaced. "Except when I get wound up, and that's a different thing."

Julia saw that he could not imagine a relationship with a woman that was not based on antagonism. She said, knowing it was useless: "Everything is so easy with Tom."

"Of course it's easy," he said angrily. "The whole damn thing is a lie from beginning to end. However, if that's what you like . . ." He shrugged, his anger evaporating. He said drily: "I imagined I was qualifying as a husband."

"Some men can't ever be husbands. They'll always be lovers."

"I thought women liked that?"

"I wasn't talking about women, I was talking about me."

"Well, I intend to get married, for all that."

After that they did not discuss it. Speaking of what they felt left them confused, angry, puzzled.

Before Tom came back Kenneth said: "I ought to leave the farm."

She did not trouble to answer, it was so insincere.

"I'll get a farm over the other side of the district."

She merely smiled. Kenneth had written long letters to Tom every week of those three years, telling him every detail of what was happening on the farm. Plans for the future were already worked out.

It was arranged that Julia should go and meet Tom in town, where they would spend some weeks before the three began life together again. As Kenneth said, sarcastically, to Julia: "It will be just like a second honeymoon."

It was. Tom returned from the desert toughened, sunburnt, swaggering a little because he was unsure of himself with Julia. But she was so happy to see him that in a few hours they were back where they had been. "About Kenneth . . ." began Tom warily, after they had edged round this subject for some days.

"Much better not talk about it," said Julia quickly.

Tom's blue eyes rested on her, not critically, but appealingly. "Is it going to be all right?" he asked after a moment. She could see he was terrified she might say that Kenneth had decided to go away. She said drily: "I didn't want you to go off to the wars like a hero, did I?"

"There's something in that," he admitted; admitting at the same time that they were quits. Actually, he was rather subdued because of his years as a soldier. He was quick to drop the subject. It would not be just yet that he would begin talking about the happiest years of his life. He had still to forget how bored he had been and how he had missed his farm.

For a few days there was awkwardness between the three. Kenneth was jealous because of the way Julia had gladly turned back to Tom. But there was so much work to do, and Kenneth and Tom were so pleased to be back together, that it was not long before everything was as easy as before. Julia thought it was easier: now that her attraction for Kenneth, and his for her, had been slaked, the restlessness that had always been between them would vanish. Perhaps not quite . . . Julia's and Kenneth's eyes would meet sometimes in that instinctive, laughing understanding that she could never have with Tom, and then she would feel guilty.

Sometimes Kenneth would "take out" a girl from a near farm; and they would afterwards discuss his getting married. "If only I could fall in love," he would complain humorously. "You are the only woman I can bear the thought of, Julia." He would say this before Tom, and Tom would laugh: they had reached such a pitch of complicity.

Very soon there were plans for expanding the farm. They bought several thousands of acres of land next door. They would grow tobacco on a large scale: this was the time of the tobacco boom. They were getting very rich.

There were two assistants on the new farm, but Tom spent most of his days there. Sometimes his nights, too. Julia, after three days spent alone with Kenneth, with the old attraction strong between them, said to him: "I wish you would let Kenneth run that farm."

Tom, who was absorbed and fascinated by the new problems, said rather impatiently: "Why?"

"Surely that's obvious."

"That's up to you, isn't it?"

"Perhaps it isn't, always."

It was the business of the war over again. He seemed a slow, deliberate man, without much fire. But he liked new problems to solve. He got bored. Kenneth, the quick, lively, impatient one, liked to be rooted in one place, liked to develop what he had.

Julia had the helpless feeling again that Tom simply didn't care about herself and Kenneth. She grew to accept the knowledge that really, it was Kenneth that mattered to him. Except for the war, they had never been separated. Tom's father had died, and his mother married Kenneth's father. Tom had always been with Ken-

neth, he could not remember a time when he had not been protec-
tively guarding him. Once Julia asked him: "I suppose you must
have been very jealous of him, that was it, wasn't it?" and she was
astonished at his quick flare of rage at the suggestion. She dropped
the thing: what did it matter now?

The two boys had gone through various schools and to university
together. They had started farming in their early twenties, when
they hadn't a penny between them, and had to borrow money to
support their mother, for whom they shared a deep love, which was
also half-exasperated admiration; she had apparently been a helpless, charming lady with many admirers who left her children to
the care of nurses.

When Tom was away one evening, and would not be back till
next day, Kenneth said brusquely, with the roughness that is the
result of conflict: "Coming to my room tonight, Julia?"

"How can I?" she protested.

"Well, I don't like the idea of coming to the marriage bed," he
said practically, and they began to laugh. To Julia, Kenneth would
always be the laughter of inevitability.

Tom said nothing, though he must have known. When Julia
again appealed that he should stay on this farm and send Kenneth
to the other, he turned away, frowning, and did not reply. His manner to her did not change. And she still felt: this is my husband,
and compared to that feeling, Kenneth was nothing. At the same
time a grim anxiety was taking possession of her: it seemed that in
some perverse way the two men were brought even closer together,
for a time, by sharing the same woman. That was how Julia put it,
to herself: the plain and brutal fact.

It was Kenneth who pulled away in the end. Not from Julia:
from the situation. There came a time when it was possible for
Kenneth to say, as he stood smiling sardonically opposite Julia and
Tom, who were sitting like an old married couple on their side of
the fire: "You know that it is quite essential I should get married.
Things can't go on like this."

"But you can't marry without being in love," protested Julia; and
immediately checked herself with an annoyed laugh—she realized
that what she was protesting against was Kenneth going away from
her.

"You must see that I should."

"I don't like the idea," said Tom, as if it were his marriage that
was under discussion.

"Look at you and Tom," said Kenneth peaceably, but not without maliciousness. "A very satisfactory marriage. You weren't in love."

"Weren't we in love, Julia?" asked Tom, rather surprised.

"Actually, I was 'in love' with Kenneth," said Julia, with the sense that this was an unnecessary thing to say.

"You wanted a wife. Julia wanted a husband. All very sensible."

"One can be 'in love' once too often," said Julia, aiming this at Kenneth.

"Are you in love with Kenneth now?"

Julia did not answer; it annoyed her that Tom should ask it, after virtually handing her over to Kenneth. After a moment she remarked: "I suppose you are right. You really ought to get married." Then, thoughtfully: "I couldn't be married to you, Kenneth. You destroy me." The word sounded heightened and absurd. She hurried on: "I didn't know it was possible to be as happy as I have been with Tom." She smiled at her husband and reached over and took his hand: he returned the pressure gratefully.

"Ergo, I have to get married," said Kenneth caustically.

"But you say so yourself."

"I don't seem to be feeling what I ought to feel," said Tom at last, laughing in a bewildered way.

"That's what's wrong with the three of us," said Julia; then, feeling as if she were on the edge of that dangerous thing that might destroy them, she stopped and said: "Let's not talk about it. It doesn't do any good to talk about it."

That conversation had taken place a month ago. Kenneth had not mentioned getting married since; and Julia had secretly hoped he had shelved it. Not long since, during that trip to town, he had spent a day away from Tom and herself—and with whom? Tomorrow he was making the trip again, and for the first time for years, since they had been together, it was not the three of them, close in understanding, but Tom and Julia, with Kenneth deliberately excluding himself and putting up barriers.

Kenneth did not open his mouth the whole evening; though both Tom and Julia waited for him to break the silence. Julia did not read; she moiled over the facts of her life unhappily; and from time to time looked over at Tom, who smiled back affectionately, knowing she wanted this of him.

In spite of the fire, that now roared and crackled in the wall, Julia was cold. The thin frosty air of the high veld was of an electric dryness in the big bare room. The roof was crackling with cold; every time the tin snapped overhead it evoked the arching, myriad-starred, chilly night outside, and the drying, browning leaves, the tall waving grass that was now a dull parched colour. Julia's skin crinkled and stung with dryness.

Suddenly she said: "It won't do, Kenneth. You can't behave like this." She got up, and stood with her back to the fire, gazing levelly at them. She felt herself to be parching and withering within; she felt no heavier than a twig; the sap did not run in her veins. Because of Kenneth's betrayal, she was wounded in some place she could not name. She had no substance. That was how she felt.

What they saw was a tall, rather broad woman, big-framed, the bones of her face strongly supporting the flesh. Her eyes were blue and candid, now clouded by trouble, but still humorously troubled. She was forcing them to look at her; to make comparisons; she was challenging them. She was forcing them even to break the habit of loyalty which, blithely tender, continually recreative, blinds the eyes of lovers to change.

They saw this strong, ageing woman, the companion of their lives, standing there in front of them, still formed in the shape of beauty, for she was pleasant to look at, but with the light of beauty gone. They remembered her, perhaps, on that afternoon by the sea when they had first encountered her, or when she was newly arrived at the farm: young, vivid, a slender and rather boyish girl, with sleek, close-cropped hair and quick amused blue eyes.

Now, around the firm and bony face the soft hair fell in dressed waves, she wore a soft flowery dress: they saw a disquieting incongruity between this expression of femininity and what they knew her to be. They were irritated. To stand there, reminding them (when they did not want to be reminded) that she was facing the sorrowful abdication of middle age, and facing it alone, seemed to them irrelevant, even unfair.

Kenneth said resentfully: "Oh, Lord, you are very much a woman, after all, Julia. Must you make a scene?"

Her quick laugh was equally resentful. "Why shouldn't I make a scene. I feel entitled to it."

Kenneth said: "We all know there's got to be a change. Can't we go through with it without this sort of thing?"

"Surely," she said helplessly, "everything can't be changed without some sort of explanation . . ." She could not go on.

"Well, what sort of explanation do you want?"

She shrugged hopelessly. After a moment she said, as if continuing an old conversation: "Perhaps I should have had children, after all?"

"I always said so," remarked Tom mildly.

"You are nearly forty," said Kenneth practically.

"I wouldn't make a good mother," she said. "I couldn't compete with yours. I wouldn't have the courage to take it on, knowing I should fail by comparison with your so perfect mother." She was being sarcastic, but there were tears in her voice.

"Let's leave our mother out of it," said Tom coldly.

"Of course, we always leave everything important out of it."

Neither of them said anything; they were closed away from her in hostility. She went on: "I often wonder, why did you want me at all, Tom? You didn't really want children particularly."

"Yes, I did," said Tom, rather bewildered.

"Not enough to make me feel you cared one way or the other. Surely a woman is entitled to that, to feel that her children matter. I don't know what it is you took me into your life *for?*"

After a moment Kenneth said lightly, trying to restore the comfortable surface of flippancy: "I have always felt that we ought to have children."

Neither Tom nor Julia responded to this appeal. Julia took a candle from the mantelpiece, bent to light it at the fire, and said: "Well, I'm off to bed. The whole situation is beyond me."

"Very well then," said Kenneth. "If you must have it: I'm getting married soon."

"Obviously," said Julia drily.

"What did you want me to say?"

"Who is it?" Tom sounded so resentful that it changed the weight of the conversation: now it was Tom and Kenneth as antagonists.

"Well, she's a girl from England. She came out here a few months ago in this scheme for importing marriageable women to the Colonies . . . well, that's what the scheme amounts to."

"Yes, but the girl?" asked Julia, amused in spite of herself at Kenneth's invincible distaste at the idea of marrying.

"Well . . ." Kenneth hesitated, his dark bright eyes on Julia's face, his mouth already beginning to twist into dry amusement. "She's fair. She's pretty. She seems capable. She wants to be married . . . what more do I want?" That last phrase was savage. They had come to a dead end.

"I'm going to bed!" exclaimed Julia suddenly, the tears pouring down her face. "I can't bear this."

Neither of them said anything to prevent her leaving. When she had gone, Kenneth made an instinctive defensive movement to-

wards Tom. After a moment Tom said irritably, but command-
ingly: "It's absurd for you to get married when there's no need."

"Obviously there's a need," said Kenneth angrily. He rose, taking
another candle from the mantelpiece. As he left the room—and it
was clear that he left in order to forestall the scene Tom was about
to make—he said: "I want to have children before I get an old
man. It seems to be the only thing left."

When Tom went into the bedroom, Julia was lying dry-eyed on
the pillow, waiting for him. She was waiting for him to comfort her
into security of feeling. He had never failed her. When he was in
bed, she found herself comforting him: it gave her such a perverse,
topsy-turvy feeling she could not sleep.

Soon after breakfast Kenneth left for town. He was dressed
smartly: normally he did not care how he looked, and his clothes
seemed to have been put on in the spirit of one picking up tools for
a job. All three acknowledged his appearance with small, con-
stricted smiles; and Kenneth reddened as he got into the car. "I
might not be back tonight," he called back, driving away without
looking back.

Tom and Julia watched the big car nose its way through the
trees, and turned back to face each other. "Like to come down the
lands with me?" he asked. "Yes, I would," she accepted gratefully.
Then she saw, and was thrown back on to herself by the knowledge
of it, that he was asking her, not for her comfort, but for his own.

It was a windy, sunlit morning, and very cold; winter had taken
possession of the veld overnight.

The house was built on a slight ridge, with the country falling
away on either side. The landscape was dulling for the dry season
into olive green and thin yellows; there was that extraordinary contrast of limpid sparkling skies, with sunshine pouring down like a
volatile spirit, and dry cold parching the face and hands that made
Julia uneasy in winter. It was as if the dryness tightened the cold
into rigid fetters on her, so that a perpetual inner shivering had to
be suppressed. She walked beside Tom over the fields with hunched
shoulders and arms crossed tight over her chest. Yet she was not
cold, not in the physical sense. Around the house the mealie fields,
now a gentle silvery-gold colour, swept into runnels of light as the
wind passed over them, and there was a dry tinkling of parched
leaves moving together, like rat's feet over grass. Tom did not
speak; but his face was heavy and furrowed. When she took his
hand he responded, but listlessly. She wanted him to turn to her, to
say: "Now he's going to make something of his own, you must

come to me, and we'll build up again." She wanted him to claim her, heal her, make her whole. But he was uneasy and restless; and she said at last diffidently: "Why should you mind so much. It ought to be me who's unhappy."

"Don't you?" he asked, sounding like a person angry at dishonesty.

"Yes, of course," she said; and tried to find the words to say that if only he could take her gently into his own security, as he had years ago, things would be right for them.

But that security no longer existed in him.

All that day they hardly spoke, not because of animosity between them, but because of a deep, sad helplessness. They could not help each other.

That night Kenneth did not come back from town. Next day Tom went off by himself to the second farm, leaving her with a gentle apologetic look, as if to say: "Leave me alone, I can't help it."

Kenneth telephoned in the middle of the morning from town. His voice was offhand; it was also subtly defensive. That small voice coming from such a distance down the wires, conjured up such a clear vision of Kenneth himself, that she smiled tenderly.

"Well?" she asked warily.

"I'll be back sometime. I don't know when."

"That means it's definite?"

"I think so." A pause. Then the voice dropped into dry humour. "She's such a nice girl that things take a long time, don't you know." Julia laughed. Quickly he added: "But she really is, you know, Julia. She's awfully nice."

"Well, you must do as you think," she said cautiously.

"How's Tom?" he asked.

"I suddenly don't know anything about Tom," she answered.

There was such a long silence that she clicked the telephone.

"I'm still here," said Kenneth. "I was trying to think of the right things to say."

"Has it come to the point where we have to think of the right things?"

"Looks like it, doesn't it?"

"Goodbye," she said quickly, putting down the receiver. "Let me know when you're coming and I'll get your things ready."

As usual in the mornings, she passed on a tour of inspection from room to room of the big bare house, where the windows stood open all day, showing blocks of blue crystal round the walls, or views of veld, as if the building, the very bricks and iron, were compounded with sky and landscape to form a new kind of home. When she had made her formal inspection, and found everything cleaned and polished and arranged, she went to the kitchen. Here she ordered the meals, and discussed the state of the pantry with her cook. Then she went back to the verandah; at this hour she would normally read, or sew, till lunchtime.

The thought came into her mind, with a destroying force, that if she were not in the house, Tom would hardly notice it, from a physical point of view: the servants would create comfort without her. She suppressed an impulse to go into the kitchen and cook, or tidy a cupboard, to find some work for the hands: that was not what she sought, a temporary salve for feeling useless. She took her large light straw hat from the nail in the bare, stone-floored passage, and went out into the garden. As she did not care for gardening, the ground about the house was arranged with groups of shrubs, so that there would be patches of blossom at any time of the year. The garden boy kept the lawns fresh and green. Over the vivid emerald grass spread the flowers of dryness, the poinsettias, loose scattering shapes of bright scarlet, creamy pink, light yellow. On the fine, shiny-brown stems fluttered light green leaves. In a swift gusty wind the quickly moving blossoms and leaves danced and shook; they seemed to her the very essence of the time of year, the essence of dry cold, of light thin sunshine, of high cold-blue skies.

She passed quietly down the path through the lawns and flowers to the farm road, and turned to look back at the house. From the outside it appeared such a large, assertive, barn of a place, with its areas of shiny tin roof, the hard pink of the walls, the glinting angled shapes of the windows. Although shrubs grew sparsely around it, and it was shaded by a thick clump of trees, it looked naked, raw, crude. "That is my home," said Julia to herself, testing the word. She rejected it. In that house she had lived ten years—more. She turned away from it, walking lightly through the sifting pink dust of the roads like a stranger. There had always been times when Africa rejected her, when she felt like a critical ghost. This was one of those times. Through the known and loved scenes of the veld she saw Buenos Aires, Rome, Cape Town—a dozen cities, large and small, merging and mingling as the country rose and fell about her. Perhaps it is not good for human beings to live in so many places? But it was not that. She was suffering from an unfamiliar dryness of the senses, an unlocated, unfocussed ache that, if she were young, would have formed itself about a person or place, but now remained locked within her. "What am I?" she kept saying to herself as she walked through the veld, in the moving patch of shade that fell from the large drooping hat. On either side the long grass moved and whispered sibilantly; the doves throbbed gently from the trees; the sky was a flower-blue arch over her—it was, as they say, a lovely morning.

She passed like a revenant along the edges of the mealie fields, watching the working gangs of natives; at the well she paused to see the women with their groups of naked children; at the cattle sheds she leaned to touch the wet noses of the thrusting soft-headed calves which butted and pushed at her legs. There she stayed for some time, finding comfort in these young creatures. She understood at last that it was nearly lunchtime. She must go home, and preside at the lunch-table for Tom, in case he should decide to return. She left the calves thinking: Perhaps I ought to have children? She knew perfectly well that she would not.

The road back to the house wound along the high hogs's-back between two vleis that fell away on either side. She walked slowly, trying to recover that soft wonder she had felt when she first arrived on the farm and learned how living in cities had cheated her of the knowledge of the shapes of sky and land. Above her, in the great bright bell of blue sky, the wind currents were marked by swirls of cloud, the backwaters of the air by heavy sculptured piles of sluggish white. Around her the skeleton of rock showed under the thin covering of living soil. The trees thickened with the fall or rise of the ground, with the running of underground rivers; the grass—the long blond hair of the grass—struggled always to heal and hold whatever wounds were made by hoof of beast or thoughtlessness of man. The sky, the land, the swirling air, closed around her in an exchange of water and heat, and the deep multitudinous murmuring of living substance sounded like a humming in her blood. She listened, half-passively, half-rebelliously, and asked: "What do I contribute to all this?"

That afternoon she walked again, for hours; and throughout the following day; returning to the house punctually for meals, and greeting Tom across the distance that puts itself between people who try to support themselves with the mental knowledge of a country, and those who work in it. Once Tom said, with tired concern, looking at her equally tired face: "Julia, I didn't know you would mind so much. I suppose it was conceit. I always thought I came first."

"You do," she said quickly, "believe me, you do."

She went to him, so that he could put his arms about her. He did, and there was no warmth in it for either of them. "We'll come right again," he promised her. But it was as though he listened to the sound of his own voice for a message of assurance.

Kenneth came back unexpectedly on the fourth evening. He was alone; and he appeared purposeful and decided. During dinner no one spoke much. After dinner, in the bare, gaunt, firelit room, the three waited for someone to speak.

At last Julia said: "Well, Kenneth?"

"We are getting married next month."

"Where?"

"In Church," he said. He smiled constrictedly. "She wants a proper wedding. I don't mind, if she likes it." Kenneth's attitude was altogether brisk, down-to-earth and hard. At the same time he looked at Julia and Tom uneasily: he hated his position.

"How old is she?" asked Julia.

"A baby. Twenty-three."

This shocked Julia. "Kenneth, you can't do that."

"Why not?"

Julia could not really see why not.

"Has she money of her own?" asked Tom practically, causing the other two to look at him in surprise. "After all," he said quickly, "we must know about her, before she comes?"

"Of course she hasn't," said Kenneth coldly. "She wouldn't be coming out to the Colonies on a subsidized scheme for importing marriageable women, would she?"

Tom grimaced. "You two are brutal," he remarked.

Kenneth and Julia glanced at each other; it was like a shrug. "I didn't mention money in the first place," he pointed out. "You did. Anyway, what's wrong with it? If I were a surplus woman in England I should certainly emigrate to find a husband. It's the only sensible thing to do."

"What is she living on now?" asked Julia.

"She has a job in an office. Some such nonsense." Kenneth dismissed this. "Anyway, why talk about money? Surely we have enough?"

"How much have we got?" asked Julia, who was always rather vague about money.

"A hell of a lot," said Tom, laughing. "The last three years we've made thousands."

"How many thousands?"

"Difficult to say, there's so much going back into the farms. Fifty thousand perhaps. We'll make a lot more this year."

Julia smiled. The words "fifty thousand" could not be made to come real in her mind. She thought of how she had earned her living for years, in offices, budgeting for everything she spent. "I suppose we could be described as rich?" she asked wonderingly at last, trying to relate this fact to the life she lived, to the country around them, to their future.

"I suppose we could," agreed Tom, snorting with amused laughter. He liked it when Julia made it possible for him to think of her as helpless. "Most of the credit goes to Kenneth," he added. "All the work he did during the war is reaping dividends now."

Julia looked at him; then sardonically at Kenneth, who was shifting uncomfortably in his chair. Tom persisted with good-natured sarcasm, getting his own back for Kenneth's gibes over the war: "This is getting quite a show-place; I got a letter from the Government asking me if they could bring a collection of distinguished visitors from Home to see it, next week. You'll have to act as hostess. They're coming to see Kenneth's war effort." He laughed. "It's also been very profitable."

Kenneth shut his mouth hard; and kept his temper. "We are discussing my future wife," he said coldly.

"So we are," said Julia.

"Well, let's finish with the thing. I shall give the girl a thumping, expensive honeymoon in the most glossy and awful hotels in the sub-continent," continued Kenneth grimly. "She'll love it."

"Why shouldn't she?" asked Julia. "I should have loved it too, at her age."

"I didn't say she shouldn't."

"And then?" asked Julia again. She was wanting to hear what sort of plans Kenneth had for another farm. He looked at her blankly. "And then what?"

"Where will you go?"

"Go?"

It came to her that he did not intend to leave the farm. This was such a shock she could not speak. She collected herself at last, and said slowly: "Kenneth, surely you don't intend to live here?"

"Why not?" he asked quickly, very much on the defensive.

The atmosphere had tightened so that Julia saw, in looking from one man to the other, that this was the real crisis of the business, something she had not expected, but which they had both been waiting, consciously or unconsciously, for her to approach.

"Good God," she said slowly, in rising anger. "Good God." She looked at Tom, who at once averted his eyes. She saw that Tom was longing uneasily for her to make it possible for Kenneth to stay.

She understood at last that, if it had occurred to either of them that another woman could not live here, it was a knowledge neither of them were prepared to face. She looked at these two men and hated them, for the way they took their women into their lives, without changing a thought or a habit to meet them.

She got up, and walked away from them slowly, standing with her back to them, gazing out of the window at the heavily-starred winter's night. She said: "Kenneth, you are marrying this girl because you intend to have a family. You don't care tuppence for her, really."

"I've got to be very fond of her," protested Kenneth.

"At bottom, you don't care tuppence."

He did not reply. "You are going to bring her here to me. She'll feel with her instinct if not with her head that she's being made use of. And you bring her here to me." It seemed to her that she had made her sense of outrage clear enough. She turned to face them.

"The prospect of bringing her 'to you' doesn't seem to me as shocking as apparently it does to you," said Kenneth drily.

"Can't you see?" she said desperately. "She couldn't compete . . ."

"You flatter yourself," said Kenneth briskly.

"Oh, I don't mean that. I mean we've been together for so long. There's nothing we don't know about each other. Have I got to say it . . ."

"No," said Kenneth quietly. "Much better not."

Through all this Tom, that large, fair, comfortable man, leaned back in his chair, looking from his wife to his half-brother with the air of one suddenly transported to a foreign country.

He said stubbornly: "I don't see why you shouldn't adjust yourself, Julia. After all, both Kenneth and I have had to adjust ourselves to . . ."

"Quite," said Kenneth quickly, "quite."

She turned on Kenneth furiously. "Why do you always cut the conversation short? Why shouldn't we talk about it? It's what's real, isn't it, for all of us?"

"No point talking about it," said Kenneth, with a sullen look.

"No," she said coldly. "No point." She turned away from them, fighting back tears. "At bottom neither of you really cared tuppence. That's what it is." At the moment this seemed to her true.

"What do you mean by 'really caring'?" asked Kenneth.

Julia turned slowly from the window, jerking the light summer curtains across the stars. "I mean, we don't care. We just don't care."

"I don't know what you are talking about," said Tom, sounding bewildered and angry. "Haven't you been happy with me? Is that what you are saying, Julia?"

At this both Kenneth and Julia began laughing with an irresistible and painful laughter.

"Of course I've been happy with you," she said flatly, at last.

"Well then?" asked Tom.

"I don't know why I was happy then and why I'm unhappy now?"

"Let's say you're jealous," said Kenneth briskly.

"But I don't think I am."

"Of course you are."

"Very well then, I am. That's not the point, though. What are we going to do to the girl?" she asked suddenly, her feeling finding expression.

"I shall make her a good husband," said Kenneth. The three of them looked at each other, with raised brows, with humorous, tightened lips.

"Very well then," amended Kenneth. "But she'll have plenty of nice children. She'll have you for company, Julia, a nice intelligent woman. And she'll have plenty of money and pretty clothes and all that sort of nonsense, if she wants them."

There was a silence so long it seemed that nothing could break it.

Julia said slowly and painfully: "I think it is terrible we shouldn't be able to explain what we feel or what we are."

"I wish you'd stop trying to," said Kenneth. "I find it unpleasant. And quite useless."

Tom said: "As for me, I would be most grateful if you'd try to explain what you are feeling, Julia. I haven't an idea."

Julia stood up with her back to the fire and began gropingly: "Look at the way we are. I mean, what do we add up to? What are we doing here, in the first place?"

"Doing where?" asked Tom kindly.

"Here, in Africa, in this district, on this land."

"Ohhh," groaned Tom humorously.

"Oh *Lord*, Julia," protested Kenneth impatiently.

"I feel as if we shouldn't be here."

"Where should we be, then?"

"We've as much right as anybody else."

"I suppose so." Julia dismissed it. It was not her point, after all, it seemed. She said slowly: "I suppose there are comparatively very few people in the world as secure and as rich as we are."

"It takes a couple of bad seasons or a change in the international set-up," said Kenneth. "We could get poor as easily as we've got rich. If you want to call it easy. We've worked hard enough, Tom and I."

"So do many other people. In the meantime we've all the money we want. Why do we never talk about money, never think about it? It's what we are."

"Speak for yourself, Julia," said Tom. "Kenneth and I spend all our days thinking and talking about nothing else. How else do you suppose we've got rich?"

"How to make it. Not what it all adds up to."

The two men did not reply; they looked at each other with resignation. Kenneth lit a cigarette, Tom a pipe.

"I've been getting a feeling of money the last few days. Perhaps not so much money as . . ." She stopped. "I can't say what I feel. It's no use. What do our lives add up to? That's what I want to know."

"Why do you expect us to tell you?" asked Kenneth curiously at last.

This was a new note. Julia looked at him, puzzled. "I don't know," she said at last. Then, very drily: "I suppose I should be prepared to take the consequences for marrying the pair of you." The men laughed uneasily though with relief that the worst seemed to be over. "If I left this place tomorrow," she said sadly, "you simply wouldn't miss me."

"Ah, you love Kenneth," groaned Tom suddenly. The groan was so sudden, coming just as the flippant note had been struck, and successfully, that Julia could not bear it. She continued quietly, lightly, to wipe away the naked pain of Tom's voice: "No, I don't. I wish you wouldn't talk about love."

"That's what all this is about," said Kenneth. "Love."

Julia looked at him scornfully. She said: "What sort of people are we? Let's use bare words for bare facts, just for once."

"Must you?" breathed Kenneth.

"Yes, I must. The fact is that I have been a sort of high-class concubine for the two of you . . ." She stopped at once. Even the beginning of the tirade sounded absurd in her own ears.

"I hope that statement has cleared your mind for you," said Kenneth ironically.

"No, it hasn't. I didn't expect it would." But now Julia was fight-

ing hard against that no-man's-land of feeling in which she had
been living for so long, that under-sea territory where one thing
confuses with another, where it is so easy to drift at ease, according
to the pull of the tides.

"I should have had children," she said at last, quietly. "That's
where we went wrong, Tom. It was children we needed."

"Ah," said Kenneth from his chair, suddenly deeply sincere,
"now you are talking sense."

"Well," said Tom, "there's nothing to stop us."

"I'm too old."

"Other women of forty have children."

"I'm too—tired. It seems to me, to have children, one
needs . . ." She stopped.

"What does one need?" asked Tom.

Julia's eyes met Kenneth's; they exchanged deep, ironic, patient
understanding.

"Thank God you didn't marry me," he said suddenly. "You were
quite right. Tom's the man for you. In a marriage it's necessary for
one side to be strong enough to create the illusion."

"What illusion?" asked Tom petulantly.

"Necessity," said Kenneth simply.

"Is that the office this girl is going to perform for you?" asked
Tom.

"Precisely. She loves me, God help her. She really does, you
know . . ." Kenneth looked at them in a manner of inviting them
to share his surprise at this fact. "And she wants children. She
knows why she wants them. She'll make me know it too, bless her.
Most of the time," he could not prevent himself adding.

Now it seemed impossible to go on. They remained silent, each
face expressing tired and bewildered unhappiness. Julia stood
against the mantelpiece, feeling the warmth of the fire running
over her body, but not reaching the chill within.

Kenneth recovered first. He got up and said: "Bed, bed for all of
us. This doesn't help. We mustn't talk. We must get on, dealing
with the next thing." He said good night, and went to the door.
There he turned, looked clear and full at Julia with his black, alert,
shrewd eyes, and remarked: "You must be nice to that girl, Julia."

"You know very well I can be 'nice' to her, but I won't be 'nice' for
her. You are deliberately submitting her to it. You won't even move
two miles away on to the next farm. You won't even take that much
trouble to make her happy. Remember that."

Kenneth flushed, said hastily: "Well, I didn't say I wouldn't go to the other farm," and went out. Julia knew that it would take a lot of unhappiness for the four of them before he would consent to move himself. He thought of this house as his home; and he could not bear to leave Tom, even now.

"Come here," said Tom gently, when Kenneth had left the room. She went to him, and slipped down beside him into his chair. "Do you find me stupid?" he asked.

"Not stupid."

"What then?"

She held him close. "Put your arms round me."

He held her; but she did not feel supported: the arms were as light as wind about her, and as unsure.

In the middle of the night she rose from her bed, slipped on her gown and went along the winding passages to Kenneth's bedroom, which was at the other end of the house.

It was filled with the brightness of moonlight. Kenneth was sitting up against his pillows; he was awake; she could see the light glinting on his eyes.

She sat herself down on the foot of his bed.

"Well, Julia? It's no good coming to me, you know."

She did not reply. The confusing dimness of the moon, which hung immediately outside the window, troubled her. She held a match to the candle, and watched a warm yellow glow fill the room, so that the moon retreated and became a small hard bright coin high among the stars.

She saw on the dressing-table a new framed photograph.

"If one acquires a wife," she said sarcastically, "one of course acquires a photo to put on one's dressing-table." She went over and picked it up and returned to the bed with it. Kenneth watched her, alertly.

Slowly Julia's face spread into a compassionate smile.

"What's the matter?" asked Kenneth quickly.

She was not twenty-three, Julia could see that. She was well over thirty. It was a pretty enough face, very English, with flat broad planes and small features. Fair neatly-waved hair fell away regularly from the forehead.

There was anxiety in those too-serious eyes; the mouth smiled carefully in a prepared sweetness for the photographer; the cheeks were thin. Turning the photograph to the light Julia could see how the neck was creased and furrowed. No, she was by no means a girl. She glanced at Kenneth; and was filled slowly by a sweet irrational tenderness for him, a delicious irresponsible gaiety.

"Why," she said, "you're in love, after all, Kenneth."

"Whoever said I wasn't?" he grinned at her, lying watchfully back in his bed and puffing at his cigarette.

She grinned back affectionately, still lifted on a wave of delight; then she turned, and felt it ebb as she looked down at the photograph, mentally greeting this other tired woman, coming to the great rich farm, like the poor girl in the fairy story.

"What are you amused at?" asked Kenneth cautiously.

"I was thinking of you as a refuge," she explained drily.

"I'm quite prepared to be."

"You'd never be a refuge for anyone."

"Not for you. But you forget she's younger." He laughed: "She'll be less critical."

She smiled, without replying, looking at the pictured face. It was such a humourless, earnest, sincere face, the eyes so serious, so searching.

Julia sighed. "I'm terribly tired," she said to Kenneth, turning back to him.

"I know you are. So am I. That's why I'm marrying."

Julia had a clear mental picture of this Englishwoman, who was soon coming to the farm. For a moment she allowed herself to picture her in various situations, arriving with nervous tact, hiding her longing for a home of her own, hoping not to find Julia an enemy. She would find not strife, or hostility, or scenes—none of the situations which she might be prepared to face. She would find three people who knew each other so well that for the most part they found it hardly necessary to speak. She would find indifference to everything she really was, a prepared, deliberate kindness. She would be like a latecomer to a party, entering a room where everyone is already cemented by hours of warmth and intimacy. She would be helpless against Kenneth's need for her to be something she could not be: a young woman, with the spiritual vitality to heal him.

Looking at the pretty girl in the frame which she held between her palms, the girl under whose surface prettiness Julia could see the anxious, haunted woman, the knowledge came to her of what word it was she sought: it was as though those carefully smiling lips formed themselves into that word. "Do you know what we are?" she asked Kenneth.

"Not a notion," he replied jauntily.

Julia accepted the word evil from that humourless, homeless

girl. Twice in her life it had confronted her; this time she took it gratefully. After all, none other had been offered.

"I know what evil is," she said to Kenneth.

"How nice for you," he returned impatiently. Then he added: "I suppose, like most women who have lived their own lives, whatever that might mean, you are now beginning to develop an exaggerated conscience. If so, we shall both find you very tedious."

"Is that what I'm doing?" she asked, considering it. "I don't think so."

He looked at her soberly. "Go to bed, my dear. Do stop fussing. Are you prepared to do anything about it? You aren't, are you? Then stop making us all miserable over impossibilities. We have a pleasant enough life, taking it for what it is. It's not much fun being the fag-end of something, but even that has its compensations."

Julia listened, smiling, to her own voice speaking. "You put it admirably," she said, as she went out of the room.

A Home for the Highland Cattle

THESE days, when people emigrate, it is not so much in search of sunshine, or food, or even servants. It is fairly safe to say that the family bound for Australia, or wherever it may be, has in its mind a vision of a nice house, or a flat, with maybe a bit of garden. I don't know how things were a hundred or fifty years ago. It seems, from books, that the colonizers and adventurers went sailing off to a new fine life, a new country, opportunities, and so forth. Now all they want is a roof over their heads.

An interesting thing, this: how is it that otherwise reasonable people come to believe that this same roof, that practically vanishing commodity, is freely obtainable just by packing up and going to another country? After all, headlines like World Housing Shortage are common to the point of tedium; and there is not a brochure or pamphlet issued by immigration departments that does not say (though probably in small print, throwing it away, as it were) that it is undesirable to leave home, without first making sure of a place to live.

Marina Giles left England with her husband in just this frame of mind. They had been living where they could, sharing flats and baths, and kitchens, for some years. If someone remarked enviously: "They say that in Africa the sky is always blue," she was likely to reply absent-mindedly: "Yes, and won't it be nice to have a proper house after all these years."

They arrived in Southern Rhodesia, and there was a choice of an immigrants' camp, consisting of mud huts with a communal water supply, or a hotel; and they chose the hotel, being what are known as people of means. That is to say, they had a few hundred pounds, with which they had intended to buy a house as soon as they arrived. It was quite possible to buy a house, just as it is in England, provided one gives up all idea of buying a home one likes, and at a reasonable price. For years Marina had been inspecting houses. They fell into two groups, those she liked, and those she could afford. Now Marina was a romantic, she had not yet fallen into that passive state of mind which accepts (as nine-tenths of the population do) that one should find a corner to live, anywhere, and then arrange one's whole life around it, schooling for one's children, one's place of work, and so on. And since she refused to accept it, she had been living in extreme discomfort, exclaiming: "Why should we spend all the capital we are ever likely to have tying ourselves down to a place we detest!" Nothing could be more reasonable, on the face of it.

But she had not expected to cross an ocean, enter a new and indubitably romantic-sounding country, and find herself in exactly the same position.

The city, seen from the air, is half-buried in trees. Sixty years ago, this was all bare veld; and even now it appears not as if the veld encloses an area of buildings and streets, but rather as if the houses have forced themselves up, under and among the trees. Flying low over it, one sees greenness, growth, then the white flash of a high building, the fragment of a street that has no beginning or end, for it emerges from trees, and is at once reabsorbed by them. And yet it is a large town, spreading wide and scattered, for here there is no problem of space: pressure scatters people outwards, it does not force them perpendicularly. Driving through it from suburb to suburb, is perhaps fifteen miles—some of the important cities of the world are not much less; but if one asks a person who lives there what the population is, he will say ten thousand, which is very little. Why do so small a number of people need so large a space? The inhabitant will probably shrug, for he has never wondered. The truth is that there are not ten thousand, but more likely 150,000, but the others are black, which means that they are not considered. The blacks do not so much *live* here, as squeeze themselves in as they can—all this is very confusing for the newcomer, and it takes quite a time to adjust oneself.

Perhaps every city has one particular thing by which it is known, something which sums it up, both for the people who live in it, and those who have never known it, save in books or legend. Three hundred miles south, for instance, old Lobengula's kraal had the Big Tree. Under its branches sat the betrayed, sorrowful, magnificent King in his rolls of black fat and beads and gauds, watching his doom approach in the white people's advance from the south, and dispensing life and death according to known and honoured customs. That was only sixty years ago . . .

This town has the *Kopje*. When the Pioneers were sent north, they were told to trek on till they reached a large and noble mountain they could not possibly mistake; and there they must stop and build their city. Twenty miles too soon, due to some confusion of mind, or perhaps to understandable exhaustion, they stopped near a small and less shapely hill. This had rankled ever since. Each year, when the ceremonies are held to honour those pioneers, and the vision of Rhodes who sent them forth, the thought creeps in that this is not really what the Founder intended . . . Standing there, at the foot of that *kopje*, the speech-makers say: Sixty years, look what we have accomplished in sixty years. And in the minds of the listeners springs a vision of that city we all dream of, that planned and shapely city without stain or slum—the city that could in fact have been created in those sixty years.

The town spread from the foot of this hill. Around it are the slums, the narrow and crooked streets where the coloured people eke out their short swarming lives among decaying brick and tin. Five minutes walk to one side, and the street peters out in long, soiled grass, above which a power chimney pours black smoke, and where an old petrol tin lies in a gulley, so that a diving hawk swerves away and up, squawking, scared out of his nature by a flash of sunlight. Ten minutes the other way is the business centre, the dazzling white blocks of concrete, modern buildings like modern buildings the world over. Here are the imported clothes, the glass windows full of cars from America, the neon lights, the counters full of pamphlets advertising flights Home—wherever one's home might be. A few blocks further on, and the business part of the town is left behind. This was once the smart area. People who have grown with the city will drive through here on a Sunday afternoon, and, looking at the bungalows raised on their foundations and ornamented with iron scrollwork, will say: In 1910 there was nothing beyond this house but bare veld.

Now, however, there are more houses, small and ugly houses, until all at once we are in the 'thirties, with tall houses eight to a block, like very big soldiers standing to attention in a small space.

The verandahs have gone. Tiny balconies project like eyelids, the roofs are like bowler hats, rimless. Exposed to the blistering sun, these houses crowd together without invitation to shade or coolness, for they were not planned for this climate, and until the trees grow, and the creepers spread, they are extremely uncomfortable. (Though, of course, very smart.) Beyond these? The veld again, wastes of grass clotted with the dung of humans and animals, a vlei that is crossed and criss-crossed by innumerable footpaths where the Africans walk in the afternoon from suburb to suburb, stopping to snatch a mouthful of water in cupped palms from pot-holes filmed with iridescent oil, for safety against mosquitoes.

Over the vlei (which is rapidly being invaded by building, so that soon there will be no open spaces left) is a new suburb. Now, this is something quite different. Where the houses, only twenty min-utes' walk away, stood eight to a block, now there are twenty tiny, flimsy little houses, and the men who planned them had in mind the cheap houses along the ribbon roads of England. Small patches of roofed cement, with room, perhaps, for a couple of chairs, call themselves verandahs. There is a hall a couple of yards square—for otherwise where should one hang one's hat? Each little house is divided into rooms so small that there is no space to move from one wall to the other without circling a table or stumbling over a chair. And white walls, glaring white walls, so that one's eyes turn in relief to the trees.

The trees—these houses are intolerable unless foliage softens and hides them. Any new owner, moving in, says wistfully: It won't be so bad when the shrubs grow up. And they grow very quickly. It is an extraordinary thing that this town, which must be one of the most graceless and inconvenient in existence, consid-ered simply as an association of streets and buildings, is so beauti-ful that no one fails to fall in love with it at first sight. Every street is lined and double-lined with trees, every house screened with bril-liant growth. It is a city of gardens.

Marina was at first enchanted. Then her mood changed. For the only houses they could afford were in those mass-produced sub-urbs, that were spreading like measles as fast as materials could be imported to build them. She said to Philip: "In England, we did not buy a house because we did not want to live in a suburb. We uproot ourselves, come to a reputedly exotic and wild country, and the only place we can afford to live is another suburb. I'd rather be dead."

Philip listened. He was not as upset as she was. They were rather different. Marina was that liberally-minded person produced so plentifully in England during the 'thirties, while Philip was a scientist, and put his faith in techniques, rather than in the inherent decency of human beings. He was, it is true, in his own way an idealist, for he had come to this continent in a mood of fine optimism. England, it seemed to him, did not offer opportunities to young men equipped, as he was, with enthusiasm and so much training. Things would be different overseas. All that was necessary was a go-ahead Government prepared to vote sufficient money to Science—this was just common sense. (Clearly, a new country was likely to have more common sense than an old one.) He was prepared to make gardens flourish where deserts had been. Africa appeared to him eminently suitable for this treatment; and the more he saw of it, those first few weeks, the more enthusiastic he became.

But he soon came to understand that in the evenings, when he propounded these ideas to Marina, her mind was elsewhere. It seemed to him bad luck that they should be in this hotel, which was uncomfortable, with bad food, and packed by fellow-immigrants all desperately searching for that legendary roof. But a house would turn up sooner or later—he had been convinced of this for years. He would not have objected to buying one of those suburban houses. He did not like them, certainly, but he knew quite well that it was not the house, as such, that Marina revolted against. Ah, this feeling we all have about the suburbs! How we dislike the thought of being just like the fellow next door! Bad luck, when the whole world rapidly fills with suburbs, for what is a British Colony but a sort of highly-flavoured suburb to England itself? Somewhere in the back of Marina's mind has been a vision of herself and Philip living in a group of amiable people, pleasantly interested in the arts, who read the *New Statesman* week by week, and held that discreditable phenomena like the colour bar and the black-white struggle could be solved by sufficient goodwill . . . a delightful picture.

Temporarily Philip turned his mind from thoughts of blossoming deserts, and so on, and tried another approach. Perhaps they could buy a house through one of the Schemes for Immigrants? He would return from this Housing Board or that, and say in a worried voice: "There isn't a hope unless one has three children." At this, Marina was likely to become depressed; for she still held the old-fashioned view that before one has children, one should have a house to put them in.

"It's all very well for you," said Marina. "As far as I can see, you'll be spending half your time gallivanting in your lorry from one end of the country to the other, visiting native reserves, and having a lovely time. I don't *mind,* but I have to make some sort of life for myself while you do it." Philip looked rather guilty; for in fact he was away three or four days a week, on trips with fellow-experts, and Marina would be very often left alone.

"Perhaps we could find somewhere temporary, while we wait for a house to turn up?" he suggested.

This offered itself quite soon. Philip heard from a man he met casually that there was a flat available for three months, but he wouldn't swear to it, because it was only an overheard remark at a sundowner party—Philip followed the trail, clinched the deal, and returned to Marina. "It's only for three months," he comforted her.

138 Cecil John Rhodes Vista was in that part of the town built before the sudden expansion in the 'thirties. These were all old houses, unfashionable, built to no important recipe, but according to the whims of the first owners. On one side of 138 was a house whose roof curved down, Chinese fashion, built on a platform for protection against ants, with wooden steps. Its walls were of wood, and it was possible to hear feet tramping over the wooden floors even in the street outside. The other neighbour was a house whose walls were invisible under a mass of golden shower—thick yellow clusters, like smokey honey, dripped from roof to ground. The houses opposite were hidden by massed shrubs.

From the street, all but the roof of 138 was screened by a tall and straggling hedge. The sidewalks were dusty grass, scattered with faggots of dogs' dirt, so that one had to walk carefully. Outside the gate was a great clump of bamboo reaching high into the sky, and all the year round weaver-birds' nests, like woven-grass cricket balls, dangled there bouncing and swaying in the wind. Near it reached the angled brown sticks of the frangipani, breaking into white and a creamy pink, as if a young coloured girl held armfuls of blossom. The street itself was double-lined with trees, first jacaranda, fine green lace against the blue sky, and behind heavy dark masses of the cedrilatoona. All the way down the street were bursts of colour, a drape of purple bougainvillaea, the sparse scarlet flowers of the hibiscus. It was very beautiful, very peaceful.

Once inside the unkempt hedge, 138 was exposed as a shallow brick building, tin-roofed, like an elongated barn, that occupied the centre of two building stands, leaving plenty of space for front and back yards. It had a history. Some twenty years back, some enterprising businessman had built the place, ignoring every known rule of hygiene, in the interests of economy. By the time the local authorities had come to notice its unfitness to exist, the roof was on. There followed a series of court cases. An exhausted judge had finally remarked that there was a housing shortage; and on this basis the place was allowed to remain.

It was really eight semi-detached houses, stuck together in such a way that, standing before the front door of any one, it was possible to see clear through the two rooms which composed each, to the back yard, where washing flapped over the woodpile. A verandah enclosed the front of the building: eight short flights of steps, eight front doors, eight windows—but these windows illuminated the front rooms only. The back room opened into a porch that was screened in by dull green mosquito gauze; and in this way the architect had achieved the really remarkable feat of producing, in a country continually drenched by sunlight, rooms in which it was necessary to have the lights burning all day.

The back yard, a space of bare dust enclosed by parallel hibiscus hedges, was a triumph of individualism over communal living. Eight separate woodpiles, eight clothes-lines, eight short paths edged with brick leading to the eight lavatories that were built side by side like segments of chocolate, behind an enclosing tin screen: the locks (and therefore the keys) were identical, for the sake of cheapness, a system which guaranteed strife among the inhabitants. On either side of the lavatories were two rooms, built as a unit. In these four rooms lived eight native servants. At least, officially there were eight, in practice far more.

When Marina, a woman who took her responsibilities seriously, as has been indicated, looked inside the room which her servant shared with the servant from next door, she exclaimed helplessly: "Dear me, how awful!" The room was very small. The brick walls were unplastered, the tin of the roof bare, focussing the sun's intensity inwards all day, so that even while she stood on the threshold, she began to feel a little faint, because of the enclosed heat. The floor was cement, and the blankets that served as beds lay directly on it. No cupboards or shelves: these were substituted by a string stretching from corner to corner. Two small, high windows, whose glass was cracked and pasted with paper. On the walls were pictures of the English royal family, torn out of illustrated magazines, and of various female film stars, mostly unclothed.

"Dear me," said Marina again, vaguely. She was feeling very guilty, because of this squalor. She came out of the room with relief, wiping the sweat from her face, and looked around the yard. Seen from the back, 138 Cecil John Rhodes Vista was undeniably picturesque. The yard, enclosed by low, scarlet-flowering hibiscus hedges, was of dull red earth; the piles of grey wood were each surrounded by a patch of scattered chips, yellow, orange, white. The colourful washing lines swung and danced. The servants, in their crisp white, leaned on their axes, or gossiped. There was a little black nurse-girl seated on one of the logs, under a big tree, with a white child in her arms. A delightful scene; it would have done as it was for the opening number of a musical comedy. Marina turned her back on it; and with her stern reformer's eye looked again at the end of the yard. In the spaces between the lavatories and the servants' rooms stood eight rubbish cans, each covered by its cloud of flies, and exuding a stale, sour smell. She walked through them into the sanitary lane. Now, if one drives down the streets of such a city, one sees the trees, the gardens, the flowering hedges; the streets form neat squares. Squares (one might suppose) filled with blossoms and greenness, in which the houses are charmingly arranged. But each block is divided down the middle by a sanitary lane, a dust lane, which is lined by rubbish cans, and in this the servants have their social life. Here they go for a quick smoke, in the middle of the day's work; here they meet their friends, or flirt with the women who sell vegetables. It is as if, between each of the streets of the white man's city, there is a hidden street, ignored, forgotten. Marina, emerging into it, found it swarming with gossiping and laughing Africans. They froze, gave her a long suspicious stare, and all at once seemed to vanish, escaping into their respective back yards. In a moment she was alone.

She walked slowly back across the yard to her back door, picking her way among the soft litter from the woodpiles, ducking her head under the flapping clothes. She was watched, cautiously, by the servants, who were suspicious of this sudden curiosity about their way of life—experience had taught them to be suspicious. She was watched, also, by several of the women, through their kitchen windows. They saw a small Englishwoman, with a neat and composed body, pretty fair hair, and a pink and white face under a large straw hat, which she balanced in position with a hand clothed in a white glove. She moved delicately and with obvious distaste through the dust, as if at any moment she might take wings and fly away altogether.

When she reached her back steps, she stopped and called: "Charlie! Come here a moment, please." It was a high voice, a little querulous. When they heard the accents of that voice, saw the white glove, and noted that *please*, the watching women found all their worst fears confirmed.

A young African emerged from the sanitary lane where he had been gossiping (until interrupted by Marina's appearance) with some passing friends. He ran to his new mistress. He wore white shorts, a scarlet American-style shirt, tartan socks which were secured by mauve suspenders, and white tennis shoes. He stopped before her with a polite smile, which almost at once spread into a grin of pure friendliness. He was an amiable and cheerful young man by temperament. This was Marina's first morning in her new home, and she was already conscious of the disproportion between her strong pity for her servant, and that inveterately cheerful face.

She did not, of course, speak any native language, but Charlie spoke English.

"Charlie, how long have you been working here?"

"Two years, madam."

"Where do you come from?"

"Madam?"

"Where is your home?"

"Nyasaland."

"Oh." For this was hundreds of miles north.

"Do you go home to visit your family?"

"Perhaps this year, madam."

"I see. Do you like it here?"

"Madam?" A pause; and he involuntarily glanced back over the rubbish cans at the sanitary lane. He hoped that his friends, who worked on the other side of the town, and whom he did not often see, would not get tired of waiting for him. He hoped, too, that this new mistress (whose politeness to him he did not trust) was not going to choose this moment to order him to clean the silver or do the washing. He continued to grin, but his face was a little anxious, and his eyes rolled continually backwards at the sanitary lane.

"I hope you will be happy working for me," said Marina.

"Oh, yes, madam," he said at once, disappointedly; for clearly she was going to tell him to work.

"If there is anything you want, you must ask me. I am new to the country, and I may make mistakes."

He hesitated, handling the words in his mind. But they were difficult, and he let them slip. He did not think in terms of countries, of continents. He knew the white man's town—this town. He knew the veld. He knew the village from which he came. He knew, from his educated friends, that there was "a big water" across which the white men came in ships: he had seen pictures of ships in old magazines, but this "big water" was confused in his mind with the great lake in his own country. He understood that these white people came from places called England, Germany, Europe, but these were names to him. Once, a friend of his who had been three years to a mission school had said that Africa was one of several continents, and had shown him a tattered sheet of paper— one half of the map of the world—saying: Here is Africa, here is England, here is India. He pointed out Nyasaland, a tiny strip of country, and Charlie felt confused and diminished, for Nyasaland was what he knew, and it seemed to him so vast. Now, when Marina used the phrase "this country" Charlie saw, for a moment, this flat piece of paper, tinted pink and green and blue—the world. But from the sanitary lane came shouts of laughter—again he glanced anxiously over his shoulder; and Marina was conscious of a feeling remarkably like irritation. "Well, you may go," she said formally; and saw his smile flash white right across his face. He turned, and ran back across the yard like an athlete, clearing the woodpile, then the rubbish cans, in a series of great bounds, and vanished behind the lavatories. Marina went inside her "flat" with what was, had she known it, an angry frown. "Disgraceful," she muttered, including in this condemnation the bare room in which this man was expected to fit his life, the dirty sanitary lane bordered with stinking rubbish cans, and also his unreasonable cheerfulness.

Inside, she forgot him in her own discomfort. It was a truly shocking place. The two small rooms were so made that the interleading door was in the centre of the wall. They were more like passages than rooms. She switched on the light in what would be the bedroom, and put her hands to her cheek, for it stung where the sun had caught her unaccustomed skin through the chinks of the straw of her hat. The furniture was really beyond description! Two iron bedsteads, on either side of the door, a vast chocolate-brown wardrobe, whose door would not properly shut, one dingy straw mat that slid this way and that over the slippery boards as one walked on it. And the front room! If possible, it was even worse. An enormous cretonne-covered sofa, like a solidified flower bed, a hard and shiny table stuck in the middle of the floor, so that one must walk carefully around it, and four straight, hard chairs, ranged like soldiers against the wall. And the pictures—she did not know such pictures still existed. There was a desert scene, done in coloured cloth, behind glass; a motto in woven straw, also framed in glass, saying: *Welcome all who come in here, Good luck to you and all good cheer.*

There was also a very large picture of highland cattle. Half a dozen of these shaggy and ferocious creatures glared down at her from where they stood knee-deep in sunset-tinted pools. One might imagine that pictures of highland cattle no longer existed outside of Victorian novels, or remote suburban boarding-houses—but no, here they were. Really, why bother to emigrate?

She almost marched over and wrenched that picture from the wall. A curious inhibition prevented her. It was, though she did not know it, the spirit of the building. Some time later she heard Mrs. Black, who had been living for years in the next flat with her husband and three children, remark grimly: "My front door handle has been stuck for weeks, but I'm not going to mend it. If I start doing the place up, it means I'm here for ever." Marina recognised her own feeling when she heard these words. It accounted for the fact that while the families here were all respectable, in the sense that they owned cars, and could expect a regular monthly income, if one looked through the neglected hedge it was impossible not to conclude that every person in the building was born sloven or slut. No one really lived here. They might have been here for years, without prospect of anything better, but they did not live here.

There was one exception, Mrs. Pond, who painted her walls and mended what broke. It was felt she let everyone else down. In front of *her* steps a narrow path edged with brick led to her segment of yard, which was perhaps two feet across, in which lilies and roses were held upright by trellis work, like a tall, green sandwich standing at random in the dusty yard.

Marina thought: well, what's the point? I'm not going to *live* here. The picture could stay. Similarly, she decided there was no sense in unpacking her nice curtains or her books. And the furniture might remain as it was, for it was too awful to waste effort on it. Her thoughts returned to the servants' rooms at the back: it was a disgrace. The whole system was disgraceful . . .

At this point, Mrs. Pond knocked perfunctorily and entered. She was a short, solid woman, tied in at the waist, like a tight sausage, by the string of her apron. She had hard red cheeks, a full, hard bosom, and energetic red hands. Her eyes were small and inquisitive. Her face was ill-tempered, perhaps because she could not help knowing she was disliked. She was used to the disapproving eyes of her fellow-tenants, watching her attend to her strip of "garden"; or while she swept the narrow strip across the back yard that was her path from the back door to her lavatory. There she stood, every morning, among the washing and the woodpiles, wearing a pink satin dressing-gown trimmed with swan's-down, among the clouds of dust stirred up by her yard broom, returning defiant glances for the disapproving ones; and later she would say: "Two rooms is quite enough for a woman by herself. I'm quite satisfied."

She had no right to be satisfied, or at any rate, to say so . . .

But for a woman contented with her lot, there was a look in those sharp eyes which could too easily be diagnosed as envy; and when she said, much too sweetly: "You are an old friend of Mrs. Skinner, maybe?" Marina recognised, with the exhaustion that comes to everyone who has lived too long in overfull buildings, the existence of conspiracy. "I have never met Mrs. Skinner," she said briefly. "She said she was coming here this morning, to make arrangements."

Now, arrangements had been made already, with Philip; and Marina knew Mrs. Skinner was coming to inspect herself; and this thought irritated her.

"She is a nice lady," said Mrs. Pond. "She's my friend. We two have been living here longer than anyone else." Her voice was sour. Marina followed the direction of her eyes, and saw a large white door set into the wall. A built-in cupboard, in fact. She had already noted that cupboard as the only sensible amenity the "flat" possessed.

"That's a nice cupboard," said Mrs. Pond.

"Have all the flats got built-in cupboards?"

"Oh, no. Mrs. Skinner had this put in special last year. She paid for it. Not the landlord. You don't catch the landlord paying for anything."

"I see," said Marina.

"Mrs. Skinner promised me this flat," said Mrs. Pond.

Marina made no reply. She looked at her wrist-watch. It was a beautiful gesture; she even felt a little guilty because of the pointedness of it; but Mrs. Pond promptly said: "It's eleven o'clock. The clock just struck."

"I must finish the unpacking," said Marina.

Mrs. Pond seated herself on the flowery sofa, and remarked: "There's always plenty to do when you move in. That cupboard will save you plenty of space. Mrs. Skinner kept her linen in it. I was going to put all my clothes in. You're Civil Service, so I hear?"

"Yes," said Marina. She could not account for the grudging tone of that last, apparently irrelevant question. She did not know that

in this country the privileged class was the Civil Service, or considered to be. No aristocracy, no class distinctions—but alas, one
must have something to hate, and the Civil Service does as well as
anything. She added: "My husband chose this country rather than
the Gold Coast, because it seems the climate is better, even though
the pay is bad."

This remark was received with the same sceptical smile that she
would have earned in England had she been tactless enough to say
to her charwoman: Death duties spell the doom of the middle
classes.

"You have to be in the Service to get what's going," said Mrs.
Pond, with what she imagined to be a friendly smile. "The Service
gets all the plums." And she glanced at the cupboard.

"I think," said Marina icily, "that you are under some misappre-
hension. My husband happened to hear of this flat by chance."

"There were plenty of people waiting for this flat," said Mrs.
Pond reprovingly. "The lady next door, Mrs. Black, would have
been glad of it. And she's got three children, too. You have no children, perhaps?"

"Mrs. Pond, I have no idea at all why Mrs. Skinner gave us this
flat when she had promised it to Mrs. Black . . ."

"Oh, no, she had promised it to me. It was a faithful promise."

At this moment another lady entered the room without knocking.
She was an ample, middle-aged person, in tight corsets, with rigidly-
waved hair, and a sharp, efficient face that was now scarlet from
heat. She said peremptorily: "Excuse me for coming in without
knocking, but I can't get used to a stranger being here when I've
lived here so long." Suddenly she saw Mrs. Pond, and at once
stiffened into aggression. "I see you have already made friends with
Mrs. Pond," she said, giving that lady a glare.

Mrs. Pond was standing, hands on hips, in the traditional attitude of combat; but she squeezed a smile on to her face and said:
"I'm making acquaintance."

"Well," said Mrs. Skinner, dismissing her, "I'm going to discuss
business with my tenant."

Mrs. Pond hesitated. Mrs. Skinner gave her a long, quelling
stare. Mrs. Pond slowly deflated, and went to the door. From the
verandah floated back the words: "When people make promises,
they should keep them, that's what I say, instead of giving it to
people new to the country, and civil servants . . ."

Mrs. Skinner waited until the loud and angry voice faded, and then said briskly: "If you take my advice, you'll have nothing to do with Mrs. Pond, she's more trouble than she's worth."

Marina now understood that she owed this flat to the fact that this highly-coloured lady decided to let it to a stranger simply in order to spite all her friends in the building who hoped to inherit that beautiful cupboard, if only for three months. Mrs. Skinner was looking suspiciously around her; she said at last: "I wouldn't like to think my things weren't looked after."

"Naturally not," said Marina politely.

"When I spoke to your husband we were rather in a hurry. I hope you will make yourself comfortable, but I don't want to have anything altered."

Marina maintained a polite silence.

Mrs. Skinner marched to the inbuilt cupboard, opened it, and found it empty. "I paid a lot of money to have this fitted," she said in an aggrieved voice.

"We only came in yesterday," said Marina. "I haven't unpacked yet."

"You'll find it very useful," said Mrs. Skinner. "I paid for it myself. Some people would have made allowances in the rent."

"I think the rent is quite high enough," said Marina, joining battle at last.

Clearly, this note of defiance was what Mrs. Skinner had been waiting for. She made use of the familiar weapon: "There are plenty of people who would have been glad of it, I can tell you."

"So I gather."

"I could let it tomorrow."

"But," said Marina, in the high formal voice, "you have in fact let it to us, and the lease has been signed, so there is no more to be said, is there?"

Mrs. Skinner hesitated, and finally contented herself by repeating: "I hope my furniture will be looked after. I said in the lease nothing must be altered."

Suddenly Marina found herself saying: "Well, I shall of course move the furniture to suit myself, and hang my own pictures."

"This flat is let furnished, and I'm very fond of my pictures."

"But you will be away, won't you?" This, a sufficiently crude way of saying: "But it is we who will be looking at the pictures, and not you," misfired completely, for Mrs. Skinner merely said: "Yes, I like my pictures, and I don't like to think of them being packed."

Marina looked at the highland cattle and, though not half an hour before she had decided to leave it, said now: "I should like to take that one down."

Mrs. Skinner clasped her hands together before her, in a pose of simple devotion, compressed her lips, and stood staring mournfully up at the picture. "That picture means a lot to me. It used to hang in the parlour when I was a child, back Home. It was my granny's picture first. When I married Mr. Skinner, my mother packed it and sent it especial over the sea, knowing how I was fond of it. It's moved with me everywhere I've been. I wouldn't like to think of it being treated bad, I wouldn't really."

"Oh, very well," said Marina, suddenly exhausted. What, after all, did it matter?

Mrs. Skinner gave her a doubtful look: was it possible she had won her point so easily? "You must keep an eye on Charlie," she went on. "The number of times I've told him he'd poke his broom-handle through that picture . . ."

Hope flared in Marina. There was an extraordinary amount of glass. It seemed that the entire wall was surfaced by angry, shaggy cattle. Accidents did happen . . .

"You must keep an eye on Charlie, anyway. He never does a stroke more than he has to. He's bred bone lazy. You'd better keep an eye on the food too. He steals. I had to have the police to him only last month, when I lost my garnet brooch. Of course he swore he hadn't taken it, but I've never laid my hands on it since. My husband gave him a good hiding, but Master Charlie came up smiling, as usual."

Marina, revolted by this tale, raised her eyebrows disapprovingly. "Indeed?" she said, in her coolest voice.

Mrs. Skinner looked at her, as if to say: "What are you making that funny face for?" she remarked: "They're all born thieves and liars. You shouldn't trust them further than you can kick them. I'm warning you. Of course, you're new here. Only last week a friend was saying, I'm surprised at you letting to people just from England, they always spoil the servants, with their ideas, and I said: 'Oh, Mr. Giles is a sensible man, I trust him.'" This last was said pointedly.

"I don't think," remarked Marina coldly, "that you would be well-advised to trust my husband to give people 'hidings.'" She delicately isolated this word. "I rather feel, in similar circumstances, that even if he did, he would first make sure whether the man had, in fact, stolen the brooch."

Mrs. Skinner disentangled this sentence and in due course gave

Marina a distrustful stare. "Well," she said, "it's too late now, and everyone has his way, but of course this is my furniture, and if it is stolen or damaged, you are responsible."

"That, I should have thought, went without saying," said Marina.

They shook hands, with formality, and Mrs. Skinner went out. She returned from the verandah twice, first to say that Marina must not forget to fumigate the native quarters once a month if she didn't want livestock brought into her own flat . . . ("Not that I care if they want to live with lice, dirty creatures, but you have to protect yourself . . ."); and the second time to say that after you've lived in a place for years, it was hard to leave it, even for a holiday, and she was really regretting the day she let it at all. She gave Marina a final accusing and sorrowful look, as if the flat had been stolen from her, and this time finally departed. Marina was left in a mood of defiant anger, looking at the highland cattle picture, which had assumed, during this exchange, the look of a battleground. "Really," she said aloud to herself. "Really! One might have thought that one would be entitled to pack away a picture, if one rents a place . . ."

Two days later she got a note from Mrs. Skinner, saying that she hoped Marina would be happy in the flat, she must remember to keep an eye on Mrs. Pond, who was a real trouble-maker, and she must remember to look after the picture—Mrs. Skinner positively could not sleep for worrying about it.

Since Marina had decided she was not living here, there was comparatively little unpacking to be done. Things were stored. She had more than ever the appearance of a migrating bird who dislikes the twig it has chosen to alight on, but is rather too exhausted to move to another.

But she did read the advertisement columns every day, which were exactly like those in the papers back home. The *accommodation wanted* occupied a full column, while the *accommodation offered* usually did not figure at all. When houses were advertised they usually cost between five and twelve thousand—Marina saw some of them. They were very beautiful; if one had five thousand pounds, what a happy life one might lead—but the same might be said of any country. She also paid another visit to one of the new suburbs, and returned shuddering. "What!" she exclaimed to Philip. "Have we emigrated in order that I may spend the rest of life gossiping and taking tea with women like Mrs. Black and Mrs. Skinner?"

"Perhaps they aren't all like that," he suggested absent-mindedly.

For he was quite absorbed in his work. This country was fascinating! He was spending his days in his Government lorry, rushing over hundreds of miles of veld, visiting native reserves and settlements. Never had soil been so misused! Thousands of acres of it, denuded, robbed, fit for nothing, cattle and human beings crowded together—the solution, of course, was perfectly obvious. All one had to do was—and if the Government had any sense—

Marina understood that Philip was acclimatized. One does not speak of the "Government" with that particular mixture of affection and exasperation unless one feels at home. But she was not at all at home. She found herself playing with the idea of buying one of those revolting little houses. After all, one has to live somewhere . . .

Almost every morning, in 138, one might see a group of women standing outside one or other of the flats, debating how to rearrange the rooms. The plan of the building being so eccentric, no solution could possibly be satisfactory, and as soon as everything had been moved around, it was bound to be just as uncomfortable as before. "If I move the bookcase behind the door, then perhaps . . ." Or: "It might be better if I put it into the bathroom . . ."

The problem was: Where should one eat? If the dining-table was in the front room, then the servant had to come through the bedroom with the food. On the other hand, if one had the front room as bedroom, then visitors had to walk through it to the living-room. Marina kept Mrs. Skinner's arrangement. On the back porch, which was the width of a passage, stood a collapsible card-table. When it was set up, Philip sat crouched under the window that opened inwards over his head, while Marina shrank sideways into the bathroom door as Charlie came past with the vegetables. To serve food, Charlie put on a starched white coat, red fez, and white cotton gloves. In between courses he stood just behind them, in the kitchen door, while Marina and Philip ate in state, if discomfort.

Marina found herself becoming increasingly sensitive to what she imagined was his attitude of tolerance. It seemed ridiculous that the ritual of soup, fish, and sweet, silver and glass and fish-knives, should continue under such circumstances. She began to wonder how it all appeared to this young man, who, as soon as their meal was finished, took an enormous pot of mealie porridge off the stove and retired with it to his room, where he shared it (eating with his fingers and squatting on the floor) with the servant from next door, and any of his friends or relatives who happened to be out of work at the time.

That no such thoughts entered the heads of the other inhabitants was clear; and Marina could understand how necessary it was to banish them as quickly as possible. On the other hand . . .

There was something absurd in a system which allowed a healthy young man to spend his life in her kitchen, so that she might do nothing. Besides, it was more trouble than it was worth. Before she and Philip rose, Charlie walked around the outside of the building, and into the front room, and cleaned it. But as the wall was thin and he energetic, they were awakened every morning by the violent banging of his broom and the scraping of furniture. On the other hand, if it were left till they woke up, where should Marina sit while he cleaned it? On the bed, presumably, in the dark bedroom, till he had finished? It seemed to her that she spent half her time arranging her actions so that she might not get in Charlie's way while he cleaned or cooked. But she had learned better than to suggest doing her own work. On one of Mrs. Pond's visits, she had spoken with disgust of certain immigrants from England, who had so far forgotten what was due to their position as white people as to dispense with servants. Marina felt it was hardly worth while upsetting Mrs. Pond for such a small matter. Particularly, of course, as it was only for three months . . .

But upset Mrs. Pond she did, and almost immediately.

When it came to the end of the month, when Charlie's wages were due, and she laid out the twenty shillings he earned, she was filled with guilt. She really could not pay him such an idiotic sum for a whole month's work. But were twenty-five shillings, or thirty, any less ridiculous? She paid him twenty-five, and saw him beam with amazed surprise. He had been planning to ask for a rise, since this woman was easy-going, and he naturally optimistic; but to get a rise without asking for it, and then a full five shillings! Why, it had taken him three months of hard bargaining with Mrs. Skinner to get raised from seventeen and sixpence to nineteen shillings. "Thank you, madam," he said hastily; grabbing the money as if at any moment she might change her mind and take it back. Later that same day, she saw that he was wearing a new pair of crimson satin garters, and felt rather annoyed. Surely those five shillings might have been more sensibly spent? What these unfortunate people needed was an education in civilised values—but before she could pursue the thought, Mrs. Pond entered, looking aggrieved.

It appeared that Mrs. Pond's servant had also demanded a rise, from his nineteen shillings. If Charlie could earn twenty-five shillings, why not he? Marina understood that Mrs. Pond was speaking for all the women in the building.

"You shouldn't spoil them," she said. "I know you are from England, and all that, but . . ."

"It seems to me they are absurdly underpaid," said Marina.

"Before the war they were lucky to get ten bob. They're never satisfied."

"Well, according to the cost-of-living index, the value of money has halved," said Marina. But as even the Government had not come to terms with this official and indisputable fact, Mrs. Pond could not be expected to, and she said crossly: "All you people are the same, you come here with your fancy ideas."

Marina was conscious that every time she left her rooms, she was followed by resentful eyes. Besides, she was feeling a little ridiculous. Crimson satin garters, really!

She discussed the thing with Philip, and decided that payment in kind was more practical. She arranged that Charlie should be supplied, in addition to a pound of meat twice a week, with vegetables. Once again Mrs. Pond came on a deputation of protest. All the natives in the building were demanding vegetables. "They aren't used to it," she complained. "Their stomachs aren't like ours. They don't need vegetables. You're just putting ideas into their heads."

"According to the regulations," Marina pointed out in that high clear voice, "Africans should be supplied with vegetables."

"Where did you get that from?" said Mrs. Pond suspiciously.

Marina produced the regulations, which Mrs. Pond read in grim silence. "The Government doesn't have to pay for it," she pointed out, very aggrieved. And then, "They're getting out of hand, that's what it is. There'll be trouble, you mark my words . . ."

Marina completed her disgrace on the day when she bought a second-hand iron bedstead and installed it in Charlie's room. That her servant should have to sleep on the bare cement floor, wrapped in a blanket, this she could no longer tolerate. As for Charlie, he accepted his good fortune fatalistically. He could not understand Marina. She appeared to feel guilty about telling him to do the simplest thing, such as clearing away cobwebs he had forgotten. Mrs. Skinner would have docked his wages, and Mr. Skinner cuffed him. This woman presented him with a new bed on the day that he broke her best cut-glass bowl.

He bought himself some new ties, and began swaggering around the back yard among the other servants, whose attitude towards him was as one might expect; one did not expect justice from the white man, whose ways were incomprehensible, but there should be a certain proportion: why should Charlie be the one to chance on an employer who presented him with a fine bed, extra meat, vegetables, and gave him two afternoons off a week instead of one? They looked unkindly at Charlie, as he swanked across the yard in his fine new clothes; they might even shout sarcastic remarks after him. But Charlie was too good-natured and friendly a person to relish such a situation. He made a joke of it, in self-defence, as Marina soon learned.

She had discovered that there was no need to share the complicated social life of the building in order to find out what went on. If, for instance, Mrs. Pond had quarrelled with a neighbour over some sugar that had not been returned, so that all the women were taking sides, there was no need to listen to Mrs. Pond herself to find the truth. Instead, one went to the kitchen window overlooking the back yard, hid oneself behind the curtain, and peered out at the servants.

There they stood, leaning on their axes, or in the intervals of pegging the washing, a group of laughing and gesticulating men, who were creating the new chapter in that perpetually unrolling saga, the extraordinary life of the white people, their masters, in 138 Cecil John Rhodes Vista . . .

February, Mrs. Pond's servant, stepped forward, while the others fell back in a circle around him, already grinning appreciatively. He thrust out his chest, stuck out his chin, and over a bad-tempered face he stretched his mouth in a smile so poisonously ingratiating that his audience roared and slapped their knees with delight. He was Mrs. Pond, one could not mistake it. He minced over to an invisible person, put on an attitude of supplication, held out his hand, received something in it. He returned to the centre of the circle, and looked at what he held with a triumphant smile. In one hand he held an invisible cup, with the other he spooned in invisible sugar. He was Mrs. Pond, drinking her tea, with immense satisfaction, in small dainty sips. Then he belched, rubbed his belly, smacked his lips. Entering into the game another servant came forward, and acted a falsely amiable woman: hands on hips, the jutting elbows, the whole angry body showing indignation, but the face was smiling. February drew himself up, nodded and smiled, turned himself about, lifted something from the air behind him, and began pouring it out: sugar, one could positively hear it trickling. He took the container, and handed it proudly to the waiting visitor. But just as it was taken from him, he changed his mind. A look of agonised greed came over his face, and he withdrew the sugar. Hastily turning himself back, throwing furtive glances over his shoulder, he poured back some of the sugar, then, slowly, as if it hurt to do it, he forced himself round, held out the sugar, and again—just as it left his hand, he grabbed it and poured back just a little more. The other servants were rolling with laughter, as the two men faced each other in the centre of the yard, one indignant, but still polite, screwing up his eyes at the returned sugar, as if there were too small a quantity to be seen, while February held it out at arm's length, his face contorted with the agony it caused him to return it at all. Suddenly the two sprang together, faced each other like a pair of angry hens, and began screeching and flailing their arms.

"February!" came a shout from Mrs. Pond's flat, in her loud, shrill voice. "February, I told you to do the ironing!"

"Madam!" said February, in his politest voice. He walked backwards to the steps, his face screwed up in a grimace of martyred suffering; as he reached the steps, his body fell into the pose of a willing servant, and he walked hastily into the kitchen, where Mrs. Pond was waiting for him.

But the other servants remained, unwilling to drop the game. There was a moment of indecision. They glanced guiltily at the back of the building: perhaps some of the other women were watching? No, complete silence. It was mid-morning, the sun poured down, the shadows lay deep under the big tree, the sap crystallised into little rivulets like burnt toffee on the wood chips, and sent a warm fragrance mingling into the odours of dust and warmed foliage. For the moment, they could not think of anything to do, they might as well go on with the wood-chopping. One yawned, another lifted his axe and let it fall into a log of wood, where it was held, vibrating. He plucked the handle, and it thrummed like a deep guitar note. At once, delightedly, the men gathered around the embedded axe. One twanged it, and the others began to sing. At first Marina was unable to make out the words. Then she heard:

> *There's a man who comes to our house,*
> *When poppa goes away,*
> *Poppa comes back, and . . .*

The men were laughing, and looking at No. 4 of the flats, where a certain lady was housed whose husband worked on the railways. They sang it again:

> *There's a man who comes to this house,*
> *Every single day,*
> *The baas comes back, and*
> *The man goes away . . .*

Marina found that she was angry. Really! The thing had turned into another drama. Charlie, her own servant, was driving an imaginary engine across the yard, chuff chuff, like a child, while two of the others, seated on a log of wood were—really, it was positively obscene!

Marina came away from the window, and reasoned with herself. She was using, in her mind, one of the formulae of the country: *What can one expect?*

At this moment, while she was standing beside the kitchen-table, arguing with her anger, she heard the shrill cry: "Peas! Nice potatoes! Cabbage! Ver' chip!"

Yes, she needed vegetables. She went to the back door. There stood a native woman, with a baby on her back, carefully unslinging the sacks of vegetables which she had supported over her shoulder. She opened the mouth of one, displaying the soft mass of green pea-pods.

"How much?"

"Only one sheeling," said the woman hopefully.

"What!" began Marina, in protest; for this was twice what the shops charged. Then she stopped. Poor woman. No woman should have to carry a heavy child on her back, and great sacks of vegetables from house to house, street to street, all day—"Give me a pound," she said. Using a tin cup, the woman ladled out a small quantity of peas. Marina nearly insisted on weighing them; then she remembered how Mrs. Pond brought her scales out to the back door, on these occasions, shouting abuse at the vendor, if there was short weight. She took in the peas, and brought out a shilling. The woman, who had not expected this, gave Marina a considering look and fell into the pose of a suppliant. She held out her hands, palms upwards, her head bowed, and murmured: "Present, missus, present for my baby."

Again Marina hesitated. She looked at the woman, with her

whining face and shifty eyes, and disliked her intensely. The phrase: What can one expect? came to the surface of her mind; and she went indoors and returned with sweets. The woman received them in open, humble palms, and promptly popped half into her own mouth. Then she said: "Dress, missus?"

"No," said Marina, with energy. Why should she?

Without a sign of disappointment, the woman twisted the necks of the sacks around her hand, and dragged them after her over the dust of the yard, and joined the group of servants who were watching this scene with interest. They exchanged greetings. The woman sat down on a log, easing her strained back, and moved the baby around under her armpit, still in its sling, so it could reach her breast. Charlie, the dandy, bent over her, and they began a flirtation. The others fell back. Who, indeed, could compete with that rainbow tie, the satin garters? Charlie was persuasive and assured, the woman bridling and laughing. It went on for some minutes until the baby let the nipple fall from its mouth. Then the woman got up, still laughing, shrugged the baby back into position in the small of her back, pulled the great sacks over one shoulder, and walked off, calling shrilly back to Charlie, so that all the men laughed. Suddenly they all became silent. The nurse-girl emerged from Mrs. Black's flat, and sauntered slowly past them. She was a little creature, a child, in a tight pink cotton dress, her hair braided into a dozen tiny plaits that stuck out all over her head, with a childish face that was usually vivacious and mischievous. But now she looked mournful. She dragged her feet as she walked past Charlie, and gave him a long reproachful look. Jealousy, thought Marina, there was no doubt of that! And Charlie was looking uncomfortable—one could not mistake that either. But surely not! Why, she wasn't old enough for this sort of thing. The phrase, *this sort of thing,* struck Marina herself as a shameful evasion, and she examined it. Then she shrugged and said to herself: All the same, where did the girl sleep? Presumably in one of these rooms, with the men of the place?

Theresa (she had been named after Saint Theresa at the mission school where she had been educated) tossed her head in the direction of the departing seller of vegetables, gave Charlie a final supplicating glance, and disappeared into the sanitary lane.

The men began laughing again, and this time the laughter was directed at Charlie, who received it grinning self-consciously.

Now February, who had finished the ironing, came from Mrs. Pond's flat and began hanging clothes over the line to air. The white things dazzled in the sun and made sharp, black shadows across the red dust. He called out to the others—what interesting events had happened since he went indoors? They laughed, shouted back. He finished pegging the clothes and went over to the others. The group stood under the big tree, talking; Marina, still watching, suddenly felt her cheeks grow hot. Charlie had separated himself off and, with a condensing, bowed movement of his body, had become the African woman, the seller of vegetables. Bent sideways with the weight of sacks, his belly thrust out to balance the heavy baby, he approached a log of wood—her own back step. Then he straightened, sprang back, stretched upward, and pulled from the tree a frond of leaves. These he balanced on his head, and suddenly Marina saw herself. Very straight, precise, finicky, with a prim little face peering this way and that under the broad hat, hands clasped in front of her, she advanced to the log of wood and stood looking downwards.

"Peas, cabbage, potatoes," said Charlie, in a shrill female voice.

"How much?" he answered himself, in Marina's precise, nervous voice.

"Ten sheelings a pound, missus, only ten sheelings a pound!" said Charlie, suddenly writhing on the log in an ecstasy of humility.

"How ridiculous!" said Marina, in that high, alas, absurdly high voice. Marina watched herself hesitate, her face showing mixed indignation and guilt and, finally, indecision. Charlie nodded twice, said nervously: "Of course, but certainly." Then, in a hurried, embarrassed way, he retreated, and came back, his arms full. He opened them and stood aside to avoid a falling shower of money. For a moment he mimed the African woman and, squatting on the ground, hastily raked in the money and stuffed it into his shirt. Then he stood up—Marina again. He bent uncertainly, with a cross, uncomfortable face, looking down. Then he bent stiffly and picked up a leaf—a single pea-pod, Marina realized—and marched off, looking at the leaf, saying: "Cheap, very cheap!" one hand balancing the leaves on his head, his two feet set prim and precise in front of him.

As the laughter broke out from all the servants, Marina, who was not far from tears, stood by the window and said to herself: Serve you right for eavesdropping.

A clock struck. Various female voices shouted from their respective kitchens:

"February!" "Noah!" "Thursday!" "Sixpence!" "Blackbird!"

The morning lull was over. Time to prepare the midday meal for the white people. The yard was deserted, save for Theresa the nurse-girl returning disconsolately from the sanitary lane, dragging her feet through the dust. Among the stiff quills of hair on her head she had perched a half-faded yellow flower that she had found in one of the rubbish-cans. She looked hopefully at Marina's flat for a glimpse of Charlie; then slowly entered Mrs. Black's.

It happened that Philip was away on one of his trips. Marina ate her lunch by herself, while Charlie, attired in his waiter's outfit, served her food. Not a trace of the cheerful clown remained in his manner. He appeared friendly, though nervous; at any moment, he seemed to be thinking, this strange white woman might revert to type and start scolding and shouting.

As Marina rose from the card-table, being careful not to bump her head on the window, she happened to glance out at the yard and saw Theresa, who was standing under the tree with the youngest of her charges in her arms. The baby was reaching up to play with the leaves. Theresa's eyes were fixed on Charlie's kitchen.

"Charlie," said Marina, "where does Theresa sleep?"

Charlie was startled. He avoided her eyes and muttered: "I don't know, madam."

"But you must know, surely," said Marina, and heard her own voice climb to that high, insistent tone which Charlie had so successfully imitated.

He did not answer.

"How old is Theresa?"

"I don't know." This was true, for he did not even know his own age. As for Theresa, he saw the spindly, little-girl body, with the sharp young breasts pushing out the pink stuff of the dress she wore; he saw the new languor of her walk as she passed him. "She is nurse for Mrs. Black," he said sullenly, meaning: "Ask Mrs. Black. What's it got to do with me?"

Marina said: "Very well," and went out. As she did so she saw Charlie wave to Theresa through the gauze of the porch. Theresa pretended not to see. She was punishing him, because of the vegetable woman.

In the front room the light was falling full on the highland cattle, so that the glass was a square, blinding glitter. Marina shifted her seat, so that her eyes were no longer troubled by it, and contemplated those odious cattle. Why was it that Charlie, who broke a quite fantastic number of cups, saucers, and vases, never—as Mrs. Skinner said he might—put that vigorously-jerking broom-handle through the glass? But it seemed he liked the picture. Marina had seen him standing in front of it, admiring it. Cattle, Marina knew from Philip, played a part in native tribal life that could only be described as religious—might it be that . . .

Some letters slapped on to the cement of the verandah, slid over its polished surface, and came to rest in the doorway. Two letters. Marina watched the uniformed postboy cycle slowly down the front of the building, flinging in the letters, eight times, slap, slap, slap, grinning with pleasure at his own skill. There was a shout of rage. One of the women yelled after him: "You lazy black bastard, can't you even get off your bicycle to deliver the letters?" The postman, without taking any notice, cycled slowly off to the next house.

This was the hour of heat, when all activity faded into somnolence. The servants were away at the back, eating their midday meal. In the eight flats, separated by the flimsy walls which allowed every sound to be heard, the women reclined, sleeping, or lazily gossiping. Marina could hear Mrs. Pond, three rooms away, saying: "The fuss she made over half a pound of sugar, you would think . . ."

Marina yawned. What a lazy life this was! She decided, at that moment, that she would put an end to this nonsense of hoping, year after year, for some miracle that would provide her, Marina Giles, with a nice house, a garden, and the other vanishing amenities of life. They would buy one of those suburban houses and she would have a baby. She would have several babies. Why not? Nursemaids cost practically nothing. She would become a domestic creature and learn to discuss servants and children with women like Mrs. Black and Mrs. Skinner. Why not? What had she expected? Ah, what had she not expected! For a moment she allowed herself to dream of that large house, that fine exotic garden, the free and amiable life released from the tensions and pressures of modern existence. She dreamed quite absurdly—but then, if no one dreamed these dreams, no one would emigrate, continents would remain undeveloped, and then what would happen to Charlie, whose salvation was (so the statesmen and newspapers continually proclaimed) contact with Mrs. Pond and Mrs. Skinner—white civilisation, in short.

But the phrase "white civilisation" was already coming to affect Marina as violently as it affects everyone else in that violent continent. It is a phrase like "white man's burden," "way of life" or "colour bar"—all of which are certain to touch off emotions better not classified. Marina was alarmed to find that these phrases were beginning to produce in her a feeling of fatigued distaste. For the liberal, so vociferously disapproving in the first six months, is quite certain to turn his back on the whole affair before the end of a year. Marina would soon be finding herself profoundly bored by politics.

But at this moment, having taken the momentous decision, she was quite light-hearted. After all, the house next door to this building was an eyesore, with its corrugated iron and brick and wood flung hastily together; and yet it was beautiful, covered with the yellow and purple and crimson creepers. Yes, they would buy a house in the suburbs, shroud it with greenery, and have four children; and Philip would be perfectly happy rushing violently around the country in a permanent state of moral indignation, and thus they would both be usefully occupied.

Marina reached for the two letters, which still lay just inside the door, where they had been so expertly flung, and opened the first. It was from Mrs. Skinner, written from Cape Town, where she was, rather uneasily, it seemed, on holiday.

> I can't help worrying if everything is all right, and the furniture. Perhaps I ought to have packed away the things, because no stranger understands. I hope Charlie is not getting cheeky, he needs a firm hand, and I forgot to tell you you must deduct one shilling from his wages because he came back late one afternoon, instead of five o'clock as I said, and I had to teach him a lesson.
>
> > Yours truly,
> > *Emily Skinner*
>
> P.S. I hope the picture is continuing all right.

The second was from Philip.

> I'm afraid I shan't be back tomorrow as Smith suggests while we are here we might as well run over to the Nwenze reserve. It's only just across the river, about seventy miles as the crow flies, but the roads are anybody's guess, after the wet season. Spent this morning as planned, trying to persuade these blacks it is better to have one fat ox than ten all skin and bone, never seen such erosion in my life, gullies twenty feet deep, and the whole tribe will starve next dry season, but you can talk till you are blue, they won't kill a beast till they're forced, and that's what it will come to, and then imagine the outcry from the people back home . . .

At this point Marina remarked to herself: Well, well; and continued:

You can imagine Screech-Jones or one of them shouting in the House: Compulsion of the poor natives. My eye. It's for their own good. Until all this mystical nonsense about cattle is driven out of their fat heads, we might as well save our breath. You should have seen where I was this morning! To get the reserve back in use, alone, would take the entire vote this year for the whole country, otherwise the whole place will be a desert, it's all perfectly obvious, but you'll never get this damned Government to see that in a hundred years, and it'll be too late in five.

In haste,
Phil

P.S. I do hope everything is all right, dear, I'll try not to be late.

That night Marina took her evening meal early so that Charlie might finish the washing-up and get off. She was reading in the front room when she understood that her ear was straining through the noise from the wirelesses all around her for a quite different sort of music. Yes, it was a banjo, and loud singing, coming from the servants' rooms, and there was a quality in it that was not to be heard from any wireless set. Marina went through the rooms to the kitchen window. The deserted yard, roofed high with moon and stars, was slatted and barred with light from the eight back doors. The windows of the four servants' rooms gleamed dully; and from the room Charlie shared with February came laughter and singing and the thrumming of the banjo.

> *There's a man who comes to our house,*
> *When poppa goes away . . .*

Marina smiled. It was a maternal smile. (As Mrs. Pond might remark, in a good mood: They are nothing but children.) She liked to think that these men were having a party. And women too: she could hear shrill female voices. How on earth did they all fit into that tiny room? As she returned through the back porch, she heard a man's voice shouting: "Shut up there! Shut up, I say!" Mr. Black from his back porch: "Don't make so much noise."

Complete silence. Marina could see Mr. Black's long, black shadow poised motionless: he was listening. Marina heard him grumble: "Can't hear yourself think with these bastards . . ." He went back into his front room, and the sound of his heavy feet on the wood floor was absorbed by their wireless playing: I love you, Yes I do, I love you . . . Slam! Mr. Black was in a rage.

Marina continued to read. It was not long before once more her distracted ear warned her that riotous music had begun again. They were singing: Congo Conga Conga, we do it in the Congo . . .

Steps on the verandah, a loud knock, and Mr. Black entered.

"Mrs. Giles, your boy's gone haywire. Listen to the din."

Marina said politely: "Do sit down, Mr. Black."

Mr. Black, who in England (from whence he had come as a child) would have been a lanky, pallid, genteel clerk, was in this country an assistant in a haberdasher's; but because of his sun-filled and energetic week-ends, he gave the impression, at first glance, of being that burly young Colonial one sees on advertisements for Empire tobacco. He was thin, bony, muscular, sunburnt; he had the free and easy Colonial manner, the back-slapping air that is always just a little too conscious. "Look," it seems to say, "in this country we are all equal (among the whites, that is—that goes without saying) and I'll fight the first person who suggests anything to the contrary." Democracy, as it were, with one eye on the audience. But alas, he was still a clerk, and felt it; and if there was one class of person he detested it was the civil servant; and if there was another, it was the person new from "Home."

Here they were, united in one person, Marina Giles, wife of Philip Giles, soil expert for the Department of Lands and Afforestation, Marina, whose mere appearance acutely irritated him, every time he saw her moving delicately through the red dust, in her straw hat, white gloves, and touch-me-not manner.

"I say!" he said aggressively, his face flushed, his eyes hot. "I say, what are you going to do about it, because if you don't, I shall."

"I don't doubt it," said Marina precisely; "but I really fail to see why these people should not have a party, if they choose, particularly as it is not yet nine o'clock, and as far as I know there is no law to forbid them."

"Law!" said Mr. Black violently. "Party! They're on our premises, aren't they? It's for us to say. Anyway, if I know anything they're visiting without passes."

"I feel you are being unreasonable," said Marina, with the intention of sounding mildly persuasive; but in fact her voice had lifted to that fatally querulous high note, and her face was as angry and flushed as his.

"Unreasonable! My kids can't sleep with that din."

"It might help if you turned down your own wireless," said Marina sarcastically.

He lifted his fists, clenching them unconsciously. "You people . . ." he began inarticulately. "If you were a man, Mrs. Giles, I tell you straight . . ." He dropped his fists and looked around wildly as Mrs. Pond entered, her face animated with delight in the scene.

"I see Mr. Black is talking to you about your boy," she began, sugarily.

"And your boy too," said Mr. Black.

"Oh, if I had a husband," said Mrs. Pond, putting on an appearance of helpless womanhood, "February would have got what's coming to him long ago."

"For that matter," said Marina, speaking with difficulty because of her loathing for the whole thing, "I don't think you really find a husband necessary for this purpose, since it was only yesterday I saw you hitting February yourself . . ."

"He was cheeky," began Mrs. Pond indignantly.

Marina found words had failed her; but none were necessary for Mr. Black had gone striding out through her own bedroom, followed by Mrs. Pond, and she saw the pair of them cross the shadowy yard to Charlie's room, which was still in darkness, though the music was at a crescendo. As Mr. Black shouted: "Come out of there, you black bastards!" the noise stopped, the door swung in, and half a dozen dark forms ducked under Mr. Black's extended arm and vanished into the sanitary lane. There was a scuffle, and Mr. Black found himself grasping, at arm's length, two people—Charlie and his own nursemaid, Theresa. He let the girl go and she ran after the others. He pushed Charlie against the wall. "What do you mean by making all that noise when I told you not to?" he shouted.

"That's right, that's right," gasped Mrs. Pond from behind him, running this way and that around the pair so as to get a good view.

Charlie, keeping his elbow lifted to shield his head, said: "I'm sorry, baas, I'm sorry, I'm sorry . . ."

"Sorry!" Mr. Black, keeping firm grasp of Charlie's shoulder, lifted his other hand to hit him; Charlie jerked his arm up over his face. Mr. Black's fist, expecting to encounter a cheek, met instead the rising arm and he was thrown off balance and staggered back. "How dare you hit me," he shouted furiously, rushing at Charlie; but Charlie had escaped in a bound over the rubbish-cans and away into the lane.

Mr. Black sent angry shouts after him; then turned and said indignantly to Mrs. Pond: "Did you see that? He hit me!"

"He's out of hand," said Mrs. Pond in a melancholy voice. "What can you expect? He's been spoilt."

They both turned to look accusingly at Marina.

"As a matter of accuracy," said Marina breathlessly, "he did not hit you."

"What, are you taking that nigger's side?" demanded Mr. Black. He was completely taken aback. He looked, amazed, at Mrs. Pond, and said: "She's taking his side!"

"It's not a question of sides," said Marina in that high, precise voice. "I was standing here and saw what happened. You know quite well he did not hit you. He wouldn't dare."

"Yes," said Mr. Black, "that's what a state things have come to, with the Government spoiling them, they can hit us and get away with it, and if we touch them we get fined."

"I don't know how many times I've seen the servants hit since I've been here," said Marina angrily. "If it is the law, it is a remarkably ineffective one."

"Well, I'm going to get the police," shouted Mr. Black, running back to his own flat. "No black bastard is going to hit me and get away with it. Besides, they can all be fined for visiting without passes after nine at night . . ."

"Don't be childish," said Marina, and went inside her rooms. She was crying with rage. Happening to catch a glimpse of herself in the mirror as she passed it, she hastily went to splash cold water on her face, for she looked—there was no getting away from it—rather like a particularly genteel school-marm in a temper. When she reached the front room, she found Charlie there throwing terrified glances out into the verandah for fear of Mr. Black or Mrs. Pond.

"Madam," he said. "Madam, I didn't hit him."

"No, of course not," said Marina; and she was astonished to find that she was feeling irritated with him, Charlie. "Really," she said, "must you make such a noise and cause all this fuss."

"But, madam . . ."

"Oh, all right," she said crossly. "All right. But you aren't supposed to . . . who were all those people?"

"My friends."

"Where from?" He was silent. "Did they have passes to be out visiting?" He shifted his eyes uncomfortably. "Well, really," she said irritably, "if the law is that you must have passes, for heaven's sake . . ." Charlie's whole appearance had changed; a moment before he had been a helpless small boy; he had become a sullen young man: this white woman was like all the rest.

Marina controlled her irritation and said gently: "Listen, Charlie, I don't agree with the law and all this nonsense about passes, but I can't change it, and it does seem to me . . ." Once again her irritation rose, once again she suppressed it, and found herself without words. Which was just as well, for Charlie was gazing at her with puzzled suspicion since he saw all white people as a sort of homogeneous mass, a white layer, as it were, spread over the mass of blacks, all concerned in making life as difficult as possible for him and his kind; the idea that a white person might not agree with passes, curfew, and so on was so outrageously new that he could not admit it to his mind at once. Marina said: "Oh, well, Charlie, I know you didn't mean it, and I think you'd better go quietly to bed and keep out of Mr. Black's way, if you can."

"Yes, madam," he said submissively. As he went, she asked: "Does Theresa sleep in the same room as Mr. Black's boy?"

He was silent. "Does she sleep in your room perhaps?" And, as the silence persisted: "Do you mean to tell me she sleeps with you and February?" No reply. "But Charlie . . ." She was about to protest again: But Theresa's nothing but a child; but this did not appear to be an argument which appealed to him.

There were loud voices outside, and Charlie shrank back: "The police!" he said, terrified.

"Ridiculous nonsense," said Marina. But looking out she saw a white policeman; and Charlie fled out through her bedroom and she heard the back door slam. It appeared he had no real confidence in her sympathy.

The policeman entered, alone. "I understand there's been a spot of trouble," he said.

"Over nothing," said Marina.

"A tenant in this building claims he was hit by your servant."

"It's not true. I saw the whole thing."

The policeman looked at her doubtfully and said: "Well, that makes things difficult, doesn't it?" After a moment he said: "Excuse me a moment," and went out. Marina saw him talking to Mr. Black outside her front steps. Soon the policeman came back. "In view of your attitude the charge has been dropped," he said.

"So I should think. I've never heard of anything so silly."

"Well, Mrs. Giles, there was a row going on, and they all ran away, so they must have had guilty consciences about something, probably no passes. And you know they can't have women in their rooms."

"The woman was Mr. Black's own nursemaid."

"He says the girl is supposed to sleep in the location with her father."

"It's a pity Mr. Black takes so little interest in his servants not to know. She sleeps here. How can a child that age be expected to walk five miles here every morning, to be here at seven, and walk five miles back at seven in the evening?"

The policeman gave her a look: "Plenty do it," he said. "It's not the same for them as it is for us. Besides, it's the law."

"The law!" said Marina bitterly.

Again the policeman looked uncertain. He was a pleasant young man, he dealt continually with cases of this kind, he always tried to smooth things over, if he could. He decided on his usual course, despite Marina's hostile manner. "I think the best thing to do," he said, "is if we leave the whole thing. We'll never catch them now, anyway—miles away by this time. And Mr. Black has dropped the charge. You have a talk to your boy and tell him to be careful. Otherwise he'll be getting himself into trouble."

"And what are you going to do about the nurse? It amounts to this: It's convenient for the Blacks to have her here, so they can go out at night, and so on, so they ask no questions. It's a damned disgrace, a girl of that age expected to share a room with the men."

"It's not right, not right at all," said the policeman. "I'll have a word with Mr. Black." And he took his leave, politely.

That night Marina relieved her feelings by writing a long letter about the incident to a friend of hers in England, full of phrases such as "police state," "despotism," and "fascism"; which caused that friend to reply, rather tolerantly, to the effect that she understood these hot climates were rather upsetting and she did so hope Marina was looking after herself, one must have a sense of proportion, after all.

And, in fact, by the morning Marina was wondering why she had allowed herself to be so angry about such an absurd incident. What a country this was! Unless she was very careful she would find herself flying off into hysterical states as easily, for instance, as Mr. Black. If one was going to make a life here, one should adjust oneself . . .

Charlie was grateful and apologetic. He repeated: "Thank you, madam. Thank you." He brought her a present of some vegetables and said: "You are my father and my mother." Marina was deeply touched. He rolled up his eyes and made a half-rueful joke: "The police are no good, madam." She discovered that he had spent the night in a friend's room some streets away for fear the police might come and take him to prison. For, in Charlie's mind, the police meant only one thing. Marina tried to explain that one wasn't put in prison without a trial of some sort; but he merely looked at her doubtfully, as if she were making fun of him. So she left it.

And Theresa? She was still working for the Blacks. A few evenings later, when Marina went to turn off the lights before going to bed, she saw Theresa gliding into Charlie's room. She said nothing about it: what could one expect?

Charlie had accepted her as an ally. One day, as he served vegetables, reaching behind her ducked head so that they might be presented, correctly, from the left, he remarked: "That Theresa, she very nice, madam."

"Very nice," said Marina, uncomfortably helping herself to peas from an acute angle, sideways.

"Theresa says, perhaps madam give her a dress?"

"I'll see what I can find," said Marina, after a pause.

"Thank you very much, thank you, madam," he said. He was grateful; but certainly he had expected just that reply: his thanks were not perfunctory, but he thanked her as one might thank one's parents, for instance, from whom one expects such goodness, even takes it a little for granted.

Next morning, when Marina and Philip lay as usual, trying to sleep through the cheerful din of cleaning from the next room, which included a shrill and sprightly whistling, there was a loud crash.

"Oh, damn the man," said Philip, turning over and pulling the clothes over his ears.

"With a bit of luck he's broken that picture," said Marina. She put a dressing-gown on, and went next door. On the floor lay fragments of white porcelain—her favourite vase, which she had brought all the way from England. Charlie was standing over it. "Sorry, madam," he said, cheerfully contrite.

Now that vase had stood on a shelf high above Charlie's head—to break it at all was something of an acrobatic feat . . . Marina pulled herself together. After all, it was only a vase. But her favourite vase, she had had it ten years: she stood there, tightening her lips over all the angry things she would have liked to say, looking at

Charlie, who was carelessly sweeping the pieces together. He glanced up, saw her face, and said hastily, really apologetic: "Sorry madam, very, very sorry, madam." Then he added reassuringly: "But the picture is all right." He gazed admiringly up at the highland cattle which he clearly considered the main treasure of the room.

"So it is," said Marina, suppressing the impulse to say: Charlie, if you break that picture I'll give you a present. "Oh, well," she said, "I suppose it doesn't matter. Just sweep the pieces up."

"Yes, missus, thank you," said Charlie cheerfully; and she left, wondering how she had put herself in a position where it became impossible to be legitimately cross with her own servant. Coming back into that room some time later to ask Charlie why the breakfast was so late, she found him still standing under the picture. "Very nice picture," he said, reluctantly leaving the room. "Six oxes. Six fine big oxes, in one picture!"

The work in the flat was finished by mid-morning. Marina told Charlie she wanted to bake; he filled the old-fashioned stove with wood for her, heated the oven and went off into the yard, whistling. She stood at the window, mixing her cake, looking out into the yard.

Charlie came out of his room, sat down on a big log under the tree, stretched his legs before him, and propped a small mirror between his knees. He took a large metal comb and began to work on his thick hair, which he endeavoured to make lie flat, white-man's fashion. He was sitting with his back to the yard.

Soon Theresa came out with a big enamel basin filled with washing. She wore the dress Marina had given her. It was an old black cocktail dress which hung loosely around her calves, and she had tied it at the waist with a big sash of printed cotton. The sophisticated dress, treated thus, hanging full and shapeless, looked grandmotherly and old-fashioned; she looked like an impish child in a matron's garb. She stood beside the washing-line gazing at Charlie's back; then slowly she began pegging the clothes, with long intervals to watch him.

It seemed Charlie did not know she was there. Then his pose of concentrated self-worship froze into a long, close inspection in the mirror, which he began to rock gently between his knees so that the sunlight flashed up from it, first into the branches over his head, then over the dust of the yard to the girl's feet, up her body: the ray of light hovered like a butterfly around her, then settled on her face. She remained still, her eyes shut, with the teasing light flickering on her lids. Then she opened them and exclaimed, indignantly: *"Hau!"*

Charlie did not move. He held the mirror sideways on his knees, where he could see Theresa, and pretended to be hard at work on his parting. For a few seconds they remained thus, Charlie staring into the mirror, Theresa watching him reproachfully. Then he put the mirror back into his pocket, stretched his arms back in a magnificent slow yawn, and remained there, rocking back and forth on his log.

Theresa looked at him thoughtfully; and—since now he could not see her—darted over to the hedge, plucked a scarlet hibiscus flower, and returned to the washing-line, where she continued to hang the washing, the flower held lightly between her lips.

Charlie got up, his arms still locked behind his head, and began a sort of shuffle dance in the sunny dust, among the fallen leaves and chips of wood. It was a crisp, bright morning, the sky was as blue and fresh as the sea: this idyllic scene moved Marina deeply, it must be confessed.

Still dancing, Charlie let his arms fall, turned himself round, and his hands began to move in time with his feet. Jerking, lolling, posing, he slowly approached the centre of the yard, apparently oblivious of Theresa's existence.

There was a shout from the back of the building: "Theresa!" Charlie glanced around, then dived hastily into his room. The girl, left alone, gazed at the dark door into which Charlie had vanished, sighed, and blinked gently at the sunlight. A second shout: "Theresa, are you going to be all day with that washing?"

She tucked the flower among the stiff quills of hair on her head and bent to the basin that stood in the dust. The washing flapped and billowed all around her, so that the small, wiry form appeared to be wrestling with the big, ungainly sheets. Charlie ducked out of his door and ran quickly up the hedge, out of sight of Mrs. Black. He stopped, watching Theresa, who was still fighting with the washing. He whistled, she ignored him. He whistled again, changing key; the long note dissolved into a dance tune, and he sauntered deliberately up the hedge, weight shifting from hip to hip with each step. It was almost a dance: the buttocks sharply protruding and then withdrawn inwards after the prancing, lifting knees. The girl stood motionless, gazing at him, tantalised. She glanced quickly over her shoulder at the building, then ran across the yard to Charlie. The two of them, safe for the moment beside the hedge, looked guiltily for possible spies. They saw Marina behind her curtain—an earnest English face, apparently wrestling with some severe moral problem. But she was a friend. Had she not saved Charlie from the police? Besides, she immediately vanished.

Hidden behind the curtain, Marina saw the couple face each other, smiling. Then the girl tossed her head and turned away. She picked a second flower from the hedge, held it to her lips, and began swinging lightly from the waist, sending Charlie provocative glances over her shoulder that were half disdain and half invitation. To Marina it was as if a mischievous black urchin was playing the part of a coquette; but Charlie was watching with a broad and appreciative smile. He followed her, strolling in an assured and masterful way, as she went into his room. The door closed.

Marina discovered herself to be furious. Really the whole thing was preposterous!

"Philip," she said energetically that night, "we should do something."

"What?" asked Philip, practically. Marina could not think of a sensible answer. Philip gave a short lecture on the problems of the indigenous African peoples who were halfway between the tribal society and modern industrialisation. The thing, of course, should be tackled at its root. Since he was a soil expert, the root, to him, was a sensible organisation of the land. (If he had been a churchman, the root would have been a correct attitude to whichever God he happened to represent; if an authority on money, a mere adjustment of currency would have provided the solution—there is very little comfort from experts these days.) To Philip, it was all as clear as daylight. These people had no idea at all how to farm. They must give up this old attitude of theirs, based on the days when a tribe worked out one piece of ground and moved on to the next; they must learn to conserve their soil and, above all, to regard cattle, not as a sort of spiritual currency, but as an organic part of farm-work. (The word *organic* occurred very frequently in these lectures by Philip.) Once these things were done, everything else would follow . . .

"But in the meantime, Philip, it is quite possible that something may *happen* to Theresa, and she can't be more than fifteen, if that . . ."

Philip looked a little dazed as he adjusted himself from the level on which he had been thinking to the level of Theresa: women always think so personally! He said, rather stiffly: "Well, old girl, in periods of transition, what can one expect?"

What one might expect did in fact occur, and quite soon. One of those long ripples of gossip and delighted indignation passed from one end to the other of 138 Cecil John Rhodes Vista. Mrs. Black's Theresa had got herself into trouble; these girls had no morals; no better than savages; besides, she was a thief. She was wearing clothes that had not been given to her by Mrs. Black. Marina paid a formal visit to Mrs. Black in order to say that she had given Theresa various dresses. The air was not at all cleared. No one cared to what degree Theresa had been corrupted, or by whom. The feeling was: if not Theresa, then someone else. Acts of theft, adultery, and so on were necessary to preserve the proper balance between black and white; the balance was upset, not by Theresa, who played her allotted part, but by Marina, who insisted on introducing these Fabian scruples into a clear-cut situation.

Mrs. Black was polite, grudging, distrustful. She said: "Well, if you've given her the dresses, then it's all right." She added: "But it doesn't alter what she's done, does it now?" Marina could make no reply. The white women of the building continued to gossip and pass judgment for some days: one must, after all, talk about something. It was odd, however, that Mrs. Black made no move at all to sack Theresa, that immoral person, who continued to look after the children with her usual good-natured efficiency, in order that Mrs. Black might have time to gossip and drink tea.

So Marina, who had already made plans to rescue Theresa when she was flung out of her job, found that no rescue was necessary. From time to time Mrs. Black overflowed into reproaches, and lectures about sin. Theresa wept like the child she was, her fists stuck into her eyes. Five minutes afterwards she was helping Mrs. Black bath the baby, or flirting with Charlie in the yard.

For the principals of this scandal seemed the least concerned about it. The days passed, and at last Marina said to Charlie: "Well and what are you going to do now?"

"Madam?" said Charlie. He really did not know what she meant.

"About Theresa," said Marina sternly.

"Theresa she going to have a baby," said Charlie, trying to look penitent, but succeeding only in looking proud.

"It's all very well," said Marina. Charlie continued to sweep the verandah, smiling to himself. "But Charlie . . ." began Marina again.

"Madam?" said Charlie, resting on his broom and waiting for her to go on.

"You can't just let things go on, and what will happen to the child when it is born?"

His face puckered, he sighed, and finally he went on sweeping, rather slower than before.

Suddenly Marina stamped her foot and said: "Charlie, this really won't do!" She was really furious.

"Madam!" said Charlie reproachfully.

"Everybody has a good time," said Marina. "You and Theresa enjoy yourselves, all these females have a lovely time, gossiping, and the only thing no one ever thinks about is the baby." After a pause, when he did not reply, she went on: "I suppose you and Theresa think it's quite all right for the baby to be born here, and then you two, and the baby, and February, and all the rest of your friends who have nowhere to go, will all live together in that room. It really is shocking, Charlie."

Charlie shrugged as if to say: "Well, what do you suggest?"

"Can't Theresa go and live with her father?"

Charlie's face tightened into a scowl. "Theresa's father, he no good. Theresa must work, earn money for father."

"I see." Charlie waited; he seemed to be waiting for Marina to solve this problem for him; his attitude said: I have unbounded trust and confidence in you.

"Are any of the other men working here married?"

"Yes, madam."

"Where are their wives?"

"At home." This meant, in their kraals, in the Native Reserves. But Marina had not meant the properly married wives, who usually stayed with the clan, and were visited by their men perhaps one month in a year, or in two years. She meant women like Theresa, who lived in town.

"Now listen, Charlie. Do be sensible. What happens to girls like Theresa when they have babies. Where do they live?"

He shrugged again, meaning: They live as they can, and is it my fault the white people don't let us have our families with us when they work? Suddenly he said grudgingly: "The nanny next door, she has her baby, she works."

"Where is her baby?"

Charlie jerked his head over at the servants' quarters of the next house.

"Does the baas know she has her baby there?"

He looked away, uncomfortably. "Well, and what happens when the police find out?"

He gave her a look which she understood. "Who is the father of that baby?"

He looked away; there was an uncomfortable silence; and then he quickly began sweeping the verandah again.

"Charlie!" said Marina, outraged. His whole body had become defensive, sullen; his face was angry. She said energetically: "You should marry Theresa. You can't go on doing this sort of thing."

"I have a wife in my kraal," he said.

"Well, there's nothing to stop you having two wives, is there?"

Charlie pointed out that he had not yet finished paying for his first wife.

Marina thought for a moment. "Theresa's a Christian, isn't she? She was educated at the mission." Charlie shrugged. "If you marry Theresa Christian-fashion, you needn't pay lobola, need you?"

Charlie said: "The Christians only like one wife. And Theresa's father, he wants lobola."

Marina found herself delighted. At any rate he had tried to marry Theresa, and this was evidence of proper feeling. The fact that whether the position was legalized or not the baby's future was still uncertain, did not at once strike her. She was carried away by moral approval. "Well, Charlie, that's much better," she said warmly.

He gave her a rather puzzled look and shrugged again.

"How much lobola does Theresa's father want for her?"

"Plenty. He wants ten cattle."

"What nonsense!" exclaimed Marina energetically. "Where does he suppose you are going to find cattle, working in town, and where's he going to keep them?"

This seemed to annoy Charlie. "In my kraal, I have fine cattle," he pointed out. "I have six fine oxes." He swept, for a while, in silence. "Theresa's father, he mad, he mad old man. I tell him I must give three oxes this year for my own wife. Where do I find ten oxes for Theresa?"

It appeared that Charlie, no more than Theresa's father, found nothing absurd about this desire for cattle on the part of an old man living in the town location. Involuntarily she looked over her shoulder as if Philip might be listening: this conversation would have plunged him into irritated despair. Luckily he was away on one of his trips, and was at this moment almost certain to be exhorting the Africans, in some distant reserve, to abandon this irrational attitude to "fine oxes" which in fact were bound to be nothing but skin and bone, and churning whole tracts of country to dust.

"Why don't you offer Theresa's father some money?" she suggested, glancing down at Charlie's garters which were, this morning, of cherry-coloured silk.

"He wants cattle, not money. He wants Theresa not to marry, he wants her to work for him." Charlie rapidly finished sweeping the verandah and moved off, with relief, tucking the broom under his arm, with an apologetic smile which said: I know you mean well, but I'm glad to end this conversation.

But Marina was not at all inclined to drop the thing. She interviewed Theresa who, amid floods of tears, said Yes, she wanted to marry Charlie, but her father wanted too much lobola. The problem was quite simple to her, merely a question of lobola; Charlie's other wife did not concern her; nor did she, apparently, share Charlie's view that a proper wife in the kraal was one thing, while the women of the town were another.

Marina said: "Shall I come down to the location and talk to your father?"

Theresa hung her head shyly, allowed the last big tears to roll glistening down her cheeks and go splashing to the dust. "Yes, madam," she said gratefully,

Marina returned to Charlie and said she would interview the old man. He appeared restive at this suggestion. "I'll advance you some of your wages and you can pay for Theresa in instalments," she said. He glanced down at his fine shirt, his gay socks, and sighed. If he were going to spend years of life paying five shillings a month, which was all he could afford, for Theresa, then his life as a dandy was over.

Marina said crossly: "Yes, it's all very well, but you can't have it both ways."

He said hastily: "I'll go down and see the father of Theresa, madam. I go soon."

"I think you'd better," she said sternly.

When she told Philip this story he became vigorously indignant. It presented in little, he said, the whole problem of this society. The Government couldn't see an inch in front of its nose. In the first place, by allowing the lobola system to continue, this emotional attitude towards cattle was perpetuated. In the second, by making no proper arrangements for these men to have their families in the towns it made the existence of prostitutes like Theresa inevitable.

"Theresa isn't a prostitute," said Marina indignantly. "It isn't her fault."

"Of course it isn't her fault, that's what I'm saying. But she will be a prostitute, it's inevitable. When Charlie's fed up with her she'll find herself another man and have a child or two by him, and so on . . ."

"You talk about Theresa as if she were a vital statistic," said Marina, and Philip shrugged. That shrug expressed an attitude of mind which Marina would very soon find herself sharing, but she did not yet know that. She was still very worried about Theresa, and after some days she asked Charlie: "Well, and did you see Theresa's father? What did he say?"

"He wants cattle."

"Well, he can't have cattle."

"No," said Charlie, brightening. "My own wife, she cost six cattles. I paid three last year. I pay three more this year, when I go home."

"When are you going home?"

"When Mrs. Skinner comes back. She no good. Not like you, madam, you are my father and mother," he said, giving her his touching, grateful smile.

"And what will happen to Theresa?"

"She stay here." After a long, troubled silence, he said: "She my town wife. I come back to Theresa." This idea seemed to cheer him up.

And it seemed he was genuinely fond of the girl. Looking out of the kitchen window, Marina could see the pair of them, during lulls in the work, seated side by side on the big log under the tree—charming! A charming picture! "It's all very well . . ." said Marina to herself, uneasily.

Some mornings later she found Charlie in the front room, under the picture, and looking at it this time, not with reverent admiration, but rather nervously. As she came in he quickly returned to his work, but Marina could see he wanted to say something to her.

"Madam . . ."

"Well, what is it?"

"This picture costs plenty money?"

"I suppose it did, once."

"Cattles cost plenty money, madam."

"Yes so they do, Charlie."

"If you sell this picture, how much?"

"But it is Mrs. Skinner's picture."

His body drooped with disappointment. "Yes, madam," he said politely, turning away.

"But wait, Charlie—what do you want the picture for?"

"It's all right, madam." He was going out of the room.

"Stop a moment—why do you want it? You do want it, don't you?"

"Oh, yes," he said, his face lit with pleasure. He clasped his hands tight, looking at it. "Oh, yes, yes, madam!"

"What would you do with it? Keep it in your room?"

"I give it to Theresa's father."

"Wha-a-a-t?" said Marina. Slowly she absorbed this idea. "I see." she said. And then, after a pause: "I see . . ." She looked at his hopeful face, thought of Mrs. Skinner, and said suddenly, filled with an undeniably spiteful delight: "I'll give it to you, Charlie."

"Madam!" exclaimed Charlie. He even gave a couple of involuntary little steps, like a dance. "Madam, thank you, thank you."

She was as pleased as he. For a moment they stood smiling delightedly at each other. "I'll tell Mrs. Skinner that I broke it," she said. He went to the picture and lifted his hands gently to the great carved frame. "You must be careful not to break it before you get it to her father." He was staggering as he lifted it down. "Wait!" said Marina suddenly. Checking himself, he stood politely: she saw he expected her to change her mind and take back the gift. "You can't carry that great thing all the way to the location. I'll take it for you in the car!"

"Madam," he said. "Madam . . ." Then, looking helplessly around him for something, someone he could share his joy with, he said: "I'll tell Theresa now . . ." And he ran from the room like a schoolboy.

Marina went to Mrs. Black and asked that Theresa might have the afternoon off. "She had her afternoon off yesterday," said that lady sharply.

"She's going to marry Charlie," said Marina.

"She can marry him next Thursday, can't she?"

"No, because I'm taking them both down in the car to the location, to her father, and . . ."

Mrs. Black said resentfully: "She should have asked me herself."

"It seems to me," said Marina in that high, acid voice, replying not to the words Mrs. Black had used, but to what she had meant: "It seems to me that if one employs a child of fifteen, and under such conditions, the very least one can do is to assume the responsibility for her; and it seems to me quite extraordinary that you never have the slightest idea what she does, where she lives, or even that she is going to get married."

"You swallowed the dictionary?" said Mrs. Black, with an ingratiating smile. "I'm not saying she shouldn't get married; she should have got married before, that's what I'm saying."

Marina returned to her flat, feeling Mrs. Black's resentful eyes on her back: *Who the hell does she think she is, anyway?*

When Marina and Philip reached the lorry that afternoon that was waiting outside the gate, Theresa and Charlie were already sitting in the back, carefully balancing the picture on their knees. The two white people got in the front and Marina glanced anxiously through the window and said to Philip: "Do drive carefully, dear, Theresa shouldn't be bumped around."

"I'd be doing her a favour if I did bump her," said Philip grimly. He was accompanying Marina unwillingly. "Well, I don't know what you think you're going to achieve by it . . ." he had said. However, here he was, looking rather cross.

They drove down the tree-lined, shady streets, through the business area that was all concrete and modernity, past the slums where the half-caste people lived, past the factory sites, where smoke poured and hung, past the cemetery where angels and crosses gleamed white through the trees—they drove five miles, which was the distance Theresa had been expected to walk every morning and evening to her work. They turned off the main road into the location, and at once everything was quite different. No tarmac road, no avenues of beautiful trees here. Dust roads, dust paths, led from all directions inwards to the centre, where the housing area was. Dust lay thick and brown on the veld trees, the great blue sky was seen through a rust-coloured haze, dust gritted on the lips and tongue, and at once the lorry began to jolt and bounce. Marina looked back and saw Charlie and Theresa jerking and sliding with the lorry, under the great picture, clinging to each other for support, and laughing because of the joy-ride. It was the first time Theresa had ridden in a white man's car; and she was waving and calling shrill greetings to the groups of black children who ran after them.

They drove fast, bumping, so as to escape from the rivers of dust that spurted up from the wheels, making a whirling red cloud behind them, from which crowds of loitering Africans ran, cursing and angry. Soon they were in an area that was like a cheap copy of the white man's town; small houses stood in blocks, intersected by dust streets. They were two-roomed shacks with tin roofs, the sun blistering off them; and Marina said angrily: "Isn't it awful, isn't it terrible?"

Had she known that these same houses represented years of campaigning by the liberals of the city, against white public opinion, which obstinately held that houses for natives were merely another manifestation of that *Fabian* spirit from England which was spoiling the fine and uncorrupted savage, she might have been more respectful. Soon they left this new area and were among the sheds and barns that housed dozens of workers each, a state of affairs which caused Marina the acutest indignation. Another glance over her shoulder showed Theresa and Charlie giggling together like a couple of children as they tried to hold the picture still on their knees, for it slid this way and that as if it had a spiteful life of its own. "Ask Charlie where wc must go," said Philip; and Marina tapped on the glass till Charlie turned his head and watched her gestures till he understood and pointed onwards with his thumb. More of these brick shacks, with throngs of Africans at their doors, who watched the car indifferently until they saw it was a Government car, and then their eyes grew wary, suspicious. And now, blocking their way, was a wire fence, and Marina looked back at Charlie for instructions, and he indicated they should stop. Philip pulled the lorry up against the fence and Charlie and Theresa jumped down from the back, came forwards, and Charlie said apologetically: "Now we must walk, madam." The four went through a gap in the fence and saw a slope of soiled and matted grass that ended in a huddle of buildings on the banks of a small river.

Charlie pointed at it, and went ahead with Theresa. He held the picture on his shoulders, walking bent under it. They passed through the grass, which smelled unpleasant and was covered by a haze of flies, and came to another expanse of dust, in which were scattered buildings—no, not buildings, shacks, extraordinary huts thrown together out of every conceivable substance, with walls perhaps of sacking, or of petrol boxes, roofs of beaten tin, or bits of scrap iron.

"And what happens when it rains?" said Marina, as they wound in and out of these dwellings, among scratching chickens and snarling native mongrels. She found herself profoundly dispirited, as if something inside her said: What's the use? For this area, officially, did not exist. The law was that all the workers, the servants should live inside the location, or in one of the similar townships.

But there was never enough room. People overflowed into such makeshift villages everywhere, but as they were not supposed to be there the police might at any moment swoop down and arrest them. Admittedly the police did not often swoop, as the white man must have servants, the servants must live somewhere—and so it all went on, year after year. The Government, from time to time, planned a new housing estate. On paper, all around the white man's city, were fine new townships for the blacks. One had even been built, and to this critical visitors (usually those *Fabians* from overseas) were taken, and came away impressed. They never saw these slums. And so all the time, every day, the black people came from their reserves, their kraals, drawn to the white man's city, to the glitter of money, cinemas, fine clothes; they came in their thousands, no one knew how many, making their own life, as they could, in such hovels. It was all hopeless, as long as Mrs. Black, Mr. Black, Mrs. Pond were the voters with the power; as long as the experts and administrators such as Philip had to work behind Mrs. Pond's back—for nothing is more remarkable than that democratic phenomenon, so clearly shown in this continent, where members of Parliament, civil servants (experts, in short) spend half their time and energy earnestly exhorting Mrs. Pond: For heaven's sake have some sense before it is too late; if you don't let us use enough money to house and feed these people, they'll rise and cut your throats. To which reasonable plea for self-preservation, Mrs. Pond merely turns a sullen and angry stare, muttering: They're getting out of hand, that's what it is, they're getting spoilt.

In a mood of grim despair. Marina found herself standing with Philip in front of a small shack that consisted of sheets of corrugated iron laid loosely together, resting in the dust, like a child's card castle. It was bound at the corners with string, and big stones held the sheet of iron that served as roof from flying away in the first gust of wind.

"Here, madam," said Charlie. He thrust Theresa forward. She went shyly to the dark oblong that was the door, leaned inwards, and spoke some words in her own language. After a moment an old man stooped his way out. He was perhaps not so old—impossible to say. He was lean and tall, with a lined and angry face, and eyes that lifted under heavy lids to peer at Marina and Philip. Towards Charlie he directed a long, deadly stare, then turned away. He wore a pair of old khaki trousers, an old, filthy singlet that left his long, sinewed arms bare: all the bones and muscles of his neck and shoulders showed taut and knotted under the skin.

Theresa, smiling bashfully, indicated Philip and Marina; the old man offered some words of greeting; but he was angry, he did not want to see them, so the two white people fell back a little.

Charlie now came forward with the picture and leaned it gently against the iron of the shack in a way which said: "Here you are, and that's all you are going to get from me." In these surroundings those fierce Scottish cattle seemed to shrink a little. The picture that had dominated a room with its expanse of shining glass, its heavy carved frame, seemed not so enormous now. The cattle seemed even rather absurd, shaggy creatures standing in their wet sunset, glaring with a false challenge at the group of people. The old man looked at the picture, and then said something angry to Theresa. She seemed afraid, and came forward, unknotting a piece of cloth that had lain in the folds at her waist. She handed over some small change—about three shillings in all. The old man took the money, shaking it contemptuously in his hand before he slid it into his pocket. Then he spat, showing contempt. Again he spoke to Theresa, in short, angry sentences, and at the end he flung out his arms, as if throwing something away; and she began to cry and shrank back to Charlie. Charlie laid his hand on her shoulder and pressed it; then left her standing alone and went forward to his father-in-law. He smiled, spoke persuasively, indicated Philip and Marina. The old man listened without speaking, his eyes lowered. Those eyes slid sideways to the big picture, a gleam came into them; Charlie fell silent and they all looked at the picture.

The old man began to speak, in a different voice, sad, and hopeless. He was telling how he had wooed his second wife, Theresa's mother. He spoke of the long courting, according to the old customs, how, with many gifts and courtesies between the clans, the marriage had been agreed on, how the cattle had been chosen, ten great cattle, heavy with good grazing; he told how he had driven them to Theresa's mother's family, carefully across the country, so that they might not be tired and thinned by the journey. As he spoke to the two young people he was reminding them, and himself, of that time when every action had its ritual, its meaning; he was asking them to contrast their graceless behaviour with the dignity of his own marriages, symbolized by the cattle, which were not to be thought of in terms of money, of simply buying a woman— not at all. They meant so much: a sign of good feeling, a token of union between the clans, an earnest that the woman would be looked after, an acknowledgment that she was someone very precious, whose departure would impoverish her family—the cattle were all these things and many more. The old man looked at Charlie and Theresa and seemed to say: "And what about you? What are you in comparison to what we were then?" Finally he spat again, lifted the picture and went into the dark of his hut. They could see him looking at the picture. He liked it: yes, he was pleased, in his way. But soon he left it leaning against the iron and returned to his former pose—he drew a blanket over his head and shoulders and squatted down inside the door, looking out, but not as if he still saw them or intended to make any further sign towards them.

The four were left standing there, in the dust, looking at each other.

Marina was feeling very foolish. Was that all? And Philip answered by saying brusquely, but uncomfortably: "Well, there's your wedding for you."

Theresa and Charlie had linked fingers and were together looking rather awkwardly at the white people. It was an awkward moment indeed—this was the end of it, the two were married, and it was Marina who had arranged the thing. What now?

But there was a more immediate problem. It was still early in the afternoon, the sun slanted overhead, with hours of light in it still, and presumably the newly-married couple would want to be together? Marina said: "Do you want to come back with us in the lorry, or would you rather come later?"

Charlie and Theresa spoke together in their own language, then Charlie said apologetically: "Thank you, madam, we stay."

"With Theresa's father?"

Charlie said: "He won't have Theresa now. He says Theresa can go away. He not want Theresa."

Philip said: "Don't worry, Marina, he'll take her back, he'll take her money all right." He laughed, and Marina was angry with him for laughing.

"He very cross, madam," said Charlie. He even laughed himself, but in a rather anxious way.

The old man still sat quite motionless, looking past them. There were flies at the corners of his eyes; he did not lift his hand to brush them off.

"Well . . ." said Marina. "We can give you a lift back if you like." But it was clear that Theresa was afraid of going back now; Mrs. Black might assume her afternoon off was over and make her work.

Charlie and Theresa smiled again and said, "Goodbye. Thank

you, madam. Thank you, baas." They went slowly off across the dusty earth, between the hovels, towards the river, where a group of tall brick huts stood like outsize sentry-boxes. There, though neither Marina nor Philip knew it, was sold illicit liquor; there they would find a tinny gramophone playing dance music from America, there would be singing, dancing, a good time. This was the place the police came first if they were in search of criminals. Marina thought the couple were going down to the river, and she said sentimentally: "Well, they have this afternoon together, that's something."

"Yes," said Philip drily. The two were angry with each other, they did not know why. They walked in silence back to the lorry and drove home, making polite, clear sentences about indifferent topics.

Next day everything was as usual. Theresa back at work with Mrs. Black, Charlie whistling cheerfully in their own flat.

Almost immediately Marina bought a house that seemed passable, about seven miles from the centre of town, in a new suburb. Mrs. Skinner would not be returning for two weeks yet, but it was more convenient for them to move into the new home at once. The problem was Charlie. What would he do during that time? He said he was going home to visit his family. He had heard that his first wife had a new baby and he wanted to see it.

"Then I'll pay you your wages now," said Marina. She paid him, with ten shillings over. It was an uncomfortable moment. This man had been working for them for over two months, intimately, in their home; they had influenced each other's lives—and now he was off, he disappeared, the thing was finished. "Perhaps you'll come and work for me when you come back from your family?" said Marina.

Charlie was very pleased. "Oh, yes, madam," he said. "Mrs. Skinner very bad, she no good, not like you." He gave a comical grimace, and laughed.

"I'll give you our address." Mariana wrote it out and saw Charlie fold the piece of paper and place it carefully in an envelope which also held his official pass, a letter from her saying he was travelling to his family, and a further letter, for which he had asked, listing various bits of clothing that Philip had given him, for otherwise, as he explained, the police would catch him and say he had stolen them.

"Well, goodbye, Charlie," said Marina. "I do so hope your wife and your new baby are all right." She thought of Theresa, but did not mention her; she found herself suffering from a curious disinclination to offer further advice or help. What would happen to Theresa? Would she simply move in with the first man who offered her shelter? Almost Marina shrugged.

"Goodbye, madam," said Charlie. He went off to buy himself a new shirt with the ten shillings, and some sweets for Theresa. He was sad to be leaving Theresa. On the other hand, he was looking forward to seeing his new child and his wife; he expected to be home after about a week's walking, perhaps sooner if he could get a lift.

But things did not turn out like this.

Mrs. Skinner returned before she was expected. She found the flat locked and the key with Mrs. Black. Everything was very clean and tidy, but—where was her favourite picture? At first she saw only the lightish square patch on the dimming paint—then she thought of Charlie. Where was he? No sign of him. She came back into the flat and found the letter Marina had left, enclosing eight pounds for the picture "which she had unfortunately broken." The thought came to Mrs. Skinner that she would not have got ten shillings for that picture if she had tried to sell it; then the phrase "sentimental value" came to her rescue, and she was furious. Where was Charlie? For, looking about her, she saw various other articles were missing. Where was her yellow earthen vase? Where was the wooden door-knocker that said *Welcome Friend?* Where was . . . she went off to talk to Mrs. Black, and quite soon all the women dropped in, and she was told many things about Marina. At last she said: "It serves me right for letting to an immigrant. I should have let it to you, dear." The dear in question was Mrs. Pond. The ladies were again emotionally united; the long hostilities that had led to the flat being let to Marina were forgotten; that they were certain to break out again within a week was not to be admitted in this moment of pure friendship.

Mrs. Pond told Mrs. Skinner that she had seen the famous picture being loaded on to the lorry. Probably Mrs. Giles had sold it— but this thought was checked, for both ladies knew what the picture was worth. No, Marina must have disposed of it in some way connected with her *Fabian* outlook—what could one expect from these white kaffirs?

Fuming, Mrs. Skinner went to find Theresa. She saw Charlie, dressed to kill in his new clothes, who had come to say goodbye to Theresa before setting off on his long walk. She flew out, grabbed him by the arm, and dragged him into the flat. "Where's my picture?" she demanded.

At first Charlie denied all knowledge of the picture. Then he said Marina had given it to him. Mrs Skinner dropped his arm and stared: "But it was my picture . . ." She reflected rapidly: that eight pounds was going to be very useful; she had returned from her holiday, as people do, rather short of money. She exclaimed instead: "What have you done with my yellow vase? Where's my knocker?"

Charlie said he had not seen them. Finally Mrs. Skinner fetched the police. The police found the missing articles in Charlie's bundle. Normally Mrs. Skinner would have cuffed him and fined him five shillings. But there was this business of the picture—she told the police to take him off.

©   ©

Now, in this city in the heart of what used to be known as the Dark Continent, at any hour of the day, women shopping, typists glancing up from their work out of the window, or the business men passing in their cars, may see (if they choose to look) a file of handcuffed Africans, with two policemen in front and two behind, followed by a straggling group of African women who are accompanying their men to the courts. These are the Africans who have been arrested for visiting without passes, or owning bicycles without lights, or being in possession of clothes or articles without being able to say how they came to own them. These Africans are being marched off to explain themselves to the magistrates. They are given a small fine with the option of prison. They usually choose prison. After all, to pay a ten-shilling fine when one earns perhaps twenty or thirty a month, is no joke, and it is something to be fed and housed, free, for a fortnight. This is an arrangement satisfactory to everyone concerned, for these prisoners mend roads, cut down grass, plant trees: it is as good as having a pool of free labour.

Marina happened to be turning into a shop one morning, where she hoped to buy a table for her new house, and saw, without really seeing them, a file of such handcuffed Africans passing her. They were talking and laughing among themselves, and with the black policemen who herded them, and called back loud and jocular remarks at their women. In Marina's mind the vision of that ideal table (for which she had been searching for some days, without success) was rather stronger than what she actually saw; and it was not until the prisoners had passed that she suddenly said to herself: "Good heavens, that man looks rather like Charlie—and that girl behind there, the plump girl with the spindly legs, there was something about the back view of that girl that was very like Theresa . . ." The file had in the meantime turned a corner and was out of sight. For a moment Marina thought: Perhaps I should follow and see? Then she thought: Nonsense, I'm seeing things, of course it can't be Charlie, he must have reached home by now . . . And she went into the shop to buy her table.

Eldorado

HUNDREDS of miles south were the gold-bearing reefs of Johannesburg; hundreds of miles north, the rich copper mines. These the two lodestars of the great central plateau, these the magnets which drew men, white and black; drew money from the world's counting-houses; concentrated streets, shops, gardens; attracted riches and misery—particularly misery.

But this, here, was farming country, true farming land, a pocket of good, dark, rich soil in the wastes of the light sandveld. A "pocket" some hundreds of miles in depth, and only to be considered in such midget terms by comparison with those eternal sandy wastes which fed cattle, though poorly, and satisfied that shallow weed tobacco. For that is how a certain kind of farmer sees it; a man of the old-fashioned sort will think of farming as the making of food, and of tobacco as a nervous, unsatisfactory crop, geared to centres in London and New York; he will watch the fields fill and crowd with new, bright leaf, and imagine it crushed through factory and warehouse to end in a wisp of pale smoke; he will not like to imagine the substance of his soil dissipating in smoke. And if sensible people argue: Yes, but people must smoke, you smoke yourself, you're not being reasonable; he is likely to reply (rather irritably perhaps): "Yes, of course, you're right—but I want to grow food, the others can grow tobacco."

When Alec Barnes came searching for a farm, he chose the rich maize soil, though cleverer, experienced men told him the big money was to be found only in tobacco. Tobacco and gold, gold and tobacco—these were the money-makers. For this country had gold too, a great deal of it; but perhaps there is only room in one's mind for one symbol, one type; and when people say "gold" they think of the Transvaal, and so it was with Alec. There were many ways of seeing this new country, and Alec Barnes chose to see it with the eye of the food producer. He had not left England, he said, to worry about money and chase success. He wanted a slow, satisfying life, taking things easy.

He bought a small farm, about two thousand acres, from a man who had gone bankrupt. There was a house already built. It was a pleasant house, in the style of the country, of light red brick with a corrugated iron roof, big, bare rooms and a wide verandah. Shrubs and creepers, now rather neglected, showed scarlet against the dull green scrub, or hung in showers of gold and purple from the trees. The rainy season had sprung new grass high and thick over paths, over flower beds. When the Barnes family came in they had to send an African ahead with a scythe to cut an opening through thickets of growth; and in the front room the bricks of the floor were being tumbled aside by the shoots from old tree-roots. There was a great deal to do before the place could be comfortable, and Maggie Barnes set herself to work. She was the daughter of a small Glasgow shopkeeper, and it might be thought that everything would be strange to her; but her grandparents had farmed, and she remembered visiting the old people as a child, playing with a shaggy old cart-horse, feeding the chickens. That way of farming could hardly be compared to this, but in a sense it was like returning to her roots. At least, that was how she thought of it. She would pause in her work, duster in hand, at a window or on the verandah, and look over the scrub to the mealie fields, and it did not seem so odd that she should be here, in this big house, with black servants to wait on her, not so outlandish that she might walk an hour across country and call the soil underfoot her soil. There was no domesticated cart-horse to take sugar from her hand, only teams of sharp-horned and wild-eyed oxen; but there were chickens and turkeys and geese—she had no intention of paying good money for what she could grow herself, not she who knew the value of money! Besides, a busy woman has no time for fainthearted comparisons, and there was so much to do; and she intended that all this activity should earn its proper reward. She had gone beyond her grandparents, with their tight, frugal farm, which earned a living but no more; had gone beyond her parents, counting their modest profits in the back rooms of the grocery shop. In a sense she included both generations, could see the merits and failings of both, but—she and her husband would "get on," they would be prosperous as the farmers around them were prosperous. It was true that when the neighbours made doubtful faces at their growing small-scale maize, and said there could be no "taking it easy" on that farm, she felt a little troubled. But she approved her husband's choice; the growing of food satisfied her ideas of what was right, and connected her with her religious and respectable grandparents. Besides, many of the things Alec said she simply did not take seriously. When he said, fiercely, how glad he was to be out of England, out of the fight for success and the struggle to be better than one's neighbours, she merely smiled: what was the matter with getting on, and bettering oneself? They were just words to her. She would say, in her bluff, affectionate way, of Alec: "He's a queer man, being English, I canna get used to the way of him." For she put down his high-flown notions to his being English. Also, he was strange to her because of his gentleness: the men of her people were outspoken and determined and did not defer to their women. Alec deferred to her. Sometimes she could not understand him; but she was happy with him, and with her son, who was still a small child.

She sent Paul out with a native servant to play in the veld, while she worked, whitewashing the house, even climbing the roof herself to see to the guttering. Paul learned a new way of playing. He spread himself, ranging over the farm, so that the native youth who had the care of him found himself kept running. His toys, the substitutes for the real thing, mechanical lorries and bricks and dolls, were left in cupboards; and he made dams in the mud of the fields, plunged fearfully on the plough behind the oxen, rode high on the sacks of the waggons. He lost the pretty, sheltered look of the child from "home," who must be nervous of streets and traffic, always conscious of the pressure of the neighbours. He grew fast and tall, big-boned and muscular, and lean and burnt. Sometimes Maggie would say, with that good-natured laugh: "Well, and I don't know myself with this change-child!" Perhaps the laugh was a little uneasy, too. For she was not as thick-fibred as she looked. She was that Scots type, rather short, but finely made, even fragile, with the great blue eyes and easily-freckling fair skin and a mass of light black curls. Even after the hard work and the sunlight, which thickened her into a sturdy, energetic body of a woman, she kept, under the appearance of strength, that fine-boned delicacy and a certain shy charm. And here was her son shooting up into a lanky, bony youngster, the whites of his eyes always a little reddened by glare, his dark hair tumbling rough over his head with rusty bleached locks where the sun had struck. She looked at him in the bath, showing smooth dark-brown all over, save for the tender, milky skin like a loincloth where the strong khaki shorts kept the sun off. She felt a little perturbed, as if in some way he was most flagrantly betraying her by growing so, away from the fair, clear, open looks of her good Scots ancestors. There was something stubborn and secretive about him—perhaps even something a little coarse. But then—she reminded herself—he was half-English, too, and Alec was tall, long-headed, with a closed English face, and slow English speech which concealed more than it said. For a time she tried to change the child, to make him more dependent, until Alec noticed it and was angry. She had never seen him so angry before. He was a mild, easy man, who noticed very little, content to work at the farm and leave the rest to her. But now they fought. "What are you coddling him for?" Alec shouted. "What's the good of bringing him here to a country where he can grow up a man if you're going to fuss and worry all the time?" She gave him back as good; for to her women friends she would expound her philosophy of men: "You've got to stand against them once in a way, it doesnae do to be too sweet to them." But these remarks, she soon understood, sounded rather foolish; for when did she need to "stand against" Alec? She had her own way over everything. Except in this, for the very country was against her. Soon she left the boy to do as he liked on the veld. He was at an age when children at "home" would be around their mothers, but at seven and eight he was quite independent, had thrown off the attendant servant, and would spend all day on the fields, coming in for meals as if—so Maggie complained in that soft, pretty, Scots voice: "As if I'm no better than a restaurant!" But she accepted it, she was not the complaining sort; it was only a comfortable grumble to her woman friends. Besides, living here had hardened her a little. Perhaps hardened was not the right word? It was a kind of fatalism, the easy atmosphere of the country, which might bring in Paul and her husband an hour late for a meal, looking at her oddly if she complained of the time. What's an hour? they seemed to be asking; even: "What's time at all?" She could understand it, she was beginning to feel a little that way herself. But in her heart she was determined that Paul would not grow up lax and happy-go-lucky, like a Colonial. Soon he would be going to school and he would "have it knocked out of him." She had that good sturdy Scottish attitude towards education. She expected children to work and win scholarships. And indeed, it would be necessary, for the farm could hardly support a son through the sort of schooling she visualised for him. She was beginning to understand that it never would. At the end of the first five years she understood that their neighbours had been right: this farm would never do more than make a scanty living.

When she spoke to Alec he seemed to turn against her, not noisily, in a healthy and understandable quarrel, but in a stubborn, silent way. Surely he wanted Paul to make something of himself? she demanded. Put like that, of course, Alec had to agree, but he agreed vaguely. It was this vagueness that upset Maggie, for there was no way of answering it. It seemed to be saying: All these things are quite irrelevant; I don't understand you.

Alec had been a clerk in a bank until the First World War. After the upheaval he could not go back into an office. He married Maggie and came to this new country. There were farmers in his family, too, a long way back, though he had only come to remember this when he felt a need to explain, even excuse, that dissident streak which had made a conventional English life impossible. He would talk of a certain great-uncle, who had ridden a wild black horse around the shires, fathering illegitimate children and drinking and behaving so that he ended in prison for smuggling. Yes, this was all very well, thought Maggie, but what has that old rascal got to do with Alec, and what with *my* son? For Alec would talk of this unsatisfactory ancestor with pride and his eyes would rest speculatively on Paul—it gave Maggie gooseflesh to see him.

Alec grew even vaguer as time went by. He used to stand at the edge of a field, gazing dimly across it at a ridge of bush which rose sharp to the great blue sky; or at the end of the big vlei, which cut across the farm in a shallow, golden swathe of rustling grasses, with a sluggish watercourse showing green down its centre. He would stand on a moonlight night staring across the fields which now appeared like a diffusing green sea, the white crests of the maize shifting like foam; or at midday, looking over the stretching acres of brown and heaving clods, warm and rich with sunlight; or at sunset, when the miles of bush flared gold and red. Distance— that was what he needed. It was what he had left England to find.

He cleared new ground every year. When he first came it was mostly bush, with a few cleared patches. The house was bedded in trees. Now one walked from the house through Maggie's pretty garden, and the mealies stood like a green wall on three sides of the homestead. From a little hillock behind the house, the swaying green showed solid and unbroken, hundreds of acres of it, beautiful to look at until one remembered that the experts were warning against this kind of planting. Better small fields with trees to guard them from wind; better girdles of grass, so that the precious soil might be held by the roots and not wash away with the flooding storm-waters. But Alec's instinct was for space, and soon half the surface of the farm was exposed, and the ploughs drove a straight line from boundary to boundary, and the labourers worked in a straight line, like an advancing army, their hoes rising and falling and flashing like spears in the sun. The vivid green of the leaves rippled and glittered, or shone soft with moonlight; or at reaping time the land lay bare and hard, and over it the tarnished litter of the fallen husks; or at planting, a wide sweep of dark-brown clods which turned to harsh red under the rain. Beautiful it was, and Maggie could understand Alec's satisfaction in it; but it was disturbing when the rains drove the soil along the gulleys; when the experts came from town and told Alec he was ruining his farm; when at the season's end the yield rose hardly at all, in spite of the constantly increased acreage. But Alec set that obstinate face of his against the experts and the evidence of the books, and cut more trees, exposing the new soil which fed fine, strong plants, showing the richness of their growth in the heavy cobs. One could mark the newly-cleared area in the great field every year; the maize stood a couple of feet shorter on the old soil. Alec sent gangs of workers into the trees, and through the dry season the dull thud-thud of axes sounded across the wide, clean air, and the trees crashed one after another into the wreckage of their branches. Always a new field, or rather, the old one extended; always fine new soil ready for the planting. But there came a time when it was not possible to cut more trees, for where would the cattle graze? There must be sufficient veld left to feed them, for without them the ploughs and waggons could not move, and there wasn't sufficient capital for a tractor. So Alec rested on his laurels for a couple of years, working the great field, and Maggie sent her son off to school in town a hundred miles away. He would return only for the holidays—would return, she hoped, brisker, with purpose, the languor of the farm driven out of him. She missed him badly, but it was a relief that he was with other children, and this relief made up for the loss. As for Alec, Paul's going made him uneasy. Now he was actually at school, he must face his responsibility for the child's future. He wandered over his farm rather less vaguely and wondered how Paul thought of the town. For that was how he saw it; not that he was at school, but in town; and it was the reason why he had been so reluctant for him to go. He did not want him to grow into an office-worker, a pen-user, a city-cypher, the sort of person he had been himself and now disowned. But what if Paul did not feel as he did? Alec would stand looking at a tree, or a stretch of water, thinking: What does this mean to Paul, what does he think when he swims here?—in the secretive, nostalgic way of parents trying to guess at their children's souls. What sort of a creature was Paul? When he came to it, he had no idea at all, although the child was so like him, a long, lean, dark, silent boy, with contemplative dark eyes and a slow way of speaking. And here was Maggie, with such plans for him, determined that he must be an engineer, a scientist, a doctor, and nothing less than famous. The fame could be discounted, tolerantly, with her maternal pride and possessiveness, but scientists of any kind are not produced on the sort of profits he was making.

He thought worriedly about the farm. Perhaps he could lease adjoining land and graze his beasts there, and leave his own good land free for cutting? But all the land was taken up. He knew quite well, too, that the problem was deeper. He should change his way of farming. There were all sorts of things he could do—*should* do, at once; but at the idea of them a lassitude crept over him and he thought, obstinately: Why should I, why fuss and worry, when I'm free of all that, free of the competition in the Old Country? I didn't come here to fight myself into a shadow over getting rich. . . . But the truth was, though he did not admit it to himself, not for a second, he was very bored. He had come to the limits of his old way, and now, to succeed, it would be going over the same ground, but in a different way—nothing *new;* that was the point. Rather guiltily he found himself daydreaming about pulling up his roots here and going off somewhere else—South America, China—why not? Then he pulled himself together. To postpone the problem he cut another small area of trees, and the cutting of them exposed all the ground to where the ridge lifted itself; they could see clear from the house across the vlei and up the other side; all mealies, all a shimmering mass of green; and on the ridge was the boundary of the next farm, a low, barbed-wire fence, and against the fence was a small mine. It was nothing very grand, just a two-stamp affair, run by a single man who got what gold he could from a poor but steady seam. The mine had been there for years. The mine-stamp thudded day and night, coming loud or soft, according to the direction of the wind. But to Alec there was something new and even terrible about seeing the black dump of the mine buildings, seeing the black smoke drifting up into the blue, fresh sky. His deep and thoughtful eyes would often turn that way. How strange that from that cluster of black ugliness, under the hanging smoke, gold should come from the earth. It was unpleasant, too. This was farming land. It was outrageous that the good soil should be covered, even for a mere five acres or so, by buildings and iron gear and the sordid mine compound.

Alec felt as he did when people urged him to grow tobacco. It would be a betrayal, though what he would be betraying he could not say. And this mine was a betrayal of everything decent. They fetched up the ore, they washed the gold out, melted it to conveniently-handled shapes, thousands of workers spent their lives on it when they might be doing something useful on the land; and ultimately the gold was shipped off to America. He often made the old joke, these days, about digging up gold from one hole in the ground and sending it to America to be buried in another. Maggie listened and wondered at him. What a queer man he was! He noticed nothing until he was faced with it. For years she had been talking about Paul's future; and only when she packed him off to school did Alec begin to talk, just as if he had only that moment come to consider it, of how he should be educated. For years he had been living a couple of miles from a mine, with the sound of it always in his ears, but it was not until he could see it clear on the next ridge that he seemed to notice it. And yet for years the old miner had been dropping in of an evening. Alec would make a polite inquiry or two and then start farm-talk, which could not possibly interest him. "Poor body," Maggie had been used to say, half-scornfully, "what's the use of talking seasons and prices to *him?*" For she shared Alec's feeling that mining was not a serious way of living—not this sort of mining, scratching in the dirt for a little gold. That was how she thought of it. But at least she had thought of it; and here was Alec like a man with a discovery.

When Paul came home for his holiday and saw the mine lifted black before him on the long, green ridge, he was excited, and made his longest journey afield. He spent a day at the mine and came home chattering about pennyweights and ounces of gold; about reefs and seams and veins; about ore and slimes and cyanide —a whole new language. Maggie poured brisk scorn on the glamour of gold; but she was secretly pleased at this practical new interest. He was at least talking about *things*, he wasn't mooning about the farm like a waif returned from exile. She dreamed of him becoming a mining engineer or a geologist. She sent to town for books about famous men of science and left them lying about. Paul hardly glanced at them. His practical experience of handling things, watching growth, seeing iron for implements shaped in a fire, made it so that his knowledge must come first-hand, and afterwards he confirmed by reading. And he was roused to quite different thoughts. He would kick at an exposed rock, so that the sparks fell dull red under his boot-soles, and say: "Daddy, perhaps this is gold rock?" Or he would come running with bits of decomposed stone that showed dull gleams of metal and say: "Look, this is gold, isn't it?"

"Maybe," said Alec, reluctantly. "This is all gold country. The prospectors used to come through here. There is a big reef running across that ridge which is exactly the same formation as one of the big reefs on the Rand; once they thought they'd find a mine as big as that one, here. But it didn't come to anything."

"Perhaps we'll find it," said Paul, obstinately.

"Perhaps," said Alec, indulgently. But he was stirred, whether he liked it or not. He thought of the old prospectors wandering over the country with their meagre equipment, panning gold from the sand of river-beds, crushing bits of rock, washing the grit for those tiny grains that might proclaim a new Rand. Sometimes, when he came on a projecting ledge of rock, instead of cursing it for being on farmland at all, he would surreptitiously examine it, thinking: That bit there looks as if it had been broken off—perhaps one of the old hands used his hammer here twenty years ago. Or he might find an old digging, half-filled in by the rains, where someone had tried his luck; and he stood looking down at the way the rock lay in folds under the earth, sometimes flat, packed tidily one above the other, sometimes slanting in a crazy plunge where the subterranean forces had pushed and squeezed. And then he would shake himself and turn back to the business of farming, to the visible surfaces, the tame and orderly top-soil that was a shallow and understandable layer responsive to light and air and wetness, where the worms and air-bringing roots worked their miracles of decomposition and growth. He put his thoughts back to this malleable surface of the globe, the soil—or imagined that he did; and suppressed his furtive speculation about the fascinating underground structures—but not altogether. There was slowly growing in him another vision, another need; and he listened to the regular thud-thud of the mine-stamps from the opposite ridge as if they were drums beating from a country whose frontier he was forbidden to cross.

One evening an old weather-stained man appeared at the door and unslung from his back a great bundle of equipment and came in for the night, assuming the traveller's privilege of hospitality. He was, in fact, one of the vanishing race of wandering prospectors; and for most of the night he talked about his life on the veld. It was like a story from a child's adventure book in its simplicities of luck and bad fortune and persistent courage rewarded only by the knowledge of right-doing. For this old man spoke of the search for gold as a scientist might of discovery, or an artist of his art. Twice he had found gold and sold his riches trustingly, so that he was tricked by unscrupulous men who were now rich, while he was as poor as he had been forty years before. He spoke of this angrily, it is true, but it was that kind of anger we maintain from choice, like a relation whose unpleasantness has become, through the years, almost a necessity. There had been one brief period of months when he was very rich indeed, and squandered he did not know how much money in the luxury hotels of the golden city. He spoke of this indifferently, as of a thing which had chosen to visit him, and then as arbitrarily chosen to withdraw. Maggie, listening, was thankful that Paul was not there. And yet this was a tale any child might remember all his life, grateful for a glimpse of one of the old kind of adventurer, bred when there were still parts of the world unknown to map-makers and instrument-users. This was a character bound to fire any boy; but Maggie thought, stubbornly: There is enough nonsense as it is. And by this she meant, making no bones about it: Alec is enough of a bad influence. For she had come to understand that if Paul was to have that purpose she wanted in him, she must plant it and nurture it herself. She did not like the way Alec listened to this old man, who might be a grand body in his way, but not in *her* way. He was listening to a siren song, she could see that in his face. And later he began talking again about that nuisance of a great-uncle of his who, in some queer way, he appeared to link with the prospector. What more did the man want? Most sensible people would think that gallivanting off to farm in Africa was adventure enough, twice as adventurous as being a mere waster and ruffian, deceiving honest girls and taking honest people's goods, and ending as a common criminal!

Maggie, that eminently sensible woman, wept a little that night when Alec was asleep, and perhaps her courage went a little numb.

Or rather, it changed its character, becoming more like a shield than a spear, a defensive, not an attacking thing. For when she thought of Alec she felt helpless; and the old man asleep in the next room made her angry. Why did he have to come to *this* farm, why not take his dangerous gleam elsewhere? Long afterwards, she remembered that night and said, tartly, to Alec: "Yes, that was when the trouble started, when that old nuisance came lolloping along here with his long tongue wagging . . ." But "the trouble" started long before; who could say when? With the war, that so unsettled men and sent them flying off to new countries, new women? With whatever forces they were that bred men's silly wars? Something in Alec himself: his long-dead ancestor stirring in him and whispering along his veins of wildness and adventure? Well, she would leave all that to Alec and see that *her* son became a respectable lawyer, or a bridge-builder. That was enough adventure for her.

When the old man left next day, trudging off through the mealie fields with his pack over his shoulder, Alec watched him from the verandah. And that evening he climbed the hillock behind the house, and saw the small red glow of a fire down in the vlei. There he was, after his day of rock-searching, rock-chipping. He would be cooking his supper, or perhaps already lying wrapped in his blanket beside the embers, a fold of it across his face so that the moon would not trouble his eyelids with its shifting, cold gleams. The old man was alone; he did not even take an African with him to interpret the veld; he no longer needed this intermediary; he understood the country as well as the black men who lived on it. Alec went slowly to bed, thinking of the old prospector who was free, bound to no one, owning nothing but a blanket and a frying-pan and his clothes.

Not long afterwards a package arrived from the station and Maggie watched Alec open it. It was a gold pan. Alec held it clumsily between his palms, as he had seen the prospector do. He had not yet got the feel of the thing. It was like a deep frying-pan, without a handle, of heavy black metal, with a fine groove round the inside of the rim. This groove was to catch the runnels of silt that should hold grains of gold, if there was any gold. Alec brought back fragments of rock from the lands and crushed them in a mortar and stood beside the water tanks swirling the muddy mixture around and around endlessly, swearing with frustration, because he was still so clumsy and could not get the movements right. Each sample took a long time, and he could not be sure, when he had finished, if it had been properly done. First the handfuls of crushed rock, as fine as face-powder, must be placed in the pan and then the water run in. Afterwards it must be shaken so that the heavy metals should sink, and then with a strong sideways movement the lighter grit and dust must be flung out, with the water. Then more water added and the shaking repeated. Finally, there should be nothing but a wash of clean water, and the loose grit and bits of metal sliding along the groove: the dull, soft black of iron, a harder shine for chrome, the false glitter of pyrites, that might be taken for gold by a greenhorn, and finally, and in almost every sample, dragging slow and heavy behind the rest, would be the few dully-shining grains of true gold. But the movements had to be learned. The secret was a subtle little sideways jerk at the end, which separated the metals from the remnants of lighter rock. So stood Alec, methodically practising, with the heavy pan between his palms, the packets of crushed rock on the ground beside him, and on the other side the dripping water-taps. He was squandering the precious water that had to be brought from the well three times a week in the water-cart. The household was always expected to be niggardly with water, and now here was Alec swilling away gallons of it every day. An aggrieved Maggie watched him through the kitchen window.

But it was still a hobby. Alec worked as usual on the farm, picking up interesting bits of rock if he came across them, and panned them at evening, or early in the morning before breakfast. The house was littered with lumps of rocks, and Maggie handled them wonderingly when she was alone, for she did not intend to encourage Alec in "this nonsense." She was fascinated by the rocks, and she did not want to be fascinated. There were round stones, worn smooth by the wash of water; red stones, marbled with black; green stones, dull like rough jade; blue stones, with a fire of metal when they were shifted against a light. They were beautiful enough to be cut and worn as jewels. Then there were lumps of rough substance, halfway between soil and rock, the colour of ox-blood; and some so rich with metal that they weighed the hand low. Most promising were the decomposing rocks, where the soft parts had been rotted out by wind and water, leaving a crumbling, veiny substance, like a skeleton of the soil, and in some of these the gold could be seen lying thick and close, like dirt along the seams of a garment.

Alec did not yet know the names of the rocks and minerals, and he was troubled by his ignorance. He sent for books; and in the meantime he moved like an explorer over the farm he imagined he knew as well as it could be known, learning to see it in a new way. That rugged jut of reef, for instance, which intersected the big vlei like the wall of a natural dam—what was the nature of that hard and determined rock, and what happened to it beneath the ground? Why was the soil dark and red at one end of the big field and a sullen orange at the other? He looked at this field when it was bared ready for the planters, and saw how the soil shaded and modulated from acre to acre, according to the varieties of rock from which it had been formed, and he no longer saw the field, he saw the reefs and shales and silts and rivers of the underworld. He lifted his eyes from this vision and saw the *kopjes* six miles away; hard granite, they were; and the foothills, tumbled outposts of granite boulders almost to his own boundary—rock from another era, mountains erupted from an older time. On another horizon could be seen the long mountain where chrome was mined and exported to the countries which used it for war. Along the flanks of the mountain showed the scars and levels of the workings—it was another knowledge, another language of labour. He felt as if he had been blind half his life and only just discovered it. And on the slopes of his own farm were the sharp quartz reefs that the prospector told him were promise of gold. Quartz, that most lovely of rocks, coloured and weathered to a thousand shapes and tints, sometimes standing cold and glittering, like miniature snow mountains; sometimes milky, like slabs of opal, or delicate pink and amber with a smoky flush in its depths, as if a fire burnt there invisibly; marbled black, or mottled blue—there was no end to the strangeness and variety of those quartz reefs which for years he had been cursing because they made whole acres of his land unfit for the plough. Now he wandered there with a prospector's hammer, watching the fragments of rock fly off like chips of ice, or like shattering jewels. When he panned these pieces they showed traces of gold. But not enough: he had already learned how to measure the richness of a sample.

He sent for a geological map and tacked it to the wall of his farm office. Maggie found it and stood in front of it, studying it when he couldn't see her. Here was Africa, but in a new aspect. Instead of the shaded greens and browns and blues of the map she was accustomed to see, the colours of earth and growth, the colours of leaf and soil and grass and moving water, now they were harsh colours, like the metallic hues of rock. An arsenic green showed the copper deposits of Northern Rhodesia, a cold yellow the gold of the Transvaal—but not only the Transvaal. She had had no idea how much gold there was, worked everywhere; the patches of yellow mottled the sub-continent. But Maggie had no feeling for gold; her sound instincts were against the useless stuff. She looked with interest at the black of the coalfields—one of the richest in the world, Alec said, and hardly touched; at the dull grey of the chrome deposits, whole mountains of it, lying unused; at the glittering light green of the asbestos, at the iron and the manganese and—but most of these names she had never heard, could not even pronounce.

When Alec's books came, she would turn over the pages curiously, gaining not so much a knowledge as an intimation of the wonderful future of this continent. Perhaps Alec should have been a scientist, she thought, and not a farmer at all? Perhaps, with this capacity of his for completely losing himself (as he had become lost) he might have been a great man? For this was how the vision narrowed down in her; all the rich potentialities of Africa she saw through her son, who might one day work with coal, or with copper; or through Alec, the man, who "might have done well for himself" if he had had a different education. Education, that was the point. And she turned her thoughts steadily towards her son. All her interests had narrowed to him. She set her will hard, like a prayer, towards him, as if her damned forces could work on him a hundred miles away at school in the city.

When he came home from school he found his father using a new vocabulary. Alec was still attending to the farm with half his attention, but his passion was directed into this business of gold-finding. He had taken half a dozen labourers from the fields and they were digging trenches along the quartz reef on the ridge. Maggie made no direct comment, but Paul could feel her disapproval. The child was torn between loyalty to his mother and fascination for this new interest, and the trenches won. For some days Maggie hardly saw him, he was with his father, or over at the mine on the ridge.

"Perhaps we'll have a mine on our farm, too," said Paul to Maggie; and then, scornfully: "But we won't have a silly mine like that one, we'll have a big one, like Johannesburg." And Maggie's heart sank, listening to him. Now was the time, she thought, to mould him, and she showed him the coloured map on the office wall and tried to make it come alive for him, as it had for her. She spoke of the need for engineers and experts, but he looked and listened without kindling. "But my bairn," said Maggie reproachfully, using the old endearment which was falling out of use now, with her other Scots ways of speech, "my bairn, it's time you were making

your mind to what you want. You must know what you want to be."
He looked sulky and said if they found "a big mine, like Johannesburg," he would be a gold-miner. "Oh, no," said Maggie indignantly.
"That's just luck. Anyone can have a stroke of luck. It takes a clever
man to be educated and know about things." So Paul evaded this
and said all right then, he'd be a tobacco farmer. "Oh, no," said
Maggie again; and wondered herself at the passion she put into it.
Why should he not be a tobacco farmer? But it wasn't what she
dreamed of for him. He would become a rich tobacco farmer? He
would make his thousands and study the international money-
juggling and buy more farms and more farms and have assistants
until he sat in an office and directed others, just as if he were a
businessman? For with tobacco there seemed to be no halfway
place, the tobacco farmers drove themselves through night-work
and long hours on the fields, as if an invisible whip threatened
them, and then they failed, or they succeeded suddenly, and paid
others to do the slaving . . . it was no sort of a life, or at least, not
for *her* son. "What's the matter with having money?" asked Paul at
last, in hostility. "Don't you see," said Maggie, desperately, trying to
convey something of her solid and honest values; "anyone can be
lucky, anyone can do it. Young men come out from England, with a
bit of money behind them, and they needn't be anything, just fools
maybe, and then the weather's with them, and the prices are good,
and they're rich men—but there's nothing in that, you want to try
something more worthwhile than that, don't you?" Paul swung the
dark and stubborn eyes on her and asked, dourly: "What do you
think of my father, then?" She caught her breath, looked at him in
amazement—surely he couldn't be criticising his father! But he
was; already his eyes were half-ashamed, however, and he said
quickly, "I'll think about it," and made his escape. He went straight
off to the diggings, and seemed to avoid his mother for a time. As
for Alec, Maggie thought he'd lost his senses. He came rushing in
and out of the house with bits of rock and announcements of imminent riches so that Paul became as bad, and spent half his day
crushing stones and watching his father panning. Soon he learned
to use the pan himself. Maggie watched the intent child at work beside the water-tanks, while the expensive water went sloshing over
to the dry ground, so that there were always puddles, in spite of the
strong heat. The tanks ran dry and Alec had to give orders for the
water-carts to make an extra journey. Yes, thought Maggie, bitterly,
all these years I've been saving water and now, over this foolish-

ness, the water-carts can make two or three extra trips a week.
Because of this, Alec began talking of sinking a new well; and
Maggie grew more bitter still, for she had often asked for a well to
be sunk close at the back of the house, and there had never been
time or money to see to it. But now, it seemed, Alec found it justified.

People who live on the veld for a long time acquire an instinct
for the places where one must sink for water. An old-timer will go
snuffing and feeling over the land like a dog, marking the fall of
the earth, the lie of a reef, the position of an anthill, and say at
last: Here is the place. Likely enough he will be right, and often
enough of course, quite wrong.

Alec went through just such a morning of scenting and testing,
through the bush at the back of the house, where the hillock
erupted its boulders. If the underground forces had broken here,
then there might be fissures where water could push its way; water
was often to be found near a place of reefs and rocks. And there
were antheaps; and ant galleries mostly ended, perhaps a hundred
feet down, in an underground river. And there was a certain promising type of tree—yes, said Alec, this would be a good place for a
well. And he had already marked the place and taken two labourers
from the farm to do the digging when there appeared yet another of
those dangerous visitors; another vagrant old man, just as stained
and weather-worn as the last; with just such a craziness about him,
only this time even worse, for he claimed he was a water-diviner
and would find Alec Barnes a well for the sum of one pound ster-
ling.

That night Paul was exposed until dawn to the snares of magical
possibilities. He could not be made to go to bed. The old man had
many tales of travel and danger; for he had spent his youth as a big-
game hunter, and later, when he was too old for that, became a
prospector; and later still, by chance, found that the forked twig of
a tree had strength in his hands. Chance!—it was always chance,
thought Maggie, listening dubiously. These men lived from one
stroke of luck to the next. It was bad luck that the elephant charged
and left the old man lame for life, with the tusk-scars showing
white from angle to groin. It was good luck that he "fell in" with old
Thompson, who had happened to "make a break" with diamonds in
the Free State. It was bad luck that malaria and then blackwater
got him, so that he could no longer sleep in the bush at nights. It
was good luck that made him try his chances with the twig, so that

now he might move from farm to farm, with an assured welcome
for a night behind mosquito netting . . . What an influence for
Paul!

Paul sat quietly beside her and missed not a word. He blinked
slow attention through those dark and watchful eyes; and he was
critical, too. He rejected the old man's boasting, his insistence on
the scientific certainties of the magic wand, all the talk of wells and
watercourses, of which he spoke as if they were a species of underground animal that could be stalked and trapped. Paul was fixed by
something else, by what kept his father still and alert all night, his
eyes fixed on his guest. That *something else*—how well Maggie
knew it! and how she distrusted it, and how she grieved for Paul,
whose heart was beating (she could positively hear it) to the pulse
of that dangerous *something else*. It was not the elephants and the
lions and the narrow escapes; not the gold; not underground rivers;
none of these things in themselves, and perhaps not even the pursuit of them. It was that oblique, unnamable quality in life which
Maggie, trying to pin it down safely in homely words, finally dismissed in the sour and nagging phrase: Getting something for
nothing. That's all they wanted, she said to herself, sadly; and
when she kissed Paul and put him to bed she said, in her sensible
voice: "There isn't anything to be proud of in getting something for
nothing." She saw that he did not know what she meant; and so she
left him.

Next morning, when they all went off to the projected well, Maggie remained a little way off, her apron lifted over her head against
the sun, arms folded on her breast, in that ancient attitude of a
patient and ironic woman; and she shook her head when the diviner offered her the twig and suggested she should try. But Paul
tried, standing on his two planted feet, elbows tight to his sides, as
he was shown, with the angles of the fork between palm and
thumb. The twig turned over for him and he cried, delightedly:
"I'm a diviner, I'm a diviner," and the old man agreed that he had
the gift.

Alec indicated the place, and the old man walked across and
around it with the twig, and at last he gave his sanction to dig—the
twig turned down, infallibly, at just that spot. Alec paid him twenty
shillings, and the old man wandered off to the next farm. Maggie
said: "In a country the like of this, where everyone is parched for
water, a man who could tell for sure where the water is would be
nothing but a millionaire. And look at this one, his coat all patches

and his boots going." She knew she might as well save her breath, for she found two pairs of dark and critical eyes fixed on her, and it was as good as if they said: Well, woman, and what has the condition of his boots got to do with it?

Late that evening she saw her husband go secretly along the path to the hillock with a twig, and later still he came back with an excited face, and she knew that he, too, "had the gift."

It was that term that Maggie got a letter from Paul's headmaster saying that Paul was not fitted for a practical education, nor yet did he have any especial facility for examinations. If he applied himself, he might win a scholarship, however, and become academically educated . . . and so on. It was a tactful letter, and its real sense Maggie preferred not to examine, for it was too wounding to her maternal pride. Its surface sense was clear: it meant that Paul was going to cost them a good deal of money. She wrote to say that he must be given special coaching, and went off to confront Alec. He was rather irritable with her, for his mind was on the slow descent of the well. He spent most of his time watching the work. And what for? Wells were a routine. One set a couple of men to dig, and if there was no water by a certain depth, one pulled them out and tried again elsewhere. No need to stand over the thing like a harassed mother hen. So thought Maggie as she watched her husband walking in his contemplative way around the well with his twig in his hands. At thirty feet they came on water. It was not a very good stream, and might even fail in the dry season, but Alec was delighted. "And if that silly old man hadnae come at all, the well would have been sunk just that place, and no fiddle-faddle with the divining rod," Maggie pointed out. Alec gave her a short answer and went off to the mine on the ridge, taking his twig with him. The miner said, tolerantly, that he could divine a well if he liked. Alec chose a place, and came home to tell Maggie he would earn a guinea if there turned out to be water. "But man," said Maggie in amazement, "you aren't going to keep the family in shoe-leather on guineas earned that way!" She asked again about the money for Paul's coaching, and Alec said: "What's the matter with the boy, he's doing all right." She persisted, and he gave in; but he seemed to resent it, this fierce determination of hers that her son must be something special in the world. But when it came to the point, Alec could not find the money, it was just not in the bank. Maggie roused herself and sold eggs and poultry to the store at the station, to earn the extra few pounds that were needed. And she went on scraping shillings together and hoarding them in a drawer, though money from chickens and vegetables would not send Paul through university.

She said to Alec: "The wages of the trench-boys would save up for Paul's education." She did not say, since she could not think of herself as a nagging woman: And if you put your mind to it there'd be more money at the end of a season. But although she did not say it, Alec heard it, and replied with an aggrieved look and dogged silence. Later he said: "If I find another Rand here the boy can go to Oxford, if you want that." There was not a grain of humour in it, he was quite in earnest.

He spent all his time at the mine while the well was being sunk. They found water and he earned his guinea, which he put carefully with the silver for paying the labourers. What Maggie did not know was that during that time he had been walking around the mine-shaft with his divining rod. It was known how the reefs lay underground, and how much gold they carried.

He remarked, thoughtfully: "Lucky the mine is just over the way for testing. The trouble with this business is it's difficult to check theories."

Maggie did not at first understand; for she was thinking of water. She began: "But the well on the mine is just the same as this one . . ." She stopped, and her face changed as the outrageous suspicion filled her. "But Alec," she began, indignantly; and saw him turning away, shutting out her carping and doubt. "But Alec," she insisted, furiously, "surely you aren't thinking of . . ."

"People have been divining for water for centuries," he said simply, "so why not gold?" She saw that it was all quite clear to him, like a religious faith, and that nothing she could say would reach him at all. She remained silent; and it was at that moment the last shreds of her faith in him dissolved; and she was filled with the bitterness of a woman who has no life of her own outside husband and children, and must see everything that she could be destroyed. For herself she did not mind; it was Paul—he would have to pay for this lunacy. And she must accept that too; she had married Alec, and that was the end of it; for the thought of leaving him did not enter her mind: Maggie was too old-fashioned for divorce. There was nothing she could do; one could not argue with a pos-sessed person, and Alec was possessed. And in this acceptance, which was like a slow shrug of the shoulders, was something deeper, as if she felt that the visionary moon-chasing quality in Alec—even though it was ridiculous—was something necessary, and that there must always be a moment when the practical-minded must pay tribute to it. From that day, Alec found Maggie willing to listen, though ironically; she might even enquire spontaneously after his "experiments." Well, why not? she would catch herself thinking; perhaps he may discover something new after all. Then she pulled herself up, rather angrily; she was becoming infected by the lunacy. In her mind she was lowering the standards she had for Paul.

When Paul next returned from school he found the atmosphere again altered. The exhilaration had gone out of Alec; the honeymoon phase of discovery was past; he was absorbed and grim. His divining rod had become an additional organ; for he was never seen without it. Now it was made of iron wire, because of some theory to do with the attraction of gold for iron; and this theory and all the others were difficult to follow. Maggie made no comment at all; and this Paul would have liked to accept at its surface value, for it would have left him free to move cheerfully from one parent to the other without feeling guilt. But he was deeply disturbed. He saw his mother, with the new eyes of adolescence, for the first time, as distinct from feeling her, as the maternal image. He saw her, critically, as a fading, tired woman, with grey hair. He watched her at evening, sitting by the lamp, with the mending on her lap, in the shabby living-room; he saw how she knitted her brows and peered to thread a needle; and how the sock or shirt might lie forgotten while she went off into some dream of her own which kept her motionless, her face sad and pinched, for half an hour at a time, while her hands rubbed unconsciously in a hard and nervous movement over the arms of the chair. It is always a bad time when a son grows up and sees his mother as an elderly lady; but this did not last longer than a few days with Paul; because at once the pathos and tiredness of her gripped him, and with it, a sullen anger against his own father. Paul had become a young man when he was hardly into his teens; he took a clear look at his father and hated him for murdering the gay and humorous Maggie. He looked at the shabby house, at the neat but faded clothes of the family, and at the neglected farm. That holiday he spent down on the lands with the labourers, trying to find out what he should do. To Maggie, the new protective gentleness of her son was sweet, and also very frightening, because she did not know how to help him. He would come to her and say: "Mother, there's a gulley down the middle of that land, what should I tell the boss-boy to do?" or "We should plant some trees, there's hardly any timber

on the place, *he's* gone and cut it all down." He referred to his
father, with hostility, as *he;* all those weeks, and Maggie said over
and over again that he should not worry, he was too young. She was
mortally afraid he would become absorbed by the farm and never
be able to escape. When he went back to school he wrote desperate
letters full of appeals like this one: "Do please, *make* him see to
that fence before the rains, please mother, don't be soft and good-
natured with him." But Alec was likely to be irritable about details
such as fences; and Maggie would send back the counter-appeal:
"Be patient, Paul. Finish your studies first, there'll be plenty of time
for farming."

He scraped through his scholarship examination with three
marks to spare, and Maggie spoke to him very seriously. He appeared to be listening and perhaps he tried to; but in the end he
broke in impatiently: "Oh, Mother, what's the use of me wasting
time on French and Latin and English Literature. It just doesn't
make sense in this country, you must see that." Maggie could not
break through this defence of impatient common sense, and
planned to write him a long, authoritative letter when he got back
to school. She still kept a touching belief in what schools could put
in and knock out of children. At school, she thought, he might be
induced into a serious consideration of his future, for the scholarship was a very small one, and would only last two years.

In the meantime he went to his father, since Maggie could not or
would not help him, for advice about the farm. But Alec hardly
listened to warnings about drains that needed digging and trees
that should be planted; and in a fit of bitter disappointment, Paul
wandered off to the mine: the boy needed a father, and had to find
one somewhere. The miner liked the boy, and spoiled him with
sweets and gave him the run of the workings, and let him take
rides in the iron lift down the mine-shaft that descended through
the soiled and sour-smelling earth. He went for a tour through the
underground passages where the mine-boys worked in sodden grey
loincloths, the water from the roof dripping and mingling with
their running sweat. The muffled thudding of their picks sounded
like marching men, a thudding that answered the beat of the mine-
stamps overhead; and the lamps on their foreheads, as they moved
cautiously through the half-dark tunnels made them seem like a
race of groping Cyclops. At evening he would watch the cage coming up to the sunlight full of labourers, soaked with dirt and sweat,
their forehead lamps blank now, their eyes blinking painfully at the
glare. Then everyone stood around expectantly for the blessing. At

the very last moment the cage came racing up, groaning with the strain, and discharged the two men who had lit the fuse; and almost at once there was a soft, vibrating roar from far under their feet, and the faces and bodies of the watchers relaxed. They yawned and stretched, and drifted off in groups for their meal. Paul would lean over the shaft to catch the acrid whiff from the blasting; and then went off to eat with James, the miner. He lived in a little house with a native woman to cook for him. It was unusual to have a woman working in the house, and this plump creature, who smiled and smiled and gave him biscuits and called him darling, fascinated Paul. It was terrible cheek for a kaffir, and a kaffir woman at that, to call him darling; and Paul would never have dreamed of telling his mother, who had become so critical and impatient, and might forbid him to come again.

Several times his father appeared from the trenches down the ridge, walking straight and fast through the bush with his divining rod in his hand. "So there you are, old son," he would say to Paul, and forgot him at once. He nodded to James, asked: "Do you mind?" and at once began walking back and forth around the mineshaft with his rod. Sometimes he was pleased, and muttered: "Looks as if I'm on the right track." Or he might stand motionless in the sun, his old hat stuck on the back of his head, eyes glazed in thought. "Contradictory," he would mutter. "Can't make it out at all." Then he said, briefly, "Thanks!" nodded again at James and Paul as if at strangers, and walked back just as fast and determined to the "experimental" trenches. James watched him expressionlessly, while Paul avoided his eyes. He knew James found his father ridiculous, and he did not intend to show that he knew it. He would stare off into the bush, chewing at a grass-stem, or down at the ground, making patterns in the dust with his toes, and his face was flushed and unhappy. James, seeing it, would say, kindly: "Your father'll make it yet, Paul."

"Do you think there could be gold?" Paul asked, eagerly, for confirmation, not of the gold, but of his father's good sense.

"Why not? There's a mine right here, isn't there? There's half a dozen small-workers round about."

"How did you find this reef?"

"Just luck. I was after a wild pig, as it happened. It disappeared somewhere here and I put my rifle down against a rock to have a smoke, and when I picked it up the rock caught my eye, and it seemed a likely bit, so I panned it and it showed up well; I dug a trench or two and the reef went down well, and—so here I am."

But Paul was still thinking of his father. He was looking away through the trees, over the wire fence to where the trenches were. "*My* father says if he proves right he'll divine mines for everyone, all over the world, and not only gold but diamonds and coal—and everything!" maintained Paul proudly, with a defiant look at the miner.

"That's right, son," said James nicely, meeting the look seriously. "Your dad's all right," he added, to comfort the boy. And Paul was grateful. He used to go over to James every day just after breakfast and return late in the evening when the sun had gone. Maggie did not know what to say to him. He could not be blamed for taking his troubles to someone who was prepared to spend time with him. It was not his fault for having Alec as a father—thus Maggie, secretly feeling disloyal.

One evening she paid a visit to Alec's trenches. The reef lay diagonally down the slope of the ridge for about a mile, jutting up slantingly, like a rough ledge. At intervals, trenches had been dug across it and in places it had been blown away by a charge of gelignite.

Maggie was astonished at the extent of the work. There were about twelve labourers, and the sound of picks on flinty earth sounded all around her. From shallow trenches protruded the shoulders and heads of some of the men, but others were out of sight, twelve or more feet down. She stood looking on, feeling sad and tired, computing what the labour must cost each month, let alone the money for gelignite and fuses and picks. Alec was moving through the scrub with his wire. He had a new way of handling it. As a novice he had gripped it carefully, elbows tight at his sides, and walked cautiously as if he were afraid of upsetting the magnetism. Now he strode fast over the ground, his loose bush-shirt flying around him, the wire held lightly between his fingers. He was zigzagging back and forth in a series of twenty-foot stretches, and Maggie saw he was tracking the course of a reef, for at the centre of each of these stretches the wire turned smartly downwards. Maggie could not help thinking there was something rather perfunctory in it. "Let me try," she asked, and for the first time she held the magic wand. "Walk along here," her husband ordered, frowning with the concentration he put into it; and she walked as bidden. It was true that the wire seemed to tug and strain her hands; but she tried again and it appeared to her that if she pulled the two ends apart, pressure tugged the point over and down, whereas if she held it without tension it remained unresponsive. Surely it could not be as simple as that? Surely Alec was not willing the wire to move as he wanted? He saw the doubt in her face and said quickly: "Perhaps you haven't the electricity in you." "I daresay not," she agreed, drily; and then asked quickly, trying to sound interested, because at once he reacted like a child to the dry note in her voice: "Is this water or a reef?"

"A reef." His face had brightened pathetically at this sign of interest, and he explained: "I've worked out that either an iron rod or a twig works equally well for water, but if you neutralize the current with an iron nut on the end there must be mineral beneath, but I don't know whether gold or just any mineral."

Maggie digested this, with difficulty, and then said: "You say an iron rod, but this is just called galvanized iron, it's just a name, it might be made of anything really, steel or tin—or anything," she concluded lamely, her list of metals running out.

His face was perturbed. She saw that this, after all, very simple idea had never occurred to him. "It doesn't matter," he said, quickly, "the point is that it works. I've proved it on the reefs at the mine." She saw that he was looking thoughtful, nevertheless, and could not prevent herself thinking sarcastically that she had given birth to a new theory, probably based on the word *galvanized*. "How do you know it isn't reacting to water? That mine is always having trouble with water, they say there's an underground river running parallel to the main reef." But this was obvious enough to be insulting, and Alec said, indignantly: "Give me credit for some sense. I checked that a long time ago." He took the wire, slipped an iron nut on each bent end and gripped the ends tight. "Like that," he said. "The iron neutralizes, do you see?" She nodded, and he took off the iron nuts and then she saw him reach into his pocket and take out his signet ring and put that on the wire.

"What are you doing?" asked Maggie, with the most curious feeling of dismay. That signet ring she had given him when they were married. She had bought it with money saved from working as a girl in her parents' shop, and it represented a great deal of sacrifice to her then. Even now, for that matter. And here he was using it as an implement, not even stopping to think how she might feel about it. When he had finished he slipped the gold ring, together with the two iron nuts, back into the pocket of his bush-shirt. "You'll lose it," she said, anxiously, but he did not hear her. "If the iron neutralizes the water, which I've proved," he said, worriedly, "then the gold ring should neutralize the gold." She did not follow the logic of this, though she could not doubt it all had been worked out most logically. He took her slowly along the great reef, talking in that slow, thoughtful way of his. She felt a thwarted misery—for what was the use of being miserable? She did not believe in emotions that were not useful in some way.

Later he began flying back and forth again over a certain vital patch of earth, and he dropped the signet ring and it rolled off among the long grasses, and she helped him to find it again. "As a matter of fact," he mused aloud, "I'll give up the trenches here, I think, and sink a proper shaft. Not here. It's had a fair chance. I'll try somewhere new."

Before they left at sundown she walked over to one of the deep trenches and stood looking down. It was like a grave, she thought. The mouth was narrow, a slit among the long, straggling grass, with the mounds of rubble banked at the ends, and the rosy evening sun glinted red on the grass-stems and flashed on the pebbles. The trees glowed, and the sky was a wash of colour. The side of the trench showed the strata of soil and stone. First a couple of feet of close, hard, reddish soil, hairy with root-structure; then a slab of pinkish stuff mixed with round white pebbles; then a narrow layer of smooth white that resembled the filling in the cake; and then a deep plunge of greyish shale that broke into flakes at the touch of the pick. There was no sign of any reef at the bottom of the trench; and as Alec looked down he was frowning; and she could see that there should have been a reef, and this trench proved something unsettling to the theory.

Some days later he remarked that he was taking the workers off the reef to a new site. She did not care to ask where; but soon she saw a bustle of activity in the middle of the great mealie field. Yes, he had decided to sink a shaft just there, he, who had once lost his temper if he found even a small stone in a furrow which might nick the ploughshares.

It was becoming a very expensive business. The cases of explosive came out from the station twice a month on the waggon; and she had to order boxes of mining candles, instead of packets, from the store. And when Alec panned the samples there were twenty or more, instead of the half-dozen, and he would be working at the water-tanks half the morning. He was very pleased with the shaft; he thought he was on the verge of success. There were always a few grains of gold in the pan, and one day a long trail of it, which he estimated at almost as much as would be worth working. He sent a sample to the Mines Department for a proper test, and it came back confirmed. But this was literally a flash in the pan, for nothing fresh happened, and soon that shaft was abandoned. Workers dragged an untidy straggle of barbed wire around the shaft so that cattle should not stray into it; and the ploughs detoured there; and in the centre of the once unbroken field stood a tall thicket of grass and scrub, which made Paul furious when he came home for the holidays. He remonstrated with his father, who replied that it had been justified, because from that shaft he had learned a great deal, and one must be prepared to pay for knowledge. He used just those words, very seriously, like a scientist. Maggie remarked that the shaft had cost at least a hundred pounds to sink, and she hoped the knowledge was worth that much. It was the sort of remark she never made these days; and she understood she had made it now because Paul was there, who supported her. As soon as Paul came home she always had the most uncomfortable feeling that his very presence tugged her away from her proper loyalty to Alec. She found herself becoming critical and nagging; while the moment Paul had gone she drifted back into a quiet acceptance, like fatalism. It was not long after that bitter remark that Alec finally lost his signet ring; and, because it was necessary to work with a gold ring, asked her for her wedding ring. She had never taken it off her finger since they married, but she slipped it off now and handed it to him without a word. As far as she was concerned it was a moment of spiritual divorce; but a divorce takes two, and if the partner doesn't even notice it, what then?

He lost that ring too, of course, but it did not matter by then, for he had amended his theory, and gold rings had become a thing of the past. He was now using a rod of fine copper wire with shreds of asbestos wound about it. Neither Maggie nor Paul asked for explanations, for there were pages of detailed notes on his farm desk, and books about magnetic fields and currents and the sympathy of metals, and they could not have understood the terms he used, for his philosophy had become the most extraordinary mixture of alchemy and magic and the latest scientific theories. His office, which for years had held nothing but a safe for money and a bookshelf of farming magazines, was now crammed with lumps of stone, crucibles, mortars, and the walls were covered with maps and diagrams, while divining rods in every kind of metal hung from nails. Next to the newest geological map from the Government office was an old map imagined by a seventeenth-century explorer, with mammoth-like beasts scrolling the border; and the names of the territories were fabulous, like El Dorado, and Golconda, and Queen Sheba's Country. There were shelves of retorts and test-tubes and chemicals, and in a corner stood the skull of an ox, for there was a period of months when Alec roamed the farm with that skull dangling from his divining rod, to test a belief that the substances of bone had affinities with probable underground deposits of lime. The books ranged from the latest Government publications to queer pamphlets with titles such as *Metallurgy and the Zodiac,* or *Gold Deposits on Venus.*

It was in this room that Maggie confronted him with a letter from Paul's headmaster. The scholarship money was finished. Was it intended that the boy should try for a fresh one to take him through university? In this case, he must change his attitude, for, while he could not be described as stupid, he "showed no real inclination for serious application." If not, there was "no immediate necessity for reviewing the state of affairs," but a list of employers was enclosed with whom Mrs. Barnes might care to communicate. In short, the headmaster thought Paul was thick-witted. Maggie was furious. *Her* son become a mere clerk! She informed Alec, peremptorily, that they must find the money to send Paul through university. Alec was engaged in making a fine diagram of his new shaft in cross-section, and he lifted a blank face to say: "Why spoon-feed the boy? If he was any good he'd work." The words struck Maggie painfully, for they summed up her own belief; but she found herself thinking that it was all Alec's fault for being English and infecting her son with laziness. She controlled this thought and said they must find the money, even if Alec curtailed his experimenting. He looked at her in amazement and anger. She saw that the anger was against her false scale of values. He was thinking: What is one child's future (even if he happens to be my own, which is a mere biological accident, after all) against a discovery which might change the future of the world? He maintained the silence necessary when dealing with little-minded people. But she would not give in. She argued and even wept, and gave him no peace, until his silence crumbled into violence and he shouted: "Oh, all right then, have it your own way."

At first Maggie thought that she should have done this before "for his own good." It was not long before she was sorry she had done it. For Alec went striding anxiously about the farm, his eyes worriedly resting on the things he had not really seen for so long— eroded soil, dragging fences, blocked drains—he had been driven out of the inward refuge where everything was clear and meaningful, and there was a cloud of fear on his face like a child with nightterrors. It hurt Maggie to look at him; but for a while she held out, and wrote a proud letter to the headmaster saying there was no need to trouble about a scholarship, they could pay the money. She wrote to Paul himself, a nagging letter, saying that his laziness was making his father ill, and the very least he could do "after all his father had done for him" was to pass his matriculation well.

This letter shocked Paul, but not in the way she had intended. He knew quite well that his father would never notice whether he passed an examination or not. His mother's dishonesty made him hate her; and he came home from school in a set and defiant mood, saying he did not want to go to university. This betrayal made Maggie frantic. Physically she was passing through a difficult time, and the boy hardly recognised this hectoring and irritable mother. For the sake of peace he agreed to go to university, but in a way which told Maggie that he had no intention at all of doing any work. But his going depended, after all, on Alec, and when Maggie confronted him with the fact that money for fees was needed, he replied, vaguely, that he would have it in good time. It was not quite the old vagueness, for there was a fever and urgency in him that seemed hopeful to Maggie, and she looked every day at the fields for signs of reorganisation. There were no changes yet. Weeks passed, and again she went to him, asking what his new plans were. Alec replied, irritably, that he was doing what he could, and what did she expect, a miracle to order? There was something familiar in this tone and she looked closely at him and demanded: "Alec, what exactly are you doing?"

He answered in the old, vague way: "I'm on to it now, Maggie, I'm certain I'll have the answer inside a month."

She understood that she had spurred him, not into working on the farm, but into putting fresh energies behind the gold-seeking. It was such a shock to her that she felt really ill, and for some days she kept to her bed. It was not real illness, but a temporary withdrawal from living. She pulled the curtains and lay in the hot half-dark. The servants took in her meals, for she could not bear the sight of either her son or her husband. When Paul entered tentatively, after knocking and getting no reply, he found her lying in her old dressing-gown, her eyes averted, her face flushed and exhausted, and she replied to his questions with nervous dislike. But it was Paul who coaxed her back into the family, with that gentle, protective sympathy which was so strange in a boy of his age. She came back because she had to; she took her place again and behaved sensibly, but in a tight and controlled way which upset Paul, and which Alec ignored, for he was quite obsessed. He would come in for meals, his eyes hot and glittering, and eat unconsciously, throwing out remarks like: Next week I'll know. I'll soon know for sure.

In spite of themselves, Paul and Maggie were affected by his certainty. Each was thinking secretly: Suppose he's right? After all, the great inventors are always laughed at to begin with.

There was a day when he came triumphantly in, loaded with pieces of rock. "Look at this," he said, confidently. Maggie handled them, to please him. They were of rough, heavy, crumbling substance, like rusty honeycomb. She could see the minerals glistening. She asked: "Is this what you wanted?"

"You'll see," said Alec, proudly, and ordered Paul to come with him to the shaft, to help bring more samples. Paul went, in his rather sullen way. He did not want to show that he half-believed his father. They returned loaded. Each piece of rock was numbered according to the part of the reef it had been taken from. Half of each piece was crushed in the mortar, and father and son stood panning all the afternoon.

Paul came to her and said, reluctantly: "It seems quite promising, Mother." He was appealing to her to come and look. Silently she rose, and went with him to the water-tanks. Alec gave her a defiant stare and thrust the pan over to her. There was the usual trail of mineral, and behind was a smear of dull gold, and behind that big grits of the stuff. She looked with listless irony over at Paul, but he nodded seriously. She accepted it from him, for he knew quite a lot by now. Alec saw that she trusted his son when she disbelieved him, and gave her a baffled and angry look. She hastened to smooth things over. "Is it a lot?" she asked.

"Quite enough to make it workable."

"I see," she said, seriously. Hope flickered in her and again she looked over at Paul. He gave an odd, humorous grimace, which meant: Don't get excited about it yet; but she could see that he was really excited. They did not want to admit to each other that they were aroused to a half-belief, so they felt awkward. If this madness turned out to be no madness at all, how foolish they would feel!

"What are you going to do now?" she asked Alec.

"I'm sending in all these samples to the Department for proper assaying."

"*All* of them . . ." she checked the protest, but she was thinking: That will cost an awful lot of money. "And when will you hear?"

"In about a week."

Again Paul and she exchanged glances, and they went indoors, leaving Alec to finish the panning. Paul said, with that grudging enthusiasm: "You know, Mother, if it's true . . ."

"If . . ." she scoffed.

"But he says if this works it means he can divine anything. He says Governments will be sending for him to divine their coalfields, water, gold—everything!"

"But Paul," she said, wearily, "they can find coalfields and minerals with scientific instruments, they don't need black magic." She even felt a little mean to damp the boy in this way. "Can they?" he asked, doubtfully. He didn't want to believe it, because it sounded so dull to him. "But Mother, even if he can't divine, and it's all nonsense, we'll have a rich mine on this farm."

"That won't satisfy your father," she said. "He'll rest at nothing less than a universal theory."

The rocks were sent off that same day to the station; and now they were restless and eager, even Maggie, who tried not to show it. They all went to examine this vital shaft one afternoon. It was in a thick patch of bush and they had to walk along a native path to reach the rough clearing, where a simple windlass and swinging iron bucket marked the shaft. Maggie leaned over. There being no gleam of water, as in a well, to mark the bottom, she could see nothing at first. For a short distance the circular hole plunged rockily, with an occasional flash of light from the faceted pebble; then a complete darkness. But as she looked there was a glow of light far below and she could see the tiny form of a man against the lit rock face. "How deep?" she asked, shuddering a little.

"Over a hundred now," said Alec, casually. "I'll go down and have a look." The Africans swung the bucket out into the centre of the shaft and Alec pulled the rope to him, so that the bucket inclined at the edge, slid in one leg and thrust himself out, so that he hung in space, clinging to the rope with one hand and using an arm and a leg to fend off the walls as the rope unwound him down into the blackness. Maggie found it frightening to watch so she pulled her head back from the shaft so as not to look; but Paul lay on his stomach and peered over.

At last Alec came up again. He scrambled lightly from the rocking bucket to safety, and Maggie suppressed a sigh of relief. "You should see that reef," he said, proudly. "It's three feet wide. I've cross-cut in three places and it doesn't break at all."

Maggie was thinking: Only three days of waiting gone! They were all waiting now, in a condition of hallucinatory calm, for the result to come back from the Assay Department. When only five

days had passed Alec said: "Let's send the boy in for the post." She
had been expecting this, and although she said "Silly to send so
soon," she was eager to do so; after all, they *might* have replied, one
never knew—and so the houseboy made the trip in to the station.
Usually they only sent twice a week for letters. Next day he went
again—nothing. And now a week had passed and the three of them
were hanging helplessly about the house, watching the road for the
postboy. Eight days: Alec could not work, could not eat; and Paul
lounged about the verandah, saying: "Won't it be funny to have a
big mine just down there, on our own farm. There'll be a town
around it, and think what this land will be worth then!"

"Don't count your chickens," said Maggie. But all kinds of half-
suppressed longings were flooding up in her. It would be nice to
have good clothes again; to buy nice linen, instead of the thin,
washed-out stuff they had been using for years. Perhaps she could
go to the doctor for her headaches, and he would prescribe a holiday, and they could go to Scotland for a holiday and see the old
people . . .

Nine days. The tension was no longer pleasant. Paul and Alec
quarrelled. Alec said he would refuse to allow a town to be built
around the mine; it would be a pity to waste good farming land.
Paul said he was mad—look at Johannesburg, the building lots
there were worth thousands the square inch. Maggie again told
them not to be foolish; and they laughed at her and said she had no
imagination.

The tenth day was a regular mail-day. If there was no letter then
Alec said he would telephone the Department; but this was a mere
threat, because the Department dealt with hundreds of samples
from hopeful gold-searchers all over the country, and could not be
expected to make special arrangements for one person. But Alec
said: "I'm surprised they haven't telephoned before. Just like a
Government department not to see the importance of something
like this." The post was late. They sat on the darkening verandah,
gazing down the road through the mealie fields, and when the man
came at last there was still no letter. They had all three expected
it.

And now there was a feeling of anti-climax, and Maggie found a
private belief confirmed: that nothing could happen to this family
in neat, tidy events; everything must always drag itself out, everything declined and decayed and muddled itself along. Even if there
is gold, she thought, secretly, there'll be all kinds of trouble with
selling it, and it'll drag out for months and months! That eleventh

day was a long torture. Alec sat in his office, anxiously checking his calculations, drinking cup after cup of strong, sweet tea. Paul pretended to read, and yawned, and watched the clock until Maggie lost her temper with him. The houseboy, now rather resentful because of these repeated trips of seven miles each way on foot, set off late after lunch to the station. They tried to sleep the afternoon away, but could not keep their eyes closed. When the sun was hanging just over the mountains, they again arranged themselves on the verandah to wait. The sun sank, and Maggie telephoned the station: Yes, the train had been two hours late. They ate supper in tense silence and went back to the verandah. The moon was up and everything flooded with that weird light which made the mealie fields lose solidity, so that there was a swaying and murmuring like a sea all around them. At last Paul shouted: "Here he comes!" And now, when they could see the swinging hurricane lamp, that sent a dim, red flicker along the earth across the bright moonlight, they could hardly bring themselves to move. They were thinking: Well, it needn't be today, after all—perhaps we'll have this waiting tomorrow, too.

The man handed in the sack. Maggie took it, removed the bundle of letters and handed them to Alec; she could see a Government envelope. She was feeling sick, and Paul was white, the bones of his face showed too sharply. Alec dropped the letters and then clumsily picked them up. He made several attempts to open the envelope and at last ripped it across, tearing the letter itself. He straightened the paper, held it steady, and—but Maggie had averted her eyes and glanced at Paul. He was looking at her with a sickly and shamed smile.

Alec held the piece of paper loose by one corner, and he was sitting rigid, his eyes dark and blank. "No good," he said at last, in a difficult, jerking voice. He seemed to have shrunk, and the flesh of his face was tight. His lips were blue. He dropped the paper and sat staring. Then he muttered: "I can't understand it, I simply can't understand it."

Maggie whispered to Paul. He jumped up, relieved to get away, and went to the kitchen and soon returned with a tray of tea. Maggie poured out a big cup, sugared it heavily and handed it to Alec. Those blue lips worried her. He put it at his side, but she took it again and held it in front of him and he drank it off, rather impatiently. It was that impatient movement which reassured her. He was now sitting more easily and his face was flushed. "I can't understand it," he said again, in an aggrieved voice, and Maggie understood that the worst was over. She was aching with pity for him and for Paul, who was pretending to read. She could see how badly the disappointment had gripped him. But he was only a child, she thought; he would get over it.

"Perhaps we should go to bed," she suggested, in a small voice; but Alec said: "That means . . ." He paused, then thought for a moment and said: "I must have been wrong over—all this time I've been over-estimating the amount in the sample. I thought that was going ounces to the ton. And it means that my theory about the copper was . . ." He sat leaning forward, arms hanging loosely before him; then he jumped up, strode through to his office and returned with a divining wire. She saw it was one of the old ones, a plain iron rod. "Have you anything gold about you?" he asked, impatiently.

She handed him a brooch her mother had given her. He took it and went towards the verandah. "Alec," she protested, "not to-night." But he was already outside. Paul put down his book and smiled ruefully at her. She smiled back. She did not have to tell him to forget all the wild-goose daydreams. Life would seem flat and grey for a while, but not for long—that was what she wanted to say to him; she would have liked, too, to add a little lecture about working for what one wanted in life, and not to trust to luck; but the words stuck. "Get yourself to bed," she suggested; but he shook his head and handed his cup for more tea. He was looking out at the moonlight, where a black, restless shape could be seen passing backwards and forwards.

She went quietly to a window and looked out, shielding herself with a curtain, though she felt ashamed of this anxious supervision which Alec would most certainly resent if he knew. But he did not notice. The moon shone monotonously down; it looked like a polished silver sixpence; and Alec's shadow jerked and lengthened over the rough ground as he walked up and down with his divining rod. Sometimes he stopped and stood thinking. She went back to sit by Paul. She slipped an arm around him, and so they remained for a time, thinking of the man outside. Later she went to the window again, and this time beckoned to Paul and he stood with her, silently watching Alec.

"He's a very brave man," she found herself saying, in a choked voice; for she found that determined figure in the moonlight unbearably pathetic. Paul felt awkward because of her emotion, and looked down when she insisted: "Your father's a very brave man and don't you ever forget it." His embarrassment sent him off to bed. He could not stand her emotion as well as his own.

Afterwards she understood that her pity for Alec was a false feeling—he did not need pity. It flashed through her mind, too—though she suppressed the thought—that words like brave were as false.

Until the moon slid down behind the house and the veld went dark, Alec remained pacing the patch of ground before the house. At last he came morosely to bed, but without the look of exposed and pitiful fear she had learnt to dread: he was safe in the orderly inner world he had built for himself. She heard him remark from the bed on the other side of the room where he was sitting smoking in the dark: "If that reef outside the front door is what I think it is, then I've found where I was wrong. Quite a silly little mistake, really."

Cautiously she enquired: "Are you going on with that shaft?"

"I'll see in the morning. I'll just check up on my new idea first." They exchanged a few remarks of this kind; and then he crushed out his cigarette and lay down. He slept immediately; but she lay awake, thinking drearily of Paul's future.

In the morning Alec went straight off down to his shaft, while Paul forced himself to go and interview the boss-boys about the farmwork. Maggie was planning a straight talk with the boy about his school, but his present mood frightened her. Several times he said, scornfully, just as if he had not himself been intoxicated: "Father's crazy. He's got no sense left." He laughed in an arrogant, half-ashamed way; and she controlled her anger at this youthful unfairness. She was tired, and afraid of her own irritability, which these days seemed to explode in the middle of the most trifling arguments. She did not want to be irritable with Paul because, when this happened, he treated her tolerantly, as a grown man would, and did not take her seriously. She waited days before the opportunity came, and then the discussion went badly after all.

"Why do you want me to be different, Mother?" he asked, sullenly, when she insisted he should study for a scholarship. "You and Father were just like everybody else, but I've got to be something high and mighty." Maggie already found herself growing angry. She said, as her mother might have done: "Everybody has the duty to better themselves and get on. If you try you can be anything you like." The boy's face was set against her. There was something in the air of this country which had formed him that made the other, older voice seem like an anachronism. Maggie persisted: "Your great-grandparents were small farmers. They rented their land from a lord. But they saved enough to give your grandfather fifty pounds to take to the city. He got his own shop by working for it. Your father was just an ordinary clerk, but he took his opportunities and made his way here. But you see no shame in accepting a nobody's job, wherever someone's kind enough to offer it to you." He seemed embarrassed, and finally remarked: "All that class business doesn't mean anything out here. Besides, my father's a small farmer, just like his grandparents. I don't see what's so new about that." At this, as if his words had released a spring marked *anger,* she snapped out: "So, if that's what you are, the way you look at things, it's a waste of time even . . ." She checked herself, but it was too late. Her loss of control had ended the contact between them. Afterwards she wondered if perhaps he was right. In a way, the wheel had come the circle: the difference between that old Scotsman and Alec was that one worked his land with his own hands; he was limited only by his own capacities; while the other worked through a large labour-force: he was as much a slave to his ill-fed, backward, and sullen labourers as they were to him. Well then, and if this were true, and Paul could see it as clearly as she did, why could he not decide to break the circle and join the men who had power because they had knowledge: the free men, that was how she saw them. Knowledge freed a man; and to that belief she clung, because it was her nature; and she was to grieve all her life because such a simple and obvious truth was not simple for Paul.

Some days later she said, tartly, to Paul: "If you're not going back to school, then you might as well put your mind to the farmwork." He replied that he was trying to; to her impatience he answered with an appeal: "It's difficult, Mother. Everything's in such a mess. I don't know where to start. I haven't the experience." Maggie tried hard to control that demon of disappointment and anger in her that made her hard, unsympathetic; but her voice was dry: "You'll get experience by working."

And so Paul went to his father. He suggested, practically, that Alec should spend a month ("only a month, Dad, it's not so long") showing him the important things. Alec agreed, but Paul could see that as they went from plough to waggon, field to grazing land, that Alec's thoughts were not with him. He would ask a question, and Alec did not hear. And at the end of three days he gave it up. The boy was seething with frustration and misery. "What do they expect me to do?" he kept muttering to himself; "what do they want?" His mother was like a cold wall; she would not love him unless he became a college boy; his father was amiably uninterested. He took himself off to neighbouring farmers. They were kind, for everyone was sorry for him. But after a week or so of listening to advice, he was more dismayed than before. "You'd better do something about your soil, lad," they said. "Your dad's worked it out." Or: "The first thing is to plant trees, the wind'll blow what soil there is away unless you do something quickly." Or: "That big vlei of yours: do you know it was dry a month before the rains last year? Your father has ploughed up the catchment area; you'd better sink some wells quickly." It meant a complete reorganisation. He could do it, of course, but . . . the truth was he had not the heart to do it, when no one was interested in him. They just don't care, he said to himself; and after a few weeks of desultory work he took himself off to James, his adopted father. Part of the day he would spend on the lands, just to keep things going, and then he drifted over to the mine.

James was a big, gaunt man, with a broad and bony face. Small grey eyes looked steadily from deep sockets, his mouth was hard. He stood loosely, bending from the shoulders, and his hands swung loose beside him so that there was something of a gorilla-look about him. Strength—that was the impression he gave, and that was what Paul found in him. And yet there was also a hesitancy, a moment of indecision before he moved or spoke, and a sardonic note in his drawl—it was strength on the defensive, a watchful and precarious strength. He smoked heavily, rough cigarettes he rolled for himself between yellow-stained fingers; and regularly drank just a little too much. He would get really drunk several times a year, but between these indulgences kept to his three whiskies at sundown. He would toss these back, standing, one after another, when he came in from work; and then give the bottle a long look, a malevolent look, and put it away where he could not see it. Then he took his dinner, without pleasure, to feed the drink; and immediately went to bed. Once Paul found him at a week-end lying sodden and asleep sprawled over the table, and he was sickened; but afterwards James was simple and kindly as always; nor did he apologise, but took it as a matter of course that man needed to drink himself blind from time to time. This, oddly enough, reassured the boy. His own father never drank, and Maggie had a puritan horror of it; though she would offer visitors a drink from politeness. It was a problem that had never touched him; and now it was presented crudely to him and seemed no problem at all.

He asked questions about James's life. James would give him that shrewd, slow look, hesitate a little, and then in a rather tired voice, as if talking were disagreeable, answer the boy's clumsy questions. He was always very patient with Paul; but behind the good-natured patience was another emotion, like a restrained cruelty; it was not a personal cruelty, directed against Paul, but the self-punishment of fatalism, in which Paul was included.

James's mother was Afrikaans and his father English. He had the practicality, the humour, the good sense of his mother's people, and the inverted and tongue-tied poetry of the English, which expressed itself in just that angry fatalism and perhaps also in the drink. He had been raised in a suburb of Johannesburg, and went early to the mines. He spoke of that city with a mixture of loathing and fascination, so that to Paul it became an epitome of all the great and glamorous cities of the world. But even while Paul was dreaming of its delights he would hear James drawl: "I got out of it in time, I had that much sense." And though he did not want to have his dream darkened, he had to listen: "When you first go down, you get paid like a prince and the world's your oyster. Then you get married and tie yourself up with a houseful of furniture on the hire-purchase and a house under a mortgage. Your car's your own, and you exchange it for a new one every year. It's a hell of a life, money pouring in and money pouring out, and your wife loves you, and everything's fine; parties and a good time for one and all. And then your best friend finds his chest is giving him trouble and he goes to the doctor, and then suddenly you find he's dropped out of the crowd; he's on half the money and all the bills to pay. His wife finds it no fun and off she goes with someone else. Then you discover it's not just one of your friends, but half the men you know are in just that position, crocks at thirty and owning nothing but the car, and they soon sell that to pay alimony. You find you drink too much—there's something on your mind, as you might say. Then, if you've got sense, you walk out while the going's good. If not, you think: It can't happen to me, and you stay on." He allowed a minute to pass while he looked at the boy to see how much had sunk in. Then he repeated, firmly: "That's not just my story, son, take it from me. It's happened to hundreds."

Paul thought it over and said: "But you didn't have a wife?"

"Oh, yes, I had a wife all right," said James, grim and humorous.

"I had a fine wife, but only while I was underground raking in the shekels. When I decided it wasn't good enough and I wanted to save my lungs, and I went on surface work at less money, she transferred to one of the can't-happen-to-me boys. She left him when the doctor told him he was fit for the scrap-heap, and then she used her brains and married a man on the stock exchange."

Paul was silent, because this bitter note against women was not confirmed by what he felt about his mother. "Do you ever want to go back?" he asked.

"Sometimes," conceded James, grudgingly. "Johannesburg's a mad-house, but it's got something—but when I get the hankering I remember I'm still alive and kicking when my crowd's mostly dead or put out to grass." He was speaking of the city as men do of the sea, or travel, or of drugs; and it gripped Paul's imagination. But James looked sharply at him and said: "Hey, sonnie, if you've got any ideas about going south to the golden city, then think again. You don't want to get any ideas about getting rich quick. If you want to mix yourself up in that racket, then you buy yourself an education and stay on the surface bossing the others, and not underground being bossed. You take it from me, son."

And Paul took it from him, though he did not want to. The golden city was shimmering in his head like a mirage. But what was the alternative? To stay on this shabby little farm? In comparison, James's life seemed daring and wonderful and dangerous. It seemed to him that James was telling him everything but what was essential; he was leaving something out—and soon he came back again for another dose of the astringent common sense that left him unfed, acknowledging it with his mind but not his imagination.

He found James sitting on a heap of shale at the shaft-head, rolling cigarettes, his back to the evening sun. Paul stepped over the long, black shadow and seated himself on the shale. It was loose and shifted under him to form a warm and comfortable hollow. He asked for a cigarette and James good-humouredly gave him one. "Are you glad you became a small-worker?" he asked at once.

There was a shrewd look and the slow reply: "No complaints, there's a living as long as the seam lasts—looks as if it won't last much longer at that." Paul ignored that last remark and persisted: "If you had your life again, how would you change it?"

James grimaced and asked: "Who's offering me my life again?"

The boy's face was stained with disappointment. "I want to know," he said, stubbornly, like a child.

"Listen, sonnie," said James, quietly, "I'm no person to ask for advice. I've nothing much to show. All I've got to pat myself on the back for is I had the sense to pull out of the big money in time to save my lungs." Paul let these words go past him and he looked up at the big man, who seemed so kindly and solid and sensible, and asked: "Are you happy?"

At last the question was out. James positively started: then he gave that small, humorous grimace and put back his head and laughed. It was painful. Then he slapped Paul's knee and said, tolerantly, still laughing: "Sonnie, you're a nice kid, don't let any of them get you down."

Paul sat there, shamefaced, trying to smile, feeling badly let down. He felt as if James, too, had rejected him. But he clung to the man, since there was no one else; he came over in the evenings to talk, while he decided to put his mind to the farm. There was nothing else to do.

Yet while he worked he was daydreaming. He imagined himself travelling south, to the Rand, and working as James had done, saving unheard-of sums of money and then leaving, a rich man, in time to save his health. Or did not leave, but was carried out on a stretcher, with his mother and James as sorrowing witnesses of this victim of the gold industry. Or he saw himself as the greatest mine expert of the continent, strolling casually among the mine-dumps and headgear of the Reef, calmly shedding his pearls of wisdom before awed financiers. Or he bought a large tobacco farm, made fifty thousand the first season and settled vast sums on James and his parents.

Then he took himself in hand, refusing himself even the relief of daydreams, and forced himself to concentrate on the work. He would come back full of hopeful enthusiasm to Maggie, telling her that he was dividing the big field for a proper rotation of crops and that soon it would show strips of colour, from the rich, dark green of maize to the blazing yellow of the sunflower. She listened kindly, but without responding as he wanted. So he ceased to tell her what he was doing—particularly as half the time he felt uneasily that it was wrong, he simply did not know. He set his teeth over his anger and went to Alec and said: "Now listen, you've got to answer a question." Alec, divining rod in hand, turned and said: "What now?" "I want to know, should I harrow the field now or wait until the rains?" Alec hesitated and said: "What do you think?" Paul shouted: "I want to know what *you* think—you've had the experience, haven't you?" And then Alec lost his temper and said: "Can't you see I'm working this thing out? Go and ask—well go and ask one of the neighbours."

Paul would not give in. He waited until Alec had finished, and then said: "Now come on, Father, you're coming with me to the field. I want to know." Reluctantly, Alec went. Day after day, Paul fought with his father; he learned not to ask for general advice, he presented Alec with a definite problem and insisted until he got an answer. He was beginning to find his way among the complexities of the place, when Maggie appealed to him: "Paul, I know you'll think I'm hard, but I want you to leave your father alone."

The boy said, in amazement: "What do you mean? I don't ask him things oftener than once or twice a day. He's got all the rest of the time to play with his toys."

Maggie said: "He should be left. I know you won't understand, but I'm right, Paul." For several days she had been watching Alec; she could see that cloud of fear in his eyes that she had seen before. When he was forced to look outside him and his private world, when he was made to look at the havoc he had created by his negligence, then he could not bear it. He lay tossing at night, complaining endlessly: "What does he want? What more can I do? He goes on and on, and he knows I'm on to the big thing. I'll have it soon, Maggie, I know I will. This new reef'll be full of gold, I am sure . . ." It made her heart ache with pity for him. She had decided, firmly, to support her husband against her son. After all, Paul was young, he'd his life in front of him. She said, quietly: "Leave him, Paul. You don't understand. When a person's a failure, it's cruel to make them see it."

"I'm not making him see anything," said Paul, bitterly. "I'm only asking for advice, that's all, that's all!" And the big boy of sixteen burst into tears of rage; and, after a helpless, wild look at his mother, ran off into the bush, stumbling as he ran. He was saying to himself: I've had enough, I'm going to run away. I'm going south . . . But after a while he quietened and went back to work. He left Alec alone. But it was not so easy. Again he said to Maggie: "He's dug a trench right across my new contour ridges; he didn't even ask me . . ." And later: "He's put a shaft clean in the middle of the sunflowers, he's ruined half an acre—can't you talk to him, Mother?" Maggie promised to talk to her husband, and when it came to the point, lost her courage. Alec was like a child, what was the use of talking?

Later still, Paul came and said: "Do you realize what he's spent this last year on his nonsense?"

"Yes, I know," sighed Maggie.

"Well, he can't spend so much, and that's all there is to it."

"What are you going to do?" said Maggie. And then quickly: "Be gentle with him, Paul. Please . . ."

Paul insisted one evening that Alec "should listen to him for a moment." He made his father sit at one end of the table while he placed books of accounts before him and stood over him while he looked through them. "You can't do it, Father," said Paul, reasonably, patiently; "you've got to cut it down a bit."

It hurt Maggie to see them. It hurt Paul, too—it was like pensioning off his own father. For he was simply making conditions, and Alec had to accept them. He was like a petitioner, saying: "You're not going to take it all away from me, are you? You can't do that?" His face was sagging with disappointment, and in the end it brightened pathetically at the concession that he might keep four labourers for his own use and spend fifty pounds a year. "Not a penny more," said Paul. "And you've got to fill in all the abandoned diggings and shafts. You can't walk a step over the farm now without risking your neck."

Maggie was tender with Alec afterwards, when he came to her and said: "That young know-all, turning everything upside down, all theories and not experience!" Then he went off to fill in the trenches and shafts, and afterwards to a distant part of the farm where he had found a new reef.

But now he tended to make sarcastic remarks to Paul; and Maggie had to be careful to keep the peace between them, feeling a traitor to both, for she would agree first with one man, then with the other—Paul was a man now, and it hurt her to see it. Sixteen, thin as a plank, sunburn dark on a strained face, much too patient with her. For Paul would look at the tired old woman who was his mother and think that by rights she should still be a young one, and he shut his teeth over the reproaches he wanted to make: Why do you support him in this craziness; why do you agree to everything he says? And so he worried through that first season; and there came the time to balance the farm books; and there happened something that no one expected.

When all the figuring and accounting was over, Alec, who had apparently not even noticed the work, went into the office and spent an evening with the books. He came out with a triumphant smile and said to Paul: "Well, you haven't done much better than I did, in spite of all your talk."

Paul glanced at his mother, who was making urgent signals at him to keep his temper. He kept it. He was white, but he was making an effort to smile. But Alec continued: "You go on at me, both of you, but when it comes to the point you haven't made any profit either." It was so unfair that Paul could no longer remain silent. "You let the farm go to pieces," he said, bitterly, "you won't even give me advice when I ask for it, and then you accuse me . . ."

"Paul," said Maggie, urgently.

"And when I find a gold mine," said Alec, magnificently, "and it won't be long now, you'll come running to me, you'll be sorry then! You can't run a farm, and you haven't got the sense to learn elementary geology from me. You've been with me all these years and you don't even know one sort of reef from another. You're too damned lazy to live." And with this he walked out of the room.

Paul was sitting still, head dropped a little, looking at the floor. Maggie waited for him to smile with her at this child who was Alec. She was arranging the small, humorous smile on her lips that would take the sting out of the scene, when Paul slowly rose, and said quietly: "Well, that's the end."

"No, Paul," cried Maggie, "you shouldn't take any notice; you can't take it seriously . . ."

"Can't I?" said Paul, bitterly. "I've had enough."

"Where are you going? What are you going to do?"

"I don't know."

"You can't leave," Maggie found herself saying. "You haven't got the education to . . ." She stopped herself, but not in time. Paul's face was so hurt and abandoned that she cried out to herself: What's the matter with me? Why did I say it? Paul said: "Well, that's that." And he went out of the room after his father.

Paul went over to the mine, found James sitting on his verandah, and said at once: "James, can I come as a partner with you?"

James's face did not change. He looked patiently at the boy and said, "Sit down." Then, when Paul had sat, and was leaning forward waiting, he said: "There isn't enough profit for a partner here, you know that. Otherwise I'd like to have you. Besides, it looks as if the reef is finished." He waited and asked: "What's gone wrong?"

Paul made an impatient movement, dismissing his parents, the farm, and his past, and said: "Why is your reef finished?"

"I told you that a long time ago."

He had, but Paul had not taken it in. "What are you going to do?" he enquired.

"Oh, I don't know," said James, comfortably, lighting a cigarette. "I'll get along."

"Yes, but . . ." Paul was very irritated. This laxness was like his father. "You've got to do something," he insisted.

"Well, what do you suggest?" asked James, humorously, with the intention of loosening the lad up. But Paul gripped his hands together and shouted: "Why should I suggest anything? Why does everyone expect me to suggest things?"

"Hey, take it easy," soothed James. "Sorry," said Paul. He relaxed and said: "Give me a cigarette." He lit it clumsily and asked: "Yes, but if there's no reef, there's no profit, so how are you going to live?"

"Oh, I'll get a job, or find another reef or something," said James, quite untroubled.

Paul could not help laughing. "Do you mean to say you've known the reef was finished and you've been sitting here without a care in the world?"

"I didn't say it was finished. It's just dwindling away. I'm not losing money and I'm not making any. But I'll pull out in a week or so, I've been thinking," said James, puffing clouds of lazy smoke.

"Going prospecting?" asked the boy, persistently.

"Why not?"

"Can I come with you?"

"What do you mean by prospecting?" temporised James. "If you think I'm going to wander around with a pan and a hammer, romantic-like, you're wrong. I like my comfort. I'll take my time and see what I can find."

Paul laughed again at James's idea of comfort. He glanced into the two little rooms behind the verandah, hardly furnished at all, with the kitchen behind where the slovenly and good-natured African woman cooked meat and potatoes, potatoes and boiled fowl, with an occasional plate of raw tomatoes as relish.

James said: "I met an old pal of mine at the station last week. He found a reef half a mile from here last month. He's starting up when he can get the machinery from town. The country's lousy with gold, don't worry."

And with this slapdash promise of a future Paul was content. But before they started prospecting James deliberately arranged a drinking session. "About time I had a holiday," he said, quite seriously. James went through four bottles of whisky in two days. He drank, slowly, and persistently, until he became maudlin and sentimental, a phase which embarrassed the boy. Then he became hectoring and noisy, and complained about his wife, the mine owners of the Rand, and his parents, who had taken him from school at fifteen to make his way as he could. Then, having worked that out of his system, nicely judging his condition, he took a final half-glass of neat whisky, lay comfortably down on the bed and passed out. Paul sat beside his friend and waited for him to wake, which he did, in five or six hours, quite sober and very depressed. Then the process was repeated.

Maggie was angry when Paul came home after three days' absence, saying that James had had malaria and needed a nurse. At the same time she was pleased that her son could sit up three nights with a sick man and then come walking quietly home across the veld, without any fuss or claim for attention, to demand a meal and eat it and then take himself off to bed; all very calm and sensible, like a grown person.

She wanted to ask him if he intended to run the farm, but did not dare. She could not blame him for feeling as he did, but she could not approve his running away either. In the end it was Alec who said to Maggie, in his son's presence: "Your precious Paul. He runs off the farm and leaves it standing while he drinks himself under the table." He had heard that James was in a drinking bout from one of the Africans.

"Paul doesn't drink," said Maggie finally, telling Alec with her eyes that she was not going to sit there and hear him run down his son. Alec looked away. But he said derisively to Paul: "Been beaten by the farm already? You can't stick it more than one season?"

Paul replied, calmly: "As you like."

"What are you going to do now?" asked Maggie, and Paul said: "You'll know in good time." To his father he could not resist saying: "You'll know soon enough for your peace of mind!"

When he had gone, Maggie sat thinking for a long time: if he was with James it meant he was going mining; he was as bad as his father, in fact. Worse, he was challenging his father. With the tired thought that she hoped at least Alec would not understand his son was challenging him, she walked down to the fields to tell her husband that he should spend a little of his time keeping the farm going. She found him at work beside his new shaft, and sat quietly on a big stone while he explained some new idea to her. She said nothing about the farm.

As for Paul, he said to James: "Let's start prospecting." James said: "There's no hurry." "Yes, there is, there is," insisted the boy, and with a shrug James went to find his hammer.

Together they spent some days working over the nearer parts of the bush. At this stage they did not go near the Barneses' farm, but

kept on the neighbouring farm. This neighbour was friendly because he hoped that a really big reef would be found and then he
could sell his land for what he chose to ask for it. Sometimes he
sent a native to tell them that there was a likely reef in such and
such a place, and the man and the boy went over to test it. Nothing
came of these suggestions. Mostly Paul slept in James's house.
Once or twice, for the sake of peace, he went home, looking defiant.
But Maggie greeted him pleasantly. She had gone beyond caring.
She was listless and ironic. All she feared was that Alec would find
out that Paul was prospecting. Once she said, trying to joke:
"What'd you do if Paul found gold?" Alex responded, magnificently: "Any fool can find gold. It takes intelligence to use the divining rod properly." Maggie smiled and shrugged. Then she found
another worry: that if Paul knew that his father did not think
enough of him to care, he might give up the search; and she felt it
better for him to be absorbed in prospecting than in running away
down South, or simply drinking his time away. She thought sadly
that Paul had made for himself an image of a cruel and heartless
father, whereas he was more like a shadow. To fight Alec was
shadow-boxing, and she remembered what she had felt over the
wedding rings. He had lost her ring, she felt as if the bottom had
dropped out of their marriage, and all he said was: "Send to town
for another one, what's in a ring, after all?" And what was in a
ring? He was right. With Alec, any emotion always ended in a
shrug of the shoulders.

And then, for a time, there was excitement. Alec found a reef
that carried gold; not much, but almost as much as the mine on the
ridge. And of course he wanted to work it. Maggie would not agree.
She said it was too risky; and anyway, where would they find the
capital? Alec said, calmly, that money could be borrowed. Maggie
said it would be hanging a millstone around their necks . . . and
so on. At last experts came from town and gave a verdict: it was
under the workable minimum. The experts went back again, but
oddly enough, Alec seemed encouraged rather than depressed.
"There you are," he said, "I always said there was gold, didn't I?"
Maggie soothed him, and he went off to try another reef.

Paul, who had not been home for a couple of weeks, got wind of
this discovery and came striding over with a fevered look to demand: "Is it true that Father's found gold?"

"No," said Maggie. And then, with sad irony: "Wouldn't you be
pleased for his sake if he did?" At that look he coloured, but he
could not bring himself to say he would be pleased. Suddenly Mag-

gie asked: "Are you drinking, Paul?" He did not look well, but that was due to the intensity of his search for gold, not to drink. James would not let him drink: "You can do what you like when you're twenty-one," he said, just like a father. "But you're not drinking when you're with me till then."

Paul did not want to tell his mother that he allowed James to order him about, and he said: "You've got such a prejudice against drink."

"Plenty of people'd be pleased if they'd been brought up with *that* prejudice," she said, drily. "Look how many ruin themselves in this country with drink."

He said, obstinately: "James is all right, isn't he? There's nothing wrong with him—and he drinks off and on."

"Can't you be 'all right' without drinking off and on?" enquired Maggie, with that listless irony that upset Paul because it was not like her. He kissed her and said: "Don't worry about me, I'm doing fine." And back he went to James.

For now he and James spent every spare moment prospecting. It was quite different from Alec's attitude. James seemed to assume that since this was gold country, gold could be found; it was merely a question of persistence. Quite calmly, he closed down his mine, and dismissed his labour force, and set himself to find another. It had a convincing ring to Paul; it was not nearly as thrilling as with Alec, who was always on the verge of a discovery that must shake the world, no less; but it was more sensible. Perhaps, too, Paul was convinced because it was necessary; and what is necessary has its own logic.

When they had covered the neighbour's farm they hesitated before crossing the boundary on to Alec's. But one evening they straddled over the barbed fence, while Paul lagged behind, feeling unaccountably guilty. James wanted to go to the quartz reef. He glanced enquiringly back at the boy, who slowly followed him, persuading himself there was no need to feel guilty. Prospecting was legal, and he had a right to it. They slowly made their way to the reef. The trenches had been roughly filled in, and the places where the stone had been hammered and blasted were already weathering over. They worked on the reef for several days, and sometimes James said, humorously: "When your father does a thing he does it thoroughly . . ." For there was hardly a piece of that mile-long reef which had not been examined. Soon they left it, and worked their way along the ridge. The ground was broken by jutting reefs, outcrops, boulders, but here, it seemed, Alec had not been.

"Well, sonnie," said James, "this looks likely, hey?"

There was no reason why it should be any more likely than any other place, but Paul was trusting to the old miner's instinct. He liked to watch him move slowly over the ground, pondering over a slant of rock, a sudden scattering of sparkling white pebbles. It seemed like a kind of magic, as ways of thinking do that have not yet been given names and classified. Yet it was based on years of experience of rock and minerals and soil; although James did not consciously know why he paused beside this outcrop and not the next; and to Paul it appeared an arbitrary process.

One morning they met Alec. At first Paul hung back; then he defiantly strode forward. Alec's face was hostile and he demanded: "What are you two doing here?"

"It's legal to prospect, Mr. Barnes," said James.

Alec frowned and said: "You didn't have the common decency to ask." He was looking at Paul and not at James. Then, when Paul could not find words, he seemed to lose interest and began moving away. They were astounded to hear him remark: "You're quite right to try here, though. It always did seem a likely spot. Might have another shot here myself one day." Then he walked slowly off.

Paul felt bad; he had been imagining his father as an antagonist. So strong was his reaction that he almost lost interest in the thing; he might even have gone back to the farm if James had not been there to keep him to it. For James was not the sort of man to give up a job once he had started.

Now he glanced at Paul and said: "Don't you worry, son. Your dad's a decent chap, when all's said. He was right, we should have asked, just out of politeness."

"It's all very well," said Paul, hugging his old resentment. "He sounds all right now, but you should have heard the things he said."

"Well, well, we all lose our tempers," said James, tolerantly.

Several days later James remarked: "This bit of rock looks quite good, let's pan it." They panned it, and it showed good gold. "Doesn't prove anything," said James. "We'd better dig a trench or two." A trench or two were dug, and James said, casually: "Looks as if this might be it." It did not immediately come home to Paul that this was James's way of announcing success. It was too unheroic. He even found himself thinking: If this is all it is, what's the point of it? *To find gold*—what a phrase it is! Impossible to hear it without a quickening of the pulse. And so through the rest: I might find gold, you could find gold; they, most certainly, always seem to find gold. But not only was it possible to drop the words, as if they were the most ordinary in the world, it did not occur to James that Paul might be disappointed. "Yes, this is it," he confirmed himself, some days later, and added immediately: "Let's get some food, no point in being uncomfortable for nothing."

So flat was the scene, just a few untidy diggings in the low greenish scrub, with the low, smokey September sky pressing down, that Paul was making the thing verbally dramatic in his mind, thus: "We have found gold. James and I have found gold. And won't my father be cross!" But it was no use at all; and he obediently followed James back to the little shack for cold meat and potatoes. It all went on for weeks, while James surveyed the whole area, digging cross trenches, sinking a small shaft. Then he sent some rocks in to the Assay people and their assessment was confirmed. Surely this should be a moment for rejoicing, but all James said was: "We won't get rich on this lot, but it could be worse." It seemed as if he might even shrug the whole thing off and start again somewhere else.

Once again the experts came out, standing over the diggings making their cautious pronouncements; city men, dressed in the crisp khaki they donned for excursions into the veld. "Yes, it was workable. Yes, it might even turn out quite prosperous, with luck." Paul felt cheated of glory, and there was no one who would understand this feeling. Not even Maggie; he tried to catch her eye and smile ruefully, but her eye would not be caught. For she was there on her son's invitation. She walked over to see Paul's triumph without telling Alec. And all the time she watched the experts, watched Paul and James, she was thinking of Alec, who would have to be told. After all these years of work with his divining rods and his theories; after all that patient study of the marsh light, gold, it seemed too cruel that his son should casually walk over the ridge he had himself prospected so thoroughly and find a reef within a matter of weeks. It was so cruel that she could not bring herself to tell him. Why did it have to be there, on that same ridge? Why not anywhere else in the thousands of acres of veld? And she felt even more sad for Alec because she knew quite well that the reef's being there, on the ridge, was part of Paul's triumph. She was afraid that Alec would see that gleam of victory in his son's eyes.

In the meantime the important piece of ground lay waiting, guarded by the prescribed pegging notices that were like signboards on which were tacked the printed linen notices listing fines and penalties against any person—even Alec himself—who came near to the still invisible gold without permission. Then out came the businessmen and the lawyers, and there was a long period of signing documents and drinking toasts to everyone concerned.

Paul came over to supper one evening, and Maggie sat in suspense, waiting for him to tell his father, waiting for the cruel blow to fall. The boy was restless, and several times opened his mouth to speak, fell silent, and in the end said nothing. When Alec had gone to his office to work out some calculations for a new reef, Maggie said: "Well, I suppose you're very pleased with yourself."

Paul grinned and said: "Shouldn't I be?"

"Your poor father—can't you see how he's going to feel about it?"

All she could get out of him was: "All right, you tell him then. I won't say anything."

"I'm glad you've got some feeling for him."

So Paul left and she was faced with the task of telling Alec. She marvelled that he did not know it already. All he had to do was lift his eyes and look close at the ridge. There, among the bare, thinned trees of the September veld, were the trenches, like new scars, and a small black activity of workers.

Then one day Paul came again and said—and now he sounded apologetic: "You'll have to tell him, you know. We're moving the heavy machinery tomorrow. He'll see for himself."

"I really will tell him," she promised.

"I don't want him to feel bad, really I don't, Mother." He sounded as insistent as a child who needs to be forgiven.

"You didn't think of it before," she said, drily.

He protested: "But surely—you've never said you were glad, not once. Don't you understand? This might turn out to be a really big thing; the experts said it might. I might be a partner of a really big mine quite soon."

"And you're not eighteen yet," she said, smiling to soften the words. She was thinking that it was a sad falling-off from what he had hoped. What was he? A small-worker. Half-educated, without ambition, dependent on the terrible thing, luck. He might be a small-worker all his life, with James for companion, drinking at week-ends, the African woman in the kitchen—oh, yes, she knew what went on, although he seemed to think she was a fool. And if they were lucky, he would become a rich man, one of the big financiers of the sub-continent. It was possible, anything was possible—she smiled tolerantly and said nothing.

That night she lay awake, trying to arouse in herself the courage to tell Alec. She could not. At breakfast she watched his absorbed, remote face, and tried to find the words. They would not come. After the meal he went into his office, and she went quickly outside. Shading her eyes she looked across the mealie fields to the ridge. Yes, there went the heavy waggons, laden with the black bulk of the headgear, great pipes, pulleys: Alec had only to look out of his window to see. She slowly went inside and said: "Alec, I want to tell you something." He did not lift his eyes. "What is it?" he asked, impatiently.

"Come with me for a minute." He looked at her, frowned, then shrugged and went after her. She pointed at the red dust track that showed in the scrub and said: "Look." Her voice sounded like a little girl's.

He glanced at the laden waggons, then slowly moved his eyes along the ridge to where the diggings showed.

"What is it?" he asked. She tried to speak and found that her lips were trembling. Inside she was crying: Poor thing; poor, poor thing! "What is it?" he demanded again. Then, after a pause: "Have they found something?"

"Yes," she brought out at last.

"Any good?"

"They said it might be very good." She dared to give him a sideways glance. His face was thoughtful, no more, and she was encouraged to say: "James and Paul are partners."

"And on that ridge," he exclaimed at last. There was no resentment in his voice. She glanced at him again. "It seems hard, doesn't it?" he said, slowly; and at once she clutched his arm and said: "Yes, my dear, it is, it is, I'm so very sorry . . ." And here she began to cry. She wanted to take him in her arms and comfort him. But he was still gazing over at the ridge. "I never tried just that place," he said, thoughtfully. She stopped crying. "Funny, I was going to sink a trench just there, and then—I forget why I didn't."

"Yes?" she said, in a little voice. She was understanding that it was all right. Then he remarked: "I always said there was gold on that ridge, and there is. I always said it, didn't I?"

"Yes, my dear, you did—where are you going?" she added, for he was walking away, the divining rod swinging from his hand.

"I'll just drop over and do a bit of work around their trenches," she heard as he went. "If they know how the reefs lie, then I can test . . ."

He vanished into the bush, walking fast, the tails of his bush-shirt flying.

When Paul saw him coming he went forward to meet him, smiling a rather sickly smile, his heart beating with guilt, and all Alec said was: "Your mother told me you'd struck it lucky. Mind if I use my rod around here for a bit?" And then, as Paul remained motionless from surprise, he said impatiently: "Come on, there's a good kid, I'm in a hurry."

And as the labourers unloaded the heavy machinery and James and Paul directed the work, Alec walked in circles and in zigzags, the rods rising and falling in his hands like a variety of trapped insects, his face rapt with thought. He was oblivious to everything. They had to pull him aside to avoid being crushed by the machinery. When, at midday, they asked him to share their cold meat, and broke it to him that they had found a second reef, even richer than the first, with every prospect of "going as deep as China," all he said was, and in a proud, pleased voice: "Well, that proves it. I told you, didn't I? I always told you so."

The Antheap

BEYOND the plain rose the mountains, blue and hazy in a strong blue sky. Coming closer they were brown and grey and green, ranged heavily one beside the other, but the sky was still blue. Climbing up through the pass the plain flattened and diminished behind, and the peaks rose sharp and dark grey from lower heights of heaped granite boulders, and the sky overhead was deeply blue and clear and the heat came shimmering off in waves from every surface. "Through the range, down the pass, and into the plain the other side—let's go quickly, there it will be cooler, the walking easier." So thinks the traveller. So the traveller has been thinking for many centuries, walking quickly to leave the stifling mountains, to gain the cool plain where the wind moves freely. But there is no plain. Instead, the pass opens into a hollow which is closely surrounded by *kopjes:* the mountains clench themselves into a fist here, and the palm is a mile-wide reach of thick bush, where the heat gathers and clings, radiating from boulders, rocking off the trees, pouring down from a sky which is not blue, but thick and low and yellow, because of the smoke that rises, and has been rising so long from this mountain-imprisoned hollow. For though it is hot and close and arid half the year, and then warm and steamy and wet in the rains, there is gold here, so there are always people, and everywhere in the bush are pits and slits where the prospectors have been, or shallow holes, or even deep shafts. They say that the Bushmen were here, seeking gold, hundreds of years ago. Perhaps, it is possible. They say that trains of Arabs came from the coast, with slaves and warriors, looking for gold to enrich the courts of the Queen of Sheba. No one has proved they did not.

But it is at least certain that at the turn of the century there was a big mining company which sunk half a dozen fabulously deep shafts, and found gold going ounces to the ton sometimes, but it is a capricious and chancy piece of ground, with the reefs all broken and unpredictable, and so this company loaded its heavy equipment into lorries and off they went to look for gold somewhere else, and in a place where the reefs lay more evenly.

For a few years the hollow in the mountains was left silent, no smoke rose to dim the sky, except perhaps for an occasional prospector, whose fire was a single column of wavering blue smoke, as from the cigarette of a giant, rising into the blue, hot sky.

Then all at once the hollow was filled with violence and noise and activity and hundreds of people. Mr. Macintosh had bought the rights to mine this gold. They told him he was foolish, that no single man, no matter how rich, could afford to take chances in this place.

But they did not reckon with the character of Mr. Macintosh, who had already made a fortune and lost it, in Australia, and then made another in New Zealand, which he still had. He proposed to increase it here. Of course, he had no intention of sinking those expensive shafts which might not reach gold and hold the dipping, chancy reefs and seams. The right course was quite clear to Mr. Macintosh, and this course he followed, though it was against every known rule of proper mining.

He simply hired hundreds of African labourers and set them to shovel up the soil in the centre of that high, enclosed hollow in the mountains, so that there was soon a deeper hollow, then a vast pit, then a gulf like an inverted mountain. Mr. Macintosh was taking great swallows of the earth, like a gold-eating monster, with no fancy ideas about digging shafts or spending money on roofing tunnels. The earth was hauled, at first, up the shelving sides of the gulf in buckets, and these were suspended by ropes made of twisted bark fibre, for why spend money on steel ropes when this fibre was offered free to mankind on every tree? And if it got brittle and broke and the buckets went plunging into the pit, then they were not harmed by the fall, and there was plenty of fibre left on the trees. Later, when the gulf grew too deep, there were trucks on rails, and it was not unknown for these, too, to go sliding and plunging to the bottom, because in all Mr. Macintosh's dealings there was a fine, easy good-humour, which meant he was more likely to laugh at such an accident than grow angry. And if someone's head got in the way of the falling buckets or trucks, then there were plenty of black heads and hands for the hiring. And if the loose, sloping bluffs of soil fell in landslides, or if a tunnel, narrow as an ant-bear's hole, that was run off sideways from the main pit like a tentacle exploring for new reefs, caved in suddenly, swallowing half a dozen men—well, one can't make an omelette without breaking eggs. This was Mr. Macintosh's favourite motto.

The Africans who worked this mine called it "the pit of death," and they called Mr. Macintosh "The Gold Stomach." Nevertheless, they came in their hundreds to work for him, thus providing free arguments for those who said: "The native doesn't understand good treatment, he only appreciates the whip, look at Macintosh, he's never short of labour."

Mr. Macintosh's mine, raised high in the mountains, was far from the nearest police station, and he took care that there was always plenty of kaffir beer brewed in the compound, and if the police patrols came searching for criminals, these could count on Mr. Macintosh facing the police for them and assuring them that such and such a native, Registration Number Y2345678, had never worked for him. Yes, of course they could see his books.

Mr. Macintosh's books and records might appear to the simple-minded as casual and ineffective, but these were not the words used of his methods by those who worked for him, and so Mr. Macintosh kept his books himself. He employed no book-keeper, no clerk. In fact, he employed only one white man, an engineer. For the rest, he had six overseers or boss-boys whom he paid good salaries and treated like important people.

The engineer was Mr. Clarke, and his house and Mr. Macintosh's house were on one side of the big pit, and the compound for the Africans was on the other side. Mr. Clarke earned fifty pounds a month, which was more than he would earn anywhere else. He was a silent, hardworking man, except when he got drunk, which was not often. Three or four times in the year he would be off work for a week, and then Mr. Macintosh did his work for him till he recovered, when he greeted him with the good-humored words: "Well, laddie, got that off your chest?"

Mr. Macintosh did not drink at all. His not drinking was a passionate business, for like many Scots people he ran to extremes. Never a drop of liquor could be found in his house. Also, he was religious, in a reminiscent sort of way, because of his parents, who had been very religious. He lived in a two-roomed shack, with a bare wooden table in it, three wooden chairs, a bed and a wardrobe. The cook boiled beef and carrots and potatoes three days a week, roasted beef three days, and cooked a chicken on Sundays.

Mr. Macintosh was one of the richest men in the country, he was more than a millionaire. People used to say of him: But for heaven's sake, he could do anything, go anywhere, what's the point of having so much money if you live in the back of beyond with a parcel of blacks on top of a big hole in the ground?

But to Mr. Macintosh it seemed quite natural to live so, and when he went for a holiday to Cape Town, where he lived in the most expensive hotel, he always came back again long before he was expected. He did not like holidays. He liked working.

He wore old, oily khaki trousers, tied at the waist with an old red tie, and he wore a red handkerchief loose around his neck over a white cotton singlet. He was short and broad and strong, with a big square head tilted back on a thick neck. His heavy brown arms and neck sprouted thick black hair around the edges of the singlet. His eyes were small and grey and shrewd. His mouth was thin, pressed tight in the middle. He wore an old felt hat on the back of his head, and carried a stick cut from the bush, and he went strolling around the edge of the pit, slashing the stick at bushes and grass or sometimes at lazy Africans, and he shouted orders to his boss-boys, and watched the swarms of workers far below him in the bottom of the pit, and then he would go to his little office and make up his books, and so he spent his day. In the evenings he sometimes asked Mr. Clarke to come over and play cards.

Then Mr. Clarke would say to his wife: "Annie, he wants me," and she nodded and told her cook to make supper early.

Mrs. Clarke was the only white woman on the mine. She did not mind this, being a naturally solitary person. Also, she had been profoundly grateful to reach this haven of fifty pounds a month with a man who did not mind her husband's bouts of drinking. She was a woman of early middle age, with a thin, flat body, a thin, colourless face, and quiet blue eyes. Living here, in this destroying heat, year after year, did not make her ill, it sapped her slowly, leaving her rather numbed and silent. She spoke very little, but then she roused herself and said what was necessary.

For instance, when they first arrived at the mine it was to a two-roomed house. She walked over to Mr. Macintosh and said: "You are alone, but you have four rooms. There are two of us and the baby, and we have two rooms. There's no sense in it." Mr. Macintosh gave her a quick, hard look, his mouth tightened, and then he began to laugh. "Well, yes, that is so," he said, laughing, and he made the change at once, chuckling every time he remembered how the quiet Annie Clarke had put him in his place.

Similarly, about once a month Annie Clarke went to his house and said: "Now get out of my way, I'll get things straight for you." And when she'd finished tidying up she said: "You're nothing but a pig, and that's the truth." She was referring to his habit of throwing his clothes everywhere, or wearing them for weeks unwashed, and also to other matters which no one else dared to refer to, even as indirectly as this. To this he might reply, chuckling with the pleasure of teasing her: "You're a married woman, Mrs. Clarke," and she said: "Nothing stops you getting married that I can see." And she walked away very straight, her cheeks burning with indignation.

She was very fond of him, and he of her. And Mr. Clarke liked and admired him, and he liked Mr. Clarke. And since Mr. Clarke and Mrs. Clarke lived amiably together in their four-roomed house, sharing bed and board without ever quarreling, it was to be presumed they liked each other too. But they seldom spoke. What was there to say?

It was to this silence, to these understood truths, that little Tommy had to grow up and adjust himself.

Tommy Clarke was three months old when he came to the mine, and day and night his ears were filled with noise, every day and every night for years, so that he did not think of it as noise, rather, it was a different sort of silence. The mine-stamps thudded gold, gold, gold, gold, gold, gold, on and on, never changing, never stopping. So he did not hear them. But there came a day when the machinery broke, and it was when Tommy was three years old, and the silence was so terrible and so empty that he went screeching to his mother: "It's stopped, it's stopped," and he wept, shivering, in a corner until the thudding began again. It was as if the heart of the world had gone silent. But when it started to beat, Tommy heard it, and he knew the difference between silence and sound, and his ears acquired a new sensitivity, like a conscience. He heard the shouting and the singing from the swarms of working Africans, reckless, noisy people because of the danger they always must live with. He heard the picks ringing on stone, the softer, deeper thud of picks on thick earth. He heard the clang of the trucks, and the roar of falling earth, and the rumbling of trolleys on rails. And at night the owls hooted and the nightjars screamed, and the crickets chirped. And when it stormed it seemed the sky itself was flinging down bolts of noise against the mountains, for the thunder rolled and crashed, and the lightning darted from peak to peak around him. It was never silent, never, save for that awful moment when the big heart stopped beating. Yet later he longed for it to stop again, just for an hour, so that he might hear a true silence. That was when he was a little older, and the quietness of his parents was beginning to trouble him. There they were, always so gentle, saying so little only: That's how things are; or: You ask so many questions; or: You'll understand when you grow up.

It was a false silence, much worse than that real silence had been.

He would play beside his mother in the kitchen, who never said anything but Yes, and No, and—with a patient, sighing voice, as if even his voice tired her: You talk so much, Tommy!

And he was carried on his father's shoulders around the big, black working machines, and they couldn't speak because of the din the machines made. And Mr. Macintosh would say: Well, laddie? and give him sweets from his pocket, which he always kept there, especially for Tommy. And once he saw Mr. Macintosh and his father playing cards in the evening, and they didn't talk at all, except for the words that the game needed.

So Tommy escaped to the friendly din of the compound across the great gulf, and played all day with the black children, dancing in their dances, running through the bush after rabbits, or working wet clay into shapes of bird or beast. No silence there, everything noisy and cheerful, and at evening he returned to his equable, silent parents, and after the meal he lay in bed listening to the thud, thud, thud, thud, thud, thud, of the stamps. In the compound across the gulf they were drinking and dancing, the drums made a quick beating against the slow thud of the stamps, and the dancers around the fires yelled, a high, undulating sound like a big wind coming fast and crooked through a cap in the mountains. That was a different world, to which he belonged as much as to this one, where people said: Finish your pudding; or: It's time for bed; and very little else.

When he was five years old he got malaria and was very sick. He recovered, but in the rainy season of the next year he got it again. Both times Mr. Macintosh got into his big American car and went streaking across the thirty miles of bush to the nearest hospital for the doctor. The doctor said quinine, and be careful to screen for mosquitoes. It was easy to give quinine, but Mrs. Clark, that tired, easy-going woman, found it hard to say: Don't, and Be in by six;

and Don't go near the water; and so, when Tommy was seven, he got malaria again. And now Mrs. Clarke was worried, because the doctor spoke severely, mentioning blackwater.

Mr. Macintosh drove the doctor back to his hospital and then came home, and at once went to see Tommy, for he loved Tommy very deeply.

Mrs. Clarke said: "What do you expect, with all these holes everywhere, they're full of water all the wet season."

"Well, lassie, I can't fill in all the holes and shafts, people have been digging up here since the Queen of Sheba."

"Never mind about the Queen of Sheba. At least you could screen our house properly."

"I pay your husband fifty pounds a month," said Mr. Macintosh, conscious of being in the right.

"Fifty pounds and a proper house," said Annie Clarke.

Mr. Macintosh gave her that quick, narrow look, and then laughed loudly. A week later the house was encased in fine wire mesh all round from roof-edge to verandah-edge, so that it looked like a new meat safe, and Mrs. Clarke went over to Mr. Macintosh's house and gave it a grand cleaning, and when she left she said: "You're nothing but a pig, you're as rich as the Oppenheimers, why don't you buy yourself some new vests at least. And you'll be getting malaria, too, the way you go traipsing about at nights."

She returned to Tommy, who was seated on the verandah behind the grey-glistening wire-netting, in a big deck-chair. He was very thin and white after the fever. He was a long child, bony, and his eyes were big and black, and his mouth full and pouting from the petulances of the illness. He had a mass of richly-brown hair, like caramels, on his head. His mother looked at this pale child of hers, who was yet so brightly coloured and full of vitality, and her tired will-power revived enough to determine a new régime for him. He was never to be out after six at night, when the mosquitoes were abroad. He was never to be out before the sun rose.

"You can get up," she said, and he got up, thankfully throwing aside his covers.

"I'll go over to the compound," he said at once.

She hesitated, and then said: "You mustn't play there any more."

"Why not?" he asked, already fidgeting on the steps outside the wire-netting cage.

Ah, how she hated these Whys, and Why nots! They tired her utterly. "Because I say so," she snapped.

But he persisted: "I always play there."

"You're getting too big now, and you'll be going to school soon."

Tommy sank on to the steps and remained there, looking away over the great pit to the busy, sunlit compound. He had known this moment was coming, of course. It was a knowledge that was part of the silence. And yet he had not known it. He said: "Why, why, why, why?" singing it out in a persistent wail.

"Because I say so." Then, in tired desperation: "You get sick from the Africans, too."

At this, he switched his large black eyes from the scenery to his mother, and she flushed a little. For they were derisively scornful. Yet she half-believed it herself, or rather, must believe it, for all through the wet season the bush would lie waterlogged and festering with mosquitoes, and nothing could be done about it, and one has to put the blame on something.

She said: "Don't argue. You're not to play with them. You're too big now to play with a lot of dirty kaffirs. When you were little it was different, but now you're a big boy."

Tommy sat on the steps in the sweltering afternoon sun that came thick and yellow through the haze of dust and smoke over the mountains, and he said nothing. He made no attempt to go near the compound, now that his growing to manhood depended on his not playing with the black people. So he had been made to feel. Yet he did not believe a word of it, not really.

Some days later, he was kicking a football by himself around the back of the house when a group of black children called to him from the bush, and he turned away as if he had not seen them. They called again and then ran away. And Tommy wept bitterly, for now he was alone.

He went to the edge of the big pit and lay on his stomach looking down. The sun blazed through him so that his bones ached, and he shook his mass of hair forward over his eyes to shield them. Below, the great pit was so deep that the men working on the bottom of it were like ants. The trucks that climbed up the almost vertical sides were like matchboxes. The system of ladders and steps cut in the earth, which the workers used to climb up and down, seemed so flimsy across the gulf that a stone might dislodge it. Indeed, falling stones often did. Tommy sprawled, gripping the earth tight with tense belly and flung limbs, and stared down. They were all like ants and flies. Mr. Macintosh, too, when he went down, which he did often, for no one could say he was a coward. And his father, and Tommy himself, they were all no bigger than little insects.

It was like an enormous ant-working, as brightly tinted as a fresh antheap. The levels of earth around the mouth of the pit were reddish, then lower down grey and gravelly, and lower still, clear yellow. Heaps of the inert, heavy yellow soil, brought up from the bottom, lay all around him. He stretched out his hand and took some of it. It was unresponsive, lying lifeless and dense on his fingers, a little damp from the rain. He clenched his fist, and loosened it, and now the mass of yellow earth lay shaped on his palm, showing the marks of his fingers. A shape like——what? A bit of root? A fragment of rock rotted by water? He rolled his palms vigorously around it, and it became smooth like a water-ground stone. Then he sat up and took more earth, and formed a pit, and up the sides flying ladders with bits of stick, and little kips of wetted earth for the trucks. Soon the sun dried it, and it all cracked and fell apart. Tommy gave the model a kick and went moodily back to the house. The sun was going down. It seemed that he had left a golden age of freedom behind, and now there was a new country of restrictions and time-tables.

His mother saw how he suffered, but thought: Soon he'll go to school and find companions.

But he was only just seven, and very young to go all the way to the city to boarding-school. She sent for school-books, and taught him to read. Yet this was for only two or three hours in the day, and for the rest he mooned about, as she complained, gazing away over the gulf to the compound, from where he could hear the noise of the playing children. He was stoical about it, or so it seemed, but underneath he was suffering badly from this new knowledge, which was much more vital than anything he had learned from the school-books. He knew the word loneliness, and lying at the edge of the pit he formed the yellow clay into little figures which he called Betty and Freddy and Dirk. Playmates. Dirk was the name of the boy he liked best among the children in the compound over the gulf.

One day his mother called him to the back door. There stood Dirk, and he was holding between his hands a tiny duiker, the size of a thin cat. Tommy ran forward, and was about to exclaim with Dirk over the little animal, when he remembered his new status. He stopped, stiffened himself, and said: "How much?"

Dirk, keeping his eyes evasive, said: "One shilling, baas."

Tommy glanced at his mother and then said, proudly, his voice high: "Damned cheek, too much."

Annie Clarke flushed. She was ashamed and flustered. She came forward and said quickly: "It's all right, Tommy, I'll give you the shilling." She took the coin from the pocket of her apron and gave it to Tommy, who handed it at once to Dirk. Tommy took the little animal gently in his hands, and his tenderness for this frightened and lonely creature rushed up to his eyes and he turned away so that Dirk couldn't see—he would have been bitterly ashamed to show softness in front of Dirk, who was so tough and fearless.

Dirk stood back, watching, unwilling to see the last of the buck. Then he said: "It's just born, it can die."

Mrs. Clarke said, dismissingly: "Yes, Tommy will look after it." Dirk walked away slowly, fingering the shilling in his pocket, but looking back at where Tommy and his mother were making a nest for the little buck in a packing-case. Mrs. Clarke made a feeding-bottle with some linen stuffed into the neck of a tomato sauce bottle and filled it with milk and water and sugar. Tommy knelt by the buck and tried to drip the milk into its mouth.

It lay trembling lifting its delicate head from the crumpled, huddled limbs, too weak to move, the big eyes dark and forlorn. Then the trembling became a spasm of weakness and the head collapsed with a soft thud against the side of the box, and then slowly, and with a trembling effort, the neck lifted the head again. Tommy tried to push the wad of linen into the soft mouth, and the milk wetted the fur and ran down over the buck's chest, and he wanted to cry.

"But it'll die, Mother, it'll die," he shouted, angrily.

"You mustn't force it,' said Annie Clarke, and she went away to her household duties. Tommy knelt there with the bottle, stroking the trembling little buck and suffering every time the thin neck collapsed with weakness, and tried again and again to interest it in the milk. But the buck wouldn't drink at all.

"Why?" shouted Tommy, in the anger of his misery. "Why won't it drink? Why? Why?"

"But it's only just born," said Mrs. Clarke. The cord was still on the creature's navel, like a shrivelling, dark stick.

That night Tommy took the little buck into his room, and secretly in the dark lifted it, folded in a blanket, into his bed. He could feel it trembling fitfully against his chest, and he cried into the dark because he knew it was going to die.

In the morning when he woke, the buck could not lift its head at all, and it was a weak, collapsed weight on Tommy's chest, a chilly weight. The blanket in which it lay was messed with yellow stuff like a scrambled egg. Tommy washed the buck gently, and wrapped it again in new coverings, and laid it on the verandah where the sun could warm it.

Mrs. Clarke gently forced the jaws open and poured down milk until the buck choked. Tommy knelt beside it all morning, suffering as he had never suffered before. The tears ran steadily down his face and he wished he could die too, and Mrs. Clarke wished very much she could catch Dirk and give him a good beating, which would be unjust, but might do something to relieve her feelings. "Besides," she said to her husband, "it's nothing but cruelty, taking a tiny thing like that from its mother."

Late that afternoon the buck died, and Mr. Clarke, who had not seen his son's misery over it, casually threw the tiny, stiff corpse to the cookboy and told him to go and bury it. Tommy stood on the verandah, his face tight and angry, and watched the cookboy shovel his little buck hastily under some bushes, and return whistling.

Then he went into the room where his mother and father were sitting and said: "Why is Dirk yellow and not dark brown like the other kaffirs?"

Silence. Mr. Clarke and Anne Clarke looked at each other. Then Mr. Clarke said: "They come different colours."

Tommy looked forcefully at his mother, who said: "He's a half-caste."

"What's a half-caste?"

"You'll understand when you grow up."

Tommy looked from his father, who was filling his pipe, his eyes lowered to the work, then at his mother, whose cheekbones held that proud, bright flush.

"I understand now," he said, defiantly.

"Then why do you ask?" said Mrs. Clarke, with anger. Why, she was saying, do you infringe the rule of silence?

Tommy went out, and to the brink of the great pit. There he lay, wondering why he had said he understood when he did not. Though in a sense he did. He was remembering, though he had not noticed it before, that among the gang of children in the compound were two yellow children. Dirk was one, and Dirk's sister another. She was a tiny child, who came toddling on the fringe of the older children's games. But Dirk's mother was black, or rather, dark-brown like the others. And Dirk was not really yellow, but light copper-colour. The colour of this earth, were it a little darker. Tommy's fingers were fiddling with the damp clay. He looked at the little figures he had made, Betty and Freddy. Idly, he smashed them. Then he picked up Dirk and flung him down. But he must have flung him down too carefully, for he did not break, and so he set the figure against the stalk of a weed. He took a lump of clay, and as his fingers experimentally pushed and kneaded it, the shape grew into the shape of a little duiker. But not a sick duiker, which had died because it had been taken from its mother. Not at all, it was a fine strong duiker, standing with one hoof raised and its head listening, ears pricked forward.

Tommy knelt on the verge of the great pit, absorbed, while the duiker grew into its proper form. He became dissatisfied—it was too small. He impatiently smashed what he had done, and taking a big heap of the yellowish, dense soil, shook water on it from an old rusty railway sleeper that had collected rainwater, and made the mass soft and workable. Then he began again. The duiker would be half life-size.

And so his hands worked and his mind worried along its path of questions: Why? Why? Why? And finally: If Dirk is half black, or rather half white and half dark-brown, then who is his father?

For a long time his mind hovered on the edge of the answer, but did not finally reach it. But from time to time he looked across the gulf to where Mr. Macintosh was strolling, swinging his big cudgel, and he thought: There are only two white men on this mine.

The buck was now finished, and he wetted his fingers in rusty rainwater, and smoothed down the soft clay to make it glisten like the surfaces of fur, but at once it dried and dulled, and as he knelt there he thought how the sun would crack and it would fall to pieces, and an angry dissatisfaction filled him and he hung his head and wanted very much to cry. And just as the first tears were coming he heard a soft whistle from behind him, and turned, and there was Dirk, kneeling behind a bush and looking out through the parted leaves.

"Is the buck all right?" asked Dirk.

Tommy said: "It's dead," and he kicked his foot at his model duiker so that the thick clay fell apart in lumps.

Dirk said: "Don't do that, it's nice," and he sprang forward and tried to fit the pieces together.

"It's no good, the sun'll crack it," said Tommy, and he began to cry, although he was so ashamed to cry in front of Dirk. "The buck's dead," he wept, "it's dead."

"I can get you another," said Dirk, looking at Tommy rather surprised. "I killed its mother with a stone. It's easy."

Dirk was seven, like Tommy. He was tall and strong, like Tommy. His eyes were dark and full, but his mouth was not full and soft, but long and narrow, clenched in the middle. His hair was very black and soft and long, falling uncut around his face, and his skin was a smooth, yellowish copper. Tommy stopped crying and looked at Dirk. He said: "It's cruel to kill a buck's mother with a stone." Dirk's mouth parted in surprised laughter over his big white teeth. Tommy watched him laugh, and he thought: Well, now I know who his father is.

He looked away to his home, which was two hundred yards off, exposed to the sun's glare among low bushes of hibiscus and poinsettia. He looked at Mr. Macintosh's house, which was a few hundred yards farther off. Then he looked at Dirk. He was full of anger, which he did not understand, but he did understand that he was also defiant, and this was a moment of decision. After a long time he said: "They can see us from here," and the decision was made.

They got up, but as Dirk rose he saw the little clay figure laid against a stem, and he picked it up. "This is me," he said at once. For crude as the thing was, it was unmistakably Dirk, who smiled with pleasure. "Can I have it?" he asked, and Tommy nodded, equally proud and pleased.

They went off into the bush between the two houses, and then on for perhaps half a mile. This was the deserted part of the hollow in the mountains, no one came here, all the bustle and noise was on the other side. In front of them rose a sharp peak, and low at its foot was a high anthill, draped with Christmas fern and thick with shrub.

The two boys went inside the curtains of fern and sat down. No one could see them here. Dirk carefully put the little clay figure of himself inside a hole in the roots of a tree. Then he said: "Make the buck again." Tommy took his knife and knelt beside a fallen tree, and tried to carve the buck from it. The wood was soft and rotten, and was easily carved, and by night there was the clumsy shape of the buck coming out of the trunk. Dirk said: "Now we've both got something."

The next day the two boys made their way separately to the antheap and played there together, and so it was every day.

Then one evening Mrs. Clark said to Tommy just as he was going to bed: "I thought I told you not to play with the kaffirs?"

Tommy stood very still. Then he lifted his head and said to her, with a strong look across at his father: "Why shouldn't I play with Mr. Macintosh's son?"

Mrs. Clarke stopped breathing for a moment, and closed her eyes. She opened them in appeal at her husband. But Mr. Clarke was filling his pipe. Tommy waited and then said good night and went to his room.

There he undressed slowly and climbed into the narrow iron bed and lay quietly, listening to the thud, thud, gold, gold, thud, thud, of the mine-stamps. Over in the compound they were dancing, and the tom-toms were beating fast, like the quick beat of the buck's heart that night as it lay on his chest. They were yelling like the wind coming through gaps in a mountain and through the window he could see the high, flaring light of the fires, and the black figures of the dancing people were wild and active against it.

Mrs. Clarke came quickly in. She was crying. "Tommy," she said, sitting on the edge of his bed in the dark.

"Yes?" he said, cautiously.

"You mustn't say that again. Not ever."

He said nothing. His mother's hand was urgently pressing his arm. "Your father might lose his job," said Mrs. Clarke, wildly. "We'd never get this money anywhere else. Never. You must understand, Tommy."

"I do understand," said Tommy, stiffly, very sorry for his mother, but hating her at the same time. "Just don't say it, Tommy, don't ever say it." Then she kissed him in a way that was both fond and appealing, and went out, shutting the door. To her husband she said it was time Tommy went to school, and next day she wrote to make the arrangements.

And so now Tommy made the long journey by car and train into the city four times a year, and four times a year he came back for the holidays. Mr. Macintosh always drove him to the station and gave him ten shillings pocket money, and he came to fetch him in the car with his parents, and he always said: "Well, laddie, and how's school?" And Tommy said: "Fine, Mr. Macintosh." And Mr. Macintosh said: "We'll make a college man of you yet."

When he said this, the flush came bright and proud on Annie Clarke's cheeks, and she looked quickly at Mr. Clarke, who was smiling and embarrassed. But Mr. Macintosh laid his hands on Tommy's shoulders and said: "There's my laddie, there's my laddie," and Tommy kept his shoulders stiff and still. Afterwards, Mrs. Clarke would say, nervously: "He's fond of you, Tommy, he'll do right by you." And once she said: "It's natural, he's got no children of his own." But Tommy scowled at her and she flushed and said: "There's things you don't understand yet, Tommy, and you'll regret it if you throw away your chances." Tommy turned away with an impatient movement. Yet it was not so clear at all, for it was almost as if he were a rich man's son, with all that pocket money, and the parcels of biscuits and sweets that Mr. Macintosh sent into school during the term, and being fetched in the great rich car. And underneath it all he felt as if he were dragged along by the nose. He felt as if he were part of a conspiracy of some kind that no one ever spoke about. Silence. His real feelings were growing up slow and complicated and obstinate underneath that silence.

At school it was not at all complicated, it was the other world. There Tommy did his lessons and played with his friends and did not think of Dirk. Or rather, his thoughts of him were proper for that world. A half-caste, ignorant, living in the kaffir location—he felt ashamed that he played with Dirk in the holidays, and he told no one. Even on the train coming home he would think like that of Dirk, but the nearer he reached home the more his thoughts wavered and darkened. On the first evening at home he would speak of the school, and how he was first in the class, and he played with this boy or that, or went to such fine houses in the city as a guest. The very first morning he would be standing on the verandah looking at the big pit and at the compound away beyond it, and his mother watched him, smiling in nervous supplication. And then he walked down the steps, away from the pit, and into the bush to the antheap. There Dirk was waiting for him. So it was every holiday. Neither of the boys spoke at first of what divided them. But, on the eve of Tommy's return to school after he had been there a year, Dirk said: "You're getting educated, but I've nothing to learn." Tommy said: "I'll bring back books and teach you." He said this in a quick voice, as if ashamed, and Dirk's eyes were accusing and angry. He gave his sarcastic laugh and said: "That's what you say, white boy."

It was not pleasant, but what Tommy said was not pleasant either, like a favour wrung out of a condescending person.

The two boys were sitting on the antheap under the fine lacy curtains of Christmas fern, looking at the rocky peak soaring into the smoky yellowish sky. There was the most unpleasant sort of annoyance in Tommy, and he felt ashamed of it. And on Dirk's face there was an aggressive but ashamed look. They continued to sit there, a little apart, full of dislike for each other, and knowing that the dislike came from the pressure of the outside world. "I said I'd teach you, didn't I?" said Tommy, grandly, shying a stone at a bush so that leaves flew off in all directions. "You white bastard," said Dirk, in a low voice, and he let out that sudden ugly laugh, showing his white teeth. "What did you say?" said Tommy, going pale and jumping to his feet. "You heard," said Dirk, still laughing. He too got up. Then Tommy flung himself on Dirk and they over-balanced and rolled off into the bushes, kicking and scratching. They rolled apart and began fighting properly, with fists. Tommy was better-fed and more healthy. Dirk was tougher. They were a match, and they stopped when they were too tired and battered to go on. They staggered over to the antheap and sat there side by side, panting, wiping the blood off their faces. At last they lay on their backs on the rough slant of the anthill and looked up at the sky. Every trace of dislike had vanished, and they felt easy and quiet. When the sun went down they walked together through the bush to a point where they could not be seen from the houses, and there they said, as always: "See you tomorrow."

When Mr. Macintosh gave him the usual ten shillings, he put them into his pocket thinking he would buy a football, but he did not. The ten shillings stayed unspent until it was nearly the end of term, and then he went to the shops and bought a reader and some exercise books and pencils, and an arithmetic. He hid these at the bottom of his trunk and whipped them out before his mother could see them.

He took them to the antheap next morning, but before he could reach it he saw there was a little shed built on it, and the Christmas fern had been draped like a veil across the roof of the shed. The bushes had been cut on the top of the anthill, but left on the sides, so that the shed looked as if it rose from the tops of the bushes. The shed was of unbarked poles pushed into the earth, the roof was of thatch, and the upper half of the front was left open. Inside there was a bench of poles and a table of planks on poles. There sat Dirk, waiting hungrily, and Tommy went and sat beside him, putting the books and pencils on the table.

"This shed is fine," said Tommy, but Dirk was already looking at the books. So he began to teach Dirk how to read. And for all that holiday they were together in the shed while Dirk pored over the books. He found them more difficult than Tommy did, because there were full of words for things Dirk did not know, like curtains or carpet, and teaching Dirk to read the word carpet meant telling him all about carpets and the furnishings of a house. Often Tommy felt bored and restless and said: "Let's play," but Dirk said fiercely: "No, I want to read." Tommy grew fretful, for after all he had been working in the term and now he felt entitled to play. So there was another fight. Dirk said Tommy was a lazy white bastard, and Tommy said Dirk was a dirty half-caste. They fought as before, evenly matched and to no conclusion, and afterwards felt fine and friendly, and even made jokes about the fighting. It was arranged that they should work in the mornings only and leave the afternoons for play. When Tommy went back home that evening his mother saw the scratches on his face and the swollen nose, and said hopefully: "Have you and Dirk been fighting?" But Tommy said no, he had hit his face on a tree.

His parents, of course, knew about the shed in the bush, but did not speak of it to Mr. Macintosh. No one did. For Dirk's very existence was something to be ignored by everyone, and none of the workers, not even the overseers, would dare to mention Dirk's name. When Mr. Macintosh asked Tommy what he had done to his face, he said he had slipped and fallen.

And so their eighth year and their ninth went past. Dirk could read and write and do all the sums that Tommy could do. He was always handicapped by not knowing the different way of living and soon he said, angrily, it wasn't fair, and there was another fight about it, and then Tommy began another way of teaching. He would tell how it was to go to a cinema in the city, every detail of it, how the seats were arranged in such a way, and one paid so much, and the lights were like this, and the picture on the screen worked like that. Or he would describe how at school they ate such things for breakfast and other things for lunch. Or tell how the man had come with picture slides talking about China. The two boys got out an atlas and found China, and Tommy told Dirk every word of what the lecturer had said. Or it might be Italy or some other country. And they would argue that the lecturer should have said this or that, for Dirk was always hotly scornful of the white man's way of looking at things, so arrogant, he said. Soon Tommy saw things through Dirk; he saw the other life in town clear and brightly-coloured and a little distorted, as Dirk did.

Soon, at school, Tommy would involuntarily think: I must remember this to tell Dirk. It was impossible for him to do anything, say anything, without being very conscious of just how it happened, as if Dirk's black, sarcastic eye had got inside him, Tommy, and never closed. And a feeling of unwillingness grew in Tommy, because of the strain of fitting these two worlds together. He found himself swearing at niggers or kaffirs like the other boys, and more violently than they did, but immediately afterwards he would find himself thinking: I must remember this so as to tell Dirk. Because of all this thinking, and seeing everything clear all the time, he was very bright at school, and found the work easy. He was two classes ahead of his age.

That was the tenth year, and one day Tommy went to the shed in the bush and Dirk was not waiting for him. It was the first day of the holidays. All the term he had been remembering things to tell Dirk, and now Dirk was not there. A dove was sitting on the Christmas fern, cooing lazily in the hot morning, a sleepy, lonely sound. When Tommy came pushing through the bushes it flew away. The mine-stamps thudded heavily, gold, gold, and Tommy saw that the shed was empty even of books, for the case where they were usually kept was hanging open.

He went running to his mother: "Where's Dirk?" he asked.

"How should I know?" said Annie Clarke, cautiously. She really did not know.

"You do know, you do!" he cried, angrily. And then he went racing off to the big pit. Mr. Macintosh was sitting on an upturned truck on the edge, watching the hundreds of workers below him, moving like ants on the yellow bottom. "Well, laddie?" he asked, amiably, and moved over for Tommy to sit by him.

"Where's Dirk?" asked Tommy, accusingly, standing in front of him.

Mr. Macintosh tipped his old felt hat even further back and scratched at his front hair and looked at Tommy.

"Dirk's working," he said, at last.

"Where?"

Mr. Macintosh pointed at the bottom of the pit. Then he said again: "Sit down, laddie, I want to talk to you."

"I don't want to," said Tommy, and he turned away and went blundering over the veld to the shed. He sat on the bench and cried, and when dinnertime came he did not go home. All that day he sat in the shed, and when he had finished crying he remained on the bench, leaning his back against the poles of the shed, and stared into the bush. The doves cooed and cooed, kru-kruuuu, kru-kruu-uuu, and a woodpecker tapped, and the mine-stamps thudded. Yet it was very quiet, a hand of silence gripped the bush, and he could hear the borers and the ants at work in the poles of the bench he sat on. He could see that although the anthill seemed dead, a mound of hard, peaked, baked earth, it was very much alive, for there was a fresh outbreak of wet, damp earth in the floor of the shed. There was a fine crust of reddish, lacey earth over the poles of the walls.

The shed would have to be built again soon, because the ants and borers would have eaten it through. But what was the use of a shed without Dirk?

All that day he stayed there, and did not return until dark, and when his mother said: "What's the matter with you, why are you crying?" he said angrily, "I don't know," matching her dishonesty with his own. The next day, even before breakfast, he was off to the shed, and did not return until dark, and refused his supper although he had not eaten all day.

And the next day it was the same, but now he was bored and lonely. He took his knife from his pocket and whittled at a stick, and it became a boy, bent and straining under the weight of a heavy load, his arms clenched up to support it. He took the figure home at suppertime and ate with it on the table in front of him.

"What's that?" asked Annie Clarke, and Tommy answered: "Dirk."

He took it to his bedroom, and sat in the soft lamp-light, working away with his knife, and he had it in his hand the following morning when he met Mr. Macintosh at the brink of the pit. "What's that, laddie?" asked Mr. Macintosh, and Tommy said: "Dirk."

Mr. Macintosh's mouth went thin, and then he smiled and said: "Let me have it."

"No, it's for Dirk."

Mr. Macintosh took out his wallet and said: "I'll pay you for it."

"I don't want any money," said Tommy, angrily, and Mr. Macintosh, greatly disturbed, put back his wallet. Then Tommy, hesitating, said: "Yes, I do." Mr. Macintosh, his values confirmed, was relieved, and he took out his wallet again and produced a pound note, which seemed to him very generous. "Five pounds," said Tommy, promptly. Mr. Macintosh first scowled, then laughed. He tipped back his head and roared with laughter. "Well, laddie, you'll make a businessman yet. Five pounds for a little bit of wood!"

"Make it for yourself then, if it's just a bit of wood."

Mr. Macintosh counted out five pounds and handed them over. "What are you going to do with that money?" he asked, as he watched Tommy buttoning them carefully into his shirt pocket. "Give them to Dirk," said Tommy, triumphantly, and Mr. Macintosh's heavy old face went purple. He watched while Tommy walked away from him, sitting on the truck, letting the heavy cudgel swing lightly against his shoes. He solved his immediate problem by thinking: He's a good laddie, he's got a good heart.

That night Mrs. Clarke came over while he was sitting over his roast beef and cabbage, and said: "Mr. Macintosh, I want a word with you." He nodded at a chair, but she did not sit. "Tommy's upset," she said, delicately, "he's been used to Dirk, and now he's got no one to play with."

For a moment Mr. Macintosh kept his eyes lowered, then he said: "It's easily fixed, Annie, don't worry yourself." He spoke heartily, as it was easy for him to do, speaking of a worker, who might be released at his whim for other duties.

That bright protesting flush came on to her cheeks, in spite of herself, and she looked quickly at him, with real indignation. But he ignored it and said: "I'll fix it in the morning, Annie."

She thanked him and went back home, suffering because she had not said those words which had always soothed her conscience in the past: You're nothing but a pig, Mr. Macintosh . . .

As for Tommy, he was sitting in the shed, crying his eyes out. And then, when there were no more tears, there came such a storm of anger and pain that he would never forget it as long as he lived. What for? He did not know, and that was the worst of it. It was not simply Mr. Macintosh, who loved him, and who thus so blackly betrayed his own flesh and blood, nor the silences of his parents. Something deeper, felt working in the substance of life as he could hear those ants working away with those busy jaws at the roots of the poles he sat on, to make new material for their different forms of life. He was testing those words which were used, or not used— merely suggested—all the time, and for a ten-year-old boy it was almost too hard to bear. A child may say of a companion one day that he hates so and so, and the next: He is my friend. That is how a relationship is, shifting and changing, and children are kept safe in their hates and loves by the fabric of social life their parents make over their heads. And middle-aged people say: This is my friend, this is my enemy, including all the shifts and changes of feeling in one word, for the sake of an easy mind. In between these ages, at about twenty perhaps, there is a time when the young people test everything, and accept many hard and cruel truths about living, and that is because they do not know how hard it is to accept them finally, and for the rest of their lives. It is easy to be truthful at twenty.

But it is not easy at ten, a little boy entirely alone, looking at words like friendship. What, then, was frieindship? Dirk was his friend, that he knew, but did he like Dirk? Did he love him? Sometimes not at all. He remembered how Dirk had said: "I'll get you an-other baby buck. I'll kill its mother with a stone." He remembered his feeling of revulsion at the cruelty. Dirk was cruel. But—and here Tommy unexpectedly laughed, and for the first time he understood Dirk's way of laughing. It was really funny to say that Dirk was cruel, when his very existence was a cruelty. Yet Mr. Macintosh laughed in exactly the same way, and his skin was white, or rather, white browned over by the sun. Why was Mr. Macintosh also en-titled to laugh, with that same abrupt ugliness? Perhaps some-where in the beginnings of the rich Mr. Macintosh there had been the same cruelty, and that had worked its way through the life of Mr. Macintosh until it turned into the cruelty of Dirk, the coloured boy, the half-caste? If so, it was all much harder to understand.

And then Tommy thought how Dirk seemed to wait always, as if he, Tommy, were bound to stand by him, as if this were a justice that was perfectly clear to Dirk; and he, Tommy, did in fact fight with Mr. Macintosh for Dirk, and he could behave in no other way. Why? Because Dirk was his friend? Yet there were times when he hated Dirk, and certainly Dirk hated him, and when they fought they could have killed each other easily, and with joy.

Well, then? Well, then? What was friendship, and why were they bound so closely, and by what? Slowly the little boy, sitting alone on his antheap, came to an understanding which is proper to middle-aged people, that resignation in knowledge which is called irony. Such a person may know, for instance, that he is bound most deeply to another person, although he does not like that person, in the way the word is ordinarily used, or the way he talks, or his politics, or anything else. And yet they are friends and will always be friends, and what happens to this bound couple affects each most deeply, even though they may be in different continents, or may never see each other again. Or after twenty years they may meet, and there is no need to say a word, everything is understood. This is one of the ways of friendship, and just as real as amiability or being alike.

Well, then? For it is a hard and difficult knowledge for any little boy to accept. But he accepted it, and knew that he and Dirk were closer than brothers and always would be so. He grew many years older in that day of painful struggle, while he listened to the mine-stamps saying gold, gold, and to the ants working away with their jaws to destroy the bench he sat on, to make food for themselves.

Next morning Dirk came to the shed, and Tommy, looking at

him, knew that he, too, had grown years older in the months of working in the great pit. Ten years old—but he had been working with men and he was not a child.

Tommy took out the five pound notes and gave them to Dirk.

Dirk pushed them back. "What for?" he asked.

"I got them from him," said Tommy, and at once Dirk took them as if they were his right.

And at once, inside Tommy, came indignation, for he felt he was being taken for granted, and he said: "Why aren't you working?"

"He said I needn't. He means, while you are having your holidays."

"I got you free," said Tommy, boasting.

Dirk's eyes narrowed in anger. "He's my father," he said, for the first time.

"But he made you work," said Tommy, taunting him. And then: "Why do you work? I wouldn't. I should say no."

"So you would say no?" said Dirk in angry sarcasm.

"There's no law to make you."

"So there's no law, white boy, no law . . ." But Tommy had sprung at him, and they were fighting again, rolling over and over, and this time they fell apart from exhaustion and lay on the ground panting for a long time.

Later Dirk said: "Why do we fight, it's silly?"

"I don't know," said Tommy, and he began to laugh, and Dirk laughed too. They were to fight often in the future, but never with such bitterness, because of the way they were laughing now.

It was the following holidays before they fought again. Dirk was waiting for him in the shed.

"Did he let you go?" asked Tommy at once, putting down new books on the table for Dirk.

"I just came," said Dirk. "I didn't ask."

They sat together on the bench, and at once a leg gave way and they rolled off on the floor laughing. "We must mend it," said Tommy. "Let's build the shed again."

"No," said Dirk at once, "don't let's waste time on the shed. You can teach me while you're here, and I can make the shed when you've gone back to school."

Tommy slowly got up from the floor, frowning. Again he felt he was being taken for granted. "Aren't you going to work on the mine during the term?"

"No, I'm not going to work on the mine again. I told him I wouldn't."

"You've got to work," said Tommy, grandly.

"So I've got to work," said Dirk, threateningly. "You can go to school, white boy, but I've got to work, and in the holidays I can just take time off to please you."

They fought until they were tired, and five minutes afterwards they were seated on the anthill talking. "What did you do with the five pounds?" asked Tommy.

"I gave them to my mother."

"What did she do with them?"

"She bought herself a dress, and then food for us all, and bought me these trousers, and she put the rest away to keep."

A pause. Then, deeply ashamed, Tommy asked: "Doesn't he give her any money?"

"He doesn't come any more. Not for more than a year."

"Oh, I thought he did still," said Tommy casually, whistling.

"No." Then, fiercely, in a low voice: "There'll be some more half-castes in the compound soon."

Dirk sat crouching, his fierce black eyes on Tommy, ready to spring at him. But Tommy was sitting with his head bowed, looking at the ground. "It's not fair," he said. "It's not fair."

"So you've discovered that, white boy?" said Dirk. It was said good-naturedly, and there was no need to fight. They went to their books and Tommy taught Dirk some new sums.

But they never spoke of what Dirk would do in the future, how he would use all this schooling. They did not dare.

That was the eleventh year.

When they were twelve, Tommy returned from school to be greeted by the words: "Have you heard the news?"

"What news?"

They were sitting as usual on the bench. The shed was newly built, with strong thatch, and good walls, plastered this time with mud, so as to make it harder for the ants.

"They are saying you are going to be sent away."

"Who says so?"

"Oh, everyone," said Dirk, stirring his feet about vaguely under the table. This was because it was the first few minutes after the return from school, and he was always cautious, until he was sure Tommy had not changed towards him. And that "everyone" was explosive. Tommy nodded, however, and asked apprehensively: "Where to?"

"To the sea."

"How do they know?" Tommy scarcely breathed the word they.

"Your cook heard your mother say so . . ." And then Dirk added with a grin, forcing the issue: "Cheek, dirty kaffirs talking about white men."

Tommy smiled obligingly, and asked: "How, to the sea, what does it mean?"

"How should we know, dirty kaffirs."

"Oh, shut up," said Tommy, angrily. They glared at each other, their muscles tensed. But they sighed and looked away. At twelve it was not easy to fight, it was all too serious.

That night Tommy said to his parents: "They say I'm going to sea. Is it true?"

His mother asked quickly: "Who said so?"

"But is it true?" Then, derisively: "Cheek, dirty kaffirs talking about us."

"Please don't talk like that, Tommy, it's not right."

"Oh, mother, please, how am I going to sea?"

"But be sensible Tommy, it's not settled, but Mr. Macin-tosh . . ."

"So it's Mr. Macintosh!"

Mrs. Clarke looked at her husband, who came forward and sat down and settled his elbows on the table. A family conference. Tommy also sat down.

"Now listen, son. Mr. Macintosh has a soft spot for you. You should be grateful to him. He can do a lot for you."

"But why should I go to sea?"

"You don't have to. He suggested it—he was in the Merchant Navy himself once."

"So I've got to go just because he did."

"He's offered to pay for you to go to college in England, and give you money until you're in the Navy."

"But I don't want to be a sailor. I've never even seen the sea."

"But you're good at your figures, and you have to be, so why not?"

"I won't," said Tommy, angrily. "I won't, I won't." He glared at them through tears. "You want to get rid of me, that's all it is. You want me to go away from here, from . . ."

The parents looked at each other and sighed.

"Well, if you don't want to, you don't have to. But it's not every boy who has a chance like this."

"Why doesn't he send Dirk?" asked Tommy, aggressively.

"Tommy," cried Annie Clarke, in great distress.

"Well, why doesn't he? He's much better than me at figures."

"Go to bed," said Mr. Clarke suddenly, in a fit of temper. "Go to bed."

Tommy went out of the room, slamming the door hard. He must be grown-up. His father had never spoken to him like that. He sat on the edge of the bed in stubborn rebellion, listening to the thudding of the stamps. And down in the compound they were dancing, the lights of the fires flickered red on his window-pane.

He wondered if Dirk were there, leaping around the fires with the others.

Next day he asked him: "Do you dance with the others?" At once he knew he had blundered. When Dirk was angry, his eyes darkened and narrowed. When he was hurt, his mouth set in a way which made the flesh pinch thinly under his nose. So he looked now.

"Listen, white boy. White people don't like us half-castes. Neither do the blacks like us. No one does. And so I don't dance with them."

"Let's do some lessons," said Tommy, quickly. And they went to their books, dropping the subject.

Later Mr. Macintosh came to the Clarkes' house and asked for Tommy. The parents watched Mr. Macintosh and their son walk together along the edge of the great pit. They stood at the window and watched, but they did not speak.

Mr. Macintosh was saying easily: "Well, laddie, and so you don't want to be a sailor."

"No, Mr. Macintosh."

"I went to sea when I was fifteen. It's hard, but you aren't afraid of that. Besides, you'd be an officer."

Tommy said nothing.

"You don't like the idea?"

"No."

Mr. Macintosh stopped and looked down into the pit. The earth at the bottom was as yellow as it had been when Tommy was seven, but now it was much deeper. Mr. Macintosh did not know how deep, because he had not measured it. Far below, in this man-made valley, the workers were moving and shifting like black seeds tilted on a piece of paper.

"Your father worked on the mines and he became an engineer working at nights, did you know that?"

"Yes."

"It was very hard for him. He was thirty before he was qualified, and then he earned twenty-five pounds a month until he came to this mine."

"Yes."

"You don't want to do that, do you?"

"I will if I have to," muttered Tommy, defiantly.

Mr. Macintosh's face was swelling and purpling. The veins along nose and forehead were black. Mr. Macintosh was asking himself why this lad treated him like dirt, when he was offering to do him an immense favour. And yet, in spite of the look of sullen indifference which was so ugly on that young face, he could not help loving him. He was a fine boy, tall, strong, and his hair was the soft, bright brown, and his eyes clear and black. A much better man than his father, who was rough and marked by the long struggle of his youth. He said: "Well, you don't have to be a sailor, perhaps you'd like to go to university and be a scholar."

"I don't know," said Tommy, unwillingly, although his heart had moved suddenly. Pleasure—he was weakening. Then he said suddenly: "Mr. Macintosh, why do you want to send me to college?"

And Mr. Macintosh fell right into the trap. "I have no children," he said, sentimentally. "I feel for you like my own son." He stopped. Tommy was looking away towards the compound, and his intention was clear.

"Very well then," said Mr. Macintosh, harshly. "If you want to be a fool."

Tommy stood with his eyes lowered and he knew quite well he was a fool. Yet he could not have behaved in any other way.

"Don't be hasty," said Mr. Macintosh, after a pause. "Don't throw away your chances, laddie. You're nothing but a lad, yet. Take your time." And with this tone, he changed all the emphasis of the conflict, and made it simply a question of waiting. Tommy did not move, so Mr. Macintosh went on quickly: "Yes, that's right, you just think it over." He hastily slipped a pound note from his pocket and put it into the boy's hand.

"You know what I'm going to do with it?" said Tommy, laughing suddenly, and not at all pleasantly.

"Do what you like, do just as you like, it's your money," said Mr. Macintosh, turning away so as not to have to understand.

Tommy took the money to Dirk, who received it as if it were his right, a feeling in which Tommy was now an accomplice, and they sat together in the shed. "I've got to be something," said Tommy angrily. "They're going to make me be something."

"They wouldn't have to make me be anything," said Dirk, sardonically. "I know what I'd be."

"What?" asked Tommy, enviously.

"An engineer."

"How do you know what you've got to do?"

"That's what I want," said Dirk, stubbornly.

After a while Tommy said: "If you went to the city, there's a school for coloured children."

"I wouldn't see my mother again."

"Why not?"

"There's laws, white boys, laws. Anyone who lives with and after the fashion of the natives is a native. Therefore I'm a native, and I'm not entitled to go to school with the half-castes."

"If you went to the town, you'd not be living with the natives so you'd be classed as a coloured."

"But then I couldn't see my mother, because if she came to town she'd still be a native."

There was a triumphant conclusiveness in this that made Tommy think: He intends to get what he wants another way . . . And then: Through me . . . But he had accepted that justice a long time ago, and now he looked at his own arm that lay on the rough plank of the table. The outer side was burnt dark and dry with the sun, and the hair glinted on it like fine copper. It was no darker than Dirk's brown arm, and no lighter. He turned it over. Inside, the skin was smooth, dusky white, the veins running blue and strong across the wrist. He looked at Dirk, grinning, who promptly turned his own arm over, in a challenging way. Tommy said, unhappily: "You can't go to school properly because the inside of your arm is brown. And that's that!" Dirk's tight and bitter mouth expanded into the grin that was also his father's, and he said: "That is so, white boy, that is so."

"Well, it's not my fault," said Tommy, aggressively, closing his fingers and banging the fist down again and again.

"I didn't say it was your fault," said Dirk at once.

Tommy said, in that uneasy, aggressive tone: "I've never even seen your mother."

To this, Dirk merely laughed, as if to say: You have never wanted to.

Tommy said, after a pause: "Let me come and see her now."

Then Dirk said, in a tone which was uncomfortable, almost like compassion: "You don't have to."

"Yes," insisted Tommy. "Yes, now." He got up, and Dirk rose too. "She won't know what to say," warned Dirk. "She doesn't speak English." He did not really want Tommy to go to the compound; Tommy did not really want to go. Yet they went.

In silence they moved along the path between the trees, in silence skirted the edge of the pit, in silence entered the trees on the other side, and moved along the paths to the compound. It was big, spread over many acres, and the huts were in all stages of growth and decay, some new, with shining thatch, some tumble-down, with dulled and sagging thatch, some in the process of being built, the peeled wands of the roof-frames gleaming like milk in the sun.

Dirk led the way to a big square hut. Tommy could see people watching him walking with the coloured boy, and turning to laugh and whisper. Dirk's face was proud and tight, and he could feel the same look on his own face. Outside the square hut sat a little girl of about ten. She was bronze, Dirk's colour. Another little girl, quite black, perhaps six years old, was squatted on a log, finger in mouth, watching them. A baby, still unsteady on its feet, came staggering out of the doorway and collapsed, chuckling, against Dirk's knees. Its skin was almost white. Then Dirk's mother came out of the hut after the baby, smiled when she saw Dirk, but went anxious and bashful when she saw Tommy. She made a little bobbing curtsey, and took the baby from Dirk, for the sake of something to hold in her awkward and shy hands.

"This is Baas Tommy," said Dirk. He sounded very embarrassed.

She made another little curtsey and stood smiling.

She was a large woman, round and smooth all over, but her legs were slender, and her arms, wound around the child, thin and knotted. Her round face had a bashful curiosity, and her eyes moved quickly from Dirk to Tommy and back, while she smiled and smiled, biting her lips with strong teeth, and smiled again.

Tommy said: "Good morning," and she laughed and said "Good morning."

Then Dirk said: "Enough now, let's go." He sounded very angry. Tommy said: "Goodbye." Dirk's mother said: "Goodbye," and made her little bobbing curtsey, and she moved her child from one arm to another and bit her lip anxiously over her gleaming smile.

Tommy and Dirk went away from the square mud hut where the variously-coloured children stood staring after them.

"There now," said Dirk, angrily. "You've seen my mother."

"I'm sorry," said Tommy uncomfortably, feeling as if the responsibility for the whole thing rested on him. But Dirk laughed suddenly and said: "Oh, all right, all right, white boy, it's not your fault."

All the same, he seemed pleased that Tommy was upset.

Later, with an affectation of indifference, Tommy asked, thinking of those new children: "Does Mr. Macintosh come to your mother again now?"

And Dirk answered "Yes," just one word.

In the shed Dirk studied from a geography book, while Tommy sat idle and thought bitterly that they wanted him to be a sailor. Then his idle hands protested, and he took a knife and began slashing at the edge of the table. When the gashes showed a whiteness from the core of the wood, he took a stick lying on the floor and whittled at it, and when it snapped from thinness he went out to the trees, picked up a lump of old wood from the ground, and brought it back to the shed. He worked on it with his knife, not knowing what it was he made, until a curve under his knife reminded him of Dirk's sister squatting at the hut door, and then he directed his knife with a purpose. For several days he fought with the lump of wood, while Dirk studied. Then he brought a tin of boot polish from the house, and worked the bright brown wax into the creamy white wood, and soon there was a bronze-coloured figure of the little girl, staring with big, curious eyes while she squatted on spindly legs.

Tommy put it in front of Dirk, who turned it around, grinning a little. "It's like her," he said at last. "You can have it if you like," said Tommy. Dirk's teeth flashed, he hesitated, and then reached into his pocket and took out a bundle of dirty cloth. He undid it, and Tommy saw the little clay figure he had made of Dirk years ago. It was crumbling, almost worn to a lump of mud, but in it was still the vigorous challenge of Dirk's body. Tommy's mind signalled recognition—for he had forgotten he had ever made it—and he picked it up. "You kept it?" he asked shyly, and Dirk smiled. They looked at each other, smiling. It was a moment of warm, close feeling, and yet in it was the pain that neither of them understood, and also the cruelty and challenge that made them fight. They lowered their eyes unhappily. "I'll do your mother," said Tommy, getting up and running away into the trees. in order to escape from the challenging closeness. He searched until he found a thorn tree, which is so hard it turns the edge of an axe, and then he took an axe and worked at the felling of the tree until the sun went down. A big stone near him was kept wet to sharpen the axe, and next day he worked on until the tree fell. He sharpened the worn axe again, and cut a length of tree about two feet, and split off the tough bark, and brought it back to the shed. Dirk had fitted a shelf against the logs of the wall at the back. On it he had set the tiny, crumbling figure of himself, and the new bronze shape of his little sister. There was a space left for the new statue. Tommy said, shyly: "I'll do it as quickly as I can so that it will be done before the terms starts." Then, lowering his eyes, which suffered under this new contract of shared feeling, he examined the piece of wood. It was not pale and gleaming like almonds, as was the softer wood. It was a gingery brown, a close-fibred, knotted wood, and down its centre, as he knew, was a hard black spine. He turned it between his hands and thought that this was more difficult than anything he had ever done. For the first time he studied a piece of wood before starting on it, with a desired shape in his mind, trying to see how what he wanted would grow out of the dense mass of material he held.

Then he tried his knife on it and it broke. He asked Dirk for his knife. It was a long piece of metal, taken from a pile of scrap mining machinery, sharpened on stone until it was razor-fine. The handle was cloth wrapped tight around.

With this new and unwieldy tool Tommy fought with the wood for many days. When the holidays were ending, the shape was there, but the face was blank. Dirk's mother was full-bodied, with soft, heavy flesh and full, naked shoulders above a tight, sideways draped cloth. The slender legs were planted firm on naked feet, and the thin arms, knotted with work, were lifted to the weight of a child who, a small, helpless creature swaddled in cloth, looked out with large, curious eyes. But the mother's face was not yet there.

"I'll finish it next holidays," said Tommy, and Dirk set it carefully beside the other figures on the shelf. With his back turned he asked cautiously: "Perhaps you won't be here next holidays?"

"Yes I will," said Tommy, after a pause. "Yes I will."

It was a promise, and they gave each other that small, warm, unwilling smile, and turned away, Dirk back to the compound and Tommy to the house, where his trunk was packed for school.

That night Mr. Macintosh came over to the Clarkes' house and spoke with the parents in the front room. Tommy, who was asleep, woke to find Mr. Macintosh beside him. He sat on the foot of the bed and said: "I want to talk to you, laddie." Tommy turned the wick of the oil-lamp, and now he could see in the shadowy light that Mr. Macintosh had a look of uneasiness about him. He was sitting with his strong old body balanced behind the big stomach, hands laid on his knees, and his grey Scots eyes were watchful.

"I want you to think about what I said," said Mr. Macintosh, in a quick, bluff good-humour. "Your mother says in two years' time you will have matriculated, you're doing fine at school. And after that you can go to college."

Tommy lay on his elbow, and in the silence the drums came tapping from the compound, and he said: "But Mr. Macintosh, I'm not the only one who's good at his books."

Mr. Macintosh stirred, but said bluffly: "Well, but I'm talking about you."

Tommy was silent, because as usual these opponents were so much stronger than was reasonable, simply because of their ability to make words mean something else. And then, his heart painfully beating, he said: "Why don't you send Dirk to college? You're so rich, and Dirk knows everything I know. He's better than me at figures. He's a whole book ahead of me, and he can do sums I can't."

Mr. Macintosh crossed his legs impatiently, uncrossed them, and said: "Now why should I send Dirk to college?" For now Tommy would have to put into precise words what he meant, and this Mr. Macintosh was quite sure he would not do. But to make certain, he lowered his voice and said: "Think of your mother, laddie, she's worrying about you, and you don't want to make her worried, do you?"

Tommy looked towards the door, under it came a thick yellow streak of light: in that room his mother and his father were waiting in silence for Mr. Macintosh to emerge with news of Tommy's sure and wonderful future.

"You know why Dirk should go to college," said Tommy in despair, shifting his body unhappily under the sheets, and Mr. Macintosh chose not to hear it. He got up, and said quickly: "You just think it over, laddie. There's no hurry, but by next holidays I want to know." And he went out of the room. As he opened the door, a brightly-lit, painful scene was presented to Tommy: his father and mother sat, smiling in embarrassed entreaty at Mr. Macintosh. The door shut, and Tommy turned down the light, and there was darkness.

He went to school next day. Mrs. Clarke, turning out Mr. Macintosh's house as usual, said unhappily: "I think you'll find everything in its proper place," and slipped away, as if she were ashamed.

As for Mr. Macintosh, he was in a mood which made others, besides Annie Clarke, speak to him carefully. His cookboy, who had worked for him twelve years, gave notice that month. He had been knocked down twice by that powerful, hairy fist, and he was not a slave, after all, to remain bound to a bad-tempered master. And when a load of rock slipped and crushed the skulls of two workers, and the police came out for an investigation, Mr. Macintosh met them irritably, and told them to mind their own business. For the first time in that mine's history of scandalous recklessness, after many such accidents, Mr. Macintosh heard the indignant words from the police officer: "You speak as if you were above the law, Mr. Macintosh. If this happens again, you'll see . . ."

Worst of all, he ordered Dirk to go back to work in the pit, and Dirk refused.

"You can't make me," said Dirk.

"Who's the boss on this mine?" shouted Mr. Macintosh.

"There's no law to make children work," said the thirteen-year-old, who stood as tall as his father, a straight, lithe youth against the bulky strength of the old man.

The word law whipped the anger in Mr. Macintosh to the point where he could feel his eyes go dark, and the blood pounding in that hot darkness in his head. In fact, it was the power of this anger that sobered him, for he had been very young when he had learned to fear his own temper. And above all, he was a shrewd man. He waited until his sight was clear again, and then asked, reasonably: "Why do you want to loaf around the compound, why not work and earn money?"

Dirk said: "I can read and write, and I know my figures better than Tommy—Baas Tommy," he added, in a way which made the anger rise again in Mr. Macintosh, so that he had to make a fresh effort to subdue it.

But Tommy was a point of weakness in Mr. Macintosh, and it was then that he spoke the words which afterwards made him wonder if he'd gone suddenly crazy. For he said: "Very well, when you're sixteen you can come and do my books and write the letters for the mine."

Dirk said: "All right," as if this were no more than his due, and walked off, leaving Mr. Macintosh impotently furious with himself. For how could anyone but himself see the books? Such a person would be his master. It was impossible, he had no intention of ever letting Dirk, or anyone else, see them. Yet he had made the promise. And so he would have to find another way of using Dirk, or—and the words came involuntarily—getting rid of him.

From a mood of settled bad temper, Mr. Macintosh dropped into one of sullen thoughtfulness, which was entirely foreign to his character. Being shrewd is quite different from the processes of thinking. Shrewdness, particularly the money-making shrewdness, is a kind of instinct. While Mr. Macintosh had always known what he wanted to do, and how to do it, that did not mean he had known why he wanted so much money, or why he had chosen these ways of making it. Mr. Macintosh felt like a cat whose nose has been rubbed into its own dirt, and for many nights he sat in the hot little house, that vibrated continually from the noise of the mine-stamps, most uncomfortably considering himself and his life. He reminded himself, for instance, that he was sixty, and presumably had not more than ten or fifteen years to live. It was not a thought that an unreflective man enjoys, particularly when he had never considered his age at all. He was so healthy, strong, tough. But he was sixty nevertheless, and what would be his monument? An enormous pit in the earth, and a million pounds' worth of property. Then how should he spend ten or fifteen years? Exactly as he had the preceding sixty, for he hated being away from this place, and this gave him a caged and useless sensation, for it had never entered his head before that he was not as free as he felt himself to be.

Well, then—and this thought gnawed most closely to Mr. Macintosh's pain—why had he not married? For he considered himself a marrying sort of man, and had always intended to find himself the right sort of woman and marry her. Yet he was already sixty. The truth was that Mr. Macintosh had no idea at all why he had not married and got himself sons; and in these slow, uncomfortable ponderings the thought of Dirk's mother intruded itself only to be hastily thrust away. Mr. Macintosh, the sensualist, had a taste for dark-skinned women; and now it was certainly too late to admit as a permanent feature of his character something he had always considered as a sort of temporary whim, or makeshift, like someone who learns to enjoy an inferior brand of tobacco when better brands are not available.

He thought of Tommy, of whom he had been used to say: "I've taken a fancy to the laddie." Now it was not so much a fancy as a deep, grieving love. And Tommy was the son of his employee, and looked at him with contempt, and he, Mr. Macintosh, reacted with angry shame as if he were guilty of something. Of what? It was ridiculous.

The whole situation was ridiculous, and so Mr. Macintosh allowed himself to slide back into his usual frame of mind. Tommy's only a boy, he thought, and he'll see reason in a year or so. And as for Dirk, I'll find him some kind of a job when the time comes . . .

At the end of the term, when Tommy came home, Mr. Macintosh asked, as usual, to see the school report, which usually filled him with pride. Instead of heading the class with approbation from the teachers and high marks in all subjects, Tommy was near the bottom, with such remarks as Slovenly, and Lazy, and Bad-mannered. The only subject in which he got any marks at all was that called Art, which Mr. Macintosh did not take into account.

When Tommy was asked by his parents why he was not working, he replied, impatiently: "I don't know," which was quite true; and at once escaped to the anthill. Dirk was there, waiting for the books Tommy always brought for him. Tommy reached at once up to the shelf where stood the figure of Dirk's mother, lifted it down and examined the unworked space which would be the face. "I know how to do it," he said to Dirk, and took out some knives and chisels he had brought from the city.

That was how he spent the three weeks of that holiday, and when he met Mr. Macintosh he was sullen and uncomfortable. "You'll have to be working a bit better," he said, before Tommy went back, to which he received no answer but an unwilling smile.

During that term Tommy distinguished himself in two ways besides being steadily at the bottom of the class he had so recently led. He made a fiery speech in the debating society on the iniquity of the colour bar, which rather pleased his teachers, since it is a well-known fact that the young must pass through these phases of rebellion before settling down to conformity. In fact, the greater the verbal rebellion, the more settled was the conformity likely to be. In secret Tommy got books from the city library such as are not usually read by boys of his age, on the history of Africa, and on comparative anthropology, and passed from there to the history of the moment—he ordered papers from the Government Stationery Office, the laws of the country. Most particularly those affecting the relations between black and white and coloured. These he bought in order to take back to Dirk. But in addition to all this ferment, there was that subject Art, which in this school meant a drawing lesson twice a week, copying busts of Julius Caesar, or it might be Nelson, or shading in fronds of fern or leaves, or copying a large vase or a table standing diagonally to the class, thus learning what he was told were the laws of Perspective. There was no modelling, nothing approaching sculpture in this school, but this was the nearest thing to it, and that mysterious prohibition which forbade him to distinguish himself in Geometry or English, was silent when it came to using the pencil.

At the end of the term his Report was very bad, but it admitted that he had An Interest in Current Events, and a Talent for Art.

And now this word Art, coming at the end of two successive terms, disturbed his parents and forced itself on Mr. Macintosh. He said to Annie Clarke: "It's a nice thing to make pictures, but the lad won't earn a living by it." And Mrs. Clarke said reproachfully to Tommy: "It's all very well, Tommy, but you aren't going to earn a living drawing pictures."

"I didn't say I wanted to earn a living with it," shouted Tommy, miserably. "Why have I got to be something, you're always wanting me to be something."

That holiday Dirk spent studying the Acts of Parliament and the Reports of Commissions and Sub-Committees which Tommy had brought him, while Tommy attempted something new. There was a square piece of soft white wood which Dirk had pilfered from the mine, thinking Tommy might use it. And Tommy set it against the walls of the shed, and knelt before it and attempted a frieze or engraving—he did not know the words for what he was doing. He cut out a great pit, surrounded by mounds of earth and rock, with the peaks of great mountains beyond, and at the edge of the pit stood a big man carrying a stick, and over the edge of the pit wound a file of black figures, tumbling into the gulf. From the pit came flames and smoke. Tommy took green ooze from leaves and mixed clay to colour the mountains and edges of the pit, and he made the little figures black with charcoal, and he made the flames writhing up out of the pit red with the paint used for parts of the mining machinery.

"If you leave it here, the ants'll eat it," said Dirk, looking with grim pleasure at the crude but effective picture.

To which Tommy shrugged. For while he was always solemnly intent on a piece of work in hand, afraid of anything that might mar it, or even distract his attention from it, once it was finished he cared for it not at all.

It was Dirk who had painted the shelf which held the other figures with a mixture that discouraged ants, and it was now Dirk who set the piece of square wood on a sheet of tin smeared with the same mixture, and balanced it in a way so it should not touch any part of the walls of the shed, where the ants might climb up.

And so Tommy went back to school, still in that mood of obstinate disaffection, to make more copies of Julius Caesar and vases of flowers, and Dirk remained with his books and his Acts of Parliament. They would be fourteen before they met again, and both knew that crises and decisions faced them. Yet they said no more than the usual: Well, so long, before they parted. Nor did they ever write to each other, although this term Tommy had a commission to send certain books and other Acts of Parliament for a purpose which he entirely approved.

Dirk had built himself a new hut in the compound, where he lived alone, in the compound but not of it, affectionate to his mother, but apart from her. And to this hut at night came certain of the workers who forgot their dislike of the half-caste, that cuckoo in their nest, in their common interest in what he told them of the Acts and Reports. What he told them was what he had learnt himself in the proud loneliness of his isolation. "Education," he said, "education, that's the key"—and Tommy agreed with him, although he had, or so one might suppose from the way he was behaving, abandoned all idea of getting an education for himself. All that term parcels came to "Dirk, c/o Mr. Macintosh," and Mr. Macintosh delivered them to Dirk without any questions.

In the dim and smokey hut every night, half a dozen of the workers laboured with stubs of pencil and the exercise books sent by Tommy, to learn to write and do sums and understand the Laws.

One night Mr. Macintosh came rather late out of that other hut, and saw the red light from a fire moving softly on the rough ground outside the door of Dirk's hut. All the others were dark. He moved cautiously among them until he stood in the shadows outside the door, and looked in. Dirk was squatting on the floor, surrounded by half a dozen men, looking at a newspaper.

Mr. Macintosh walked thoughtfully home in the starlight. Dirk, had he known what Mr. Macintosh was thinking, would have been very angry, for all his flaming rebellion, his words of resentment were directed against Mr. Macintosh and his tyranny. Yet for the first time Mr. Macintosh was thinking of Dirk with a certain rough, amused pride. Perhaps it was because he was a Scot, after all, and in every one of his nation is an instinctive respect for learning and people with the determination to "get on." A chip off the old block, thought Mr. Macintosh, remembering how he, as a boy, had laboured to get a bit of education. And if the chip was the wrong colour—well, he would do something for Dirk. Something, he would decide when the time came. As for the others who were with Dirk, there was nothing easier than to sack a worker and engage another. Mr. Macintosh went to his bed, dressed as usual in vest and pyjama trousers, unwashed and thrifty in candlelight.

In the morning he gave orders to one of the overseers that Dirk should be summoned. His heart was already soft with thinking about the generous scene which would shortly take place. He was going to suggest that Dirk should teach all the overseers to read and write—on a salary from himself, of course—in order that these same overseers should be more useful in the work. They might learn to mark pay-sheets, for instance.

The overseer said that Baas Dirk spent his days studying in Baas Tommy's hut—with the suggestion in his manner that Baas Dirk could not be disturbed while so occupied, and that this was on Tommy's account.

The man, closely studying the effect of his words, saw how Mr. Macintosh's big, veiny face swelled, and he stepped back a pace. He was not one of Dirk's admirers.

Mr. Macintosh, after some moments of heavy breathing, allowed his shrewdness to direct his anger. He dismissed the man, and turned away.

During that morning he left his great pit and walked off into the bush in the direction of the towering blue peak. He had heard vaguely that Tommy had some kind of a hut, but imagined it as a child's thing. He was still very angry because of that calculated "Baas Dirk." He walked for a while along a smooth path through the trees, and came to a clearing. On the other side was an anthill, and on the anthill a well-built hut, draped with Christmas fern around the open front, like curtains. In the opening sat Dirk. He wore a clean white shirt, and long smooth trousers. His head, oiled and brushed close, was bent over books. The hand that turned the pages of the books had a brass ring on the little finger. He was the very image of an aspiring clerk: that form of humanity which Mr. Macintosh despised most.

Mr. Macintosh remained on the edge of the clearing for some time, vaguely waiting for something to happen, so that he might fling himself, armoured and directed by his contemptuous anger, into a crisis which would destroy Dirk for ever. But nothing did happen. Dirk continued to turn the pages of the book, so Mr. Macintosh went back to his house, where he ate boiled beef and carrots for his dinner.

Afterwards he went to a certain drawer in his bedroom, and from it took an object carelessly wrapped in cloth which, exposed, showed itself as that figure of Dirk the boy Tommy had made and sold for five pounds. And Mr. Macintosh turned and handled and pored over that crude wooden image of Dirk in a passion of curiosity, just as if the boy did not live on the same square mile of soil with him, fully available to his scrutiny at most hours of the day.

If one imagines a Judgment Day with the graves giving up their dead impartially, black, white, bronze, and yellow, to a happy reunion, one of the pleasures of that reunion might well be that people who have lived on the same acre or street all their lives will look at each other with incredulous recognition. "So that is what you were like," might be the gathering murmur around God's heaven. For the glass wall between colour and colour is not only a barrier against touch, but has become thick and distorted, so that black men, white men, see each other through it, but see—what? Mr. Macintosh examined the image of Dirk as if searching for some final revelation, but the thought that came persistently to his mind was that the statue might be of himself as a lad of twelve. So after a few moments he rolled it again in the cloth and tossed it back into the corner of a drawer, out of sight, and with it the unwelcome and tormenting knowledge.

Late that afternoon he left his house again and made his way towards the hut on the antheap. It was empty, and he walked through the knee-high grass and bushes till he could climb up the hard, slippery walls of the antheap and so into the hut.

℮   ℮

First he looked at the books in the case. The longer he looked, the faster faded that picture of Dirk as an oiled and mincing clerk, which he had been clinging to ever since he threw the other image into the back of a drawer. Respect for Dirk was reborn. Complicated mathematics, much more advanced than he had ever done. Geography. History. "The Development of the Slave Trade in the Eighteenth Century." "The Growth of Parliamentary Institutions in Great Britain." This title made Mr. Macintosh smile—the freebooting buccaneer examining a coastguard's notice perhaps. Mr. Macintosh lifted down one book after another and smiled. Then, beside these books, he saw a pile of slight, blue pamphlets, and he examined them. "The Natives Employment Act." "The Natives Juvenile Employment Act." "The Native Passes Act." And Mr. Macintosh flipped over the leaves and laughed, and had Dirk heard that laugh it would have been worse to him than any whip.

For as he patiently explained these laws and others like them to his bitter allies in the hut at night, it seemed to him that every word he spoke was like a stone thrown at Mr. Macintosh, his father. Yet Mr. Macintosh laughed, since he despised these laws, although in a different way, as much as Dirk did. When Mr. Macintosh, on his rare trips to the city, happened to drive past the House of Parliament, he turned on it a tolerant and appreciative gaze. "Well, why not?" he seemed to be saying. "It's an occupation, like any other."

So to Dirk's desperate act of retaliation he responded with a smile, and tossed back the books and pamphlets on the shelf. And then he turned to look at the other things in the shed, and for the first time he saw the high shelf where the statuettes were arranged. He looked, and felt his face swelling with that fatal rage. There was Dirk's mother, peering at him in bashful sensuality from over the baby's head, there the little girl, his daughter, squatting on spindly legs and staring. And there, on the edge of the shelf, a small, worn shape of clay which still held the vigorous strength of Dirk. Mr. Macintosh, breathing heavily, holding down his anger, stepped back to gain a clearer view of those figures, and his heel slipped on a slanting piece of wood. He turned to look, and there was the picture Tommy had carved and coloured of his mine. Mr. Macintosh saw the great pit, the black little figures tumbling and sprawling over into the flames, and he saw himself, stick in hand, astride on his two legs at the edge of the pit, his hat on the back of his head.

And now Mr. Macintosh was so disturbed and angry that he was driven out of the hut and into the clearing, where he walked back and forth through the grass, looking at the hut while his anger growled and moved inside him. After some time he came close to the hut again and peered in. Yes, there was Dirk's mother, peering bashfully from her shelf, as if to say: Yes, it's me, remember? And there on the floor was the square tinted piece of wood which said what Tommy thought of him and his life. Mr. Macintosh took a box of matches from his pocket. He lit a match. He understood he was standing in the hut with a lit match in his hand to no purpose. He dropped the match and ground it out with his foot. Then he put a pipe in his mouth, filled it and lit it, gazing all the time at the shelf and at the square carving. The second match fell to the floor and lay spurting a small white flame. He ground his heel hard on it. Anger heaved up in him beyond all sanity, and he lit another match, pushed it into the thatch of the hut, and walked out of it and so into the clearing and away into the bush. Without looking behind him he walked back to his house where his supper of boiled beef and carrots was waiting for him. He was amazed, angry, resentful. Finally he felt aggrieved, and wanted to explain to someone what a monstrous injustice was Tommy's view of him. But there was no one to explain it to; and he slowly quietened to a steady dulled sadness, and for some days remained so, until time restored him to normal. From this condition he looked back at his behaviour and did not like it. Not that he regretted burning the hut, it seemed to him unimportant. He was angry at himself for allowing his anger to dictate his actions. Also he knew that such an act brings its own results.

So he waited, and thought mainly of the cruelty of fate in denying him a son who might carry on his work—for he certainly thought of his work as something to be continued. He thought sadly of Tommy, who denied him. And so, his affection for Tommy was sprung again by thinking of him, and he waited, thinking of reproachful things to say to him.

When Tommy returned from school he went straight to the clearing and found a mound of ash on the antheap that was already sifted and swept by the wind. He found Dirk, sitting on a tree-trunk in the bush waiting for him.

"What happened?" asked Tommy. And then, at once: "Did you save your books?"

Dirk said: "He burnt it."

"How do you know?"

"I know."

Tommy nodded. "All your books have gone," he said, very grieved, and as guilty as if he had burnt them himself.

"Your carvings and your statues are burnt too."

But at this Tommy shrugged, since he could not care about his things once they were finished. "Shall we build the hut again now?" he suggested.

"My books are burnt," said Dirk, in a low voice, and Tommy, looking at him, saw how his hands were clenched. He instinctively moved a little aside to give his friend's anger space.

"When I grow up I'll clear you all out, all of you, there won't be one white man left in Africa, not one."

Tommy's face had a small, half-scared smile on it. The hatred Dirk was directing against him was so strong he nearly went away. He sat beside Dirk on the tree-trunk and said: "I'll try and get you more books."

"And then he'll burn them again."

"But you've already got what was in them inside your head," said Tommy, consolingly. Dirk said nothing, but sat like a clenched fist, and so they remained on the tree-trunk in the quiet bush while the doves cooed and the mine-stamps thudded, all that hot morning. When they had to separate at midday to return to their different worlds, it was with deep sadness, knowing that their childhood was finished, and their playing, and something new was ahead.

And at the meal Tommy's mother and father had his school report on the table, and they were reproachful. Tommy was at the foot of his class, and he would not matriculate that year. Or any year if he went on like this.

"You used to be such a clever boy," mourned his mother, "and now what's happened to you?"

Tommy, sitting silent at the table, moved his shoulders in a hunched, irritable way, as if to say: Leave me alone. Nor did he feel himself to be stupid and lazy, as the report said he was.

In his room were drawing blocks and pencils and hammers and chisels. He had never said to himself he had exchanged one purpose for another, for he had no purpose. How could he, when he had never been offered a future he could accept? Now, at this time, in his fifteenth year, with his reproachful parents deepening their reproach, and the knowledge that Mr. Macintosh would soon see that report, all he felt was a locked stubbornness, and a deep strength.

In the afternoon he went back to the clearing, and he took his chisels with him. On the old, soft, rotted tree-trunk that he sat on that morning, he sat again, waiting for Dirk. But Dirk did not come. Putting himself in his friend's place he understood that Dirk could not endure to be with a white-skinned person—a white face, even that of his oldest friend, was too much the enemy. But he waited, sitting on the tree-trunk all through the afternoon, with his chisels and hammers in a little box at his feet in the grass, and he fingered the soft, warm wood he sat on, letting the shape and texture of it come into the knowledge of his fingers.

Next day, there was still no Dirk.

Tommy began walking around the fallen tree, studying it. It was very thick, and its roots twisted and slanted into the air to the height of his shoulder. He began to carve the root. It would be Dirk again.

That night Mr. Macintosh came to the Clarkes' house and read the report. He went back to his own, and sat wondering why Tommy was set so bitterly against him. The next day he went to the Clarkes' house again to find Tommy, but the boy was not there.

He therefore walked through the thick bush to the antheap, and found Tommy kneeling in the grass working on the tree root.

Tommy said: "Good morning," and went on working, and Mr. Macintosh sat on the trunk and watched.

"What are you making?" asked Mr. Macintosh.

"Dirk," said Tommy, and Mr. Macintosh went purple and almost sprang up and away from the tree-trunk. But Tommy was not looking at him. So Mr. Macintosh remained, in silence. And then the useless vigour of Tommy's concentration on that rotting bit of root goaded him, and his mind moved naturally to a new decision.

"Would you like to be an artist?" he suggested.

Tommy allowed his chisel to rest, and looked at Mr. Macintosh as if this were a fresh trap. He shrugged, and with the appearance of anger, went on with his work.

"If you've a real gift, you can earn money by that sort of thing. I had a cousin back in Scotland who did it. He made souvenirs, you know, for travellers." He spoke in a soothing and jolly way.

Tommy let the souvenirs slide by him, as another of these impositions on his independence. He said: "Why did you burn Dirk's books?"

But Mr. Macintosh laughed in relief. "Why should I burn his books?" It really seemed ridiculous to him, his rage had been against Tommy's work, not Dirk's.

"I know you did," said Tommy. "I know it. And Dirk does too."

Mr. Macintosh lit his pipe in good humour. For now things seemed much easier. Tommy did not know why he had set fire to the hut, and that was the main thing. He puffed smoke for a few moments and said: "Why should you think I don't want Dirk to study? It's a good thing, a bit of education."

Tommy stared disbelievingly at him.

"I asked Dirk to use his education, I asked him to teach some of the others. But he wouldn't have any of it. Is that my fault?"

Now Tommy's face was completely incredulous. Then he went scarlet, which Mr. Macintosh did not understand. Why should the boy be looking so foolish? But Tommy was thinking: We were on the wrong track . . . And then he imagined what his offer must have done to Dirk's angry, rebellious pride, and he suddenly understood. His face still crimson, he laughed. It was a bitter, ironical laugh, and Mr. Macintosh was upset—it was not a boy's laugh at all.

Tommy's face slowly faded from crimson, and he went back to work with his chisel. He said, after a pause: "Why don't you send Dirk to college instead of me? He's much more clever than me. I'm not clever, look at my report."

"Well, laddie . . ." began Mr. Macintosh reproachfully—he had been going to say: "Are you being lazy at school simply to force my hand over Dirk?" He wondered at his own impulse to say it; and slid off into the familiar obliqueness which Tommy ignored: "But you know how things are, or you ought to by now. You talk as if you didn't understand."

But Tommy was kneeling with his back to Mr. Macintosh, working at the root, so Mr. Macintosh continued to smoke. Next day he returned and sat on the tree-trunk and watched. Tommy looked at him as if he considered his presence an unwelcome gift, but he did not say anything.

Slowly, the big fanged root which rose from the trunk was taking Dirk's shape. Mr. Macintosh watched with uneasy loathing. He did not like it, but he could not stop watching. Once he said: "But if there's a veld fire, it'll get burnt. And the ants'll eat it in any case." Tommy shrugged. It was the making of it that mattered, not what happened to it afterwards, and this attitude was so foreign to Mr. Macintosh's accumulating nature that it seemed to him that Tommy was touched in the head. He said: "Why don't you work on something that'll last? Or even if you studied like Dirk it would be better."

Tommy said: "I like doing it."

"But look, the ants are already at the trunk—by the time you get back from your school next time there'll be nothing left of it."

"Or someone might set fire to it," suggested Tommy. He looked steadily at Mr. Macintosh's reddening face with triumph. Mr. Macintosh found the words too near the truth. For certainly, as the days passed, he was looking at the new work with hatred and fear and dislike. It was nearly finished. Even if nothing more were done to it, it could stand as it was, complete.

Dirk's long, powerful body came writhing out of the wood like something struggling free. The head was clenched back, in the agony of the birth, eyes narrowed and desperate, the mouth—Mr. Macintosh's mouth—tightened in obstinate purpose. The shoulders were free, but the hands were held; they could not pull themselves out of the dense wood, they were imprisoned. His body was free to the knees, but below them the human limbs were uncreated, the natural shapes of the wood swelled to the perfect muscled knees.

Mr. Macintosh did not like it. He did not know what art was, but he knew he did not like this at all, it disturbed him deeply, so that when he looked at it he wanted to take an axe and cut it to pieces. Or burn it, perhaps . . .

As for Tommy, the uneasiness of this elderly man who watched him all day was a deep triumph. Slowly, and for the first time, he saw that perhaps this was not a sort of game that he played, it might be something else. A weapon—he watched Mr. Macintosh's reluctant face, and a new respect for himself and what he was doing grew in him.

At night, Mr. Macintosh sat in his candlelit room and he thought or rather *felt*, his way to a decision.

There was no denying the power of Tommy's gift. Therefore, it was a question of finding the way to turn it into money. He knew nothing about these matters, however, and it was Tommy himself who directed him, for towards the end of the holidays he said: "When you're so rich you can do anything. You could send Dirk to college and not even notice it."

Mr. Macintosh, in the reasonable and persuasive voice he now always used, said, "But you know these coloured people have nowhere to go."

Tommy said: "You could send him to the Cape. There are coloured people in the university there. Or Johannesburg." And he insisted against Mr. Macintosh's silence: "You're so rich you can do anything you like."

But Mr. Macintosh, like most rich people, thought not of money as things to buy, things to do, but rather how it was tied up in buildings and land.

"It would cost thousands," he said. "Thousands for a coloured boy."

But Tommy's scornful look silenced him, and he said hastily: "I'll think about it." But he was thinking not of Dirk, but of Tommy. Sitting alone in his room he told himself it was simply a question of paying for knowledge.

So next morning he made his preparations for a trip to town. He shaved, and over his cotton singlet he put a striped jacket, which half concealed his long, stained khaki trousers. This was as far as he ever went in concessions to the city life he despised. He got into his big American car and set off.

In the city he took the simplest route to knowledge.

He went to the Education Department, and said he wanted to see the Minister of Education. "I'm Macintosh," he said, with perfect confidence; and the pretty secretary who had been patronising his clothes, went at once to the Minister and said: "There is a Mr. Macintosh to see you." She described him as an old, fat, dirty man with a large stomach, and soon the doors opened and Mr. Macintosh was with the spring of knowledge.

He emerged five minutes later with what he wanted, the name of a certain expert. He drove through the deep green avenues of the city to the house he had been told to go to, which was a large and well-kept one, and comforted Mr. Macintosh in his faith that art properly used could make money. He parked his car in the road and walked in.

On the verandah, behind a table heaped with books, sat a middle-aged man with spectacles. Mr. Tomlinson was essentially a scholar with working hours he respected, and he lifted his eyes to see a big, dirty man with black hair showing above the dirty whiteness of his vest, and he said sharply: "What do you want?"

"Wait a minute, laddie," said Mr. Macintosh easily, and he held out a note from the Minister of Education, and Mr. Tomlinson took it and read it, feeling reassured. It was worded in such a way that his seeing Mr. Macintosh could be felt as a favour he was personally doing the Minister.

"I'll make it worth your while," said Mr. Macintosh, and at once distaste flooded Mr. Tomlinson, and he went pink, and said: "I'm afraid I haven't the time."

"Damn it, man, it's your job, isn't it? Or so Wentworth said."

"No," said Mr. Tomlinson, making each word clear, "I advise on ancient Monuments."

Mr. Macintosh stared, then laughed, and said: "Wentworth said you'd do, but it doesn't matter, I'll get someone else." And he left.

Mr. Tomlinson watched this hobo go off the verandah and into a magnificent car, and his thought was: "He must have stolen it." Then, puzzled and upset, he went to the telephone. But in a few moments he was smiling. Finally he laughed. Mr. Macintosh was the Mr. Macintosh, a genuine specimen of the old-timer. It was the phrase "old-timer" that made it possible for Mr. Tomlinson to relent. He therefore rang the hotel at which Mr. Macintosh, as a rich man, would be bound to be staying, and he said he had made an error, he would be free the following day to accompany Mr. Macintosh.

And so next morning Mr. Macintosh, not at all surprised that the expert was at his service after all, with Mr. Tomlinson, who preserved a tolerant smile, drove out to the mine.

They drove very fast in the powerful car, and Mr. Tomlinson held himself steady while they jolted and bounced, and listened to

Mr. Macintosh's tales of Australia and New Zealand, and thought of him rather as he would of an ancient Monument.

At last the long plain ended, and foothills of greenish scrub heaped themselves around the car, and then high mountains piled with granite boulders, and the heat came in thick, slow waves into the car, and Mr. Tomlinson thought: I'll be glad when we're through the mountains into the plain. But instead they turned into a high, enclosed place with mountains all around, and suddenly there was an enormous gulf in the ground, and on one side of it were two tiny tin-roofed houses, and on the other acres of kaffir huts. The mine-stamps thudded regularly, like a pulse of the heart, and Mr. Tomlinson wondered how anybody, white or black, could bear to live in such a place.

He ate boiled beef and carrots and greasy potatoes with one of the richest men in the sub-continent, and thought how well and intelligently he would use such money if he had it—which is the only consolation left to the cultivated man of moderate income. After lunch, Mr. Macintosh said: "And now, let's get it over."

Mr. Tomlinson expressed his willingness, and, smiling to himself, followed Mr. Macintosh off into the bush on a kaffir path. He did not know what he was going to see. Mr. Macintosh had said: "Can you tell if a youngster has got any talent just by looking at a piece of wood he has carved?"

Mr. Tomlinson said he would do his best.

Then they were beside a fallen tree-trunk, and in the grass knelt a big lad, with untidy brown hair falling over his face, labouring at the wood with a large chisel.

"This is a friend of mine," said Mr. Macintosh to Tommy, who got to his feet and stood uncomfortably, wondering what was happening. "Do you mind if Mr. Tomlinson sees what you are doing?"

Tommy made a shrugging movement and felt that things were going beyond his control. He looked in awed amazement at Mr. Tomlinson, who seemed to him rather like a teacher or professor, and certainly not at all what he imagined an artist to be.

"Well?" said Mr. Macintosh to Mr. Tomlinson, after a space of half a minute.

Mr. Tomlinson laughed in a way which said: "Now don't be in such a hurry." He walked around the carved tree root, looking at the figure of Dirk from this angle and that.

Then he asked Tommy: "Why do you make these carvings?"

Tommy very uncomfortably shrugged, as if to say: What a silly question; and Mr. Macintosh hastily said: "He gets high marks for Art at school."

Mr. Tomlinson smiled again and walked around to the other side of the trunk. From here he could see Dirk's face, flattened back on the neck, eyes half-closed and strained, the muscles of the neck shaped from natural veins of the wood.

"Is this someone you know?" he asked Tommy in an easy, intimate way, one artist to another.

"Yes," said Tommy, briefly; he resented the question.

Mr. Tomlinson looked at the face and then at Mr. Macintosh. "It has a look of you," he observed dispassionately, and coloured himself as he saw Mr. Macintosh grow angry. He walked well away from the group, to give Mr. Macintosh space to hide his embarrassment. When he returned, he asked Tommy: "And so you want to be a sculptor?"

"I don't know," said Tommy, defiantly.

Mr. Tomlinson shrugged rather impatiently, and with a nod at Mr. Macintosh suggested it was enough. He said goodbye to Tommy, and went back to the house with Mr. Macintosh.

There he was offered tea and biscuits, and Mr. Macintosh asked: "Well, what do you think?"

But by now Mr. Tomlinson was certainly offended at this casual cash-on-delivery approach to art, and he said: "Well, that rather depends, doesn't it?"

"On what?" demanded Mr. Macintosh.

"He seems to have talent," conceded Mr. Tomlinson.

"That's all I want to know," said Mr. Macintosh, and suggested that now he could run Mr. Tomlinson back to town.

But Mr. Tomlinson did not feel it was enough, and he said: "It's quite interesting, that statue. I suppose he's seen pictures in magazines. It has quite a modern feeling."

"Modern?" said Mr. Macintosh. "What do you mean?"

Mr. Tomlinson shrugged again, giving it up. "Well," he said, practically, "what do you mean to do?"

"If you say he has talent, I'll send him to the university and he can study art."

After a long pause, Mr. Tomlinson murmured: "What a fortunate boy he is." He meant to convey depths of disillusionment and irony, but Mr. Macintosh said: "I always did have a fancy for him."

He took Mr. Tomlinson back to the city, and as he dropped him on his verandah, presented him with a cheque for fifty pounds, which Mr. Tomlinson most indignantly returned. "Oh, give it to charity," said Mr. Macintosh impatiently, and went to his car, leaving Mr. Tomlinson to heal his susceptibilities in any way he chose.

When Mr. Macintosh reached his mine again it was midnight, and there were no lights in the Clarkes' house, and so his need to be generous must be stifled until the morning.

Then he went to Annie Clarke and told her he would send Tommy to university, where he could be an artist, and Mrs. Clarke wept with gratitude, and said that Mr. Macintosh was much kinder than Tommy deserved, and perhaps he would learn sense yet and go back to his books.

As far as Mr. Macintosh was concerned it was all settled.

He set off through the trees to find Tommy and announce his future to him.

But when he arrived at seeing distance there were two figures, Dirk and Tommy, seated on the trunk talking, and Mr. Macintosh stopped among the trees, filled with such bitter anger at this fresh check to his plans that he could not trust himself to go on. So he returned to his house, and brooded angrily—he knew exactly what was going to happen when he spoke to Tommy, and now he must make up his mind, there was no escape from a decision.

And while Mr. Macintosh mused bitterly in his house, Tommy and Dirk waited for him; it was now all as clear to them as it was to him.

Dirk had come out of the trees to Tommy the moment the two men left the day before. Tommy was standing by the fanged root, looking at the shape of Dirk in it, trying to understand what was going to be demanded of him. The word "artist" was on his tongue, and he tasted it, trying to make the strangeness of it fit that powerful shape struggling out of the wood. He did not like it. He did not want—but what did he want? He felt pressure on himself, the faint beginnings of something that would one day be like a tunnel of birth from which he must fight to emerge; he felt the obligations working within himself like a goad which would one day be a whip perpetually falling behind him so that he must perpetually move onwards.

His sense of fetters and debts was confirmed when Dirk came to stand by him. First he asked: "What did they want?"

"They want me to be an artist, they always want me to be something," said Tommy sullenly. He began throwing stones at the tree and shying them off along the tops of the grass. Then one hit the figure of Dirk, and he stopped.

Dirk was looking at himself. "Why do you make me like that?" he asked. The narrow, strong face expressed nothing but that familiar, sardonic antogonism, as if he said: "You, too—just like the rest!"

"Why, what's the matter with it?" challenged Tommy at once.

Dirk walked around it, then back. "You're just like all the rest," he said.

"Why? Why don't you like it?" Tommy was really distressed. Also, his feeling was: What's it got to do with him? Slowly he understood that his emotion was that belief in his right to freedom which Dirk always felt immediately, and he said in a different voice: "Tell me what's wrong with it?"

"Why do I have to come out of the wood? Why haven't I any hands or feet?"

"You have, but don't you see . . ." But Tommy looked at Dirk standing in front of him and suddenly gave an impatient movement: "Well, it doesn't matter, it's only a statue."

He sat on the trunk and Dirk beside him. After a while he said: "How should you be, then?"

"If you made yourself, would you be half wood?"

Tommy made an effort to feel this, but failed. "But it's not me, it's you." He spoke with difficulty, and thought: But it's important, I shall have to think about it later. He almost groaned with the knowledge that here it was, the first debt, presented for payment.

Dirk said suddenly: "Surely it needn't be wood. You could do the same thing if you put handcuffs on my wrists." Tommy lifted his head and gave a short, astonished laugh. "Well, what's funny?" said Dirk, aggressively. "You can't do it the easy way, you have to make me half wood, as if I was more a tree than a human being."

Tommy laughed again, but unhappily. "Oh, I'll do it again," he acknowledged at last. "Don't fuss about that one, it's finished. I'll do another."

There was a silence.

Dirk said: "What did that man say about you?"

"How do I know?"

"Does he know about art?"

"I suppose so."

"Perhaps you'll be famous," said Dirk at last. "In that book you gave me, it said about painters. Perhaps you'll be like that."

"Oh, shut up," said Tommy, roughly. "You're just as bad as he is."

"Well, what's the matter with it?"

"Why have I got to be something? First it was a sailor, and then it was a scholar, and now it's an artist."

"They wouldn't have to make me be anything," said Dirk sarcastically.

"I know," admitted Tommy grudgingly. And then, passionately: "I shan't go to university unless he sends you too."

"I know," said Dirk at once, "I know you won't."

They smiled at each other, that small, shy, revealed smile, which was so hard for them because it pledged them to such a struggle in the future.

Then Tommy asked: "Why didn't you come near me all this time?"

"I get sick of you," said Dirk. "I sometimes feel I don't want to see a white face again, not ever. I feel that I hate you all, every one."

"I know," said Tommy, grinning. Then they laughed, and the last strain of dislike between them vanished.

They began to talk, for the first time, of what their lives would be.

Tommy said: "But when you've finished training to be an engineer, what will you do? They don't let coloured people be engineers."

"Things aren't always going to be like that," said Dirk.

"It's going to be very hard," said Tommy, looking at him questioningly, and was at once reassured when Dirk said, sarcastically: "Hard, it's going to be hard? Isn't it hard now, white boy?"

Later that day Mr. Macintosh came towards them from his house.

He stood in front of them, that big, shrewd, rich man, with his small, clever grey eyes, and his narrow, loveless mouth; and he said aggressively to Tommy: "Do you want to go to the university and be an artist?"

"If Dirk comes too," said Tommy immediately.

"What do you want to study?" Mr. Macintosh asked Dirk, direct.

"I want to be an engineer," said Dirk at once.

"If I pay your way through the university then at the end of it I'm finished with you. I never want to hear from you and you are never to come back to this mine once you leave it."

Dirk and Tommy both nodded, and the instinctive agreement between them fed Mr. Macintosh's bitter unwillingness in the choice, so that he ground out viciously: "Do you think you two can be to-

gether in the university? You don't understand. You'll be living separate, and you can't go around together just as you like."

The boys looked at each other, and then, as if some sort of pact
had been made between them, simply nodded.

"You can't go to university anyway, Tommy, until you've done a
bit better at school. If you go back for another year and work you
can pass your matric, and go to university, but you can't go now,
right at the bottom of the class."

Tommy said: "I'll work." He added at once: "Dirk'll need more
books to study here till we can go."

The anger was beginning to swell Mr. Macintosh's face, but
Tommy said: "It's only fair. You burnt them, and now he hasn't
any at all."

"Well," said Mr. Macintosh heavily. "Well, so that's how it is!"

He looked at the two boys, seated together on the tree-trunk.
Tommy was leaning forward, eyes lowered, a troubled but determined look on his face. Dirk was sitting erect, looking straight at
his father with eyes filled with hate.

"Well," said Mr. Macintosh, with an effort at raillery which
sounded harsh to them all: "Well, I send you both to university and
you don't give me so much as a thank-you!"

At this, both faced towards him, with such bitter astonishment
that he flushed.

"Well, well," he said. "Well, well . . ." And then he turned to
leave the clearing, and cried out as he went, so as to give the appearance of dominance: "Remember, laddie, I'm not sending you
unless you do well at school this year . . ."

And so he left them and went back to his house, an angry old
man, defeated by something he did not begin to understand.

As for the boys, they were silent when he had gone.

The victory was entirely theirs, but now they had to begin again,
in the long and difficult struggle to understand what they had won
and how they would use it.

Hunger

It is dark inside the hut, and very cold. Yet around the oblong shape that is the doorway where a sack hangs, for the sake of comely decency, is a diffusing yellow glare, and through holes in the sack come fingers of yellow warmth, nudging and prodding at Jabavu's legs. "Ugh," he mutters, drawing up his feet and kicking at the blanket to make it stretch over him. Under Jabavu is a reed mat, and where its coolness touches him he draws back, grumbling in his sleep. Again his legs sprawl out, again the warm fingers prod him, and he is filled with a rage of resentment. He grabs at sleep, as if a thief were trying to take it from him; he wraps himself in sleep like a blanket that persists in slipping off; there is nothing he has ever wanted, nothing he will ever want again as he wants sleep at this moment. He leans as greedily towards it as towards a warm drink on a cold night. He drinks it, guzzles it, and is sinking contentedly into oblivion when words come dropping through it like stones through thick water. "Ugh!" mutters Jabavu again. He lies as still as a dead rabbit. But the words continue to fall into his ears, and although he has sworn to himself not to move, not to sit up, to hold to this sleep which they are trying to take from him, he nevertheless sits up, and his face is surly and unwilling.

His brother, Pavu, on the other side of the dead ashes of the fire which is in the middle of the mud floor, also sits up. He, too, is sulking. His face is averted and he blinks slowly as he rises to his feet, lifting the blanket with him. Yet he remains respectfully silent while his mother scolds.

"Children, your father has already been waiting for you as long as it takes to hoe a field." This is intended to remind them of their duty, to put back into their minds what their minds have let slip— that already, earlier, they have been awakened, their father laying his hand silently first on one shoulder and then on another.

Pavu guiltily folds his blanket and lays it on the low earth mound on one side of the hut, and then stands waiting for Jabavu.

But Jabavu is leaning on his elbow by the ashen smudge of last night's fire, and he says to his scolding mother: "Mother, you make as many words as the wind brings grains of dust." Pavu is shocked. He would never speak any way but respectfully to his parents. But also, he is not shocked, for this is Jabavu the Big Mouth. And if the parents say with sorrow that in their day no child would speak to his parents as Big Mouth speaks, then it is true, too, that now there are many children who speak thus—and how can one be shocked by something that happens every day?

Jabavu says, breaking into a shrill whirl of words from the mother: "Ah, Mother, *shut up!*" The words "shut up" are in English. And now Pavu is really shocked, with the whole of himself, not merely with that part of him that pays tribute to the old forms of behaviour. He says, quickly, to Jabavu: "And now that is enough. Our father is waiting." He is so ashamed that he lifts the sacking from the door and steps outside, blinking into the sunlight. The sun is pale bright gold, and quickly gathering heat. Pavu moves his stiff limbs in it as if it were hot water, and then stands beside his father. "Good morning, my father," he says; and then the old man greets him: "Good morning, my son."

The old man wears a brown blanket striped with red, folded over his shoulder and held with a large steel safety-pin. He carries a hoe for the fields, and the spear of his forefathers with which to kill a rabbit or buck if one should show itself. The boy has no blanket. He wears a vest that is rubbed into holes tucked into a loincloth. He also carries a hoe.

From inside the hut come voices. The mother is still scolding. They can hear scraping sounds and the small knock of wood—she is kneeling to remove the dead ash and to build the new fire. It is as if they can see her crouching there, coaxing the new day's fire to life. And it is as if they can see Jabavu huddled on his mat, his face sullenly turned away from her while she scolds.

They look at each other, ashamed; then they look away past the little huts of the native village; they see disappearing among the trees a crowd of their friends and relatives from these huts. The other men are already on their way to the fields. It is nearly six in the morning. The father and Pavu, avoiding each other's eyes because of their shame, move off after them. Jabavu must come by himself—if he comes at all. Once the men from this hut were first at the fields, once their fields were first hoed, first planted, first reaped. Now they were last, and it is because of Jabavu who works or does not work as he feels inclined.

Inside the hut the mother kneels at the fire, watching a small glow of flame rise inside the hollow of her sheltering hand. The warmth contents her, melts her bitterness.

"Ah, my Big Mouth, get up now," she says with tender reproach. "Are you going to lie there all day while your father and brother work?" She lifts her face, ready to smile forgiveness at the bad son. But Jabavu leaps from the blanket as if he had found a snake there, and roars: "My name is Jabavu, not Big Mouth. Even my own, my given name, you take from me!" He stands there stiff, accusing, his eyes quivering with unhappy anger. And his mother slowly drops her eyes, as if guilty.

Now this is strange, for Jabavu is a hundred times in the wrong; while she has always been a proper mother, a good wife. Yet for that moment it is between these two, mother and son, as if she has done wrong and he is justly accusing her. Soon his body loses the stiffness of anger and he leans idly against the wall, watching her; and she turns towards the crescent-shaped earth shelf behind her for a pot. Jabavu watches intently. Now there is a new thought, a new need—which kind of utensil will she bring out? When he sees what it is, he quivers out a sigh of relief, and his mother hears that sigh and wonders and marvels. She had brought out not the cooking pot for the morning porridge, but the petrol tin in which she heats water for washing.

The father and Pavu, all the men of the village, will wash when they return from the fields for the first meal, or in the river by the place where they work. But Jabavu's whole being, every atom of his brain and body is concentrated on the need that she should serve him thus—should warm water especially so that he may wash in it now. And yet at other times Jabavu is careless of his cleanness.

The mother sets the half-tin on the stones in the clump of red and roaring flames, and almost at once a wisp of blueish steam curls off the rocking water. She hears Jabavu sigh again. She keeps her head lowered, wondering. She is thinking that it is as if inside Jabavu, her son, some kind of hungry animal is living, looking out of his eyes, speaking from his mouth. She loves Jabavu. She thinks of him as brave, affectionate, clever, strong, and respectful. She believes that he is all these things, that the fierce animal which has made its lair inside Jabavu is not her son. And yet her husband, her other children, and indeed the whole village call him Jabavu the Big Mouth, Jabavu the greedy, the boastful, the bad son, who will certainly one day run off to the white man's town and become one of the matsotsis, the criminal youth. Yes, that is what they say, and she knows it. There are even times when she says so herself. And yet—fifteen years ago there was a year of famine. It was not a famine as is known in other countries that this woman has never heard of, China perhaps, or India. But it was a season of drought, and some people died, and many were hungry.

The year before the drought they sold their grain as was usual to the African store, keeping sufficient for themselves. They were given the prices that were fair for that year. The white man at that store, a Greek, stored the grain, as was his custom, for resale to these same natives when they ran short, as they often did—a shiftless lot, always ready to sell more than they should for the sake of the glittering shillings with which they could buy head-cloths or bangles or cloth. And that year, in the big markets in America and Europe there was a change of prices. The Greek sold all the maize he had to the big stores in town, and sent his men around the native villages, coaxing them to sell everything they had. He offered a little more money than they had been used to get. He was buying at half of what he could get in the city. And all would have been well if there had not been that season of drought. For the mealies wilted in the fields, the cobs struggled towards fullness, but remained as small as a fist. There was panic in the villages and people came streaming towards the Greek store and to all the other African stores all over the country. The Greek said Yes, Yes, he had the maize, he always had the maize, but of course at the new price laid down by the Government. And of course the people did not have the money to buy this newly expensive maize.

So in the villages there was a year of hunger. That year, Jabavu's elder sister, three years old, came running playfully to her mother's teats, and found herself smacked off, like a troublesome puppy. The mother was still feeding Jabavu, who had always been a demanding, hungry child, and there was a new baby a month old. The winter was cold and dusty. The men went hunting for hares and buck, the women searched through the bush all day for greens and roots, and there was hardly any grain for the porridge. The dust filled the villages, the dust hung in sullen clouds in the air, blew into the huts and into the nostrils of the people. The little girl died—it was said because she had breathed too much dust. And the mother's breasts hung limp, and when Jabavu came tugging at her dress she smacked him off. She was sick with grief because of the death of the child, and also with fear for the baby. For now the buck and hares were scarce, they had been hunted so relentlessly, and one cannot keep life on leaves and roots. But Jabavu did not relinquish his mother's breasts so easily. At night, as she lay on her mat, the new baby beside her, Jabavu came pushing and struggling to her milk, and she woke, startled, saying: "Ehhh, but this child of mine is strong." He was only a year old, yet she had to use all her strength to fend him off. In the dark of the hut her husband woke and lifted Jabavu, screaming and kicking, away from her, and away from the tender new baby. That baby died, but by then Jabavu had turned sullen and was fighting like a little leopard for what scraps of food there were. A little skeleton he was, with loose brown skin and enormous, frantic eyes, nosing around in the dust for fallen mealies or a scrap of sour vegetable.

This is what the mother thinks of as she crouches watching the wisps of steam curl off the water. For her Jabavu is three children, she loves him still with all the bereaved passion of that terrible year. She thinks: It was then, when he was so tiny, that Jabavu the Big Mouth was made—yes, the people called him the Big Mouth even then. Yes, it is the fault of the Long Hunger that Jabavu is as he is.

But even while she is excusing him thus, she cannot help remembering how he was as a new baby. The women used to laugh as they watched him suck. "That one was born hungry," they said, "that one will make a big man!" For he was such a big child, so fierce in his sucking, always crying for food . . . and again she excuses him, fondly: If he had not been so, if he had not fed his strength from the time he was born, he too would have died, like the others. And at this thought she lifts her eyes, filled with love and pride—but she lowers them again quickly. For she knows that a big lad, like Jabavu, who is nearly seventeen years old, resents it when a mother looks at him, remembering the baby he was. Jabavu only knows what he is, and that very confusedly. He is still leaning against the mud wall. He does not look at his mother, but at the water which is heating for his use. And inside there is such a storm of anger, love, pain, and resentment: he feels so much, and all at once, that it is as if a wind-devil had got into him. He knows quite well that he does not behave as he ought, yet there is no other way he can behave; he knows that among his own people he is like a black bull in a herd of goats—yet he was bred from them; he wants only the white man's town, yet he knows nothing of it save what he has heard from travellers. And suddenly into his head comes the thought: If I go to the white man's town my mother will die of grief.

Now he looks at his mother. He does not think of her as young, old, pretty, ugly. She is his mother, who came properly endowed to her husband, after a proper amount of cattle had been paid for her. She has borne five children, three of whom live. She is a good cook and respectful to her husband. She is a mother, as a mother should be, according to the old ideas. Jabavu does not despise these ideas: simply, they are not for him. There is no need to despise something from which one is already freed. Jabavu's wife will not be like his mother: he does not know why, but he knows it.

His mother is, in fact, according to the new ideas, not yet thirty-five years old, a young woman who would still look pretty in a dress such as the townswomen wear. But she wears some cotton stuff, blue, bound around her breasts leaving her shoulders bare, and a blue cotton skirt bunched in such a way that the heat will not scorch her legs. She has never thought of herself as old, young, modern or old-fashioned. Yet she, too, knows that Jabavu's wife will not be as she is, and towards this unknown woman her mind lifts in respectful but fearful wonder. She thinks: Perhaps if this son of mine finds a woman who is like him, then he will no longer be like a wild bull among oxen . . . this thought comforts her; she allows her skirt to fall as it will, steps back from the scorching heat, and lifts the tin off the flames. "Now you may wash, my son," she says. Jabavu grabs the tin, as if it might run away from him, and carries it outside. And then he stops and slowly sets it down. Sullenly, as if ashamed of this new impulse, he goes back into the hut, lifts his blanket which lies where he let it drop, folds it and lays it on the earthen shelf. Then he rolls his reed mat, sets it against the wall, and also rolls and places his brother's mat. He glances at his mother, who is watching him in silence, sees her soft and compassionate eyes . . . but this he cannot bear. Rage fills him; he goes out.

She is thinking: See, this is my son! How quickly and neatly he folds the blanket, sets the mats against the wall. How easily he lifts the tin of heavy water! How strong he is, and how kind! Yes, he thinks of me, and returns to tidy the hut, he is ashamed of his thoughtlessness. So she muses, telling herself again and again how kind her Jabavu is, although she knows he is not kind, and particularly not to himself; and that when a kind impulse takes him, such as it has now, Jabavu behaves as if he has performed a bad deed and not a good one. She knows that if she thanks him he will shout at her. She glances through the door of the hut and sees her son, strong and powerful, his bronze skin shining with health in the new morning's sun. But his face is knotted with anger and resentment. She turns away so as not to see it.

Jabavu carries the tin of water to the shade of a big tree, strips off his loincloth and begins to wash. The comforting hot water flows over him, he liked the tingle of the strong soap: Jabavu was the first in all the village to use the white man's soap. He thinks: I, Jabavu, wash in good, warmed water, and with proper soap. Not even my father washes when he wakes . . . He sees some women walking past, and pretends he does not see them. He knows what they are thinking, but says to himself: Stupid kraal women, they don't know anything. But I know that Jabavu is like a white man, who washes when he leaves his sleep.

The women slowly go past and their faces are sorrowful. They look at the hut where his mother is kneeling to cook, and they shake their heads and speak their compassion for this poor woman, their friend and sister, who has bred such a son. But in their voices is another note of emotion, and Jabavu knows it is there, though he cannot hear them speak. Envy? Admiration? Neither of these. But it is not the first time a child like Jabavu has been bred by the villages. And these women know well that the behaviour of Jabavu can be understood only by thinking of the world of white man. The white man has brought evil and good, things to admire and things to fear, and it is hard to know one from the other. But when an aeroplane flies far overhead like a shining beetle through the air, and when the big motorcars drive past on the road North, they think also of Jabavu and of the young people like him.

Jabavu has finished washing. He stands idle under the big tree, his back turned to the huts of the village, quite naked, covering what should not be seen of his body with his cupped hand. The yellow patches of sunlight tremble and sway on his skin. He feels the shifting warmth and begins to sing with pleasure. Then an unpleasant thought stops the singing: he has nothing to wear but the loincloth which is the garb of a kraal-boy. He owns an old pair of shorts which were too small for him years ago. They once belonged to the son of the Greek at the store when that son was ten years old.

Jabavu takes the shorts from the crotch of the tree and tries to tug them over his hips. They will not go. Suddenly they split behind. Cautiously he twists himself to see how big the tear is. His buttock is sticking out of the material. He frowns, takes a big needle such as is used for sewing grain sacks, threads it with fine strands of fibre stripped from under the bark of a tree, and begins to make a lace-work of the fibre across his behind. He does this without taking the shorts off: he stands twisted, using the needle with one hand and holding the edges of frayed material with the other. At last it is done. The shorts decently cover him. They are old, they grip him as tight as the bark of a tree grips the white wood underneath, but they are trousers and not a loincloth.

Now he carefully slides the needle back under the bark of the tree, rolls his loincloth into the crotch of the trunk, then lifts down a comb from where it is laced through a frond of leaves. He kneels before a tiny fragment of mirror that he found in a rubbish-heap behind the Greek store, and combs his thick hair. He combs until his arm is tired, but at last the parting shows clear down his scalp. He sticks the steel comb jauntily at the back of his head, like the comb of a fine cock, and looks at himself happily in the mirror. Now his hair is done like a white man's.

He lifts the tin and throws the water in a fine, gleaming curve over the bushes, watching the drops fall in a glittering shower; and an old hen, which was seeking shelter from the heat, runs away squawking. He roars with laughter, seeing that flapping old hen. Then he tosses the tin away into the bushes. It is new and glints among the green leaves. He looks at the tin, while an impulse stirs in him——that same impulse that always hurts him so, leaving him limp and confused. He is thinking that his mother, who paid a shilling for the tin in the Greek store, will not know where it is. Secretly, as if he were doing something wicked, he lifts the tin, carries it to the door of the hut and, stretching his hand carefully around the opening, sets it inside. His mother, who is stirring meal into boiling water for the porridge, does not turn around. Yet he knows that she knows what he is doing. He waits for her to turn—if she does and thanks him, then he will shout at her; already he feels the anger crowding his throat. And when she does not turn he feels even more anger, and a hot blackness rocks across his eyes. He cannot endure that anyone, not even his mother, should understand why he creeps like a thief to do a kind thing. He walks swaggering back to the shade of the tree, muttering: I am Jabavu, I am Jabavu —as if this were the answer to any sad look or reproachful words or understanding silence.

He squats under the tree, but carefully, so that his trousers may not fall completely to pieces. He looks at the village. It is a native kraal, such as one may see anywhere in Africa, a casual arrangement of round mud huts with conical grass roofs. A few are square, influenced by the angled dwellings of the white man. Beyond the kraal is a belt of trees, and beyond them, the fields. Jabavu thinks: This is my village—and immediately his thoughts leave it and go to the white man's town. Jabavu knows everything about this town, although he has never been there. When someone returns, or passes through this village, Jabavu runs to listen to the tales of the wonderful living, the adventure, the excitement. He has a very clear picture in his mind of the place. He knows the white man's house is always of brick, not of mud. He has seen such a house. The Greek at the store has a brick house, two fine rooms, with chairs in them, and tables, and beds lifted off the floor on legs. Jabavu knows the white man's town will be of such houses, many many houses, perhaps as many as will reach from where he is sitting to the big road going north that is half a mile away. His mind is bright with wonder and excitement as he imagines it, and he looks at his village with impatient dissatisfaction. The village is for the old people, it is right for them. And Jabavu can remember no time when he has not felt as he does now; it is as if he were born with the knowledge that the village was his past, not his future. Also, that he was born longing for the moment when he could go to the town. A hunger rages in him for that town. What is this hunger? Jabavu does not know. It is so strong that a voice speaks in his ear, I want, I want, as if his fingers curl graspingly in a movement, We want, as if every fibre of his body sings and shouts, I want, I want, I want . . .

He wants everything and nothing. He does not say to himself: I want a motorcar, an aeroplane, a house. Jabavu is intelligent, and knows that the black man does not own such things. But he wants to be near them, to see them, touch them, perhaps serve them. When he thinks of the white man's town he sees something beautiful, richly coloured, strange. A rainbow to him means the white man's town, or a fine warm morning, or a clear night when there is a dancing. And this exciting life waits for him, Jabavu, he was born for it. He imagines a place of light and warmth and laughter, and people saying: *Hau!* Here is our friend Jabavu! Come, Jabavu, and sit with us.

This is what he wants to hear. He does not want to hear any longer the sorrowful voices of the old people: The Big Mouth, look at the Big Mouth, listen to the Big Mouth hatching out words again.

He wants so terribly that his body aches with wanting. He begins to day-dream. This is his dream, slipping, half-ashamed, through his mind. He sees himself walking to town, he enters the town, a black policeman greets him: "Why, Jabavu, so there you are, I come from your village, do you remember me?" "My friend," answers Jabavu, "I have heard of you from our brothers, I have been told that you are now a son of the Government." "Yes, Jabavu, now I serve the Government. See, I have a fine uniform, and a place to sleep, and friends. I am respected both by the white people and the black. I can help you." This son of the Government takes Jabavu to his room and gives him food—bread perhaps, white bread, such as the white man eats, and tea with milk. Jabavu has heard of such food from people returning to the village. Then the son of the Government takes Jabavu to the white man whom he serves. "This is Jabavu," he says, "my friend from my village." "So this is Jabavu," says the white man. "I heard of you, my son. But no one told me how strong you were, how clever. You must put on this uniform and become a son of the Government." Jabavu has seen such policemen, because once a year they come gathering taxes from the villages. Big men, important men, black men in uniform . . . Jabavu sees himself in this uniform, and his eyes dazzle with wanting. He sees himself walking around the white man's town. Yes, Baas, no Baas; and to his own people he is very kind. They say, Yes, that is our Jabavu, from our village, do you remember? He is our good brother, he helps us . . .

Jabavu's dream has flown so high that it crashes and he blinks his eyes in waking. For he has heard things about the town which tell him this dream is nonsense. One does not become a policeman and a son of the Government so easily. One must be clever indeed and Jabavu gets up and goes to a big, flat stone, first looking around in case anyone is watching. He flips the stone over, brings from under it a roll of paper, quickly replaces the stone and sits on it. He has taken the paper off parcels of things he has bought from the Greek store. Some are all print, some have little coloured pictures, many together, making a story. The bright sheets of pictures are what he likes best.

They have taught Jabavu to read. He spreads them out on the

ground and bends over them, his lips forming the words. The very first picture shows a big white man on a big black horse, with a great gun that spits red fire. "Bang!" say the letters above. "Bang," says Jabavu slowly. "B-a-n-g." That was the first word he learned. The second picture shows a beautiful white girl, with her dress slipping off her shoulder, her mouth open. "Help!" say the letters. "Help," says Jabavu, "help, help." He goes on to the next. Now the big white man has caught the girl around the waist and is lifting her on to the horse. Some wicked white men with big black hats are pointing guns at the girl and the good white man. "Hold me, honey," say the letters. Jabavu repeats the words. He slowly works his way to the foot of the page. He knows this story by heart and loves it. But the story on the next page is not so easy. It is about some yellow men with small, screwed-up faces. They are wicked. There is another big white man who is good and carries a whip. It is that whip that troubles Jabavu, for he knows it; he was slashed himself by the Greek at the store for being cheeky. The words say: "Grrrrrr, you Gooks, this'll teach you!" The white man beats the little yellow men with the whip, and Jabavu feels nothing but confusion and dismay. For in the first story he is the white man on the horse who rescues the beautiful girl from the bad men. But in this story he cannot be the white man because of the whip . . . Many many hours has Jabavu spent puzzling over that story, and particularly over the words which say: "You little yellow snakes . . ." There goes the whip-lash curling over the picture, and for a long time Jabavu thought the word snake meant that whip. Then he saw the yellow men were the snakes . . . And in the end, just as he has done often before, he turns the page, giving up that difficult story, and goes to another.

Jabavu cannot merely read the stories in pictures, but also simple print. On the rubbish heap behind the Greek store he once found a child's alphabet, or rather, half of one. It was a long time before he understood it was half only. He used to sit, hour after hour, fitting the letters in the alphabet to words like Bang! and later, to English words he already knew, from the sorrowful, admiring stories that were told about the white men. Black, white, colour, native, kaffir, mealiemeal, smell, bad, dirty, stupid, work. These were some of the words he knew how to speak before he could read them. After a long time he completed the alphabet for himself. A very long time—it took him over a year of sitting under that tree thinking and thinking while the people of the village laughed and called him lazy. Later still he tried the print without pictures. And it was so hard it was as if he had learned nothing. Months passed. Slowly, very slowly, the sheet of black letters put on meaning. Jabavu will never forget, as long as he lives, that day when he first puzzled out a whole sentence. This was the sentence. "The African must eat beans and vegetables as well as meat and nuts to keep him healthy." When he understood that long and difficult sentence, he rolled on the ground with pride, laughing and saying: "The white men write that we must eat these things all the time! That's what I shall eat when I go to white man's town."

Some of the words he cannot understand, no matter how hard he tries. "Any person who contravenes any provision of any of the regulations (which contain fifty clauses) is liable to a fine of £25 or three months' imprisonment." Jabavu has spent many hours over that sentence, and it still means nothing to him. Once he walked five miles to the next village to ask a clever man who knew English what it meant. He did not know either. But he taught Jabavu a great deal of English to speak. Jabavu speaks it now quite well. And he has marked all the difficult words on the newspaper with a piece of charcoal, and will ask someone what they mean, when he finds such a person. Perhaps when a traveller returns for a visit from the town? But there is no one expected. One of the young men, the son of Jabavu's father's brother, was to have come, but he went to Johannesburg instead. Nothing has been heard of him for a year. In all, there are seven young men from this village working in the town, and two in Johannesburg at the mines. Any one of them may come next week or perhaps next year . . . The hunger in Jabavu swells and mutters: When will I go, when, when, when? I am sixteen, I am a man. I can speak English, I can read the newspaper. I can understand the pictures—but at this thought he reminds himself he does not understand all the pictures. Patiently he turns back the sheet and goes to the story about the little yellow men. What have they done to be beaten with the whip? Why are some men yellow, some white, some black, some bronze, like himself? Why is there a war in the country of the little yellow men? Why are they called snakes and Gooks? Why, why, why? But Jabavu cannot frame the questions to which he needs the answers, and the frustration feeds that hunger in him. I must go to the white man's town, there I will know, there I will learn.

He thinks, half-heartedly: Perhaps I should go by myself? But it is a frightening thought, he does not have the courage. He sits loose and listless under the tree, letting his hand stir patterns in the dust, and thinks: Perhaps someone will return soon from the town and I may go back with him? Or perhaps I can persuade Pavu to come with me? But his heart stirs painfully at the thought: surely his mother and father will die of grief if both sons go at once! For their daughter left home three years before to work as a nanny at the farm twenty miles away, so that they only see her two or three times a year, and that only for a day.

But the hunger swells up until his regret for his parents is consumed by it, and he thinks: I shall speak to Pavu. I shall make him come with me.

Jabavu is still sitting under the tree thinking when the men come back from the fields, his father and brother with them. At the sight of them he at once gets up and goes to the hut. Now his hunger is for food, or rather that he should be there first and be served first.

His mother is laying the white porridge on each plate. The plates are of earthenware, made by herself, and decorated with black patterns on the red. They are beautiful, but Jabavu longs for tin plates such as he has seen in the Greek store. The spoons are of tin, and it gives him pleasure to touch them.

After she has slapped the porridge on to the plates, she carefully smooths the surfaces with the back of the spoon to make them nice and shiny. She has cooked a stew of roots and leaves from the bush, and she pours a little of this over each white mound. She sets the plates on a mat on the floor. Jabavu at once begins to eat. She looks at him; she wants to ask: Why do you not wait, as is proper, until your father is eating? She does not say it. When the father and brother come in, setting their hoes and the spear against the wall, the father looks at Jabavu, who is eating in disagreeable silence, eyes lowered, and says: "One who is too tired to work is not too tired to eat."

Jabavu does not reply. He has almost finished the porridge. He is thinking that there is enough for another big plateful. He is consumed with a craving to eat and eat until his belly is heavy. He hastily gulps down the last mouthfuls and pushes his plate towards his mother. She does not at once take it up to refill it, and rage surges in Jabavu, but before the words can come bubbling out of his mouth, the father, who has noticed, begins to talk. Jabavu lets his hands fall and sits listening.

The old man is tired and speaks slowly. He has said all this very often before. His family listen yet do not listen. What he says already exists, like words on a piece of paper, to be read or not, to be listened to or not.

"What is happening to our people?" he asks, sorrowfully. "What is happening to our children? Once, in our kraals, there was peace, there was order. Every person knew what it was they should do and how that thing should be done. The sun rose and sank, the moon changed, the dry season came, then the rains, a man was born and lived and died. We knew, then, what was good and what was evil."

His wife, the mother, thinks: He longs so much for the old times, which he understood, that he has forgotten how one tribe harried another, he has forgotten that in this part of the country we lived in terror because of the tribes from the South. Half our lives were spent like rabbits in the *kopjes,* and we women used to be driven off like cattle to make wives for men of other tribes. She says nothing of what she thinks, only: "Yes, yes, my husband, that is very true." She lifts more porridge from the pot and lays it on his plate, although he has hardly touched his food. Jabavu sees this; his muscles tighten and his eyes, fixed on his mother, are hungry and resentful.

The old man goes on: "And now it is as if a great storm is among our people. The men go to the towns and to the mines and farms, they learn bad ways, and when they return to us they are strangers, with no respect for their elders. The young women become prostitutes in the towns, they dress like white women, they will take any man for husband, regardless of the laws of relationship. And the white man uses us for servants, and there is no limit set to this time of bondage."

Pavu has finished his porridge. He looks at his mother. She lays some porridge on his plate and pours vegetable relish over it. Now, having served the men who work, she serves the one who has not. She gives Jabavu what is left, which is not much, and scrapes out what is left of the relish. She does not look at him. She knows of the pain, a child's pain, that sears him because she served him last. And Jabavu does not eat it, simply because he was served last. His stomach does not want it. He sits, sullenly, and listens to his father. What the old man says is true, but there is a great deal he does not say, and can never say, because he is old and belongs to the past. Jabavu looks at his brother, sees the thoughtful, frowning face, and knows that Pavu's thoughts are his own.

"What will become of us? When I look into the future it is as if I see a night that has no end. When I hear the tales that are brought from the white man's towns my heart is dark as a valley under a raincloud. When I hear how the white man corrupts our children it is as if my head were filled with a puddle of muddy water, I cannot think of these things, they are too difficult."

Jabavu looks at his brother and makes a small movement of his head. Pavu excuses himself politely to his father and his mother, and this politeness must be enough for both, for Jabavu says nothing at all.

The old man stretches himself on his mat in the sun for half an hour's rest before returning to the fields. The mother takes the plates and pot to wash them. The young men go out to the big tree.

"It was heavy work without you, my brother," are the reproachful words that Jabavu hears. He has been expecting them, but he frowns, and says: "I have been thinking." He wants his brother to ask eagerly after these important and wonderful thoughts, but Pavu goes on: "There is half a field to finish, and it is right that you should work with us this afternoon."

Jabavu feels that extraordinary resentment rising in him, but he manages to shut it down. He understands that it is not reasonable to expect his brother to see the importance of the pictures on the paper and words that are printed. He says: "I have been thinking about the white man's town." He looks importantly at his brother, but all Pavu says is: "Yes, we know that it will soon be time for you to leave us."

Jabavu is indignant that his secret thoughts should be spoken of so casually. "No one has said I must leave. Our father and mother speak all the time, until their jaws must ache with saying it, that good sons stay in the village."

Pavu says gently, with a laugh: "Yes, they talk like all the old people, but they know that the time will come for both of us to go."

First Jabavu frowns and stares; then he exults: "You will come with me!"

But Pavu lets his head droop. "How can I come with you," he temporises. "You are older, it is right that you should go. But our father cannot work the fields by himself. I may come later, perhaps."

"There are other fathers who have sons. Our father talks of the custom, but if a custom is something that happens all the time, then it is now a custom with us that young men leave the villages and go to the city."

Pavu hesitates, his face puckered with distress. He wants to go to the city. Yet he is afraid. He knows Jabavu will go soon, and travelling with his big, strong, clever brother will take the fear from it.

Jabavu can see it all on his face, and suddenly he feels nervous, as if a thief were abroad. He wonders if this brother dreams and plans for the white man's city as he does; and at the thought he stretches out his arms in a movement which suggests he is keeping something for himself. He feels that his own wanting is so strong that nothing less than the whole of the white man's city will be enough for him, not even some left over for his brother! But then his arms fall and he says, cunningly: "We will go together. We will help each other. We will not be alone in that place where travellers say a stranger may be robbed and even killed."

He glances at Pavu, who looks as if he were listening to lovers' talk.

"It is right for brothers to be together. A man who goes alone is like a man who goes hunting alone into dangerous country. And when we are gone, our father will not need to grow so much food, for he will not have our stomachs to fill. And when our sister marries, he will have her cattle and her lobola money . . ." He talks on and on, trying to keep his voice soft and persuasive, although it keeps rising on waves of passionate desire for those good things in the city. He tries to talk as a reasonable man talks of serious things, but his hands twitch and his legs will not keep still.

He is still making words while Pavu listens when the father comes out of the hut and looks across at them. Both rise and follow him to the fields. Jabavu goes because he wants to win Pavu over, for no other reason, and he talks softly to him as they wind through the trees.

There are two rough patches in the bush. Mealies grow there and between the mealies are pumpkins. The plants are straggly, the pumpkins few. Not long ago a white man came from the city in a car, and was angry when he saw these fields. He said they were farming like ignorant people, and that in other parts of the country the black people were following the advice of the white, and in consequence their crops were thick and fruitful. He said that the soil was poor because they kept too many cattle on it—but at this their ears were closed to his talk. It was well known in the villages that when the white men said they should reduce their cattle to benefit the soil, it was only because they wanted these cattle themselves. Cattle were wealth, cattle were power; it was the thought of an alien mind that one good cow is worth ten poor ones. Because of this misunderstanding over the cattle the people of this village are suspicious of everything they hear from the sons of the Government black or white. This suspicion is a terrible burden, like a cloud on their lives. And it is being fed by every traveller from the towns. There are whispers and rumours of new leaders, new thoughts, a new anger. The young people, like Jabavu, and even Pavu, in his own fashion, listen as if this is nothing terrible, but the old people are frightened.

When the three reach the field they are to hoe, the old man makes a joke about the advice given them by the man from the city; Pavu laughs politely, Jabavu says nothing. It is part of his impatience with his life here that the father insists on the old ways of farming. He has seen the new ways in the village five miles distant. He knows that the white man is right in what he says.

He works beside Pavu and mutters: "Our father is stupid. This field would grow twice as much if we did what the sons of the Government tell us."

Pavu says gently: "Quiet, he will hear. Leave him to his own knowledge. An old ox follows the path to water that he learned as a calf."

"Ah, *shut up*," mutters Jabavu, and he quickens his work so as to be by himself. What is the use of taking a child like this brother to the city? he is asking himself, crossly. Yet he must, for he is afraid. And he tries to make it up, to attract Pavu's attention so they may work together. And Pavu pretends not to notice, but works quietly beside the father.

Jabavu hoes as if there is a devil in him. He has finished as much as a third more than the others when the sun goes down. The father says approvingly: "When you work, my son, you work as if you were fed only on meat."

Pavu is silent. He is angry with Jabavu, but also he is waiting, half with longing, half with fear, for the moment when the sweet and dangerous talk begins again. And after the evening meal the brothers go out into the dark and stroll among the cooking fires, and Jabavu talks and talks. And so it is for a long time, a week passes and then a month. Sometimes Jabavu loses his temper and Pavu sulks. Then Jabavu comes back, making his words quiet and gentle. Sometimes Pavu says, "Yes," then again he says "No, and how can we both leave our father?" And still Jabavu the Big Mouth talks, his eyes restless and glittering, his body tense with eagerness. During this time the brothers are together more than they have been in years. They are seen under the tree at night, walking among the huts, sitting at the hut door. There are many people who say: Jabavu is talking so that his brother may go with him.

Yet Jabavu does not know that what he is doing is clear to others, since he never thinks of the others—he sees only himself and Pavu.

There comes a day when Pavu agrees, but only if they first tell their parents; he wishes this unpleasantness to be softened by at least the forms of obedience. Jabavu will not hear of it. Why? He does not know himself, but it seems to him that this flight into the new life will be joyless unless it is stolen. Besides, he is afraid that his father's sorrow will weaken Pavu's intention. He argues. Pavu argues. Then they quarrel. For a whole week there is an ugly silence between them, broken only by intervals of violent words. And the whole village is saying: "Look—Pavu the good son is resisting the talk of Jabavu the Big Mouth." The only person who does not know is the father, and this is perhaps because he does not wish to know anything so terrible.

On the seventh day Jabavu comes in the evening to Pavu and shows him a bundle which he has ready. In it is his comb, his scraps of paper with words and pictures, a piece of soap. "I shall go tonight," he says to Pavu, and Pavu replies: "I do not believe it." Yet he half believes it. Jabavu is fearless, and if he takes the road by himself there may never be another chance for Pavu. Pavu seats himself in the door of the hut, and his face shows the agony of his indecision. Jabavu sits near him saying, "And now my brother you must surely make up your mind, for I can wait no longer."

It is then that the mother comes and says: "And so my sons, you are going to the city?" She speaks sadly, and at the tone of her voice the younger brother wishes only to assure her that the thought of leaving the village has never entered his mind. But Jabavu shouts, angrily: "Yes, yes, we are leaving. We cannot live any longer in this village where there are only children and women and old men."

The mother glances to where the father is seated with some friends at a fire by another hut. They make dark shapes against the red fire, and the flames scatter sparks up into the blackness. It is a dark night, good for running away. She says: "Your father will surely die." She thinks: He will not die, any more than the other fathers whose sons go to the towns.

Jabavu shouts: "And so we must be shut here in this village until we die, because of the foolishness of an old man who can see nothing in the life of the white men but what is bad."

She says, quietly: "I cannot prevent you from leaving, my sons. But if you go, go now, for I can no longer bear to see you quarrelling and angry day after day." And then, because her sorrow is filling her throat, she quickly lifts a pot and walks off with it, pretending she needs to fetch water for the cooking. But she does not go further than the first patch of deep shadow under the big tree. She stands there, looking into the dim and flickering lights that come from the many fires, and at the huts which show sharp and black, and at the far glow of the stars. She is thinking of her daughter. When the girl left she, the mother, wept until she thought she would die. Yet now she is glad she left. She works for a kind white woman, who gives her dresses, and she hopes to marry the cook, who earns good money. The life of this daughter is something far beyond the life of the mother, who knows that if she were younger she, too, would go to the town. And yet she wishes to weep from misery and loneliness. She does not weep. Her throat aches because of the tears locked in it.

She looks at her two sons, who are talking fast and quiet, their heads close together.

Jabavu is saying: "Now, let us go. If we do not, our mother will tell our father and he will prevent us." Pavu rises slowly to his feet. He says: "Ah, Jabavu, my heart is weak for this thing."

Jabavu knows that this is the moment of final decision. He says: "Now consider, our mother knows of our leaving and she is not angry, and we can send back money from the city to soften the old age of our parents."

Pavu enters the hut, and from the thatch takes his mouth organ, and from the earthen shelf his hatchet. He is ready. They stand in the hut looking fearfully at each other, Jabavu in his torn shorts, naked from the waist, Pavu in his loincloth and his vest with holes in it. They are thinking that they will be figures of fun when they reach the town. All the tales they have heard of the matsotsis who thieve and murder, the tales of the recruiting men for the mines, the stories of the women of the towns who are like no women they have ever met—these crowd into their seething heads and they cannot move. Then Jabavu says jauntily: "Come now, my brother. This will not carry our feet along the road." And they leave the hut.

They do not look at the tree where their mother is standing. They walk past like big men, swinging their arms. And then they hear quick steps, their mother runs to them and says: "Wait, my sons." They feel how she fumbles for their hands, and in them they feel something hard and cold. She has given them each a shilling. "This is for your journey. And wait—" Now, in each hand is a little bundle, and they know she has cooked them food for the journey and kept it for the moment.

The brother turns his face away in shame and sorrow. Then he embraces his mother and hurries on. Jabavu is filled first with gratitude, then with resentment—again his mother has understood him too well, and he dislikes her for it. He is stuck to the piece of ground where he stands. He knows if he says one word he will weep like a little child. His mother says, softly, out of the darkness: "Do not let your brother come to harm. You are headstrong and fearless and may go into danger where he may not." Jabavu shouts: "My brother is my brother, but he is also a man—" Her eyes glint softly at him from the dark, and then he hears the apologetic words: "And your father, he will surely die if he does not hear word of you. You must not do as so many of the children do—send us word through the Native Commissioner what has happened to you." And Jabavu shouts: "The Native Commissioner is for the baboons and the ignorant. I can write letters and you will have letters from me two—no, three times a week!" At this boast the mother sighs, and Jabavu, although he had no intention of doing any such thing, grabs her hand, clings to it, then gives it a little push away from him as if it were her desire to clasp his hand—and so he walks away, whistling, through the shadows of the trees.

The mother watches him until she can see her sons walking together, then waits a little, then turns towards the light of the fires, wailing first softly, then, as her sorrow grows strength with use, very loudly. She is wailing that her sons have left the kraal for the wickedness of the city. This is for her husband, and with him she will mourn bitterly, and for many days. She saw their backs as they stole away with their bundles—so she will say, and her voice will be filled with a bitter reproach and anguish. For she is a wife as well as a mother, and a woman feels one thing as a mother, another as wife, and both may be true and heartfelt.

As for Jabavu and Pavu, they walk in silence and fear because of the darkness of the bush till on the very outskirts of the village they see a hut that has been abandoned. They do not like to walk at night; their plan had been to leave at dawn; and so now they creep into this hut and lie there, sleepless, until the light comes first grey and then yellow.

The road runs before them fifty miles to the city; they intend to reach it by night, but the cold shortens their steps. They walk, crouching their loins and shoulders against it, and their teeth are clenched so as not to confess their shivering. Around them the grass is tall and yellow, and hung with throngs of glittering diamonds that slowly grow few and then are gone, and now the sun is very hot on their bodies. They straighten, the skin of their shoulders loosens and breathes. Now they swing easily along, but in silence. Pavu turns his narrow, cautious face this way and that for new sights, new sounds. He is arming his courage to meet them, for he is afraid. Already his thoughts have returned to the village for comfort: Now my father will be walking alone to the fields, slowly, because of the weight of grief in his legs; now my mother will be settling water to heat on the fire for the porridge . . .

Jabavu walks confidently. His mind is entirely on the big city. Jabavu! he hears, look, here is Jabavu come to the town!

A roar grows in their ears, and they have to leap aside to avoid a great lorry. They land in the thick grass on hands and knees, so violently did they have to jump. They look up open-mouthed, and see the white driver leaning out and grinning at them. They do not understand that he has swerved his lorry so that they have to jump for his amusement. They do not know he is laughing now because he thinks they look very funny, crouching in the grass, staring like yokels. They stand up and watch the lorry disappearing in clouds of pale dust. The back of it is filled with black men, some of them shout, some wave and laugh. Jabavu says: "*Hau!* But that was a big lorry." His throat and chest are filled with wanting. He wants to touch the lorry, to look at the wonder of its construction, perhaps even to drive it . . . There he stands, his face tense and hungry, when there is a roar, a shrill sound like the crowing of a cock—and again the brothers jump aside, this time landing on their feet, while the dust eddies and swirls about them.

They look at each other, then drop their eyes so as not to confess they do not know what to think. But they are wondering: Are those lorries trying to frighten us on purpose? But why? They do not understand. They have heard tales of how an unpleasant white man may make a fool of a black one, so that he may laugh, but that is quite different from what has just happened. They think: We were walking along, we mean no harm, and we are rather frightened, so why does he frighten us even more? But now they are walking slowly, glancing back over their shoulders so as not to be taken by surprise. And when a car or lorry comes up behind they move away on to the grass and stand waiting until it has gone. There are few cars, but many lorries, and these are filled with black men. Jabavu thinks: Soon, maybe tomorrow when I have a job, I will be carried in such a lorry . . . He is so impatient for this wonderful thing to happen that he walks quickly, and once again has to make a sudden jump aside when a lorry screeches at him.

They have been walking for perhaps an hour when they overtake a man who is travelling with his wife and children. The man walks in front with a spear and an axe, the woman behind, carrying the cooking pots and a baby on her back, and another little child holds her skirt. Jabavu knows that these people are not from the town, but travelling from one village to another, and so he is not afraid of them. He greets them, the greetings are returned, and they go together, talking.

When Jabavu says he is making the long journey to the city, the man says: "Have you never been before?" Jabavu, who cannot bear to confess his ignorance says: "Yes, many times," and the reply is: "Then there is no need to warn you against the wickedness of the place." Jabavu is silent, regretting he had not told the truth. But it is too late, for a path leads off the road, and the family turn on to it. As they are making their goodbyes, another lorry sweeps by, and the dust swirls up around them. The man looks after the lorry and shakes his head. "Those are the lorries that carry our brothers to the mines," he says, brushing the dust from his face and shaking it from his blanket. "It is well you know the dangers of the road, for otherwise by now you would be in one of them, filling the mouths of honest people with dust, and laughing when they shake with fright because of the loud noise of the horn." He has settled his blanket again over his shoulders and now he turns away, followed by his wife and children.

Jabavu and Pavu slowly walk on, and they are thinking: How often have they heard of the recruiters of the mines! Yet these stories, coming through many mouths, grow into something like the ugly pictures that flit through sleep when it is difficult and uneasy. It is hard to think of them now, with the sun shining down. And yet this companion of the road spoke with horror of these lorries? Jabavu is tempted; he thinks: This man is a village man and, like my father, he sees only the bad things. Perhaps I and my brother may travel on one of these lorries to the city? And then the fear swells up in him and so his feet are slow with indecision, and when another lorry comes sweeping past he is standing on the very edge of the road, looking after it with big eyes, as if he wishes it to stop. And when it slows, his heart beats so fast he does not know whether it is with fear, excitement, or desire. Pavu tugs at his arm and says: "Let us run quickly," and he replies: "You are afraid of everything, like a child who still smells the milk of its mother."

The white man who drives the lorry puts his head out and looks back. He looks long at Jabavu and at his brother, and then his head goes inside. Then a black man gets out of the front and walks back. He wears clothes like the white men and walks jauntily. Jabavu, seeing this smart fellow, thinks of his own torn trousers and he hugs his elbows around his hips to hide them. But the smart fellow advances, grinning, and says: "Yes, yes—you boys there! Want a lift?"

Jabavu takes a step forward, and feels Pavu clutching his elbow from behind. He takes no notice of that clutching grip, but it is like a warning, and he stands still and plants his two feet hard in the dust like the feet of an ox who resists the yoke.

"How much?" he asks, and the smart fellow laughs and says: "You clever boy, you! No money. Lift to town. And you can put your name on a piece of paper like a white man and travel in the big lorry and there will be a fine job for you." He laughs and swaggers and his white teeth glisten. He is a very fine fellow indeed, and Jabavu's hunger is like a hand clutching at his heart as he thinks that he, too, will be like this man. "Yes," he says, eagerly, "I can make my name, I can write and I can read, too, and with the pictures."

"So," says the fine fellow, laughing more than ever. "Then you are a clever, clever boy. And your job will be a clever one, with writing in an office, with nice white man, plenty money—ten pounds, perhaps fifteen pounds a month!"

Jabavu's brain goes dark, it is as if his thoughts run into water. His eyes have a yellow dazzling in them. He finds he has taken another step forward and the fine fellow is holding out a sheet of paper covered all over with letters. Jabavu takes the paper and tries to make out the words. Some he knows, others he has never seen. He stands for a long time looking at the paper.

The fine fellow says: "Now, you clever boy, do you want to understand that all at once? And the lorry is waiting. Now just put your cross at the foot there and come quickly to the lorry."

Jabavu says, resentfully: "I can make my name like a white man and I do not need to make a cross. My brother will make a cross and I will make my own name, Jabavu." And he kneels on the ground, and puts the paper on a stone, and takes the stub of pencil that the fine fellow is holding out to him, and then thinks where to put the first letter of his name. And then he hears that the fine fellow is saying: "Your brother is not strong enough for this work." Jabavu, turning around, sees that Pavu's face is yellow with fear, but also very angry. He is looking with horror at Jabavu. Jabavu rests his pencil and thinks: Why is my brother not big enough?

Many of us go to town when we are still children, and work. A memory comes into his head of how someone has told him that when they recruit for the mines they take only strong men with fine shoulders. He, Jabavu, has the bulky strength of a young bull—he is filled with pride: Yes, he will go to the mines, why not? But then, how can he leave his brother? He looks up at the fine fellow, who is now impatient, and showing it; he looks at the black men in the back of the lorry. He sees one of these men shake his head at him as if in warning. But others are laughing. It seems to Jabavu that it is a cruel laughter, and suddenly he gets to his feet, hands the paper back to the fine fellow, and says: "My brother and I travel together. Also you try to cheat me. Why did you not tell me this lorry was for the mines?"

And now the fine fellow is very angry. His white teeth are hidden behind a closed mouth. His eyes flash. "You ignorant nigger," he says. "You waste my time, you waste my bosses' time, I'll get the policeman to you!" He takes a big step forward and his fists are raised. Jabavu and his brother turn as if their four legs were on a single body, and they rush off into the trees. As they go they hear a roar of laughter from the men on the lorry, and they see the fine fellow going back to the lorry. He is very angry—the two brothers see that the men are laughing at him, and not at them, and they crouch in the bushes, well hidden, thinking about the meaning of these things. When the lorry has sped off into its dust, Jabavu says: "He called us nigger, and yet his skin is like ours. That is not easy to understand."

Pavu speaks for the first time: "He says I was not strong enough for the work!" Jabavu looks at him in surprise. He sees that his brother is offended. "I am fifteen years old, so the Native Commissioner has said, and for five years already I have been working for my father. And yet this man says I am not strong enough." Jabavu sees that the fear and the anger in his brother are having a fight, and it is by no means certain which will win. He says: "Did you understand, my brother, that this was a recruiter for the mines in Johannesburg?"

Pavu is silent. Yes, he understood it, but his pride is speaking too loudly to allow any other voice to be heard. Jabavu decides to say nothing. For his own thoughts are moving too fast. First he thinks: That was a fine fellow with his smart white clothes! Then he thinks: Am I mad to be thinking of the mines? For this city we are going to is hard and dangerous, yet it is small in comparison with Johannesburg, or so the travellers tell us—and now my brother who has the heart of a chicken is so wounded in his pride that he is ready not only for the small city, but for Johannesburg!

The brothers linger under the bushes, though the road is empty. The sun comes from overhead and their stomachs begin to speak of food. They open the bundles their mother has made for them and find small, flat cakes of mealie-meal, baked in the ashes. They eat the cakes, and their stomachs are only half silenced. They are a long way from proper food and the city, and yet they stay in the safety of the bushes. The sun has shifted so that it strikes on their right shoulders when they come out of the bushes. They walk slowly, and every time a lorry passes they turn their faces away as they walk through the grass at the edge of the road. Their faces are so firmly turned that it is a surprise to them when they understand that another lorry has stopped, and they peer cautiously around to see yet another fine fellow grinning at them.

"Want a nice job?" he says, smiling politely.

"We do not wish to go to the mines," says Jabavu.

"Who said the mines?" laughs the man. "Job in office, with pay seven pounds a month, perhaps ten, who knows?" His laughter is not the kind one may trust, and Jabavu's eyes lift from the beautiful black boots this dandy is wearing, and he is about to say "No," when Pavu asks, suddenly: "And there is a job for me also?"

The fellow hesitates, and it is for as long as it would take him to say "Yes" several times. Jabavu can see the pride strong on Pavu's face.

Then the fellow says: "Yes, yes, there is a job for you also. In time you will grow to be as strong as your brother." He is looking at Jabavu's shoulders and thick legs. He brings out a piece of paper and hands it to the brother, not to Jabavu. And Pavu is ashamed because he has never held a pencil and the paper feels light and difficult to him, and he clutches it between his fingers as if it might blow away. Jabavu is glowing with anger. It is he who should have been asked; he is the older, and the leader, and he can write. "What is written on this paper?" he asks.

"The job is written on this paper," says the fellow, as if it were of no importance.

"Before we put our names on the paper we shall see what this job is," says Jabavu, and the fellow's eyes shift, and then he says: "Your brother has already made his cross, so now you make your name also, otherwise you will be separated." Jabavu looks at Pavu, who is smiling a half-proud, half-sickly smile, and he says softly:

"That was a foolish thing, my brother, the white man makes an important thing of such crosses."

Pavu looks in fear at the paper where he has put his cross, and the fine fellow rocks on his feet with laughter and says: "That is true. You have signed this paper, and so have agreed to work for two years at the mines, and if you do not it means a broken contract, and that is prison. And now"—this he says to Jabavu—"you sign also, for we shall take your brother in the lorry, since he has signed the paper."

Jabavu sees that the hand of the fine fellow is reaching out to grasp Pavu's shoulder. In one movement he butts his head into the fellow's stomach and pushes Pavu away, and then both turn and run. They run leaping through the bushes till they have run a long way. Fearful glances over their shoulders show that the fine fellow does not attempt to chase them, but stands looking after them, for the breath being shaken from his stomach has darkened his eyes. After a while they hear the lorry growl, then rumble, then purr into silence along the road.

Jabavu says, after a long time of thinking: "It is true that when our people go to the city they change so that their own family would not know them. That man, he who told us the lies, would he have been such a skellum in his own village?" Pavu does not reply, and Jabavu follows his thoughts until he begins to laugh. "Yet we were cleverer than he was!" he says, and as he remembers how he butted his head into the fine fellow's stomach he rolls on the ground with laughing. Then he sits up again—for Pavu is not laughing, and on his face is a look that Jabavu knows well. Pavu is still so frightened that he is trembling all over, and his face is turned away so that Jabavu may not see it. Jabavu speaks to him as gently as a young man to a girl. But Pavu has had enough. It is in his mind to go back home, and Jabavu knows it. He pleads until the darkness comes filtering through the trees and they must find a place to sleep. They do not know this part of the country, it is more than six hours' walking from home. They do not like to sleep in the open where the light of their fire might be seen, but they find some big rocks with a cleft between, and here they build a fire and light it as their fathers did before them, and they lie down to sleep, cold because of their naked shoulders and legs, very hungry, and no prospect of waking to a meal of good, warm porridge. Jabavu falls asleep thinking that when they wake in the morning with the sun falling kindly through the trees, Pavu will have regained his courage and forgotten the recruiter. But when he wakes, Jabavu is alone. Pavu has run away very early, as soon as the light showed, as much afraid of Jabavu the Big Mouth's clever tongue as he is of the recruiters. By now he will have run halfway back along the road home. Jabavu is so angry that he flings stones at the trees, calling the trees Pavu. He is so angry that he exhausts himself with dancing and shouting, and finally he quietens and wonders whether he should run after his brother and make him turn around. Then he says to himself it is too late, and that anyway Pavu is nothing but a frightened child and no help to a brave man like himself. For a moment he thinks that he too will return home, because of his very great fear of going on to the city alone. And then he decides to go alone, and immediately: he, Jabavu, is afraid of nothing.

And yet it is not so easy to leave the sheltering trees and take the road. He lingers there, encouraging himself, saying that yesterday he outwitted the recruiters when so many fail. I am Jabavu, he says, I am Jabavu, who is too clever for the tricks of bad white men and bad black men. He thumps himself on the chest. He dances a little, kicking up the leaves and grass until they make a little whirlpool around him. "I am Jabavu, the Big Mouth . . ." It turns into a song.

> *Here is Jabavu,*
> *Here is the Big Mouth of the clever true words.*
> *I am coming to the city,*
> *To the big city of the white man.*
> *I walk alone, hau! hau!*
> *I fear no recruiter,*
> *I trust no one, not even my brother.*
> *I am Jabavu, who goes alone.*

And with this he leaves the bush and takes the road, and when he hears a lorry he runs into the bush and waits until it has gone past.

Because he has so often to hide in the bush his progress is very slow, and when the sun turns red that evening he has still not reached the city. Perhaps he has taken the wrong road? He does not dare ask anyone. If someone walks along the road and greets him he remains silent, for fear of a trap. He is so hungry that it can no longer be called hunger. His stomach has got tired of speaking to him of its emptiness and has become silent and sulky, while his legs tremble as if the bones inside have gone soft, and his head is

big and light as if a wind has got into it. He creeps off into the bush
to look for roots and leaves, and he gnaws at them, while his stomach mutters: Eh, Jabavu! So you offer me leaves after so long a
fasting? Then he crouches under a tree, his head lowered, hands
dangling limp, and for the first time his fear of what he might find
in the big city goes through him again and again like a spear and he
wishes he had not left home. Pavu will be sitting by the fire now,
eating the evening meal . . .. The dusk settles, the trees first loom
huge and black, then settle into general darkness, and from quite
close Jabavu sees a glow of fire. Caution stiffens his limbs. Then he
drags himself to his feet and walks towards the fire as carefully as
if he were stalking a hare. From a safe distance he kneels to peer
through the leaves at the fire. Three people, two men and a woman,
sit by it, and they are eating. Jabavu's mouth fills with water like a
tin standing in heavy rain. He spits. His heart is hammering at
him: Trust no one, trust no one! Then his hunger yawns inside him
and he thinks: With us it has always been that a traveller may ask
for hospitality at a fire—it cannot be that everyone has become cold
and unfriendly. He steps forward, his hunger pushing him, his fear
dragging him back. When the three people see him they stiffen and
stare and speak together, and Jabavu understands that they are
afraid he comes for harm. Then they look at his torn trousers—no
longer so tight on him now, and they greet him kindly, as one from
the villages. Jabavu returns the greetings and pleads: "My brothers, I am very hungry."

The woman at once lays out for him some white, flat cakes, and
some pieces of yellowish substance, which Jabavu eats like a hungry dog, and when his sick hunger has quietened he asks what they
were, and they tell him this is food from the city, he has eaten fish
and buns. Jabavu now looks at them and sees that they are dressed
well, they wear shoes—even the woman—they have proper shirts
and trousers and the woman has a red dress with a yellow crocheted cap on her head. For a moment the fear returns: These are
people from the city, perhaps skellums? His muscles tense, his eyes
glare, but they speak to him, laughing, telling him they are respectable people. Jabavu is silent, for he is wondering why they travel
on foot like village people, instead of by train or lorry service, as is
usual for city people. Also, he is annoyed that they have so quickly
understood what he is thinking. But his pride is soothed when they
say: "When people from the villages first come to the city they see
a skellum in every person. But that is much wiser than trusting
everyone. You do well to be cautious."

They pack away what food is left in a square, brown case that has a shiny metal clasp. Jabavu is fascinated to see how it works, and asks if he may also move the clasp, and they smile and say he may. Then they pile more wood on the fire and they talk quietly while Jabavu listens. What they say is only half-understood by him. They are speaking of the city and of the white man, not as do the people of the villages, with voices that are sad, admiring, fearful. Nor do they speak as Jabavu feels, as of a road to an exciting new country where everything is possible. No, they measure their words, and there is a quiet bitterness that hurts Jabavu, for it says to him: What a fool you are with your big hopes and dreams.

He understands that the woman is wife to one of the men, Mr. Samu, and sister to the other. This woman is like no woman he has met or heard about. When he tries to measure her difference he cannot, because of his inexperience. She wears smart clothes, but she is not a coquette, as he has heard are all the women of the towns. She is young and newly married, but she is serious and speaks as if what she says is as important as what the men say, and she does not use words like Jabavu's mother: Yes, my husband, that is true, my husband, no, my husband. She is a nurse at the hospital for women in the Location at the city, and Jabavu's eyes grow big when he hears it. She is educated! She can read and write! She understands the medicine of the white man! And Mr. Samu and the other are also educated. They can read, not only words like yes, no, good, bad, black, and white, but also long words like regulation and document. As they talk, words such as these fill their mouths, and Jabavu decides he will ask them what mean the words on the paper in his bundle which he has marked with charcoal. But he is ashamed to ask, and continues to listen. It is Mr. Samu who speaks most, but it is all so difficult that Jabavu's brain grows heavy and he pokes the edges of the fire with a green twig, listening to the sizzle of the sap, watching the sparks snap up and fade into the dark. The stars are still and brilliant overhead. Jabavu thinks, sleepily, that the stars perhaps are the sparks from all the fires people make—they drift up and up until they come against the sky and there they must remain like flies crowding together looking for a way out.

He shakes himself awake and gabbles: "Sir, will you explain to me . . ." He has taken the folded, stained piece of paper from his pocket and, kneeling, spreads it before Mr. Samu, who has stopped talking and is perhaps a little cross at being interrupted so irreverently.

He reads the difficult words. He looks at Jabavu. Then, before explaining, he asks questions. How did Jabavu learn to read? Was he all by himself? He was? Why did he want to read and write? What does he think of what he reads?—Jabavu answers clumsily, afraid of the laughter of these clever people. They do not laugh. They lean on their elbows looking at him, and their eyes are soft. He tells of the torn alphabet, how he finished the alphabet himself, how he learned the words that explained the pictures, and finally the words that are by themselves without pictures. As he speaks, his tongue slips into English, out of sympathy with what he is saying, and he tells of the hours and weeks and months of years he has spent, beneath the big tree, teaching himself, wondering, asking questions.

The three clever people look at each other, and their eyes say something Jabavu does not at once understand. And then Mrs. Samu leans forward and explains what the difficult sentence means, very patiently, in simple words, and also how the newspapers are, some for white people, some for black. She explains about the story of the little yellow people, and how wicked a story it is—and it seems to Jabavu that he learns more in a few minutes from this woman about the world he lives in, than he has in all his life. He wants to say to her: Stop, let me think about what you have said, or I shall forget it. But now Mr. Samu interrupts, leaning forward, speaking to Jabavu. After some moments of talking, it seems to Jabavu that Mr. Samu sees not only him, but many other people —his voice has lifted and grown strong, and his sentences swing up and down, as if they have been made often before, and in exactly the same way. So strong is this feeling that Jabavu looks over his shoulder to see if perhaps there are people behind him, but no, there is nothing but darkness and the trees showing a glint of starlight on their leaves.

"This is a sad and terrible time for the people of Africa," Mr. Samu is saying. "The white man has settled like a locust over Africa, and, like the locusts in early morning, cannot take flight for the heaviness of the dew on their wings. But the dew that weights the white man is the money that he makes from our labour. The white man is stupid or clever, brave or cowardly, kind or cruel, but all, all say one thing, if they say it in different ways. They may say that the black man has been chosen by God to serve as a drawer of water and a hewer of wood until the end of time; they may say that the white man protects the black from his own ignorance until that ignorance is lightened; two hundred years, five hundred, or a thou-

sand—he will only be allowed free when he has learned to stand on
his two feet like a child who lets go his mother's skirts. But whatever they say, their actions are the same. They take us, men and
women, into their houses to cook, clean, and tend their children;
into their factories and mines; their lives are built on our work, and
yet every day and every hour of every day they insult us, call us
pigs and kaffirs or children, lazy, stupid, and ignorant. Their ugly
names for us are as many as leaves on that tree, and every day the
white people grow more rich and the black more poor. Truly, it is
an evil time, and many of our people become evil, they learn to
steal and to murder, they learn the ways of easy hatred, they become the pigs the white man says they are. And yet, though it is a
terrible time, we should be proud that we live now, for our children
and the children of our children will look back and say: if it were
not for them, those people who lived in the terrible time, and lived
with courage and wisdom, our lives would be the lives of slaves.
We are free because of them."

The first part of this speech Jabavu has understood very well, for
he has often heard it before. So does his father speak, so all the
travellers who come from the city. He was born with such words in
his ears. But now they are becoming difficult. In a different tone
does the voice of Mr. Samu continue, his hand is lifting and falling,
he says trade union, organisation, politics, committee, reaction,
progress, society, patience, education. And as each new and heavy
word enters Jabavu's mind he grabs at it, clutches it, examines it,
tries to understand—and by that time a dozen such words have
flown past his ears, and he is lost in bewilderment. He looks daz-
edly at Mr. Samu, who is leaning forward, that hand rising and
falling, his steady, intent eyes fixed on his own, and it seems to him
that those eyes sink into him, searching for his secret thoughts. He
turns his own away, for he wishes them to remain secret. In the
kraal I was always hungry, always waiting for when I would reach
the plenty of the white man's town. All my life my body has been
speaking with the voices of hunger: I want, I want, I want. I want
excitement and clothes and food, such as the fish and buns I have
eaten tonight; I want a bicycle and the women of the town; I want,
I want . . . And if I listen to these clever people, straight away
my life will be bound to theirs, and it will not be dancing and music
and clothes and food, but work, work, work, and trouble, danger
and fear. For Jabavu has only just understood that these people
travel so, at night, through the bush on foot, because they are going

to another town with books, which speak of such matters as committees and organisation, and these books are not liked by the police.

These clever people, rich people, good people, with clothes on their bodies and nice food in their bellies, travel like village natives on foot—the hunger in Jabavu rises and says in a loud voice: No, not for Jabavu.

Mr. Samu sees his face and stops. Mrs. Samu says, pleasantly: "My husband is so used to making speeches that he cannot stop himself." The three laugh, and Jabavu laughs with them. Then Mr. Samu says it is very late and they should sleep. But first he writes on a piece of paper and gives it to Jabavu, saying: "I have written here the name of a friend of mine, Mr. Mizi, who will help you when you reach the city. He will be very impressed when you tell him you learned to read and write all by yourself in the kraal." Jabavu thanks him and puts the paper in his bundle, and then they all four lie around the fire to sleep. The others have blankets. Jabavu is cold, and the flesh of his chest and back is tight with shivering. Even his bones seem to shiver. The lids of his eyes, weighted with sleep, fly open in protest at the cold. He puts more wood on the fire and then looks at the shape of the woman huddled under her blanket. He suddenly desires her. That's a silly woman, he thinks. She needs a man like me, not a man who talks only. But he does not believe in this thought, and when the woman moves he hastily turns his eyes away in case she sees what is in them and is angry. He looks at the brown suitcase on the other side of the fire, lying on the grass. The metal clasp glints and glimmers in the flickering red glow. It dazzles Jabavu. His lids sink. He is asleep. He dreams.

Jabavu is a policeman in a fine uniform with bright brass buttons. He walks down the road swinging a whip. He sees the three ahead of him, the woman carrying the suitcase. He runs after them, catches the woman by the shoulder and says: "So, you have stolen that suitcase. Open it, let me see what is inside." She is very frightened. The other two men have run away. She opens the suitcase. Inside are buns and fish, and a big black book with the name *Jabavu* written on it. Jabavu says: "You have stolen my book. You are a thief." He takes her to the Native Commissioner who punishes her.

Jabavu wakes. The fire has sunk low, a heap of grey with red glimmering beneath. The clasp on the suitcase no longer shines. Jabavu crawls on his belly through the grass until he reaches the suitcase. He lays his hand on it, looks around. No one has moved. He lifts it, rises soundlessly to his feet and steals away down the path into the dark. Then he runs. But he does not run far. He stops, for it is very dark and he is afraid of the dark. He asks himself suddenly: Jabavu, why have you stolen this case? They are good people who wish only to help you and they gave you food when you were sick with hunger. But his hand tightens on the case as if it spoke a different language. He stands motionless in the dark, his whole being clamorous with desire for the suitcase, while small, frightened thoughts go through his mind. It will be four or five hours before the sun comes, and all that time he will be alone in the bush. He shivers with terror. Soon his body is clenched in cold and fear. He wishes he still lies beside the fire, he wishes he never touched the case. Kneeling in the dark, his knees painful on rough grass, he opens the case and feels inside it. There are the soft, damp shapes of food, and the hard shapes of books. It is too dark to see, he can only feel. For a long time he kneels there. Then he fastens the case and creeps back until he can see the faint glow of the fire and three bodies, quite still. He moves like a wild cat across the ground, lays the case down where it was, and then lies down himself. "Jabavu is not a thief," he says, proudly. "Jabavu is a good boy." He sleeps and dreams, but he does not know what he dreams, and wakes suddenly, alert, as if there were an enemy close by. A grey light is struggling through the trees, showing a heap of grey ashes and the three sleepers. Jabavu's body is aching with cold, and his skin is rough like soil. He slowly rises, remains poised for a moment in the attitude of a runner about to take the first great leap. The hunger in him is now saying: "Get away, Jabavu, quickly, before you too become like these, and live in terror of the police." He springs away through the bushes with big, flying leaps, and the dew soaks him in clinging cold. He runs until he has reached the road, which is deserted because it is so early. Then, when the first cars and lorries come, much later, he moves a little way into the bush beside the road, and so travels out of sight. Today he will reach the city. Each time he climbs a rise he looks for it: surely it must appear, a bright dream of richness over the hill! And towards the middle of the morning he sees a house. Then another house. The houses continue, scattered, at small distances, for half an hour's walking. Then he climbs a rise, and down the other side of it he sees—but Jabavu stands still and his mouth falls open.

Ah, but it is beautiful, how beautiful is the city of the white man!

Look how the houses run in patterns, the smooth grey streets making patterns between them like the marks of a clever finger. See how the houses rise, white and coloured, the sun shining on them so that they dazzle. And see how big they are, why, the house of the Greek is the house of a dog compared with them. Here the houses rise as if three or four were on top of each other, and gardens lie around each with flowers of red and purple and gold, and in the gardens are stretches of water, gleaming dark, and on the water flowers are floating. And see how this city stretches down the valley and even up the other side! Jabavu walks on, his feet putting themselves down one after the other with no help from his eyes, so that he goes straying this way and that until there is a shriek of warning from a car, and once again he leaps aside and stands staring, but now there is no dust, only smooth, warm asphalt. He walks on slowly, down the slope, up the other side, and then he reaches the top of the next rise, and now he stands for a long time. For the houses continue as far as he can see in front of him, and also to either side. There is no end to the houses. A new feeling has come into him. He does not say he is afraid, but his stomach is heavy and cold. He thinks of the village, and Jabavu, who has longed for so many years for just this moment, believing he has no part in the village, now hears it saying softly to him: Jabavu, Jabavu, I made you, you belong to me, what will you do in this great and bewildering city that must surely be greater than every other city. For by now he has forgotten that this is nothing compared with Johannesburg and other cities in the South, or rather, he does not dare to remember it, it is too frightening.

The houses are now of different kinds, some big, some as flimsy as the house of the Greek. There are different kinds of white men, says Jabavu's brain slowly, but it is a hard idea to absorb all at once. He had thought of them, until now, as all equally rich, powerful, clever.

Jabavu says to his feet: Now walk on, walk. But his feet do not obey him. He stands there while his eyes move over the streets of houses, and they are the eyes of a small child. And then there is a slurring sound, wheels of rubber slowing, and beside him is an African policeman on a bicycle. He rests one foot on the road and looks at Jabavu. He looks at the old, torn trousers and at the unhappy face. He says, kindly: "Have you lost your way?" He speaks in English.

At first Jabavu says no, because even at this moment it goes against the grain not to know everything. Then he says sullenly: "Yes, I do not know where to go."

"And you are looking for work?"

"Yes, son of the Government, I seek work." He speaks in his own language, the policeman, who is from another district, does not understand, and Jabavu speaks again in English.

"Then you must go to the office for passes and get a pass to seek work."

"And where is this office?"

The policeman gets off his bicycle and, taking Jabavu's arm, speaks to him for a long time, thus: "Now you must go straight on for half a mile, and then where the five roads meet turn left, and then turn again and go straight on and . . ." Jabavu listens and nods and says Yes and Thank you, and the policeman bicycles away and Jabavu stands helplessly, for he has not understood. And then he walks on, and he does not know whether his legs tremble from fear or from hunger. When he met the policeman, the sun came from behind on his back, and when his legs stop on their own accord, from weakness, the sun is overhead. The houses are all around him, and white women sit on the verandahs with their children, and black men work in the gardens, and he sees more in the sanitary lanes talking and laughing. Sometimes he understands what they say, and sometimes not. For in this city are people from Nyasaland and from Northern Rhodesia and from the country of the Portuguese, and not one word of their speech does he know, and he fears them. But when he hears his own tongue he knows that these people point at his torn trousers and his bundle, and laugh, saying: "Look at the raw boy from kraal."

He stands where two streets cross, looking this way and that way. He has no idea where the policeman told him to go. He walks on a little, then sees a bicycle leaning against a tree. There is a basket at the back, and in it are loaves of bread and buns, such as he has eaten the night before. He looks at them, while his mouth fills with water. Suddenly his hand reaches out and takes a bun. He looks around. No one has seen. He puts the bun in his pocket and moves away. When he has left that street behind, he takes it out and walks along eating the bun. But when it is finished his stomach seems to say: What, one small bun after being empty all morning! Better that you give me nothing!

Jabavu walks on, looking for another basket on a bicycle. Several times he turns up a street after one that looks the same but is not.

It is a long time before he finds what he wants. And now it is not easy as before. Then his hand went out by itself and took the bun, while his mind is warning him: Be careful, Jabavu, careful! He is standing near the basket, looking around, when a white woman in her garden shouts at him over the hedge, and he runs until he has turned a corner and is in another street. There he leans against a tree, trembling. It is a narrow street, full of trees, quiet and shady. He can see no one. Then a nanny comes out of a house with her arms full of clothes, and she hangs them on a line, looking over the hedge at Jabavu. "Hi, kraal boy, what do you want?" she shouts at him, laughing; "look at the stupid kraal boy." "I am not a kraal boy," he says, sullenly, and she says: "Look at your trousers—ohhhhh, what can I see there!" and she goes inside, looking scornful. Jabavu remains leaning against a tree, looking at his trousers. It is true that they are nearly falling off him. But they are still decent.

There is nothing to be seen. The street seems empty. Jabavu looks at the clothes hanging on the line. There are many: dresses, shirts, trousers, vests. He thinks: That girl was cheeky . . . he is shocked at what she said. Again he clasps his elbows, crouching, around his hips to cover his trousers. His eyes are on the clothes—then Jabavu has leapt over the hedge and is tugging at a pair of trousers. They will not come off the line, there is a little wooden stick holding them. He pulls, the stick falls off, and he holds the trousers. They are hot and smooth, they have just been ironed. He pulls at a yellow shirt, the cloth tears under the wooden peg, but it comes free, and in a moment he has leapt back over the hedge and is running. At the turn of the street he glances back; the garden is quiet and empty, it appears no one has seen him. Jabavu walks soberly along the street, feeling the fine warm cloth of the shirt and trousers. His heart is beating, first like a small chicken tottering as it comes out of the shell, then, as it strengthens, like a strong wind banging against a wall. The violence of his heart exhausts Jabavu and he leans against a tree to rest. A policeman comes slowly past on a bicycle. He looks at Jabavu. Then he looks again, makes a wide circle and comes to rest beside him. Jabavu says nothing, he only stares.

"Where did you get those clothes?" asks the policeman.

Jabavu's brain whirls and from his mouth come words: "I carry them for my master."

The policeman looks at Jabavu's torn shorts and his bundle.

"Where does your master live?" he asks cunningly. Jabavu points ahead. The policeman looks where Jabavu is pointing and then at Jabavu's face. "What is the number of your master's house?"

Again Jabavu's brain faints and comes to life. "Number three." he says.

"And what is the name of the street?"

And now nothing comes from Jabavu's tongue. The policeman is getting off his bicycle in order to look at Jabavu's papers, when suddenly there is a commotion in the street which Jabavu has come from. The theft has been discovered. There are voices scolding, high and shrill, it is the white mistress telling the nanny to fetch the missing clothes, the nanny is crying, and there is the word police repeated many times. The policeman hesitates, looks at Jabavu, looks back at the other street, and then Jabavu remembers the recruiter. He butts his head into the policeman's stomach, the bicycle falls over on top of him, and Jabavu leaps away and into a sanitary lane, vaults over a rubbish bin, then another, darts across a garden which is empty, then over another which is not, so that people start up and stare at him, then over into another sanitary lane and comes to rest between a rubbish bin and the wall of a lavatory. There he quickly pulls off his shorts, pulls on the trousers. They are long, grey, of fine stuff such as he has never seen. He pulls on the yellow shirt, but it is difficult, since he has never worn one, and it gets caught around the arms before he discovers the right hole in which to put his head. He stuffs the shirt, which is too small for him, inside the trousers, which are a little too long, thinking sadly of the hole in the shirt, which is due entirely to his ignorance about those little wooden pegs. He quickly pushes the torn shorts under the lid of a rubbish bin and walks up the sanitary lane, careful not to run, although his feet are itching to run. He walks until that part of the city is well left behind, and then he thinks: Now I am safe; with so many people, no one will notice grey trousers and a yellow shirt. He remembers how the policeman looked at the bundle, and he puts the soap and the comb into his pockets, together with the papers, and stuffs the rag of the bundle under the low branches of a hedge. And now he is thinking: I came to this city only this morning and already I have grey trousers like a white man, and a yellow shirt, and I have eaten a bun. I have not spent the shilling my mother gave me. Truly it is possible to live well in the white man's town! And he lovingly handles the hard shape of the shilling. At this moment, for no reason that he understands, comes into his head a memory of the three he met last

night, and suddenly Jabavu is muttering: Skellums! Bad people!
Damn, hell, bloody. For these are words he knows of the white people's swearing, and he thinks them very wicked. He says them
again and again, till he feels like a big man, and not like the little
boy at whom his mother used to look, saying sorrowfully: Ah, Jabavu, my Big Mouth, what white man's devil has got into you!

Jabavu swaggers himself into such a condition of pride that
when a policeman stops him and asks for his pass, Jabavu cannot
at once stop swaggering, but says haughtily: "I am Jabavu."

"So you are Jabavu," said the policeman, at once getting in front
of him. "So, my fine, clever boy. And who is Jabavu and where is
his pass?"

The madness of pride sinks in Jabavu, and he says humbly: "I
have no pass yet. I have come to seek work."

But the policeman looks more suspicious than ever. Jabavu
wears very fine clothes, although there is one small rent in the
shirt, and he speaks good English. How then can he have just arrived from the kraals? So he looks at Jabavu's situpa, which is the
paper that every African native must carry all the time, and he
reads: Native Jabavu. District so-and-so. Kraal so-and-so. Registration Certificate No. Xo78910312. He copies this down in a little
book, and gives the situpa to Jabavu saying: "Now I shall tell you
the way to the Pass Office, and if by this time tomorrow you have
no pass to seek work, then there will be big trouble for you." He
goes away.

Jabavu follows the streets which have been shown to him and
soon he comes to a poor part of the town, full of houses like that of
the Greek, and in them are people of half-colour, such as he has
heard about but never seen, who are called in this country the Coloured People. And soon he comes to a big building, which is the
Pass Office, with many black people waiting in long files that lead
to windows and doors in the building. Jabavu joins one of these
files, thinking that they are like cattle waiting to enter the dip, and
then he waits. The file moves very slowly. The man in front of him
and the woman behind him do not understand his questions, until
he speaks in English, and then he finds he is in the wrong file and
must go to another. And now he goes politely to a policeman who is
standing by to see there is no trouble or fighting, and he asks for
help and is put in the right queue. And now he waits again, and
because he must stand, without moving, he has time to hear the
voices of his hunger, and particularly the hunger of his stomach,
and soon it seems as if darkness and bright light are moving like

shifting water across his brain, and his stomach says again that since he left home, three days ago, he has eaten very little, and Jabavu tries to quieten the pain in his stomach by saying I shall eat soon, I shall eat soon, but the light swirls violently across his eyes, is swallowed by heavy, nauseating blackness, and then he finds he is lying on a cold, hard floor, and there are faces bending over him, some white, some dark.

He has fainted and has been carried inside the Pass Office. The faces are kind, but Jabavu is terrified and scrambles to his feet. Arms support him, and he is helped into an inner room, which is where he must wait to be examined by a doctor before he may receive a pass to seek work. There are many other Africans there, and they have no clothes on at all. He is told to take off his clothes, and everyone turns to look at him, amazed, because he clutches his arms across his chest, protecting the clothes, imagining they will be taken from him. His eyes roll in despair, and it is some time before he understands and takes them off and waits, naked, in a line with the others. He is cold because of his hunger, although outside the sun is at its hottest. One after another the Africans go up to be examined and the doctor puts a long, black thing to their chests and handles their bodies. Jabavu's whole being is crying out in protest, and there are many voices. One says: Am I an ox to be handled as that white doctor handles us? Another says, anxiously: If I had not been told that the white men have many strange and wonderful things in their medicine I would think that black thing he listens through is witchcraft. And the voice of his stomach says again and again, not at all discouraged, that he is hungry and will faint again soon if food does not come.

At last Jabavu reaches the doctor, who listens to his chest, taps him, looks in his throat and eyes and armpits and groin, and peers at the secret parts of Jabavu's body in a way that makes anger mutter in him like thunder. He wishes to kill the white doctor for touching him and looking at him so. But there is also a growing patience in him, which is the first gift of the white man's city to the black man. It is patience against anger. And when the doctor has said that Jabavu is strong as an ox and fit for work, he may go. The doctor has said, too, that Jabavu has an enlarged spleen, which means he has had malaria and will have it again, that he probably has bilharzia, and there is a suspicion of hookworm. But these are too common for comment, and what the doctor is looking for are diseases which may infect the white people if he works in their houses.

Then the doctor, as Jabavu is turning away, asks him why the blackness came into him so that he fell down, and Jabavu says simply that he is hungry. At this a policeman comes forward and asks why he is hungry. Jabavu says because he has had nothing to eat. At this the policeman says impatiently: "Yes, yes, but have you no money?"—for if not, Jabavu will be sent to a camp where he will get a meal and shelter for that night. But Jabavu says Yes, he has a shilling. "Then why do you not buy food?" "Because I must keep the shilling to buy what I need." "And do you not need food?"

People are laughing because a man who has a shilling in his pocket allows himself to fall down to the ground with hunger, but Jabavu remains silent.

"And now you must leave here and buy yourself some food and eat it. Have you a place to sleep tonight?"

"Yes," says Jabavu, who is afraid of this question.

The policeman then gives Jabavu a pass that allows him to seek work for a fortnight. Jabavu has put back his clothes, and now he takes from the pocket the roll of papers that includes his situpa, in order to put the new pass with them. And as he fumbles with them a piece of paper flutters to the floor. The policeman quickly bends down, picks it up and looks at it. On it is written: Mr. Mizi, No. 33 Tree Road, Native Township. The policeman looks with suspicion at Jabavu. "So Mr. Mizi is a friend of yours?"

"No," says Jabavu.

"Then why have you a piece of paper with his name on it?"

Jabavu's tongue is locked. After another question he mutters: "I do not know."

"So you do not know why you have that piece of paper? You know nothing of Mr. Mizi?" The policeman continues to make such sarcastic questions, and Jabavu lowers his eyes and waits patiently for him to stop. The policeman takes out a little book, makes a long note about Jabavu, tells him that it would be wise for him to go to the camp for people newly come to town. Jabavu again refuses, repeating that he has friends with whom to sleep. The policeman says Yes, he can see what his friends are—a remark which Jabavu does not understand—and so at last he is free to leave.

Jabavu walks away from the Pass Office, very happy because of this new pass which allows him to stay in the city. He does not suspect that the first policeman who took his name will hand it in to the office whose business it is, saying that Jabavu is probably a thief, and that the policeman in the Pass Office will give his name and number as a man who is a friend of the dangerous agitator Mr.

Mizi. Yes, Jabavu is already well-known in this city after half a day, and yet as he walks out into the street he feels as lost and lonely as an ox that has strayed from the herd. He stands at a corner watching the crowds of Africans streaming along the roads to the Native Township, on foot and on bicycle, talking, laughing, singing. Jabavu thinks he will go and find Mr. Mizi. And so he joins the crowds, walking very slowly because of the many new things there are to see. He stares at everything, particularly at the girls, who seem to him unbelievably beautiful in their smart dresses, and after a time he feels as if one of them is looking at him. But there are so many of them that he cannot keep any particular one in his mind. And in fact many are gazing at him, because he is very handsome in his fine yellow shirt and new trousers. Some even call out to him, but he cannot believe it is meant for him, and looks away.

After some time, he becomes certain that there is one girl who has walked past him, then come back, and is now walking past him again. He is certain because of her dress. It is bright yellow with big red flowers on it. He stares around him and can see no other dress like it, so it must be the same girl. For the third time she saunters by, close on the pavement, and he sees she has smart green shoes on her feet and wears a crocheted cap of pink wool, and she carries a handbag like a white woman. He is shy, looking at this smart girl, yet she is giving him glances he cannot mistake. He asks himself, distrustfully: Should I talk to her? Yet everyone says how immodest are these women of the towns, I should wait until I understand how to behave with her. Shall I smile, so that she will come to me? But the smile will not come to his face. Does she like me? The hunger rises in Jabavu and his eyes go dark. But she will want money and I have only one shilling.

The girl is now walking beside him at the distance of a stretched arm. She asks softly: "Do you like me, handsome, yes?" It is in English, and he replies: "Yes, very much I like."

"Then why do you frown and look so cross?"

"I do not," says Jabavu.

"Where do you live?"—and now she is so close he can feel her dress touching him.

"I do not know," he says, abashed.

At this she laughs and laughs, rolling her eyes about: "You are a funny, clever man, yes that's true!" And she laughs some more, in a loud, hard way that surprises him, for it does not sound like laughter.

"Where can I find a place to sleep, for I do not wish to go to the camp run by the Native Commissioner," he asks politely, breaking into the laughter, and she stops and looks at him in real surprise.

"You are from the country?" she asks, after a long time, looking at his clothes.

"I came today from my village, I have got a pass for looking for work, I am very hungry and I know nothing," he says, his voice falling into a humble tone, which annoys him, for he wishes to act the big man with this girl, and now he is speaking like a child. Anger at himself makes a small, feeble movement and then lies quiet: he is too hungry and lost. As for her, she has moved away to the edge of the pavement, and there walks in silence, frowning. Then she says: "Did you learn to speak English at a mission?"

"No," says Jabavu, "in my kraal."

Again she is silent. She does not believe him. "And where did you get that fine smart shirt and the white-man trousers just like new?"

Jabavu hesitates, then with a swagger says: "I took them this morning from a garden as I went past."

And now again the girl laughs, rolls her eyes, and says: "Heh, heh, what a clever boy, he comes straight from the kraal and steals so clever!" At once she stops laughing, for she has said this to gain time; she has not believed him. She walks on, thinking. She is a member of a gang who look out for such raw country boys, steal from them, make use of them as is necessary for their work. But she spoke to him because she liked him—it was a holiday from her work. But now what should she do? For it seems that Jabavu is a member of another gang, or perhaps works by himself, and if so, her own gang should know about it.

Another glance at him shows her that he walks along with a serious face, apparently indifferent to her—she goes up to him swiftly, eyes flashing, teeth showing: "You lie! You tell me big lie, that's the truth!"

Jabavu shrinks away—*hau!* but what women these are! "I do not lie," he says, angrily. "It is as I have said." And he begins to walk away from her, thinking: I was a fool to speak to her, I do not understand the ways of these girls.

And she, watching him, notices his feet, which are bare, and they have certainly never worn shoes—he is telling the truth. And in this case—she makes up her mind in a flash. A raw boy who can come to town, steal so cleverly without being caught, this is talent that can be turned to good use. She goes after him, says politely: "Tell me how you did the stealing, it was very cunning."

And Jabavu's vanity spurs him to tell the story exactly as it happened, while she listens thoughtfully. "You should not be wearing those clothes now," she says at last. "For the white missus will have told the police, and they will be watching the boys new to town in case they have the clothes."

Jabavu asks in surprise: "How can they find one pair of trousers and one shirt in a city full of shirts and trousers?"

She laughs and says: "You know nothing, there are as many police watching us as flies around porridge; you come with me, I will take those clothes and give you others, as good as those, but different." Jabavu thanks her politely but edges away. He has understood she is a thief. And he does not think of himself as a thief—he has stolen today, but he hardly gives it that name. Rather he feels as if he has helped himself to crumbs from the rich man's table. After a pause he enquires: "Do you know Mr. Mizi of 33 Tree Road?"

For the second time she is surprised into silence; then distrust fills her, and she thinks: This man either knows nothing at all or he is very cunning. She says, sarcastically, in the same tone that the policeman in the Pass Office used: "You have fine friends. And how should I know a great man like Mr. Mizi?"

But Jabavu tells her of the encounter at night in the bush, of Mr. and Mrs. Samu and the other, of what they said, and how they admired him for learning to read and write by himself, and gave him Mr. Mizi's name.

At last this girl believes him, and understands, and she thinks: "Certainly I must not let him slip away. He will be of great help in our work." And there is another thought, even more powerful: Heh! but he is handsome . . .

Jabavu asks, politely: "And do you like these people, Mr. Samu and Mrs. Samu and Mr. Mizi?"

She laughs scornfully and with disappointment, for she wishes him only to think of her. "You mad? You think I am mad too? Those people stupid. They call themselves leaders of the African people, they talk and talk, they write letters to the Government: Please Sir, Please. Give us food, give us houses, let us not carry passes all the time. And the Government throws them a shilling after years of asking and they say, Thank you, sir. They are fools." And then she sidles up to him, lays her hand inside his elbow, and says: "Besides, they are skellums—did you not see that? You come with me, I help you."

Jabavu feels the warm hand inside his bare arm, and she swings her hips and makes her eyes soft. "You like me, handsome?" And

Jabavu says: "Yes, very much," and so they walk down the road to the Native Township and she talks of the fine things there are to do, of the films and the dances and the drinking. She is careful not to talk of the stealing or of the gang, in case he should be frightened. And there is another reason: there is a man who leads the gang who frightens her. She thinks: If this new clever man likes me, I will make him marry me, I will leave the gang and work with him alone.

Because her words are one thing and what she is thinking another, there is something in her manner that confuses Jabavu, and he does not trust her; besides, that dizziness is coming back in waves, and there are moments when he does not hear what she says.

"What is the matter?" she asks at last, when he stops and closes his eyes.

"I have told you that I am hungry," he says out of the darkness around him.

"But you must be patient," she says lightly, for it is such a long time since she has been hungry she has forgotten how it feels. She becomes irritated when he walks slowly, and even thinks: This man is no good, he's not strong for a girl like me—and then she notices that Jabavu is staring at a bicycle with a basket on the back, and as he is reaching out his arm for the bread in the basket, she strikes down his arm.

"You crazy?" she asks in a high, scared voice, glancing around. For there are people all around them. "I am hungry," he says again, staring at the loaves of bread. She quickly takes some money from a place in front of her dress, gives it to the vendor, and hands a loaf of bread to Jabavu. He begins to eat as he stands, so hungrily that people turn to stare and laugh, and she gazes at him with shocked, big eyes and says: "You are a pig, not a smart boy for me." And she walks away ahead of him thinking: This is nothing but a raw kraal boy. I am crazy to like him. But Jabavu does not care at all. He eats the bread and feels the strength coming back to him, and the thoughts begin to move properly through his mind. When he has finished the bread he looks for the girl, but all he can see is a yellow dress far down the road, and the skirt of the dress is swinging in a way that reminds him of the mockery of her words: You are a pig . . . Jabavu walks fast to catch her; he comes up beside her and says: "Thank you, my friend, for the bread. I was very hungry." She says, without looking around, "Pig, dog without manners." He says: "No, that is not true. When a man is so hungry, one cannot talk of manners." "Kraal boy," she says, swinging her hips, but thinking: "It does no harm to show him I know more than he does." And then says Jabavu, full of bread and new strength: "You are nothing but a bitch woman. There are many smart girls in this city, and as pretty as you." And with this he marches off ahead of her and is looking around for another pretty girl when she runs up to him.

"Where are you going?" she asks, smiling. "Did I not say I would help you?"

"You shall not call me kraal boy," says Jabavu magnificently, and with real strength, since he truly does not care for her more than the others he sees about him, and so she gives him a quick, astonished look and is silent.

Now that Jabavu's stomach is filled he is looking around him with interest again, and so he asks questions continually and she answers him pleasantly. "What are these big houses with smoke coming out?" "They are factories." "What is this place full of little bits of garden with crosses and stone shaped like children with wings?" "It is the cemetery for the white people." So, having walked a long way, they turn off the main road into the Native Township, and the first thing Jabavu notices is that while in the city of the white people the soil lies hidden under grass and gardens or asphalt, here it billows up in thick red clouds, gives the sun a dulled and sullen face, and makes the trees look as if a swarm of locusts had passed, so still and heavy with dust are they. Also, there are now such swarms of Africans all around him that he has to make himself strong, like a rock in the middle of a swift river. And still he asks questions, and is told that this big, empty place is for playing football, and this for wrestling, and then they come to the buildings. Now these are like the house of the Greek, small, ugly, bare. But there are very many, and close together. The girl strolls along calling out greetings in her high, shrill voice, and Jabavu notices that sometimes she is called Betty, sometimes Nada, sometimes Eliza. He asks: "Why do you have so many names?" And she laughs and says: "How do you know I am not many girls?" And now, and for the first time, he laughs as she does, high and hard, doubling up his body, for it seems to him a very good joke. Then he straightens and says: "I shall call you Nada," and she says quickly: "My village name for a village boy!" At once he says: "No, I like Betty," and she presses her thigh against his and says: "My good friends call me Betty."

He says he wishes to see all this town now, before it grows dark, and she says it will not take long. "The white man's town is very big and it takes many days to see it. But our town is small, though we are ten, twenty, a hundred times as many." Then she adds: "That is what they call justice," and looks to see the effect of the word. But Jabavu remembers that when Mr. Samu used it it sounded different, and he frowns, and seeing his frown she leads him forward, talking of something else. For if he does not understand her, she understands that what the men of light—for this is how they are called—have said to Jabavu marked his mind deeply, and she thinks: If I am not careful he will go to Mr. Mizi and I will lose him and the gang will be very angry.

When they pass Mr. Mizi's house, number 33 Tree Road, she makes some rude jokes about him, but Jabavu is silent, and Betty thinks: Perhaps I should let him go to Mr. Mizi? For if he goes later, it may be dangerous. Yet she cannot bear to let him go, already her heart is soft and heavy for Jabavu. She leads him through the streets very kindly and politely, answering all his questions, though their foolishness often makes her impatient. She explains that the better houses, which have two rooms and a kitchen, are for the rich Africans, and the big, strangely-shaped houses are called Nissen huts, where twenty single men sleep, and these old shacks are called the Old Bricks, and they are for those who earn only a little, and this building here is the Hall, for meetings and dances. Then they reach a big open space which is filled with people. It is the market, and policemen are everywhere, walking with whips in their hands. Jabavu is thinking that one small loaf of bread, although it was white and fine to eat, was not much for a stomach as long empty as his, and he is looking at the various foodstuffs when Betty says: "Wait, we shall eat better than this later." And Jabavu looks at the people who buy some groundnuts or a few cooked maize-cobs for their supper, and already feels superior to them because of what Betty says.

Soon she pulls him away, for she has lived so long here that she cannot find interest, as he does, in watching the people; and now they walk away from the centre and she says: "Now we are going to Poland." Her face is ready for laughter, Jabavu sees it is a joke and asks: "And what is the joke in Poland?"

She says, quickly, before her laughter gets too strong: "In the war of the white people that has just finished, there was a country called Poland, and there was a terrible fight, with many bombs, and so now we call where we are going Poland because of the fights and the trouble there." She lets her laughter loose, but stops when she sees Jabavu stern and silent. He is thinking: I do not want fighting and trouble. Then she says in a little, foolish voice, like a child: "And so now we are going to Johannesburg," and he, not wanting to appear afraid, asks: "What is the joke in this?" She says: "This place is also called Johannesburg because there are fights and trouble in the townships of Johannesburg." And now she bends double with laughing, and Jabavu laughs from politeness. Then, seeing it is only politeness, she says, wishing to impress him, and with a big, important sigh: "Ah, yes, these white people, they tell us: See how we have saved you from the wicked fighting of the tribes; we have brought you peace—and yet see how they make wars and kill so many people one cannot understand the numbers when they are written in the newspaper." This she has heard Mr. Mizi say at a meeting; and when she notices that Jabavu is impressed, she goes on proudly: "Yes, and that is what they call civilisation!" At this Jabavu asks: "I do not understand, what is civilisation?" And she says, like a teacher: "It is how the white men live, with houses and bioscope and cowboys and food and bicycles." "Then I like civilisation," says Jabavu, from the pulse of his deepest hunger, and Betty laughs amiably and says: "Heh, but you are one big fool my friend, I like you."

They are now in an evil-looking place where there are many tall brick shelters crowded together in rows, and shacks made of petrol tins beaten flat, or of sacks and boxes, and there is a foul smell. "This is Poland Johannesburg," says Betty, walking carefully in her nice shoes through the filth and ordure. And the staring and horrified eyes of Jabavu see a man lying huddled in the grass. "Has he nowhere to sleep?" he asks, stupidly, but she pulls at his arm and says: "Fool, leave him, he is sick with the drink." For now he is on her territory, and afraid, she uses a more casual tone with him, she is his superior. Jabavu follows her, but his eyes cannot leave that man who looks as if he were dead. And his heart, as he follows Betty, is heavy and anxious. He does not like this place, he is scared.

But when they turn into a small house that stands a little by itself, he is reassured. The room they stand in is of bare red brick, with a bench around the walls and some chairs at one end. The floor is of red cement, and there are streamers of coloured paper festooned from nails in the rafters. There are two doors, and one of these opens and a woman appears. She is very fat, with a broad, shiny black face and small, quick eyes. She wears a white cloth bound round her head, and her dress is of clean pink cotton. She holds a nice clean little boy by one hand. She looks in enquiry at Betty, who says: "I am bringing Jabavu, my friend, to sleep here tonight." The woman nods and gazes at Jabavu, who smiles at her. For he likes her, and thinks: "This is a nice woman of the old kind, decent and respectable, and that is a nice little boy."

He goes into a room off the big one with Betty, and it is as well he does not say what he is thinking, for it is probable that she would have given him up as a fool beyond teaching, for while it is true that this woman, Mrs. Kambusi, is kind in her way, and respectable in her way, it is also true that her cleverness has enabled her to run the most profitable shebeen in the city for many years, and only once has she been taken to the courts, and that in the capacity of a witness. She has four children, by different fathers, and the three elder children have been sent by this wise and clever woman far away to Roman school where they will grow up educated with no knowledge of this place where the money comes for their schooling. And the little boy will be going next year also, before he is old enough to understand what Mrs. Kambusi does. Later she intends that the children will go to England and become doctors and lawyers. For she is very, very rich.

The room where he stands makes Jabavu feel cramped and restless. It is so small that there is room for one narrow bed—a bed on legs, with a space around it for walking. Some dresses hang on a nail on the wall from wooden sticks. Betty sits on the bed and looks provocatively at Jabavu. But he remains still, rolling his eyes at the low ceiling and the narrow walls, while he thinks: My fathers! But how can I live in boxes like a chicken!

Seeing his absence of mind, she says softly: "Perhaps you would like to eat now?" and his eyes return to her and he says: "Thanks, I am still very hungry."

"I will tell Mrs. Kambusi," she says, in a soft, meek voice that he does not altogether like, and goes out. After a little while she calls him to follow her, so he leaves the tiny room, crosses the big one, and goes through the second doorway into a room which makes him stare in admiration. It has a table with a real cloth on it, and many chairs around the table, and a big stove after the fashion of the white man. Never has Jabavu sat on a chair, but he does so now, and thinks: Soon I, too, will have such chairs for the comfort of my body.

Mrs. Kambusi is busy at the stove, and wonderful smells come from the pots on it. Betty puts knives and forks on the table, and Jabavu wonders how he will dare to use them without appearing ignorant. The little boy sits opposite and gazes with big, solemn eyes, and Jabavu feels inferior even to this child, who understands chairs and forks and knives.

When the food is ready, they eat. Jabavu makes his thick fingers handle the difficult knife and fork as he sees the others do, and his discomfort is soon forgotten in his delight at this delicious new food. There is fish again, which comes all the way from the big lakes in Nyasaland, and there are vegetables in a thick and savoury liquid, and there are sweet, soft cakes with pink sugar on them. Jabavu eats and eats until his stomach is heavy and comfortable, and then he sees that Mrs. Kambusi is watching him. "You have been very hungry," she observes pleasantly, speaking in his own tongue. It seems to Jabavu that he has not heard it for many months, instead of only three days, and he says gratefully: "Ah, my friend, you are of my people."

"I was," says Mrs. Kambusi, with a smile that has a certain quality, and again discomfort fills him. There is a hardness in her, and yet the hardness is not meant as cruelty against him. Her eyes are quick and shrewd, like black sparks, and she says: "Now I will give you a little lesson, listen. In the villages we may enter and greet our brothers, and take hospitality from them by right of blood and kinship. This is not the case here, and every man is a stranger until he has proved himself a friend. And every woman, too," she adds, glancing at Betty.

"This I have heard, my mother," says Jabavu, gratefully.

"What have I been telling you? I am not your mother."

"And yet," says Jabavu, "I come to the city and who sets food before me but a woman from my own people?"

And changing to English she says, quietly: "You will pay for your food, also, you come here as Betty's friend and not as my friend."

Jabavu's spirits are chilled by this coldness, and because he has no money for the food. Then he sees again the clever eyes of this woman, and knows this is meant as kindness.

Speaking in their mutual tongue she continues: "And now listen to me. This girl here, whose name I will not say so that she does not know we are speaking of her, has told me your story. She has told me of your meeting with the men of light in the bush at night, and how they took a liking to you and gave you the name of their friend here—I will not say the name, for the people who are friends of the girl who sits here trying to understand what we say do not like the men of light. You will understand why not when you have been in the city a little longer. But what I wish to tell you is this. It is probable that like most boys who come newly to the city you have many fine ideas about the life, and what you will do. Yet it is a hard life, much harder than you now know. My life has been hard, and still is, though I have done very well because I use my head. And if I were given the chance to begin again, knowing what I know now, I would not lightly throw away that piece of paper with the name written on it. It means a great deal to enter that house as a friend, to be the friend of that man—remember it."

Jabavu listens, his eyes lowered. It seems that there are two different voices speaking inside him. One says: This is a woman of great experience, do as she says, she means you well. Another says: So! Here is another busybody giving you advice; an old woman who has forgotten the excitements of being young, who wishes you to be as quiet and sleepy as herself.

She continues, leaning forward, her eyes fixed on his: "Now listen. When I heard you had fallen in with the men of light before you even entered the city, I asked myself what kind of good luck it was that you carry with you! And then I remembered that from their hands you had fallen into those which we now see lying on the table, twitching crossly because what we say is not understood. Your luck is very mixed, my friend. And yet it is very powerful, for many thousands of our people enter this city and know nothing of either the men of light or the men of darkness—for whom this very bad girl sitting here works—save what they hear through other mouths. But since it has fallen out that you have a choice to make, I wish to tell you, speaking now as one of your own people, and as your mother, that you are a fool if you do not leave this girl and go immediately to the house whose number you know."

She ceases speaking, rises, and says: "And now we shall have some tea." She pours out cups of very strong, sweet tea, and for the first time Jabavu tastes it, and it seems very good to him. He drinks it, keeping his eyes lowered for fear of seeing the eyes of Betty. For he can feel that she is angry. Also, he does not want Mrs. Kambusi to see what he is thinking, which is that he does not want to leave Betty—later, perhaps, not at once. For now that his body is fed and rested his desire is reaching out for the girl. When they both rise he still keeps his eyes lowered, and so watches how Betty puts money on the table for the meal. But what money! It is four shillings each, and wonder fills him at these women who handle such sums so casually. And then a quick glance at Mrs. Kambusi shows him that she watches him with a heavy, ironical look, as if she understands quite well everything in his mind. "Thank you for what you have told me," he says, since he does not want to lose her favour; and she replied: "It will be time to thank me when you have profited by it," and without looking his way again, reaches for a book, lifts her child on her knee, and so sits teaching the child from the book as the young people go out, saying good night.

"What did she say to you?" asks Betty, as soon as the door is closed.

"She gave me good advice about the city," says Jabavu, and then says, wishing to be told about her: "She is a kind and clever woman." But Betty laughs scornfully: "She is the biggest skellum in the city." "And how is that?" he asks, startled; but she flaunts her hips a little and says: "You will see." Jabavu does not believe her. They reach her room, and now Jabavu pushes her on to the bed and puts his arm around her so that his hand is on her breast.

"And how much?" she asks, with contempt that is meant to goad him.

Jabavu sees how her eyes are heavy, and says simply: "You know from my own mouth that I have no money."

She lies loosely in his arms and says laughing, to tease him: "I want five shillings, perhaps fifteen."

Jabavu says, scornfully: "And perhaps fifteen pounds."

"For you no money," she says, sighing; and Jabavu takes her for his own pleasure, allowing hers to look after itself, until he has had enough and lies sprawled across the bed, half-naked, and thinks: This is my first day in the city, and what have I not done? Truly Mrs. Kambusi is right when she says I have powerful luck with me. I have even had one of these smart town girls, and without paying. The words turn into a song.

> Here is Jabavu in the city,
> He has a yellow shirt and new trousers,
> He has eaten food like a lion,
> He has filled a woman of the town with his strength.
> Jabavu is stronger than the city.
> He is stronger than a lion.
> He is stronger than the women of the town.

This song moves sleepily through his mind and dies in sleep, and he wakes to find the girl sitting on the foot of the bed, looking impatiently at him and saying: "You sleep like a chicken with the setting of the sun." He says, lazily: "I am tired with the journey from my kraal."

"But I am not tired," she says lightly, and adds: "I shall dance tonight, if not with you, with someone else." But Jabavu says nothing, only yawns and thinks: This girl is only a woman like any other. Now I have had her I do not care. There are many in the city.

And so after a while she says, in that sweet, humble voice: "I was teasing you only. Now get up, lazy dog. Do you not want to see the dancing?" She adds, cunningly: "And to see also how the clever Mrs. Kambusi runs a shebeen."

But by now Mrs. Kambusi and what she has said seem unimportant to Jabavu. He yawns, gets off the bed, puts on his trousers, and then combs his hair. She watches him with bitterness and admiration. "Kraal boy," she says, in a soft voice, "you have been in the city half a day, and already you behave as if you were tired of it." This pleases him, as it was meant to do, and so he fondles her breasts a little, and then her buttocks, until she slaps him with pleasure and laughs, and so they go together into the other room. And now it is full of people sitting around the walls on the benches, while there are some men with things to make music sitting on the chairs at the end. Through the open door is the dark night, and continually more people enter.

"So this is a shebeen?" says Jabavu, doubtfully, for it looks very respectable, and she replies: "You will see what it is." The music begins. The band is a saxophone, a guitar, a petrol tin for a drum, a trumpet, and two tins to bang together. Jabavu does not know this music. And to begin with the people do not dance. They sit with tin mugs in their hands, and allow their limbs to move, while their heads and shoulders begin to nod and jerk as the music enters them.

Then the other door opens and Mrs. Kambusi comes in. She looks the same, clean and nice in her pink dress. She carries a very big jug in her hand, and moves around from mug to extended mug, pouring in liquor from the jug and holding out her free hand for the money. A little boy follows her. It is not her own child, who is asleep in the room next door and forbidden ever to see what happens in this room. No, this is a child whom Mrs. Kambusi hires from a poor family, and his work is to run out into the darkness where there is a drum of skokiaan buried, to bring supplies as needed, so that if the police should come it will not be found in the house, and also to take the money and put it in a safe place under the walls.

Skokiaan is a wicked and dangerous drink, and it is illegal. It is made quickly, in one day, and may contain many different substances. On this night it has mealiemeal, sugar, tobacco, methylated spirits, boot polish, and yeast. Some skokiaan queens use magic, such as the limb of a dead person, but Mrs. Kambusi does not believe in magic. She makes plenty of money without it.

When she reaches Jabavu she asks in a low voice in their language: "And so you wish to drink?"

"Yes, my mother," he says, humbly, "I wish to taste it."

She says: "Never have I drunk it, though I make it every day. But I will give you some." She pours him out half a cup instead of filling it, and Jabavu says, in the voice of his surly, hungry, angry youth: "I will have it full." And she stops in the act of turning away and gives him a glare of bitter contempt. "You are a fool," she says. "Clever people make this poison for fools to drink. And you are one of the fools." But she pours out more skokiaan until it slops over, smiling so that no one may know how angry she is, and moves on up the line of seated men and women, making jokes and laughing, while the little boy behind her holds out a tray full of sweets and nuts and fish and cakes with the sugar on top.

Betty asks, jealously: "What did she say to you?"

Jabavu says: "She gives me the drink for nothing because we come from the same district." And it is true she has forgotten to take money from Jabavu.

"She likes you," says Betty, and he is pleased to see she is jealous. Well, he thinks, these clever town women are as simple as the village girls! And with this thought he gives a certain smile across the room to Mrs. Kambusi, but he sees how Mrs. Kambusi only looks contemptuous, and so Betty laughs at him. Jabavu leaps to his feet to hide his shame and begins to dance. He has always been a great dancer.

He dances invitingly around the girl, throwing out his legs, until she laughs and rises and joins him, and in a moment the room is full of people who wriggle and stamp and shout, and the air fills with dust and the roof shakes and even the walls seem to tremble. Soon Jabavu is thirsty and dives towards his mug on the bench. He takes a big mouthful—and it is as if fire entered him. He coughs and chokes while Betty laughs. "Kraal boy," she says, but in a soft, admiring voice. And Jabavu, taunted, lifts the mug and drains it, and it sinks through him, lighting his limbs and belly and brain with madness. And now Jabavu really dances, first like a bull, standing over the girl with his head lowered and shoulders hunched forward, sniffing at her breasts while she shakes them at him, and then like a cock, on the tips of his toes with his arms held out, lifting his knees and scraping his heels, and all the time the girl wriggles and shakes in front of him, her hips writhing, her breasts shaking, the sweat trickling down her. And soon Jabavu grabs her, swings her through the dancers into the other room, and there he flings her on the bed. Afterwards they return and continue to dance.

Later Mrs. Kambusi comes round with the big white jug, and when he holds out his mug, she refills it saying, with a bright, hard smile: "That's right, my clever friend, drink, drink as much as you can." This time she holds out her hand for money, and Betty puts money into it. He swallows it all in a gulp, so that he staggers with the power of it, and the room swings around him. Then he dances in the packed mass of sweating, leaping people, he dances like a devil and there is the light of madness on his face. Later, but he does not know how long afterwards, there is Mrs. Kambusi's voice calling "Police!" Betty grabs him and pulls him to the bench, and they sit, and through a haze of drink and sickness he sees that everyone has drained his mug empty and that the child is quickly refilling them with lemonade. Then, at a signal from Mrs. Kambusi, three couples rise and dance, but in a different way. When two black policemen enter the room there is no skokiaan, the dancing is quiet, and the men of the band are playing a tune that has no fire in it.

Mrs. Kambusi, as calm as if she were grinding meal in her village, is smiling at the policemen. They go round looking at the mugs, but they know they will not find skokiaan for they have raided this place often. It is almost as if old friends enter it. But when they have finished the search for the skokiaan they begin to look for people who have no passes; and it is at this point that two men duck quickly under their arms and out of the door, while Mrs. Kambusi smiles and shrugs as if to say: Well, is it my fault they have no passes?

When the policemen reach Jabavu he shows them the pass for seeking work and his situpa, and they ask, When did he come to town, and he says: "This morning," and they look at each other. Then one asks: "Where did you get those smart clothes?" Jabavu's eyes roll, his feet tense, he is about to spring towards the door in flight when Mrs. Kambusi comes forward and says that she gave him the smart clothes. The policemen shrug, and one says to Jabavu: "You have done well for one day in town." It is said with unpleasantness, and Jabavu feels Betty's hand on his arm saying to him: Be quiet, do not speak.

He remains silent, and when the policemen go they take with them four men and one woman who have not had the right passes. Mrs. Kambusi follows them outside the door and slips a pound into the hand of each; they exchange formalities with good humour, and Mrs. Kambusi returns, smiling.

For Mrs. Kambusi has run this shebeen so long and so profitably not only because she is clever at arranging that the skokiaan and the large sums of money are never found in the house, but also because of the money she pays the police. And she makes it easy for them to leave her alone. As far as such places can be called orderly, hers is orderly. If the police are searching for a criminal they go first to the other skokiaan queens; and often Mrs. Kambusi sends them a message: You are looking for so-and-so who was fighting last night? Well, you will find him in such a place. This arrangement is helpful for everybody, except perhaps the people who drink the skokiaan, but it is not Mrs. Kambusi's fault that there are so many fools.

After a few minutes' quiet, for the sake of caution, Mrs. Kambusi nods at the band, and the music changes in rhythm and the dancing goes on. But now Jabavu is no longer conscious of what he is doing. Other people see him dancing and shouting and drinking, but he remembers nothing after the police left. When he wakes he is lying on the bed, and it is midday, because the slant and colour of the light says it is. Jabavu moves his head and lets it fall back with a groan that is torn out of him. Never has he felt as he does now. Inside his head there is something heavy and loose which rolls as he moves it, and each movement sends waves of terrible sickness through him. It is as if his very flesh were dissolving, yet struggling not to dissolve, and pain moves through him like knives, and where it moves his limbs hang heavy and powerless. And so he lies, suffering and wishing himself dead, and sometimes darkness comes into his eyes then goes in a dazzle of light, and after a long time he feels there is a heavy weight on his arm and remembers that there is also a girl. And she, too, lies and suffers and groans, and so they remain for a long time. It is late afternoon when they sit up and look at each other. The light still flickers inside their eyes, and so it is not at once that they can see properly. Jabavu thinks: This woman is very ugly. And she thinks the same of him, and staggers off the bed and towards the window where she leans, swaying.

"Do you often drink this stuff," asks Jabavu in wonder.

"You get used to it," she says, sullenly.

"But how often?"

Instead of replying directly, she says: "What are we to do? There is one hall for all of us and there are many thousands of us. Into the hall only perhaps three or four hundred may go. And there they sell bad beer, made by white men, who cannot make our beer. And the police watch us like children. What do they expect?"

These bitter words do not affect Jabavu at all because they are not what she feels to be true, but are what she had heard people say in speeches. Besides, he is lost in wonder that she often drinks this poison and survives. He leans his head in his hand and rocks back and forth gently, groaning. Then the rocking makes him sick and so he keeps still. Again the time goes past, and the dark begins to settle outside.

"Let us walk a little," she says, "it will relieve the sickness."

Jabavu staggers off the bed and out into the other room, and she follows. Mrs. Kambusi, hearing them, puts her head through her door and enquires, in a sweet, polite, contemptuous voice: "Well, my fine friend, and how do you like skokiaan?" Jabavu lowers his eyes and says: "My mother, I shall never taste this bad drink again." She looks at him, as if to say: "We shall see!" and then asks: "Do you wish to eat?" and Jabavu shudders and says, through a wave of sickness: "My mother, I shall never eat again!" But the girl says: "You know nothing. Yes, we shall eat. It will help the sickness."

Mrs. Kambusi nods and goes back inside her door; the two go outside to walk, moving like sick hens through the shanties of tin and sacking, and then out to the area of bedraggled and dirty grass.

"It is a bad drink," she says, indifferently, "but if you do not drink it every day it does no harm. I have lived here now for four years and I drink perhaps two or three times in a month. I like the white man's drink, but it is against the law to buy it, for they say it may teach us bad ways, and so we have to pay much money to the coloured people who buy it for us."

And now they feel their legs will not go any further, and they stand, while the evening wind sweeps into their faces, coming from far over the bush and the *kopjes* which can be seen many miles away, massed dark against the young stars. The wind is fresh, the sickness lies quiet in them and so they go back, walking slowly but more strongly. In one of the doorways of the brick sheds a man lies motionless, and now Jabavu does not need to ask what is wrong with him. Yet he halts, in an impulse to help him, for there is blood on his clothes. The girl gives him a quick, anxious look, and says: "Are you crazy? Leave him," and she pulls him away. Jabavu follows her, looking back at the hurt man, and he says: "In this city it is true that we are all strangers!" His voice is low and troubled, and Betty says quickly, for she knows he is ashamed: "And is it my fault? If we are seen near that man, people may think we hurt him . . ." And then, since Jabavu still looks sullen and unhappy, she says in a changed voice, full of sadness: "Ah, my mother! Sometimes I ask myself what it is I do here, and how my life is running away with fools and skellums. I was educated in a mission with the Roman sisters, and now what is it I am doing?" She glances at Jabavu to see how he takes her sadness, but he is not affected by it. His smile makes anger rise in her and she shouts: "Yes, it is because men are such liars and cheats, every one. Five times has a man promised to marry me so that I may live properly in a house such as they rent to married people. Five times has this man gone away, and after I have bought him clothes and food and spent much money on him." Jabavu walks quietly along, frowning, and she continues, viciously: "Yes, and you too—you kraal boy, will you marry me? You have slept with me not once, but six, seven times, and in one night, and you have spent not one penny of money, though I see you have a shilling in your pocket, for I looked while you slept, and I have given you food and drink and helped you." She has come close to him, eyes narrow and black with hate, and now Jabavu's mouth falls open with surprise, for she has opened her handbag and taken out a knife, and she moves the knife cunningly so that a pale gleam from the sky shows on it. *Hau!* thinks Jabavu, I have lain all night beside a woman who searches my pockets and carries a knife in her handbag. But he remains silent, while she comes so close her shoulders are against his chest and he feels the point of the knife pressing to his stomach. "You will marry me or I kill you," she says, and Jabavu's legs go weak. Then the courage comes to him with his contempt for her and he takes her wrist and twists it so that the knife falls to the ground. "You are a bad girl," he says, "I not marry a bad girl with a knife and ugly tongue."

And now she begins to cry while she kneels and scuffles after the knife in the dust. She rises, putting the knife carefully in her bag, and she says: "This is a bad town and the life here is bad and difficult." Jabavu does not soften, for inside him is a voice saying the same thing, and he does not want to believe it, since his hunger for the good things of the town is as strong as ever.

For the second time he sits at Mrs. Kambusi's table and eats. There are potatoes fried with fat and salt, and then boiled mealies with salt and oil, and then more of the little cakes with pink sugar that he likes so much, and finally cups of the hot, sweet tea. Afterwards he says: "What you say is true—the sickness is gone."

"And now you are ready to drink skokiaan again?" asks Mrs. Kambusi, politely. Jabavu glances quickly at her, for the quality of her politeness has changed. It seems to him that her eyes are very frightening, for now they are saying, in that cool, quietly bitter look: Well, my friend, you may kill yourself with skokiaan, you may spend your strength on this girl until you have none left, and I do not care. You may even learn sense and become one of the men of light—I do not care about that either. I simply do not care. I have seen too much. She rests her bulky body against the back of her chair, stirs her tea round and round with a fine, shiny spoon, and smiles with her cool, shrewd eyes until Jabavu rises and says: "Let us go." Betty also rises, pays eight shillings as she did the night before and, having said good night, they go out.

"Not only have I paid much money for your food," says Betty, bitterly, "but you sleep in my room, and your nice Mrs. Kambusi, who you call your mother, charges me a fine rent for it, I can tell you."

"And what do you do in your room?" asks Jabavu, laughing, and Betty hits him. He holds her wrists, but with one hand, and puts his other on her breasts, and she says: "I do not like you," and he lets her go, laughing, and says: "That I can see." He goes into her room and lies on her bed as if this were his right, and she comes meekly after him and lies beside him. He is thinking, and besides even his bones are tired and aching, but she wishes to make love and begins to tease him with her hand, but he pushes it away and says: "I wish only to sleep." At this she rises angrily from beside him and says: "You are a man? No, you are only a kraal boy." This he cannot bear, so he gets up, throws her down and makes love to her until she no longer moves or speaks; and then he says, with swaggering contempt: "Now you shut up." But in spite of his pride in his knowledge of the nature of women it is a bad time for Jabavu, and sleep will not come. There is a fight going on inside him. He thinks of the advice Mrs. Kambusi has given him, then, when it seems difficult to follow, he tells himself she is nothing but a skellum and a skokiaan queen. He thinks of Mr. and Mrs. Samu and their friend, and how they liked him and thought him clever, and just as he decides to go to them he groans with the thought of the hardness of their life. He thinks of this girl, and how she is a bad girl, without modesty or even beauty, except what the smart clothes give her, and then the pride rises in him and a song forms itself: I am Jabavu, I have the strength of a bull, I can quieten a noisy woman with my strength, I can . . .

And then he remembers he has one shilling only and that he must earn some more. For Jabavu still thinks that he will do proper work for his money, he does not think of thieving. And so, though only half an hour before he made the girl sleep, he now shakes her, and she wakes reluctantly, crinkling the skin around her eyes against the glare from the unshaded yellow bulb that hangs from the roof. "I want to know what work is paid best in this city?" he demands.

At first her face is foolish, then when she understands she laughs derisively, and says: "You still do not know what work pays the best?" She closes her eyes and turns away from him. He shakes her again and now she is angry. "Ah, be still, kraal boy, I will show you in the morning."

"Which work is the most money?" he insists. And now she turns back, leans on her elbow and looks at him. Her face is bitter. It is not the truthful bitterness that can be seen on Mrs. Kambusi's face, but rather the self-pity of a woman. After a while she says: "Well, my big fool, you can work in the white people's houses, and if you behave well and work many years you may earn two or three pounds a month." She laughs, because of the smallness of the sum. But Jabavu thinks it is a great deal. For a moment he remembers that the food he has eaten with Mrs. Kambusi cost four shillings, but he thinks: She is a skellum after all, and probably cheats me. His confusion is really because he cannot believe that he, Jabavu, will not have what he wants simply by putting out his hand and taking it. He has dreamed so long and so passionately about this town, and the essence of a dream is that it must come disguised, smiling brightly, its dark side hidden where is written: This is what you must pay—

"And in the factories?" asks Jabavu.

"Perhaps one pound a month and your food."

"Then tomorrow I shall go to the houses of the white men, three pounds is better than one."

"Fool, you have to work months or years to earn three pounds."

But Jabavu, having settled his own mind, falls asleep at once, and now she lies awake, thinking she is a fool to take up with a man from the kraals who knows nothing about the city; then she is sad, with an old sadness, because it is in her nature to love the indifference of men, and it is by no means the first time she has lain awake beside a sleeping man, thinking how he will leave her. Then she is frightened, because soon she must tell her gang about Jabavu, and there is the one man, who calls himself Jerry, clever enough to know that her interest in Jabavu is a good deal more than professional.

Finally, seeing no way out of her troubles, she drifts into the bitterness which is not her own, but learned from what others say; and she repeats that the white men are wicked and make the black live like pigs, and there is no justice, and it is not her fault she is a bad girl—and many things of this sort, until her mind loses interest in them and she falls asleep at last. She wakes in the morning to see Jabavu combing his hair, looking very handsome in the yellow shirt. She thinks, maliciously: The police will be looking for that shirt, and he will get into trouble. But it appears her desire to hurt him is not as strong as she thinks; for she pulls a suitcase from under the bed, takes out a pink shirt, throws it at him and says: "Wear this, otherwise you will be caught."

Jabavu thanks her, but as if he expects such attention, then says: "Now you will show me where to go to find good work."

She says: "I will not come with you. I must earn money for myself today. I have spent so much on you I have none left."

"I did not ask you to spend money on me," says Jabavu, cruelly, and she flashes out her knife again, threatening him with it. But he says: "Stop being a stupid woman. I am not afraid of your knife." So she begins to cry. And now Jabavu's manhood, which has been fed with pride so much that he feels there is nothing he cannot do, tells him that he should comfort her, so he puts his arm around her and says: "Do not cry," and "You are a nice girl, though foolish," and also, "I love you." And she weeps and says: "I know about men, you will never come back to me," and he smiles and says: "Perhaps I will, perhaps not." And saying this, he rises and goes out, and the last thing she sees of him that morning are his white teeth flashing in a gay smile. And so for a while she weeps, then she grows angry, then she goes in search of Jerry and the gang, thinking all the time of that impudent smile and how she may speak to them so that they make Jabavu one of the gang.

Jabavu goes from the place which is called Poland and Johannesburg, walks through the Native Township, along the busy road to the white man's city, and so to where the fine houses are. And here he saunters along, choosing which house he likes best. For his success since he came to the city has given him such a swelled head he imagines the first he enters will open its doors saying: Ah, here is Jabavu, I have been waiting for you! When he has made up his mind, he walks in through the gate and stands looking around, and an old white woman who is cutting at some flowers with a shiny pair of scissors says, in a sharp voice: "What do you want?" He says: "I want work." She says: "Go to the back of the house. What cheek!" He stands insolently in front of her, till she shouts: "Did you hear? Get to the back; since when do you come to the front of a house asking for work?" And so he walks out of the garden, cursing her to himself, listening to how she grumbles and mutters about spoilt kaffirs, and goes to the back of the house, where a servant tells him that here there is no work for him. Jabavu is angry. He strolls into the sanitary lane, letting his anger make words of hatred: White bitch, filthy woman, white people all pigs. Then he goes to the back part of another house. There is a big garden here, with vegetables, a cat sitting fat and happy on a green lawn, and a baby in a basket under a tree. But there is no one to be seen. He waits, he walks about, he looks through the windows carefully, the baby coos in its basket, waving its legs and arms, and then Jabavu sees there are a row of shoes on the back verandah waiting to be cleaned. He cannot help looking at the shoes. He measures them with his eyes against his feet. He glances around— still no one in sight. He snatches up the biggest pair of shoes and goes into the sanitary lane. He cannot believe it is so easy, his flesh is prickling with fear of hearing angry voices or feet running after him. But nothing happens, so he sits down and puts on the shoes. Since he has never worn any, he does not know whether his discomfort is because they are too small or because his feet are not used to them. He walks on them and his legs make small, mincing steps of pain, but he is very proud. Now he is dressed, even his feet like a white man.

He goes into the back of another house, and this time the woman there asks him what work he knows. He says, "Everything." She asks him: "Are you cook or houseboy?" And now he is silent. She asks: "What money did you earn before?" And when he is still silent she asks to see his situpa. As soon as she looks at it, she says angrily: "Why do you tell me lies? You are a raw boy." And so he goes out into the sanitary lane, angry and sore, but thinking of what he has learned, and when he goes to the next house and a woman asks what he knows, he puts on a humble look and says in a cringing voice that he has not worked in a white house before, but that he will learn quickly. He is thinking: I look so fine in my clothes, this woman will like a smart man like me. But she says she does not want a boy without experience. And now, as Jabavu walks away, his heart is cold and unhappy and he feels that no one in the whole world wants him. He whistles jauntily, making his fine new shoes stamp, and says he will surely find a good job with much money soon, but in the next house the woman says she will take him for rough work at twelve shillings a month. And Jabavu says he will not take twelve shillings. And she hands him back his situpa and says, pleasantly enough, that he will not get more than twelve shillings without experience. Then she goes back into the house. This happens several times until in the afternoon Jabavu goes to a man chopping wood in a garden, whom he has heard speaking his own language, and he asks for advice. This man is friendly and tells him that he will not earn more than twelve or thirteen shillings a month until he has learned the work, and then, after many months, a pound. He will be given mealiemeal every day to make his porridge with, and meat once or twice a week, and he will sleep in a small room like a box at the back of the house with the other servants. Now all this Jabavu knows, for he has heard it often from people passing through the village, but he has not known it for himself; he has always thought: For me it will be different.

He thanks the friendly man and wanders on through the sanitary lanes, careful not to stop or loiter, otherwise a policeman may notice him. He is wondering: What is this experience? I, Jabavu, am the strongest of the young men in my village. I can hoe a field in half the time it takes any other; I can dance longer than anyone without tiring; all the girls like me best and smile as I go past; I came to this city two days ago and already I have clothes, and I can treat one of the clever women of the town like a servant and she loves me. I am Jabavu! I am Jabavu, come to the white man's town. He dances a little, shuffling through the leaves in the sanitary lane, but then he sees dust filming his new shoes, and so he stops. The sun will soon be sinking; he has not eaten since last night, and he wonders whether he should return to Betty. But he thinks: There are other girls, and he goes slowly through the sanitary lanes looking over the hedges into the gardens, and where there is a nanny hanging up clothes or playing with children, he looks carefully at her. He tells himself that he wants just such another girl as Betty, yet he sees one with her look of open and insolent attraction, and though he hesitates, he moves on, until at last he sees a girl standing by a white baby in a small cart on wheels, and he stops. She has a pleasant, round face, and eyes that are careful of what they say. She wears a white dress and has a dark-red cloth bound round her head. He watches her for a time and then says, in English: "Good morning." She does not at once answer, but looks at him first. "Can you help me?" he asks again. Then she says: "What can I tell you?"

From the sound of her voice he thinks she may be from his district, and he speaks to her in his language, and she answers him, smiling, and they move close and speak over the hedge. They discover that her village is not more than an hour's walking from his, and because the old traditions of hospitality are stronger than the new fear in both of them, she asks him to her room, and he goes. There, while the baby sleeps in its carriage, they talk, and Jabavu, forgetting how he has learned to speak to Betty, treats this girl as respectfully as he would one in the village.

She tells him he may sleep here tonight, having first said that she is bound to a man in Johannesburg, whom she will marry, so that Jabavu may not mistake her intention. She leaves him for a time, to help her mistress put the baby to bed. Jabavu is careful not to show himself, but sits in a corner, for Alice has said that it is against the law for him to be there, and if the police should come he must try and run away, for her mistress is kind and does not deserve trouble from the police.

Jabavu sits quietly, looking at the little room, which is the same size as Betty's and has the same brick walls and floor and tin roof, and sees that three people sleep here, for their bedding is rolled into separate corners, and he tells himself he will not be a houseboy. Soon Alice returns with food. She has cooked mealiemeal porridge, not as well as his mother would do, for that needs time, and it must be done on the mistress's stove. But there is plenty of it, and there is some jam her mistress has given her. As they eat they speak of their villages and of the life here. Alice tells him she earns a pound a month and the mistress gives her clothes and plenty of mealiemeal. She speaks with great affection of this woman, and for a time Jabavu is tempted to change his mind and find just such another for himself. But a pound a month—no, not for Jabavu, who despises Alice for being satisfied with so little. Yet he looks kindly at her and thinks her very pretty. She has stuck a candle in its own grease on the door-sill, and it gives a nice light, and her cheeks and eyes and teeth glisten. Also she has a soft, modest voice, which pleases him after the way Betty uses hers. Jabavu warms to her and feels her answering warmth for him. Soon there is a silence and Jabavu tries to approach her, but with respect, not as he would handle Betty. She allows him, and sits within his arm and tells him of the man who promised her marriage and then went to Johannesburg to earn money for the lobola. At first he wrote and sent money, but now there has been silence for a year. He has another woman now, so travellers have told her. Yet she believes he will come back, for he was a good man. "So Johannesburg is not all bad?" asks Jabavu, thinking of the many different things he has heard. "It seems that many like it, for they go once and then go again and again," she says, but with reluctance, for it is not a thought she enjoys. Jabavu comforts her; she weeps a little, then he takes her, but with gentleness. Afterwards he asks her what would happen if there was a baby. She says that there are many children in the city who do not know their fathers; and then she tells him things that make him dizzy with astonishment and admiration. So that is why the white women have one or two or three children or none at all? Alice tells him of the things a woman may use, and a man may use; she says that many of the more simple people do not know of them, or fear them as witchcraft, but the wise people protect themselves against children for whom there are no fathers or homes. Then she sighs and says how much she longs for children and a husband, but Jabavu interrupts her to ask how he may obtain these things she has spoken about, and she tells him it is best to ask a kind white person to buy them, if one knows such a white person, or one may buy them from the coloured people who traffic in more things than liquor, or if one is brave enough to face a snubbing, one may go and ask in a white man's shop—there are some traders who will sell to the black people. But these things are expensive, she says, and need care in use, and . . . she continues to talk, and Jabavu learns another lesson for life in the big city, and he is grateful to her. Also he is grateful and warm to her because here is a girl who keeps her gentleness and her knowledge of what is right even in the city. In the morning he thanks her many times and says goodbye to her and to the two other men who came in to sleep in the room late at night, after visiting, and while she thanks him also, for politeness's sake, her eyes tell him that if he wished he could take the place of the man in Johannesburg. But Jabavu had already learned to be afraid of the way every woman in the city longs only for a husband, and he adds that he wishes for the early return of her promised husband so that she may be happy. He leaves her, and

before he has reached the end of the sanitary lane is thinking what
he should do next, while she looks after him and thinks sadly of
him for many days.

It is early in the morning, the sun is newly risen, and there are
few people in the streets. Jabavu walks for a long time around the
houses and gardens, learning how the city is planned, but he does
not ask for work. When he has understood enough of the place to
find his way without asking questions at every corner he goes to the
part of the town where the shops are, and examines them. Never
has he imagined such richness and variety. Half of what he sees he
does not understand, and he wonders how these things are used,
but in spite of his wonder he never stands still before a window; he
makes his legs move on even when they would rather stop, in order
that the police may not notice him. And then, when he has seen
windows of food and of clothes, and many other strange articles, he
goes to the place where the Indian shops are for natives to buy, and
there he mixes with the crowds, listens to the gramophones playing
music, and keeps his ears attentive so that he may learn from what
people say, and so the afternoon slowly passes in learning and listening. When he grows hungry he watches until he sees a cart with
fruit on it, he walks quickly past and takes half a dozen bananas
with a skill that seems to have been born in his fingers, for he is
astonished himself at their cunning. He walks down a side-street
eating the bananas as if he had paid money for them, quite openly;
and he is thinking what he should do next. Return to Betty? He
does not like the thought. Go to Mr. Mizi, as Mrs. Kambusi says he
should? But he shrinks from it—later, later, he thinks, when I have
tasted all the excitements of the town. And in the meantime, he
still owns one shilling, nothing else.

And so he begins to dream. It is strange that when he was in the
village and made such dreams they were far less lofty and demanding than the one he makes now; yet, even in the ignorance of the
village, he was ashamed of those small and childish dreams, while
now, although he knows quite well what he is thinking is nonsense,
the bright pictures moving through his mind grip him so fast he
walks like a mad person, open-mouthed, his eyes glazed. He sees
himself in one of the big streets where the big houses are. A white
man stops him and says: I like you, I wish to help you. Come to my
house. I have a fine room which I do not use. You may live in it, and
you may eat at my table and drink tea when you like. I will give you
money when you need it. I have many books; you may read them
all and become educated . . . I am doing this because I do not

agree with the colour bar and wish to help your people. When you know everything that is in the books, then you will be a man of light, just the same as Mr. Mizi, whom I respect very much. Then I will give you enough money to buy a big house, and you may live in it and be a leader of the African people, like Mr. Samu and Mr. Mizi . . .

This dream is so sweet and so strong that Jabavu at last stands under a tree, gazing at nothing, quite bewildered. Then he sees a policeman cycling slowly past and looking at him, and it does not mix well with the dream, and so he makes his feet walk on. The dream's sad and lovely colours are all around him still, and he thinks: The white people are so rich and powerful, they would not miss the money to give me a room and books to read. Then a voice says: But there are many others beside me, and Jabavu shakes himself crossly because of that voice. He cannot bear to think of others, his hunger for himself is so strong. Then he thinks: Perhaps if I go to school in the Township and tell them how I learned to read and write by myself they will take me in . . . But Jabavu is too old for school, and he knows it. Slowly, slowly, the foolish sweetness of the dreaming leaves him, and he walks soberly down to the road to the Township. He has no idea at all of what he will do when he gets there, but he thinks something will happen to help him.

It is now early in the evening, about five, and it is a Saturday. There is an air of festivity and freedom, for yesterday was pay-day, and people are looking how best to spend their money. When he reaches the market he lingers there, tempted to spend his shilling on some proper food. But now it has become important to him, like a little piece of magic. It seems to him he has been in the city for a very long time, although it is only four days, and all that time the shilling has been in his pocket. He has the feeling that if he loses it he will lose his luck. Also there is another thought—it took his mother so long to save it. He wonders that in the kraal a shilling is such a lot of money, whereas here he could spend it on a few boiled mealies and a small cake. He is angry with himself because of this feeling of pity for his mother, and mutters: "You big fool, Jabavu," but the shilling stays in his pocket and he wanders on, thinking how he may find something to eat without asking Betty, until he reaches the Recreation Hall, which has people surging all around it.

It is too early for the Saturday dancing, and so he loiters through the crowd to see what is happening. Soon he sees Mr. Samu with some others at a side door, and he goes closer with the feeling: Ah, here is someone who will help me. Mr. Samu talks to a friend, in the way in which Jabavu recognises, as if that friend is not one person but many; and Mr. Samu's eyes move from one face near to him to another, and then on, always moving, as if it is with his eyes that he holds them, gathers them in, makes them one. And his eyes rest on Jabavu's face, and Jabavu smiles and steps forward—but Mr. Samu, still talking, is looking at someone else. Jabavu feels as if something cold hit his stomach. He thinks, and for the first time: Mr. Samu is angry because I ran away this morning; and at once he walks jauntily away, saying to himself: Well, I don't care about Mr. Samu, he's nothing but a big talker, these men of light, they are just fools, saying Please, Please to the Government! Yet he has not gone a hundred yards when his feet slow, he stops, and then his feet seem to turn him around so that he must go back to the hall. Now the people are crowding in at the big door, Mr. Samu has gone inside, and Jabavu follows at the back of the crowd. By the time he has got inside the hall is full, and so he stands at the back against the wall.

On the platform are Mr. Samu, the other man who was with him in the bush, and a third man, who is almost at once introduced as Mr. Mizi. Jabavu's eyes, dazed with so many people all together, hardly see Mr. Mizi's face, but he understands this is a man of great strength and cleverness. He stands as straight and tall as he can so that Mr. Samu may see him, but Mr. Samu's eyes again move past without seeing, and Jabavu thinks: But who is Mr. Samu? Nothing besides Mr. Mizi . . . And then he looks how these men are dressed, and sees their clothes are dark and some-times old, sometimes even with patches on them. There is no one in this hall who has as bright and smart clothes as Jabavu himself, and so the small, unhappy child in Jabavu quietens, appeased, and he is able to stand quietly listening.

Mr. Mizi is talking. His voice is powerful, and the people in the benches sit motionless, leaning forward, and their faces are full of longing, as if they are listening to a beautiful story. Yet what Mr. Mizi says is not at all beautiful. Jabavu cannot understand, and asks a man near him what this meeting is. The man says that the men on the platform are the leaders for the League for the Advancement of the African People; that they are now discussing the laws which treat Africans differently from the white people . . . they are very clever, he says; and can understand the laws as they are written, which it takes many years to do. Later the meeting will be told about the management of land in the reserves, and how the Government wishes to reduce the cattle owned by the African people, and about the pass-laws, and also many other things. Jabavu is shown a piece of paper with numbers 1, 2, 3, 4, 5, and 6, and opposite these numbers are written words like Destocking of Cattle. He is told this piece of paper is an Agenda.

First Mr. Mizi speaks for a long time, then Mr. Samu, then Mr. Mizi again, and sometimes the people in the hall seem to growl with anger, sometimes they sigh and call out "Shame!" and these feelings, which are like the feelings of one person, become Jabavu's also, and he, too, claps and sighs and calls out "Shame, Shame!" Yet he hardly understands what is said. After a long time Mr. Mizi rises to speak on a subject which is called Minimum Wage, and now Jabavu understands every word. Mr. Mizi says that not long ago a member of the white man's Parliament asks for a law which would make one pound a month a minimum wage for African workers, but the other members of Parliament said "No," it would be too much. And now Mr. Mizi says he wishes every person to sign a petition to the members of the Parliament to reconsider this cruel decision. And when he says this, every man and woman in the hall roars out "Yes, yes," and they clap so long that Jabavu's hands grow tired. And now he is looking at those great and wise men on the platform, and with every nerve of his body longs to be like them. He sees himself standing on a platform while hundreds of people sigh and clap and cry "Yes, yes!"

And suddenly, without knowing how it has happened, his hand is raised and he has called out, "Please, I want to speak." Everybody in the hall has turned to look, and they are surprised. There is complete silence in the hall. Then Mr. Samu stands up quickly and says, after a long look at Jabavu: "Please, this is a young friend of mine, let him speak." He smiles and nods at Jabavu, who is filled with immense pride, as if a great hawk carried him into the sky on its wings. He swaggers a little as he stands. Then he speaks of how he came from his kraal only four days ago, how he outwitted the recruiters who tried to cheat him, how he had no food and fainted with hunger and was handled like an ox by the white doctor, how he has searched for work . . . The words flow into Jabavu's tongue as if someone very clever stood behind his shoulder and whispered them into his ear. Some things this clever person does not mention, such as how he stole clothes and shoes and food, and how he fell in with Betty and spent the night at the shebeen. But he tells how in the white woman's garden he has been rudely ordered to the back, "which is the right place for niggers"—and this Jabavu tells with great bitterness—and how he has been offered twelve shillings a month and his food. And as Jabavu speaks the people in the hall murmur, "Yes, yes."

Jabavu is still full of words when Mr. Samu stands up, interrupting him, saying: "We are grateful to our young friend for what he has said. His experiences are typical for young men coming to town. We all know from our own lives that what he says is true, but it does no harm to hear it again." And with this he quietly introduces the next subject, which is how terrible it is that Africans must carry so many passes, and the meeting goes on. Jabavu is upset, for he feels that it is not right the meeting should simply go on to something else after the ugly things he has told them. Also, he has seen that some of the people, in turning back to the platform, have smiled at each other, and that smile stung his pride. He glances at the man next to him, who says nothing. Then, since Jabavu continues to look and smile, as if wanting words, the man says pleasantly: "You have a big mouth, my friend." At this, such rage fills Jabavu that his hand lifts by itself, and very nearly hits the man, who swiftly clasps Jabavu's wrist and murmurs: "Quiet, you will make big trouble for yourself. We do not fight here." Jabavu mutters in anguish: "My name is Jabavu, not Big Mouth," and the man says: "I did not speak of your name, I do not know it. But in this place we do not fight, for the men of light have trouble enough without that."

Jabavu struggles his way towards the door, for it is as if his ears were full of mocking laughter, and Big Mouth, Big Mouth, repeated often. Yet the people are standing packed in the door and he cannot go out, though he tries so that he disturbs them, and they ask him to be quiet. And while Jabavu stands there, angry and unhappy, a man says to him: "My friend, what you said spoke to my heart. It is very true." And Jabavu forgets his bitterness and at once is calm and full of pride; for he cannot know that this man spoke only so as to see his face clearly, for he comes to all such meetings pretending to be like the others in order to return later to the Government office which wishes to know who of the Africans are trouble-makers and seditious. Before the meeting is over, Jabavu has told this friendly man his name and his village, and how much he admires the men of light, information which is very welcome.

When Mr. Samu declares the meeting closed, Jabavu slips out as quickly as he can and goes out to the other door where the speakers will come. Mr. Samu smiles and nods when he sees him, and shakes his hand, and introduces him to Mr. Mizi. None congratulate him on what he has said, but rather look at him like village elders who think: That child may grow up to be useful and clever if his parents are strict with him. Mr. Samu says: "Well, well, my young friend, you haven't had good luck since you came to the city, but you made a mistake if you think yours is an exceptional case." Then, seeing Jabavu's dismayed face, he says, kindly: "But why did you run away so early, and why did you not go to Mr. Mizi who is glad to help people who need help?" Jabavu hangs his head and says that he ran away so early because he wished to reach the city soon and did not want to disturb their sleep for nothing, and that he could not find Mr. Mizi's house.

Mr. Mizi says: "Then come with us now, and you will find it." Mr. Mizi is a big man, strong, heavy-shouldered. If Jabavu is like a young bull, clumsy with his own strength, then Mr. Mizi is like an old bull who is used to his power. His face is not one a young man may easily love, for there is no laughter in it, no easy warmth. He is stern and thoughtful and his eyes see everything. But if Jabavu does not love Mr. Mizi, he admires him, and at every moment he feels more like a small boy, and as this feeling of dependence, which is one he hates and makes him angry, grows in him, he does not know whether to run away or stay where he is. He stays, however, and walks with a group of others to Mr. Mizi's house.

It is a house similar to that of the Greek. Jabavu knows now that compared with the houses of the white men it is nothing, but the front room seems very fine to him. There is a big mirror on the wall, and a big table covered with soft green stuff that has thick, silky tassels dangling, and around this table, many chairs. Jabavu sits on the floor as a mark of respect, but Mrs. Mizi, who is welcoming her guests, says kindly: "My friend, sit on this chair," and pushes it forward for him. Mrs. Mizi is a tiny woman, with a merry face and eyes that dart everywhere looking for something to laugh at. It seems that there is so much laughter in Mrs. Mizi that there is no room for it in Mr. Mizi, while Mr. Mizi thinks so much he has taken all thought from Mrs. Mizi. Seeing Mrs. Mizi alone it is hard to believe she should have a big, stern, clever husband; while seeing Mr. Mizi, one would not think of his wife as small and laughing. Yet together they fit each other, as if they make one person.

Jabavu is so full of awe at being here that he knocks over the chair and feels he would like to die of shame, but Mrs. Mizi laughs at him with such good nature that he begins to laugh too, and only stops when he sees that this gathering of friends is not only for friendship, but also for serious talking.

Seated around the table are Mr. Samu and Mrs. Samu and the brother, and Mr. Mizi and Mrs. Mizi and a young boy who is the Mizis' son. Mrs. Mizi sets tea on the table, in nice white cups, and plenty of little cakes with pink sugar. The young boy drinks one cup of tea quickly, and then says he wishes to study and goes next door with a cake in his hand, while Mrs. Mizi rolls up her eyes and complains that he will study himself to death. Mr. Mizi, however, tells her not to be a foolish woman, and so she sits down, smiling, to listen.

Mr. Mizi and Mr. Samu talk. It appears that they talk to each other, yet sometimes they glance at Jabavu, for what they are saying is not just what comes into their heads, but is chosen to teach Jabavu what it is good for him to know.

Jabavu does not at once understand this, and when he does that familiar storm of resentment clouds his hearing; one voice says: I, Jabavu, treated like a small child; while the other says: These are good people, listen. So it is only in fragments that their words enter his mind, and there they form a strange and twisted idea that would surprise these wise and clever men if they could see it. But perhaps it is a weakness of such men, who spend their lives studying and thinking and saying things such as: The movement of history, or the development of society, that they forget the childhood of their own minds, when such phrases have a strange and even terrible sound.

So there sits Jabavu at the table, eating the cakes which Mrs. Mizi presses on him, and his face is first sullen and unwilling, then bright and eager, and sometimes his eyes are lowered to hide what he thinks, and then they flash up, saying: Yes, yes, that is true!

Mr. Mizi is saying how hard it is for the African when he first comes to the town knowing nothing save that he must leave everything he has learned in the kraal behind him. He says that such a young man must be forgiven if out of confusion he drifts into the wrong company.

And here Jabavu instinctively lifts his arms to cross them over his bright new shirt, and Mrs. Mizi smiles at him and refills his cup.

Then Mr. Samu says that such a young man has the choice of a short life, with money and a good time, before prison or drink or sickness overtake him, or he may work for the good of his people and . . . but here Mrs. Mizi lets out a yell of laughter and says: "Yes, yes, but that may be a short life too, and prison, just as much."

Mr. Mizi smiles patiently and says that his wife likes a good joke, and there is a difference between prison for silly things like stealing, and prison for a good cause. Then he goes on to say that a young man of intelligence will soon understand that the company of the matsotsis leads only to trouble, and will devote himself to study. Further, he will soon understand that it is foolish to work as a cook or houseboy or office-boy, for such people are never more than one or two or three together, but he will go into a factory, or even to the mines, because . . . But for the space of perhaps ten minutes Jabavu understands not one word, since Mr. Mizi is using such phrases as the development of industry, the working class, and historical mission. When what Mr. Mizi says becomes again easy to follow, it is that Jabavu must become such a worker that everyone trusts him, and at night he will study on his own or with others, for a man who wishes to lead others must not only be better than they, but also know more . . . and here Mrs. Mizi giggles and says that Mr. Mizi has a swelled head, and he is only a leader because he can talk louder than anyone else. At which Mr. Mizi smiles fondly, and says a woman should respect her husband.

Jabavu, breaking into this flirtation between Mr. Mizi and Mrs. Mizi, asks, suddenly: "Tell me, please, how much money will I earn in a factory?" And there is the hunger in his voice so that Mr. Mizi frowns a little, and Mrs. Mizi makes a little grimace and a shake of the head.

Mr. Mizi says: "Not much money. Perhaps a pound a month. But . . ."

And here Mrs. Mizi laughs irrepressibly and says: "When I was a girl at the Roman school, I heard nothing but God, and how I must be good, and sin is evil, and how wicked to want to be happy in this life, and how I must think only of heaven. Then I met Mr. Mizi and he told me there is no God, and I thought: Ah, now I shall have a fine, handsome man for a husband, and no Church and plenty of fun and dancing and good times. But what I find is that even though there is no God, still I have to be good and not think of dancing or a good time, but only of the time when there is a heaven on earth—sometimes I think these clever men are just as bad as the preachers." And at this she shakes with laughter so much she puts her hand over her mouth, and she makes big eyes at her husband over her hand, and he sighs and says, patiently: "There is a certain amount of truth in what you say. There was once a time in the development of society when religion was progressive and held all the goodness of mankind, but now that goodness and hope belongs to the movements of the people everywhere in the world."

These words make no sense to Jabavu and he looks at Mrs. Mizi for help, like a small child at its mother. And it is true that she knows more of what is passing through his mind than either of the two clever men or even Mrs. Samu, who has none of the child left in her.

Mrs. Mizi sees Jabavu's eyes, demanding love from her, and protection from the harshness of the men, and she nods and smiles at him, as if to say: Yes, I laugh, but you should listen, for they are right in what they say. And Jabavu drops his head and thinks: For the whole of my life I must work for one pound a month and study at nights and have no fine clothes or dancing . . . and he feels his old hunger raging in him, saying: Run, run quickly, before it is too late.

But the men of light see so clearly what should be Jabavu's proper path that to them it seems no more needs to be said, and they go on to discuss how a leader should arrange his life, just as if Jabavu were already a leader. They say that such a man must behave so that no one may say: He is a bad man. He must be sober and law-abiding, he must be careful never to infringe even the slightest of the pass-laws, nor forget to have a light on his bicycle or be out after curfew, for—and here they smile as if it were the best of jokes—they get plenty of attention from the police as things are. If they are entrusted with money they must be able to account for every penny—"As if," says Mizi, giggling, "it were money from heaven which God will ask them to account for." And they must each have one wife only, and be faithful to her—but here Mrs. Mizi says, playfully, that even without these considerations Mr. Mizi would have one woman only, and so he needn't blame that on the evils of the time.

At this, everyone laughs a great deal, even Mr. Mizi; but they see Jabavu does not laugh at all, but sits silent, face puckered with difficult thought. And then Mr. Samu tells the following story, for the proper education of Jabavu, while the voices bicker and argue inside him so loudly he can hardly hear Mr. Samu's voice above them.

"Mr. Mizi," says Mr. Samu, "is an example to all who wish to lead the African people to a better life. He was once a messenger at the Office of the Native Commissioner, and even an interpreter, and so was respected and earned a good salary. Yet, because he was forbidden, as employee of the Government, to talk at meetings or even be a member of the League, he saved his money, which took him many years, until he had enough to buy a little store in the Township, and so he left his employment and became independent. Yet now he must struggle to make a living, for it would be a terrible thing for the League if a leader should be accused of charging high prices or cheating, and this means that the other stores always make more money than the store of Mr. and Mrs. Mizi, and so . . ."

Very late, Jabavu is asked if he will sleep there for that night, and in the morning work will be found for him in a factory. Jabavu thanks Mr. Mizi, then Mr. Samu, but in a low and troubled voice. He is taken to the kitchen, where the son is still sitting over his books. There is a bed in the kitchen for his son, and a mattress is put on the floor for Jabavu. Mrs. Mizi says to her son: "Now that is enough studying, go to bed," and he rises unwillingly from his books and leaves the kitchen to wash before sleeping. And Jabavu stands awkwardly beside the mattress and watches Mrs. Mizi arrange the bedclothes of the son more comfortably; and he feels a strong desire to tell her everything, how he longs to devote himself to becoming a man of light, while at the same time he dreads it; but he does not, for he is ashamed. Then Mrs. Mizi straightens herself and looks kindly at him. She comes to him and puts her hand on his arm, saying: "Now, my son, I tell you a little secret. Mr. Mizi and Mr. Samu are not so alarming as they sound." Here she giggles, while she keeps giving him concerned glances, and pushes his arm once or twice as if to say: Laugh a little, then things will seem easier! But Jabavu cannot laugh. Instead, his hand goes into his pocket and he brings out the shilling, and before he knows what he is doing he has pushed it into her hand. "Now, what is this?" she asks, astonished. "It is a shilling. For the work." And now he longs above all that she should take the shilling and understand what he is saying. And at once she does. She stands there, looking at the shilling in her palm, then at Jabavu, and then she nods and smiles. "That is well, my son," she says, in a soft voice. "That is very well. I shall give it to Mr. Mizi and tell him you have given your last shilling to the work he does." And she again puts her two hands on his arms and presses them warmly, then bids him good night and goes out.

Almost at once the son comes back and, having shut the doors so that his mother will not see and scold him, goes back to the books.

Jabavu lies on his mattress, and his heart is warm and big with love for Mrs. Mizi and her kindness, also his good intentions for the future. And then, lying warm and idle there, he sees how the son's eyes are thick and red with studying, how he is serious and stern, just like his father, and yet he is the same age as Jabavu, and a cold dismay enters Jabavu, in spite of his desire to live like a good man, and he cannot help thinking: And must I also be like this, working all day and then at night as well, and all this for other people? It is in the misery of his thought that he falls asleep and dreams, and although he does not know what it is he dreams, he struggles and calls out, so loudly that Mrs. Mizi, who has crept to the door to make sure her son has been sensible and gone to bed, hears him and clicks her tongue in compassion. Poor boy, she thinks, poor boy . . . And so goes again to her bed, praying, as is her habit before sleep, but secretly, for Mr. Mizi would be angry if he knew. She prays, as she has been taught in the Mission School of the Romans, for the soul of Jabavu, who needs help in his struggle against the temptations of the shebeens and matsotsis, and she prays for her son, of whom she is rather afraid, since he is so serious all the time and has always known exactly what he intends to become.

She prays so long, sitting in her bed, that Mr. Mizi wakes and says: "Eh, now, my wife, and what is this you are doing?" And she says meekly: "But nothing at all." And he says gruffly: "And now sleep; that is better for our work than praying." And she says: "Surely times are so bad for our people that praying can do no harm, at least." And he says: "You are nothing but a child—sleep." And so she lies down, and husband and wife go to sleep in great contentment with each other and with Jabavu. Mr. Mizi is already planning how he will first test Jabavu for loyalty, and then train him, and then teach him how to speak at meetings, and then . . .

Jabavu wakes from a bad dream when a cold, grey glimmer is already coming through the small window. The son is lying across his bed, asleep, still fully dressed, he has been too tired to remove his clothes.

He rises, light as a wild-cat, and goes to the table where the books lie tumbled, and looks at them. The words on them are so long and difficult he does not know what they mean. There he stands, silently, stiffly, in the small, cold kitchen, his hands clenched, his eyes rolling this way and that, first towards the clever and serious young man, who is worn out with his studying, and then towards the window, where the morning light is coming. For a very long time does Jabavu stand there, suffering with the violence of his feelings. Ah, he does not know what to do. First he takes a step towards the window, then he moves towards his mattress as if to lie down, and all the time his hunger roars and burns in him like a fire. He hears voices saying: Jabavu, Jabavu—but he does not know whether they commend a rich man with smart clothes or a man of light with knowledge and a strong, persuasive voice.

And then the storm dies in him and he is empty, all feeling gone. He tiptoes to the window, slips the catch up, and is over the sill and out. There is a small bush beneath, and he crouches behind it, looking around him. Houses and trees seem to rise from shadows of night into morning, for the sky is clear and grey, flushed pink in long streaks, and yet there are street-lamps glimmering pale above dim roads. And along these narrow roads move an army of people going to work, although Jabavu had imagined everything would still be deserted. If he had known, he would never have risked running away; but now he must somehow get from the bush to the road without being seen. There he crouches, shivering with cold, watching the people go past, listening to the thudding of their feet, and then it seems to him as if one of them is looking at him. It is a young man, slim, with a narrow, alert head, and eyes which look everywhere. He is one of the matsotsis, for his clothes say so. His trousers are narrow at the bottom, his shoulders are sharp, he wears a scarf of bright red. Over this scarf, it seems, his eyes peer at the bush where Jabavu is. Yet it is impossible, for Jabavu has never seen him before. He straightens himself, pretends he has been urinating into the bush, and walks calmly out into the road. And at once the young man moves over and walks beside him. Jabavu is afraid and he does not know why, and he says nothing, keeping his eyes fixed in front of him.

"And how is the clever Mr. Mizi?" enquires the strange young man at last, and Jabavu says: "I do not know who you are."

At this the young man laughs and says: "My name is Jerry, so now you know me." Jabavu's steps quicken, and Jerry's feet move faster also.

"And what will clever Mr. Mizi say when he knows you climbed out of his window?" asks Jerry, in his light, unpleasant voice, and he begins to whistle softly, with a smile on his face, as if he finds his own whistling very nice.

"I did not," says Jabavu, and his voice quivers with fear.

"Well, well. Yet last night I saw you go into the house with Mr. Mizi and Mr. Samu, and this morning you climb out of the window, how is that?" asks Jerry, in the same light voice, and Jabavu stops in the middle of the road and asks: "Why do you watch me?"

"I watch you for Betty," says Jerry, gaily, and continues to whistle. Jabavu slowly goes on, and he is wishing with all his heart he is back on Mrs. Mizi's mattress in the kitchen. He can see that this is very bad for him, but he does not yet know why. And so he thinks: Why am I afraid? What can this Jerry do? I must not be like a small child. And he says: "I do not know you, I do not want to see Betty, so now go away from me."

Jerry says, making his voice ugly and threatening: "Betty will kill you. She told me to tell you she will come with her knife and kill you."

And Jabavu suddenly laughs, saying truthfully: "I am not afraid of Betty's knife. She talks too much of it."

Jerry is quiet for a few breaths, he is looking at Jabavu in a new way. Then he, too, laughs and says: "Quite right, my friend. She is silly girl."

"She is very silly girl," agrees Jabavu, heartily, and both laugh and move closer together as they walk.

"What will you do next?" asks Jerry, softly, and Jabavu answers: "I do not know." He stops again, thinking: If I return quickly I can climb back through the window before anyone wakes, and no one will know I climbed out. But Jerry seems to know what he is thinking, for he says: "It is a good joke you climb out of Mr. Mizi's window like a thief," and Jabavu says quickly: "I am not a thief." Jerry laughs and says: "You are a big thief, Betty told me. You are very clever she says. You steal quickly so that no one knows." He laughs a little and says: "And what will Mr. Mizi say if I tell him how you steal?"

Jabavu asks, foolishly: "And will you tell him?" Again Jerry laughs, but does not answer, and Jabavu walks on silently. It takes some time for the truth to come into his head, and even then it is hard to believe. Then Jerry asks, still light and gay: "And what did Mr. Mizi say when you told him you had been at the shebeen and about Betty?"

"I told him nothing," says Jabavu, sullenly, then he understands at last why Jerry is doing this, and he says eagerly: "I told him nothing at all, nothing, and that is the truth."

Jerry only walks on, smiling unpleasantly. Then Jabavu says: "And why are you afraid of Mr. Mizi . . ." But he cannot finish for Jerry has whipped round and glares at him: "Who has told you I am afraid? I am afraid of that . . . skellum." And he calls Mr. Mizi names Jabavu has never heard in his life.

"Then I do not understand you," says Jabavu, in his simplicity, and Jerry says: "It is true you understand nothing. Mr. Mizi is a dangerous man. Because the police do not like him for what he does, he is very quick to tell the police if he knows of a theft or a fight. And he is making big trouble. Last month he held a meeting in the hall, and he spoke about crime. He said it was the duty of every African to prevent skokiaan drinking and fighting and stealing, and to help the police close the shebeens and clean up Poland Johannesburg." Jerry speaks with great contempt, and Jabavu thinks suddenly: Mr. Mizi does not like enjoying himself so he stops other people doing it. But he is half-ashamed of this thought; first he says to himself: Yes, it would be good if Poland Joahnnesburg were cleaned up, then he says, hungrily: But I like dancing very much . . .

"And so," Jerry goes on calmly, "we do not like Mr. Mizi."

Jabavu wishes to say that he likes Mr. Mizi very much, and yet he cannot. Something stops him. He listens while Jerry talks on and on about Mr. Mizi, calling him those names that are new to Jabavu, and he can think of nothing to say. And then Jerry changes his voice and asks, threateningly: "What did you steal from Mr. Mizi?"

"I steal from Mr. Mizi?" says Jabavu, amazed. "But why should I steal there?" Jerry grabs his arm, stops him, and says: "That is rich man, he has a store, he has a good house. And you tell me you stole nothing? Then you are a fool, and I do not believe you." Jabavu stands helpless because of his surprise while he feels Jerry's quick fingers moving as light as wind through his pockets. Then Jerry stands away from him, in complete astonishment, and, unable to believe what his own fingers have told him, goes through every pocket again. For there is nothing there but a comb, a mouth-organ, and a piece of soap. "Where have you hidden it?" asks Jerry, and Jabavu stares at him. For this is the beginning of that inability to understand each other which will one day, and not so long distant, lead to bad trouble. Jerry simply cannot believe that Jabavu let an opportunity for stealing go past; while Jabavu could no more steal from the Mizis or the Samus than he could from his parents or his brother. Then Jerry decides to put on a show of belief, and says: "Well, I have been told they are rich. They have all the money from the League in their house." Jabavu is silent. Jerry says: "And did you not see where it is hidden?" Jabavu makes an unwilling movement of his shoulders and looks about for escape. They have reached a cross-roads, and Jabavu stops. He is so simple that he thinks of turning to the right, on the road that leads to the city, with the idea that he may return to Alice and ask her help. But one look at Jerry's face tells him it is not possible, and so he walks beside him on the other road that leads towards Poland Johannesburg. "Let us go and see Betty," says Jerry. "She is a silly girl, but she's nice too." He looks at Jabavu to make him laugh, and Jabavu laughs in just the way he wants; and in a few moments the two young men are saying of Betty that she is like this and like that, her body is so, her breasts so, and anyone looking at the two young men as they walk along, laughing, would think they are good friends, happy to be together.

And it is true that there is a part of Jabavu that is excited at the idea he will soon be in the shebeens and with Betty, although he comforts himself that soon he will run away from Jerry and go back to the Mizis', and he even believes it.

He expects they will go to Betty's room in Mrs. Kambusi's house, but they go past it and down a slope towards a small river, and up the other side, and there is an old shack of a building which looks as if it were disused. There are trees and bushes all around it, and they go quickly through these, and to the back of the place, and through a window which looks as if it were locked, but opens under the pressure of Jerry's knife, which he slides up against the latch. And inside Jabavu sees not only Betty, but half a dozen others, young men and a girl; and as he stands in fear, wondering what will happen, and looking crookedly at Betty, Jerry says in a cheerful voice: "And this is the friend Betty told you about," and winks, but so Jabavu does not see. And they greet him, and he sits down beside them. It is an empty room which was once a store, but now has some boxes for chairs and a big packing-case in the middle where there are candles stuck in their grease, and packs of cards, and bottles of various kinds of drink. No one is drinking, but they offer Jabavu food, and he eats. Betty is quiet and polite, and yet when he looks at her eyes he knows she likes him as much as before, and this makes him uneasy, and he is altogether uncomfortable and full of fear because he does not know what they want with him. Yet as time passes he loses his fear. They seem full of laughter, and without violence. Betty's knife does not leave her handbag, and all that happens is that she comes to sit near him and says, with rolling eyes: "Are you pleased to see me again?" and Jabavu says that he is, and it is true.

Later they go to the Township and see the film show, and Jabavu is lifted clean out of his fear into a state so delirious that he does not notice how the others look at each other and smile. For it is a film of cowboys and Indians and there is much shooting and yelling and riding about on horses, and Jabavu imagines himself shooting and yelling and prancing about on a horse as he sees it on the screen. He wishes to ask how the pictures are made, but he does not want to show his ignorance to the others who take it all for granted. Afterwards it is midday and they go back, but in ones and twos, secretly to the disused store, and play cards. And by now Jabavu has forgotten that part of himself that wishes to become like Mr. Mizi and be Mrs. Mizi's son. It seems natural that he should play cards and sometimes put his hand on Betty's breasts, and drink. They are drinking kaffir beer, properly made, which means it is illegal, since no African is allowed to make it in the Township for sale. And when evening comes Jabavu is drunk, but not unpleasantly so, and his scruples about being here seem unimportant and even childish, and he whispers to Betty that he wishes to come to her room. Betty glances at Jerry, and for a moment rage fills Jabavu, for he thinks that perhaps Jerry, too, sleeps with Betty when he wishes—yet this morning he knew it, for Jerry said so, and then he did not mind, he and Jerry were calling her names and a whore. Now it is all different, and he does not like to remember it. But Betty says meekly, Yes, he may come, and he goes out with her, but not before Jerry has told him to meet him next morning so that they may work together. At the word "work" everyone laughs, and Jabavu too. Then he goes with Betty to her room, and is careful to slip in through the big room filled with dancers at a time when Mrs. Kambusi is not in it, for he is ashamed to see her, and Betty humours him in everything he does and takes him to her bed as if she has been thinking of nothing else ever since he left. Which is nearly true, but not quite; she has been made to think by Jerry, and very disagreeably indeed, of her disloyalty and folly in becoming involved with Jabavu. When she first told him he was much angrier than she had expected, although she knew he would be angry. He beat her and threatened her and questioned her so long and brutally that she lost her head, which is never very strong at any time, and told all sorts of lies so conflicting that even now Jerry does not know what is the truth.

First she said she did not know Jabavu knew Mr. Mizi, then she said she thought it would be useful to have someone in the gang who could tell them at any time what Mr. Mizi's plans were—but at this Jerry slapped her and she began to cry. Then she lost her head and said she intended to marry Jabavu and they would have a gang of their own—but it was not long before she was very very sorry indeed she had said that. For Jerry took out his knife, which unlike hers was meant for use and not show, and in a few moments she was writhing with inarticulate terror. So Jerry left her, with clear and certain orders which even her foolish head could not mistake.

But Jabavu, on this evening, is thinking only that he is jealous of Jerry, and will not support that another man sleeps with Betty. And he talks so long of it that she tells him, sulkily, that he has learned nothing yet, for surely he can see by looking at Jerry that he is not interested in women at all? This subtlety of the towns is so strange to Jabavu that it is some time before he understands it, and when he does he is filled with contempt for Jerry, and from this contempt makes a resolution that it is folly to be afraid of him, and he will go to the Mizis'.

In the morning Betty wakes him early and tells him he must go and meet Jerry in such and such a place; and Jabavu says he does not wish to go, but will return instead to the men of light. And at this Betty springs up and leans towards him with frightened eyes and says: "Have you not understood that Jerry will kill you?" And Jabavu says: "I will have reached the Mizis' house before he can kill me," and she says: "Do not be like a child. Jerry will not allow it." And Jabavu says: "I do not understand this feeling about Mr. Mizi—he does not like the police either." And she says: "Perhaps it is because once Jerry himself stole money from Mr. Samu that belonged to the League, and . . ." But Jabavu laughs at this and embraces her into compliance, and whispers to her that he will go to the Mizis' and change his life and become honest, and then he will marry her. He does not mean to do this, but Betty loves him, and between her fear of Jerry and love for Jabavu, she can only cry, lying on the bed, her face hidden. Jabavu leans over her and says that he longs only for that night so that he may see her again, a thing that he heard a cowboy say on the pictures which they all visited together, and then he kisses her long and hard, exactly as he saw a kiss done between that cowboy and the lovely girl, and with this he goes out, thinking he will go quickly to Mr. Mizi's house. But almost at once he sees Jerry waiting for him behind one of the tall brick huts.

Jabavu greets Jerry as if he were not at all surprised to see him there, which does not deceive Jerry in the least, and the two young men go towards the market, which is already open for buying, although it is so early, because the sellers sleep on their places at night, and they buy some cold boiled mealies and eat them walking along the road to the city. They walk in company with many others, some on bicycles. It is now about seven in the morning. The house-boys and cooks and nannies have gone to work a good hour since, these are the workers for the factories, and Jabavu sees their ragged clothes, and how poor they are, and how much less clever than Jerry, and cannot help feeling pleased he is not one of them. So resentful is he against Mr. Mizi for wanting him to go into a factory, he begins to make fun of the men of light again, and Jerry laughs and applauds, and every now and again says a little bit more to spur Jabavu on.

So begins the most bewildering, frightening and yet exciting day Jabavu has ever known. Everything that happens shocks him, makes him tremble, and yet—how can he not admire Jerry, who is so cool, so quick, so fearless? He feels like a child beside him, and this happens before they have even begun their "work."

For Jerry takes him first to the back room of an Indian trader. This is a shop for Africans to buy in, and they may enter it easily with all the others who move in and out and loiter on the pavements. They stand for a while in the shop, listening to a gramophone playing jazz music, and then the Indian himself looks at them in a certain way, and the two young men slip unnoticed into a side room and through that into the back room. It is heaped with every kind of thing: second-hand clothes, new clothes, watches, and clocks, shoes—but there is no end to them. Jerry tells Jabavu to take off his clothes. They both do so, and put on ordinary clothes, so that they may look like everyone else; khaki shorts, and Jabavu's have a patch at the back, and rather soiled white shirts. No tie and only canvas sandals for their feet. Jabavu's feet are very happy to be released from the thick leather shoes, yet Jabavu mourns to part with them, even for a time.

Then Jerry takes a big basket, which has a few fresh vegetables in it, and they leave the back room, but this time through the door into the street. Jabavu asks who the Indian is, but Jerry says, curtly, that he is an Indian who helps them in their work, which tells Jabavu nothing. They walk up through the area of kaffir shops and Indian stores, and Jabavu looks marvelling at Jerry, who seems to be quite different, like a rather simple country boy, with a fresh and open face. Only his eyes are still the same, quick, cunning, narrow. They come to a street of white people's houses, and Jerry and Jabavu go to a back door and call out that they have vegetables

for sale. A voice shouts at them to go away. Jerry glances quickly
around: there is a table on the back verandah with a pretty cloth on
it, and he whisks it off, rolls it so fast that Jabavu can scarcely see
his fingers move, and it vanishes under the vegetables. The two
walk slowly away, just like respectable vegetable sellers. And in the
next house, the white woman buys a cabbage, and while she is
fetching money from inside, Jerry takes, through an open window,
a clock and an ashtray, and these are hidden under the vegetables.
In the next house there is nothing to be stolen, for the woman is
sitting on her back verandah knitting where she may see everything, but in the next there is another cloth.

Then there is a moment which makes Jabavu feel very bad,
though to Jerry it is a matter for great laughter: a policeman asks
them what they carry in the basket, but Jerry tells him a long, sad
story, very confused, about how they are for the first time in the
city and cannot find their way, and so the policeman is very kind
and helps them with good advice.

When Jerry has finished laughing at the policeman, he says:
"And now we will do something hard, everything we have done so
far has been work for children." Jabavu says he does not want to
get into trouble, but Jerry says he will kill Jabavu if he does not do
as he is told. And this troubles Jabavu for he never knows, when
Jerry laughs and speaks in such a way, whether he means it or not.
One minute he thinks: Jerry is making a joke; the next he is trembling. Yet there are moments, when they make jokes together,
when he feels Jerry likes him—altogether, he is more confused
about Jerry than about anyone he has known. One may say: Betty
is like this or that, Mr. Mizi is like this, but about Jerry there is
something difficult, shadowy, and even in the moments when Jabavu cannot help liking him.

They go into a shop for white people. It is a small shop, very
crowded. There is a white man serving behind the counter, and he
is busy all the time. There are several women waiting to buy. One
of them has a baby in a carriage and she has put her handbag at
the foot of this carriage. Jerry glances at the bag and then at Jabavu, who knows quite well what is meant. His heart goes cold, but
Jerry's eyes are so frightening that he knows he must take it.

The woman is talking to a friend and swinging the carriage a
little way forwards, a little back, while the baby sleeps. Jabavu
feels a cold wetness running down his back, his knees are soft. But
he waits for when the white man has turned to reach something
down from a shelf and the woman is laughing with her friend, and

he nips the bag quickly out and walks through the door with it. There Jerry takes it and slips it under the vegetables. "Do not run," says Jerry, quietly. His eyes are darting everywhere, though his face is calm. They walk quickly around a corner and go into another shop. In this shop they steal nothing, but buy sixpence worth of salt. Afterwards Jerry says to Jabavu, and with real admiration: "You are very good at this work. Betty told the truth. I have seen no one before who is so good so soon after beginning." And Jabavu cannot help feeling proud, for Jerry is not one who gives praise easily.

They leave that part of the town and do a little more stealing in another, collecting another clock, some spoons and forks, and then, but by chance, a second handbag which is left on a table in a kitchen.

And then they return to the Indian shop. There Jerry bargains with the Indian, who gives them two pounds for the various articles, and there is five pounds from the two handbags. Jerry gives Jabavu one-third of the money, but Jabavu is suddenly so angry that Jerry pretends to laugh, and says he was only joking, and gives Jabavu the half that is due to him. And then Jerry says: "It is now two o'clock in the afternoon. In these few hours we have each earned three pounds. The Indian takes the risk of selling those things that were stolen and might be recognised. We are safe. And now—what do you think of this work?"

Jabavu says, after a pause that is a little too long, for Jerry gives him a quick, suspicious look: "I think it is very fine." Then he says timidly: "Yet my pass for seeking work is only for fourteen days, and some of those have gone."

"I will show you what to do," says Jerry, carelessly. "It is easy. Living here is very easy for those who use their heads. Also, one must know when to spend money. Also, there are other things. It is useful to have a woman who makes a friend of a policeman. With us, there are two such women. Each has a policeman. If there should be trouble, those two policemen would help us. Women are very important in this work."

Jabavu thinks about this, and then says quickly: "And is Betty one of the women?"

Jerry, who has been waiting for this, says calmly: "Yes, Betty is very good for the police." And then he says: "Do not be a big fool. With us, there is no jealousy. I do not allow it. I would not have women in the gang, since they are foolish with the work, except they are useful for the police. And I tell you now, I will have no trouble over the policeman. If Betty says to you: Tonight there is my policeman coming, then you say nothing. Otherwise . . ." And Jerry slips the half of his knife a little way from his pocket so that Jabavu may see it. Yet he remains smiling and friendly, as if it is all a joke. And Jabavu walks on in silence. For the first time he understands clearly that he is now one of the gang, that Jerry is his leader, that Betty is his woman. And this state of affairs will continue—but for how long? Is there no way of escaping? He asks, timidly: "How long has there been this gang?"

Jerry does not reply at once. He does not trust Jabavu yet. But since that morning he has changed his mind about him, for he had planned to make Jabavu steal and then see that he got into trouble with the police in such a way that would implicate no one else, thus removing him as a danger. Yet he is so impressed with Jabavu's quickness and cleverness at the "work" that he wishes to keep him. He thinks: After another week of our good life, when he has stolen several times and perhaps been in a fight or two, he will be too frightened to go near Mr. Mizi. He will be one of us, and in perfect safety for us all. He says: "I have been leader of this gang for two years. There are seven in the gang, two women, five men. The men do the stealing, as we have this morning. The women are friends of the police, they make a friend of anyone who might be dangerous. Also, they pick up kraal boys who come to the town and steal from them. We do not allow the women to go into the streets or shops for stealing, because they are no good. Also, we do not tell the women the business of the gang, because they talk and because they do foolish things." Here there is a pause, and Jabavu knows that Jerry is thinking that he himself is just such a foolish thing that Betty did. But he is flattered because Jerry tells him things the women are not told. He asks: "And I would like to know other matters: supposing one of us gets caught, what would happen then?" And Jerry replies: "In the two years I have been leader not one has been caught. We are very careful. But if you are caught, then you will not speak of the others, otherwise something will happen you won't like." Again he slips up the haft of his knife, and again he is smiling as if it is all a joke. When Jabavu asks another question, he says: "That is enough for today. You will learn the business of the gang in good time."

And Jabavu, thinking about what he has been told, understands that in fact he knows very little and that Jerry does not trust him. With this, his longing for Mr. Mizi returns, and he curses himself bitterly for running away. And he thinks sadly of Mr. Mizi all the way along the road, and hardly notices where they are going.

They have turned off to a row of houses where the coloured people live. The house they enter is full of people, children everywhere, and they go through to the back and enter a small, dirty room that is dark and smells bad. A coloured man is lying on a bed in a corner, and Jabavu can hear the breath wheezing through his chest before he is even inside the door. He rises, and in the dimness of the room Jabavu sees a stooping, lean man, yellow with sickness beyond his natural colour, his eyes peering through the whitish gum that is stuck around the lashes, his mouth open as the breath heaves in and out. And as soon as he sees Jerry he slaps Jerry on the shoulder, and Jerry slaps him, but too hard for the sickness, for he reels back, coughing and spluttering, gripping his arms across his painful chest, but he laughs as soon as he has breath. And Jabavu wonders at this terrible laughter which comes so often with these people, for what is funny about what is happening now? Surely it is ugly and fearful that this man is so sick and the room is dirty and evil, with the dirty, ragged children running and screaming along the passages outside? Jabavu is stunned with the horror of the place, but Jerry laughs some more and calls the coloured man some rude and cheerful names, and the man calls Jerry bad names and laughs. Then they look at Jabavu and Jerry says: "Here is another cookboy for you," and at this they both rock with laughter until the man begins coughing again, and at last is exhausted and leans against the wall, his eyes shut, while his chest heaves. Then he gasps out, smiling painfully: "How much?" and Jerry begins to bargain, as Jabavu has heard him with the Indian. The coloured man, through coughing and wheezing, sticks to his point, that he wants two pounds for pretending to employ Jabavu, and that every month; but Jerry says ten shillings, and at last they agree on one pound, which Jabavu can see was understood from the first—so why these long minutes of bargaining through the ugly, hurtful coughing and smell of sickness? Then the coloured man gives Jabavu a note saying he wishes to employ him as a cook, and writes his name in Jabavu's situpa. And then, peering close, showing his broken, dirty teeth, he wheezes out: "So you will be a good cook, hee, hee, hee . . ." And at this they go out, both young men, shutting the door behind them, and down the dim passage through the children, and so out into the fresh and lovely sunshine, which has the power of making that ugly, broken house seem quite pleasant among its bushes of hibiscus and frangipani. "That man will die soon," says Jabavu, in a small, dispirited voice; but all he hears from Jerry is: "Well, he will last the month at least, and there are others who will do you this favour for a pound."

And Jabavu's heart is so heavy with fear of the sickness and the ugliness that he thinks: I will go now, I cannot stay with these people. When Jerry tells him he must go to the Pass Office to have his employment registered, he thinks: And now I shall take this chance to run to Mr. Mizi. But Jerry has no intention of letting Jabavu have any such chance. He strolls with him to the Pass Office, on the way buying a bottle of white man's whisky from another coloured man who does this illegal trade, and while Jabavu stands in the queue of waiting people at the Pass Office Jerry waits cheerfully, the bottle under his coat, and even chats with the policeman.

When at last Jabavu has had his situpa examined and the business is over, he comes back to Jerry thinking: *Hau*, but this Jerry is brave. He fears nothing, not even talking to a policeman while he has a bottle of whisky under his coat.

They walk together back to the Native Township, and Jerry says, laughing: "And now you have a job and are a very good boy." Jabavu laughs too, as loudly as he can. Then Jerry says: "And so your great friend Mr. Mizi can be pleased with you. You are a worker and very respectable." They both laugh again, and Jerry gives Jabavu a quick look from his cold, narrow eyes, for he is above all not a fool, and Jabavu's laughter is rather as if he wishes to cry. He is thinking how best to handle Jabavu when chance helps him, for Mrs. Samu crosses their path, in her white dress and white cap, on her way to the hospital, where she is on duty. She first looks at Jabavu as if she does not know him at all; then she gives him a small, cold smile, which is the most her goodness of heart can do, and is more the goodness of Mrs. Mizi's heart, who has been saying: "Poor boy, he cannot be blamed, only pitied," and things of that sort. Mrs. Samu has much less heart than Mrs. Mizi, but much more head, and it is hard to know which is most useful; but in this case she is thinking: Surely there are better things to worry about than a little skellum of a matsotsi? And she goes on to the hospital, thinking about a woman who has given birth to a baby who has an infection of the eyes.

But Jabavu's eyes are filled with tears and he longs to run after Mrs. Samu and beg for her protection. Yet how can a woman protect him against Jerry?

Jerry begins to talk about Mrs. Samu, and in a clever way. He laughs and says what hypocrites! They talk about goodness and crime, and yet Mrs. Samu is Mr. Samu's second wife, and Mr. Samu treated his first wife so badly she died of it, and now Mrs. Samu is nothing but a bitch who is always ready, why she even made advances to Jerry himself at a dance; he could have had her by pushing her over . . . Then Jerry goes on to Mr. Mizi and says he is a fool for trusting Mrs. Mizi, whose eyes invite everybody, and there is not a soul in the Township who does not know she sleeps with Mrs. Samu's brother. All these men of light are the same, their women are light, and they are like a herd of baboons, no better . . . and Jerry continues to speak thus, laughing about them, until Jabavu, remembering the coldness of Mrs. Samu's smile, half-heartedly agrees, and then he makes a rude joke about Mrs. Samu's uniform, which is very tight across her buttocks, and suddenly the two young men are roaring with laughter and saying women are this and that. And so they return to the others, who are not in the empty store now, for it does not do to be in one place too often, but in one of the other shebeens, which is much worse than Mrs. Kambusi's. There they spend the evening, and Jabavu again drinks skokiaan, but with discretion, for he fears what he will feel next day. And as he drinks he notices that Jerry also drinks no more than a mouthful, but pretends to be drunk, and is watching how Jabavu drinks. Jerry is pleased because Jabavu is sensible, yet he does not altogether like it, for it is necessary for him to think that he is the only one stronger than the others. And for the first time it comes into his head that perhaps Jabavu is a little too strong, too clever, and may be a challenge to himself some day. But all these thoughts he hides behind his narrow, cold eyes, and only watches, and late that night he speaks to Jabavu as an equal, saying how they must now see that these fools get to bed without harm. Jabavu takes Betty and two of the young men to Betty's room, where they fall like logs across the floor, snoring off the skokiaan, and Jerry takes one girl and the other men to a place he knows, an old hut of straw on the edge of the veld.

In the morning Jerry and Jabavu wake clear-headed, leaving the others to sleep off their sickness, and they go together to the town, where they steal very well and cleverly, another clock and two pairs of shoes and a baby's pillow from under its head, and also, and most important, some trinkets which Jerry says are gold. When these things are taken by the Indian, he offers much money for them. Jerry says as they walk back to the Township: "And on the

second day we each make five pounds . . ." and looks hard at Jabavu so that he may not miss what he means. And Jabavu today is
easier about Mr. Mizi, for he admires himself for not drinking the
skokiaan, and for working with Jerry so cleverly that there is no
difference between them.

That night they all go to the deserted store where they drink
whisky, which is better than the skokiaan, for it does not make
them sick. They play cards and eat well; and all the time Jerry
watches Jabavu, and with very mixed thoughts. He sees that he
does as he pleases with Betty, although never before has Betty been
so humble and anxious with a man. He sees how he is careful what
he drinks—and never has he seen a boy raw from the kraals learning sense so quickly with the drink. He sees how the others already,
after two days, speak to Jabavu with almost the respect they have
for him. And he does not like this at all. Nothing of what he is
thinking does he show, and Jabavu feels more and more that Jerry
is a friend. And next day they go again to the white streets and
steal, and afterwards drink whisky and play cards. The next day
also, and so a week passes. All that time Jerry is soft-speaking,
polite, smiling; his cold, watchful eyes hooded in discretion and
cunning, and Jabavu is speaking freely of what he feels. He has
told of his love for Mrs. Mizi, his admiration for Mr. Mizi. He has
spoken with the free confidence of a little child, and Jerry has listened, leading him on with a soft, sly word or a smile, until by the
end of that week there is a strange way of speaking indeed. Jerry
will say: "And about the Mizis . . ." And Jabavu will say: "Ah,
they are clever, they are brave." And Jerry will say, in a soft, polite
voice: "You think that is so?" And Jabavu will say: "Ah, my friend,
those are men who think only of others." And Jerry will say: "You
think so?" But in that soft, deadly, polite voice. And then he will
talk a little, as if he does not care at all, about the Mizis or the
Samus, how once they did this or that, and how they are cunning,
and then state suddenly and with violence: "Ah, what a skellum!"
or "Now that is a bitch." And Jabavu will laugh and agree. It is as if
there are two Jabavus, and one of them is brought into being by the
clever tongue of Jerry. But Jabavu himself is hardly aware of it. For
it may seem strange that a man can spend his time stealing and
drinking and making love to a woman of the town and yet think of
himself as something quite different—a man who will become a
man of light, yet this is how things are with Jabavu. So confused is
he, so bound up in the cycle of stealing, and then good food and
drink, then more stealing, then Betty at night, that he is like a

young, powerful, half-broken ox, being led to work by a string around his horns which the man hardly allows him to feel. Yet there are moments when he feels it.

There is a day when Jerry asks casually, as if he does not mind at all: "And so you will leave us and join the men of light?" And Jabavu says, with the simplicity of a child: "Yes, that is what I wish to do." And Jerry allows himself to laugh, and for the first time. And fear goes through Jabavu like a knife, so that he thinks: I am a fool to speak thus to Jerry. And yet in a moment Jerry is making jokes again and saying, "Those skellums," as if he is amused at the folly of the men of light, and Jabavu laughs with him. For above all Jerry is cunning in the use of laughter with Jabavu. He leads Jabavu gently onwards, with jokes, until he becomes serious, and in one moment, and says: "And so you will leave us when you are tired of us and go to Mr. Mizi?" And the seriousness makes Jabavu's tongue stick in his mouth, so that he says nothing. He is like the ox who has been led so softly to the edge of the field, and now there is a pressure around the base of his horns and he thinks: But surely this man cannot mean to make a fool of me? And because he does not wish to understand he stands motionless, his four feet stubborn on the earth, blinking his foolish eyes, and the man watches him thinking: In a moment there will be the fighting, when this stupid ox bellows and roars and leaps into the air, not knowing it is all useless since I am so much more clever than he is.

Jerry, however, does not think of Jabavu quite as the man thinks of the ox. For while he is in every way more cunning and more experienced than Jabavu, yet there is something in Jabavu he cannot handle. There are moments when he wonders: Perhaps it would be better if I let this fool go to Mr. Mizi, why not? I shall threaten to kill him if he speaks of us and our work . . . Yet it is impossible, precisely because of this other Jabavu which is brought into being by the jokes. Once with the Mizis, will not Jabavu have times when he longs for the richness and excitement of the stealing and the shebeens and the women? And at those moments will he not feel the need to call the matsotsis bad names, and perhaps even tell the police? Of course he will. And what will he not be able to tell the police? The names of all the gang, and the coloured men who help them, and the Indian who helps them . . . Jerry wishes bitterly that he had put a knife into Jabavu long ago, when he first heard of him from Betty. Now he cannot, because Betty loves Jabavu, and therefore is dangerous. Ah, how Jerry wishes he had never allowed women into the work; how he wishes he could kill them both . . . Yet he never kills, unless it is really necessary and certainly not two killings at once. But his hatred for Jabavu, and more particularly Betty, grows and deepens, until it is hard for him to shut it down and appear smiling and cool and friendly.

But he does so, and gently he leads Jabavu along the path of dangerous laughter. The jokes they make are frightening, and when Jabavu is frightened by them, he has to say: "Well, but it is a joke only." For they speak of things which would have made him tremble only a few weeks before. First he learns to laugh at the richness of Mr. Mizi, and how this clever skellum hides money in his house and so cheats all the people who trust him. Jabavu does not believe it, but he laughs, and even goes on with the joke, saying: "What fools they are," or "It is more profitable to run a League for the Advancement of the African People than to run a shebeen." And when Jerry speaks of how Mrs. Mizi sleeps with everyone or how Mrs. Samu is in the movement only because of the young men whom she may meet, Jabavu says Mrs. Samu reminds him of the advertisement in the white man's papers: Drink this and you will sleep well at night. Yet all the time Jabavu does not believe any of these things, and he sincerely admires the men of light, and wishes only to be with them.

Later Jerry tightens the leash and says: "One day the men of light will be killed because they are sure skellums," and he makes a joke about such a killing. It takes a few days before Jabavu is ready to laugh, but at last it seems unimportant and a joke only, and he laughs. And then Jerry speaks of Betty and says how once he killed a woman who had become dangerous, and he laughs and says a stupid woman is as bad as a dangerous one, and it would be a good idea to kill Betty. Many days pass before Jabavu laughs, and this is because the idea of Betty being dead makes his heart leap with joy. For Betty has become a burden on his nights so that he dreads them. All night she will wake him, saying: "And now marry me and we will run away to another town," or "Let us kill Jerry, and you may be leader of this gang," or "Do you love me? Do you love me? Do you love me?"—and Jabavu thinks of the women of the old kind who do not talk of love day and night: women with dignity; but at last he laughs. The two young men laugh together, reeling across the road, sometimes, as they speak of Betty, and of women and how they are this and that, until things have changed so that Jabavu laughs easily when Jerry speaks of killing Betty, or any other member of the gang, and they speak with contempt of the others, how they are fools and not clever in the work, and the only two with any sense are Jerry and Jabavu.

Yet underneath the friendship both are very frightened, and both know that something must happen soon, and they watch each other, sideways, and hate each other, and Jabavu thinks all the time of how he may run to Mr. Mizi, while Jerry dreams at night of the police and prison, and often of killing, Jabavu mostly, but Betty too, for his dislike of Betty is becoming like a fever. Sometimes, when he sees how Betty rubs her body against Jabavu, or kisses him, like the cinema, and in front of the others, and how she never takes her eyes away from Jabavu, his hand goes secretly to the knife and fingers it, itching with the need to kill.

The gang itself is confused, for it is as if they have two leaders. Betty stays always beside Jabavu, and her deference towards him influences the others. Also, Jerry has owed his leadership to the fact that he is always clear-headed, never drunk, stronger than anyone else. But now he is not stronger than Jabavu. It is as if some fast-working yeast of dissolution were in the gang, and Jerry names this yeast Mr. Mizi.

There comes a day when he decides to get rid of Jabavu finally one way or the other, although he is so clever with the stealing.

First he speaks persuasively of the mines in Johannesburg, saying how good the life is there, and how much money for people like themselves. But Jabavu listens indifferently, saying: "Yes," and "Is that so?" For why should a man make the dangerous and difficult journey south to the richness of the City of Gold when life is rich where he is? So Jerry drops that plan and tries another. It is a dangerous one, and he knows it. He wishes to make a last attempt to weaken Jabavu by skokiaan. And for six nights he leads them to the shebeens, although usually he discourages his gang from drinking the bad stuff because it muffles their will and their thinking. On the first night things are as usual, the rest drink, but Jerry and Jabavu do not. On the second it is the same. On the third, Jerry challenges Jabavu to a contest and Jabavu first refuses, then consents. For he has reached a state of mind which he by no means understands—it is as if he is ceasing to care what happens. So Jabavu and Jerry drink, and it is Jerry who succumbs first. He wakes on the fourth afternoon to find his gang playing cards, while Jabavu sits against a wall, staring at nothing, already recovered. And now Jerry is filled with hatred against Jabavu such as he has never known before. For Jabavu's sake he has drunk himself stupid, so that he has lain for hours weak and out of his mind, even while his gang play cards and probably laugh at him. It is as if Jabavu is now the leader and not himself. As for Jabavu, his unhappiness has reached a point where something very strange is happening to him. It is as if very slowly he, the real Jabavu, is moving away from the thief and the skellum who drinks and steals, and watches with calm interest, not caring. He thinks there is no hope for him now. Never can he return to Mr. Mizi; never can he be a man of light. There is no future. And so he stares at himself and waits, while a dark grey cloud of misery settles on him.

Jerry comes to him, concealing what he is thinking, and sits by him and congratulates him on having a stronger head. He flatters Jabavu, and then makes jokes at the expense of the others which they cannot hear. Jabavu assents without interest. Then he begins calling Betty names, and then all women names, for it is in these moments,when they are hating women, that they are most nearly good friends. Jabavu joins in the game, indifferently at first, and then with more will. And soon they are laughing together, and Jerry congratulates himself on his cunning. Betty does not like this, and comes to them, and is pushed aside by both, and returns to the others, filled with bitterness, calling them names. And Jerry says how Betty is a dangerous woman, and then tells how once before he killed a girl in the gang who fell in love with a policeman she was supposed to be keeping sweet and friendly. He tells Jabavu this partly to frighten him, partly to see how he will react now at the thought of Betty being killed. And into Jabavu's mind again flickers the thought how pleasant if Betty were no longer there, always boring him with her demands and her complaints, but he pushes it away. And when Jerry sees him frown he swiftly changes the joke into that other about how funny it would be to rob Mr. Mizi. Jabavu sits silent, and for the first time he begins to understand about laughter and jokes, how it is that people laugh most at what they fear, and how a joke is sometimes more like a plan for what will some day be the truth. And he thinks: Perhaps all this time Jerry really was planning to kill, and even to rob Mr. Mizi? And the thought of his own foolishness is so terrible that the misery, which has lifted in the moment of comradeship with Jerry, returns, and he leans silent against the wall, and nothing matters. But this is better for Jerry than he knows, for when he suggests they go to the shebeens, Jabavu rises at once. On that fourth night Jabavu drinks skokiaan and for the first time willingly, and with pleasure, since he came to the Township and drank it a Mrs. Kambusi's. Jerry does not drink, but watches, and he feels an immense relief. Now, he thinks, Jabavu will take to skokiaan like the others, and that will make him weak like the others, and Jerry will lead him like the rest.

On the fifth day Jabavu sleeps till late, and wakes as it grows dark, and finds that the others are already talking about going to the shebeen. But the sickness in him rises at the thought and he says he will not go to the shebeen, but will stay while the others go. And with this he turns his face to the wall, and although Jerry jokes with him and cajoles and jokes, he does not move. But Jerry cannot tell the others that he wishes them to go to the shebeen only for the sake of Jabavu, and so he has to go with them, cursing and bitter, for Jabavu remains in the disused store. So the next day is the sixth, and by now the gang are sodden and sick and stupid with the skokiaan, and Jerry can hardly control them. And Jabavu is bored and calm and sits in his place against the wall, looking at his thoughts, which must be so sad and dark, for his face is heavy with them. Jerry thinks: It was in such a mood that he agreed to drink the night before last, and woos Jabavu to drink again, and Jabavu does. That is the sixth night. Jabavu gets drunk as before, with the others, while Jerry does not. And on the seventh day Jerry thinks: Now this will be the last. If Jabavu does not come willingly to the shebeen tonight, I will give up this plan and try another.

On that seventh day Jerry is truly desperate, though it does not show on his face. There he sits against the wall, while his hands deal out the cards and gather them in, and his eyes watch those cards as if nothing else interested them. Yet from time to time they glance quickly at Jabavu, who is sitting, without moving, opposite him. The others are still not conscious, but are lying on the floor, groaning and complaining in thick voices.

Betty is lying close by Jerry, in a loose, disgusting heap, and he looks at her and hates her. He is full of hate. He is thinking that two months ago he was running the most profitable gang in the Township, there was no danger, the police were controlled sufficiently, there seemed no reason why it should not all go on for a long time. Yet all at once Betty takes a liking to this Jabavu, and now it is at an end, the gang restless, Jabavu dreaming of Mr. Mizi, and nothing is clear or certain.

It is Betty's fault—he hates her. It is Jabavu's fault—ah, how he hates Jabavu! It is Mr. Mizi's fault—if he could he would kill Mr. Mizi, for truly he hates Mr. Mizi more than anyone in the world. But to kill Mr. Mizi would be foolish—for that matter, to kill anyone is foolish, unless there is need for it. He must not kill needlessly. But his mind is filled with thoughts of killing, and he keeps looking at Betty, rolling drunkenly by him, and wishing he could kill her for starting all this trouble, and as the cards go flick! flick! flick! each sharp, small noise seems to him like the sound of a knife.

Then all at once Jerry takes a tight hold of himself and says: I am crazy. What is this? Never in all my life have I done a thing without thought or cause, and now I sit here without a plan, waiting for something to happen—this man Jabavu has surely made me mad!

He looks across at Jabavu and asks, pleasantly: "Will you come to the shebeen tonight for some fun, hey?"

But Jabavu says: "No, I shall not go. That is four times I have drunk the skokiaan and now what I say is true. I shall never drink it again."

Jerry shrugs, and lets his eyes drop. So! he thinks. Well, that has failed. Yet it succeeded in the past. But if it has failed, then I must now think and decide what to do—there must be a way, there is always a way. But what? Then he thinks: Well, and why do I sit here? Before there was just such a matter, when things got too difficult, but that was in another town, and I left that town and came here. It is easy. I can go south to another city. There are always fools, and always work for people like myself. And then, just as this plan is becoming welcome in his mind, he is stung by a foolish vanity: And so I should leave this city, where I have contacts, and know sufficient police, and have an organisation, simply because of this fool Jabavu? I shall not.

And so he sits, dealing the cards, while these thoughts go through his mind, and his face shows nothing, and his anger and fear and spiteful vanity see inside him. Something will happen, he thinks. Something. Wait.

He waits, and soon it grows dark. Through the dirty window-panes comes a flare of reddish light from the sunset which makes blotches and pools of dark red on the floor. Jerry looks at it. Blood, he thinks, and an immense longing fills him. Without thinking, he slides up his knife a little, lovingly fingering the haft of it. He sees that Jabavu is looking at him, and suddenly Jabavu shudders. An immense satisfaction fills Jerry. Ah, how he loves that shudder. He slides up the knife a little further and says: "You have not yet learned to be afraid of this as you should." Jabavu looks at the knife, then at Jerry, then drops his eyes. "I'm afraid," says Jabavu, simply, and Jerry lets the knife slide back. For a moment the thought slides into him: This is nothing but madness. Then it goes again.

Jerry's own feet are now lying in a pool of reddish light from the window, and he quickly moves them back, rises, takes candles from the top of the wall where they lie hidden, sticks them in their grease on the packing-cases, and lights them. The reddish light has gone. Now the room is lit by the warm yellow glow of candles, showing packing-cases, bottles stacked in corners, the huddled bodies of the drunken, and sheets of spider web across the rafters. It is the familiar scene of companionship in drink and gambling, and the violent longing to kill sinks inside Jerry. Again he thinks: I must make a plan, not wait for something to happen. And then, one after another, the bodies move, groaning, and sit up, holding their heads. Then they begin to laugh weakly. When Betty heaves herself up from the floor she sees she is some way from Jabavu, and she crawls to him and falls across his knees, but he quietly pushes her aside. And this sight, for some reason, fills Jerry with irritation. But he suppresses it and thinks: I must make these stupid fools sensible, and wait until they have come out of the skokiaan, and then: Then I shall make a plan.

He fills a large tin with fresh tea from the kettle that boils on the fire he has made on the floor, and gives mugs of it to everyone, including Jabavu, who simply sets it down without touching it. This annoys Jerry, but he says nothing. The others drink, and it helps their sickness, and they sit up, still holding their heads.

"I want to go to the shebeen," says Betty, rocking sideways, back and forth, "I want to go to the shebeen." And the others, taking up her voice without thought, say: "Yes, yes, the shebeen." Jerry whips round, glaring at them. Then he holds down his irritation. And as easily as the desire came into them, it goes. They forget about the shebeen, and drink their tea. Jerry makes more, even stronger, and refills their mugs. They drink. Jabavu watches this scene as if it were a long way from him. He remarks, in a quiet voice: "Tea is not strong enough to silence the anger of the skokiaan. I know. The times I have drunk it, it was as if my body wanted to fall to pieces. Yet they have drunk it each night for a week." Jerry stands near Jabavu, and his face is twitching. Into him has come again that violent need to kill; and yet again he stops it. He thinks: Better if I leave all these fools now . . . But this sensible thought is drowned by a flood of rising vanity. He thinks: I can make them do what I want. Always they do as I say.

He says calmly: "Better if you each take a piece of bread and eat it." In a low voice to Jabavu he says: "Shut up. If you speak again I will kill you." Jabavu makes that indifferent movement of his shoulders and continues to watch. There is a blank look in the darkness of his eyes that frightens Jerry.

Betty staggers to her feet and walks, knees rocking, to the wall where a mirror is hanging on a nail. But before she gets there she says: "I want to go to the shebeen." Again the others repeat the words, and they rise, planting their feet firmly so as not to fall down.

Jerry shouts: "Shut up. You will not go to the shebeen tonight."

Betty laughs, in a high, weak way, and says: "Yes, the shebeen. Yes, yes, I want that badly, to go to the shebeen . . ." The words having started to make themselves, they are likely to continue, and Jerry takes her by her shoulders and shakes her. "Shut up," he says. "Did you hear what I said?"

And Betty laughs, and sways, and puts her arms around him and says: "Nice Jerry, handsome Jerry, oh, please Jerry . . ." She is speaking in a voice like a child trying to get its way. Jerry, who has stood rigid under her touch, eyes fixed and black with anger, shakes her again and flings her off. She goes staggering backwards till she reaches the other wall, and there she sprawls, laughing and laughing, till she straightens again and goes staggering forward towards Jerry, and the others see what she is doing, and it seems very funny to them and they go with her, so that in a moment Jerry is surrounded by them, and they put their arms around his neck and pat his shoulders, and all say, in high, childish voices, laughing as if laughter in them is a kind of a spring, bubbling up and up and forcing its way out of their lips: "Nice Jerry, yes, handsome, please, clever Jerry."

And Jerry snaps out: "Shut up. Get back. I'll kill you all . . ."

His voice surprises them into silence for one moment. It is high, jerky, crazy. And his face twitches and his lips quiver. They stand there around him, looking at him, then at each other, blinking their eyes so that the cloud of skokiaan may clear, then all move back and sit down, save Betty, who stands in front of him. Her mouth stretched in such a way across her face that it might be either laughter or the sound of weeping that will come from it, but it is laughter again, and with a high, cackling sound, just like a hen, she rocks forward, and for the third time her arms go around Jerry and she begins pressing her body against his. Jerry stands quite still. The others, watching, see nothing but that Betty is hugging and squeezing him, with her body and her arms, while she laughs and laughs. Then she stops laughing and her hands loosen and then fall and swing by her side. Jerry holds her with his hand across her back. They set up a yell of laughter because it seems to them very funny. Betty is making some sort of funny joke, and so they must laugh.

But Jerry, in a flush of anger and hatred such as he has never known before, has slipped his knife into Betty, and the movement gave him such joy as he has not felt in all his life. And so he stands, holding Betty, while for a moment he does not think at all. And then the madness of anger and joy vanishes and he thinks: I am truly mad. To kill a person, and for nothing, and in anger . . . He stands holding her, trying to make a plan quickly, and then he sees how Jabavu, just beside him on the floor, is looking up, blinking his eyes in slow wonder, and at once the plan comes to him. He allows himself to stagger a little, as if Betty's weight is too much, then he falls sideways, with Betty, across Jabavu, and there he makes a scuffling movement and rolls away.

Jabavu, feeling a warm wetness come from Betty, thinks: He has killed her and now he will say I killed her. He stands up slowly, and Jerry shouts: "Jabavu has killed her, look, he has killed Betty because he was jealous."

Jabavu does not speak. The thought in his mind is one that shocks him. It is an immense relief that Betty is dead. He had not known how tired he was of this woman, how she weighed on him, knowing that he would never be able to shake her off. And now she lies dead in front of him.

"I did not kill her," he says. "I did not."

The others are standing and staring, like so many chickens. Jerry is shouting: "That skellum—he has killed Betty."

Then Jabavu says: "But I did not."

Their eyes go first to Jerry, and they believe him, then they go to Jabavu, and they believe him.

Jerry stops saying it. He understands they are too stupid to hold any thoughts in their heads longer than a moment.

He seats himself on a packing-case and looks at Betty, while he thinks fast and hard.

Jabavu, after a long, long silence while he looks at Betty, seats himself on another. A feeling of despair is growing so strong in him that his limbs will hardly move. He thinks: And now there is nothing left. Jerry will say I killed her; there is no one who will believe me. And—but here is that terrible thought—I was pleased he killed her. Pleased. I am pleased now. And from here his mind goes darkly into the knowledge: It is just. It is a punishment. And he sits there, passive, while his hands dangle loosely and his eyes go blank.

Slowly the others seat themselves on the floor, huddling together for comfort in this killing they do not understand. All they know is that Betty is dead, and their goggling, empty eyes are fixed on Jerry, waiting for him to do something.

And Jerry, after sorting out his various plans, lets his tense body ease, and tries to put quietness and confidence into his eyes. First he must get rid of the body. Then it will be time to think of the next thing.

He turns to Jabavu and says, in a light, friendly voice: "Help me put this stupid girl outside into the grass."

Jabavu does not move. Jerry repeats the words, and still Jabavu is motionless. Jerry gets up, stands in front of him, and orders him. Jabavu slowly lifts his eyes and then shakes his head.

And now Jerry comes close to Jabavu, his back to the others, and in his hand he holds his knife, and this knife he presses very lightly against Jabavu. "Do you think I'm afraid to kill you too?" he asks, so low only Jabavu can hear. The others cannot see the knife, only that Jerry and Jabavu are thinking how to dispose of Betty. They begin to cry a little, whimpering.

Jabavu shakes his head again. Then he looks down, feeling the pressure of the knife. Its point is at his flesh, he can feel a slight cold sting. And into his mind comes the angry thought: He is cutting my smart coat. His eyes narrow, and he says furiously: "You are cutting my coat."

He's mad, thinks Jerry, but it is the moment of weakness that he knows and understands. And now, using every scrap of his will, he narrows his eyes, stares down into Jabavu's empty eyes, and says: "Come now, and do as I say."

And Jabavu slowly rises and, at a sign from Jerry, lifts Betty's feet. Jerry takes the shoulders. They carry her to the door, and then Jerry says, shouting loudly so that it will be strong enough to get inside the fog of drink: "Put out the candles." No one moves. Then Jerry shouts again, and the young man who sleeps at night with Jerry gets up and slowly pinches out the candles. The room is now all darkness and there is a whimper of fear, but Jerry says: "You will not light the candles. Otherwise the police will get you. I am coming back." The whimper stops. They can hear hard, frightened breathing, but no one moves. And now they move from the blackness of the room to the blackness of the night. Jerry puts down the body and locks the door, and then goes to the window and wedges it with stones. Then he comes back and lifts the shoulders of the body. It is very heavy and it rolls between their gripping hands. Jerry says not a word, and Jabavu is also silent. They carry her a long way, through grass and bushes, never on the paths, and throw her at last into a deep ditch just behind one of the shebeens. She will not be found until morning, and then it will be the people who have been drinking in the shebeen who will be suspected, not Jerry or Jabavu. Then they run very quickly back to the disused store, and as they enter they hear the others wailing and keening in their terror of the darkness and their muddled understanding. A window-pane has been smashed where someone tried to get out, but the wedged stones held the frame. They are crowded in a bunch against the wall, with no sense or courage in them. Jerry lights the candles and says: "Shut up!" He shouts it again, and they are quiet. "Sit down!" he shouts, and they sit. He also sits against the wall, takes up his cards, and pretends to play.

Jabavu is looking down at his coat. It is soaked with blood. Also, as he pulls the cloth over his chest, there is a small cut, where the point of the knife pressed. He is asking himself why he is so stupid as to mind about a coat. What does a coat matter? Yet, even at that moment, Jerry nods at a hook on the wall, where there hang several coats and jackets, and Jabavu goes to the hook, takes down a fine blue jacket, and then looks again at Jerry. And now their eyes stare hard across the space between them. Jabavu's eyes drop. Jerry says: "Take off your shirt and your vest." Jabavu does so. Jerry says: "Put on the vest and shirt you will find among the others in that packing-case." Jabavu goes as if he has no will, to the packing-case, finds a vest and a shirt that will fit him, puts them on, and puts on the blue jacket. Now Jerry quickly rises, strips off his own jacket and shirt, which have blood on them, wipes his knife carefully on them, and then gives the bundle to Jabavu.

"Take my things out with yours and bury them in the ground," he says. Again the two pairs of eyes stare at each other, and Jabavu's eyes drop. He takes all the bloodied things and goes out. He makes his way in the darkness to a place where the bushes grow close, and then he digs, using a sharp stick. He buries the clothes, and then goes back to the store. And as he enters he knows that Jerry has been talking, talking, talking to the others, explaining how he, Jabavu, killed Betty. And he can see from the way their frightened eyes look at him that they believe it.

But it is as if in burying the soiled and cut clothes he also buried his weakness towards Jerry. He says, quietly: "I did not kill Betty," and with this he goes to the wall and seats himself, and gives himself up to whatever may happen. For he does not care. Most deeply he does not care. And Jerry, seeing this deep lassitude, misunderstands it entirely. He thinks: Now I can do what I like with this one. Perhaps it was a good thing I killed that stupid woman. For at last Jabavu will do as I tell him.

But he ignores Jabavu, whom he thinks is safe, and goes to the others and tries to calm them. They are weeping and crying out, and sometimes they call out for skokiaan as a remedy for the fear of this terrible night. But Jerry speaks firmly to them, and makes more strong tea, and gives each a piece of bread and makes them eat it, and finally tells them to sleep. But they cannot. They huddle in a group, talking about the police, and how they will all be blamed for the murder, until at last Jerry makes them drink some tea in which he has put some stuff he bought from an Indian, which is to make people sleep. Soon everyone is lying again on the floor, but this time in a sleep which will heal them and drive away the sickness of the long skokiaan drinking.

For all the long hours of the night they lie, groaning sometimes, sometimes calling out, making thick, frightened words. And Jerry sits and plays cards and watches Jabavu, who does not move.

Jerry is now full of confidence. He makes plans, examines them, alters them; all night his mind is busy, and all the fear and weakness has gone. He decides that killing Betty was the only clever thing he has ever done without planning it.

The night struggles on in the flick of the playing cards and groans from the sleepers. The light comes grey through the dirty window, then rose and gold as the sun rises, then strengthens to a steady, warm yellow. And when the day is truly there, Jerry kicks the sleepers awake, but so that when they sit up they will not know they have been kicked.

They sit up, to see Jerry playing cards and Jabavu slumped against the wall, staring. And into each mind comes a wild, confused memory of murder and fighting, and they look at each other and see that the memory shows in every face. Then they look towards Jerry for an explanation. But Jerry is looking at Jabavu. And they remember that Jabavu has killed Betty, and their faces turn greyish and their breath comes with difficulty. Yet they are no longer stupid with skokiaan, only weak and tired and frightened. Jerry has no fear at all that he may not be able to handle them.

When they are properly awake and he can see the knowledge in their faces he begins to talk. He explains, in a quiet and offhand way, what happened last night, saying that Jabavu has killed Betty, and Jabavu says nothing at all.

It is only the silence of Jabavu that upsets Jerry for he has not expected it. But he is so confident that he takes no notice. He explains that according to the rules of the gang, if suspicion should fall on them, Jabavu must give himself up to the police, saying nothing of the others. But if the trouble should pass, they must all keep silence and continue as if nothing has happened. Jerry speaks so lightly that they are reassured, and one slips out to buy some bread and some milk for tea, and they eat and drink together, even laughing when Jerry makes a joke. The laughter is not very deep, but it helps them. And all this time Jabavu sits against the wall, apart, saying nothing.

Jerry has now made his plans. They are very simple. If the police show signs that day of finding out who killed Betty, he will quickly slip away, go to people he knows who will help him, and travel south, with papers that have a different name, leaving all the trouble behind him. But he has very little money left, after the week of drinking. Perhaps five shillings. His friends may give him a little more. Jerry does not like to think of going all the way to Johannesburg with so little. He wants some more. If the police do not know on whom to put the blame, Jerry will stay here, in this store, with Jabavu and the others, until the evening. And then—but now the plan is so audacious that Jerry laughs inside himself, longing to tell the others, because it is such a good joke. Jerry plans nothing else than to go to Mr. Mizi's house, take the money that will be there, and with it run away to the south. He believes that there is money in the house, and a great deal. When he robbed Mr. Samu, five years ago, and in another town, he took nineteen pounds. Mr. Samu had the money in a big tin that once held tobacco, and it was in the grass roof of a hut. Jerry believes that he has only to go to Mr. Mizi's house to find enough money to take him in luxury and safety, with plenty of funds for bribery, to Johannesburg. And he will take Jabavu with him. Jabavu is now safe, sullen, and too afraid to tell Mr. Mizi. Also, he must know where the money is.

It is all very simple. As soon as Jabavu has given the money to Jerry, Jerry will tell him to go back to the others and wait for his return. They will wait. It will be some days before they understand he has tricked them, and by then he will be in Johannesburg.

Towards midday, Jerry brings out the last bottle of whisky and gives everyone a little of it. Jabavu refuses, with a small shake of the head. Jerry ignores him. So much the better.

But he takes care that all the group are sitting playing cards, drinking a little whisky, and that they have plenty to eat. He wishes them to like him and trust him before explaining his plan, which might frighten them in their condition of being softened by the drinking and the murder.

In the middle of the afternoon he slips out again and mingles with the people in the market, where he hears much talk of the killing. The police have questioned a lot of people, but no one has been arrested. This will be a case like so many others—yet another of the matsotsis killed in a brawl, and no one cares much about that. The newspapers will print a paragraph; perhaps a preacher will make a sermon. Mr. Mizi might make another speech about the corruption of the African people through poverty. At this last idea Jerry laughs to himself and returns to the others in a very good humour indeed.

He tells them that everything will be safe, and then speaks of Mr. Mizi, half as part of his plan, but partly because of the pleasure it gives him. He gives a fine imitation of Mr. Mizi making a speech about corruption and degradation. Jabavu does not stir through this, or even lift his eyes. Then Jerry makes a lot of jokes about Mrs. Mizi and Mrs. Samu and how they are immoral, and everyone laughs except Jabavu.

And everyone, including Jerry, misunderstands this silence of Jabavu. They think that he is afraid, and above all afraid of them because they know he has killed Betty, for now they all believe it; they even believe they saw it.

They do not understand that what is happening in Jabavu is something very old. His mind is darkening in despair, in accepting of what destiny has willed for him, and is turning towards death. This feeling of destiny, of fate, is very strong in the life of the tribe where guilt and responsibility for evil is decided by the old ways of magic. Perhaps if these young people had not lived so long in the white man's city they might understand what they see now in Jabavu. Even Jerry does not, although there are moments when this long silence annoys him. He would like to see Jabavu a little more afraid, and respectful.

Late in the afternoon Jerry takes his last five shillings, gives it to the girl who worked with Betty, and who is more troubled than the rest, and tells her that because of her cleverness she is the one chosen again to go to the market and buy food. She is pleased, and

returns in half an hour with bread and cold boiled mealies, saying
that people are no longer speaking of the murder. Jerry urges them
all to eat. It is very important that they must be full and comfortable, and when they are, he speaks of his plan. "And now I must tell
you a good joke," he says, laughing already. "Tonight we shall rob
from the house of Mr. Mizi; he is very rich. And Jabavu will do the
stealing with me."

For a second there is uncertainty. Then they look at each other,
see Jabavu's heavy eyes, lifted painfully towards them, and then
they roll on the floor with laughing and do not stop for a long time.
But Jerry is looking at Jabavu. He decides to taunt him a little:
"You kraal nigger," he says. "You're scared."

Jabavu sighs, but does not move, and panic moves through Jerry.
Why does Jabavu not cry out, protest, show fear?

He decides to wait for a show of strength until the moment itself.
As the others cease laughing and look at him for the next good joke
he makes a grimace towards Jabavu, inviting their complicity, and
they grin and look at each other. He lights the candles, and makes
them come together in a small, lit space around a packing-case,
with Jabavu outside in the shadow, and there they all play cards,
with much noise and laughter, and Jerry coaxes their excitement
into the cards so that their attention is not on Jabavu. And all the
time he is thinking of every detail of the plan, and his mind is set
hard on his purpose.

At midnight, with a wink at the others, he gets up and goes to
Jabavu. He is sweating with the effort of his will. "It is time," he
says, lightly, and fixes his eyes on Jabavu. Jabavu does not lift his
eyes, or move. Jerry kneels, very swiftly, and exactly as he did the
night before, keeping his back to the others, he presses the tip of
his knife lightly against Jabavu's chest. He stares hard, hard at
Jabavu, and he whispers: "I am cutting the coat." He narrows his
eyes, forcing their pressure at Jabavu, and says again: "I am cutting the coat, soon the knife will go into you." Jabavu lifts his eyes.
"Get up," says Jerry, and Jabavu rises like a drugged man. Jerry is a
little dizzy with the relief of that victory, but resting his hand
against the wall he turns and says to the others: "And now listen to
what I shall tell you. We two go now to Mr. Mizi's house. Blow the
candles out and wait in darkness—no, you may keep one candle,
but set it on the floor so that no sign of light may show. I know that
there is a great sum of money hidden in Mr. Mizi's house. This we
shall bring back. If there is trouble, I shall go quickly to one of our
friends. There I shall stay perhaps one day, perhaps two. Jabavu

will return here. If I am not here by tomorrow morning, then you may leave here one by one, not together. Do not work together for a few days, and do not go near the shebeens, and I forbid you to touch skokiaan again until I say. I shall tell you when it is safe for us to meet again. But all this is if there is trouble, and there is no need for it. Jabavu and I will be back in three-quarters of an hour with the money. Then we shall share it out between us. It will mean there is no need to work for a week, and by that time the police will have forgotten the murder."

For the first time Jabavu speaks. "Mr. Mizi is not rich and he has no money in his house." Jerry frowns, and then swiftly draws Jabavu after him into the darkness. The candles flicker out in the room behind. There is dark everywhere, the trees are swinging in a fast, cool wind, mounds of thick cloud move across the sky, showing damp, weak stars between. It is a good night for stealing.

Jerry thinks: "Why does he say that? It is strange." But what is strange is that in all these weeks Jerry has believed Jabavu is lying about the money, and Jabavu has never understood that Jerry truly thinks there is money.

"Come," says Jerry, quietly. "It will be over soon. And now, as we go, think of what you saw in the Mizis' house, and where the money will be hidden."

Suddenly across Jabavu's mind flickers a picture, then another. He sees how on that evening Mr. Mizi went to the corner of the room, lifted a piece of plank from the flooring, and leaned down into the dark hole underneath to bring up books. That is where he keeps books which the police might take away from him. But following this picture comes another, which he has not seen at all, but which his mind creates. He sees Mr. Mizi reaching up at a large tin filled with rolls of paper money. Yes, Jerry is very clever, for the old hunger in Jabavu raises its head and almost speaks. Then the pictures vanish from his mind, and the hunger with them. He plods along beside Jerry, thinking only: We are going to Mr. Mizi. Somehow I will speak to him when we get there. He will help me. Jerry says, in a loud voice: "Don't stamp so loud, you fool." Jabavu does not change the way he walks. Jerry glances all around him through the dark, thinking nervously: Surely Jabavu is not mad? Or perhaps he has some drug I know nothing of? For his behaviour is very strange. Then he comforts himself: See how the killing of Betty turned out well, although it was not meant. See how this night is so good for stealing, although I did not choose it. My luck is very strong. Everything will be all right . . . And so he does not again tell Jabavu about walking quietly, for the wind is swishing the branches back and forth and raising swirls of dust and leaves around their feet. It is very dark. The lights are out in the houses, for now they are walking in the respectable part of the city where people rise early for work and so must sleep early. Then Jabavu stumbles over a stone and there is a big noise, and Jerry whips out his knife and nudges Jabavu with his elbow until he turns and looks. "I'll stick this into you if you call out or run away," he says, softly, but Jabavu says nothing. He is thinking that Jerry is very strange indeed. Why does he go to Mr. Mizi for money? Why does he take him, Jabavu? Perhaps the killing of Betty hurt his mind and he has gone crazy? And then Jabavu thinks: Yet it is not so strange. He made jokes about killing Betty and then he killed her, and he made jokes about stealing from Mr. Mizi and now we are doing that too . . . And so Jabavu plods on, through the noise of the wind and the blackness that is full of dust and moving leaves, and his head is empty and he does not feel. Only he is very heavy in his limbs, for he is tired with so little sleep, and then the nights of dancing and the skokiaan, and above all, he is tired from the despair, which tells him all the time: There is nothing for you, you will die, Jabavu. You will die. Words of a song form themselves, a sad, slow song, as for someone who has died. "Eh, but see Jabavu, there he goes the big thief. The knife has spoken, and it says: See the murderer, Jabavu, he who creeps through the dark to rob his friend. See Jabavu, whose hands are red with blood. Eh, Jabavu, but now we are coming for you. We are coming Jabavu, there is no escape from us . . ."

Under the street-lights, but at great distances, since there are few lamps in the Native Township, shed small patches of yellow glimmer. Jabavu blunders straight into such a patch of light. "Be careful, fool," says Jerry, in a violent, frightened voice. He drags Jabavu aside, and then stops. He is thinking: Perhaps this man is mad? How, otherwise, could he behave like this? How can I take a mad fool on a dangerous job like this? Perhaps I had better not go to the house . . . Then he looks at Jabavu, who is standing quiet and patient beside him, and he thinks: No, it is simply that he is so afraid of me. So he goes on walking, gripping Jabavu by the wrist.

Then Jabavu laughs out loud and says: "I can see the Mizis' house, and there is a light in the window."

"Shut up," says Jerry, and Jabavu goes on: "The men of light study, at night. There are things you know nothing of."

Jerry slams his hand over Jabavu's mouth, and Jabavu bites the hand. Jerry jerks it away and for a moment stands trembling with the desire to slip his knife sweetly home between Jabavu's ribs. But he keeps himself tight and controlled. He stands there, quietly shaking his bitten hand, looking at the light in the Mizis' house. Now he can almost see the money, and the desire for it grows strong in him. He cannot bear to stop now, to turn back, to change the plan. It is so easy simply to go forward, the money will be his inside five minutes, then he will give Jabavu the slip and in another fifteen minutes he will be in the house of that friend who will shelter him safely till morning. It is all so easy, so easy. And to go back difficult and, above all, shameful. So he shuts his teeth close and promises himself: You wait, my fine kraal nigger. In a moment I'll have got the money, and you might be caught. And even if you're not, what will you do without me? You'll go back to the gang, and without me they're like a lot of chickens, and you'll be in trouble with the police inside a week. The thought gives him great pleasure, so strong he nearly laughs, and in good humour he takes Jabavu's wrist and pulls him forward.

They walk until they are ten paces from the window, just beyond where the light falls dimly, showing the ground, rough and broken, and the bush under the window standing dense and black. The damp and windy dark is loud in their ears. They can see how Mr. Mizi's son lies sprawled on his bed, still dressed. He has fallen asleep with a book in his hand.

Jerry thinks rapidly, then he says: "You will climb quickly in at the window. Do not try to be clever. I can throw a knife as well as I can use it close, so . . ." He wriggles it lightly against the cloth of Jabavu's coat and with what exultation feels Jabavu move away! It is strange that Jabavu has no fear for himself, but it hurts him even now to imagine his jacket cut and spoilt. He has moved away instinctively, almost with irritation, as if a fly were pestering him, yet he moved, and he hears Jerry's voice, now strong and confident: "You will keep away from the door into the other room. You will stand against the wall, with your back to it, and reach out your arm sideways and switch the light off. You needn't think you can be clever, for I shall keep my torch on you, so . . ." And he switches on the tiny torch he has in the palm of his hand, that sends a single, strong beam of light, as narrow as a pencil. He switches it off and grips his teeth tight, against the desire to curse, because the blood where Jabavu bit him is making the torch slippery. "Then I shall come into the room and tie that fool on the bed quickly, and then you will show me the money."

Jabavu is silent, and then he says: "But this money. I have told you there is no money. Why do you really come to this house?"

Jerry grips his arm and says: "It's time to stop joking."

Jabavu says: "Sometimes I said that there was money, but it was when we were making jokes. Surely you understood . . ." He stops, thinking about the nature of those jokes. Then he thinks: It does not matter, for when I am inside I shall call the Mizis.

Jerry says: "And how could there not be money? Where does he keep the money for the League? Did you not see the place where such people keep what is forbidden? When I took money from Mr. Samu it was in such a place . . ." But Jabavu has pulled his arm free and is walking forward through the light to the window, making no effort to quieten his steps. Jerry hisses after him: "Quiet, quiet, you fool."

Then Jabavu pushes his heavy shoulder against the window so that it slides up with a bang, and he climbs in. Behind him Jerry is dancing and swearing with rage. For a second he wavers with the thought of running away. Then it is as if he sees a big tin full of money, and he flings himself across the lit space after Jabavu and climbs in the window.

The two young men have climbed in at a window filled with light, and made a great deal of noise. The boy on the bed stirs, but Jerry has leaned over him, tangled his eyes in a cloth and stuffed into his mouth a handkerchief into which is kneaded some wet dough, while in the same movement he has knelt on his legs. He ties him with some thick string and in a moment the boy cannot move or see or cry out. But when Jabavu sees Mr. Mizi's son lying tied up on the bed, something inside him moves and speaks, the heavy load of fatalistic indifference lifts, and he raises his voice and shouts: "Mr. Mizi, Mrs. Mizi!" It is the voice of a terrified child, for his terror of Jerry has returned. Jerry whips round, cursing, and lifts his arm with the knife in it. Jabavu jumps forward and grabs his wrist. The two stand swaying together under the light, their arms straining for the knife, when there is a noise in the room behind. Jerry springs aside, very quickly, so that Jabavu staggers, and then he jumps away and out of the window. As the door opens Jabavu is staggering back against the door with the knife in his hand.

It is Mr. Mizi and Mrs. Mizi, and when they see him Mr. Mizi leaps forward and grips his arms to his body with his own, and Jabavu says: "No, no, I am your friend."

Mr. Mizi speaks over his shoulder to Mrs. Mizi: "Leave that boy.

Give me some cloth to tie this one with." For Mrs. Mizi is moaning with fear over her son who is lying helpless and half-suffocated under the cloth. And Jabavu stands limp under Mr. Mizi's hands and says: "I am not a thief, I called you, but believe me, Mr. Mizi, I wanted to warn you." Mr. Mizi is too angry to listen. He grips Jabavu's wrists and watches Mrs. Mizi let her son loose.

Then Mrs. Mizi turns to Jabavu and says, half crying: "We helped you, you came to our house, and now you steal from us."

"No, no, Mrs. Mizi, it is not so, I will tell you."

"You will tell the police," says Mr. Mizi roughly. And Jabavu, looking at the hard, angry face of Mr. Mizi, feels that he has been betrayed. Somewhere inside him that well of despair slowly begins to fill again.

The boy who is now sitting on the bed holding his jaw, which has been wrenched with the big lump of dough, says: "Why did you do it? Have we harmed you?"

Jabavu says: "It was not I, it was the other."

But the son has had cloth wound over his eyes before he even opened them, and has seen nothing.

Then Mr. Mizi looks at the knife lying on the ground and says: "You are a murderer as well as thief." There is blood on the floor. Jabavu says: "No, the blood must be from Jerry's hand, which I bit." Already his voice is sullen.

Mrs. Mizi says, with contempt: "You think we are fools. Twice you have run away. Once from Mr. and Mrs. Samu when they helped you in the bush. Then from us, when we helped you. All these weeks you have been with the matsotsis, and now you come here with a knife and expect us to say nothing when you tie our son and fill his mouth with uncooked bread?"

Jabavu goes quite limp in Mr. Mizi's grip. He says, simply: "You do not believe me." Despair goes through his veins like a dark poison. For the second time that despair takes the people with him by surprise. Mr. Mizi lets go his grip and Mrs. Mizi, who is crying bitterly, says: "And a knife, Jabavu, a knife!"

Mr. Mizi picks up the knife, sees there is no blood on it, looks at the blood on the floor, and says: "One thing is true. The blood does not come from a knife wound." But Jabavu's eyes are on the floor, and his face is heavy and indifferent.

Then the police come, all at once, some climbing through the window, some from the front of the house. The police put handcuffs on Jabavu and take a statement from Mr. Mizi. Mrs. Mizi is still crying and fluttering around her son.

Only once does Jabavu speak. He says: "I am not a thief. I came here to tell you. I wish to live honestly."

And at this the policemen laugh and say that Jabavu, after only a few weeks in the Township, is known as one of the cleverest thieves and a member of the worst gang. And now, because of him, they will all be caught and put into prison.

Jabavu hears this with indifference. He looks at Mrs. Mizi, and it is with the bitter look of a child whose mother has betrayed him. Then he looks at Mr. Mizi, and it is the same look. They look in a puzzled way at Jabavu. But Mr. Mizi is thinking: All my life I try to live in such a way to keep out of sight of the police, and now this little fool is going to make me waste time in the courts and get a name for being in trouble.

Jabavu is taken to the police van, and is driven to the prison. There he lies that night, and sleeps with the dark, dreamless sleep of a man who has gone beyond hope. The Mizis have betrayed him. There is nothing left.

In the morning he expects to be taken to the court, but he is transferred to another cell in the prison. He thinks this must be very serious indeed, for it is a cell to himself, a small brick room with a stone floor and a window high up with bars.

A day passes, then another. The warders speak to him and he does not answer. Then a policeman comes to ask him questions, and Jabavu does not say a word. The policeman is first patient, then impatient, and finally threatening. He says the police know everything and Jabavu will gain nothing by keeping quiet. But Jabavu is silent because he does not care. He wishes only the policeman would go away, which at last he does.

They bring him food and water, but he does not eat or drink unless he is told to do so, and then he eats or drinks automatically, but is likely to forget, and sit immobile, with a piece of bread or the mug in his hand. And he sleeps and sleeps as if his soul is drugging itself so that he may slip easily into death. He does not think of death, but it is there with him, in his cell, like a big, black shadow.

And so a week passes, though Jabavu does not know it.

On the eighth day the door opens and a white preacher comes in. Jabavu is asleep, but the warder kicks him till he wakes, then gives him a shake so that he stands up, and finally he sits when the preacher tells him to sit. He does not look at the preacher.

This man is a Mr. Tennent from the Church of England, who visits the prisoners once a week. He is a tall man, lean, grey, stooping. He moves slowly, speaks slowly, and gives an impression of distrusting even the words he chooses to use.

He is a deeply doubting man, as are so many of his persuasion. Perhaps, if he were from another church, that which the Africans call the Romans, he would enter his cell in a different way. Sin is this, a soul is that, there would be definite things to say, and his words would have the ring of a faith which does not change with changing life.

But Mr. Tennent's church allows him much latitude in belief. Also, he has been working with the poorer Africans of this city for many years, and he sees Jabavu rather as Mr. Mizi sees him. First, there is an economic process, and caught in it like a leaf in a whirlpool, there is Jabavu. He believes that to call a child like Jabavu sinful is lack of charity. On the other hand, a man who believes in God, if not the devil, must put the blame on something or someone—and what or who should it be? He does not know. His view of Jabavu robs him of comfort, even for himself.

This man, who comes to the prison every week, hates this work from the bottom of his heart because he does not trust himself. He enters Jabavu's cell taking himself to task for lack of sympathy, and at the first glance towards Jabavu he hardens himself. He has often seen such prisoners weeping like children and calling on their mothers, a sign which is deeply distasteful to him because he is English and despises such shows of emotion. He has seen them stubborn and indifferent and bitter. This is bad, but better than the weeping. He has also, and very often, seen them as Jabavu is, silent, motionless, their eyes lacking sight. It is a condition he dislikes more than any other, because it is foreign to his own being. He has seen prisoners condemned to death as Jabavu is today; they are dead long before the noose goes round their neck. But Jabavu is not going to be hung, his offence is comparatively light, and so this despair is altogether irrational, and Mr. Tennent knows by experience that he is not equipped to deal with it.

He seats himself on an uncomfortable chair that the warder has brought in, and wonders why he finds it hard to speak of God. Jabavu is not a Christian, as can be seen from his papers, but should that prevent a man of God from speaking of Him? After a long silence he says: "I can see that you are very unhappy. I should like to help you."

The words are flat and thin and weak, and Jabavu does not move.

"You are in great trouble. But if you spoke of it, it might ease you."

Not a sound from Jabavu, and his eyes do not move.

For the hundredth time Mr. Tennent thinks that it would be better if he resigned from this work and let one of his colleagues do it who do not think of better housing and bigger wages rather than of God. But he continues in his mild, patient voice: "Perhaps things are better than you think. You seem to be too unhappy for the trouble you are in. There will be only light charges against you. Housebreaking and being without proper employment, and that is not so serious."

Jabavu remains motionless.

"There has been such a long delay in the case because of the number of people involved in it. Your accomplice, the man they call Jerry, has been denounced by his gang as the person who incited you to rob the Mizis' house."

At the name Mizi, Jabavu stirs slightly, then remains still.

"Jerry will be charged with organising the robbery, for carrying a knife, and for being in the city without proper employment. The police suspect he has been involved in many other things, but nothing can be proved. He will get a fairly heavy sentence—that is to say, he will if he is caught. They think he is on his way to Johannesburg. When they catch him he will be put in prison. They have also caught a coloured man who has been giving Africans, you among them, false employment. But this man is very ill in hospital and is not expected to live. As regards the other members of the gang, the police will charge them with being without proper employment, but that is all. There has been such a cloud of lies and counter-charges that it has been a very difficult case for the police. But you must remember it is your first offence, and you are very young, and things will not go badly for you."

Silence from Jabavu. Then Mr. Tennent thinks: Why should I comfort this boy as if he were innocent? The police tell me they know him to have been involved with all kinds of wickedness, even if they cannot prove it. He changes his voice and says, sternly: "I am not saying the fact that you were known to be a member of a gang will not influence your sentence. You will have to pay the penalty for breaking the law. It is thought you may get a year in prison . . ."

He stops, for he can see that if he said ten years it would be the same to Jabavu. He remains silent for some time, thinking, for

he has a choice to make which is not easy. That morning Mr. Mizi
came to his house and asked him if he intended to visit the prison.
When he said Yes, Mr. Mizi asked him if he would take a letter to
Jabavu. Now, it is against the rules to take letters to prisoners. Mr.
Tennent has never broken the law. Also, he dislikes Mr. Mizi, because he dislikes all politics and politicians. He thinks Mr. Mizi
is nothing but a loud-voiced, phrase-making demagogue out for
power and self-glory. Yet he cannot disapprove of Mr. Mizi entirely,
who asks nothing for his people but what he, Mr. Tennent, sincerely believes to be just. At first he refused to take the letter, then
he stiffly said Yes, he would try . . . The letter is in his pocket
now.

At last he takes the letter from his pocket and says: "I have a letter for you." Jabavu still does not move.

"You have friends waiting to help you," he says, loudly, trying
to make his words pierce Jabavu's apathy. Jabavu lifts his eyes.
After a long pause he says: "What friends?"

It gives Mr. Tennent a shock to hear his voice, after such a silence. "It is from Mr. Mizi," he says stiffly.

Jabavu snatches it, scrambles up and stands under the light that
falls from the small, high window. He tears off the envelope, and
it falls to the floor. Mr. Tennent picks it up and says: "I am not
really supposed to give you letters," and understands that his voice
sounds angry. And this is unjust, for it is his own responsibility
that he agreed. He does not like injustice, and he controls his
voice and says: "Read it quickly and then give it back to me. That
is what Mr. Mizi asked."

Jabavu is staring at the letter. It begins: "My son . . ." And at
this the tears begin to roll down his cheeks. And Mr. Tennent is
embarrassed and put out, and he thinks: "Now we are going to
have one of these unpleasant displays, I suppose." Then he chides
himself again for lacking Christian charity, and turns his back so
as not to be offended by Jabavu's tears. Also it is necessary to watch
the door in case the warder should come in too soon.

Jabavu reads:

I wish to tell you that I believe you told the truth when you
said you came unwillingly to my house, and that you wished
to warn us. What I do not understand is what you expected us
to do then. For certain members of the gang have come to me
saying that you told them you expected me to find you employment and look after you. They came to me thinking I would

then defend them to the police. This I shall not do. I have no time for criminals. If I do not understand this case, neither does anyone else. For a whole week the police have been interviewing these people and their accomplices, and very little can be proved, except that the brain was the man Jerry, and that he used some kind of pressure on you. They appear to be afraid of him, and also of you, for it seems to me there are things you might tell the police if you wished.

And now you must try to understand what I am going to say. I am writing only because Mrs. Mizi persuaded me to write. I tell you honestly I have no sympathy with you . . .

And here Jabavu lets the paper fall, and the coldness begins to creep around his heart. But Mr. Tennent, tense and nervous at the door, says: "Quickly, Jabavu. Read it quickly."

And so Jabavu continues to read, and slowly the coldness dissolves, leaving behind it a feeling he does not understand, but it is not a bad feeling.

Mrs. Mizi tell me I think too much from the head and too little from the heart. She says you are nothing but a child. This may be so, but you do not behave like a child, and so I shall speak to you as a man and expect you to act like one. Mrs. Mizi wishes me to go to the Court and say we know you, and that you were led astray by evil companions, and that you are good at heart. Mrs. Mizi uses words like good and evil with ease, and perhaps it is because of her mission education, but as for me, I distrust them, and I shall leave them to the Reverend Mr. Tennent, who I hope will bring you this letter.

I know only this, that you are very intelligent and gifted and that you could make good use of your gifts if you wanted. I know also that until now you have acted as if the world owes you a good time for nothing. But we are living in a very difficult time, when there is much suffering, and I can see no reason why you should be different from everyone else. Now, I shall have to come to Court as a witness, because it was my house that was broken into. But I shall not say I knew you before, save casually, as I know hundreds of people—and this is true, Jabavu . . .

Once again the paper drops, and a feeling of resentment surges through Jabavu. For harder than any other will be this lesson for Jabavu, that he is one of many others and not something special and apart from them.

He hears Mr. Tennent's urgent voice: "Go on, Jabavu, you can think about it afterwards." And he continues:

Our opponents take every opportunity to blacken us and our movement, and they would be delighted if I said I was a friend of a man whom everyone knows is a criminal even if they cannot prove it. So far, and with great effort, I have kept a very good character with the police as an ordinary citizen. They know I do not thieve or lie or cheat. I am what they call respectable. I do not propose to change this for your sake. Also, in my capacity as leader of our people, I have a bad character, so if I spoke for you, it would have a double meaning for the police. Already they have been asking questions which make it clear that they think you are one of us, have been working with us, and I have denied it absolutely. Also, it is true that you have not.

And now, my son, like my wife, Mrs. Mizi, you will think I am a hard man, but you must remember I speak for hundreds of people, who trust me, and I cannot harm them for the sake of one very foolish boy. When you are in Court I will speak sternly, and I will not look at you. Also, I shall leave Mrs. Mizi at home, for I fear her goodness of heart. You will be in prison for perhaps a year, and your sentence will be shortened if you behave well. It will be a hard time for you. You will be with other criminals who may tempt you to return to the life, you will do very hard work, and you will have bad food. But if there are opportunities for study, take them. Do not attract attention to yourself in any way. Do not speak of me. When you come out of prison come to see me, but secretly, and I will help you, not because of what you are, but because your respect for me was a respect for what I stand for, which is bigger than either of us. While you are in prison, think of the hundreds and thousands of our people who are in prison in Africa, voluntarily, for the sake of freedom and justice, in that way you will not be alone, for in a difficult and round-about way I believe you to be one of them.

I greet you on behalf of myself and Mrs. Mizi and our son, and Mr. Samu and Mrs. Samu, and others who are waiting to trust you. But this time, Jabavu, you must trust us. We greet you . . .

Jabavu lets the paper drop and stands staring. The word that has meant most to him of all the many words written hastily on that paper is We. We, says Jabavu. We, Us. Peace flows into him.

For in the tribe and the kraal, the life of his fathers was built on the word We. Yet it was never for him. And between then and now has been a harsh and ugly time when there was only the word I, I, I—as cruel and sharp as a knife. The word We has been offered to him again, accepting all his goodness and his badness, demanding everything he can offer. We, thinks Jabavu, We . . . And for the first time that hunger in him, which has raged like a beast all his life, swells up, unrefused, and streams gently into the word We.

There are steps outside clattering on the stone.

Mr. Tennent says: "Give me the letter." Jabavu hands it to him and it slides quickly into Mr. Tennent's pocket. "I will give it back to Mr. Mizi and say you have read it."

"Tell him I have read it with all my understanding, and that I thank him and will do what he says and he may trust me. Tell him I am no longer a child, but a man, and that his judgment is just, and it is right I should be punished."

Mr. Tennent looks in surprise at Jabavu and thinks, bitterly, that he, the man of God, is a failure; that an intemperate and godless agitator may talk of justice, and of good and evil, and reach Jabavu where he is afraid to use these terms. But he says, with scrupulous kindness: "I shall visit you in prison, Jabavu. But do not tell the warder or the police I brought you that letter."

Jabavu thanks him and says: "You are kind, sir."

Mr. Tennent smiles his dry, doubting smile, and goes out, and the warder locks the door.

Jabavu seats himself on the floor, his legs stretched out. He no longer sees the grey walls of the cell, he does not even think of the Court or of the prison afterwards.

We, says Jabavu over and over again, We. And it is as if in his empty hands are the warm hands of brothers.

The Words He Said

ON THE morning of the *braavleis*, Dad kept saying to Moira, as if he thought it was a joke, "Moy, it's going to rain." First she did not hear him, then she turned her head slowly and deliberately and looked at him so that he remembered what she had said the day before; and he got red in the face and went indoors, out of her way. The day before he had said to her, speaking to me, "What's Moy got into her head? Is the *braavleis* for her engagement or what?"

It was because Moira spent all morning cooking her lemon cake for the *braavleis*, and she went over to Sam the butcher's to order the best ribs of beef and best rump steak.

All the cold season she was not cooking, she was not helping Mom in the house at all, she was not taking an interest in life; and Dad was saying to Mom: "Oh, get the girl to town or something; don't let her moon about here. Who does she think she is?"

Mom just said, quiet and calm, the way she was with Dad when they did not agree: "Oh, let her alone, Dickson." When Mom and Dad were agreeing, they called each other Mom and Dad; when they were against each other, it was Marion and Dickson. And that is how it was for the whole of the dry season, and Moira was pale and mooney and would not talk to me. It was no fun for me, I can tell you.

"What's this for?" Dad said once about halfway through the

season, when Moira stayed in bed three days and Mom let her.
"Has he said anything to her or hasn't he?"

Mom just said: "She's sick, Dickson."

But I could see what he said had gone into her, because I was in
our bedroom when Mom came to Moira.

Mom sat down on the bed, but at the bottom of it, and she was
worried. "Listen, girl," said Mom, "I don't want to interfere, I don't
want to do that, but what did Greg say?" Moira was not properly
in bed, but in her old pink dressing-gown that used to be Mom's,
and she was lying under the quilt. She lay there, not reading or
anything, watching out of the window over at the big water tanks
across the railway lines. Her face looked bad, and she said: "Oh,
leave me alone, Mom."

Mom said: "Listen, dear, just let me say something. You don't
have to follow what I say, do you?"

But Moira said nothing.

"Sometimes boys say a thing, and they don't mean it the way we
think. They feel they have to say it. It's not they don't mean it, but
they mean it different."

"He didn't say anything at all," said Moira. "Why should he?"

"Why don't you go into town and stay with Auntie Nora awhile?
You can come back for the holidays when Greg comes back."

"Oh, let me alone," said Moira, and she began to cry. That was
the first time she cried. At least, in front of Mom. I used to hear
her cry at night when she thought I was asleep.

Mom's face was tight and patient, and she put her hand on
Moira's shoulder, and she was worried I could see. I was sitting on
my bed pretending to do my stamps, and she looked over at me
and seemed to be thinking hard.

"He didn't say anything, Mom," I said. "But I know what happened."

Moira jerked her head up and she said: "Get that kid away from
me."

They could not get me away from Moira because there were
only two bedrooms, and I always slept with Moira. But she would
not speak to me that night at all; and Mom said to me, "Little pitch-
ers have big ears."

It was the last year's *braavleis* it happened. Moira was not keen
on Greg then; I know for a fact because she was sweet on Jordan.
Greg was mostly at the Cape in college; but he came back for
the first time in a year, and I saw him looking at Moira. She was
pretty then, because she had finished school and spent all her time

making herself pretty. She was eighteen, and her hair was wavy because the rains had started. Greg was on the other side of the bonfire, and he came walking around it through the sparks and the white smoke, and up to Moira. Moira smiled out of politeness, because she wanted Jordan to sit by her, and she was afraid he wouldn't if he saw her occupied by Greg.

"Moira Hughes?" he said. Moira smiled, and he said: "I wouldn't have known you."

"Go on," I said, "you've known us always."

They did not hear me. They were just looking. It was peculiar. I knew it was one of the peculiar moments of life because my skin was tingling all over, and that is how I always know.

Because of how she was looking at him, I looked at him too, but I did not think he was handsome. The holidays before, when I was sweet on Greg Jackson, I naturally thought he was handsome, but now he was just ordinary. He was very thin, always, and his hair was ginger, and his freckles were thick, because naturally the sun is no good for people with white skin and freckles.

But he wasn't bad, particularly because he was in his sensible mood. Since he went to college he had two moods, one noisy and sarcastic; and then Moira used to say, all lofty and superior: "Medical students are always rowdy. It stands to reason because of the hard life they have afterwards." His other mood was when he was quiet and grown-up; and some of the gang didn't like it, because he was better than us—he was the only one of the gang to go to university at the Cape.

After they had finished looking, he just sat down in the grass in the place Moira was keeping for Jordan, and Moira did not once look around for Jordan. They did not say anything else, just went on sitting, and when the big dance began, with everyone holding hands around the bonfire, they stood at one side watching.

That was all that happened at the *braavleis*, and that was all the words he said. Next day Greg went on a shooting trip with his father, who was the man at the garage. They went right up the Zambesi valley, and Greg did not come back to our station during those holidays or the holidays after.

I knew Moira was thinking of a letter, because she bought some of Croxley's best blue at the store, and she always went herself to the post office on mail-days. But there was no letter. But after that she said to Jordan, "No thanks, I don't feel like it," when he asked her to go into town to the pictures.

She did not take any notice of any of the gang after that, though before she was leader of the gang, even over the boys.

That was when she stopped being pretty again; she looked as she did before she left school and was working hard at her studies. She was too thin; the curl went out of her hair, and she didn't bother to curl it, either.

All that dry season she did nothing and hardly spoke and did not sing, and I knew it was because of that minute when Greg and she looked at each other—that was all; and when I thought of it, I could feel the cold-hot down my back.

Well, on the day before the *braavleis,* as I said, Moira was on the verandah, and she had on her the dress she wore last year to the *braavleis.* Greg had come back for the holidays the night before; we knew he had, because his mother said so when Mom met her at the store. But he did not come to our house. I did not like to see Moira's face, but I had to keep on looking at it—it was so sad, and her eyes were sore. Mom kissed her, putting both her arms around her, but Moira gave a hitch of her shoulders like a horse with a fly bothering it.

Mom sighed, and then I saw Dad looking at her, and the look they gave each other was most peculiar; it made me feel very peculiar again. And then Moira started in on the lemon cake, and went to the butcher's, and that was when Dad said that about the *braavleis* being for the engagement. Moira looked at him, with her eyes all black and sad, and said: "Why have you got it in for me, Dad? What have I done?"

Dad said: "Greg's not going to marry you. Now he's got to college, and going to be a doctor, he won't be after you."

Moira was smiling, her lips small and angry.

Mom said: "Why, Dickson, Moira's got her diploma and she's educated. What's got into your head?"

Dad said: "I'm telling you, that's all."

Moira said, very grown-up and quiet: "Why are you trying to spoil it for me, Dad? I haven't said anything about marrying, have I? And what have I done to you, anyway?"

Dad didn't like that. He went red and he laughed, but he didn't like it. And he was quiet, for a bit at least.

After lunch, when she'd finished with the cakes, she was sitting on the verandah when Jordan went past across to the store, and she called out: "Hi, Jordan, come and talk to me."

Now I know for a fact that Jordan wasn't sweet on Moira any

more. He was sweet on Beth from the store, because I know for a fact he kissed her at the last station dance; I saw him. And he shouted out, "Thanks, Moy, but I'm on my way."

"Oh, please yourself then," said Moira, friendly and nice, but I knew she was cross, because she was set on it.

Anyway, he came in, and I've never seen Moira so nice to anyone, not even when she was sweet on him, and certainly never to Greg. Well, Jordan was embarrassed, because Moira was not pretty that season and all the station was saying she had gone off. She took Jordan into the kitchen to see the lemon cake and dough all folded, ready for the sausage rolls, and she said, slow and surprised, "But we haven't enough bread for the sandwiches, Mom. What are you thinking of?"

Mom said, quick and cross, because she was proud of her kitchen, "What do you mean? No one's going to eat sandwiches with all that meat you've ordered. And it'll be stale by tomorrow."

"I think we need more bread," said Moira. And she said to me in the same voice, slow and lazy, "Just run over to the Jacksons' and see if they can let us have some bread."

At this I didn't say anything, and Mom did not say anything either, and it was lucky Dad didn't hear. I looked at Mom, and she made no sign; so I went out across the railway lines to the garage. At the back of the garage was the Jacksons' house, and there was Greg Jackson reading a book about the body because he was going to be a doctor.

"Mom says," I said, "can you let us have some bread for the *braavleis?*"

He put down the book and said, "Oh, hullo, Betty."

"Hullo," I said.

"But the store will be open tomorrow," he said. "Isn't the *braavleis* tomorrow?"

"It's Sunday tomorrow," I said.

"But the store's open now."

"We want some stale bread," I said. "Moy's making some stuffing for the chicken; our bread's all fresh."

"Mom's at the store," he said, "but help yourself."

So I went into the pantry and got half a stale loaf, and came out and said, "Thanks," and walked past him.

He said, "Don't mention it." Then, when I was nearly gone, he said, "And how's Moy?" And I said, "Fine, thanks, but I haven't seen much of her this vacation because she's busy with Jordan."

And I went away, and I could feel my back tingling; and sure enough there he was coming up behind me. And then he was beside me, and my side was tingling.

"I'll drop over and say hello," said Greg; and I felt peculiar, I can tell you, because what I was thinking was: Well! If this is love.

When we got near our house, Moira and Jordan were side by side on the verandah wall, and Moy was laughing; and I knew she had seen Greg coming because of the way she laughed.

Dad was not on the verandah, so I could see Mom had got him to stay indoors.

"I've got you the bread, Moy," I said, and with this I went into the kitchen, and there was Mom, and she was looking more peculiar than I've ever seen her. I could have bet she wanted to laugh; but she was sighing all the time. Because of the sighing I knew she had quarrelled with Dad. "Well, I don't know," she said, and she threw the bread I'd fetched into the waste-bucket.

There sat Mom and I in the kitchen, smiling at each other off and on in a peculiar way, and Dad was rattling his paper in the bedroom where she had made him go. He was not at the station that day because the train had come at nine o'clock and there wasn't another one coming. When we looked out on the verandah in about half an hour Jordan was gone, and Greg and Moira were sitting on the verandah wall. And I can tell you she looked so pretty again—it was peculiar her getting pretty like that so suddenly.

That was about five, and Greg went back to supper at home. Moira did not eat anything; she was in our room curling her hair, because she and Greg were going for a walk.

"Don't go too far; it's going to rain," Mom said, but Moira said, sweet and dainty, "Don't worry, Mom, I can look after myself."

Mom and Dad said nothing to each other all the evening.

I went to bed early for a change, so I'd be there when Moy got in, although I was thirteen that season and now my bedtime was up to ten o'clock.

Mom and Dad went to bed, although I could see Mom was worried because there was a storm blowing up; the dry season was due to end, and the lightning kept spurting all over the sky.

I lay awake saying to myself, Sleep sleep, go away, come again another day. But I went to sleep, and when I woke up, the room was full of the smell of rain, of the earth wet with rain, and the light was on and Moira was in the room.

"Have the rains come?" I said, and then I woke right up and

saw of course they hadn't, because the air was as dry as sand, and Moira said, "Oh, shut up and go to sleep."

She did not look pretty as much as being different from how I'd seen her; her face was soft and smiling, and her eyes were different. She had blue eyes most of the time, but now they seemed quite black. And now that her hair was all curled and brushed, it looked pretty, like golden syrup. And she even looked a bit fatter. Usually when she wasn't too thin, she was rather fat, and when she was one of the gang we used to call her Pudding. That is, until she passed her J.C., and then she fought everyone, and the boys, too, so that she could be called Moy. So no one had called her Pudding for years now except Dad, to make her cross. He used to say, "You're going to make a fine figure of a woman like your mother." That always made Moy cross, I can tell you, because Mom was very fat, and she wore proper corsets these days, except just before the rains when it was so hot. I remember the first time the corsets came from the store, and she put them on. Moy had to lace her in, and Mom laughed so much Moy couldn't do the laces; and anyway she was cross because Mom laughed, and she said to me afterwards, "It's disgusting, letting yourself go—I'm not going to let myself go."

So it would have been more than my life was worth to tell her she was looking a bit fatter already, or to tell her anything at all, because she sat smiling on the edge of her bed, and when I said, "What did he say, Moy?" she just turned her head and made her eyes thin and black at me, and I saw I'd better go to sleep. But I knew something she didn't know I knew, because she had some dead jacaranda flowers in her hair; that meant she and Greg had been at the water tanks. There were only two jacaranda trees at our station, and they were at the big water tanks for the engines; and if they were at the water tanks, they must have been kissing, because it was romantic at the tanks. It was the end of October, and the jacarandas were shedding, and the tanks looked as if they were standing in pools of blue water.

Well, next morning Moy was already up when I woke, and she was singing, and even before breakfast she began ironing her muslin dress that she had made for last Christmas.

Mom said nothing; Dad kept rustling his newspaper; and I wouldn't have dared open my mouth. Besides, I wanted to find out what Greg had said. After breakfast, we sat around, because of its being Sunday; Dad didn't have to be at the station office because there weren't any trains on Sundays. And Dad kept grinning at Moira and saying: "I think it's going to rain," and she pretended she didn't know what he meant, until at last she jumped when he said it and turned herself and looked at him just the way she had the day before. That was when he got red in the face and said: "Can't you take a joke these days?" and Moira looked away from him with her eyebrows up, and Mom sighed, and then he said, very cross, "I'll leave you all to it, just tell me when you're in a better temper," and with this he took the newspaper inside to the bedroom.

Anybody could see it wasn't going to rain properly that day, because the clouds weren't thunderheads, but great big white ones, all silver and hardly any black in them.

Moy didn't eat any dinner, but went on sitting on the verandah, wearing her muslin dress, white with red spots and big puffed sleeves and a red sash around her waist.

After dinner, time went very slowly, and it was a long time before Greg came down off the Jacksons' verandah and came walking slowly along the gum-tree avenue. I was watching Moy's face, and she couldn't keep the smile off it. She got paler and paler until he got underneath our verandah, and she was looking at him so that I had gooseflesh all over.

Then he gave a jump up our steps to the verandah and said, "Hoy, Moy, how's it?" I thought she was going to fall right off the verandah wall, and her face had gone all different again.

"How are you, Gregory?" said Moira, all calm and proud.

"Oh, skidding along," he said; and I could see he felt awkward, because he hadn't looked at her once, and his skin was all red around the freckles. She didn't say anything, and she was looking at him as if she couldn't believe it was him.

"I hope the rain will keep off for the *braavleis*," said Mom, in her visiting voice; and she looked hard at me, and I had to get up and go inside with her. But I could see Greg didn't want us to go at all, and I could see Moy knew it; her eyes were blue again, a pale thin blue, and her mouth was small.

Well, Mom went into the kitchen to make the sausage rolls; and I went into our bedroom, because I could see what went on on the verandah from behind the curtains.

Greg sat on the verandah wall and whistled. He was whistling "I Love You, Yes I Do"; and Moira was gazing at him as if he were a Christmas beetle she had just noticed. And then he began whis-

tling "Three Little Words"; and suddenly Moira got down off the
wall and stretched herself like a cat when it's going to walk off
somewhere, and Greg said, "Skinny!"

At this she made her eyebrows go up, and I've never seen such a
look.

And he was getting redder in the face, and he said: "You'd better not wear that dress to the *braavleis;* it's going to rain."

Moira didn't say a word for what seemed about half an hour,
and then she said, in that lazy sort of voice, "Well, Greg Jackson,
if you've changed your mind, it's O.K. with me."

"Changed my mind?" he said, very quickly, and he looked scared;
and she looked scared, and she asked: "What did you say all
those things for last night?"

"Say what?" he asked, more scared than ever; and I could see
he was trying to remember what he'd said.

Moira was just looking at him, and I wouldn't have liked to be
Greg Jackson just then, I can tell you. Then she walked off the
verandah, letting her skirt swish slowly, and through the kitchen,
and into our room, and then she sat on the bed.

"I'm not going to the *braavleis,* Mom," she said, in that sweet,
slow voice like Mom uses when she's got visitors and she wishes
they'd go.

Mom just sighed and slapped the dough about on the kitchen-
table. Dad made the springs of the bed creak, and he said half
aloud, "Oh, my God, preserve me!"

Mom left the pastry and glared through the door of their bedroom at Dad, and then came into our room. There was Moira sitting all lumped up on her bed as if she had a pain, and her face was
like pastry dough. Mom said nothing to Moira, but went on to the
verandah. Greg was still sitting there, looking sick.

"Well, son," Mom said, in her easy voice, the voice she has when
she was tired of everything, but keeping up, "well, son, I think
Moy's got a bit of a headache from the heat."

As I've said, I wasn't sweet on Greg that vacation; but if I was
Moy I would have been, the way he looked just then—all sad,
but grown-up, like a man—when he said: "Mrs. Hughes, I don't
know what I've done." Mom just smiled and sighed. "I can't marry,
Mrs. Hughes. I've got five years' training ahead of me."

Mom smiled and said, "Of course, son, of course."

I was lying on my bed with my stamps; and Moira was on her
bed, listening, and the way she smiled gave me a bad shiver.

"Listen to him," she said, in a loud slow voice. "Marry? Why does everyone go on about marrying? They're nuts. I wouldn't marry Greg Jackson, anyway, if he were the last man on a desert island."

Outside, I could hear Mom sigh hard; then her voice, quick and low; and then the sound of Greg's feet crunching off over the cinders of the path.

Then Mom came back into our room, and Moira said, all despairing, "Mom, what made you say that about marrying?"

"He said it, my girl, I didn't."

"Marrying!" said Moira, laughing hard.

Mom said, "What did he say then—you talked about him saying something?"

"Oh, you all make me sick," said Moira, and she lay down on her bed, turned away from us. Mom hitched her head at me, and we went out. By then it was five in the afternoon and the cars would be leaving at six, so Mom finished the sausage rolls in the oven, and packed the food, and then she took off her apron and went across to Jordan's house. Moira did not see her go, because she was still lost to the world in her pillow.

Soon Mom came back and put the food into the car. Then Jordan came over with Beth from the store and said to me, "Betty, my mom says, will you and Moy come in our car to the *braavleis,* because your car's full of food?"

"I will," I said, "but Moira's got a headache."

But at this moment Moira called out from our room, "Thanks, Jordan, I'd like to come."

So Mom called to Pop, and they went off in our car together, and I could see she was talking to him all the time, and he was just pulling the gears about and looking resigned to life.

Moira and I went with Jordan and Beth in their car. I could see Jordan was cross because he wanted to be with Beth; and Beth kept smiling at Moira with her eyebrows up, to tell her she knew what was going on; and Moira smiled back and talked a lot in her visiting voice.

The *braavleis* was at a high place at the end of a vlei, where it rose into a small hill full of big boulders. The grass had been cut that morning by natives of the farmer who always let us use his farm for the *braavleis.* It was pretty, with the hill behind and the moon coming up over it, and then the cleared space, and the vlei sweeping down to the river, and the trees on either side. The moon was just over the trees when we got there, so the trees looked black and big, and the boulders were big and looked as if they might topple over, and the grass was silvery; but the great bonfire was roaring up twenty feet, and in the space around the fire it was all hot and red. The trench of embers where the spits were for the meat was on one side, and as soon as she arrived Moira went there and helped with the cooking.

Greg was not there, and I thought he wouldn't come; but much later, when we were all eating the meat, and laughing because it burned our fingers it was so hot, I saw him on the other side of the fire talking to Mom. Moira saw him talking, and she didn't like it, but she pretended not to see.

By then we were seated in a half-circle on the side of the fire the wind was blowing, so that the red flames were sweeping off away from us. There were about fifty people from the station and some farmers from round about. Moira sat by me, quiet, eating grilled ribs and sausage rolls; and for once she was pleased I was there, so that she wouldn't seem to be by herself. She had changed her dress again, and it was the dress she had worn last year for the *braavleis;* it was blue with pleats, and it was the dress she had for best the last year at school, so it wasn't very modern any more. Across the fire, I could see Greg. He did not look at Moira, and she did not look at him. Except that this year Jordan did not want to sit by Moira but by Beth, I kept feeling peculiar, as if this year were really last year, and in a minute Greg would walk across past the fire, and say: "Moira Hughes? I wouldn't have known you."

But he stayed where he was. He was sitting on his legs, with his hands on his knees. I could see his legs and knees and his big hands all red from the fire and the yellow hair glinting in the firelight. His face was red, too, and wet with the heat.

Then everyone began singing. We were singing "Sarie Marais," and "Sugar Bush," and "Henrietta's Wedding" and "We don't want to go home." Moira and Greg were both singing as hard as they could.

It was getting late. The natives were damping down the cooking trench with earth and looking for scraps of meat and bits of sausage roll, and the big fire was sinking down. It would be time in a minute for the big dance in a circle around the fire.

Moira was just sitting. Her legs were tucked under her sideways, and they had got scratched from the grass—I could see the white dry scratches across the sunburn—and I can tell you it was a good thing she hadn't worn her best muslin because there wouldn't have been much left of it. Her hair, that she had curled yesterday, was tied back in a ribbon, so that her face looked small and thin.

I said, "Here, Moy, don't look like your own funeral"; and she said, "I will if I like." Then she gave me a bit of a grin, and she said: "Let me give you a word of warning for when you're grown-up: Don't believe a word men say, I'm telling you."

But I could see she was feeling better just then.

At that very moment the red light of the fire on the grass just in front of us went out and someone sat down. I hoped it was Greg, and it was. They were looking at each other again; but my skin didn't tingle at all, so I looked at his face and at her face, and they were both quiet and sensible.

Then Moira reached out for a piece of grass, pulled it clean and neat out of the socket, and began nibbling at the soft piece at the end; and it was just the way Mom reached out for her knitting when she was against Dad. But of course Greg did not know the resemblance.

"Moy," he said, "I want to talk to you."

"My name is Moira," said Moira, looking him in the eyes.

"Oh heck, Moira," he said, sounding exasperated, just like Dad.

I wriggled back away from the two of them into the crowd that was still singing softly "Sarie Marais" and looking at the way the fire was glowing low and soft, ebbing red and then dark as the wind came up from the river. The moon was half-covered with the big, soft, silvery clouds, and the red light was strong on our faces.

I could just hear what they said. I wasn't going to move too far off, I can tell you.

"I don't know what I've said," said Greg.

"It doesn't matter in the slightest," said Moira.

"Moira, for crying out loud!"

"Why did you say that about marrying?" said Moira, and her voice was shaky. She was going to cry if she didn't watch out.

"I thought you thought I meant. . . ."

"You think too much," said Moira, tossing her head carefully so that her long tail of hair should come forward and lie on her shoulder. She put up her hand and stroked the curls smooth.

"Moira, I've got another five years at university. I couldn't ask you to be engaged for five years."

"I never said you should," said Moira, calm and lofty, examining the scratches on her legs.

The way she was sitting, curled up sideways, with her hair lying forward like syrup on her shoulder—it was pretty, it was as pretty as I've ever seen, and I could see his face, sad and almost sick.

"You're so pretty, Moy," he said, jerking it out.

Moira seemed not to be able to move. Then she turned her head slowly and looked at him. I could see the beginning of something terrible on her face. The shiver had begun under my hair at the back of my neck and was slowly moving down to the small of my back.

"You're so beautiful," he said, sounding angry, leaning forward with his face almost against hers.

And now she looked the way she had last night, when I was not awake and asked was it raining outside.

"When you look like that," he said, quite desperate about everything, "it makes me feel. . . ."

People were getting up now all around us. The fire had burned right down; it was a low wave of red heat coming out at us. The redness was on our shoulders and legs, but our faces were having a chance to cool off. The moon had come out again, full and bright, and the cloud had rolled on. It was funny the way the light was red to their shoulders, and the white of the moon on their faces, and their eyes glistening. I didn't like it; I was shivering; it was the most peculiar moment of all my life.

"Well," said Moira, and she sounded just too tired even to try to understand, "that's what you said last night, wasn't it?"

"Don't you see," he said, trying to explain, his tongue all mixed up, "I can't help—I love you, I don't know. . . ."

Now she smiled, and I knew the smile at once, it was the way Mom smiled at Dad when if he had any sense he'd shut up. It was sweet and loving, but it was sad, and as if she were saying, Lord, you're a fool, Dickson Hughes!

Moira went on smiling like that at Greg, and he was sick and angry and not understanding a thing.

"I love you," he said again.

"Well, I love you—and what of it?" said Moira.

"But it will be five years."

"And what has that got to do with anything?" At this she began to laugh.

"But Moy. . . ."

"My name is Moira," she said, once and for all.

For a moment they were both white and angry, their eyes glimmering in the light of the big white moon over them.

There was a shout and a hustle; and suddenly all the people

were in the big circle around the big low heap of fire; and they were whirling around and around, yelling and screaming. Greg and Moira stayed where they were, just outside the range of the feet, and they didn't hear a thing.

"You're so pretty," he was saying, in that rough, cross, helpless voice. "I love you, Moira. There couldn't ever be anyone but you."

She was smiling, and he went on saying: "I love you. I see your face all the time; I see your hair and your face and your eyes."

And I wished he'd go on, the poor sap, just saying it, for every minute it was more like last night when I woke up and I thought it had rained—the feeling of the dry earth with the rain just on it, that was how she was, and she looked as if she would sit there and listen and listen forever to the words he said, and she didn't want to hear him saying, "Why don't you say something, Moy? You don't say anything; you do understand, don't you?—It's not fair, it isn't right to bind you when we're so young." But he started saying it in just a minute, and then she smiled her visiting smile, and she said: "Gregory Jackson, you're a fool."

Then she got up off the grass and went across to Mom to help load the car, and she never once looked at Greg again, not for the rest of the holidays.

Lucy Grange

THE farm was fifty miles from the nearest town, in a maize-growing district. The mealie lands began at a stone's throw from the front door of the farmhouse. At the back were several acres of energetic and colourful domestic growth: chicken runs, vegetables, pumpkins. Even on the verandah there were sacks of grain and bundles of hoes. The life of the farm, her husband's life, washed around the house, leaving old scraps of iron on the front step where the children played wagon-and-driver, or a bottle of medicine for a sick animal on her dressing-table among the bottles of Elizabeth Arden.

One walked straight from the verandah of this gaunt, iron-roofed, brick barracks of a house into a wide drawing-room that was shaded in green and orange Liberty linens.

"Stylish?" said the farmers' wives when they came on formal calls, asking the question of themselves while they discussed with Lucy Grange the price of butter and servants' aprons and their husbands discussed the farm with George Grange. They never "dropped over" to see Lucy Grange; they never rang her up with invitations to "spend the day." They would finger the books on child psychology, politics, art; gaze guiltily at the pictures on her walls, which they felt they ought to be able to recognise; and say: "I can see you are a great reader, Mrs. Grange."

There were years of discussing her among themselves before their voices held the good-natured amusement of acceptance: "I found Lucy in the vegetable patch wearing gloves full of cold cream." "Lucy has ordered another dress pattern from town." And later still, with self-consciously straightened shoulders, eyes directly primly before them, discreet non-committal voices: "Lucy is very attractive to men."

One can imagine her, when they left at the end of those mercifully short visits, standing on the verandah and smiling bitterly after the satisfactory solid women with their straight tailored dresses, made by the Dutchwoman at the store at seven-and-six a time, buttoned loosely across their well-used breasts; with their untidy hair permanent-waved every six months in town; with their femininity which was asserted once and for all by a clumsy scrawl of red across the mouth. One can imagine her clenching her fists and saying fiercely to the mealie fields that rippled greenly all around her, cream-topped like the sea: "I won't. I simply won't. He needn't imagine that I will!"

"Do you like my new dress, George?"

"You're the best-looking woman in the district, Lucy." So it seemed, on the face of it, that he didn't expect, or even want, that she should. . . .

Meanwhile she continued to order cookbooks from town, to make new recipes of pumpkin and green mealies and chicken, to put skin food on her face at night; she constructed attractive nursery furniture out of packing-cases enameled white—the farm wasn't doing too well; and discussed with George how little Betty's cough was probably psychological.

"I'm sure you're right, my dear."

Then the rich, over-controlled voice: "Yes, darling. No, my sweetheart. Yes, of course, I'll play bricks with you, but you must have your lunch first." Then it broke, hard and shrill: *"Don't* make all that noise, darling. I can't stand it. Go on, go and play in the garden and leave me in peace."

Sometimes, storms of tears. Afterwards: "Really, George, didn't your mother ever tell you that all women cry sometimes? It's as good as a tonic. Or a holiday." And a lot of high laughter and gay explanations at which George hastened to guffaw. He liked her gay. She usually was. For instance, she was a good mimic. She would "take off," deliberately trying to relieve his mind of farm worries, the visiting policemen, who toured the district once a month to see if the natives were behaving themselves, or the Government agricultural officials.

"Do you want to see my husband?"

That was what they had come for, but they seldom pressed the point. They sat far longer than they had intended, drinking tea, talking about themselves. They would go away and say at the bar in the village: "Mrs. Grange is a smart woman, isn't she?"

And Lucy would be acting, for George's benefit, how a khaki-clad, sun-raw youth had bent into her room, looking around him with comical surprise; had taken a cup of tea, thanking her three times; had knocked over an ashtray, stayed for lunch and afternoon tea, and left saying with awkward gallantry: "It's a real treat to meet a lady like you who is interested in things."

"You shouldn't be so hard on us poor Colonials, Lucy."

Finally one can imagine how cne day, when the houseboy came to her in the chicken runs to say that there was a baas waiting to see her at the house, it was no sweating policeman, thirsty after fifteen dusty miles on a motorcycle, to whom she must be gracious.

He was a city man, of perhaps forty or forty-five, dressed in city clothes. At first glance she felt a shudder of repulsion. It was a coarse face, and sensual; and he looked like a patient vulture as the keen, heavy-lidded eyes travelled up and down her body.

"Are you looking for my husband, perhaps? He's in the cow-sheds this morning."

"No, I don't think I am. I was."

She laughed. It was as if he had started playing a record she had not heard for a long time, and which started her feet tapping. It was years since she had played this game. "I'll get you some tea," she said hurriedly and left him in her pretty drawing-room.

Collecting the cups, her hands were clumsy. Why, Lucy! she said to herself, archly. She came back, very serious and responsible, to find him standing in front of the picture that filled half the wall at one end of the room. "I should have thought you had sunflowers enough here," he said, in his heavy, over-emphasised voice, which made her listen for meanings behind his words. And when he turned away from the wall and came to sit down, leaning forward, examining her, she suppressed an impulse to apologise for the picture: Van Gogh is obvious, but he's rather effective, she might have said; and she felt that the whole room was that: effective but obvious. But she was pleasantly conscious of how she looked: graceful and cool in her green linen dress, with her corn-coloured hair knotted demurely on her neck. She lifted wide, serious eyes to his face and asked, "Milk? Sugar?" and knew that the corners of her mouth were tight with self-consciousness.

When he left, three hours later, he turned her hand over and lightly kissed the palm. She looked down at the greasy dark head, the red folded neck, and stood rigid, thinking of the raw, creased necks of vultures.

Then he straightened up and said with simple kindliness, "You must be lonely here, my dear"; and she was astounded to find her eyes full of tears.

"One does what one can to make a show of it." She kept her lids lowered and her voice light. Inside she was weeping with gratitude. Embarrassed, she said quickly, "You know, you haven't yet said what you came for."

"I sell insurance. And besides, I've heard people talk of you."

She imagined the talk and smiled stiffly. "You don't seem to take your work very seriously."

"If I may, I'll come back another time and try again?"

She did not reply. He said, "My dear, I'll tell you a secret: one of the reasons I chose this district was because of you. Surely there aren't so many people in this country one can really talk to that we can afford not to take each other seriously?"

He touched her cheek with his hand, smiled, and went.

She heard the last thing he had said like a parody of the things she often said and felt a violent revulsion.

She went to her bedroom, where she found herself in front of the mirror. Her hands went to her cheeks and she drew in her breath with the shock. "Why, Lucy, whatever is the matter with you?" Her eyes were dancing, her mouth smiled irresistibly. Yet she heard the archness of her "Why, Lucy," and thought: I'm going to pieces. I must have gone to pieces without knowing it.

Later she found herself singing in the pantry as she made a cake, stopped herself; made herself look at the insurance salesman's face against her closed eyelids; and instinctively wiped the palms of her hands against her skirt.

He came three days later. Again, in the first shock of seeing him stand at the door, smiling familiarly, she thought, It's the face of an old animal. He probably chose this kind of work because of the opportunities it gives him.

He talked of London, where he had lately been on leave; about the art galleries and the theatres.

She could not help warming, because of her hunger for this kind of talk. She could not help an apologetic note in her voice, because she knew that after so many years in this exile she must seem provincial. She liked him because he associated himself with her abdication from her standards by saying: "Yes, yes, my dear, in a country like this we all learn to accept the second-rate."

While he talked his eyes were roving. He was listening. Outside the window the turkeys were scraping in the dust and gobbling. In the next room the houseboy was moving; then there was silence because he had gone to get his midday meal. The children had had their lunch and gone off to the garden with the nurse.

No, she said to herself. No, no, no.

"Does your husband come back for lunch?"

"He takes it on the lands at this time of the year, he's so busy."

He came over and sat beside her. "Well, shall we console each other?" She was crying in his arms. She could feel their impatient and irritable tightening.

In the bedroom she kept her eyes shut. His hand travelled up and down her back. "What's the matter, little one? What's the matter?"

His voice was a sedative. She could have fallen asleep and lain there for a week inside the anonymous, comforting arms. But he was looking at his watch over her shoulder. "We'd better get dressed, hadn't we?"

"Of course."

She sat naked on the bed, covering herself with her arms, looking at his white hairy body in loathing, and then at the creased red neck. She became extremely gay; and in the living-room they sat side by side on the big sofa, being ironical. Then he put his arm around her, and she curled up inside it and cried again. She clung to him and felt him going away from her; and in a few minutes he stood up, saying, "Wouldn't do for your old man to come in and find us like this, would it?" Even while she was hating him for the "old man," she put her arms around him and said, "You'll come back soon."

"I couldn't keep away." The voice purred caressingly over her head, and she said: "You know, I'm very lonely."

"Darling, I'll come as soon as I can. I've a living to make, you know."

She let her arms drop, and smiled, and watched him drive away down the rutted red-rust farm road, between the rippling sea-coloured mealies.

She knew he would come again, and next time she would not cry; she would stand again like this, watching him go, hating him, thinking of how he had said: In this country we learn to accept the second-rate. And he would come again and again and again; and she would stand here, watching him go and hating him.

A Mild Attack of Locusts

THE rains that year were good; they were coming nicely just as the crops needed them—or so Margaret gathered when the men said they were not too bad. She never had an opinion of her own on matters like the weather, because even to know about what seems a simple thing like the weather needs experience. Which Margaret had not got. The men were Richard her husband, and old Stephen, Richard's father, a farmer from way back; and these two might argue for hours whether the rains were ruinous or just ordinarily exasperating. Margaret had been on the farm three years. She still did not understand how they did not go bankrupt altogether, when the men never had a good word for the weather, or the soil, or the Government. But she was getting to learn the language. Farmers' language. And they neither went bankrupt nor got very rich. They jogged along doing comfortably.

Their crop was maize. Their farm was three thousand acres on the ridges that rise up toward the Zambesi escarpment—high, dry windswept country, cold and dusty in winter, but now, in the wet season, steamy with the heat rising in wet soft waves off miles of green foliage. Beautiful it was, with the sky blue and brilliant halls of air, and the bright green folds and hollows of country beneath, and the mountains lying sharp and bare twenty miles off across the rivers. The sky made her eyes ache; she was not used to it. One does not look so much at the sky in the city she came from. So that evening when Richard said: "The Government is sending out warnings that locusts are expected, coming down from the breeding grounds up North," her instinct was to look about her at the trees. Insects—swarms of them—horrible! But Richard and the old man had raised their eyes and were looking up over the mountain. "We haven't had locusts in seven years," they said. "They go in cycles, locusts do." And then: "There goes our crop for this season!"

But they went on with the work of the farm just as usual until one day they were coming up the road to the homestead for the midday break, when old Stephen stopped, raised his finger and pointed: "Look, look, there they are!"

Out ran Margaret to join them, looking at the hills. Out came the servants from the kitchen. They all stood and gazed. Over the rocky levels of the mountain was a streak of rust-coloured air. Locusts. There they came.

At once Richard shouted at the cookboy. Old Stephen yelled at the houseboy. The cookboy ran to beat the old ploughshare hanging from a tree branch, which was used to summon the labourers at moments of crisis. The houseboy ran off to the store to collect tin cans, any old bit of metal. The farm was ringing with the clamour of the gong; and they could see the labourers come pouring out of the compound, pointing at the hills and shouting excitedly. Soon they had all come up to the house, and Richard and old Stephen were giving them orders—Hurry, hurry, hurry.

And off they ran again, the two white men with them, and in a few minutes Margaret could see the smoke of fires rising from all around the farmlands. Piles of wood and grass had been prepared there. There were seven patches of bared soil, yellow and oxblood color and pink, where the new mealies were just showing, making a film of bright green; and around each drifted up thick clouds of smoke. They were throwing wet leaves on to the fires now, to make it acrid and black. Margaret was watching the hills. Now there was a long, low cloud advancing, rust-colour still, swelling forward and out as she looked. The telephone was ringing. Neighbours—quick, quick, there come the locusts. Old Smith had had his crop eaten to the ground. Quick, get your fires started. For of course, while every farmer hoped the locusts would overlook his farm and go on to the next, it was only fair to warn each other; one must play fair. Everywhere, fifty miles over the countryside, the smoke was rising from myriads of fires. Margaret answered the telephone calls, and between calls she stood watching the locusts. The air was darkening. A strange darkness, for the sun was blazing—it was like the darkness of a veld fire, when the air gets thick with smoke. The sunlight comes down distorted, a thick, hot orange. Oppressive it was, too, with the heaviness of a storm. The locusts were coming fast. Now half the sky was darkened. Behind the reddish veils in front, which were the advance guards of the swarm, the main swarm showed in dense black cloud, reaching almost to the sun itself.

Margaret was wondering what she could do to help. She did not know. Then up came old Stephen from the lands. "We're finished, Margaret, finished! Those beggars can eat every leaf and blade off the farm in half an hour! And it is only early afternoon—if we can make enough smoke, make enough noise till the sun goes down, they'll settle somewhere else perhaps. . . ." And then: "Get the kettle going. It's thirsty work, this."

So Margaret went to the kitchen, and stoked up the fire, and boiled the water. Now, on the tin roof of the kitchen she could hear the thuds and bangs of falling locusts, or a scratching slither as one skidded down. Here were the first of them. From down on the lands came the beating and banging and clanging of a hundred gasoline cans and bits of metal. Stephen impatiently waited while one gasoline can was filled with tea, hot, sweet and orange-coloured, and the other with water. In the meantime, he told Margaret about how twenty years back he was eaten out, made bankrupt, by the locust armies. And then, still talking, he hoisted up the gasoline cans, one in each hand, by the wood pieces set cornerwise across each, and jogged off down to the road to the thirsty labourers. By now the locusts were falling like hail on to the roof of the kitchen. It sounded like a heavy storm. Margaret looked out and saw the air dark with a criss-cross of the insects, and she set her teeth and ran out into it—what the men could do, she could. Overhead the air was thick, locusts everywhere. The locusts were flopping against her, and she brushed them off, heavy red-brown creatures, looking at her with their beady old-men's eyes while they clung with hard, serrated legs. She held her breath with disgust and ran through into the house. There it was even more like being in a heavy storm. The iron roof was reverberating, and the clamour of iron from the lands was like thunder. Looking out, all the trees were queer and still, clotted with insects, their boughs weighed to the ground. The earth seemed to be moving, locusts crawling everywhere, she could not see the lands at all, so thick was the swarm. Towards the mountains it was like looking into driving rain—even as she watched, the sun was blotted out with a fresh onrush of them. It was a half-night, a perverted blackness. Then came a sharp crack from the bush—a branch had snapped off. Then another. A tree down the slope leaned over and settled heavily to the ground. Through the hail of insects a man came running. More tea, more water was needed. She supplied them. She kept the fires stoked and filled cans with liquid, and then it was four in the afternoon, and the locusts had been pouring across overhead for a couple of hours. Up came old Stephen again, crunching locusts underfoot with every step, locusts clinging all over him; he was cursing and swearing, banging with his old hat at the air. At the doorway he stopped briefly, hastily pulling at the clinging insects and throwing them off, then he plunged into the locust-free living-room.

"All the crops finished. Nothing left," he said.

But the gongs were still beating, the men still shouting, and Margaret asked: "Why do you go on with it, then?"

"The main swarm isn't settling. They are heavy with eggs. They are looking for a place to settle and lay. If we can stop the main body settling on our farm, that's everything. If they get a chance to lay their eggs, we are going to have everything eaten flat with hoppers later on." He picked a stray locust off his shirt and split it down with his thumbnail—it was clotted inside with eggs. "Imagine that multiplied by millions. You ever seen a hopper swarm on the march? Well, you're lucky."

Margaret thought an adult swarm was bad enough. Outside now the light on the earth was a pale, thin yellow, clotted with moving shadows; the clouds of moving insects thickened and lightened like driving rain. Old Stephen said, "They've got the wind behind them, that's something."

"Is it very bad?" asked Margaret fearfully, and the old man said emphatically: "We're finished. This swarm may pass over, but once they've started, they'll be coming down from the North now one after another. And then there are the hoppers—it might go on for two or three years."

Margaret sat down helplessly, and thought: Well, if it's the end, it's the end. What now? We'll all three have to go back to town. . . . But at this, she took a quick look at Stephen, the old man who had farmed forty years in this country, been bankrupt twice, and she knew nothing would make him go and become a clerk in the city. Yet her heart ached for him, he looked so tired, the worry lines deep from nose to mouth. Poor old man. . . . He had lifted up a locust that had got itself somehow into his pocket, holding it in the air by one leg. "You've got the strength of a steel-spring in those legs of yours," he was telling the locust, good-humouredly.

Then, although he had been fighting locusts, squashing locusts, yelling at locusts, sweeping them in great mounds into the fires to burn for the last three hours, nevertheless he took this one to the door and carefully threw it out to join its fellows, as if he would rather not harm a hair of its head. This comforted Margaret; all at once she felt irrationally cheered. She remembered it was not the first time in the last three years the man had announced their final and irremediable ruin.

"Get me a drink, lass," he then said, and she set the bottle of whisky by him.

In the meantime, out in the pelting storm of insects, her husband was banging the gong, feeding the fires with leaves, the insects clinging to him all over—she shuddered. "How can you bear to let them touch you?" she asked. He looked at her, disapproving. She felt suitably humble—just as she had when he had first taken a good look at her city self, hair waved and golden, nails red and pointed. Now she was a proper farmer's wife, in sensible shoes and a solid skirt. She might even get to letting locusts settle on her—in time.

Having tossed back a whisky or two, old Stephen went back into the battle, wading now through glistening brown waves of locusts.

Five o'clock. The sun would set in an hour. Then the swarm would settle. It was as thick overhead as ever. The trees were ragged mounds of glistening brown.

Margaret began to cry. It was all so hopeless—if it wasn't a bad season, it was locusts; if it wasn't locusts, it was army-worm or veld fires. Always something. The rustling of the locust armies was like a big forest in the storm; their settling on the roof was like the beating of the rain; the ground was invisible in a sleek, brown, surging tide—it was like being drowned in locusts, submerged by the loathsome brown flood. It seemed as if the roof might sink in under the weight of them, as if the door might give in under their pressure and these rooms fill with them—and it was getting so dark . . . she looked up. The air was thinner; gaps of blue showed in the dark, moving clouds. The blue spaces were cold and thin—the sun must be setting. Through the fog of insects she saw figures approaching. First old Stephen, marching bravely along, then her husband, drawn and haggard with weariness. Behind them the servants. All were crawling all over with insects. The sound of the gongs had stopped. She could hear nothing but the ceaseless rustle of a myriad wings.

The two men slapped off the insects and came in.

"Well," said Richard, kissing her on the cheek, "the main swarm has gone over."

"For the Lord's sake," said Margaret angrily, still half-crying, "what's here is bad enough, isn't it?" For although the evening air was no longer black and thick, but a clear blue, with a pattern of insects whizzing this way and that across it, everything else—trees, buildings, bushes, earth, was gone under the moving brown masses.

"If it doesn't rain in the night and keep them here—if it doesn't rain and weight them down with water, they'll be off in the morning at sunrise."

"We're bound to have some hoppers. But not the main swarm—that's something."

Margaret roused herself, wiped her eyes, pretended she had not been crying, and fetched them some supper, for the servants were too exhausted to move. She sent them down to the compound to rest.

She served the supper and sat listening. There is not one maize plant left, she heard. Not one. The men would get the planters out the moment the locusts had gone. They must start all over again.

But what's the use of that, Margaret wondered, if the whole farm was going to be crawling with hoppers? But she listened while they discussed the new government pamphlet that said how to defeat the hoppers. You must have men out all the time, moving over the farm to watch for movement in the grass. When you find a patch of hoppers, small lively black things, like crickets, then you dig trenches around the patch or spray them with poison from pumps supplied by the Government. The Government wanted them to co-operate in a world plan for eliminating this plague forever. You should attack locusts at the source. Hoppers, in short. The men were talking as if they were planning a war, and Margaret listened, amazed.

In the night it was quiet; no sign of the settled armies outside, except sometimes a branch snapped, or a tree could be heard crashing down.

Margaret slept badly in the bed beside Richard, who was sleeping like the dead, exhausted with the afternoon's fight. In the morning she woke to yellow sunshine lying across the bed—clear sunshine, with an occasional blotch of shadow moving over it. She went to the window. Old Stephen was ahead of her. There he stood outside, gazing down over the bush. And she gazed, astounded—

and entranced, much against her will. For it looked as if every tree, every bush, all the earth, were lit with pale flames. The locusts were fanning their wings to free them of the night dews. There was a shimmer of red-tinged gold light everywhere.

She went out to join the old man, stepping carefully among the insects. They stood and watched. Overhead the sky was blue, blue and clear.

"Pretty," said old Stephen, with satisfaction.

Well, thought Margaret, we may be ruined, we may be bankrupt, but not everyone has seen an army of locusts fanning their wings at dawn.

Over the slopes, in the distance, a faint red smear showed in the sky, thickened and spread. "There they go," said old Stephen. "There goes the main army, off south."

And now from the trees, from the earth all round them, the locusts were taking wing. They were like small aircraft, manoeuvring for the take-off, trying their wings to see if they were dry enough. Off they went. A reddish-brown steam was rising off the miles of bush, off the lands, the earth. Again the sunlight darkened.

And as the clotted branches lifted, the weight on them lightening, there was nothing but the black spines of branches, trees. No green left, nothing. All morning they watched, the three of them, as the brown crust thinned and broke and dissolved, flying up to mass with the main army, now a brownish-red smear in the southern sky. The lands which had been filmed with green, the new tender mealie plants, were stark and bare. All the trees stripped. A devastated landscape. No green, no green anywhere.

By midday the reddish cloud had gone. Only an occasional locust flopped down. On the ground were the corpses and the wounded. The African labourers were sweeping these up with branches and collecting them in tins.

"Ever eaten sun-dried locust?" asked old Stephen. "That time twenty years ago, when I went broke, I lived on mealie meal and dried locusts for three months. They aren't bad at all—rather like smoked fish, if you come to think of it."

But Margaret preferred not even to think of it.

After the midday meal the men went off to the lands. Everything was to be replanted. With a bit of luck another swarm would not come travelling down just this way. But they hoped it would rain very soon, to spring some new grass, because the cattle would die otherwise—there was not a blade of grass left on the farm. As for

Margaret, she was trying to get used to the idea of three or four years of locusts. Locusts were going to be like bad weather, from now on, always imminent. She felt like a survivor after war—if this devastated and mangled countryside was not ruin, well, what then was ruin?

But the men ate their supper with good appetites.

"It could have been worse," was what they said. "It could be much worse."

Flavours of Exile

AT THE foot of the hill, near the well, was the vegetable garden, an acre fenced off from the Big Field where the earth was so rich that mealies grew there, year after year, ten feet tall. Nursed from that fabulous soil, carrots, lettuces, beets, tasting as I have never found vegetables taste since, loaded our table and the tables of our neighbours. Sometimes, if the garden boy was late with the supply for lunch, I would run down the steep pebbly path through the trees at the back of the hill and along the red dust of the waggon road until I could see the windlass under its shed of thatch. There I stopped. The smell of manure, of sun on foliage, of evaporating water, rose to my head; two steps farther, and I could look down into the vegetable garden enclosed within its tall pale of reeds—rich chocolate earth studded emerald green, frothed with the white of cauliflowers, jewelled with the purple globes of eggplant and the scarlet wealth of tomatoes. Around the fence grew lemons, pawpaws, bananas—shapes of gold and yellow in their patterns of green.

In another five minutes I would be dragging from the earth carrots ten inches long, so succulent they snapped between two fingers. I ate my allowance of these before the cook could boil them and drown them in the white flour sauce without which—and unless they were served in the large china vegetable dishes brought from that old house in London—they were not carrots to my mother.

For her, that garden represented a defeat.

When the family first came to the farm, she built vegetable beds on the *kopje* near the house. She had in her mind, perhaps, a vision of the farmhouse surrounded by outbuildings and gardens like a hen sheltering its chicks.

The *kopje* was all stone. As soon as the grass was cleared off its crown where the house stood, the fierce rains beat the soil away. Those first vegetable beds were thin sifted earth walled by pebbles. The water was brought up from the well in the water-cart.

"Water is gold," grumbled my father, eating peas which, he reckoned, must cost a shilling a mouthful. "Water is gold!" he came to shout at last, as my mother toiled and bent over those reluctant beds. But she got more pleasure from them than she ever did from the exhaustless plenty of the garden under the hill.

At last, the spaces in the bush where the old beds had been were seeded by wild or vagrant plants, and we children played there. Someone must have thrown away gooseberries, for soon the low-spreading bushes covered the earth. We used to creep under them, William MacGregor and I, lie flat on our backs, and look through the leaves at the brilliant sky, reaching around us for the tiny sharp-sweet yellow fruits in their jackets of papery white. The smell of the leaves was spicy. It intoxicated us. We would laugh and shout, then quarrel; and William, to make up, shelled a double-handful of the fruit and poured it into my skirt, and we ate together, pressing the biggest berries on each other. When we could eat no more, we filled baskets and took them to the kitchen to be made into that rich jam, which, if allowed to burn just the right amount on the pan, is the best jam in the world—clear sweet amber, with lumps of sticky sharpness in it, as if the stings of bees were preserved in honey.

But my mother did not like it. "Cape gooseberries!" she said bitterly. "They aren't gooseberries at all. Oh, if I could let you taste a pie made of real English gooseberries."

In due course, the marvels of civilisation made this possible; she found a tin of gooseberries in the Greek store at the station and made us a pie.

My parents and William's ate the pie with a truly religious emotion.

It was this experience with the gooseberries that made me cautious when it came to Brussels sprouts. Year after year my mother yearned for Brussels sprouts, whose name came to represent to me something exotic and forever unattainable. When at last she managed to grow half a dozen spikes of this plant in one cold winter that offered us sufficient frost, she of course sent a note to the Mac-

Gregors, so that they might share the treat. They came from Glasgow, they came from Rome, and they could share the language of nostalgia. At the table the four grownups ate the bitter little cabbages and agreed that the soil of Africa was unable to grow food that had any taste at all. I said scornfully that I couldn't see what all the fuss was about. But William, three years older than myself, passed the plate up and said he found them delicious. It was like a betrayal; and afterwards I demanded how he could like such flavourless stuff. He smiled at me and said it cost us nothing to pretend, did it?

That smile, so gentle, a little whimsical, was a lesson to me; and I remembered it when it came to the affair of the cherries. She found a tin of cherries at the store, we ate them with cream; and while she sighed over memories of barrows loaded with cherries in the streets of London, I sighed with her, ate fervently, and was careful not to meet her eyes.

And when she said: "The pomegranates will be fruiting soon," I offered to run down and see how they progressed. I returned from the examination saying: "It won't be long now, really it won't— perhaps next year."

The truth was, my emotion over the pomegranates was not entirely due to the beautiful lesson in courtesy given me by William. Brussels sprouts, cherries, English gooseberries—they were my mother's; they recurred in her talk as often as "a real London pea-souper," or "chestnuts by the fire," or "cherry blossom at Kew." I no longer grudged these to her; I listened and was careful not to show that my thoughts were on my own inheritance of veld and sun. But pomegranates were an exotic for my mother; and therefore more easily shared with her. She had been in Persia, where, one understood, pomegrante juice ran in rivers. The wife of a minor official, she had lived in a vast stone house cooled by water trickling down a thousand stone channels from the mountains; she had lived among roses and jasmine, walnut trees and pomegranates. But, unfortunately, for too short a time.

Why not pomegranates here, in Africa? Why not?

The four trees had been planted at the same time as the first vegetable beds; and almost at once two of them died. A third lingered on for a couple of seasons and then succumbed to the white ants. The fourth stood lonely among the Cape gooseberry bushes, bore no fruit, and at last was forgotten.

Then one day my mother was showing Mrs. MacGregor her chickens; and as they returned through tangles of grass and weed, their skirts lifted high in both hands, my mother exclaimed: "Why, I do believe the pomegranate is fruiting at last. Look, look, it is!" She called to us, the children, and we went running, and stood around a small thorny tree, and looked at a rusty-red fruit the size of a child's fist. "It's ripe," said my mother, and pulled it off.

Inside the house we were each given a dozen small seeds on saucers. They were bitter, but we did not like to ask for sugar. Mrs. MacGregor said gently: "It's wonderful. How you must miss all that!"

"The roses!" said my mother. "And sacks of walnuts . . . and we used to drink pomegranate juice with the melted snow water . . . nothing here tastes like that. The soil is no good."

I looked at William, sitting opposite to me. He turned his head and smiled. I fell in love.

He was then fifteen, home for the holidays. He was a silent boy, thoughtful; and the quietness in his deep grey eyes seemed to me like a promise of warmth and understanding I had never known. There was a tightness in my chest, because it hurt to be shut out from the world of simple kindness he lived in. I sat there, opposite to him, and said to myself that I had known him all my life and yet until this moment had never understood what he was. I looked at those extraordinarily clear eyes, that were like water over grey pebbles; I gazed and gazed, until he gave me a slow, direct look that showed he knew I had been staring. It was like a warning, as if a door had been shut.

After the MacGregors had gone, I went through the bushes to the pomegranate tree. It was about my height, a tough, obstinate-looking thing; and there was a round yellow ball the size of a walnut hanging from a twig.

I looked at the ugly little tree and thought, Pomegranates! Breasts like pomegranates and a belly like a heap of wheat! The golden pomegranates of the sun, I thought . . . pomegranates like the red of blood.

I was in a fever, more than a little mad. The space of thick grass and gooseberry bushes between the trees was haunted by William; and his deep, calm, grey eyes looked at me across the pomegranate tree.

Next day I sat under the tree. It gave no shade, but the acrid sunlight was barred and splotched under it. There was hard, cracked, red earth beneath a covering of silvery dead grass. Under the grass I saw grains of red and half a hard brown shell. It seemed that a fruit had ripened and burst without our knowing it—yes, everywhere in the soft old grass lay the tiny crimson seeds. I tasted one; warm sweet juice flooded my tongue. I gathered them up and ate them until my mouth was full of dry seeds. I spat them out and thought that a score of pomegranate trees would grow from that mouthful.

As I watched, tiny black ants came scurrying along the roots of the grass, scrambling over the fissures in the earth, to snatch away the seeds. I lay on my elbow and watched. A dozen of them were levering at a still unbroken seed. Suddenly the frail tissue split as they bumped it over a splinter, and they were caught in a sticky red ooze.

The ants would carry these seeds for hundreds of yards; there would be an orchard of pomegranates. William MacGregor would come visiting with his parents and find me among the pomegranate trees; I could hear the sound of his grave voice mingled with the tinkle of camel bells and the splashing of falling water.

I went to the tree every day and lay under it, watching the single yellow fruit ripening on its twig. There would come a moment when it must burst and scatter crimson seeds; I must be there when it did; it seemed as if my whole life was concentrated and ripening with that single fruit.

It was very hot under the tree. My head ached. My flesh was painful with the sun. Yet there I sat all day, watching the tiny ants at their work, letting them run over my legs, waiting for the pomegranate fruit to ripen. It swelled slowly; it seemed set on reaching perfection, for when it was the size that the other had been picked, it was still a bronzing yellow, and the rind was soft. It was going to be a big fruit, the size of both my fists.

Then something terrifying happened. One day I saw that the twig it hung from was splitting off the branch. The wizened, dry little tree could not sustain the weight of the fruit it had produced. I went to the house, brought down bandages from the medicine chest, and strapped the twig firm and tight to the branch, in such a way that the weight was supported. Then I wet the bandage, tenderly, and thought of William, William, William. I wet the bandage daily, and thought of him.

What I thought of William had become a world, stronger than anything around me. Yet, since I was mad, so weak, it vanished at a touch. Once, for instance, I saw him, driving with his father on the waggon along the road to the station. I remember I was ashamed that that marvellous feverish world should depend on a half-grown boy in dusty khaki, gripping a piece of grass between

his teeth as he stared ahead of him. It came to this—that in order
to preserve the dream, I must not see William. And it seemed he
felt something of the sort himself, for in all those weeks he never
came near me, whereas once he used to come every day. And yet I
was convinced it must happen that William and the moment when
the pomegranate split open would coincide.

I imagined it in a thousand ways, as the fruit continued to grow.
Now, it was a clear bronze yellow with faint rust-coloured streaks.
The rind was thin, so soft that the swelling seeds within were shaping it. The fruit looked lumpy and veined, like a nursing breast.
The small crown where the stem fastened on it, which had been the
sheath of the flower, was still green. It began to harden and turn
back into iron-grey thorns.

Soon, soon, it would be ripe. Very swiftly, the skin lost its smooth
thinness. It took on a tough, pored look, like the skin of an old
weather-beaten countryman. It was a ruddy scarlet now, and hot to
the touch. A small crack appeared, which in a day had widened so
that the packed red seeds within were visible, almost bursting out. I
did not dare leave the tree. I was there from six in the morning
until the sun went down. I even crept down with the candle at
night, although I argued it could not burst at night, not in the cool
of the night; it must be the final unbearable thrust of the hot sun
that would break it.

For three days nothing happened. The crack remained the same.
Ants swarmed up the trunk, along the branches, and into the fruit.
The scar oozed red juice in which black ants swarm and struggled.
At any moment it might happen. And William did not come. I was
sure he would; I watched the empty road helplessly, waiting for
him to come striding along, a piece of grass between his teeth, to
me and the pomegranate tree. Yet he did not. In one night, the
crack split another half-inch. I saw a red seed push itself out of the
crack and fall. Instantly it was borne off by the ants into the grass.

I went up to the house and asked my mother when the Mac-
Gregors were coming to tea.

"I don't know, dear. Why?"

"Because. I just thought. . . ."

She looked at me. Her eyes were critical. In one moment, she
would say the name "William." I struck first. To have William and
the moment together, I must pay fee to the family gods. "There's a
pomegranate nearly ripe, and you know how interested Mrs. Mac-
Gregor is. . . ."

She looked sharply at me. "Pick it, and we'll make a drink of it."

"Oh, no, it's not quite ready. Not altogether. . . ."

"Silly child," she said at last. She went to the telephone and said: "Mrs. MacGregor, this daughter of mine, she's got it into her head —you know how children are."

I did not care. At four that afternoon I was waiting by the pomegranate tree. Their car came thrusting up the steep road to the crown of the hill. There was Mr. MacGregor in his khaki, Mrs. MacGregor in her best afternoon dress—and William. The adults shook hands, kissed. William did not turn round and look at me. It was not possible, it was monstrous, that the force of my dream should not have had the power to touch him at all, that he knew nothing of what he must do.

Then he slowly turned his head and looked down the slope to where I stood. He did not smile. It seemed he had not seen me, for his eyes travelled past me, and back to the grownups. He stood to one side while they exchanged their news and greetings; and then all four laughed, and turned to look at me and my tree. It seemed for a moment they were all coming. At once, however, they went into the house, William trailing after them, frowning.

In a moment he would have gone in; the space in front of the old house would be empty. I called "William!" I had not known I would call. My voice sounded small in the wide afternoon sunlight.

He went on as if he had not heard. Then he stopped, seemed to think, and came down the hill towards me while I anxiously examined his face. The low tangle of the gooseberry bushes was around his legs, and he swore sharply.

"Look at the pomegranate," I said. He came to a halt beside the tree, and looked. I was searching those clear grey eyes now for a trace of that indulgence they had shown my mother over the Brussels sprouts, over that first unripe pomegranate. Now all I wanted was indulgence; I abandoned everything else.

"It's full of ants," he said at last.

"Only a little, only where it's cracked."

He stood, frowning, chewing at his piece of grass. His lips were full and thin-skinned; and I could see the blood, dull and dark around the pale groove where the grass stem pressed.

The pomegranate hung there, swarming with ants.

"Now," I thought wildly, "now—crack now."

There was not a sound. The sun came pouring down, hot and

yellow, drawing up the smell of the grasses. There was, too, a faint sour smell from the fermenting juice of the pomegranate.

"It's bad," said William, in that uncomfortable, angry voice. "And what's that bit of dirty rag for?"

"It was breaking, the twig was breaking off—I tied it up."

"Mad," he remarked, aside, to the afternoon. "Quite mad." He was looking about him in the grass. He reached down and picked up a stick.

"No," I cried out, as he hit at the tree. The pomegranate flew into the air and exploded in a scatter of crimson seeds, fermenting juice, and black ants.

The cracked empty skin, with its white, clean-looking inner skin faintly stained with juice, lay in two fragments at my feet.

He was poking sulkily with the stick at the little scarlet seeds that lay everywhere on the earth.

Then he did look at me. Those clear eyes were grave again, thoughtful, and judging. They held that warning I had seen in them before.

"That's your pomegranate," he said at last.

"Yes," I said.

He smiled, "We'd better go up, if we want any tea."

We went together up the hill to the house, and as we entered the room where the grownups sat over the teacups, I spoke quickly, before he could. In a bright, careless voice I said: "It was bad, after all; the ants had got at it. It should have been picked before."

Getting Off the Altitude

THAT night of the dance, years later, when I saw Mrs. Slatter come into the bedroom at midnight, not seeing me because the circle of lamplight was focussed low, with a cold and terrible face I never would have believed could be hers after knowing her so long during the day-times and the visits—that night, when she dragged herself out of the room again, still not knowing I was there, I went to the mirror to see my own face. I held the lamp as close as I could and looked into my face. For I had not known before that a person's face could be smooth and comfortable, though often sorrowful, like Molly Slatter's had been all those years, and then hard-set, in the solitude away from the dance and the people (that night they had drunk a great deal and the voices of the singing reminded me of when dogs howl at the full moon), into an old and patient stone. Yes, her face looked like white stone that the rain has trickled over and worn through the wet seasons.

My face, that night in the mirror, dusted yellow from the lamplight, with the dark watery spaces of the glass behind, was smooth and enquiring, with the pert, flattered look of a girl in her first long dress and dancing with the young people for the first time. There was nothing in it, a girl's face, empty. Yet I had been crying just before, and I wished then I could go away into the dark and stay there forever. Yet Molly Slatter's terrible face was familiar to me, as if it were her own face, her real one. I seemed to know it. And that meant that the years I had known her, comfortable and warm in spite of all her troubles, had been saying something else to me about her. But only now I was prepared to listen.

I left the mirror, set the lamp down on the dressing-table, went out into the passage, and looked for her among the people; and there she was in her red satin dress, looking just as usual, talking to my father, her hand on the back of his chair, smiling down at him.

"It hasn't been a bad season, Mr. Farquar," she was saying. "The rains haven't done us badly at all."

Driving home in the car that night, my mother asked, "What was Molly saying to you?"

And my father said, "Oh I don't know, I really don't know." His voice was sad and angry.

She said, "That dress of hers. Her evening dresses look like a cheap night club."

He said, troubled and sorrowful, "Yes. Actually I said something to her."

"Somebody should."

"No," he said, quick against the cold criticising voice. "No. It's a—pretty colour. But I said to her, 'There's not much to that dress, is there?' "

"What did she say?"

"She was hurt. I was sorry I said anything."

"H'mm," said my mother, with a little laugh.

He turned his head from his driving, so that the car lights swung wild over the rutted track for a moment, and said direct at her: "She's a good woman. She's a nice woman."

But she gave another offended gulp of laughter. As a woman insists in an argument because she won't give in, even when she knows she is wrong.

As for me, I saw that dress again, with its criss-cross of narrow, sweat-darkened straps over the ageing white back; and I saw Mrs. Slatter's face when my father criticised her. I might have been there, I saw it so clearly. She coloured, lifted her head, lowered her lids so that the tears would not show, and she said, "I'm sorry you feel like that, Mr. Farquar." It was with dignity. Yes. She had put on that dress in order to say something. But my father did not approve. He had said so.

She cared what my father said. They cared very much for each other. She called him Mr. Farquar always, and he called her Molly; and when the Slatters came over to tea, and Mr. Slatter was being brutal, there was a gentleness and a respect for her in my father's manner that made even Mr. Slatter feel it and even, sometimes, repeat something he had said to his wife in a lower voice, although it was still impatient.

The first time I knew my father felt for Molly Slatter and that my mother grudged it to her was when I was perhaps seven or eight. Their house was six miles away over the veld, but ten by the road. Their house, like ours, was on a ridge. At the end of the dry season, when the trees were low and the leaves thinning, we could see their lights flash out at sundown, low and yellow across the miles of country. My father, after coming back from seeing Mr. Slatter about some farm matter, stood by our window looking at their lights, and my mother watched him. Then he said, "Perhaps she should stand up to him? No, that's not it. She does, in her way. But Lord, he's a tough customer—Slatter."

My mother said, her head low over her sewing: "She married him."

He let his eyes swing around at her, startled. Then he laughed. "That's right, she married him."

"Well?"

"Oh, come off it, old girl," he said, almost gay, laughing and hard. Then, still laughing angrily, he went over and kissed her on the cheek.

"I like Molly," she said, defensive. "I like her. She hasn't got what you might call conversation, but I like her."

"Living with Slatter, I daresay she's got used to keeping her mouth shut."

When Molly Slatter came over to spend the day with my mother the two women talked eagerly for hours about household things. Then, when my father came in for tea or dinner, there was a lock of sympathies and my mother looked ironical while he went to sit by Mrs. Slatter, even if only for a minute, saying: "Well, Molly? Everything all right with you?"

"I'm very well, thank you, Mr. Farquar, and so are the children."

Most people were frightened of Mr. Slatter. There were four Slatter boys, and when the old man was in a temper and waving the whip he always had with him, they ran off into the bush and stayed there until he had cooled down. All the natives on their farm were afraid of him. Once when he knew their houseboy had stolen some soap he tied him to a tree in the garden without food and water all of one day, and then through the night, and beat him with his whip every time he went past, until the boy confessed. And once, when he had hit a farm boy, and the boy complained to the police, Mr.

Slatter tied the boy to his horse and rode it at a gallop to the police station twelve miles off and made the boy run beside, and told him if he complained to the police again he would kill him. Then he paid the ten-shilling fine and made the boy run beside the horse all the way back again.

I was so frightened of him that I could feel myself begin trembling when I saw his car turning to come up the drive from the farmlands.

He was a square, fair man, with small sandy-lashed blue eyes and small puffed cracked lips and red ugly hands. He used to come up the wide red shining steps of the verandah, grinning slightly, looking at us. Then he would take a handful of towhair from the heads of whichever of his sons were nearest, one in each fist, and tighten his fists slowly, not saying a word, while they stood grinning back and their eyes filled slowly. He would grin over their heads at Molly Slatter, while she sat silent, saying nothing. Then, one or the other of the boys would let out a sound of pain, and Mr. Slatter showed his small discoloured teeth in a grin of triumphant good humour and let them both go. Then he stamped off in his big farm boots into the house.

Mrs. Slatter would say to her sons, "Don't cry. Your father doesn't know his own strength. Don't cry." And she went on sewing, composed and pale.

Once, at the station, the Slatter car and ours were drawn up side by side outside the store. Mrs. Slatter was sitting in the front seat, beside the driver's seat. In our car my father drove and my mother was beside him. We children were in the back seats. Mr. Slatter came out of the bar with Mrs. Pritt and stood on the store verandah talking to her. He stood before her, legs apart, in his way of standing, head back on his shoulders, eyes narrowed, grinning, red fists loose at his sides, and talked on for something like half an hour. Meanwhile Mrs. Pritt let her weight slump on to one hip and lolled in front of him. She wore a light, shrill green dress, so short it showed the balls of her thin knees.

And my father leaned out of our car window, though we had all our stores in and might very well leave for home now, and talked steadily and gently to Mrs. Slatter, who was quiet, not looking at her husband, but making conversation with my father and across him to my mother. And so they went on talking until Mr. Slatter left Mrs. Pritt and slammed himself into the driver's seat and started the car.

I did not like Mrs. Pritt and I knew neither of my parents did.

She was a thin, wiry, tall woman with black, short, jumpy hair. She had a sharp, knowing face and a sudden laugh like the scream of a hen caught by the leg. Her voice was always loud, and she laughed a great deal.

But seeing Mr. Slatter with her was enough to know that they fitted. She was not gentle and kindly like Mrs. Slatter. She was as tough in her own way as Mr. Slatter. And long before I ever heard it said I knew well enough that, as my mother said primly, they liked each other. I asked her, meaning her to tell the truth, "Why does Mr. Slatter always go over when Mr. Pritt is away?" And she said, "I expect Mr. Slatter likes her."

In our district, with thirty or forty families on the farms spread over a hundred square miles or so, nothing happened privately. That day at the station I must have been ten years old, or eleven; but it was not the first or the last time I heard the talk between my parents:

My father: "I daresay it could make things easier for Molly."

She, then: "Do you?"

"But, if he's got to have an affair, he might at least not push it down our throats, for Molly's sake."

And she: "Does he have to have an affair?"

She said the word "affair" with difficulty. It was not her language. Nor, and that was what she was protesting against, my father's. For they were both conventional and religious people. Yet at moments of crisis, at moments of scandal and irregularity, my father spoke this other language, cool and detached, as if he were born to it.

"A man like Slatter," he said thoughtfully, as if talking to another man, "it's obvious. And Emmy Pritt. Yes. Obviously, obviously! But it depends on how Molly takes it. Because if she doesn't take it the right way, she could make it hell for herself."

"Take it the right way," said my mother, with bright protesting eyes, and my father did not answer.

I used to stay with Mrs. Slatter sometimes during the holidays. I went across country over the kaffir paths, walking or on my bicycle, with some clothes in a small suitcase.

The boys were, from having to stand up to Mr. Slatter, tough and indifferent boys, and went about the farm in a closed gang. They did man's work, driving tractors and superintending the gangs of boys before they were in their teens. I stayed with Mrs. Slatter. She cooked a good deal and sewed and gardened. Most of the day she sat on the verandah, sewing. We did not talk much. She used to make her own dresses, cotton prints and pastel linens, like all the women of the district wore. She made Mr. Slatter's khaki farm-shirts and the boys' shirts. Once she made herself a petticoat that was too small for her to get into, and Mr. Slatter saw her struggling with it in front of the mirror, and he said, "What size do you think you are, Bluebell?" in the same way he would say, as we sat down to table, "What have you been doing with your lily-white hands to-day, Primrose?" To which she would reply, pleasantly, as if he had really asked a question, "I've made some cakes." Or, "I got some salt meat from the butcher at the station today, fresh out of the pickle." About the petticoat she said, "Yes, I must have been put-ting on more weight than I knew."

When I was twelve or thereabouts, I noticed that the boys had turned against their mother, not in the way of being brutal to her, but they spoke to her as their father did, calling her Bluebell, or the Fat Woman at the Fair. It was odd to hear them, because it was as if they said, simply, Mum, or Mother. Not once did I hear her lose her temper with them. I could see she had determined to herself not to make them any part of what she had against Mr. Slatter. I knew she was pleased to have me there, during that time, with the five men coming in only for meals.

One evening during a long stay, the boys as usual had gone off to their rooms to play when supper was done, and Mr. Slatter said to his wife: "I'm off. I'll be back tomorrow for breakfast." He went out into the dark and the wet. It was raining hard that night. The win-dow-panes were streaked with rain and shaking with the wind. Mrs. Slatter looked across at me and said—and this was the first time it had been mentioned how often he went off after dinner, coming back as the sun rose, or sometimes not for two or three days: "You must remember something. There are some men, like Mr. Slatter, who've got more energy than they know what to do with. Do you know how he started? When I met him and we were courting he was a butcher's boy at the corner. And now he's worth as much as any man in the district."

"Yes," I said, understanding for the first time that she was very proud of him.

She waited for me to say something more, and then said: "Yes, we have all kinds of ideas when we're young. But Mr. Slatter's a man that does not know his own strength. There are some things he doesn't understand, and it all comes from that. He never under-stands that other people aren't as strong as he is."

We were sitting in the big living-room. It had a stone floor with

rugs and skins on it. A boot clattered on the stone and we looked up
and there was Mr. Slatter. His teeth were showing. He wore his big
black boots, shining now from the wet, and his black oilskin glis-
tened. "The boss-boy says the river's up," he said. "I won't get
across tonight." He took off his oilskin there, scattering wet on Mrs.
Slatter's polished stone floor; tugged off his boots; and reached out
through the door to hang his oilskin in the passage and set his boots
under it; and came back.

There were two rivers between the Slatters' farm and the Pritts'
farm, twelve miles off; and when the water came down they could
be impassable for hours.

"So I don't know my own strength?" he said to her, direct, and it
was a soft voice, more frightening than I had ever heard from him,
for he bared grinning teeth as usual, and his big fists hung at his
sides.

"No," she said steadily, "I don't think you do." She did not lift her
eyes, but stayed quiet in the corner of the sofa under the lamp. "We
aren't alone," she added quickly, and now she did look warningly
at him.

He turned his head and looked towards me. I made fast for the
door. I heard her say, "Please. I'm sorry about the river. But leave
me alone, please."

"So you're sorry about the river?"

"Yes."

"And I don't know my own strength?"

I shut the door. But it was a door that was never shut, and it
swung open again and I ran down the passage away from it, as he
said: "So that's why you keep your bedroom door locked, Lady
Godiva, is that it?"

And she screamed out: "Ah, leave me alone. I don't care what you
do. I don't care now. But you aren't going to make use of me. *I
won't let you make use of me.*"

It was a big house, rooms sprawling everywhere. The boys had
two rooms and a playroom off at one end of a long stone passage.
Dairies and larders and kitchen opened off the passage. Then a
dining-room and some offices and a study. Then the living-room.
And another passage off at an angle, with the room where I slept
and beside it Mrs. Slatter's big bedroom with the double bed and
after that a room they called the workroom, but it was an ordinary
room and Mr. Slatter's things were in it, with a bed.

I had not thought before that they did not share a bedroom. I
knew no married people in the district who had separate rooms,

and that is why I had not thought about the small room where Mr. Slatter slept.

Soon after I had shut the door on myself, I heard them come along the passage outside, I heard voices in the room next door. Her voice was pleading, his loud; and he was laughing a lot.

In the morning at breakfast I looked at Mrs. Slatter, but she was not taking any notice of us children. She was pale. She was helping Mr. Slatter to his breakfast. He always had three or four eggs on thick slabs of bacon, and then slice after slice of toast, and half a dozen cups of tea as black as it would come from the pot. She had some toast and a cup of tea and watched him eat. When he went out to the farm-work he kissed her, and she blushed.

When we were on the verandah after breakfast, sewing, she said to me, apologetically and pink-cheeked: "I hope you won't think anything about last night. Married people often quarrel. It doesn't mean anything."

My parents did not quarrel. At least, I had not thought of them as quarrelling. But because of what she said I tried to remember times when they disagreed and perhaps raised their voices and then afterwards laughed and kissed each other. Yes, I thought, it is true that married people quarrel, but that doesn't mean they aren't happy together.

That night after supper, when the boys had gone to their room, Mr. Slatter said, "The rivers are down; I'm off." Mrs. Slatter, sitting quiet under the lamp, kept her eyes down and said nothing. He stood there staring at her, and she said: "Well, you know what that means, don't you?"

He simply went out, and we heard the lorry start up; and the headlights swung up against the window-panes a minute, so that they dazzled up gold and hard and went black again.

Mrs. Slatter said nothing, so that my feeling that something awful had happened slowly faded. Then she began talking about her childhood in London. She was a shop assistant before she met Mr. Slatter. She often spoke of her family, and the street she lived in, so I wondered if she were homesick, but she never went back to London so perhaps she was not homesick at all.

Soon after that Emmy Pritt got ill. She was not the sort of woman one thought of as being ill. She had some kind of operation; and they all said she needed a holiday, she needed to get off the altitude. Our part of Central Africa was high, nearly four thousand feet; and we all knew that when a person got run down they needed a rest from the altitude in the air at sea level. Mrs. Pritt went down to the Cape; and soon after Mr. and Mrs. Slatter went, too, with the four children, and they all had a holiday together at the same hotel.

When they came back, the Slatters brought a farm assistant with them. Mr. Slatter could not manage the farm-work, he said. I heard my father say that Slatter was taking things a bit far; he was over at the Pritts' every week-end from Friday night to Monday morning and nearly every night from after supper until morning. Slatter, he said, might be as strong as a herd of bulls, but no one could go on like that; and in any case, one should have a sense of proportion. Mr. Pritt was never mentioned, though it was not for years that I thought to consider what this might mean. We used to see him about the station, or at gymkhanas. He was an ordinary man, not like a farmer, as we knew farmers—men who could do anything; he might have been anybody, or an office person. He was ordinary in height, thinnish, with his pale hair leaving his narrow forehead high and bony. He was an accountant as well. People used to say that Charlie Slatter helped Emmy Pritt run their farm, and most of the time Mr. Pritt was off staying at neighbouring farms doing their accounts.

The new assistant was Mr. Andrews; and, as Mrs. Slatter said to my mother when she came over for tea, he was a gentleman. He had been educated at Cambridge in England. He came of a hard-up family, though, for he had only a few hundred pounds of capital of his own. He would be an assistant for two years and then start his own farm.

For a time I did not go to stay with Mrs. Slatter. Once or twice I asked if she had said anything to my mother about my coming, and she said in a dry voice, meaning to discourage me, "No, she hasn't said anything." I understood when I heard my father say: "Well, it might not be such a bad thing. For one thing, he's a nice lad; and for another, it might make Slatter see things differently." And another time: "Perhaps Slatter would give Molly a divorce? After all, he practically lives at the Pritts'! And then Molly could have some sort of a life at last."

"But the boy's not twenty-five," said my mother. And she was really shocked, as distinct from her obstinate little voice when she felt him to be wrong-headed or loose in his talk—a threat of some kind. "And what about the children? Four children!"

My father said nothing to this, but after some minutes he came off some track of thought with: "I hope Molly's taking it sensibly. I do hope she is. Because she could be laying up merry hell for herself if she's not."

I saw George Andrews at a gymkhana, standing at the rail with Mrs. Slatter. Although he was an Englishman he was already brown; and his clothes were loosened up and easy, as our men's clothes were. So there was nothing to dislike about him on that score. He was rather short, not fat, but broad, and you could see he would be fat. He was healthy-looking above all, with a clear, reddish face the sun had laid a brown glisten over; and very clear blue eyes; and his hair was thick and short, glistening like fur. I wanted to like him and so I did. I saw the way he leaned beside Mrs. Slatter, with her dust coat over his arm, holding out his programme for her to mark. I could understand that, after Mr. Slatter, she would like a gentleman who would open doors for her and stand up when she came into the room. I could see she was proud to be with him. And so I liked him, though I did not like his mouth; his lips were pink and wettish. I did not look at his mouth again for a long time. And because I liked him I was annoyed with my father when he said, after that gymkhana, "Well, I don't know. I don't think I like it after all. He's a bit of a young pup, Cambridge or no Cambridge."

Six months after George Andrews came to the district there was a dance for the young people at the Slatters'. It was the first dance. The two older boys were eighteen and seventeen and they had girls. The two younger boys were fifteen and thirteen and they despised girls. I was fifteen then, and all these boys were too young for me, and the girls of the two older boys were nearly twenty. There were about sixteen of us, and the married people thirty or forty, as usual. The married people sat in the living-room and danced in it, and we were on the verandahs. Mr. Slatter was dancing with Emmy Pritt, and sometimes another woman; and Mrs. Slatter was busy being a hostess and dancing with George Andrews. I was still in a short dress and unhappy because I was in love with one of the assistants from the farm between the rivers; and I knew very well that until I had a long dress he would not see me. I went into Mrs. Slatter's bedroom latish because it seemed the only room empty, and I looked out of the window at the dark wet night. It was the rainy season, and we had driven over the swollen noisy river and all the way the rainwater was sluicing under our tires. It was still raining, and the lamplight gilded streams of rain so that as I turned my head slightly this way and that, the black and the gold rods shifted before me, and I thought (and I had never thought so simply before about these things): "How do they manage? With all these big boys in the house? And they never go to bed before eleven or half-past these days, I bet, and with Mr. Slatter coming home unexpectedly from Emmy Pritt—it must be difficult. I suppose he has to wait until everyone's alseep. It must be horrible, wondering all the time if the boys have noticed something. . . ." I turned from the window and looked from it into the big, low-ceilinged, comfortable room with its big low bed covered over with pink roses, the pillows propped high in pink frilled covers; and although I had been in that room during visits for years of my life, it seemed strange to me, and ugly. I loved Mrs. Slatter. Of all the women in the district she was the kindest, and she had always been good to me. But at that moment I hated her and I despised her.

I started to leave the bedroom, but at the door I stopped, because Mrs. Slatter was in the passage, leaning against the wall, and George Andrews had his arms around her, and his face in her neck. She was saying, "Please don't, George, please don't, please; the boys might see." And he was swallowing her neck and saying nothing at all. She was twisting her face and neck away and pushing him off. He staggered back from her, as though she had pushed him hard, but it was because he was drunk and had no balance, and he said: "Oh, come on into your bedroom a minute. No one will know." She said, "No, George. Why should we have to snatch five minutes in the middle of a dance, like—"

"Like what?" he said, grinning. I could see how the light that came down the passage from the big room made his pink lips glisten.

She looked reproachfully at him, and he said: "Molly, this thing is getting a bit much, you know. I have to set my alarm clock for one in the morning, and then I'm dead beat. I drag myself out of my bed, and then you've got your clock set for four, and God knows working for your old man doesn't leave one with much enthusiasm for bouncing about all night." He began to walk off towards the big room where the people were dancing. She ran after him and grabbed at his arm. I retreated backward towards Mr. Slatter's room, but almost at once she had got him and turned him around and was kissing him. The people in the big room could have seen if they had been interested.

That night Mrs. Slatter had on an electric blue crepe dress with diamonds on the straps and in flower patterns on the hips. There was a deep V in front which showed her breasts swinging loose under the crepe, though usually she wore strong corsets. And the back was cut down to the waist. As the two turned and came along, he put his hand into the front of her dress, and I saw it lift out her left breast, and his mouth was on her neck again. Her face was desperate; but that did not surprise me, because I knew she must be ashamed. I despised her, because her white, long breast, lying in his hand like a piece of limp, floured dough, was not like Mrs. Slatter who called men Mister even if she had known them twenty years, and was really very shy, and there was nothing Mr. Slatter liked more than to tease her because she blushed when he used bad language.

"What did you make such a fuss for?" George Andrews was saying in a drunken sort of way. "We can lock the door, can't we?"

"Yes, we can lock the door," she answered in the same way, laughing.

I went back into the crowd of married people, where the small children also were, and sat beside my mother; and it was only five minutes before Mrs. Slatter came back looking as usual, from one door, and then George Andrews, in at another.

I did not go to the Slatters' again for some months. For one thing, I was away at school; and for another people were saying that Mrs. Slatter was run down and she should get off the altitude for a bit. My father was not mentioning the Slatters by this time, because he had quarrelled with my mother over them. I knew they had, because whenever Molly Slatter was mentioned, my mother tightened her mouth and changed the subject.

And so a year went by. At Christmas they had a dance again, and I had my first long dress, and I went to that dance not caring if it was at the Slatters' or anywhere else. It was my first dance as one of the young people. And so I was on the verandah dancing most of the evening, though sometimes the rain blew in on us, because it was raining again, being the full of the rainy season, and the skies were heavy and dark, with the moon shining out like a knife from the masses of the clouds and then going in again leaving the verandah with hardly light enough to see each other. Once I went down to the steps to say goodbye to some neighbours who were going home early because they had a new baby, and coming back up the steps there was Mr. Slatter and he had Mrs. Slatter by the arm. "Come here, Lady Godiva," he said. "Give us a kiss."

"Oh, go along," she said, sounding good-humoured. "Go along with you and leave me in peace."

He was quite drunk, but not very. He twisted her arm around. It looked like a slight twist but she came up sudden against him, in a bent-back curve, her hips and legs against him, and he held her there. Her face was sick, and she half-screamed, "You don't know your own strength." But he did not slacken the grip, and she stayed there, and the big sky was filtering a little stormy moonlight and I could just see their faces, and I could see his grinning teeth. "Your bloody pride, Lady Godiva," he said. "Who do you think you're doing in? Who do you think is the loser over your bloody locked door?" She said nothing and her eyes were shut. "And now you've frozen out George, too? What's the matter, isn't he good enough for you either?" He gave her arm a wrench, and she gasped, but then shut her lips again, and he said: "So now you're all alone in your tidy bed, telling yourself fairy stories in the dark. Sister Theresa, the little flower."

He let her go suddenly, and she staggered, so he put out his other hand to steady her, and held her until she was steady. It seemed odd to me that he should care that she shouldn't fall to the ground, and that he should put his hand like that to stop her falling.

And so I left them and went back on to the verandah. I was dancing all the night with the assistant from the farm between the rivers. I was right about the long dress. All those months, at the station or at gymkhanas, he had never seen me at all. But that night he saw me, and I was wanting him to kiss me. But when he did I slapped his face. Because then I knew that he was drunk. I had not thought he might be drunk, though it was natural he was, since everybody was. But the way he kissed me was not at all what I had been thinking. "I beg your pardon I'm sure," he said, and I walked past him into the passage, and then into the living-room. But there were so many people and my eyes were stinging, so I went through into the other passage, and there, just like last year, as if the whole year had never happened, were Mrs. Slatter and George Andrews. I did not want to see it, not the way I felt.

"And why not?" he was saying, biting into her neck.

"Oh, George, that was all ended months ago, months ago!"

"Oh, come on, Moll, I don't know what I've done. You never bothered to explain."

"No." And then, crying out, "*Mind my arm.*"

"What's the matter with your arm?"

"I fell and sprained it."

So he let go of her, and said, "Well, thanks for the nice interlude, thanks anyway, old girl." I knew that he had been meaning to hurt her, because I could feel what he said hurting me. He went off into the living-room by himself, and she went off after him, but to talk to someone else, and I went into her bedroom. It was empty. The lamp was on a low table by the bed, turned down; and the sky through the windows was black and wet and hardly any light came from it.

Then Mrs. Slatter came in and sat on the bed and put her head in her hands. I did not move.

"Oh my God!" she said. "Oh my God, my God!" Her voice was strange to me. The gentleness was not in it, though it was soft, but it was soft from breathlessness.

"Oh my God!" she said, after a long long silence. She took up one of the pillows from the bed, and wrapped her arms around it, and laid her head down on it. It was quiet in this room, although from the big room came the sound of singing, a noise like howling, because people were drunk, or part-drunk, and it had the melancholy savage sound of people singing when they are drunk. An awful sound, like animals howling.

Then she put down the pillow, tidily, in its proper place, and swayed backward and forward and said: "Oh God, make me old soon, make me old. I can't stand this, I can't stand this any longer."

And again the silence, with the howling sound of the singing outside, and the footsteps of the people who were dancing scraping on the cement of the verandah.

"I can't go on living," said Mrs. Slatter, into the dark above the small glow of lamplight. She bent herself up again, double, as if she were hurt physically, her hands gripped around her ankles, holding herself together; and she sat crunched up, her face looking straight in front at the wall, level with the lamplight. So now I could see her face. I did not know that face. It was stone, white stone, but her eyes gleamed out of it black, and with a flicker in them. And her black shining hair that was not grey at all yet had loosened and hung in streaks around the white stone face.

"I can't stand it," she said again. The voice she used was strange to me. She might have been talking to someone. For a moment I even thought she had seen me and was talking to me, explaining herself to me. And then, slowly, she let herself unclench and she went out into the dance again.

I took up the lamp and held it as close as I could to the mirror and bent in and looked at my face. But there was nothing to my face.

Next day I told my father I had heard Mrs. Slatter say she could not go on living. He said, "Oh Lord, I hope it's not because of what I said about her dress"; but I said no, it was before he said he didn't like the dress. "Then if she was upset," he said, "I expect what I said made her feel even worse." And then: "Oh poor woman, poor woman!" He went into the house and called my mother and they talked it over. Then he got onto the telephone and I heard him asking Mrs. Slatter to drop in next time she was going past to the station. And it seemed she was going in that morning, and before lunchtime she was on our verandah talking to my father. My mother was not there, although my father had not asked her in so many words not to be there. As for me, I went to the back of the verandah where I could hear what they said.

"Look, Molly," he said, "we are old friends. You're looking like hell these days. Why don't you tell me what's wrong? You can say anything to me, you know."

After quite a time she said, "Mr. Farquar, there are some things you can't say to anybody. Nobody."

"Ah, Molly," he said, "if there's one thing I've learned—and I learned it early on, when I was a young man and I had a bad time —it's this. Everybody's got something terrible, Molly. Everybody has something awful they have to live with. We all live together and we see each other all the time, and none of us knows what awful thing the other person might be living with."

And then she said, "But Mr. Farquar, I don't think that's true. I know people who don't seem to have anything private to make them unhappy."

"How do you know, Molly? How do you know?"

"Take Mr. Slatter," she said. "He's a man who does as he likes. But he doesn't know his own strength. And that's why he never seems to understand how other people feel."

"But how do you know, Molly? You can live next to someone for fifty years and still not know. Perhaps he's got something that gives him hell when he's alone, like all the rest of us?"

"No, I don't think so, Mr. Farquar."

"Molly," he said, appealing suddenly, and very exasperated. "You're too hard on yourself, Molly."

She didn't say anything.

He said, "Listen, why don't you get away for a while, get yourself down to the sea? This altitude drives us all quietly crazy. You get down off the altitude for a bit."

She still said nothing, and he lowered his voice, and I could imagine how my mother's face would have gone stiff and cold had she heard what he said: "And have a good time while you're there. Have a good time and let go a bit."

"But, Mr. Farquar, I don't want a good time." The words, a good time, she used as if they could have nothing to do with her.

"If we can't have what we want in this world, then we should take what we can get."

"It wouldn't be right," she said at last, slowly. "I know people have different ideas, and I don't want to press mine on anyone."

"But *Molly*—" he began, exasperated, or so it sounded, and then he was silent.

From where I sat I could hear the grass chair creaking; she was getting out of it. "I'll take your advice," she said. "I'll get down to the sea and I'll take the children with me. The two younger ones."

"To hell with the kids for once. Take your old man with you and see that Emmy Pritt doesn't go with you this time."

"Mr. Farquar," she said, "if Mr. Slatter wants Emmy Pritt, he can have her. He can have either one or the other of us. But not both. If I took him to the sea he would be over at her place ten minutes after we got back."

"Ah, Molly, you women can be hell. Have some pity on him for once."

"Pity? Mr. Slatter's a man who needs nobody's pity. But thank you for your good advice, Mr. Farquar. You are always very kind, you and Mrs. Farquar."

And she said goodbye to my father, and when I came forward she kissed me and asked me to come and see her soon, and she went to the station to get the stores.

And so Mrs. Slatter went on living. George Andrews bought his own farm and married and the wedding was at the Slatters'. Later on Emmy Pritt got sick again and had another operation and died. It was a cancer. Mr. Slatter was ill for the first time in his life from grief, and Mrs. Slatter took him to the sea, by themselves, leaving the children, because they were grown-up anyway. For this was years later, and Mrs. Slatter's hair had gone grey and she was fat and old, as I had heard her say she wanted to be.

A Road to the Big City

THE train left at midnight, not at six. Jansen's flare of temper at the clerk's mistake died before he turned from the counter; he did not really mind. For a week he had been with rich friends, in a vacuum of wealth, politely seeing the town through their eyes. Now, for six hours, he was free to let the dry and nervous air of Johannesburg strike him direct. He went into the station buffet. It was a bare place, with shiny brown walls and tables arranged regularly. He sat before a cup of strong orange-coloured tea; and because he was in the arrested, dreamy frame of mind of the uncommitted traveller, he was the spectator at a play that could not hold his attention. He was about to leave, in order to move by himself through the streets, among the people, trying to feel what they were in this city, what they had which did not exist, perhaps, in other big cities—for he believed that in every place there dwelt a demon that expressed itself through the eyes and voices of those who lived there—when he heard someone ask: "Is this place free?" He turned quickly, for there was a quality in the voice which could not be mistaken. Two girls stood beside him, and the one who had spoken sat down without waiting for his response; there were many empty tables in the room. She wore a tight, short, black dress, several brass chains, and high-heeled, shiny, black shoes. She was a tall, broad girl with colourless hair ridged tightly round her head, but given a bright surface so that it glinted like metal. She immediately lighted a cigarette and said to her companion, "Sit down, for

God's sake." The other girl shyly slid into the chair next to Jansen, averting her face as he gazed at her, which he could not help doing —she was so different from what he expected. Plump, childish, with dull hair bobbing in fat rolls on her neck, she wore a flowered and flounced dress and flat white sandals on bare and sunburnt feet. Her face had the jolly friendliness of a little dog. Both girls showed Dutch ancestry in the broad blunt planes of cheek and forehead; both had small blue eyes, though one pair was surrounded by sandy lashes and the other by black varnished fringes.

The waitress came for an order. Jansen was too curious about the young girl to move away. "What will you have?" he asked. "Brandy," said the older one at once. "Two brandies," she added, with another impatient look at her sister—there could be no doubt that they were sisters.

"I haven't never drunk brandy," said the younger with a giggle of surprise. "Except when Mom gave me some sherry at Christmas." She blushed as the older said despairingly, half under her breath: "Oh God preserve me from it!"

"I came to Johannesburg this morning," said the little one to Jansen confidingly. "But Lilla has been here earning a living for a year."

"My God!" said Lilla again. "What did I tell you? Didn't you hear what I told you?" Then, making the best of it, she smiled professionally at Jansen and said, "Green! You wouldn't believe it if I told you. I was green when I came, but compared with Marie. . . ." She laughed angrily.

"Have you been to Joburg before this day?" asked Marie in her confiding way.

"You are passing through," stated Lilla, with a glance at Marie. "You can tell easy if you know how to look."

"You're quite right," said Jansen.

"Leaving tomorrow perhaps?" asked Lilla.

"Tonight," said Jansen.

Instantly Lilla's eyes left Jansen and began to rove about her, resting on one man's face and then the next. "Midnight," said Jansen, in order to see her expression change.

"There's plenty time," she said, smiling.

"Lilla promised I could go to the bioscope," said Marie, her eyes becoming large. She looked around the station buffet, and because of her way of looking, Jansen tried to see it differently. He could not. It remained for him a bare, brownish, dirty sort of place, full of badly-dressed and dull people. He felt as one does with a child whose eyes widen with terror or delight at the sight of an old woman muttering down the street, or a flowering tree. What hunched black crone from a fairy tale, what celestial tree does the child see? Marie was smiling with charmed amazement.

"Very well," said Jansen, "let's go to the movies."

For a moment Lilla calculated, her hard blue glance moving from Jansen to Marie. "You take Marie," she suggested, direct to Jansen, ignoring her sister. "She's green, but she's learning." Marie half-rose, with a terrified look. "You can't leave me," she said.

"Oh my God!" said Lilla resignedly. "Oh, all right. Sit down, baby. But I've a friend to see. I told you."

"But I only just came."

"All right, all right. Sit down, I said. He won't bite you."

"Where do you come from?" asked Jansen.

Marie said a name he had never heard.

"It's not far from Bloemfontein," explained Lilla.

"I went to Bloemfontein once," said Marie, offering Jansen this experience. "The bioscope there is big. Not like near home."

"What is home like?"

"It's small," said Marie.

"What does your father do?"

"He works on the railway," Lilla said quickly.

"He's a ganger," said Marie, and Lilly rolled her eyes up and sighed.

Jansen had seen the gangers' cottages, the frail little shacks along the railway lines, miles from any place, where the washing flapped whitely on the lines over patches of garden, and the children ran out to wave to the train that passed shrieking from one wonderful fabled town to the next.

"Mom is old-fashioned," said Marie. She said the word old-fashioned carefully; it was not hers, but Lilla's; she was tasting it, in the way she sipped at the brandy, trying it out, determined to like it. But the emotion was all her own; all the frustration of years was in her, ready to explode into joy. "She doesn't want us to be in Joburg. She says it is wrong for girls."

"Did you run away?" asked Jansen.

Wonder filled the child's face. "How did you guess I ran away?" she said, with a warm admiring smile at Lilla. "My sister sent me the money. I didn't have none at all. I was alone with Mom and Dad, and my brothers are working on the copper mines."

"I see." Jansen saw the lonely girl in the little house by the railway lines, helping with the chickens and the cooking, staring hope-

lessly at the fashion papers, watching the trains pass, too old now
to run out and wave and shout, but staring at the fortunate people
at the windows with grudging envy, and reading Lilla's letters week
after week: "I have a job in an office. I have a new dress. My young
man said to me . . ." He looked over the table at the two fine
young South African women, with their broad and capable look,
their strong bodies, their health, and he thought: Well, it happens
every day. He glanced at his watch and Marie said at once:
"There's time for the bioscope, isn't there?"

"You and your bioscope," said Lilla. "I'll take you tomorrow afternoon." She rose, said to Jansen in an offhand way: "Coming?" and
went to the door. Jansen hesitated, then followed Marie's uncertain
but friendly smile.

The three went into the street. Not far away shone a large white
building with film stars kissing between thin borders of coloured
shining lights. Streams of smart people went up the noble marble
steps where splendid men in uniform welcomed them. Jansen,
watching Marie's face, was able to see it like that. Lilla laughed
and said: "We're going home, Marie. The pictures aren't anything
much. There's better things to do than pictures." She winked at
Jansen.

They went to a two-roomed flat in a suburb. It was over a grocery
store called Mac's Golden Emporium. It had canned peaches, dried
fruit, dressed dolls and rolls of cotton goods in the window. The flat
had new furniture in it. There was a sideboard with bottles and
a radio. The radio played: "Or would you like to swing on a star,
carry moonbeams home in a jar, and be better off than you
are . . ."

"I like the words," said Marie to Jansen, listening to them with
soft delight. Lilla said, "Excuse me, but I have to phone my friend,"
and went out.

Marie said, "Have a drink." She said it carefully. She poured
brandy, the tip of her tongue held between her teeth, and she
spilled the water. She carried the glass to Jansen, and smiled in
unconscious triumph as she set it down by him. Then she said:
"Wait," and went into the bedroom. Jansen adjusted himself on the
juicy upholstery of a big chair. He was annoyed to find himself
here. What for? What was the good of it? He looked at himself in
the glass over a sideboard. He saw a middle-aged gentleman, with a
worn, indulgent face, dressed in a grey suit and sitting uncomfortably in a very ugly chair. But what did Marie see when she looked
at him? She came back soon, with a pair of black shiny shoes on

her broad feet, and a tight red dress, and a pretty face painted over her own blunt honest face. She sat herself down opposite him, as she had seen Lilla sit, adjusting the poise of her head and shoulders. But she forgot her legs, which lay loosely in front of her, like a schoolgirl's.

"Lilla said I could wear her dresses," she said, lingering over her sister's generosity. "She said today I could live here until I earned enough to get my own flat. She said I'd soon have enough." She caught her breath. "Mom would be mad."

"I expect she would," said Jansen drily, and saw Marie react away from him. She spread her red skirts and faced him politely, waiting for him to make her evening.

Lilla came in, turning her calculating, good-humoured eyes from her sister to Jansen, smiled, and said: "I'm going out a little. Oh, keep your hair on. I'll be back soon. My friend is taking me for a walk."

The friend came in and took Lilla's arm; he was a large, handsome sunburnt man who smiled with a good-time smile at Marie. She responded with such a passion of admiration in her eyes that Jansen understood at once what she did not see when she looked at himself. "My, my," said this young man with easy warmth to Marie. "You're a fast learner, I can see that."

"We'll be back," said Lilla to Marie. "Remember what I said." Then, to Jansen, like a saleswoman: "She's not bad. Anyhow she can't get herself into any trouble here at home." The young man slipped his arm around her and reached for a glass off the sideboard with his free hand. He poured brandy, humming with the radio: "In a shady nook, by a babbling brook. . . ." He threw back his head, poured the brandy down, smiled broadly at Jansen and Marie, winked and said: "Be seeing you. Don't forget to wind up the clock and put the cat out." Outside on the landing he and Lilla sang, "Carry moonbeans home in a jar, be better off than you are. . . ." They sang their way down to the street. A car door slammed; an engine roared. Marie darted to the window and said bitterly, "They've gone to the pictures."

"I don't think so," said Jansen. She came back, frowning, preoccupied with responsibility. "Would you like another drink?" she asked, remembering what Lilla had told her. Jansen shook his head and sat still for a moment, weighted with inertia. Then he said, "Marie, I want you to listen to me." She leaned forward dutifully, ready to listen. But this was not as she had gazed at the other man —the warm, generous, laughing, singing young man. Jansen found many words ready on his tongue, disliked them, and blurted: "Marie, I wish you'd let me send you back home tonight." Her face dulled. "No, Marie, you really must listen." She listened politely, from behind her dull resistance. He used words carefully, out of the delicacy of his compassion, and saw how they faded into meaninglessness in the space between him and Marie. Then he grew brutal and desperate, because he had to reach her. He said, "This sort of life isn't as much fun as it looks"; and "Thousands of girls all over the world choose the easy way because they're stupid, and afterward they're sorry." She dropped her lids, looked at her feet in her new high-heeled shoes, and shut herself off from him. He used the words whore and prostitute; but she had never heard them except as swear words and did not connect them with herself. She began repeating, over and over again: "My sister's a typist; she's got a job in an office."

He said angrily, "Do you think she can afford to live like this on a typist's pay?"

"Her gentleman friend gives her things—he's generous, she told me so," said Marie doubtfully.

"How old are you, Marie?"

"Eighteen," she said, turning her broad freckled wrist, where Lilla's bracelet caught the light.

"When you're twenty-five you'll be out on the streets picking up any man you see, taking them to hotels. . . ."

At the word "hotel" her eyes widened; he remembered she had never been in a hotel; they were something lovely on the cinema screen.

"When you're thirty you'll be an old woman."

"Lilla said she'd look after me. She promised me faithfully," said Marie, in terror at his coldness. But what he was saying meant nothing to her, nothing at all. He saw that she probably did not know what the word prostitute meant; that the things Lilla had told her meant only lessons in how to enjoy the delights of this city.

He said, "Do you know what I'm here for? Your sister expects you to take off your clothes and get into bed and. . . ." He stopped. Her eyes were wide open, fastened on him, not in fear, but in the anxious preoccupation of a little girl who is worried she is not behaving properly. Her hands had moved to the buckle of her belt, and she was undoing it.

Jansen got up, and without speaking he gathered clothes that were obviously hers from off the furniture, from off the floor. He went into the bedroom and found a suitcase and put her things into it. "I'm putting you on the train tonight," he said.

"My sister won't let you," she cried out. "She'll stop you."

"Your sister's a bad girl," said Jansen, and saw, to his surprise, that Marie's face showed fear at last. Those two words, "bad girl," had had more effect than all his urgent lecturing.

"You shouldn't say such things," said Marie, beginning to cry. "You shouldn't never say someone's a bad girl." They were her mother's words, obviously, and had hit her hard where she could be reached. She stood listless in the middle of the floor, weeping, making no resistance. He tucked her arm under his and led her downstairs. "You'll marry a nice man soon, Marie," he promised. "You won't always have to live by the railway lines."

"I don't never meet no men, except Dad," she said, beginning to tug at his arm again.

He held her tight until they were in a taxi. There she sat crouched on the edge of the seat, watching the promised city sweep past. At the station, keeping a firm hold on her, he bought her a ticket and gave her five pounds, and put her into a compartment and said: "I know you hate me. One day you'll know I'm right, and you'll be glad." She smiled weakly and huddled herself into her seat, like a cold little animal, staring sadly out of the window.

He left her, running, to catch his own train, which already stood waiting on the next platform.

As it drew out of the station he saw Marie waddling desperately on her tall heels along the platform, casting scared glances over her shoulder. Their eyes met; she gave him an apologetic smile and ran on. With the pound notes clutched loosely in her hand she was struggling her way through the crowds back to the lights, the love, the joyous streets of the promised city.

Flight

ABOVE the old man's head was the dovecote, a tall wire-netted shelf on stilts, full of strutting, preening birds. The sunlight broke on their grey breasts into small rainbows. His ears were lulled by their crooning; his hands stretched up towards his favourite, a homing pigeon, a young plump-bodied bird, which stood still when it saw him and cocked a shrewd bright eye.

"Pretty, pretty, pretty," he said, as he grasped the bird and drew it down, feeling the cold coral claws tighten around his finger. Content, he rested the bird lightly on his chest and leaned against a tree, gazing out beyond the dovecote into the landscape of a late afternoon. In folds and hollows of sunlight and shade, the dark red soil, which was broken into great dusty clods, stretched wide to a tall horizon. Trees marked the course of the valley; a stream of rich green grass the road.

His eyes travelled homewards along this road until he saw his grand-daughter swinging on the gate underneath a frangipani tree. Her hair fell down her back in a wave of sunlight; and her long bare legs repeated the angles of the frangipani stems, bare, shining brown stems among patterns of pale blossoms.

She was gazing past the pink flowers, past the railway cottage where they lived, along the road to the village.

His mood shifted. He deliberately held out his wrist for the bird to take flight, and caught it again at the moment it spread its wings. He felt the plump shape strive and strain under his fingers;

and, in a sudden access of troubled spite, shut the bird into a small box and fastened the bolt. "Now you stay there," he muttered and turned his back on the shelf of birds. He moved warily along the hedge, stalking his grand-daughter, who was now looped over the gate, her head loose on her arms, singing. The light happy sound mingled with the crooning of the birds, and his anger mounted.

"Hey!" he shouted, and saw her jump, look back, and abandon the gate. Her eyes veiled themselves, and she said in a pert, neutral voice, "Hullo, Grandad." Politely she moved towards him, after a lingering backward glance at the road.

"Waiting for Steven, hey?" he said, his fingers curling like claws into his palm.

"Any objection?" she asked lightly, refusing to look at him.

He confronted her, his eyes narrowed, shoulders hunched, tight in a hard knot of pain that included the preening birds, the sunlight, the flowers, herself. He said, "Think you're old enough to go courting, hey?"

The girl tossed her head at the old-fashioned phrase and sulked, "Oh, Grandad!"

"Think you want to leave home, hey? Think you can go running around the fields at night?"

Her smile made him see her, as he had every evening of this warm end-of-summer month, swinging hand in hand along the road to the village with that red-handed, red-throated, violent-bodied youth, the son of the postmaster. Misery went to his head and he shouted angrily: "I'll tell your mother!"

"Tell away!" she said, laughing, and went back to the gate.

He heard her singing, for him to hear:

> *"I've got you under my skin,*
> *I've got you deep in the heart of . . ."*

"Rubbish," he shouted. "Rubbish. Impudent little bit of rubbish!"

Growling under his breath, he turned towards the dovecote, which was his refuge from the house he shared with his daughter and her husband and their children. But now the house would be empty. Gone all the young girls with their laughter and their squabbling and their teasing. He would be left, uncherished and alone, with that square-fronted, calm-eyed woman, his daughter.

He stooped, muttering, before the dovecote, resenting the absorbed, cooing birds.

From the gate the girl shouted: "Go and tell! Go on, what are you waiting for?"

Obstinately he made his way to the house, with quick, pathetic, persistent glances of appeal back at her. But she never looked around. Her defiant but anxious young body stung him into love and repentance. He stopped. "But I never meant. . . ." he muttered, waiting for her to turn and run to him. "I didn't mean. . . ."

She did not turn. She had forgotten him. Along the road came the young man Steven, with something in his hand. A present for her? The old man stiffened as he watched the gate swing back and the couple embrace. In the brittle shadows of the frangipani tree his grand-daughter, his darling, lay in the arms of the postmaster's son, and her hair flowed back over his shoulder.

"I see you!" shouted the old man spitefully. They did not move. He stumped into the little whitewashed house, hearing the wooden verandah creak angrily under his feet. His daughter was sewing in the front room, threading a needle held to the light.

He stopped again, looking back into the garden. The couple were now sauntering among the bushes, laughing. As he watched he saw the girl escape from the youth with a sudden mischievous movement and run off through the flowers with him in pursuit. He heard shouts, laughter, a scream, silence.

"But it's not like that at all," he muttered miserably. "It's not like that. Why can't you see? Running and giggling, and kissing and kissing. You'll come to something quite different."

He looked at his daughter with sardonic hatred, hating himself. They were caught and finished, both of them, but the girl was still running free.

"Can't you see?" he demanded of his invisible grand-daughter, who was at that moment lying in the thick green grass with the postmaster's son.

His daughter looked at him and her eyebrows went up in tired forbearance.

"Put your birds to bed?" she asked, humouring him.

"Lucy," he said urgently. "Lucy. . . ."

"Well, what is it now?"

"She's in the garden with Steven."

"Now you just sit down and have your tea."

He stumped his feet alternately, thump, thump, on the hollow wooden floor and shouted: "She'll marry him. I'm telling you, she'll be marrying him next!"

His daughter rose swiftly, brought him a cup, set him a plate.

"I don't want any tea. I don't want it, I tell you."

"Now, now," she crooned. "What's wrong with it? Why not?"

"She's eighteen. Eighteen!"

"I was married at seventeen, and I never regretted it."

"Liar," he said. "Liar. Then you should regret it. Why do you make your girls marry? It's you who do it. What do you do it for? Why?"

"The other three have done fine. They've three fine husbands. Why not Alice?"

"She's the last," he mourned. "Can't we keep her a bit longer?"

"Come, now, Dad. She'll be down the road, that's all. She'll be here every day to see you."

"But it's not the same." He thought of the other three girls, transformed inside a few months from charming, petulant, spoiled children into serious young matrons.

"You never did like it when we married," she said. "Why not? Every time, it's the same. When I got married you made me feel like it was something wrong. And my girls the same. You get them all crying and miserable the way you go on. Leave Alice alone. She's happy." She sighed, letting her eyes linger on the sunlit garden. "She'll marry next month. There's no reason to wait."

"You've said they can marry?" he said incredulously.

"Yes, Dad. Why not?" she said coldly and took up her sewing.

His eyes stung, and he went out on to the verandah. Wet spread down over his chin, and he took out a handkerchief and mopped his whole face. The garden was empty.

From around the corner came the young couple; but their faces were no longer set against him. On the wrist of the postmaster's son balanced a young pigeon, the light gleaming on its breast.

"For me?" said the old man, letting the drops shake off his chin. "For me?"

"Do you like it?" The girl grabbed his hand and swung on it. "It's for you, Grandad. Steven brought it for you." They hung about him, affectionate, concerned, trying to charm away his wet eyes and his misery. They took his arms and directed him to the shelf of birds, one on each side, enclosing him, petting him, saying wordlessly that nothing would be changed, nothing could change, and that they would be with him always. The bird was proof of it, they said, from their lying happy eyes, as they thrust it on him. "There, Grandad, it's yours. It's for you."

They watched him as he held it on his wrist, stroking its soft, sun-warmed back, watching the wings lift and balance.

"You must shut it up for a bit," said the girl intimately, "until it knows this is its home."

"Teach your grandmother to suck eggs," growled the old man.

Released by his half-deliberate anger, they fell back, laughing at him. "We're glad you like it." They moved off, now serious and full of purpose, to the gate, where they hung, backs to him, talking quietly. More than anything could, their grown-up seriousness shut him out, making him alone; also, it quietened him, took the sting out of their tumbling like puppies on the grass. They had forgotten him again. Well, so they should, the old man reassured himself, feeling his throat clotted with tears, his lips trembling. He held the new bird to his face, for the caress of its silken feathers. Then he shut it in a box and took out his favourite.

"Now you can go," he said aloud. He held it poised, ready for flight, while he looked down the garden towards the boy and the girl. Then, clenched in the pain of loss, he lifted the bird on his wrist and watched it soar. A whirr and a spatter of wings, and a cloud of birds rose into the evening from the dovecote.

At the gate Alice and Steven forgot their talk and watched the birds.

On the verandah, that woman, his daughter, stood gazing, her eyes shaded with a hand that still held her sewing.

It seemed to the old man that the whole afternoon had stilled to watch his gesture of self-command, that even the leaves of the trees had stopped shaking.

Dry-eyed and calm, he let his hands fall to his sides and stood erect, staring up into the sky.

The cloud of shining silver birds flew up and up, with a shrill cleaving of wings, over the dark ploughed land and the darker belts of trees and the bright folds of grass, until they floated high in the sunlight, like a cloud of motes of dust.

They wheeled in a wide circle, tilting their wings so there was flash after flash of light, and one after another they dropped from the sunshine of the upper sky to shadow, one after another, returning to the shadowed earth over trees and grass and field, returning to the valley and the shelter of night.

The garden was all a fluster and a flurry of returning birds. Then silence, and the sky was empty.

The old man turned, slowly, taking his time; he lifted his eyes to smile proudly down the garden at his grand-daughter. She was staring at him. She did not smile. She was wide-eyed and pale in the cold shadow, and he saw the tears run shivering off her face.

Plants and Girls

THERE was a boy who lived in a small house in a small town in the centre of Africa.

Until he was about twelve, this house had been the last in the street, so that he walked straight from the garden, across a railway line, and into the veld. He spent most of his time wandering by himself through the vleis and the *kopjes*. Then the town began to grow, so that in the space of a year a new suburb of smart little houses lay between him and the grass and trees. He watched this happening with a feeling of surprised anger. But he did not go through the raw new streets to the vlei where the river ran and the little animals moved. He was a lethargic boy, and it seemed to him as if some spell had been put on him, imprisoning him forever in the town. Now he would walk through the new streets, looking down at the hard glittering tarmac, thinking of the living earth imprisoned beneath it. Where the veld trees had been allowed to stay, he stood gazing, thinking how they drew their strength through the layers of rubble and broken brick, direct from the breathing soil and from the invisibly running underground rivers. He would stand there, staring; and it would seem to him that he could see those fresh, subtly running streams of water moving this way and that beneath the tarmac; and he stretched out his fingers like roots towards the earth. People passing looked away uncomfortably. Children called out: "Mooney, Mooney, mooning again!" Particularly the children from the house opposite laughed and teased him.

They were a large, noisy family, solid in the healthy strength of their numbers. He could hardly distinguish one from another; he felt that the house opposite was filled like a box with plump, joyous, brown-eyed people whose noisy, cheerful voices frightened him.

He was a lanky, thin-boned youth whose face was long and unfinished-looking; and his eyes were enormous, blue, wide, staring, with the brilliance of distance in them.

His mother, when he returned to the house, would say tartly: "Why don't you go over and play with the children? Why don't you go into the bush like you used to? Why don't you. . . ."

He was devoted to his mother. He would say vaguely, "Oh, I don't know," and kick stones about in the dust, staring away over the house at the sky, knowing that she was watching him through the window as she sewed, and that she was pleased to have him there, in spite of her tart, complaining voice. Or he would go into the room where she sat sewing, and sit near her, in silence, for hours. If his father came into the room he began to fidget and soon went away. His father spoke angrily about his laziness and his unnatural behaviour.

He made the mother fetch a doctor to examine the boy. It was from this time that Frederick took the words "not normal" as his inheritance. He was not normal; well, he accepted it. They made a fact of something he had always known because of the way people looked at him and spoke to him. He was neither surprised nor dismayed at what he was. And when his mother wept over him, after the doctor left, he scarcely heard the noise of her tears; he smiled at her with the warm childish grin that no one else had ever seen, for he knew he could always depend on her.

His father's presence was a fact he accepted. On the surface they made an easy trio, like an ordinary family. At meals they talked like ordinary people. In the evenings his father sometimes read to him, for Frederick found it hard to read, although he was now halfway through his teens; but there were moments when the old man fell silent, staring in unconcealable revulsion at this son he had made; and Frederick would let his eyes slide uncomfortably away, but in the manner of a person who is embarrassed at someone else's shortcomings. His mother accepted him; he accepted himself; that was enough.

When his father died he was sorry and cried with his fists in his eyes like a baby. At the graveside the neighbours looked at this great shambling child, with his colourless locks of hair and the big red fists rubbing at his eyes, and felt relieved at the normal outburst of grief. But afterwards it was he and his mother alone in the small suburban house; and they never spoke of the dead father who had vanished entirely from their lives, leaving nothing behind him. She lived for her son, waiting for his return from school, or from his rambles around the streets; and she never spoke of the fact that he was in a class with children five years his junior or that he was always alone at week-ends and holidays, never with other children.

He was a good son. He took her tea in the mornings at the time the sun rose and watched her crinkled old face light up from the pillow as he set down the tray by her knees. But he did not stay with her then. He went out again quickly, shutting the door, his eyes turned from the soft, elderly white shoulders, which were not, for him, his mother. This is how he saw her: in her dumpy flowered apron, her brown sinewy arms setting food before him, her round spectacles shining, her warm face smiling. Yet he did not think of her as an old lady. Perhaps he did not see her at all. He would sometimes put out his great lank hand and stroke her apron. Once he went secretly into her bedroom and took her hairbrush off the dressing-table and brushed the apron, which was lying on the bed; and he put the apron on and laughed out loud at the sight of himself in the mirror.

Later, when he was seventeen, a very tall, awkward youth with the strange-lighted blue eyes, too old to be put to bed with a story after supper, he wandered about by himself through that area of ugly new houses that seemed to change under the soft brightness of the moon into a shadowy beauty. He walked for hours, or stood still gazing dimly about him at the deep starry sky or at the soft shapes of trees.

There was a big veld tree that stood a short way from their gate in a space between two street-lamps, so that there was a well of shadow beneath it which attracted him very much. He stood beneath the tree, listening to the wind moving gently in the leaves and feeling it stir his hair like fingers. He would move slowly in to the tree until his long fingers met the rough bark; and he stroked the tree curiously, learning it, thinking: under this roughness and hardness moves the sap, like rivers under the earth. He came to spend his evenings there, instead of walking among the houses and looking in with puzzled, unenvious eyes through the windows at the other kind of people. One evening an extraordinarily violent spasm shook him, so that he found himself locked about that harsh strong trunk, embracing it violently, his arms and thighs knotted about it, sobbing and muttering angry words. Afterwards he slowly went home, entering the small, brightly lighted room shamedly; and his great blue eyes sought his mother's, and he was surprised that she did not say anything, but smiled at him as usual. Always there was this assurance from her; and as time went past, and each night he returned to the tree, caressing and stroking it, murmuring words of love, he would come home simply, smiling his wide childish smile, waiting for her to smile back, pleased with him.

But opposite was still that other house full of people; the children were growing up; and one evening when he was leaning against the tree in deep shadow, his arm loosely about it, as if around a tender friend, someone stopped outside the space of shadow and peered in saying: "Why, Mooney, what are you doing here by yourself?" It was one of the girls from that house, and when he did not reply she came towards him, finally putting out her hand to touch his arm. The touch struck cruelly through him, and he moved away; and she said with a jolly laugh: "What's the matter? I won't eat you." She pulled him out into the yellowy light from the street-lamp and examined him. She was a fattish, untidy, bright girl, one of the middle children, full of affection for everything in the world; and this odd, silent youth standing there quite still between her hands affected her with amused astonishment, so that she said, "Well, you are a funny boy, aren't you?" She did not know what to do with him, so at last she took him home over the street. He had never been inside her house before, and it was like a foreign country. There were so many people, so much noise and laughter, and the wireless was shouting out words and music. He was silent and smiling in this world which had nothing to do with himself.

His passive smile piqued the girl, and later when he got up saying: "My mother's waiting for me," she replied, "Well, at any rate you can take me to the movies tomorrow."

He had never taken a girl out; had never been to the movies save with his parents, as a child is taken; and he smiled as at a ridiculous idea. But next evening she came and made him go with her.

"What's the matter, Mooney?" she asked, taking his arm. "Don't you like me? Why don't you take girls out? Why do you always stay around your mother? You aren't a baby any longer."

These words he listened to smiling; they did not make him angry, because she could not understand that they had nothing to do with him.

He sat in the theatre beside the girl and waited for the picture to be over. He would not have been in the least surprised if the building and the screen and the girl had vanished, leaving him lying under a tree with not a house in sight, nothing but the veld— the long grasses, the trees, the birds and the little animals. Afterwards they walked home, and he listened to her chattering, scolding voice without replying. He did not mind being with her; but he forgot her as soon as she had gone in at her gate. He wandered back across the street to his own gate and looked at the tree standing in its gulf of shadow with the moonlight on its branches. He took two steps towards it and stopped; another step, and stopped again; and finally turned with a bolting movement, as if in fear, and shambled quickly in to his mother. She glanced up at him with a tight, suspicious face; and he knew she was angry, though she did not speak. Soon he went to bed, unable to bear this unspoken anger. He slept badly and dreamed of the tree. And next night he went to it as soon as it was dark, and stood holding the heavy dark trunk in his arms.

The girl from opposite was persistent. Soon he knew, because of the opposition of his mother, that he had a girl, as ordinary young men have girls.

Why did she want him? Perhaps it was just curiosity. She had been brought up in all that noise and warm quarrelling and laughter; and so Frederick, who neither wanted her nor did not want her, attracted her. She scolded him and pleaded with him: "Don't you love me? Don't you want to marry me?"

At this he gave her his rambling, confused grin. The word marriage made him want to laugh. It was ridiculous. But to her there was nothing ridiculous in it. In her home, marriages took place between boys and girls, and there were always festivals and lovemaking and new babies.

Now he would take her in his arms beside the tree outside the gate, embracing her as he had embraced the tree, forgetting her entirely, murmuring strangely over her head among the shadows. She hated it and she loved it; for her, it was like being hypnotised. She scolded him, stayed away, returned; and yet he would not say he would marry her.

This went on for some time; though for Frederick it was not a question of time. He did not mind having her in his arms under the tree, but he could not marry her. He was driven, night after night, to the silent love-making, with the branches of the tree between him and the moon; and afterwards he went straight to his room, so as not to face his mother.

Then she got ill. Instead of going with the girl at night, he stayed at home, making his mother drinks, silently sitting beside her, putting wet handkerchiefs on her forehead. In the mornings the girl looked at him over the hedge and said, "Baby! Baby!"

"But my mother's sick," he said, finding these words with difficulty from the dullness of his mind. At this she only laughed. Finally she left him. It was like a tight string snapping from him, so that he reeled back into his own house with his mother. He watched the girl going in and out of her house with her sisters, her brothers, her friends, her young men; at night he watched her dancing on the verandah to the gramophone. But she never looked back at him. His mother was still an invalid and kept to her chair; and he understood she was now getting old, but it did not come into his head that she might die. He looked after her. Before going off to the office at the railways, where he arranged luggage under the supervision of another clerk, he would lift his mother from her bed, turn away from her while she painfully dressed herself, support her into a chair by the window, fetch her food, and leave her for the day. At night he returned directly to her from work and sat beside her until it was time to sleep. Sometimes, when the desire for the shadowy street outside became too strong, he would go out for a little time and stand beside his tree. He listened to the wind moving in the branches and thought: It's an old tree, it's too old. If a leaf fell in the darkness he thought: The leaves are falling— it's dying; it's too old to live.

When his mother at last died, he could not understand that she was dead. He stood at her graveside in the efficient, cared-for cemetery of this new town, with its antiseptic look because of the neatness of the rows of graves and the fresh clean sunlight, and gazed down at the oblong hole in the red earth, where the spades had smoothed the steep sides into shares of glistening hardness, and saw the precisely fitting black box at the bottom of the hole, and lifted his head to stare painfully at the neighbours, among whom was the girl from opposite, although he did not see her.

He went home to the empty house that was full of his mother. He left everything as it was. He did not expand his life to fill the space she had used. He was still a child in the house, while her chair stood empty, and her bed had pillows stacked on it, and her clothes hanging over the foot.

There was very little money. His affairs were managed by a man at the bank in whose custody he had been left, and he was told how much he could spend. That margin was like a safety line around his life; and he liked taking his small notebook where he wrote down every penny he spent at each month's end to the man at the bank.

He lived on, knowing that his mother was dead, but only because people had said she was. After a time he was driven by his pain down to the cemetery. The grave was a mound of red earth. The flowers of the funeral had died long ago. There was a small head-stone of granite. A bougainvillaea creeper had been planted on the grave; it spread its glossy green branches over the stone in layers of dark shining green and clusters of bleeding purple flowers. The first time he visited the cemetery he stood staring for a long time. Later he would sit by the headstone, fingering the leaves of the plant. Slowly he came to understand that his mother lay under-neath where he sat. He saw her folded in the earth, her rough brown forearms crossed comfortably on her breast, her flowered apron pulled down to her fat knees, her spectacles glinting, her wrinkled old face closed in sleep. And he fingered the smooth hard leaves, noting the tiny working veins, thinking: They feed on her. The thought filled him with panic and drove him from the grave. Yet he returned again and again, to sit under the pressure of the heavy yellow sunlight, on the rough warm stone, looking at the red and purple flowers, feeling the leaves between his fingers.

One day, at the grave, he broke off a branch of the bougain-villaea plant and returned with it to the house, where he set it in a vase by his bed. He sat beside it, touching and smoothing the leaves. Slowly the branch lost its colour and the clusters of flowers grew limp. A spray of stiff, dead, pale leaves stood up out of the vase; and his eyes rested on it, brilliant, vague, spectral, while his face contracted with pain and with wonder.

During the long solitary evenings he began again to stand at his gate, under the stars, looking about him in the darkness. The big tree had been cut down; all the wild trees in that street were gone, because of the danger from the strong old roots to the bricks of the foundations of the houses. The authorities had planted new saplings, domestic and educated trees like bauhinia and jacaranda. Immediately outside his gate, where the old tree had been, was one of these saplings. It grew quickly: one season it was a tiny plant in a little leaning shed of grass; the next it was as high as his head. There was an evening that he went to it, leaning his forehead against it, not thinking, his hands sliding gently and unsurely up and down the long slim trunk. This taut supple thing was nothing he had known; it was strange to him; it was too slight and weak and there was no shadow around it. And yet he stood there night after night, unconscious of the windows about him where people might be looking out, unconscious of passers-by, feeling and fumbling at the tree, letting his eyes stray past to the sky or to the lines of bushy little saplings along the road or to the dusty crowding hedges.

One evening he heard a bright, scornful voice say: "What do you think you're doing?" and he knew it was the girl from opposite. But the girl from opposite had married long ago and was now an untidy, handsome matron with children of her own; she had left him so far behind that she could now nod at him with careless kindness, as if to say: Well, well, so you're still there, are you?

He peered and gawked at the girl in his intense ugly way that was yet attractive because of his enormous lighted eyes. Then, for him, the young and vigorous creature who was staring at him with such painful curiosity became the girl from opposite. She was in fact the other girl's sister, perhaps ten years her junior. She was the youngest of that large, pulsing family, who were all married and gone, and she was the only one who had known loneliness. When people said, with the troubled callousness, the necessary callousness that protects society against its rotten wood: "He's never been the same since the death of his mother; he's quite crazy now," she felt, not merely an embarrassed and fundamentally indifferent pity, but a sudden throb of sympathy. She had been watching Frederick for a long time. She was ready to defend him against people who said, troubled by this attraction of the sick for the healthy, "For God's sake what do you see in him, can't you do better than that?"

As before, he did as she wanted. He would accompany her to the movies. He would come out of his house at her call. He went walking with her through the dark streets at night. And before parting from her he took her into his arms against the sapling that swayed and slipped under their weight and kissed her with a cold persistence that filled her with horror and with desire, so that she ran away from him, sobbing, saying she would never see him again, and returned inevitably the next evening. She never entered his house; she was afraid of the invisibly present old woman. He seemed not to mind what she did. She was driven wild because she knew that if she did not seek him out, the knowledge of loss would never enter him; he would merely return to the lithe young tree, mumbling fierce, thick, reproachful words to it in the darkness.

As he grew to understand that she would always return no matter how she strove and protested, he would fold her against him, not hearing her cries, and as she grew still with chilled fear, she would hear through the darkness a dark sibilant whispering: "Your hair, your hair, your teeth, your bones." His fingers pressed and probed into her flesh. "Here is the bone, under is nothing only bone," and the long urgent fingers fought to defeat the soft envelope of flesh, fought to make it disappear, so that he could grasp the bones of her arm, the joint of her shoulder; and when he had pressed and probed and always found the flesh elastic against his hands, pain flooded along her as the teeth closed in on her neck, or while his fist suddenly drove inward, under her ribs, as if the tension of flesh were not there. In the morning she would be bruised. She avoided the eyes of her family and covered up the bruises. She was learning, through this black and savage initiation, a curious strength. She could feel the bones standing erect through her body, a branching undefeatable tree of strength; and when the hands closed in on her, stopping the blood, half-choking her, the stubborn half-conscious thought remained: You can't do it; you can't do it, I'm too strong.

Because of the way people looked in at them, through the darkness, as they leaned and struggled against the tree, she made him go inside the hedge of the small neglected garden, and there they lay together on the lawn, for hour after hour, with the cold high moon standing over them, sucking the warmth from their flesh, so they embraced in a cold, lethal ecstasy of pain, knowing only the cold, greenish light, feeling the bones of their bodies cleave and knock together while he grasped her so close that she could scarcely draw each breath. One night she fainted, and she came to herself to find him still clasping her, in a cold strong clasp, his teeth bared against her throat, so that a suffocating black pressure came over her brain in wave after wave; and she fought against him, making him tighten his grip and press her into the soil, and she felt the rough grasses driving up into her flesh.

A flame of self-preservation burned up into her brain, and she fought until he came to himself and his grip loosened. She said,

"I won't. I won't let you. I won't come back again." He lay still, breathing like a deep sleeper. She did not know if he had heard her. She repeated hurriedly, already uncertain, "I won't let you." He got up and staggered away from her, and she was afraid because of the destructive light in the great eyes that glinted at her in the moonlight.

She ran away and locked herself in her bedroom. For several days she did not return. She watched him from her window as he strode huntedly up and down the street, lurking around the young tree, sometimes shaking it so that the leaves came spinning down around him. She knew she must return; and one evening she drifted across the street and came on him standing under the lithe young tree that held its fine glinting leaves like a spray of tinted water upward in the moonlight over the fine slender trunk.

This time he reached out and grasped her and carried her inside to the lawn. She murmured helplessly, in a dim panic, "You mustn't. I won't."

She saw the hazy brilliant stars surge up behind his black head, saw the greenish moonlight pour down the thin hollows of his cheeks, saw the great crazy eyes immediately above hers. The cages of their ribs ground together; and she heard: "Your hair, dead hair, bones, bones, bones."

The bared desperate teeth came down on her throat, and she arched back as the stars swam and went out.

When people glanced over the hedge in the strong early sunlight of next morning they saw him half-lying over the girl, whose body was marked by blood and by soil; and he was murmuring: "Your hair, your leaves, your branches, your rivers."

The Sun Between Their Feet

THE ROAD from the back of the station went to the Roman Catholic Mission, which was a dead end, being in the middle of a Native Reserve. It was a poor mission, with only one lorry, so the road was always deserted, a track of sand between long or short grasses. The station itself was busy with trains and people, and the good country in front was settled thick with white farmers, but all the country behind the station was unused because it was granite boulders, outcrops, and sand. The scrub cattle from the Reserve strayed there. There were no human beings. From the track it seemed the hills of boulders were so steep and laced with vines and weed there would be no place to go between them. But you could force your way in, and there it became clear that in the past people had made use of this wilderness. For one thing there were the remains of earth and rock defences built by the Mashona against the Matabele when they came raiding after cattle and women before Rhodes put an end to all that. For another, the undersurfaces of the great boulders were covered with Bushman paintings. After a hundred yards or so of clambering and squeezing there came a flattish sandy stretch before the boulders erupted again. In this space, at the time of the raiding, the women and the cattle would have been kept while the men held the surrounding defences. From this space, at the time of the Bushmen, small hunting men took coloured clays, and earths, and plant juices for their pictures.

It had rained last night and the low grass was still wet around my ankles and the early sun had not dried the sand. There was a sharp upjut of rock in the middle of the space. The rock was damp, and I could feel the wet heat being dragged up past my bare legs.

Sitting low here, the encircling piles of boulders seemed like mountains, heightening the sky on tall horizons. The rocks were dark grey, but stained with lichens. The trees between the boulders were meagre, and several were lightning-struck, no more than black skeletons. This was hungry country, growing sand and thin grass and rocks and heat. The sun came down hard between heat-conserving rocks. After an hour of sun the sand between the grasses showed a clean dry glistening surface, and a dark wet underneath.

The Reserve cattle must have moved here since the rains last night, for there were a score of fresh cow pats laid on the grass. Big blue flies swore and tumbled over them, breaking the crust the sun had baked. The air was heavy and sweet. The buzzing of the flies, the tiny sucking sound of the heat, the cooing of the pigeons, made a morning silence.

Hot, and silent; and save for the flies, no movement anywhere, for what winds there were blew outside this sheltered space.

But soon there was new movement. Where the flies had broken the crust of the nearest dung clot, two beetles were at work. They were small, dusty, black, round-bodied beetles. One had set his back legs over a bit of dung and was heaving and levering at it. The other, with a fast rolling movement, the same that a hen makes settling roused feathers over eggs, was using his body to form the ball even before it was heaved clear of the main lump of matter. As soon as the piece was freed, both beetles assaulted it with legs and bodies, modelling fast, frantic with creation, seizing it between their back legs, spinning it, rolling it under them, both tugging and pushing it through the thick encumbering grass stems that rose over them like forest trees until at last the ball rolled away from them into a plain, or glade, or inch-wide space of sand. The two beetles scuttled about among the stems, looking for their property. They were on the point of starting again on the mother-pile of muck, when one of them saw the ball lying free in the open, and both ran after it.

All over the grassy space, around the cow pats, dung beetles were at work, the blowflies hustled and buzzed, and by night all the new cow-stomach-worked grass would be lifted away, rolled away, to feed flies, beetles and new earth. That is, unless it rained hard again, when everything would be scattered by rods of rain.

But there was no sign of rain yet. The sky was the clear slow blue of African mornings after night storms. My two beetles had the sky on their side. They had all day.

The book says that dung beetles form a ball of dung, lay their eggs in it, search for a gentle slope, roll the ball up it, and then allow it to roll down again so that in the process of rolling "the pellet becomes compacted."

Why must the pellet be compacted? Presumably so that the blows of sun and rain do not beat it to fragments. Why this complicated business of rolling up and rolling down?

Well, it is not for us to criticise the processes of nature; so I sat on top of the jutting rock, and watched the beetles rolling the ball towards it. In a few minutes of work they had reached it, and had hurled themselves and the dung ball at its foot. Their momentum took them a few inches up the slope, then they slipped, and ball and beetles rolled back to the flat again.

I got down off the rock, and sat in the grass behind them to view the ascent through their eyes.

The rock was about four feet long and three feet high. It was a jutting slab of granite, weeded and lichened, its edges blunted by rain and by wind. The beetles, hugging their ball between legs and bellies, looked up to a savage mountain, whose first slopes were an easy foot-assisting invitation. They rolled their ball, which was now crusted with dirt, to a small ridge under the foothills, and began, this time with slow care, to hitch it up from ridge to ridge, from one crust of lichen to the next. One beetle above, one below, they cherished their ball upwards. Soon they met the obstruction that had defeated them before: a sudden upswelling in the mountain wall. This time, one remained below the ball, holding its weight on its back legs, while the other scouted off sideways to find an easier path. It returned, gripped the ball with its legs, and the two beetles resumed their difficult, sideways scrambling progress, up around the swell in the rock into a small valley which led, or so it seemed, into the second great stage of the ascent. But this valley was a snare, for there was a crevasse across it. The mountain was riven. Heat and cold had split it to its base, and the narrow crack sloped down to a mountain lake full of warm fresh water over a bed of wind-gathered leaves and grass. The dung ball slipped over the edge of the crevasse into the gulf, and rolled gently into the lake where it was supported at its edge by a small

fringe of lichen. The beetles flung themselves after it. One, strad-
dling desperate legs from a raft of reed to the shore, held the ball
from plunging into the depths of the lake. The other, gripping fast
with its front legs to a thick bed of weed onshore, grappled the ball
with its back legs, and together they heaved and shoved that precious dung out of the water and back into the ravine. But now
the mountain walls rose high on either side, and the ball lay between them. The beetles remained still a moment. The dirt had
been washed from the dung, and it was smooth and slippery.

They consulted. Again one remained on guard while the other
scouted, returning to report that if they rolled the ball clear
along the bottom of the ravine, this would in due course narrow,
and they could, by use of legs and shoulders and backs, lift the
ball up the crack to a new height on the mountain and, by crossing another dangerous shoulder, attain a gentle weed-roughed
slope that led to the summit. This they tried. But on the dangerous
shoulder there was a disaster. The lake-slippery ball left their
grasp and plunged down the mountainside to the ground, to the
point they had started from half an hour before. The two beetles
flung themselves after it, and again they began their slow difficult
climb. Again their dung ball fell into the crevasse, rolled down into
the lake, and again they rescued it, at the cost of infinite resource
and patience, again they pushed and pulled it up the ravine, again
they maneuvered it up the crack, again they tried to roll it around
the mountain's sharp shoulder, and again it fell back to the foot
of the mountain, and they plunged after it.

"The dung beetle, *Scarabaeus* or *Aleuchus sacer,* lays its eggs
in a ball of dung, then chooses a gentle slope, and compacts the
pellet by pushing it uphill backwards with its hind legs and allowing it to roll down, eventually reaching its place of deposit."

I continued to sit in the low hot grass, feeling the sun first on my
back, then hard down on my shoulders, and then direct from above
on my head. The air was dry now, all the moisture from the night
had gone up into the air. Clouds were packing the lower skies. Even
the small pool in the rock was evaporating. Above it the air quivered with steam. When, for the third time, the beetles lost their
ball in the mountain lake, it was no lake, but a spongy marsh, and
getting it out involved no danger or difficulty. Now the ball was
sticky, had lost its shape, and was crusted with bits of leaf and
grass.

At the fourth attempt, when the ball rolled down to the starting
point and the beetles bundled after it, it was past midday, my head

ached with heat, and I took a large leaf, slipped it under the ball of dung and the beetles, and lifted this unit away to one side, away from the impossible and destructive mountain.

But when I slid the leaf from under them, they rested a moment in the new patch of territory, scouted this way and that among the grass stems, found their position, and at once rolled their ball back to the foot of the mountain where they prepared another ascent.

Meanwhile, the cow pats on the grass had been dismantled by flies and other dung beetles. Nothing remained but small grassy fragments, or dusty brown stains on the lifting stems. The buzzing of the flies was silenced. The pigeons were stilled by the heat. Far away thunder rolled, and sometimes there was the shriek of a train at the station or the puffing and clanging of shunting engines.

The beetles again got the ball up into the ravine, and this time it rolled down, not into a marsh, but into a damp bed of leaves. There they rested awhile in a steam of heat.

Sacred beetles, these, the sacred beetles of the Egyptians, holding the symbol of the sun between their busy stupid feet. Busy, silly beetles, mothering their ball of dung again and again up a mountain when a few minutes' march to one side would take them clear of it.

Again I lifted them, dung and beetles, away from the precipice, to a clear place where they had the choice of a dozen suitable gentle slopes, but they rolled their ball patiently back to the mountain's foot.

"The slope is chosen," says the book, "by a beautiful instinct, so that the ball of dung comes to rest in a spot suitable for the hatching of the new generation of sacred insect."

The sun had now rolled past midday position and was shining onto my face. Sweat scattered off me. The air snapped with heat. The sky where the sun would go down was banked high with darkening cloud. Those beetles would have to hurry not to get drowned.

They continued to roll the dung up the mountain, rescue it from the dried bed of the mountain lake, force it up to the exposed dry shoulder, where it rolled down and they plunged after it. Again and again and again, while the ball became a ragged drying structure of fragmented grass clotted with dung. The afternoon passed. The sun was low in my eyes. I could hardly see the beetle or the dung because of the glare from a black pack of clouds which were red-rimmed from the lowering sun behind. The red streaming rays came down and the black beetles and their dung ball on the mountainside seemed dissolved in sizzling light.

It was raining away on the far hills. The drumming of the rain and the drumming of the thunder came closer. I could see the skirmishing side lances of an army of rain pass half a mile away beyond the rocks. A few great shining drops fell here, and hissed on burning sand and on the burning mountainside. The beetles laboured on.

The sun dropped behind the piled boulders and now this glade rested in a cool spent light, the black trees and black boulders standing around it, waiting for the rain and for the night. The beetles were again on the mountain. They had the ball tight between their legs, they clung on to the lichens, they clung on to rock wall and their treasure with the desperation of stupidity.

Now the hard red glare was gone it was possible to see them clearly. It was difficult to imagine the perfect shining globe the ball had been—it was now nothing more than a bit of refuse. There was a clang of thunder. The grasses hissed and swung as a bolt of wind came fast from the sky. The wind hit the ball of dung, it fell apart into a small puff of dusty grass, and the beetles ran scurrying over the surface of the rock looking for it.

Now the rain came marching towards us, it reached the boulders in a grey envelopment of wet. The big shining drops, outrunners of the rain army, reached the beetles' mountain and one, two! the drops hit the beetles smack, and they fell off the rock into the already seething wet grasses at its foot.

I ran out of the glade with the rain sniping at my heels and my shoulders, thinking of the beetles lying under the precipice up which, tomorrow, after the rain had stopped, and the cattle had come grazing, and the sun had come out, they would again labour and heave a fresh ball of dung.

A Letter from Home

. . . *Ja,* but that isn't why I'm writing this time. You asked about Dick. You're worrying about him?—man! But he's got a poetry scholarship from a Texas university and he's lecturing the Texans about letters and life too in Suid Afrika, South Africa to you (forgive the hostility), and his poems are read, so they tell me, wherever the English read poetry. He's fine, man, but I thought I'd tell you about Johannes Potgieter, remember him? Remember the young poet, The Young Poet? He was around that winter you were here. Don't tell me you've forgotten those big melting brown eyes and those dimples. About ten years ago (*ja,* times flies) he got a type of unofficial grace-gift of a job at St. ———— University on the strength of those poems of his, and—God—they were good. Not that you or any other English-speaking *domkop* will ever know, because they don't translate out of Afrikaans. Remember me telling you and everyone else (give me credit for that at least; I give the devil his due, when he's a poet) what a poet he was, how blerry good he was—but several people tried to translate Hans's poems, including me, and failed. Right. *Goed.* Meanwhile a third of the world's population—or is it a fifth, or to put it another way, X_5Y_{59} million people—speak English (and it's increasing by six births a minute) but one million people speak Afrikaans, and though I say it in a whisper, man, only a fraction of them can read it, I mean to read it. But Hans is still a great poet. Right.

He wasn't all that happy about being a sort of unofficial laureate at that university. It's no secret some poets don't make laureates. At the end of seven months he produced a book of poems which had the whole God-fearing place sweating and sniffing out heresy of all kinds, sin, sex, liberalism, brother love, and so forth and so on; but of course in a civilised country (I say this under my breath, or I'll get the sack from my university, and I've got four daughters these days, had you forgotten?) no one would see anything in them but good poetry. Which is how Hans saw them, poor innocent soul. He was surprised at what people saw in them, and he was all upset. He didn't like being called all those names, and the good country boys from their fine farms and the smart town boys from their big houses all started looking sideways, making remarks, and our Hans, he was reduced to pap, because he's not a fighter, Hans; he was never a taker of positions on the side of justice, freedom, and the rest, for tell you the truth, I don't think he ever got round to defining them. *Goed.* He resigned, in what might be called a dignified silence, but his friends knew it was just plain cowardice or, if you like, incomprehension about what the fuss was over, and he went to live in Blagspruit in the Orange Free, where his Tantie Gertrude had a house. He helped her in her store. *Ja,* that's what he did. What did we all say to this? Well, what do you think? The inner soul of the artist (et cetera) knows what is best, and he probably *needed* the Orange Free and his Auntie's store for his development. Well, something like that. To tell the truth, we didn't say much; he simply dropped out. And time passed. *Ja.* Then they made me editor of *Onwards,* and thinking about our indigenous poets, I remembered Johannes Potgieter, and wrote "What about a poem from you?"—feeling bad because when I counted up the years, it was eight since I'd even thought of him, even counting those times when one says drunk at dawn: Remember Hans? Now, there was a poet. . . .

No reply, so I let an editorial interval elapse and I wrote again, and I got a very correct letter back. Well phrased. Polite. But not just that, it took me an hour to work out the handwriting—it was in a sort of Gothic print, each letter a work of art, like a medieval manuscript. But all he said, in that beautiful black art-writing was: he was very well, he hoped I was very well, the weather was good, except the rains were late, his Tantie Gertie was dead, and he was running the store. "*Jou vriend,* Johannes Potgieter."

Right. *Goed.* I was taking a trip up to Joburg, so I wrote and said I'd drop in at Blagspruit on my way back, and I got another Manuscript, or Missal, saying he hoped to see me, and he would pre-

pare Esther for my coming. I thought, he's married, poor *kerel*,
and it was the first time I'd thought of him as anything but a born
bachelor, and I was right—because when I'd done with Joburg, not
a moment too soon, and driven down to the Orange Free, and arrived on the doorstep, there was Hans, but not a sign of a wife,
and Esther turned out to be—but first I take pleasure in telling
you that the beautiful brown-eyed poet with his noble brow and
pale dimpled skin was bald—he has a tonsure, I swear it—and he's
fat, a sort of smooth pale fat. He's like a monk, lard-coloured
and fat and smooth. Esther is the cook, or rather, his jailor. She's
a Zulu, a great fat woman, and I swear she put the fear of God
into me before I even got into the house. Tantie Gertie's house is
a square brick four-roomed shack, you know the kind, with an iron
roof and verandahs—well, what you'd expect in Blagspruit. And
Esther stood about six feet high in a white apron and a white
doekie and she held a lamp up in one great black fist and looked
into my face and sighed and went off into her kitchen singing
"Rock of Ages." *Ja*, I promise you. And I looked at Hans, and all he
said was "It's O.K., man. She likes you. Come in."

She gave us a great supper of roast mutton and pumpkin fritters
and samp, and then some preserved fruit. She stood over us, arms
folded, as we ate, and when Johannes left some mutton fat, she
said in her mellow hymn-singing voice: "Waste not, want not, Master Johannes." And he ate it all up. *Ja*. She told me I should have
some more peaches for my health, but I defied her and I felt as
guilty as a small kicker, and I could see Hans eyeing me down the
table and wondering where I got the nerve. She lives in the *kia* at
the back, one small room with four children by various fathers, but
no man, because God is more than enough for her now, you can
see, with all those kids and Hans to bring up the right way. Auntie's
store is a Drapery and General Goods in the main street, called
Gertie's Store, and Hans was running it with a coloured man. But I
heard Esther with my own ears at supper saying to his bowed bald
shamed head: "Master Johannes, I heard from the cook at the
predikant's house today that the dried peaches have got worms in
them." And Hans said: "O.K., Esther, I'll send them up some of the
new stock tomorrow."

Right. We spent all that evening talking, and he was the same
old Hans. You remember how he used to sit, saying not a blerry
word, smiling that sweet dimpled smile of his, listening, listening,
and then he'd ask a question, remember? Well, *do* you? Because it's
only just now *I'm* beginning to remember. People'd be talking about

I don't know what—the Nats or the weather or the grape crop, anything—and just as you'd start to get nervous because he never said
anything, he'd lean forward and start questioning, terribly serious,
earnest, about some detail, something not quite central, if you
know what I mean. He'd lean forward, smiling, smiling, and he'd
say: "You really mean that? It rained all morning? It rained all
morning? Is that the truth?" That's right, you'd say, a bit uneasy,
and he'd say, shaking his head: "God, man, it rained all morning,
you say. . . ." And then there'd be a considerable silence till things
picked up again. And half an hour later he'd say: "You really mean
it? The hanepoort grapes are good this year?"

Right. We drank a good bit of brandewyn that night, but in a
civilised way—you know: "Would you like another little drop, Mr.
Martin?" "*Ja*, just a small tot, Hans, thank you"—but we got pretty
pickled, and when I woke Sunday morning, I felt like death, but
Esther was setting down a tray of tea by my bed, all dressed up in
her Sunday hat and her black silk saying: "*Goeie môre*, Master du
Preez, it's nearly time for church," and I nearly said: "I'm not a
churchgoer, Esther," but I thought better of it, because it came to
me, can it be possible, has our Hans turned a God-fearing man
in Blagspruit? So I said, "*Goed*, Esther. Thanks for telling me, and
now just get out of here so that I can get dressed." Otherwise she'd
have dressed me, I swear it. And she gave me a majestic nod,
knowing that God had spoken through her to send me to church,
sinner that I was and stinking of cheap *dop* from the night before.

Right. Johannes and I went to *kerk*, he in a black Sunday suit, if
you'd believe such a thing, and saying: "Good morning, Mr. Stein.
Goeie môre, Mrs. Van Esslin," a solid and respected member of the
congregation, and I thought, poor *kerel*, there but for the grace of
God go I, if I had to live in this godforsaken dorp stuck in the
middle of the Orange Free State. And he looked like death after the
brandewyn, and so did I, and we sat there swaying and sweating in
that blerry little church through a sermon an hour and a half long,
while all the faithful gave us nasty curious looks. Then we had a
cold lunch, Esther having been worshipping at the Kaffir church
down in the Location, and we slept it all off and woke covered with
flies and sweating, and it was as hot as hell, which is what Blagspruit is, hell. And he'd been there ten years, man, ten years. . . .

Right. It is Esther's afternoon off, and Johannes says he will
make us some tea, but I see he is quite lost without her, so I say:
"Give me a glass of water, and let's get out from under this iron,
that's all I ask." He looks surprised, because his hide is hardened to

it, but off we go, through the dusty little garden full of marigolds and zinnias, you know those sun-baked gardens with the barbed-wire fences and the gates painted dried-blood colour in those little dorps stuck in the middle of the veld, enough to make you get drunk even to think of them, but Johannes is sniffling at the marigolds, which stink like turps, and he sticks an orange zinnia in his lapel, and says: "Esther likes gardening." And there we go along the main street, saying good afternoon to the citizens, for half a mile, then we're out in the veld again, just the veld. And we wander about, kicking up the dust and watching the sun sink, because both of us have just one idea, which is: how soon can we decently start sundowning?

Then there was a nasty stink on the air, and it came from a small bird impaled on a thorn on a thorn tree, which was a butcherbird's cache, have you ever seen one? Every blerry thorn had a beetle or a worm or something stuck on it, and it made me feel pretty sick, coming on top of everything, and I was just picking up a stone to throw at the damned thorn tree, to spite the butcherbird, when I saw Hans staring at a lower part of this tree. On a long black thorn was a great big brown beetle, and it was waving all its six legs and its two feelers in rhythm, trying to claw the thorn out of its middle, or so it looked, and it was writhing and wriggling, so that at last it fell off the thorn, which was at right angles, so to speak, from the soil, and it landed on its back, still waving its legs, trying to up itself. At which Hans bent down to look at it for some time, his two monk's hands on his upper thighs, his bald head sweating and glowing red in the last sunlight. *Then he bent down, picked up the beetle and stuck it back on the thorn.* Carefully, you understand, so that the thorn went back into the hole it had already made. You could see he was trying not to hurt the beetle. I just stood and gaped, like a *domkop,* and for some reason I remembered how one used to feel when he leaned forward and said, all earnest and involved: "You say the oranges are no good this year? Honestly, is that really true?" Anyway, I said: "Hans, man, for God's sake!" And then he looked at me, and he said, reproachfully: "The ants would have killed it, just look!" Well, the ground was swarming with ants of one kind or another, so there was logic in it, but I said: "Hans, let's drink, man, let's drink."

Well, it was Sunday, and no bars open. I took a last look at the beetle, the black thorn through its oozing middle, waving its black legs at the setting sun, and I said: "Back home, Hans, and to hell with Esther. We're going to get drunk."

Esther was in the kitchen, putting out cold meat and tomatoes, and I said: "Esther, you can take the evening off."

She said: "Master Hans, I have had all the Sunday afternoon off talking to Sister Mary." Hans looked helpless at me, and I said: "Esther, I'm giving you the evening off. Good night."

And Hans said, stuttering and stammering: "That's right, Esther, I'll give you the evening off. Good night, Esther."

She looked at him. Then at me. Hey, what a woman. Hey, what a queen, man! She said, with dignity: "Good night, Mr. Johannes. Good night, Mr. du Preez." Then she wiped her hands free of evil on her white apron, and she strode off, singing "All things bright and beautiful," and I tell you we felt as if we weren't good enough to wash Esther's *broekies,* and that's the truth.

Goed. We got out the brandy, never mind about the cold meat and the tomatoes, and about an hour later I reached my point at last, which was, what about the poems, and the reason I'd taken so long was I was scared he'd say: "Take a look at Blagspruit, man. Take a look. Is this the place for poems, Martin?" But when I asked, he leaned forward and stared at me, all earnest and intent, then he turned his head carefully to the right, to see if the door into the kitchen was shut, but it wasn't; and then left at the window, and that was open too, and then past me at the door to the verandah. Then he got up on tiptoes and very carefully shut all three, and then he drew the curtains. It gave me the *skriks,* man, I can tell you. Then he went to a great old black chest and took out a Manuscript, because it was all in the beautiful black difficult writing, and gave it to me to read. And I sat and slowly worked it out, letter by letter, while he sat opposite, sweating and totting, and giving fearful looks over his shoulders.

What was it? Well, I was drunk, for one thing, and Hans sitting there all frightened scared me, but it was good, it was good, I promise you. A kind of chronicle of Blagspruit it was, the lives of the citizens—well, need I elaborate, since the lives of citizens are the same everywhere in the world, but worse in Suid Afrika, and worse a million times in Blagspruit. The Manuscript gave off a stink of church and right-doing, with the sin and the evil underneath. It had a medieval stink to it, naturally enough, for what is worse than the *kerk* in this our land? But I'm saying this to you, remember, and I never said it, but what is worse than the stink of the *kerk* and the God-fearing in this our feudal land?

But the poem. As far as I can remember, because I was full as a tick, it was a sort of prose chronicle that led up to and worked into the poems; you couldn't tell where they began or ended. The prose was stiff and old-fashioned, and formal, monk's language, and the poems too. But I knew when I read it it was the best I'd read in years—since I read those poems of his ten years before, man, not since then. And don't forget, God help me, I'm an editor now, and I read poems day and night, and when I come on something like Hans's poems that night I have nothing to say but—*Goed*.

Right. I was working away there an hour or more because of that damned black ornamented script. Then I put it down and I said: "Hans, can I ask you a question?" And he looked this way and that over his shoulder first, then leaned forward, the lamplight shining on his pate, and he asked in a low trembling sinner's voice: "What do you want to ask me, Martin?"

I said, "Why this complicated handwriting? What for? It's beautiful, but why this monkey's puzzle?"

And he lowered his voice and said: "It's so that Esther can't read it."

I said: "And what of it, Hans? Why not? Give me some more brandewyn and tell me."

He said: "She's a friend of the predikant's cook, and her sister Mary works in the Mayor's kitchen."

I saw it all. I was drunk, so I saw it. I got up, and I said: "Hans, you're right. You're right a thousand times. If you're going to write stuff like this, as true and as beautiful as God and all his angels, then Esther mustn't read it. But why don't you let me take this back with me and print it in *Onwards*?"

He went white and looked as if I might knife him there and then like a *totsti*. He grabbed the Manuscript from me and held it against his fat chest, and he said: "They mustn't see it."

"You're right," I said, understanding him completely.

"It's dangerous keeping it here," he said, darting fearful looks all around.

"Yes, you're right," I said, and I sat down with a bump in my *rimpie* chair, and I said: "*Ja*, if they found that, Hans . . ."

"They'd kill me," he said.

I saw it, completely.

I was drunk. He was drunk. We put the Manuscript *boekie* on the table and we put our arms around each other and we wept for the citizens of Blagspruit. Then we lit the hurricane lamp in the kitchen, and he took his *boekie* under his arm, and we tiptoed out into the moonlight that stank of marigolds, and out we went down the main street, all dark as the pit now because it was after twelve and the citizens were asleep, and we went staggering down the tarmacked street that shone in the moonlight between low dark houses, and out into the veld. There we looked sorrowfully at each other and wept some sad brandy tears, and right in front of us, the devil aiding us, was a thorn tree. All virgin it was, its big black spikes lifted up and shining in the devil's moon. And we wept a long time more, and we tore out the pages from his Manuscript and we made them into little screws of paper and we stuck them all over the thorns, and when there were none left, we sat under the thorn tree in the moonlight, the black spiky thorns making thin purplish shadows all over us and over the white sand. Then we wept for the state of our country and the state of poetry. We drank a lot more brandy, and the ants came after it and us, so we staggered back down the gleaming sleeping main street of Blagspruit, and that's all I remember until Esther was standing over me with a tin tray that had a teapot, teacup, sugar and some condensed milk, and she was saying: "Master du Preez, where is Master Hans?"

I saw the seven o'clock sun outside the window, and I remembered everything, and I sat up and I said: "My God!"

And Esther said: "God has not been in this house since half-past five on Saturday last." And went out.

Right. I got dressed, and went down the main street, drawing looks from the Monday-morning citizens, all of whom had probably been watching us staggering along last night from behind their black drawn curtains. I reached the veld and there was Hans. A wind had got up, a hot dust-devilish wind, and it blew about red dust and bits of grit, and leaves, and dead grass into the blue sky, and those pale dry bushes that leave their roots and go bouncing and twirling all over the empty sand, like dervishes, round and round, and then up and around, and there was Hans, letting out yelps and cries and shouts, and he was chasing about after screws of paper that were whirling around among all the dust and stuff.

I helped him. The thorn tree had three squirls of paper tugging and blowing from spikes of black thorn, so I collected those, and we ran after the blowing white bits that had the black beautiful script on them, and we got perhaps a third back. Then we sat under the thorn tree, the hard sharp black shadows over us and the sand, and we watched a dust devil whirling columns of yellow sand and his poems up and off into the sky.

I said: "But Hans, you could write them down again, couldn't you? You couldn't have forgotten them, surely?"

And he said: "But, Martin, anyone can read them now. Don't you see that, man? Esther could come out here next afternoon off, and pick any one of those poems up off the earth and read it. Or suppose the predikant or the Mayor got their hands on them?"

Then I understood. I promise you, it had never crossed my *domkop* mind until that moment. I swear it. I simply sat there, sweating out guilt and brandy, and I looked at that poor madman, and then I remembered back ten years and I thought: You idiot. You fool.

Then at last I got intelligent and I said: "But, Hans, even if Esther and the predikant and the Mayor did come out here and pick up your poems, like leaves, off the bushes? They couldn't understand one word, because they are written in that *slim* black script you worked out for yourself."

I saw his poor crazy face get more happy, and he said: "You think so, Martin? Really? You really think so?"

I said: "*Ja,* it's the truth." And he got all happy and safe, while I thought of those poems whirling around forever, or until the next rainstorm, around the blue sky with the dust and the bits of shining grass.

And I said: "Anyway, at the best only perhaps a thousand, or perhaps two thousand, people would understand that beautiful *boekie.* Try to look at it that way, Hans, it might make you feel better."

By this time he looked fine; he was smiling and cheered up.

Right.

We got up and dusted each other off, and I took him home to Esther. I asked him to let me take the poems we'd rescued back to publish in *Onwards,* but he got desperate again and said: "No, no. Do you want to kill me? Do you want them to kill me? You're my friend, Martin, you can't do that."

So I told Esther that she had a great man in her charge, through whom Heaven Itself spoke, and she was right to take such care of him. But she merely nodded her queenly white-*doekied* head and said: "Goodbye, Master du Preez, and may God be with you."

So I came home to Kapstaad.

A week ago I got a letter from Hans, but I didn't see at once it was from him; it was in ordinary writing, like yours or mine, but rather unformed and wild, and it said: "I am leaving this place. They know me now. They look at me. I'm going north to the river. Don't tell Esther. *Jou vriend,* Johannes Potgieter."

Right.

Jou vriend,
Martin du Preez

The New Man

ABOUT three miles on the track to the station a smaller overgrown road branched to the Manager's House. This house had been built by the Rich Mitchells for their manager. Then they decided to sell a third of their farm, with the house ready for its owner. It stood empty a couple of years, with sacks of grain and oxhides in it. The case had been discussed and adjudicated on the verandahs of the district: no, Rich Mitchell was not right to sell that part of his farm, which was badly watered and poorish soil, except for 100 acres or so. At the very least he should have thrown in a couple of miles of his long vlei with the lands adjacent to it. No wonder Rich Mitchell was rich (they said); and when they met him their voices had a calculated distance: "Sold your new farm yet, Mitch?" No, he hadn't sold it, nor did he, for one year, then another. But the rich can afford to wait. (As they said on the verandahs.)

The farm was bought by a Mr. Rooyen who had already gone broke farming down Que Que way. The Grants went to visit, Mrs. Grant in her new silk, Mr. Grant grumbling because it was the busy season. The small girl did not go, she refused, she wanted to stay in the kitchen with old Tom the cookboy, where she was happy, watching him make butter.

That evening, listening with half an ear to the parents' talk, it was evident things weren't too good. Mr. Rooyen hadn't a penny of his own; he had bought the farm through the Land Bank, and was working on an £800 loan. What it amounted to was, it was a gamble on the first season. "It's all very well," said Mr. Grant, summing up with the reluctant critical note in his voice that meant he knew he would have to help Mr. Rooyen, would do so, but found it all too much. And sure enough, in the dry season the Rooyen cattle were running on Grant land and using the Grant well. But Mr. Rooyen had become "the new man in the Manager's House."

The first season wasn't too bad, so the small girl gathered from the talk on the verandahs, and Mr. Rooyen might make out after all. But he was very poor. Mrs. Grant, when they had too much cheese or butter or baked, sent supplies over by the cook. In the second year Mr. Grant lent Mr. Rooyen £200 to tide him over. The small girl knew that the new neighbour belonged forever to that category of people who, when parting from the Grants, would wring their hands and say in a low, half-ashamed voice: "You've been very good to me and I'll never forget it."

The first time she saw the new farmer, who never went any-where, was when the Grants went into the station and gave Mr. Rooyen a lift. He could not afford a car yet. He stood on the track waiting for the Grants, and behind him the road to his house was even more overgrown with bushes and grass, like a dry river-bed between the trees. He sat in the back, answering Mr. Grant's ques-tions about how things were going. She did not notice him much, or rather refused to notice him, because she definitely did not like him, although he was nothing she had not known all her life. A tallish man, dressed in bush khaki, blue eyes inflamed by the sun, he was burned—not a healthy reddish brown, but a mahogany colour—because he was never out of the sun, never stopped work-ing. This colour in a white man, the small girl already knew, meant a desperate struggling poverty and it usually preceded going broke or getting very ill. But the reason she did not like him, or that he scared her, was the violence of his grievance. The hand which lay on the back of the car seat behind Mr. Grant trembled slightly; his voice trembled as he spoke of Rich Mitchell, his neighbour, who had a vlei seven miles long and would neither sell nor rent him any of it. "It isn't right," he kept saying. "He doesn't make use of my end. Perhaps his cattle graze there a couple of weeks in the dry season, but that's all." All this meant that his cattle would be run-ning with the Grants' again when the grass was low. More: that he was appealing, through Mr. Grant, for justice, to the unconstituted council of farmers who settled these matters on their verandahs.

That night Mr. Grant said: "It's all very well!" a good many times. Then he rang up Mr. Matthews (Glasgow Bob) from the

Glenisle Farm; and Mr. Paynter (Tobacco Paynter) from Bellevue; and Mr. Van Doren (the Dutchman) from Blue Hills. Their farms adjoined Rich Mitchell's.

Soon after, the Grants went into the station again. At the last minute they had remembered to ring up and ask Mr. Rooyen if he wanted a lift. He did. It wasn't altogether convenient, particularly for the small girl, because two-thirds of the back seat was packed to the roof with plough parts being sent into town for repair. And beside Mrs. Grant on the front seat was a great parcel full of dead chickens ready for sale to the hotel. "It's no bother," said Mrs. Grant to Mr. Rooyen, "the child can sit on your knee."

The trouble was that the small girl was definitely not a child. She was pretty certain she was no longer a small girl either. For one thing, her breasts had begun to sprout, and while this caused her more embarrassment than pleasure, she handled her body in a proud, gingerly way that made it impossible, as she would have done even a season before, to snuggle in onto the grownup's lap. She got out of the car in a mood of fine proud withdrawal, not looking at Mr. Rooyen as he fitted himself into the narrow space on the back seat. Then, with a clumsy fastidiousness, she perched on the very edge of his bare bony knees and supported herself with two hands on the back of the front seat. Mr. Rooyen's arms were about her waist, as if she were indeed a child, and they trembled, as she had known they would—as his voice still trembled, talking about Rich Michell. But soon he stopped talking.

The car sped forward through the heavy, red-dust-laden trees, rocking and bouncing over the dry ruts, and she was jerked back to fit against the body of Mr. Rooyen, whose fierceness was that of lonely tenderness, as she knew already, though never before in her life had she met it. She longed for the ride to be over, while she sat squeezed, pressed, suffering, in the embrace of Mr. Rooyen, a couple of feet behind the Grants. She ignored, so far as was possible, with politeness; was stiff with resistance; looked at the backs of her parents' heads and marvelled at their blindness. "If you only knew what your precious Mr. Rooyen was doing to your precious daughter . . ."

When it was time to come home from the station, she shed five years and became petulant and wilful: she would sit on her mother's knee, not on Mr. Rooyen's. Because now the car was stacked with groceries, and it was a choice of one knee or the other. "Why, my dear child," said the fond Mrs. Grant, pleased at this rebirth of the charming child in her daughter. But the girl sat as stiffly on her mother's knee as she had on the man's, for she felt his eyes continually returning to her, over her mother's shoulder, in need or in fear or in guilt.

When the car stopped at the turning to the Manager's House, she got off her mother's knee and would not look at Mr. Rooyen. Who then did something really not allowable, not in the code, for he bent, squeezed her in his great near-black hairy arms and kissed her. Her mother laughed, gay and encouraging. Mr. Grant said merely: "Goodbye, Rooyen," as the tall forlorn fierce man walked off to his house along the grass-river road.

The girl got into the back seat, silent. Her mother had let her down, had let her new breasts down by that gay social laugh. As for her father, she looked at his profile, absorbed in the business of starting the car and setting it in motion, but the profile said nothing. She said, resentful: "Who does he think he *is*, kissing me?" And Mrs. Grant said briskly: "My dear child, why ever not?" At which Mr. Grant gave his wife a quick grave look, but remained silent. And this comforted the girl, supported her.

She thought about Mr. Rooyen. Or rather she felt him—felt the trembling of his arms, felt as if he were calling to her. One hot morning, saying she was going for a walk, she set off to his house. When she got there she was overheated and tired and needed a drink. Of course there was no one there. The house was two small rooms, side by side under corrugated iron, with a lean-to kitchen behind. In front was a narrow brick verandah with pillars. Plants stood in painted paraffin tins, and they were dry and limp. She went into the first room. It had two old leather armchairs, a sideboard with a mirror that reflected trees and blue sky and long grass from the low window, and an eating table. The second room had an iron bed and a chest of drawers. She looked, long and thoughtful, at the narrow bed, and her heart was full of pity because of the lonely trembling of Mr. Rooyen's arms. She went into the tiny kitchen. It had an iron Carron Dover stove, where the fire was out. A wooden table had some cold meat on it with a piece of gauze over it. The meat smelled sourish. Flies buzzed. Up the legs of the table small black ants trickled. There was no servant visible. After getting herself a glass of tepid-tasting water from the filter, she walked very slowly through the house again, taking in everything, then went home.

At supper she said, casual: "I went to see Mr. Rooyen today."

Her father looked quickly at her mother, who dropped her eyes and crumbled bread. That meant they had discussed the incident of the kiss. "How is he?" asked Mrs. Grant, casual and bright.

"He wasn't there." Her father said nothing.

Next day she lapsed back into her private listening world. In the afternoon she read, but the book seemed childish. She wept enjoyably, alone. At supper she looked at her parents from a long way off, and knew it was a different place, where she had never been before. They were smaller, definitely. She saw them clear: the rather handsome phlegmatic man at one end of the table, brown in his khaki (but not mahogany, he could afford not to spend every second of his waking hours in the sun). And at the other end a brisk, airy, efficient woman in a tailored striped dress. The girl thought: "I came out of them," and shrank away in dislike from knowing how she had. She looked at these two strange people and felt Mr. Rooyen's arms call to her across three miles of veld. Before she went to bed she stood for a long time gazing at the small light from his house.

Next morning she went to his house again. She wore a new dress, which her mother had made. It was a childish dress that ignored her breasts, which is why she chose it. Not that she expected to see Mr. Rooyen. She wanted to see the small, brick, ant-and-fly-ridden house, walk through it and come home again.

When she got there, there was not a sign of anyone. She fetched water in a half-paraffin tin from the kitchen and soaked the half-dead plants. Then she sat on the edge of the brick verandah with her feet in the hot dust. Quite soon Mr. Rooyen came walking up through the trees from the lands. He saw her, but she could not make out what he thought. She said, girlish: "I've watered your plants for you."

"The boy's supposed to water them," he said, sounding angry. He strode onto the verandah, into the room behind, and out at the back in three great paces shouting: "Boy! Boy!" A shouting went on, because the cook had gone to sleep under a tree. The girl watched the man run himself a glass of water from the filter, gulp it down, run another, gulp that. He came back to the verandah. Standing like a great black hot tower over her, he demanded: "Does your father know you're here?"

She shook her head, primly. But she felt he was unfair. He would not have liked her father to know how his arms had trembled and pressed her in the car.

He returned to the room, and sat, knees sprawling apart, his arms limp, in one of the big ugly leather chairs. He looked at her steadily, his mouth tight. He had a thin mouth. The lips were burned and black from the sun, and the cracks in them showed white and unhealthy.

"Come here," he said, softly. It was tentative and she chose not to hear it, remained sitting with her back to him.

Over her shoulder she asked, one neighbour to another: "Have you fixed up your vlei with Mr. Mitchell yet?" He sat looking at her, his head lowered. His eyes were really ugly, she thought, red with sun glare. He was an ugly man, she thought. For now she was wishing—not that she had not come, but that he had not come. Then she could have walked, secretly and delightfully, through the house and gone secretly. And tomorrow she could have come and watered his plants again. She imagined saying to him, meeting him by chance somewhere: "Guess who was watering your plants all that time?"

"You're a pretty little girl," he said. He was grinning. The grin had no relation to the lonely hunger of his touch on her in the car. Nor was it a grin addressed to a pretty little girl—far from it. She looked at the grin, repudiating it for her future, and was glad that she wore this full, childish dress.

"Come and sit on my knee," he tried again, in the way people had been saying through her childhood: Come and sit on my knee. She obligingly went, like a small girl, and balanced herself on a knee that felt all bone under her. His hands came out and gripped her thin arms. His face changed from the ugly grin to the look of lonely hunger. She was sitting upright, using her feet as braces on the floor to prevent herself being pulled into the trembling man's body. Unable to pull her, he leaned his face against her neck, so that she felt his eyelashes and eyebrows hairy on her skin, and he muttered: "Maureen, Maureen, Maureen, my love."

She stood up, smoothing down her silly dress. He opened his eyes, sat still, hands on his knees. His mouth was half open, he breathed irregularly, and his eyes stared, not at her, but at the brick floor where tiny black ants trickled.

She sat herself on the chair opposite, tucking her dress well in around her legs. In the silence the roof cracked suddenly overhead from the heat. There was the sound of a car on the main road half a mile off. The car came nearer. Neither the girl nor the man moved. Their eyes met from time to time, frowning, serious, then moved away to the ants, to the window, anywhere. He still breathed fast. She was full of revulsion against his body, yet she remembered the heat of his face, the touch of his lashes on her neck, and his loneliness spoke to her through her dislike of him, so that she longed to assuage him. The car stopped outside the house. She saw, without surprise, that it was her father. She remained where she was as Mr. Grant stepped out of the car and came in, his eyes narrowed because of the glare and the heat under the iron roof. He nodded at his daughter, and said: "How do you do, Rooyen?" There being only two chairs, the men were standing; but the girl knew what she had to do, so she went out onto the verandah, and sat on the hot rough brick, spreading her blue skirts wide so that air could come under them and cool her thighs.

Now the two men were sitting in the chairs.

"Like some tea, Mr. Grant?"

"I could do with a cup."

Mr. Rooyen shouted: "Tea, boy!" and a shout came back from the kitchen. The girl could hear the iron stove being banged and blown into heat. It was nearly midday and she wondered what Mr. Rooyen would have for lunch. That rancid beef? She thought: If I were Maureen I wouldn't leave him alone, I'd look after him. I suppose she's some silly woman in an office in town. . . . But since he loved Maureen, she became her and heard his voice saying: Maureen, Maureen, my love. Simultaneously she held her thin brown arms into the sun and felt how they were dark dry brown and she felt the flesh melting off hard lank bones.

"I spoke to Tobacco Paynter last night on the telephone, and he said he thinks Rich Mitchell might very well be in a different frame of mind by now, he's had a couple of good seasons."

"If a couple of good seasons could make any difference to Mr. Mitchell," came Mr. Rooyen's hot resentful voice. "But thank you, Mr. Grant. Thank you."

"He's close," said her father. "Near. Canny. Careful. Those North Country people are, you know." He laughed. Mr. Rooyen laughed too, after a pause—he was a Dutchman and had to work out the unfamiliar phrase "North Country."

"If I were you," said Mr. Grant, "I'd get the whole of the lands on either side of the vlei under mealies the first season. Rich has never had it under cultivation, and the soil'd go sixteen bags to the acre for the first couple of seasons."

"Yes, I've been thinking that's what I should do."

She heard the sounds of tea being brought in.

Mr. Rooyen said to her through the door: "Like a cup?" but she shook her head. She was thinking that if she were Maureen she'd fix up the house for him. Her father's next remark was therefore no surprise to her.

"Thought of getting married, Rooyen?"

He said bitterly: "Take a look at this house, Mr. Grant."

"Well you could build on a couple of rooms for about thirty pounds, I reckon; I'll lend you my building boy. And a wife'd get it all spick and span in no time."

Soon the two men came out, and Mr. Rooyen stood on the verandah as she and her father got into the car and drove off. She waved to him, politely, with a polite smile.

She waited for her father to say something, but although he gave her several doubtful looks, he did not. She said: "Mr. Rooyen's in love with a girl called Maureen."

"Did he say so?"

"Yes, he did."

"Well," he said, talking to her, as was his habit, one grown person to another, "I'd say it was time he got married."

"Yes."

"Everything all right?" he inquired, having worked out exactly the right words to use.

"Yes, thank you."

"Good."

That season Rich Mitchell leased a couple of miles of his big vlei to Mr. Rooyen, with a promise of sale later. Tobacco Paynter's wife got a governess from England, called Miss Betty Blunt, and almost at once Mr. Rooyen and she were engaged. Mrs. Paynter complained that she could never keep a governess longer than a couple of months, they always got married; but she couldn't have been too angry about it, because she laid on a big wedding for them, and all the district was there. The girl was asked if she would be a bridesmaid, but she very politely refused. On the track to the station there was a new signpost pointing along a well-used road which said: THE BIG VLEI FARM. C. ROOYEN.

The Story of Two Dogs

GETTING a new dog turned out to be more difficult than we thought, and for reasons rooted deep in the nature of our family. For what, on the face of it, could have been easier to find than a puppy once it had been decided: "Jock needs a companion, otherwise he'll spend his time with those dirty Kaffir dogs in the compound"? All the farms in the district had dogs who bred puppies of the most desirable sort. All the farm compounds owned miserable beasts kept hungry so that they would be good hunters for their meat-starved masters; though often enough puppies born to the cage-ribbed bitches from this world of mud huts were reared in white houses and turned out well. Jacob our builder heard we wanted another dog, and came up with a lively puppy on the end of a bit of rope. But we tactfully refused. The thin flea-bitten little object was not good enough for Jock, my mother said; though we children were only too ready to take it in.

Jock was a mongrel himself, a mixture of Alsatian, Rhodesian ridgeback, and some other breed—terrier?—that gave him ears too cocky and small above a long melancholy face. In short, he was nothing to boast of, outwardly: his qualities were all intrinsic or bestowed on him by my mother who had given this animal her heart when my brother went off to boarding school.

In theory Jock was my brother's dog. Yet why give a dog to a boy at that moment when he departs for school and will be away from home two-thirds of the year? In fact my brother's dog was his substitute; and my poor mother, whose children were always away being educated, because we were farmers, and farmers' children had no choice but to go to the cities for their schooling—my poor mother caressed Jock's too-small intelligent ears and crooned: "There, Jock! There, old boy! There, good dog, yes, you're a *good* dog, Jock, you're such a *good* dog. . . ." While my father said, uncomfortably: "For goodness' sake, old girl, you'll ruin him, that isn't a house pet, he's not a lapdog, he's a farm dog." To which my mother said nothing, but her face put on a most familiar look of misunderstood suffering, and she bent it down close so that the flickering red tongue just touched her cheeks, and sang to him: "Poor old Jock then, yes, you're a poor old dog, you're not a rough farm dog, you're a good dog, and you're not strong, no you're delicate."

At this last word my brother protested; my father protested; and so did I. All of us, in our different ways, had refused to be "delicate" —had escaped from being "delicate"—and we wished to rescue a perfectly strong and healthy young dog from being forced into invalidism, as we all, at different times, had been. Also of course we all (and we knew it and felt guilty about it) were secretly pleased that Jock was now absorbing the force of my mother's pathetic need for something "delicate" to nurse and protect.

Yet there was something in the whole business that was a reproach to us. When my mother bent her sad face over the animal, stroking him with her beautiful white hands on which the rings had grown too large, and said: "There, good dog, yes Jock, you're such a gentleman"—well, there was something in all this that made us, my father, my brother and myself, need to explode with fury, or to take Jock away and make him run over the farm like the tough young brute he was, or go away ourselves forever so that we didn't have to hear the awful yearning intensity in her voice. Because it was entirely our fault that note was in her voice at all; if we had allowed ourselves to be delicate, and good, or even gentlemen or ladies, there would have been no need for Jock to sit between my mother's knees, his loyal noble head on her lap, while she caressed and yearned and suffered.

It was my father who decided there must be another dog, and for the expressed reason that otherwise Jock would be turned into a "sissy." (At this word, reminder of a hundred earlier battles, my brother flushed, looked sulky, and went right out of the room.) My mother would not hear of another dog until her Jock took to sneaking off to the farm compound to play with the Kaffir dogs. "Oh you bad dog, Jock," she said sorrowfully, "playing with those nasty dirty dogs, how could you, Jock!" And he would playfully, but in an agony of remorse, snap and lick at her face, while she bent the whole force of her inevitably betrayed self over him, crooning: "How could you, oh how could you, Jock?"

So there must be a new puppy. And since Jock was (at heart, despite his temporary lapse) noble and generous and above all well-bred, his companion must also possess these qualities. And which dog, where in the world, could possibly be good enough? My mother turned down a dozen puppies; but Jock was still going off to the compound, slinking back to gaze soulfully into my mother's eyes. This new puppy was to be my dog. I decided this: if my brother owned a dog, then it was only fair that I should. But my lack of force in claiming this puppy was because I was in the grip of abstract justice only. The fact was I didn't want a good noble and well-bred dog. I didn't know what I did want, but the idea of such a dog bored me. So I was content to let my mother turn down puppies, provided she kept her terrible maternal energy on Jock, and away from me.

Then the family went off for one of our long visits in another part of the country, driving from farm to farm to stop at night, or a day, or a meal, with friends. To the last place we were invited for the weekend. A distant cousin of my father, "a Norfolk man" (my father was from Essex), had married a woman who had nursed in the war (First World War) with my mother. They now lived in a small brick and iron house surrounded by granite *kopjes* that erupted everywhere from thick bush. They were as isolated as any people I've known, eighty miles from the nearest railway station. As my father said, they were "not suited," for they quarrelled or sent each other to Coventry all the weekend. However, it was not until much later that I thought about the pathos of these two people, living alone on a minute pension in the middle of the bush, and "not suited"; for that weekend I was in love.

It was night when we arrived, about eight in the evening, and an almost full moon floated heavy and yellow above a stark granite-bouldered *kopje*. The bush around was black and low and silent, except that the crickets made a small incessant din. The car drew up outside a small boxlike structure whose iron roof glinted off moonlight. As the engine stopped, the sound of crickets swelled up, the moonlight's cold came in a breath of fragrance to our faces; and there was the sound of a mad wild yapping. Behold, around the corner of the house came a small black wriggling object that hurled itself towards the car, changed course almost on touching it, and hurtled off again, yapping in a high delirious yammering which, while it faded behind the house, continued faintly, our ears, or at least mine, straining after it.

"Take no notice of that puppy," said our host, the man from Norfolk. "It's been stark staring mad with the moon every night this last week."

We went into the house, were fed, were looked after; I was put to bed so that the grownups could talk freely. All the time came the mad high yapping. In my tiny bedroom I looked out onto a space of flat white sand that reflected the moon between the house and the farm buildings, and there hurtled a mad wild puppy, crazy with joy of life, or moonlight, weaving back and forth, round and round, snapping at its own black shadow and tripping over its own clumsy feet—like a drunken moth around a candle flame, or like . . . like nothing I've ever seen or heard of since.

The moon, large and remote and soft, stood up over the trees, the empty white sand, the house which had unhappy human beings in it; and a mad little dog yapping and beating its course of drunken joyous delirium. That, of course, was my puppy; and when Mr. Barnes came out from the house saying: "Now, now, come now, you lunatic animal . . ." finally almost throwing himself on the crazy creature, to lift it in his arms still yapping and wriggling and flapping around like a fish, so that he could carry it to the packing case that was its kennel, I was already saying, as anguished as a mother watching a stranger handle her child: Careful now, careful, that's my dog.

Next day, after breakfast, I visited the packing case. Its white wood oozed out resin that smelled tangy in hot sunlight, and its front was open and spilling out soft yellow straw. On the straw a large beautiful black dog lay with her head on outstretched forepaws. Beside her a brindled pup lay on its fat back, its four paws sprawled every which way, its eyes rolled up, as ecstatic with heat and food and laziness as it had been the night before from the joy of movement. A crust of mealie porridge was drying on its shining black lips that were drawn slightly back to show perfect milk teeth. His mother kept her eyes on him, but her pride was dimmed with sleep and heat.

I went inside to announce my spiritual ownership of the puppy. They were all around the breakfast table. The man from Norfolk was swapping boyhood reminiscences (shared in space, not time) with my father. His wife, her eyes still red from the weeping that had followed a night quarrel, was gossiping with my mother about the various London hospitals where they had ministered to the wounded of the war they had (apparently so enjoyably) shared.

My mother at once said: "Oh my dear, no, not that puppy, didn't you see him last night? We'll never train him."

The man from Norfolk said I could have him with pleasure.

My father said he didn't see what was wrong with the dog, if a dog was healthy that was all that mattered: my mother dropped her eyes forlornly, and sat silent.

The man from Norfolk's wife said she couldn't bear to part with the silly little thing, goodness knows there was little enough pleasure in her life.

The atmosphere of people at loggerheads being familiar to me, it was not necessary for me to know *why* they disagreed, or in what ways, or what criticisms they were going to make about my puppy. I only knew that inner logics would in due course work themselves out and the puppy would be mine. I left the four people to talk about their differences through a small puppy, and went to worship the animal, who was now sitting in a patch of shade beside the sweet-wood-smelling packing case, its dark brindled coat glistening, with dark wet patches on it from its mother's ministering tongue. His own pink tongue absurdly stuck out between white teeth, as if he had been too careless or lazy to withdraw it into its proper place under his equally pink wet palate. His brown buttony beautiful eyes . . . but enough, he was an ordinary mongrelly puppy.

Later I went back to the house to find out how the battle balanced: my mother had obviously won my father over, for he said he thought it was wiser not to have that puppy: "Bad blood tells, you know."

The bad blood was from the father, whose history delighted my fourteen-year-old imagination. This district being wild, scarcely populated, full of wild animals, even leopards and lions, the four policemen at the police station had a tougher task than in places nearer town; and they had bought half a dozen large dogs to (a) terrorise possible burglars around the police station itself and (b) surround themselves with an aura of controlled animal savagery. For the dogs were trained to kill if necessary. One of these dogs, a big ridgeback, had "gone wild." He had slipped his tether at the station and taken to the bush, living by himself on small buck, hares, birds, even stealing farmers' chickens. This dog, whose proud lonely shape had been a familiar one to farmers for years, on moonlit nights, or in grey dawns and dusks, standing aloof from

human warmth and friendship, had taken Stella, my puppy's
mother, off with him for a week of sport and hunting. She simply
went away with him one morning; the Barneses had seen her go;
had called after her; she had not even looked back. A week later
she returned home at dawn and gave a low whine outside their
bedroom window, saying: I'm home; and they woke to see their
errant Stella standing erect in the paling moonlight, her nose
pointed outwards and away from them towards a great powerful
dog who seemed to signal to her with his slightly moving tail before
fading into the bush. Mr. Barnes fired some futile shots into the
bush after him. Then they both scolded Stella who in due time produced seven puppies, in all combinations of black, brown and gold.
She was no pure-bred herself, though of course her owners thought
she was, or ought to be, being their dog. The night the puppies were
born, the man from Norfolk and his wife heard a sad wail or cry,
and arose from their beds to see the wild police dog bending his
head in at the packing-case door. All the bush was flooded with a
pinkish-gold dawn light, and the dog looked as if he had an aureole
of gold around him. Stella was half wailing, half growling her welcome, or protest, or fear at his great powerful reappearance and his
thrusting muzzle so close to her seven helpless pups. They called
out, and he turned his outlaw's head to the window where they
stood side by side in striped pyjamas and embroidered pink silk. He
put back his head and howled, he howled, a mad wild sound that
gave them gooseflesh, so they said: but I did not understand that
until years later when Bill the puppy "went wild" and I saw him
that day on the antheap howling his pain of longing to an empty
listening world.

The father of her puppies did not come near Stella again; but a
month later he was shot dead at another farm, fifty miles away,
coming out of a chicken run with a fine white Leghorn in his
mouth; and by that time she had only one pup left, they had
drowned the rest. It was bad blood, they said, no point in preserving it, they had only left her that one pup out of pity.

I said not a word as they told this cautionary tale, merely preserved the obstinate calm of someone who knows she will get her
own way. Was right on my side? It was. Was I owed a dog? I was.
Should anybody but myself choose my dog? No, but . . . very well
then, I had chosen. I chose this dog. I chose it. Too late, I *had*
chosen it.

Three days and three nights we spent at the Barneses' place. The
days were hot and slow and full of sluggish emotions; and the two

dogs slept in the packing case. At night, the four people stayed in the living room, a small brick place heated unendurably by the paraffin lamp whose oily yellow glow attracted moths and beetles in a perpetual whirling halo of small moving bodies. They talked, and I listened for the mad far yapping, and then I crept out into the cold moonlight. On the last night of our stay the moon was full, a great perfect white ball, its history marked on a face that seemed close enough to touch as it floated over the dark cricket-singing bush. And there on the white sand yapped and danced the crazy puppy, while his mother, the big beautiful animal, sat and watched, her intelligent yellow eyes slightly anxious as her muzzle followed the erratic movements of her child, the child of her dead mate from the bush. I crept up beside Stella, sat on the still-warm cement beside her, put my arm around her soft furry neck, and my head beside her alert moving head. I adjusted my breathing so that my rib cage moved up and down beside hers, so as to be closer to the warmth of her barrelly furry chest, and together we turned our eyes from the great staring floating moon to the tiny black hurtling puppy who shot in circles from near us, so near he all but crashed into us, to two hundred yards away where he just missed the wheels of the farm waggon. We watched, and I felt the chill of moonlight deepen on Stella's fur, and on my own silk skin, while our ribs moved gently up and down together, and we waited until the man from Norfolk came to first shout, then yell, then fling himself on the mad little dog and shut him up in the wooden box where yellow bars of moonlight fell into black dog-smelling shadow. "There now, Stella girl, you go in with your puppy," said the man, bending to pat her head as she obediently went inside. She used her soft nose to push her puppy over. He was so exhausted that he fell and lay, his four legs stretched out and quivering like a shot dog, his breath squeezed in and out of him in small regular wheezy pants like whines. And so I left them, Stella and her puppy, to go to my bed in the little brick house which seemed literally crammed with hateful emotions. I went to sleep, thinking of the hurtling little dog, now at last asleep with exhaustion, his nose pushed against his mother's breathing black side, the slits of yellow moonlight moving over him through the boards of fragrant wood.

We took him away next morning, having first locked Stella in a room so that she could not see us go.

It was a three-hundred-mile drive, and all the way Bill yapped and panted and yawned and wriggled idiotically on his back on the lap of whoever held him, his eyes rolled up, his big paws lolling.

He was a full-time charge for myself and my mother, and, after the city, my brother, whose holidays were starting. He, at first sight of the second dog, reverted to the role of Jock's master, and dismissed my animal as altogether less valuable material. My mother, by now Bill's slave, agreed with him, but invited him to admire the adorable wrinkles on the puppy's forehead. My father demanded irritably that both dogs should be "thoroughly trained."

Meanwhile, as the nightmare journey proceeded, it was noticeable that my mother talked more and more about Jock, guiltily, as if she had betrayed him. "Poor little Jock, what will he say?"

Jock was in fact a handsome young dog. More Alsatian than anything, he was a low-standing, thick-coated animal of a warm gold colour, with a vestigial "ridge" along his spine, rather wolflike, or foxlike, if one looked at him frontways, with his sharp cocked ears. And he was definitely not "little." There was something dignified about him from the moment he was out of puppyhood, even when he was being scolded by my mother for his visits to the compound.

The meeting, prepared for by us all with trepidation, went off in a way which was a credit to everyone, but particularly Jock, who regained my mother's heart at a stroke. The puppy was released from the car and carried to where Jock sat, noble and restrained as usual, waiting for us to greet him. Bill at once began weaving and yapping around the rocky space in front of the house. Then he saw Jock, bounded up to him, stopped a couple of feet away, sat down on his fat backside and yelped excitedly. Jock began a yawning, snapping movement of his head, making it go from side to side in half-snarling, half-laughing protest, while the puppy crept closer, right up, jumping at the older dog's lifted wrinkling muzzle. Jock did not move away; he forced himself to remain still, because he could see us all watching. At last he lifted up his paw, pushed Bill over with it, pinned him down, examined him, then sniffed and licked him. He had accepted him, and Bill had found a substitute for his mother who was presumably mourning his loss. We were able to leave the child (as my mother kept calling him) in Jock's infinitely patient care. "You are such a good dog, Jock," she said, overcome by this scene, and the other touching scenes that followed, all marked by Jock's extraordinary forbearance for what was, and even I had to admit it, an intolerably destructive little dog.

Training became urgent. But this was not at all easy, due, like the business of getting a new puppy, to the inner nature of the family.

To take only one difficulty: dogs must be trained by their masters, they must owe allegiance to one person. And who was Jock to obey? And Bill: I was his master, in theory. In practice, Jock was. Was I to take over from Jock? But even to state it is to expose its absurdity: what I adored was the graceless puppy, and what did I want with a well-trained dog? Trained for *what*?

A watchdog? But all our dogs were watchdogs. "Natives"—such was the article of faith—were by nature scared of dogs. Yet everyone repeated stories about thieves poisoning fierce dogs, or making friends with them. So apparently no one really believed that watchdogs were any use. Yet every farm had its watchdog.

Throughout my childhood I used to lie in bed, the bush not fifty yards away all around the house, listening to the cry of the nightjar, the owls, the frogs and the crickets; to the tom-toms from the compound; to the mysterious rustling in the thatch over my head, or the long grass it had been cut from down the hill; to all the thousand noises of the night on the veld; and every one of these noises was marked also by the house dogs, who would bark and sniff and investigate and growl at all these; and also at starlight on the polished surface of a leaf, at the moon lifting itself over the mountains, at a branch cracking behind the house, at the first rim of hot red showing above the horizon—in short at anything and everything. Watchdogs, in my experience, were never asleep; but they were not so much a guard against thieves (we never had any thieves that I can remember) as a kind of instrument designed to measure or record the rustlings and movements of the African night that seemed to have an enormous life of its own, but a collective life, so that the falling of a stone, or a star shooting through the Milky Way, the grunt of a wild pig, and the wind rustling in the mealie field were all evidences and aspects of the same truth.

How did one "train" a watchdog? Presumably to respond only to the slinking approach of a human, black or white. What use is a watchdog otherwise? But even now, the most powerful memory of my childhood is of lying awake listening to the sobbing howl of a dog at the inexplicable appearance of the yellow face of the moon; of creeping to the window to see the long muzzle of a dog pointed black against a great bowl of stars. We needed no moon calendar with those dogs, who were like traffic in London: to sleep at all, one had to learn not to hear them. And if one did not hear them, one would not hear the stiff warning growl that (presumably) would greet a marauder.

At first Jock and Bill were locked up in the dining room at night. But there were so many stirrings and yappings and rushings from window to window after the rising sun or moon, or the black shadows which moved across whitewashed walls from the branches of the trees in the garden, that soon we could no longer stand the lack of sleep, and they were turned out on to the verandah. With many hopeful injunctions from my mother that they were to be "good dogs": which meant that they should ignore their real natures and sleep from sundown to sunup. Even then, when Bill was just out of puppyhood, they might be missing altogether in the early mornings. They would come guiltily up the road from the lands at breakfast time, their coats full of grass seeds, and we knew they had rushed down into the bush after an owl, or a grazing animal, and, finding themselves farther from home than they had expected in a strange nocturnal world, had begun nosing and sniffing and exploring in practice for their days of wildness soon to come.

So they weren't watchdogs. Hunting dogs perhaps? My brother undertook to train them, and we went through a long and absurd period of "Down, Jock," "To heel, Bill," while sticks of barley sugar balanced on noses, and paws were offered to be shaken by human hands, etc., etc. Through all this Jock suffered, bravely, but saying so clearly with every part of him that he would do anything to please my mother—he would send her glances half proud and half apologetic all the time my brother drilled him, that after an hour of training my brother would retreat, muttering that it was too hot, and Jock bounded off to lay his head on my mother's lap. As for Bill he never achieved anything. Never did he sit still with the golden lumps on his nose, he ate them at once. Never did he stay to heel. Never did he remember what he was supposed to do with his paw when one of us offered him a hand. The truth was, I understood then, watching the training sessions, that Bill was stupid. I pretended of course that he despised being trained, he found it humiliating; and that Jock's readiness to go through with the silly business showed his lack of spirit. But alas, there was no getting around it, Bill simply wasn't very bright.

Meanwhile he had ceased to be a fat charmer; he had become a lean young dog, good-looking, with his dark brindled coat, and his big head that had a touch of Newfoundland. He had a look of puppy about him still. For just as Jock seemed born elderly, had respectable white hairs on his chin from the start, so Bill kept something young in him; he was a young dog until he died.

The training sessions did not last long. Now my brother said the dogs would be trained on the job: this to pacify my father, who kept saying that they were a disgrace and "not worth their salt."

There began a new regime, my brother, myself, and the two dogs. We set forth each morning, first, my brother, earnest with responsibility, his rifle swinging in his hand, at his heels the two dogs. Behind this time-honoured unit, myself, the girl, with no useful part to play in the serious masculine business, but necessary to provide admiration. This was a very old role for me indeed: to walk away on one side of the scene, a small fierce girl, hungry to be part of it, but knowing she never would be, above all because the heart that had been put to pump away all her life under her ribs was not only critical and intransigent, but one which longed so bittery to melt into loving acceptance. An uncomfortable combination, as she knew even then—yet I could not remove the sulky smile from my face. And it *was* absurd: there was my brother, so intent and serious, with Jock the good dog just behind him; and there was Bill the bad dog intermittently behind him, but more often than not sneaking off to enjoy some side path. And there was myself, unwillingly following, my weight shifting from hip to hip, bored and showing it.

I knew the route too well. Before we reached the sullen thickets of the bush where game and birds were to be found, there was a long walk up the back of the *kopje* through a luxuriant pawpaw grove, then through sweet-potato vines that tangled our ankles, and tripped us, then past a rubbish heap whose sweet rotten smell was expressed in a heave of glittering black flies, then the bush itself. Here it was all dull green stunted trees, miles and miles of the smallish, flattish, msasa trees in their second growth: they had all been cut for mine furnaces at some time. And over the flat ugly bush a large overbearing blue sky.

We were on our way to get food. So we kept saying. Whatever we shot would be eaten by "the house," or by the house's servants, or by "the compound." But we were hunting according to a newer law than the need for food, and we knew it and that was why we were always a bit apologetic about these expeditions, and why we so often chose to return empty-handed. We were hunting because my brother had been given a new and efficient rifle that would bring down (infallibly, if my brother shot) birds, large and small; and small animals, and very often large game like koodoo and sable. We were hunting because we owned a gun. And because we owned a gun, we should have hunting dogs, it made the business less ugly for some reason.

We were on our way to the Great Vlei, as distinct from the Big Vlei, which was five miles in the other direction. The Big Vlei was burnt out and eroded, and the water holes usually dried up early. We did not like going there. But to reach the Great Vlei, which was beautiful, we had to go through the ugly bush "at the back of the *kopje*." These ritual names for parts of the farm seemed rather to be names for regions in our minds. "Going to the Great Vlei" had a fairy-tale quality about it, because of having to pass through the region of sour ugly frightening bush first. For it did frighten us, always, and without reason: we felt it was hostile to us and we walked through it quickly, knowing that we were earning by this danger the water-running peace of the Great Vlei. It was only partly on our farm; the boundary between it and the next farm ran invisibly down its centre, drawn by the eye from this outcrop to that big tree to that pothole to that antheap. It was a grassy valley with trees standing tall and spreading on either side of the watercourse which was a half-mile width of intense greenness broken by sky-reflecting brown pools. This was old bush, these trees had never been cut: the Great Vlei had the inevitable look of natural bush—that no branch, no shrub, no patch of thorn, no outcrop, could have been in any other place or stood at any other angle.

The potholes here were always full. The water was stained clear brown, and the mud bottom had a small movement of creatures, while over the brown ripples skimmed blue jays and hummingbirds and all kinds of vivid flashing birds we did not know the names of. Along the lush verges lolled pink and white water lilies on their water-gemmed leaves.

This paradise was where the dogs were to be trained.

During the first holidays, long ones of six weeks, my brother was indefatigable, and we set off every morning after breakfast. In the Great Vlei I sat on a pool's edge under a thorn tree, and day-dreamed to the tune of the ripples my swinging feet set moving across the water, while my brother, armed with the rifle, various sizes of stick, and lumps of sugar and biltong, put the two dogs through their paces. Sometimes, roused perhaps because the sun that fell through the green lace of the thorn was burning my shoulders, I turned to watch the three creatures, hard at work a hundred yards off on an empty patch of sand. Jock, more often than not, would be a dead dog, or his nose would be on his paws while his attentive eyes were on my brother's face. Or he would be sitting up, a dog statue, a golden dog, admirably obedient. Bill, on the other hand, was probably balancing on his spine, all four paws in the air, his throat back so that he was flat from nose to tailtip, receiving the hot sun equally over his brindled fur. I would hear, through my own lazy thoughts: "Good dog, Jock, yes good dog. Idiot Bill, fool dog, why don't you work like Jock?" And my brother, his face reddened and sweaty, would come over to flop beside me, saying: "It's all Bill's fault, he's a bad example. And of course Jock doesn't see why he should work hard when Bill just plays all the time." Well, it probably was my fault that the training failed. If my earnest and undivided attention had been given, as I knew quite well was being demanded of me, to this business of the boy and the two dogs, perhaps we would have ended up with a brace of efficient and obedient animals, ever ready to die, to go to heel, and to fetch it. Perhaps.

By next holidays, moral disintegration had set in. My father complained the dogs obeyed nobody, and demanded training, serious and unremitting. My brother and I watched our mother petting Jock and scolding Bill, and came to an unspoken agreement. We set off for the Great Vlei but once there we loafed up and down the water holes, while the dogs did as they liked, learning the joys of freedom.

The uses of water, for instance. Jock, cautious as usual, would test a pool with his paw, before moving in to stand chest-deep, his muzzle just above the ripples, licking at them with small yaps of greeting or excitement. Then he walked gently in and swam up and down and around the brown pool in the green shade of the thorn trees. Meanwhile Bill would have found a shallow pool and be at his favourite game. Starting twenty yards from the rim of a pool he would hurl himself, barking shrilly, across the grass, then across the pool, not so much swimming across it as bounding across it. Out the other side, up the side of the vlei, around in a big loop, then back, and around again . . . and again and again and again. Great sheets of brown water went up into the sky above him, crashing back into the pool while he barked his exhaustion.

That was one game. Or they chased each other up and down the four-mile-long valley like enemies, and when one caught the other there was a growling and a snarling, and a fighting that sounded genuine enough. Sometimes we went to separate them, an interference they suffered; and the moment we let them go one or another would be off, his hind quarters pistoning, with the other in pursuit, fierce and silent. They might race a mile, two miles, before one leaped at the other's throat and brought him down. This game too, over and over again, so that when they did go wild, we knew how they killed the wild pig and the buck they lived on.

On frivolous mornings they chased butterflies, while my brother and I dangled our feet in a pool and watched. Once, very solemnly, as it were in parody of the ridiculous business (now over, thank goodness) of "fetch it" and "to heel, " Jock brought us in his jaws a big orange and black butterfly, the delicate wings all broken, and the orange bloom smearing his furry lips. He laid it in front of us, held the still fluttering creature flat with a paw, then lay down, his nose pointing at it. His brown eyes rolled up, wickedly hypocritical, as if to say: "Look, a butterfly, I'm a *good* dog." Meanwhile, Bill leaped and barked, a small black dog hurling himself up into the great blue sky after floating coloured wings. He had taken no notice at all of Jock's captive. But we both felt that Bill was much more likely than Jock to make such a seditious comment, and in fact my brother said: "Bill's corrupted Jock. I'm sure Jock would never go wild like this unless Bill was showing him. It's the blood coming out." But alas, we had no idea yet of what "going wild" could mean. For a couple of years yet it still meant small indisciplines, and mostly Bill's.

For instance, there was the time Bill forced himself through a loose plank in the door of the store hut, and there ate and ate, eggs, cake, bread, a joint of beef, a ripening guinea fowl, half a ham. Then he couldn't get out. In the morning he was a swollen dog, rolling on the floor and whining with the agony of his overindulgence. "Stupid dog, Bill, Jock would never do a thing like that, he'd be too intelligent not to know he'd swell up if he ate so much."

Then he ate eggs out of the nest, a crime for which on a farm a dog gets shot. Very close was Bill to this fate. He had actually been seen sneaking out of the chicken run, feathers on his nose, egg smear on his muzzle. And there was a mess of oozing yellow and white slime over the straw of the nests. The fowls cackled and raised their feathers whenever Bill came near. First, he was beaten, by the cook, until his howls shook the farm. Then my mother blew eggs and filled them with a solution of mustard and left them in the nests. Sure enough, next morning, a hell of wild howls and shrieks: the beatings had taught him nothing. We went out to see a black dog running and racing in agonised circles with his tongue hanging out, while the sun came up red over black mountains—a splendid backdrop to a disgraceful scene. My mother took the poor inflamed jaws and washed them in warm water and said: "Well now Bill, you'd better learn, or it's the firing squad for you."

He learned, but not easily. More than once my brother and I, having arisen early for the hunt, stood in front of the house in the dawn hush, the sky a high far grey above us, the edge of the mountains just reddening, the great spaces of silent bush full of the dark of the night. We sniffed at the small sharpness of the dew, and the heavy somnolent night-smell off the bush, felt the cold heavy air on our cheeks. We stood, whistling very low, so that the dogs would come from wherever they had chosen to sleep. Soon Jock would appear, yawning and sweeping his tail back and forth. No Bill—then we saw him, sitting on his haunches just outside the chicken run, his nose resting in a loop of the wire, his eyes closed in yearning for the warm delicious ooze of fresh egg. And we would clap our hands over our mouths and double up with heartless laughter that had to be muffled so as not to disturb our parents.

On the mornings when we went hunting, and took the dogs, we knew that before we'd gone half a mile either Jock or Bill would dash off barking into the bush; the one left would look up from his own nosing and sniffing and rush away too. We would hear the wild double barking fade away with the crash and the rush of the two bodies, and, often enough, the subsidiary rushings away of other animals who had been asleep or resting and just waiting until we had gone away. Now we could look for something to shoot which probably we would never have seen at all had the dogs been there. We could settle down for long patient stalks, circling around a grazing koodoo, or a couple of duikers. Often enough we would lie watching them for hours, afraid only that Jock and Bill would come back, putting an end to this particular pleasure. I remember once we caught a glimpse of a duiker grazing on the edge of a farmland that was still half dark. We got onto our stomachs and wriggled through the long grass, not able to see if the duiker was still there. Slowly the field opened up in front of us, a heaving mass of big black clods. We carefully raised our heads, and there, at the edge of the clod sea, a couple of arm's lengths away, were three little duikers, their heads turned away from us to where the sun was about to rise. They were three black, quite motionless silhouettes. Away over the other side of the field, big clods became tinged with reddish gold. The earth turned so fast towards the sun that the light came running from the tip of one clod to the next across the field like flames leaping along the tops of long grasses in front of a strong wind. The light reached the duikers and outlined them with warm gold. They were three glittering little beasts on the edge of an imminent sunlight. They then began to butt each other, lifting their hind quarters and bringing down their hind feet in clicking leaps like dancers. They tossed their sharp little horns and made short half-angry rushes at each other. The sun was up. Three little buck danced on the edge of the deep green bush where we lay hidden, and there was a weak sunlight warming their gold hides. The sun separated itself from the line of the hills, and became calm and big and yellow; a warm yellow colour filled the world, the little buck stopped dancing, and walked slowly off, frisking their white tails and tossing their pretty heads, into the bush.

We would never have seen them at all, if the dogs hadn't been miles away.

In fact, all they were good for was their indiscipline. If we wanted to be sure of something to eat, we tied ropes to the dogs' collars until we actually heard the small clink-clink-clink of guinea fowl running through the bush. Then we untied them. The dogs were at once off after the birds who rose clumsily into the air, looking like flying shawls that sailed along, just above grass level, with the dogs' jaws snapping underneath them. All they wanted was to land unobserved in the long grass, but they were always forced to rise painfully into the trees, on their weak wings. Sometimes, if it was a large flock, a dozen trees might be dotted with the small black shapes of guinea fowl outlined against dawn or evening skies. They watched the barking dogs, took no notice of us. My brother or I—for even I could hardly miss in such conditions— planted our feet wide for balance, took aim at a chosen bird and shot. The carcase fell into the worrying jaws beneath. Meanwhile a second bird would be chosen and shot. With the two birds tied together by their feet, the rifle, justified by utility, proudly swinging, we would saunter back to the house through the sun-scented bush of our enchanted childhood. The dogs, for politeness' sake, escorted us part of the way home, then went off hunting on their own. Guinea fowl were very tame sport for them, by then.

It had come to this, that if we actually wished to shoot something, or to watch animals, or even to take a walk through bush where every animal for miles had not been scared away, we had to lock up the dogs before we left, ignoring their whines and their howls. Even so, if let out too soon, they would follow. Once, after we had walked six miles or so, a leisurely morning's trek towards the mountains, the dogs arrived, panting, happy, their pink wet tongues hot on our knees and forearms, saying how delighted they were to have found us. They licked and wagged for a few moments—then off they went, they vanished, and did not come home until evening. We were worried. We had not known that they went so far from the farm by themselves. We spoke of how bad it would be if they took to frequenting other farms—perhaps other chicken runs? But it was all too late. They were too old to train. Either they had to be kept permanently on leashes, tied to trees outside the house, and for dogs like these it was not much better than being dead—either that, or they must run free and take their chances.

We got news of the dogs in letters from home and it was increasingly bad. My brother and I, at our respective boarding schools where we were supposed to be learning discipline, order, and sound characters, read: "The dogs went away a whole night, they only came back at lunchtime." "Jock and Bill have been three days and nights in the bush. They've just come home, worn out." "The dogs must have made a kill this time and stayed beside it like wild animals, because they came home too gorged to eat, they just drank a lot of water and fell off to sleep like babies. . . ." "Mr. Daly rang up yesterday to say he saw Jock and Bill hunting along the hill behind his house. They've been chasing his oxen. We've got to beat them when they get home because if they don't learn they'll get themselves shot one of these dark nights. . . ."

They weren't there at all when we went home for the holidays. They had already been gone for nearly a week. But, or so we flattered ourselves, they sensed our return, for back they came, trotting gently side by side up the hill in the moonlight, two low black shapes moving above the accompanying black shapes of their shadows, their eyes gleaming red as the shafts of lamplight struck them. They greeted us, my brother and me, affectionately enough, but at once went off to sleep. We told ourselves that they saw us as creatures like them, who went off on long exciting hunts: but we knew it was sentimental nonsense, designed to take the edge off the hurt we felt because our animals, *our* dogs, cared so little about us. They went away again that night, or, rather, in the first dawnlight. A week later they came home. They smelled foul, they must have been chasing a skunk or a wildcat. Their fur was matted with grass seeds and their skin lumpy with ticks. They drank water heavily, but refused food: their breath was foetid with the smell of meat.

They lay down to sleep and remained limp while we, each taking an animal, its sleeping head heavy in our laps, removed ticks, grass seeds, blackjacks. On Bill's forepaw was a hard ridge which I thought was an old scar. He sleep-whimpered when I touched it. It was a noose of plaited grass, used by Africans to snare birds. Luckily it had snapped off. "Yes," said my father, "that's how they'll end, both of them, they'll die in a trap, and serve them both right, they won't get any sympathy from me!"

We were frightened into locking them up for a day; but we could not stand their misery, and let them out again.

We were always springing gametraps of all kinds. For the big buck, the sable, the eland, the koodoo, the Africans bent a sapling across a path, held it by light string, and fixed on it a noose of heavy wire cut from a fence. For the smaller buck there were low traps with nooses of fine baling wire or plaited tree fibre. And at the corners of the cultivated fields or at the edges of water holes, where the birds and hares came down to feed, were always a myriad of tiny tracks under the grass, and often across every track hung a small noose of plaited grass. Sometimes we spent whole days destroying these snares.

In order to keep the dogs amused, we took to walking miles every day. We were exhausted, but they were not, and simply went off at night as well. Then we rode bicycles as fast as we could along the rough farm tracks, with the dogs bounding easily beside us. We wore ourselves out, trying to please Jock and Bill, who, we imagined, knew what we were doing and were trying to humour us. But we stuck at it. Once, at the end of a glade, we saw the skeleton of a large animal hanging from a noose. Some African had forgotten to visit his traps. We showed the skeleton to Jock and Bill, and talked and warned and threatened, almost in tears, because human speech was not dogs' speech. They sniffed around the bones, yapped a few times up into our faccs—out of politeness, we felt; and were off again into the bush.

At school we heard that they were almost completely wild. Sometimes they came home for a meal, or a day's sleep, "treating the house," my mother complained, "like a hotel."

Then fate struck, in the shape of a bucktrap.

One night, very late, we heard whining, and went out to greet them. They were crawling towards the front door, almost on their bellies. Their ribs stuck out, their coats stared, their eyes shone unhealthily. They fell on the food we gave them; they were starved. Then on Jock's neck, which was bent over the food bowl, showed the explanation: a thick strand of wire. It was not solid wire, but made of a dozen twisted strands, and had been chewed through, near the collar. We examined Bill's mouth: chewing the wire through must have taken a long time, days perhaps: his gums and lips were scarred and bleeding, and his teeth were worn down to stumps, like an old dog's teeth. If the wire had not been stranded, Jock would have died in the trap. As it was, he fell ill, his lungs were strained, since he had been half strangled with the wire. And Bill could no longer chew properly, he ate uncomfortably, like an old person. They stayed at home for weeks, reformed dogs, barked around the house at night, and ate regular meals.

Then they went off again, but came home more often than they had. Jock's lungs weren't right: he would lie out in the sun, gasping and wheezing, as if trying to rest them. As for Bill, he could only eat soft food. How, then, did they manage when they were hunting?

One afternoon we were shooting, miles from home, and we saw them. First we heard the familiar excited yapping coming towards us, about two miles off. We were in a large vlei, full of tall whitish grass which swayed and bent along a fast regular line: a shape showed, it was a duiker, hard to see until it was close because it was reddish brown in colour, and the vlei had plenty of the pinkish feathery grass that turns a soft intense red in strong light. Being near sunset, the pale grass was on the verge of being invisible, like wires of white light; and the pink grass flamed and glowed; and the fur of the little buck shone red. It swerved suddenly. Had it seen us? No, it was because of Jock who had made a quick maneuvering turn from where he had been lying in the pink grass, to watch the buck, and behind it, Bill, pistoning along like a machine. Jock, who could no longer run fast, had turned the buck into Bill's jaws. We saw Bill bound at the little creature's throat, bring it down and hold it until Jock came in to kill it: his own teeth were useless now.

We walked over to greet them, but with restraint, for these two growling snarling creatures seemed not to know us, they raised eyes glazed with savagery, as they tore at the dead buck. Or, rather, as Jock tore at it. Before we went away we saw Jock pushing over lumps of hot steaming meat towards Bill, who otherwise would have gone hungry.

They were really a team now; neither could function without the other. So we thought.

But soon Jock took to coming home from the hunting trips early, after one or two days, and Bill might stay out for a week or more.

Jock lay watching the bush, and when Bill came, he licked his ears and face as if he had reverted to the role of Bill's mother.

Once I heard Bill barking and went to see. The telephone line ran through a vlei near the house to the farm over the hill. The wires hummed and sang and twanged. Bill was underneath the wires, which were a good fifteen feet over his head, jumping and barking at them: he was playing, out of exuberance, as he had done when a small puppy. But now it made me sad, seeing the strong dog playing all alone, while his friend lay quiet in the sun, wheezing from damaged lungs.

And what did Bill live on, in the bush? Rats, birds' eggs, lizards, anything *soft* enough? That was painful too, thinking of the powerful hunters in the days of their glory.

Soon we got telephone calls from neighbours: Bill dropped in, he finished off the food in our dog's bowl. . . . Bill seemed hungry, so we fed him. . . . Your dog Bill is looking very thin, isn't he? . . . Bill was around our chicken run—I'm sorry, but if he goes for the eggs, then . . .

Bill had puppies with a pedigreed bitch fifteen miles off: her owners were annoyed: Bill was not good enough for them, and besides there was the question of his "bad blood." All the puppies were destroyed. He was hanging around the house all the time, although he had been beaten, and they had even fired shots into the air to scare him off. Was there anything we could do to keep him at home? they asked; for they were tired of having to keep their bitch tied up.

No, there was nothing we could do. Rather, there was nothing we *would* do; for when Bill came trotting up from the bush to drink deeply out of Jock's bowl, and to lie for a while nose to nose with Jock, well, we could have caught him and tied him up, but we did not. "He won't last long anyway," said my father. And my mother told Jock that he was a sensible and intelligent dog; for she again sang praises of his nature and character just as if he had never spent so many glorious years in the bush.

I went to visit the neighbour who owned Bill's mate. She was tied to a post on the verandah. All night we were disturbed by a wild sad howling from the bush, and she whimpered and strained at her rope. In the morning I walked out into the hot silence of the bush, and called to him: Bill, Bill, it's me. Nothing, no sound. I sat on the slope of an antheap in the shade, and waited. Soon Bill came into view, trotting between the trees. He was very thin. He looked gaunt, stiff, wary—an old outlaw, afraid of traps. He saw me, but stopped about twenty yards off. He climbed halfway up another anthill and sat there in full sunlight, so I could see the harsh patches on his coat. We sat in silence, looking at each other. Then he lifted his head and howled, like the howl dogs give to the full moon, long, terrible, lonely. But it was morning, the sun calm and clear, and the bush without mystery. He sat and howled his heart out, his muzzle pointed away towards where his mate was chained. We could hear the faint whimperings she made, and the clink of her metal dish as she moved about. I couldn't stand it. It made my flesh cold, and I could see the hairs standing up on my forearm. I went over to him and sat by him and put my arm around his neck as once, so many years ago, I had put my arm around his mother that moonlit night before I stole her puppy away from her. He put his muzzle on my forearm and whimpered, or rather cried. Then he lifted it and howled. . . . "Oh my God, Bill, don't do that, please don't, it's not the slightest use, please, dear Bill. . . ." But he went on, until suddenly he leaped up in the middle of a howl, as if his pain were too strong to contain in sitting, and he sniffed at me, as if to say: That's you, is it, well, goodbye— then he turned his wild head to the bush and trotted away.

Very soon he was shot, coming out of a chicken run early one morning with an egg in his mouth.

Jock was quite alone now. He spent his old age lying in the sun, his nose pointed out over the miles and miles of bush between our house and the mountains where he had hunted all those years with Bill. He was really an old dog, his legs were stiff, and his coat was rough, and he wheezed and gasped. Sometimes, at night, when the moon was up, he went out to howl at it, and we would say: He's missing Bill. He would come back to sit at my mother's knee, resting his head so that she could stroke it. She would say: "Poor old Jock, poor old boy, are you missing that bad dog Bill?"

Sometimes, when he lay dozing, he started up and went trotting on his stiff old legs through the house and the outhouses, sniffing everywhere and anxiously whining. Then he stood, upright, one paw raised, as he used to do when he was young, and gazed over the bush and softly whined. And we would say: "He must have been dreaming he was out hunting with Bill."

He got ill. He could hardly breathe. We carried him in our arms down the hill into the bush, and my mother stroked and patted him while my father put the gun barrel to the back of his head and shot him.

The Story of
a Non-marrying Man

I MET Johnny Blakeworthy at the end of his life. I was at the beginning of mine, about ten or twelve years old. This was in the early Thirties, when the Slump had spread from America even to us, in the middle of Africa. The very first sign of the Slump was the increase in the number of people who lived by their wits, or as vagrants.

Our house was on a hill, the highest point of our farm. Through the farm went the only road, a dirt track, from the railway station seven miles away, our shopping and mail centre, to the farms farther on. Our nearest neighbours were three, four, and seven miles away. We could see their roofs flash in the sunlight, or gleam in the moonlight across all those trees, ridges, and valleys.

From the hill we could see the clouds of dust that marked the passage of cars or wagons along the track. We would say: 'That must be so-and-so going to fetch his mail.' Or: 'Cyril said he had to get a spare part for the plough, his broke down, that must be him now.'

If the cloud of dust turned off the main road and moved up through the trees towards us, we had time to build up the fire and put on the kettle. At busy times for the farmers, this happened seldom. Even at slack times, there might be no more than three or four cars a week, and as many wagons. It was mostly a white man's road, for the Africans moving on foot used their own quicker, short-cutting paths. White men coming to the house on foot were rare, though less rare as the Slump set in. More and more often, coming through the trees up the hill, we saw walking towards us a man with a bundle of blankets over his shoulder, a rifle swinging in his hand. In the blanket roll were always a frying pan and a can of water, sometimes a couple of tins of bully beef, or a Bible, matches, a twist of dried meat. Sometimes this man had an African servant walking with him. These men always called themselves Prospectors, for that was a respectable occupation. Many did prospect, and nearly always for gold.

One evening, as the sun was going down, up the track to our house came a tall stooped man in shabby khaki with a rifle and a bundle over one shoulder. We knew we had company for the night. The rules of hospitality were that no one coming to our homes in the bush could be refused; every man was fed, and asked to stay as long as he wanted.

Johnny Blakeworthy was burned by the suns of Africa to a dark brown, and his eyes in a dried wrinkled face were grey, the whites much inflamed by the glare. He kept screwing up his eyes, as if in sunlight, and then, in a remembered effort of will, letting loose his muscles, so that his face kept clenching and unclenching like a fist. He was thin: he spoke of having had malaria recently. He was old: it was not only the sun that had so deeply lined his face. In his blanket-roll he had, as well as the inevitable frying pan, an enamel one-pint saucepan, a pound of tea, some dried milk, and a change of clothing. He wore long, heavy khaki trousers for protection against lashing grasses and grass-seeds, and a khaki bush-shirt. He also owned a washed-out grey sweater for frosty nights. Among these items was a corner of a sack full of maize-meal. The presence of the maize-flour was a statement, and probably unambiguous, for the Africans ate maize-meal porridge as their staple food. It was cheap, easily obtainable, quickly cooked, nourishing, but white men did not eat it, at least, not as the basis of their diet, because they did not wish to be put on the same level as Africans. The fact that this man carried it, was why my father, discussing him later with my mother, said: 'He's probably gone native.'

This was not a criticism. Or rather, while with one part of the collective ethos the white men might say, He's gone native! and in anger; with a different part of their minds, or at different times it could be said in bitter envy. But that is another story . . .

Johnny Blakeworthy was of course asked to stay for supper and for the night. At the lamplit table, which was covered with every sort of food, he kept saying how good it was to see so much real food again, but it was in a vaguely polite way, as if he was having to remind himself that this was how he should feel. His plate was loaded with food, and he ate, but kept forgetting to eat, so that my mother had to remind him, putting a little bit more of nice under-cut, a splash of gravy, helpings of carrots and spinach from the garden. But by the end he had eaten very little, and hadn't spoken much either, though the meal gave an impression of much conver-sation and interest and eating, like a feast, so great was our hunger for company, so many were our questions. Particularly the two children questioned and demanded, for the life of such a man, walking quietly by himself through the bush, sometimes twenty miles or more a day, sleeping by himself under the stars, or the moon, or whatever weather the seasons sent him, prospecting when he wished, stopping to rest when he needed—such a life, it goes without saying, set us restlessly dreaming of lives different from those we were set towards by school and by parents.

We did learn that he had been on the road for 'some time, yes, some time now, yes'. That he was sixty. That he had been born in England, in the South, near Canterbury. That he had been adven-turing up and down and around Southern Africa all his life—but adventure was not the word he used, it was the word we children repeated until we saw that it made him uncomfortable. He had mined: had indeed owned his own mine. Had farmed, but had not done well. Had done all kinds of work, but 'I like to be my own master.' He had owned a store, but 'I get restless, and I must be on the move.'

Now there was nothing in this we hadn't heard before—every time, indeed, that such a wanderer came to our door. There was nothing out of the ordinary in his extraordinariness, except, per-haps, as we remembered later, sucking all the stimulation we could out of the visit, discussing it for days, he did not have a prospector's pan, nor had he asked my father for permission to prospect on this farm. We could not remember a prospector who had failed to become excited by the farm, for it was full of chipped rocks and reefs, trenches and shafts, which some people said went back to the Phoenicians. You couldn't walk a hundred yards without seeing signs ancient and modern of the search for gold. The district was called 'banket' because it had running through it reefs of the same formation as reefs on the Rand called Banket. The name alone was like a signpost.

But Johnny said he liked to be on his way by the time the sun was up. I saw him leave, down the track that was sunflushed, the trees all rosy on one side. He shambled away out of sight, a tall, much too thin, rather stooping man in washed-out khaki and soft hide shoes.

Some months later, another man, out of work and occupying himself with prospecting, was asked if he had ever met up with Johnny Blakeworthy, and he said yes, he had indeed! He went on with indignation to say that 'he had gone native' in the Valley. The indignation was false, and we assumed that this man too might have 'gone native', or that he wished he had, or could. But Johnny's lack of a prospecting pan, his maize meal, his look at the supper table of being out of place and unfamiliar—all was explained. 'Going native' implied that a man would have a 'bush wife', but it seemed Johnny did not.

'He said he's had enough of the womenfolk, he's gone to get out of their way,' said this visitor.

I did not describe, in its place, the thing about Johnny's visit that struck us most, because at the time it did not strike us as more than agreeably quaint. It was only much later that the letter he wrote us matched up with others, and made a pattern.

Three days after Johnny's visit to us, a letter arrived from him. I remember my father expected to find that it would ask, after all, for permission to prospect. But any sort of letter was odd. Letter writing equipment did not form part of a tramp's gear. The letter was on blue Croxley writing paper, and in a blue Croxley envelope, and the writing was as neat as a child's. It was a 'bread and butter' letter. He said that he had very much enjoyed our kind hospitality, and the fine cooking of the lady of the house. He was grateful for the opportunity of making our acquaintance. 'With my best wishes, yours very truly, Johnny Blakeworthy.'

Once he had been a well-brought-up little boy from a small English country town. 'You must always write and say thank you after enjoying hospitality, Johnny.'

We talked about the letter for a long time. He must have dropped in at the nearest store after leaving our farm. It was twenty miles away. He probably bought a single sheet of paper and a lone envelope. This meant that he had got them from the African part of the store, where such small retailing went on—at vast profit, of course, to the storekeeper. He must have bought one stamp, and walked across to the post office to hand the letter over the counter. Then, due having been paid to his upbringing, he moved back to the African tribe where he lived beyond post offices, letter writing, and the other impedimenta that went with being a white man.

The next glimpse I had of the man, I still have no idea where to fit into the pattern I was at last able to make.

It was years later. I was a young woman at a morning tea party. This one, like all the others of its kind, was an excuse for gossip, and most of that was—of course, since we were young married women, about men and marriage. A girl, married not more than a year, much in love, and unwilling to sacrifice her husband to the collective, talked instead about her aunt from the Orange Free State. 'She was married for years to a real bad one, and then up he got and walked out. All she heard from him was a nice letter, you know, like a letter after a party or something. It said Thank you very much for the nice time. Can you beat that? And later still she found she had never been married to him because all the time he was married to someone else.'

'Was she happy?' one of us asked, and the girl said, 'She was nuts all right, she said it was the best time of her life.'

'Then what was she complaining about?'

'What got her was, having to say Spinster, when she was as good as married all those years. And that letter got her goat, I feel I must write and thank you for . . . something like that.'

'What was his name?' I asked, suddenly understanding what was itching at the back of my mind.

'I don't remember. Johnny something or other.'

That was all that came out of that most typical of South African scenes, the morning tea party on the deep shady veranda, the trays covered with every kind of cake and biscuit, the gossiping young women, watching their offspring at play under the trees, filling in a morning of their lazy lives before going back to their respective homes where they would find their meals cooked for them, the table laid, and their husbands waiting. That tea party was thirty years ago, and still that town has not grown so wide that the men can't drive home to take their midday meals with their families. I am talking of white families, of course.

The next bit of the puzzle came in the shape of a story which I read in a local paper, of the kind that gets itself printed in the spare hours of presses responsible for much more renowned newspapers. This one was called the *Valley Advertiser*, and its circulation might have been ten thousand. The story was headed: Our Prize-winning story, The Fragrant Black Aloe. By our new Discovery, Alan McGinnery.

'When I have nothing better to do, I like to stroll down the Main Street, to see the day's news being created, to catch fragments of talk, and to make up stories about what I hear. Most people enjoy coincidences, it gives them something to talk about. But when there are too many, it makes an unpleasant feeling that the long arm of coincidence is pointing to a region where a rational person is likely to feel uncomfortable. This morning was like that. It began in a flower shop. There a woman with a shopping list was saying to the salesman: "Do you sell black aloes?" It sounded like something to eat.

' "Never heard of them," said he. "But I have a fine range of succulents. I can sell you a miniature rock garden on a tray."

' "No, no, no. I don't want the ordinary aloes. I've got all those. I want the Scented Black Aloe."

'Ten minutes later, waiting to buy a toothbrush at the cosmetic counter at our chemist, Harry's Pharmacy, I heard a woman ask for a bottle of Black Aloe.

'Hello, I thought, black aloes have suddenly come into my life!

' "We don't stock anything like that," said the salesgirl, offering rose, honeysuckle, lilac, white violets and jasmine, while obviously reflecting that black aloes must make a bitter kind of perfume.

'Half an hour later I was in a seedshop, and when I heard a petulant female voice ask: "Do you stock succulents?" then I knew what was coming. This had happened to me before, but I couldn't remember where or when. Never before had I heard of the Scented Black Aloe, and there it was, three times in an hour.

'When she had gone I asked the salesman, "Tell me, is there such a thing as the Scented Black Aloe?"

' "Your guess is as good as mine," he said. "But people always want what's difficult to find."

'And at that moment I remembered where I had heard that querulous, sad, insistent hungry note in a voice before (voices, as it turned out!) the note that means that the Scented Black Aloe represents, for that time, all the heart's desire.

'It was before the war. I was in the Cape and I had to get to Nairobi. I had driven the route before, and I wanted to get it over. Every couple of hours or so you pass through some little dorp, and they are all the same. They are hot, and dusty. In the tearoom there is a crowd of youngsters eating ice-cream and talking about motor cycles and film stars. In the bars men stand drinking beer. The restaurant, if there is one, is bad, or pretentious. The waitress longs only for the day when she can get to the big city, and she says the name of the city as if it was Paris, or London, but when you reach it, two hundred or five hundred miles on, it is a slightly larger dorp, with the same dusty trees, the same tearoom, the same bar, and five thousand people instead of a hundred.

'On the evening of the third day I was in the Northern Transvaal, and when I wanted to stop for the night, the sun was blood-red through a haze of dust, and the main street was full of cattle and people. There was the yearly Farmers' Show in progress, and the hotel was full. The proprietor said there was a woman who took in people in emergencies.

'The house was by itself at the end of a straggling dust street, under a large jacaranda tree. It was small, with chocolate-coloured trellis-work along the veranda, and the roof was sagging under scarlet bougainvillaea. The woman who came to the door was a plump, dark-haired creature in a pink apron, her hands floury with cooking.

'She said the room was not ready. I said that I had come all the way from Bloemfontein that morning, and she said, "Come in, my second husband was from there when he came here in the beginning."

'Outside the house was all dust, and the glare was bad, but inside it was cosy, with flowers and ribbons and cushions and china behind glass. In every conceivable place were pictures of the same man. You couldn't get away from them. He smiled down from the bathroom wall, and if you opened a cupboard door, there he was, stuck up among the dishes.

'She spent two hours cooking a meal, said over and over again how a woman has to spend all her day cooking a meal that is eaten in five minutes, enquired after my tastes in food, offered second helpings. In between, she talked about her husband. It seemed that four years ago a man had arrived in the week of the Show, asking for a bed. She never liked taking in single men, for she was a widow living alone, but she did like the look of him, and a week later they were married. For eleven months they lived in a dream of happiness. Then he walked out and she hadn't heard of him since, except for one letter, thanking her for all her kindness. That letter was like a slap in the face, she said. You don't thank a wife for being kind, like a hostess, do you? Nor do you send her Christmas cards. But he had sent her one the Christmas after he left, and there it was, on the mantelpiece. With Best Wishes for a Happy Christmas. But he was so good to me, she said. He gave me every penny he ever earned, and I didn't need it, because my first hubby left me provided for. He got a job as a ganger on the railways. She could never look at another man after him. No woman who knew anything about life would. He had his faults of course, like everyone. He was restless and moody, but he loved her honestly, she could see that, and underneath it all, he was a family man.

'That went on until the cocks began to crow and my face ached with yawning.

'Next morning I continued my drive North, and that night, in Southern Rhodesia, I drove into a small town full of dust and people standing about in their best clothes among milling cattle. The hotel was full. It was Show time.

'When I saw the house, I thought time had turned back twenty-four hours, for there were the creepers weighing down the roof, and the trellised veranda, and the red dust heaped all around it. The attractive woman who came to the door was fair-haired. Behind her, through the door, I saw a picture on the wall of the same handsome blond man with his hard grey eyes that had sun-marks raying out from around them into the sunburn. On the floor was playing a small child, obviously his.

'I said where I had come from that morning, and she said wistfully that her husband had come from there three years before. It was all just the same. Even the inside of the house was like the other, comfortable and frilly and full. But it needed a man's attention. All kinds of things needed attention. We had supper and she talked about her "husband"—he had lasted until the birth of the baby and a few weeks beyond it—in the same impatient, yearning, bitter urgent voice of her sister of the evening before. As I sat there listening. I had the ridiculous feeling that in hearing her out so sympathetically I was being disloyal to the other deserted "wife" four hundred miles South. Of course he had his faults, she said. He drank too much sometimes, but men couldn't help being men. And sometimes he went into a daydream for weeks at a stretch and didn't hear what you said. But he was a good husband, for all that. He had got a job in the Sales Department of the Agricultural Machinery Store, and he had worked hard. When the little boy was born he was so pleased . . . and then he left. Yes, he did write once, he wrote a long letter saying he would never forget her "affectionate kindness". That letter really had upset her. It was a funny thing to say, wasn't it?

'Long after midnight I went to sleep under such a large tinted picture of the man that it made me uncomfortable. It was like having someone watching you sleep.

'Next evening, when I was about to drive out of Southern Rhodesia into Northern Rhodesia, I was half looking for a little town full of clouds of reddish dust and crowding cattle, the small house, the waiting woman. There seemed no reason why this shouldn't go on all the way to Nairobi.

'But it was not until the day after that, on the Copper Belt in

Northern Rhodesia, that I came to a town full of cars and people. There was going to be a dance that evening. The big hotels were full. The lady whose house I was directed to was plump, red-haired, voluble. She said she loved putting people up for the night, though there was no need for her to do it since while her husband might have his faults (she said this with what seemed like hatred) he made good money at the garage where he was a mechanic. Before she was married, she had earned her living by letting rooms to travellers, which was how she had met her husband. She talked about him while we waited for him to come in to supper. "He does this every night, every night of my life! You'd think it wasn't much to ask, to come in for meals at the right time, instead of letting everything spoil, but once he gets into the bar with the men, there is no getting him out."

'There wasn't a hint in her voice of what I had heard in the voices of the other two women. And I have often wondered since if in her case too absence would make the heart grow fonder. She sighed often and deeply, and said that when you were single you wanted to be married, and when you were married, you wanted to be single, but what got her was, she had been married before, and she ought to have known better. Not that this one wasn't a big improvement on the last, whom she had divorced.

'He didn't come in until the bar closed, after ten. He was not as good-looking as in his photographs, but that was because his overalls were stiff with grease, and there was oil on his face. She scolded him for being late, and for not having washed, but all he said was: "Don't try to housetrain me." At the end of the meal she wondered aloud why she spent her life cooking and slaving for a man who didn't notice what he ate, and he said she shouldn't bother, because it was true, he didn't care what he ate. He nodded at me, and went out again. It was after midnight when he came back, with a stardazed look, bringing a cold draught of night air into the hot lamplit room.

' "So you've decided to come in?" she complained.

' "I walked out into the veld a bit. The moon is strong enough to read by. There's rain on the wind." He put his arm around her waist and smiled at her. She smiled back, her bitterness forgotten. The wanderer had come home.'

I wrote to Alan McGinnery and asked him if there had been a model for his story. I told him why I wanted to know, told him of the old man who had walked up to our house through the bush, fifteen years before. There was no reason to think it was the same man, except for that one detail, the letters he wrote, like 'bread and butter' letters after a party or a visit.

I got this reply: 'I am indebted to you for your interesting and informative letter. You are right in thinking my little story had its start in real life. But in most ways it is far from fact. I took liberties with the time of the story, moving it forward by years, no, decades, and placing it in a more modern setting. For the times when Johnny Blakeworthy was loving and leaving so many young women—I'm afraid he was a very bad lot!—are now out of the memory of all but the elderly among us. Everything is so soft and easy now. "Civilization" so-called has overtaken us. But I was afraid if I put my "hero" into his real setting, it would seem so exotic to present-day readers that they would read my little tale for the sake of the background, finding that more interesting than my "hero".

'It was just after the Boer War. I had volunteered for it, as a young man does, for the excitement, not knowing what sort of war it really was. Afterwards I decided not to return to England. I thought I would try the mines, so I went to Johannesburg, and there I met my wife, Lena. She was the cook and housekeeper in a men's boarding-house, a rough job, in rough days. She had a child by Johnny, and believed herself to be married to him. So did I. When I made enquiries, I found she had never been married, the papers he had produced at the office were all false. This made things easy for us in the practical sense, but made them worse in some ways. For she was bitter and I am afraid never really got over the wrong done to her. But we married, and I became the child's father. She was the original of the second woman in my story. I describe her as home-loving, and dainty in her ways. Even when she was cooking for all those miners, and keeping herself and the boy on bad wages, living in a room not much bigger than a dog's kennel, it was all so neat and pretty. That was what took my fancy first. I daresay it was what took Johnny's too, to begin with, at any rate.

'Much later—very much later, the child was almost grown, so it was after the Great War, I happened to hear someone speak of Johnny Blakeworthy. It was a woman who had been "married" to him. It never crossed our minds to think—Lena and me—that he had betrayed more than one woman. After careful thought, I decided never to tell her. But I had to know. By then I had done some careful field work. The trial began, or at least, began for me, in Cape Province, with a woman I had heard spoken of, and had then tracked down. She was the first woman in my story, a little plump pretty thing. At the time Johnny married her, she was the daughter of a Boer farmer, a rich one. I don't have to tell you that this marriage was unpopular. It took place just before the Boer War, that nasty time was to come, but she was a brave girl to marry an Englishman, a *roinek*. Her parents were angry, but later they were kind and took her back when he left her. He did really marry her, in Church, everything correct and legal. I believe that she was his first love. Later she divorced him. It was a terrible thing, a divorce for those simple people. Now things have changed so much, and people wouldn't believe how narrow and churchbound they were then. That divorce hurt her whole life. She did not marry again. It was not because she did not want to! She had fought with her parents, saying she must get a divorce, because she wanted to be married. But no one married her. In that old-fashioned rural community, in those days, she was a Scarlet Woman. A sad thing, for she was a really nice woman. What struck me was that she spoke of Johnny with no bitterness at all. Even twenty years later, she loved him.

'From her, I followed up other clues. With my own wife, I found four women in all. I made it three in my little story: life is always much more lavish with coincidence and drama than any fiction writer dares to be. The red-headed woman I described was a barmaid in a hotel. She hated Johnny. But there was little doubt in my mind what would happen if he walked in through that door.

'I told my wife that I had been big game hunting. I did not want to stir up old unhappiness. After she died I wrote the story of the journey from one woman to another, all now of middle age, all of whom had been "married" to Johnny. But I had to alter the settings of the story. How fast everything has changed! I would have had to describe the Boer family on their farm, such simple and old-fashioned, good and bigoted people. And their oldest daughter—the "bad" one. There are no girls like that now, not even in convents. Where in the world now would you find girls brought up as strictly and as narrowly as those on those Boer farms, fifty years ago? And *still* she had the courage to marry her Englishman, that is the marvellous thing. Then I would have had to describe the mining camps of Johannesburg. Then the life of a woman married to a storekeeper in the bush. Her nearest neighbor was fifty miles away and they didn't have cars in those days. Finally, the early days of Bulawayo, when it was more like a shanty town than a city. No, it was Johnny that interested me, so I decided to make the story modern, and in that way the reader would not be distracted by what is past and gone.'

It was from an African friend who had known the village in which Johnny died that I heard of his last years. Johnny walked into the village, asked to see the Chief, and when the Chief assembled with his elders, asked formally for permission to live in the village, as an African, not as a white man.: All this was quite correct, and polite, but the elders did not like it. This village was a long way from the centres of white power, up towards the Zambesi. The traditional life was still comparatively unchanged, unlike the tribes near the white cities, whose structure had been smashed for ever. The people of this tribe cherished their distance from the white man, and feared his influence. At least, the older ones did. While they had nothing against this white man as a man—on the contrary, he seemed more human than most—they did not want a white man in their life. But what could they do? Their traditions of hospitality were strong: strangers, visitors, travellers, must be sheltered and fed. And they were democratic: a man was as good as his behavior, it was against their beliefs to throw a person out for a collective fault. And perhaps they were, too, a little curious. The white men these people had seen were the tax-collectors, the policemen, the Native Commissioners, all coldly official or arbitrary. This white man behaved like a suppliant, sitting quietly on the outskirts of the village, beyond the huts, under a tree, waiting for the council to make up its mind. Finally they let him stay, on condition that he shared the life of the village in every way. This proviso they probably thought would soon get rid of him. But he lived there until he died, six years, with short trips away to remind himself, perhaps, of the strident life he had left. It was on such a trip that he had walked up to our house and stayed the night.

The Africans called him Angry Face. This name implied that it was only the face which was angry. It was because of his habit of screwing up and then letting loose his facial muscles. They also called him Man Without a Home, and The Man Who Has no Woman.

The women found him intriguing, in spite of his sixty years. They hung about his hut, gossiped about him, brought him presents. Several made offers, even young girls.

The Chief and his elders conferred again, under the great tree in the centre of the village, and then called him to hear their verdict.

'You need a woman,' they said, and in spite of all his protests, made it a condition of his staying with them, for the sake of the tribe's harmony.

They chose for him a woman of middle age whose husband had died of the blackwater fever, and who had had no children. They said that a man of his age could not be expected to give the patience and attention that small children need. According to my friend who as a small boy had heard much talk of this white man who had preferred their way of life to his own, Johnny and his new woman 'lived together in kindness'.

It was while I was writing this story that I remembered something else. When I was at school in Salisbury there was a girl called Alicia Blakeworthy. She was fifteen, a 'big girl' to me. She lived with her mother on the fringes of the town. Her step-father had left them. He had walked out.

Her mother had a small house, in a large garden, and she took in paying guests. One of these guests had been Johnny. He had been working as a game warden up towards the Zambesi river, and had had malaria badly. She nursed him. He married her and took a job as a counter hand in the local grocery store. He was a bad husband to Mom, said Alicia. Terrible. Yes, he brought in money, it wasn't that. But he was a cold hard-hearted man. He was no company for them. He would just sit and read, or listen to the radio, or walk around by himself all night. And he never appreciated what was done for him.

Oh how we schoolgirls all hated this monster! What a heartless beast he was.

But the way *he* saw it, he had stayed for four long years in a suffocating town house surrounded by a domesticated garden. He had worked from eight to four selling groceries to lazy women. When he came home, this money, the gold he had earned by his slavery, was spent on chocolates, magazines, dresses, hair-ribbons for his townified step-daughter. He was invited, three times a day, to sit down at a table crammed with roast beef and chickens and puddings and cakes and biscuits.

He used to try and share his philosophy of living.

'I used to feed myself for ten shillings a week!'

'But why? What for? What's the point?'

'Because I was free, that's the point! If you don't spend a lot of money then you don't have to earn it and you are free. Why do you have to spend money on all this rubbish? You can buy a piece of rolled brisket for three shillings, and you boil it with an onion and you can live off it for four days! You can live off mealiemeal well enough. I often did, in the bush.'

'Mealiemeal! I'm not going to eat native food!'

'Why not? What's wrong with it?'

'If you can't see why not, then I'm afraid I can't help you.'

Perhaps it was here, with Alicia's mother, that the idea of 'going native' had first come into his head.

'For crying out aloud, why cake all the time, why all these new dresses, why do you have to have new curtains, why do we have to have curtains at all, what's wrong with the sunlight? What's wrong with the starlight? Why do you want to shut them out? Why?'

That 'marriage' lasted four years, a fight all the way.

Then he drifted North, out of the white man's towns, and up into those parts that had not been 'opened up to white settlement', and where the Africans were still living, though not for long, in their traditional ways. And there at last he found a life that suited him, and a woman with whom he lived in kindness.

Spies I Have Known

I DON'T want you to imagine that I am drawing any sort of comparison between Salisbury, Rhodesia, of thirty years ago, a one-horse town then, if not now, and more august sites. God forbid. But it does no harm to lead into a weighty subject by way of the miniscule.

It was in the middle of the Second World War. A couple of dozen people ran a dozen or so organizations, of varying degrees of leftwingedness. The town, though a capital city, was still in that condition when 'everybody knows everybody else'. The white population was about ten thousand; the number of black people, then as now, only guessed at. There was a Central Post Office, a rather handsome building, and one of the mail sorters attended the meetings of The Left Club. It was he who explained to us the system of censorship operated by the Secret Police. All the incoming mail for the above dozen organizations was first put into a central box marked CENSOR and was read—at their leisure, by certain trusted citizens. Of course all this was as to be expected, and what we knew must be happening. But there were other proscribed organizations, like the Watchtower, a religious sect for some reason suspected by governments up and down Africa (perhaps because they prophesied the imminent end of the world?) and some fascist organizations—reasonably enough in a war against fascism. There were organizations of obscure aims and

perhaps five members and a capital of five pounds, and also in-
dividuals whose mail had first to go through the process, as it
were, of decontamination, or defusing It was this last list of a
hundred or so people which was the most baffling. What did they
have in common, these sinister ones whose opinions were such a
threat to the budding Southern Rhodesian State, then still in the
Lord Malvern phase of the Huggins/Lord Malvern/Welenski/Gar-
field Todd/Winston Field/Smith succession? After months, indeed,
years, of trying to understand what could unite them, we had
simply to give up. Of course, half were on the left, kaffir lovers and
so on, but what of the others? It was when a man wrote a letter
to the *Rhodesia Herald* in solemn parody of Soviet official style—
as heavy then as now, urging immediate extermination by firing
squad of our government, in favour of a team from the Labour
Opposition, and we heard from our contact in the Post Office that
his name was now on the Black List, that we began to suspect the
truth.

Throughout the war, this convenient arrangement continued.
Our Man in the Post Office—by then several men, but it doesn't
sound so well, kept us informed of what and who was on the
Black List. And if our mail was being held up longer than we
considered reasonable, the censors being on holiday, or lazy,
authority would be gently prodded to hurry things up a little.

This was my first experience of Espionage.

Next was when I knew someone who knew someone who had
told him of how a certain Communist Party Secretary had been
approached by the man whose occupation it was to tap communist
telephones—we are now in Europe. Of course, the machinery for
tapping was much more primitive then. Probably by now they
have dispensed with human intervention altogether, and a machine
judges the degree of a suspicious person's disaffection by the
tones of his voice. Then, and in that country, they simply played
back records of conversation. This professional had been in the
most intimate contact with communism and communists for years,
becoming involved with shopping expeditions, husbands late from
the office, love affairs, a divorce or so, children's excursions. He
had been sucked into active revolutionary politics through the
keyhole.

'I don't think you ought to let little Jackie go at all. He'll be
in bed much too late, and you know how bad tempered he gets
when he is overtired.'

'She said to me No, she said. That's final. If you want to do a thing like that, then you must do it yourself. You shouldn't expect other people to pull your chestnuts out of the fire, she said. If he was rude to you, then it's your place to tell him so.'

He got frustrated, like an intimate friend or lover with paralysis of the tongue. And there was another thing, his involvement was always at a remove. He was listening to events, emotions, several hours old. Sometimes weeks old, as for instance when he went on leave and had to catch up with a month's dangerous material all in one exhausting twenty-four hours. He found that he was getting possessive about certain of his charges, resented his colleagues listening in to 'my suspects'. Once he had to wrestle with temptation because he longed to seek out a certain woman on the point of leaving her husband for another man. Due to his advantageous position he knew the other man was not what she believed. He imagined how he would trail her to the café which he knew she frequented, sit near her, then lean over and ask: 'May I join you? I have something of importance to divulge.' He knew she would agree: he knew her character well. She was unconventional, perhaps not as responsible as she ought to be, careless for instance about the regularity of meals, but fundamentally, he was sure, a good girl with the potentiality of good wifehood. He would say to her: 'Don't do it, my dear! No, don't ask me how I know, I can't tell you that. But if you leave your husband for that man, you'll regret it!' He would press her hands in his, looking deeply into her eyes—he was sure they were brown, for her voice was definitely the voice of a brown-eyed blonde—and then stride for ever out of her life. Afterwards he could check on the success of his intervention through the tapes.

To cut a process short that took some years, he at last went secretly to a communist bookshop, bought some pamphlets, attended a meeting or two, and discovered that he would certainly become a Party Member if it were not that his job, and a very well paid one with good prospects, was to spy on the Communist Party. He felt in a false position. What to do? He turned up at the offices of the Communist Party, asked to see the Secretary, and confessed his dilemma. Roars of laughter from the Secretary.

These roars are absolutely obligatory in this convention, which insists on a greater degree of sophisticated understanding between professionals, even if on opposing sides, even if at war—Party officials, government officials, top ranking soldiers and the like— than the governed, ever a foolish, trusting and sentimental lot.

First, then, the roar. Then a soupçon of whimsicality: alas for this badly-ordered world where men so well-equipped to be friends must be enemies. Finally, the hard offer.

Our friend the telephone-tapper was offered a retaining fee by the Communist Party, and their provisional trust, on condition that he stayed where he was, working for the other side. Of course, what else had he expected? Nor should he have felt insulted, for in such ways are the double agents born, those rare men at an altogether higher level in the hierarchies of espionage than he could ever aspire to reach. But his finer feelings had been hurt by the offer of money, and he refused. He went off and suffered for a week or so, deciding that he really did have to leave his job with the Secret Police—an accurate name for what he was working for, though of course the name it went under was much blander. He returned to the Secretary in order to ask for the second time to become just a rank and file Communist Party member. This time there was no roar of laughter, not even a chuckle, but the frank (and equally obligatory) I-am-concealing-nothing statement of the position. Which was that he surely must be able to see their point of view—The Communist Party's. With a toehold in the enemy camp (a delicate way of describing his salary and his way of life) he could be of real use. To stay where he was could be regarded as a real desire to serve the People's Cause. To leave altogether, becoming just honest John Smith might satisfy his conscience (a subjective and conditioned organ as he must surely know by now if he had read those pamphlets properly) but would leave behind him an image of the capricious, or even the unreliable. What had he planned to tell his employers? 'I am tired of tapping telephones, it offends me!' Or: 'I regard this as an immoral occupation!'—when he had done nothing else for years? Come, come, he hadn't thought it out. He would certainly be under suspicion for ever more by his ex-employers. And of course he could not be so innocent, after so long spent in that atmosphere of vigilance and watchfulness not to expect the communists to keep watch on himself? No, his best course would be to stay exactly where he was, working even harder at tapping telephones. If not, then his frank advice (the Secretary's) could only be that he must become an ordinary citizen, as far from any sort of politics as possible, for his own sake, the sake of the Service he had left, and the sake of the Communist Party—which of *course* they believed he now found his spiritual home.

But the trouble was that he did want to join it. He wanted nothing more than to become part of the world of stern necessities he had followed for so long, but as it were from behind a one-way pane of glass. Integrity had disenfranchised him. From now on he could not hope to serve humanity except through the use of the vote.

His life was empty. His resignation had cut off his involvement, like turning off the television on a soap opera, with the deathless real-life dramas of the tapes.

He felt that he was useless. He considered suicide, but thought better of it. Then, having weathered a fairly routine and unremarkable nervous breakdown, became a contemplative monk—high Church of England.

Another spy I met at a cocktail party, said in the course of chat about this or that—it was in London, in the late Fifties—that at the outbreak of the Second World War he had been in Greece, or perhaps it was Turkey, where at another cocktail party, over the canapes, an official from the British Embassy invited him to spy for his country.

'But I can't,' said this man. 'You must know that perfectly well.'

'But why ever not?' inquired the official. A Second Secretary, I think he was.

'Because, as of course you must know, I am a Communist Party Member.'

'Indeed? How interesting? But surely that is not going to stand in the way of your desire to serve your country?' said the official, matching ferocious honesty with bland interest.

Cutting this anecdote short—it comes, after all, from a pretty petty level in the affairs of men, this man went home, and spent a sleepless night weighing his allegiances, and decided by morning that of course the Second Secretary was right. He would like to serve his country, which was after all engaged in a war against Fascism. He explained his decision to his superiors in the Communist Party, who agreed with him, and to his wife and his comrades. Then, meeting the Second Secretary at another cocktail party, he informed him of the decision he had taken. He was then invited to attach himself to a certain Army Unit, in some capacity to do with the Ministry of Information. He was to await orders. In due course they came, and he discovered that it was his task to spy on the Navy, or rather, that portion of it operating near him. Our Navy, of course. He was always unable to work out the ideology of this. That a communist should not be set to spy on, let's say, Russia, seemed to him fair and reasonable, but why was he deemed suitable material to spy on his own side? He found

it all baffling, and indeed rather lowering. Then, at a cocktail
party, he happened to meet a naval officer with whom he proceeded
to get drunk, and they both suddenly understood on a wild hunch
that they were engaged on spying on each other, one for the Navy,
and one for the Army. Both found this work without much uplift,
they were simply not able to put their hearts into it, apart from
the fact that they had been in the same class at prep school and
had many other social ties. Not even the fact that they weren't
being paid, since it was assumed by their superiors—quite correctly of course—that they would be happy to serve their countries for nothing, made them feel any better. They developed
the habit of meeting regularly in a café where they drank wine
and coffee and played chess in a vine-covered arbour overlooking
a particularly fine bit of the Mediterranean where, without going
through all the tedious effort of spying on each other, they simply
gave each other relevant information. They were found out. Their
excuse that they were fighting the war on the same side was
deemed inadequate. They were both given the sack as spies, and
transferred to less demanding work. But until D-Day and beyond,
the British Army spied on the British Navy, and vice versa. They
probably all still do.

The fact that human beings, given half a chance, start seeing
each other's points of view seems to me the only ray of hope there
is for humanity, but obviously this tendency must be one to cause
anguish to seniors in the diplomatic corps and the employers of
your common or garden spy—not the high level spies, but of that
in a moment. Diplomats, until they have understood why, always
complain that as soon as they understand a country and its
language really well, hey presto, off they are whisked to another
country. But diplomacy could not continue if the opposing fac-
totums lost a proper sense of national hostility. Some diplomatic
corps insist that their employees must only visit among each other,
and never fraternize with the locals, obviously believing that understanding with others is inculcated by a sort of osmosis. And
of course, any diplomat that shows signs of going native, that is to
say really enjoying the manners and morals of a place, must be
withdrawn at once.

Not so the masters among the spies: one dedicated to his country's deepest interests must be worse than useless. The rarest spirits
must be those able to entertain two or three allegiances at once;
the counter spies, the double and triple agents. Such people are
not born. It can't be that they wake up one morning at the age of
thirteen crying: Eureka, I've got it, I want to be a double agent!

That's what I was born to do! Nor can there be a training school for multiple spies, a kind of top class that promising pupils graduate towards. Yet that capacity which might retard a diplomat's career, or mean death to the small fry among spies, must be precisely the one watched out for by the Spymasters who watch and manipulate in the high levels of the world's thriving espionage systems. What probably happens is that a man drifts, even unwillingly, into serving his country as a spy—like my acquaintance of the cocktail party who then found himself spying on the Senior Service of his own side. Then, whether there through a deep sense of vocation or without enthusiasm, he must begin by making mistakes, sometimes pleased with himself and sometimes not; he goes through a phase of wondering whether he would not have done better to go into the Stock Exchange, or whatever his alternative was—and then suddenly there comes that moment, fatal to punier men but a sign of his own future greatness, when he is invaded by sympathy for the enemy. Long dwelling on what X is doing, likely to be doing, or thinking, or planning, makes X's thoughts as familiar and as likeable as his own. The points of view of the nation he spends all his time trying to undo, are comfortably at home in a mind once tuned only to those of his own dear Fatherland. He is thinking the thoughts of those he used to call enemies before he understands that he is already psychologically a double agent, and before he guesses that those men who must always be on the watch for such precious material have noticed, perhaps even prognosticated, his condition.

On those levels where the really great spies move, whose names we never hear, but whose existence we have to deduce, what fantastic feats of global understanding must be reached, what metaphysical heights of international brotherhood!

It is of course not possible to do more than take the humblest flights into speculation, while making do with those so frequent and highly publicized spy dramas, for some reason or other so very near to farce, that do leave obscurity for our attention.

It can't be possible that the high reaches of espionage can have anything in common with, for instance, this small happening.

A communist living in a small town in England, who had been openly and undramatically a communist for years, and for whom the state of being a communist had become rather like the practice of an undemanding religion—this man looked out of his window one fine summer afternoon to see standing in the street outside his house a car of such foreignness and such opulence that he was embarrassed, and at once began to work out what excuses he could use to his working-class neighbours whose cars, if any, would be dust in comparison. Out of this monster of a car came two large smiling Russians, carrying a teddy bear the size of a sofa, a bottle of vodka, a long and very heavy roll, which later turned out to be a vast carpet with a picture of the Kremlin on it, and a box of chocolates of British make, with a pretty lady and a pretty dog.

Every window in the street already had heads packed behind the curtains.

'Come in,' said he, 'but I don't think I have the pleasure of knowing who . . .'

The roll of carpet was propped in the hall, the three children sent off to play with the teddy bear in the kitchen, and the box of chocolates set aside for the lady of the house, who was out doing the week's shopping in the High Street. The vodka was opened at once.

It turned out that it was his wife they wanted: they were interested in him only as a go-between. They wished him to ask his wife, who was an employee of the town council, to get hold of the records of the Council's meetings, and to pass these records on to them. Now, this wasn't London, or even Edinburgh. It was a small unimportant North of England town, in which it would be hard to imagine anything ever happening that could be of interest to anyone outside it, let alone the agents of a Foreign Power. But, said he, these records are open, anyone could go and get copies—you, for instance—'Comrades, I shall be delighted to take you to the Town Hall myself.'

No, what they had been instructed to do was to ask his wife to procure them minutes and records, nothing less would do.

A long discussion ensued. It was all no use. The Russians could not be made to see that what they asked was unnecessary. Nor could they understand that to arrive in a small suburban street in a small English town in a car the length of a battleship, was to draw the wrong sort of attention.

'But why is that?' they enquired. 'Representatives of the country where the workers hold power should use a good car. Of course, comrade. You have not thought it out from a class position!'

The climax came when, despairing of the effects of rational argument, they said: 'And comrade, these presents, the bear, the carpet, the chocolates, the vodka, are only a small token in appreciation of your work for our common cause. Of course you will be properly recompensed.'

At which point he was swept by, indeed taken over entirely by, atavistic feelings he had no idea were in him at all. He stood up and pointed a finger shaking with rage at the door: 'How dare you imagine,' he shouted, 'that my wife and I would take money. If I were going to spy, I'd spy for the love of mankind, for duty, and for international socialism. Take those bloody things out of here, wait I'll get that teddy bear from the kids. And you can take your bloody car out of here too.'

His wife, when she came back from the supermarket and heard the story, was even more insulted than he was.

But emotions like these are surely possible only in the lowest possible levels of spy material—in this case so low they didn't qualify for the first step, entrance into the brotherhood.

Full circle back to Our Man in the Post Office, or rather, the first of three.

After sedulous attendance at a lot of left-wing meetings, semi-private and public—for above all Tom was a methodical man who, if engaged in a thing always gave it full value—he put his hand up one evening in the middle of a discussion about Agrarian Reform in Venezuela, and said: 'I must ask permission to ask a question.'

Everyone always laughed at him when he did this, put up his hand to ask for permission to speak, or to leave, or to have opinions about something. Little did we realize that we were seeing here not just a surface mannerism, or habit, but his strongest characteristic.

It was late in the meeing, at that stage when the floor is well-loaded with empty coffee cups, beer glasses, and full ash trays. Some people had already left.

He wanted to know what he ought to do: 'I want to have the benefit of your expert advice.' As it happened he had already taken the decision he was asking about.

After some two years of a life not so much double—the word implies secrecy—as dual, his boss in the Central Post Office called him to ask how he was enjoying his life with the Left. Tom was as doggedly informative with him as he was with us, and said that we were interesting people, well-informed, and full of a high-class brand of idealism which he found inspiring.

'I always feel good after going to one of their meetings,' he reported he had said. 'It takes you right out of yourself and makes you think.'

His chief said that he, for his part, always enjoyed hearing about idealism and forward-looking thought, and invited Tom to turn in reports about our activities, our discussions, and most particularly our plans for the future, as well in advance as possible.

Tom told us that he said to his boss that 'he didn't like the idea of doing that sort of thing behind our backs, because say what you like about the reds, they are very hospitable'.

The chief had said that it would be for the good of his country.

Tom came to us to say that he had told his boss that he had agreed, because he wanted to be of assistance to the national war effort.

It was clear to everyone that having told us that he had agreed to spy on us, he would, since that was his nature, most certainly go back to his boss and tell him that he had told us that he had agreed to spy. After which he would come back to us to tell us that he had told his boss that . . . and so on. Indefinitely, if his boss didn't get tired of it. Tom could not see that his chief would shortly find him unsuitable material for espionage, and might even dismiss him from being a sorter in the Post Office altogether—a nuisance for us. After which he, the chief, would probably look for someone else to give him information.

It was Harry, one of the other two Post Office employees attending Left Club meetings, who suggested that it would probably be himself who would next be invited to spy on us, now that Tom had 'told'. Tom was upset, when everybody began speculating about his probable supercession by Harry or even Dick. The way he saw it was that his complete frankness with both us and his chief was surely deserving of reward. He ought to be left in the job. God knows how he saw the future. Probably that both his boss and ourselves would continue to employ him. We would use him to find out how our letters were slowly moving through the toils of censorship, and to hurry them on, if possible; his chief would use him to spy on us. When I say employ, I don't want anyone to imagine this implies payment. Or at least, certainly not from our side. Ideology had to be his spur, sincerity his reward.

It will by now have been noticed that our Tom was not as bright as he might have been. But he was a pleasant enough youth. He was rather good-looking too, about twenty-two. His physical characteristic was neatness. His clothes were always just so; he had a small alert dark moustache; he had glossy dark well-brushed hair. His rather small hands were well-manicured—the latter trait bound to be found offensive by good colonials, whose eye for such anti-masculine evidence—as they were bound to see it, then if not now—was acute. But he was a fairly recent immigrant, from just before the war, and had not yet absorbed the mores. He probably had not noticed that real Rhodesians, in those days at least, did not like men who went in for a careful appearance.

Tom, in spite of our humorous forecast that he would be bound to tell his boss that he had told us, and his stiff and wounded denials that such a thing was possible, found himself impelled to do just that. He reported back that his chief had 'lost his rag with him'.

But that was not the end. He was offered the job of learning how to censor letters. He had said to his boss that he felt in honour bound to tell us, and his boss said: 'Oh for Christ's sake. Tell them anything you damned well like. You won't be choosing what is to be censored.'

As I said, this was an unsophisticated town in those days, and the condition of 'everybody knowing everybody else' was bound to lead to such warm human situations.

He accepted the offer because: 'My mother always told me that she wanted me to do well for myself, and I'll increase my rating into Schedule Three as soon as I start work on censoring, and that means an increment of £50 a year.'

We congratulated him, and urged him to keep us informed about how people were trained as censors, and he agreed to do this. Shortly after that the war ended, and all the wartime cameraderie of wartime ended as the Cold War began. The ferment of Left activity ended too.

We saw Tom no more, but followed his progress, steady if slow, up the Civil Service. The last I heard he was heading a Department among whose duties is censorship. I imagine him, a man in his fifties, husband and no doubt a father, looking down the avenues of lost time to those dizzy days when he was a member of a dangerous revolutionary organization. 'Yes,' he must often say, 'you can't tell me anything about them. They are idealistic, I can grant you so much, but they are dangerous. Dangerous and wrong-headed! I left them as soon as I understood what they really were.'

But of our three Post Office spies Harry was the one whose career, for a while at least, was the most rewarding for humanist idealists.

He was a silent, desperately shy schoolboy who came to a public meeting and fell madly in love for a week or so with the speaker, a girl giving her first public speech and as shy as he was.

His father had died and his mother, as the psychiatrists and welfare workers would say, was 'inadequate'. That is to say, she was not good at being a widow, and was frail in health. What little energy she had went into earning enough money for her and two younger sons to live on. She nagged at Harry for not having ambition, and for not studying for the examinations which would take him up the ladder into the next grade in the Post Office—and for wasting time with the reds. He longed to be of use. For three years he devoted all his spare time to organization on the Left, putting up exhibitions, hiring halls and rooms, decorating ballrooms for fund-raising dances, getting advertisements for our socialist magazine—circulation two thousand, and laying it out and selling it. He argued principle with town councillors: 'But it's not *fair* not to let us have the hall, this is a democratic country isn't it?'—and spent at least three nights a week discussing world affairs in smoke-filled rooms.

At the time we would have dismissed as beyond redemption anyone who suggested it, but I daresay now that the main function of those gatherings was social. Southern Rhodesia was never exactly a hospitable country for those interested in anything but sport and the sundowner, and the fifty or so people who came to the meetings were all, whether in the Forces, or refugees from Europe, or simply Rhodesians, souls in need of congenial company. And they were friendly occasions, those meetings, sometimes going on till dawn.

A girl none of us had seen before came to a public meeting. She saw Harry, a handsome confident, loquacious, energetic, efficient young man. Everyone relied on him.

She fell in love, took him home, and her father, recognizing one of the world's born organizers, made him manager in his hardware shop.

Which leaves the third, Dick. Now there are some people who should not be allowed anywhere near meetings, debates, or similar intellect-fermenting agencies. He came to two meetings. Harry brought him, describing him as 'keen'. It was Harry who was keen. Dick sat on the floor on a cushion. Wild bohemian ways, these, for well-brought up young whites. His forehead puckered like a puppy's while he tried to follow wild unRhodesian thought. He, like Tom, was a neat, well-set-up youth. Perhaps the Post Office, or at least in Rhodesia, is an institution that attracts the well-ordered? I remember he reminded me of a boiled sweet, bland sugar with a chemical tang. Or perhaps he was like a bulldog, all sleek latent ferocity, with its little bulging eyes, its little snarl. Like Tom, he was one for extracting exact information. 'I take it you people believe that human nature can be changed?'

At the second meeting he attended, he sat and listened as before. At the end he enquired whether we thought socialism was a good thing in this country where there was the white man's burden to consider.

He did not come to another meeting. Harry said that he had found us seditious and unRhodesian. Also insincere. We asked Harry to go and ask Dick why he thought we were insincere, and to come back and tell us. It turned out that Dick wanted to know why The Left Club did not take over the government of the country and run it, if we thought the place ill run. But we forgot Dick, particularly as Harry, at the zenith of his efficiency and general usefulness, was drifting off with his future wife to become a hardware store manager. And by then Tom was lost to us.

Suddenly we heard that 'The Party for Democracy, Liberty, and Freedom' was about to hold a preliminary mass meeting. One of us was delegated to go along and find out what was happening. This turned out to be me.

The public meeting was in a sideroom off a ballroom in one of the town's three hotels. It was furnished with a sideboard to hold the extra supplies of beer and sausage rolls and peanuts consumed so plentifully during the weekly dances, a palm in a pot so tall the top fronds were being pressed down by the ceiling, and a dozen stiff dining-room chairs ranged one by one along the walls. There were eleven men and women in the room, including Dick. Unable to understand immediately why this gathering struck me as so different from the ones in which I spent so much of my time, I then saw it was because there were elderly people present. Our gatherings loved only the young.

Dick was wearing his best suit in dark grey flannel. It was a very hot evening. His face was scarlet with endeavour and covered with sweat, which he kept sweeping off his forehead with impatient fingers. He was reading an impassioned document in tone rather like the Communist Manifesto, which began: 'Fellow Citizens of Rhodesia! Sincere Men and Women! This is the Time for Action! Arise and look about you and enter into your Inheritance! Put the forces of International Capital to flight.'

He was standing in front of one of the chairs, his well-brushed little head bent over his notes, which were handwritten and in places hard to read, so that these inflammatory sentiments were being stammered and stumbled out, while he kept correcting himself, wiping off sweat, and then stopping with an appealing circular glance around the room at the others. Towards him were lifted ten earnest faces, as if at a saviour or a party leader.

The programme of this nascent Party was simple. It was to 'take over by democratic means but as fast as possible' all the land and the industry of the country 'but to cause as little inconvenience as possible' and 'as soon as it was feasible' to institute a régime of true equality and fairness in this 'land of Cecil Rhodes'.

He was intoxicated by the emanations of admiration from his audience. Burning, passionate faces like these (alas, and I saw how far away we had sunk away from fervour) were no longer to be seen at our Left Club meetings, which long ago had sailed away on the agreeable tides of debate and intellectual speculation.

The faces belonged to a man of fifty or so, rather grey and beaten, who described himself as a teacher 'planning the total reform of the entire educational system'; a woman of middle age, a widow, badly dressed and smoking incessantly, who looked as if she had long since gone beyond what she was strong enough to bear from life; an old man with an angelic pink face fringed with white tufts who said he was named after Keir Hardie; three schoolboys, the son of the widow and his two friends; the woman attendant from the ladies' cloakroom who had unlocked this room to set out the chairs and then had stayed out of interest, since it was her afternoon off; two aircraftsmen from the R.A.F.; Dick the convenor; and a beautiful young woman no one had ever seen before who, as soon as Dick had finished his manifesto, stood up to make a plea for vegetarianism. She was ruled out of order. 'We have to get power first, and then we'll simply do what the majority wants.' As for me, I was set apart from them by my lack of fervour, and by Dick's hostility.

This was in the middle of the Second World War, whose aim it was to defeat the hordes of National Socialism. The Union of Soviet Socialist Republics was thirty years old. It was more than a hundred and fifty years after the French Revolution, and rather more than that after the American Revolution which overthrew the tyrannies of Britain. The Independence of India would shortly be celebrated. It was twenty years after the death of Lenin. Trotsky still lived.

One of the schoolboys, a friend of the widow's son, put up his hand to say timidly, instantly to be shut up, that 'he believed there might be books which we could read about socialism and that sort of thing.'

'Indeed there are,' said the namesake of Keir Hardie, nodding his white locks, 'but we needn't follow the writ that runs in other old countries, when we have got a brand new one here.'

(It must be explained that the whites of Rhodesia, then as now, are always referring to 'this new country'.)

'As for books,' said Dick, eyeing me with all the scornful self-command he had acquired since leaving his cushion weeks before on the floor of our living-room, 'books don't seem to do some people any good, so why do we need them? It is all perfectly simple. It isn't right for a few people to own all the wealth of a country. It isn't fair. It should be shared out among everybody, equally, and then that would be a democracy.'

'Well obviously,' said the beautiful girl.

'Ah yes,' sighed the poor tired woman, emphatically crushing out her cigarette and lighting a new one.

'Perhaps it would be better if I just moved that palm a little,' said the cloakroom attendant, 'it does seem to be a little in your way perhaps.' But Dick did not let her show her agreement in this way.

'Never mind about the palm,' he said. 'It's not important.'

And this was the point when someone asked: 'Excuse me, but where do the Natives come in?' (In those days, the black inhabitants of Rhodesia were referred to as the Natives.)

This was felt to be in extremely bad taste.

'I don't really think that is applicable,' said Dick hotly. 'I simply don't see the point of bringing it up at all—unless it is to make trouble.'

'They do live here,' said one of the R.A.F.

'Well I must withdraw altogether if there's any likelihood of us getting mixed up with kaffir trouble,' said the widow.

'You can be assured that there will be nothing of that,' said Dick, firmly in control, in the saddle, leader of all, after only half an hour of standing up in front of his mass meeting.

'I don't see that,' said the beautiful girl. 'I simply don't see that at all! We must have a policy for the Natives.'

Even twelve people in one small room, whether starting a mass Party or not, meant twelve different, defined, passionately held viewpoints. The meeting at last had to be postponed for a week to allow those who had not had a chance to air their views to have their say. I attended this second meeting. There were fifteen people present. The two R.A.F. were not there, but there were six white trade unionists from the railways who, hearing of the new party, had come to get a resolution passed. 'In the opinion of this meeting, the Native is being advanced too fast towards civilization and in his own interests the pace should be slowed.'

This resolution was always being passed in those days, on every possible occasion. It probably still is.

But the nine from the week before were already able to form a solid block against this influx of alien thought—not as champions of the Natives, of course not, but because it was necessary to attend to first things first. 'We have to take over the country first, by democratic methods. That won't take long, because it is obvious our programme is only fair, and after that we can decide what to do about the Natives.' The six railway workers then left, leaving the nine from last week, who proceeded to form their Party for Democracy Liberty and Freedom. A steering committee of three was appointed to draft a constitution.

And that was the last anyone ever heard of it, except for one cyclostyled pamphlet which was called 'Capitalism is Unfair! Let's Join Together to Abolish It! This Means You!'

The war was over. Intellectual ferments of this sort occurred no more. Employees of the Post Office, all once again good citizens properly employed in sport and similar endeavours, no longer told the citizens in what ways they were censored and when.

Dick did not stay in the Post Office. That virus, politics, was in his veins for good. From being a spokesman for socialism for the whites, he became, as a result of gibes that he couldn't have socialism that excluded most of the population, an exponent of the view that Natives must not be advanced too fast in their own interests, and from there he developed into a Town Councillor, and from there into a Member of Parliament. And that is what he still is, a gentleman of distinguished middle age, an indefatigable server on Parliamentary Committees and Commissions, particularly those to do with the Natives, on whom he is considered an authority.

An elderly bulldog of the bulldog breed he is, every inch of him.